A WILD SHEEP CHASE
&
DANCE DANCE DANCE

Haruki Murakami was born in Kyoto in 1949 and lives near Tokyo. His work has been translated into thirty-four languages, and the most recent of his many honours is the Yomiuri Literary Prize, whose previous recipients include Yukio Mishima, Kenzaburo Ōe and Kobo Abe.

Alfred Birnbaum was born in Washington D.C. in 1957 and grew up in Tokyo. He has also translated Murakami's novel *Hard-boiled Wonderland and the End of the World* and works by Natsuki Ikezawa, Kyoji Kobayashi, Miyuki Miyabe, Tatsuhiko Shibusawa and Gen'ichiro Takahashi and compiled the anthology *Monkey Brain Sushi: New Tastes in Japanese Fiction.*

ALSO BY HARUKI MURAKAMI

Fiction

The Elephant Vanishes

Hard-boiled Wonderland and the End of the World

Norwegian Wood

The Wind-Up Bird Chronicle

South of the Border, West of the Sun

Sputnik Sweetheart

After the Quake

Kafka on the Shore

Blind Willow, Sleeping Woman

Non-Fiction

Underground: The Tokyo Gas Attack and the Japanese Psyche

Edited

Birthday Stories

TWO NOVELS BY

Haruki Murakami

A Wild Sheep Chase
&
Dance Dance Dance

TRANSLATED FROM THE JAPANESE BY
Alfred Birnbaum

VINTAGE BOOKS
London

Published by Vintage 2006

2 4 6 8 10 9 7 5 3 1

A Wild Sheep Chase first published in 1982 with the title
Hitsuji o meguro bōken by Kodansha Ltd, Tokyo
A Wild Sheep Chase first published in Great Britain in 2000 by
The Harvill Press

Dance, Dance Dance first published in 1988 with the title
Dansu Dansu Dansu by Kodansha Ltd, Tokyo
Dance Dance Dance first published in Great Britain in 2002 by
The Harvill Press

Vintage
Random House, 20 Vauxhall Bridge Road,
London SW1V 2SA

Random House Australia (Pty) Limited
20 Alfred Street, Milsons Point, Sydney,
New South Wales 2061, Australia

Random House New Zealand Limited
18 Poland Road, Glenfield, Auckland 10, New Zealand

Random House (Pty) Limited
Isle of Houghton, Corner of Boundary Road & Carse O'Gowrie,
Houghton, 2198, South Africa

Random House Publishers India Private Limited
301 World Trade Tower, Hotel Intercontinental Grand Complex,
Barakhamba Lane, New Delhi 110 001, India

The Random House Group Limited Reg. No. 954009
www.randomhouse.co.uk/vintage

A CIP catalogue record for this book
is available from the British Library

ISBN 9780099507079 (from Jan 2007)
ISBN 0099507072

Papers used by Random House are natural,
recyclable products made from wood grown in sustainable forests.
The manufacturing processes conform to the environmental
regulations of the country of origin

Printed and bound in Great Britain by
Mackays of Chatham plc, Chatham, Kent

A Wild Sheep Chase

PART ONE

A PRELUDE

1

Wednesday Afternoon Picnic

It was a short one-paragraph item in the morning edition. A friend rang me up and read it to me. Nothing special. Something a rookie reporter fresh out of college might've written for practice.

The date, a street corner, a person driving a truck, a pedestrian, a casualty, an investigation of possible negligence.

Sounded like one of those poems on the inner flap of a magazine.

"Where's the funeral?" I asked.

"You got me," he said. "Did she even have family?"

Of course she had a family.

I called the police department to track down her family's address and telephone number, after which I gave them a call to get details of the funeral.

Her family lived in an old quarter of Tokyo. I got out my map and marked the block in red. There were subway and train and bus lines everywhere, overlapping like some misshapen spiderweb, the whole area a maze of narrow streets and drainage canals.

The day of the funeral, I took a streetcar from Waseda. I got off near the end of the line. The map proved about as helpful as a globe would have been. I ended up buying pack after pack of cigarettes, asking directions each time.

It was a wood-frame house with a brown board fence around it. A small yard, with an abandoned ceramic brazier filled with standing rainwater. The ground was dark and damp.

She'd left home when she was sixteen. Which may have been reason why the funeral was so somber. Only family present, nearly everyone older. It was presided over by her older brother, barely thirty, or maybe it was her brother-in-law.

Her father, a shortish man in his mid-fifties, wore a black armband of mourning. He stood by the entrance and scarcely moved. Reminded me of a street washed clean after a downpour.

On leaving, I lowered my head in silence, and he lowered his head in return, without a word.

I met her in autumn nine years ago, when I was twenty and she was seventeen.

There was a small coffee shop near the university where I hung out with friends. It wasn't much of anything, but it offered certain constants: hard rock and bad coffee.

She'd always be sitting in the same spot, elbows planted on the table, reading. With her glasses—which resembled orthodontia—and skinny hands, she seemed somehow endearing. Always her coffee would be cold, always her ashtray full of cigarette butts.

The only thing that changed was the book. One time it'd be Mickey Spillane, another time Kenzaburo Oe, another time Allen Ginsberg. Didn't matter what it was, as long as it was a book. The students who drifted in and out of the place would lend her books, and she'd read them clean through, cover to cover. Devour them, like so many ears of corn. In those days, people lent out books as a matter of course, so she never wanted for anything to read.

Those were the days of the Doors, the Stones, the Byrds, Deep Purple, and the Moody Blues. The air was alive, even as everything seemed poised on the verge of collapse, waiting for a push.

She and I would trade books, talk endlessly, drink cheap whiskey, engage in unremarkable sex. You know, the stuff of everyday. Meanwhile, the curtain was creaking down on the shambles of the sixties.

I forget her name.

I could pull out the obituary, but what difference would it make now. I've forgotten her name.

Suppose I meet up with old friends and mid-swing the conversation turns to her. No one ever remembers her name either. Say, back then there was this girl who'd sleep with anyone, you know, what's-her-face, the name escapes me, but I slept with her lots of times, wonder what she's doing now, be funny to run into her on the street.

"Back then, there was this girl who'd sleep with anyone." That's her name.

Of course, strictly speaking, she didn't sleep with just anyone. She had standards.

Still, the fact of the matter is, as any cursory examination of the evidence would suffice to show, that she was quite willing to sleep with almost any guy.

Once, and only once, I asked her about these standards of hers.

"Well, if you must know . . . ," she began. A pensive thirty seconds went by. "It's not like anybody will do. Sometimes the whole idea turns me off. But you know, maybe I want to find out about a lot of different people. Or maybe that's how my world comes together for me."

"By sleeping with someone?"

"Uh-huh."

It was my turn to think things over.

"So tell me, has it helped you make sense of things?"

"A little," she said.

From the winter through the summer I hardly saw her. The university was blockaded and shut down on several occasions, and in any case, I was going through some personal problems of my own.

When I visited the coffee shop again the next autumn, the

clientele had completely changed, and she was the only face I recognized. Hard rock was playing as before, but the excitement in the air had vanished. Only she and the bad coffee were the same. I plunked down in the chair opposite her, and we talked about the old crowd.

Most of the guys had dropped out, one had committed suicide, one had buried his tracks. Talk like that.

"What've you been up to this past year?" she asked me.

"Different things," I said.

"Wiser for it?"

"A little."

That night, I slept with her for the first time.

About her background I know almost nothing. What I do know, someone may have told me; maybe it was she herself when we were in bed together. Her first year of high school she had a big falling out with her father and flew the coop (and high school too). I'm pretty sure that's the story. Exactly where she lived, what she did to get by, nobody knew.

She would sit in some rock-music café all day long, drink cup after cup of coffee, chain-smoke, and leaf through books, waiting for someone to come along to foot her coffee and cigarette bills (no mean sum for us types in those days), then typically end up sleeping with the guy.

There. That's everything I know about her.

From the autumn of that year on into the spring of the next, once a week on Tuesday nights, she'd drop in at my apartment outside Mitaka. She'd put away whatever simple dinner I cooked, fill my ashtrays, and have sex with me with the radio tuned full blast to an FEN rock program. Waking up Wednesday mornings, we'd go for a walk through the woods to the ICU campus and have lunch in the dining hall. In the afternoon, we'd have a weak cup of coffee in the student lounge, and if the weather was good, we'd stretch out on the grass and gaze up at the sky.

Our Wednesday afternoon picnic, she called it.

"Everytime we come here, I feel like we're on a picnic."

"Really? A picnic?"

"Well, the grounds go on and on, everyone looks so happy . . ."

She sat up and fumbled through a few matches before lighting a cigarette.

"The sun climbs high in the sky, then starts down. People come, then go. The time breezes by. That's like a picnic, isn't it?"

I was twenty-one at the time, about to turn twenty-two. No prospect of graduating soon, and yet no reason to quit school. Caught in the most curiously depressing circumstances. For months I'd been stuck, unable to take one step in any new direction. The world kept moving on; I alone was at a standstill. In the autumn, everything took on a desolate cast, the colors swiftly fading before my eyes. The sunlight, the smell of the grass, the faintest patter of rain, everything got on my nerves.

How many times did I dream of catching a train at night? Always the same dream. A nightliner stuffy with cigarette smoke and toilet stink. So crowded there was hardly standing room. The seats all caked with vomit. It was all I could do to get up and leave the train at the station. But it was not a station at all. Only an open field, with not a house light anywhere. No stationmaster, no clock, no timetable, no nothing—so went the dream.

I still remember that eerie afternoon. The twenty-fifth of November. Gingko leaves brought down by heavy rains had turned the footpaths into dry riverbeds of gold. She and I were out for a walk, hands in our pockets. Not a sound to be heard except for the crunch of the leaves under our feet and the piercing cries of the birds.

"Just what is it you're brooding over?" she blurted out all of a sudden.

"Nothing really," I said.

She kept walking a bit before sitting down by the side of the path and taking a drag on her cigarette.

"You always have bad dreams?"

"I *often* have bad dreams. Generally, trauma about vending machines eating my change."

She laughed and put her hand on my knee, but then took it away again.

"You don't want to talk about it, do you?"

"Not today. I'm having trouble talking."

She flicked her half-smoked cigarette to the dirt and carefully ground it out with her shoe. "You can't bring yourself to say what you'd really like to say, isn't that what you mean?"

"I don't know," I said.

Two birds flew off from nearby and were swallowed up into the cloudless sky. We watched them until they were out of sight. Then she began drawing indecipherable patterns in the dirt with a twig.

"Sometimes I get real lonely sleeping with you."

"I'm sorry I make you feel that way," I said.

"It's not your fault. It's not like you're thinking of some other girl when we're having sex. What difference would that make anyway? It's just that—" She stopped mid-sentence and slowly drew three straight lines on the ground. "Oh, I don't know."

"You know, I never mean to shut you out," I broke in after a moment. "I don't understand what gets into me. I'm trying my damnedest to figure it out. I don't want to blow things out of proportion, but I don't want to pretend they're not there. It takes time."

"How much time?"

"Who knows? Maybe a year, maybe ten."

She tossed the twig to the ground and stood up, brushing the dry bits of grass from her coat. "Ten years? C'mon, isn't that like forever?"

"Maybe," I said.

We walked through the woods to the ICU campus, sat down in the student lounge, and munched on hot dogs. It was two in the afternoon, and Yukio Mishima's picture kept flashing on the lounge TV. The volume control was broken so we could hardly make out what was being said, but it didn't matter to us one way or the other. A student got up on a chair and tried fooling with the volume, but eventually he gave up and wandered off.

"I want you," I said.

"Okay," she said.

So we thrust our hands back into our coat pockets and slowly walked back to the apartment.

I woke up to find her sobbing softly, her slender body trembling under the covers. I turned on the heater and checked the clock. Two in the morning. A startlingly white moon shone in the middle of the sky.

I waited for her to stop crying before putting the kettle on for tea. One teabag for the both of us. No sugar, no lemon, just plain hot tea. Then lighting up two cigarettes, I handed one to her. She inhaled and spat out the smoke, three times in rapid succession, before she broke down coughing.

"Tell me, have you ever thought of killing me?" she asked.

"You?"

"Yeah."

"Why're you asking me such a thing?"

Her cigarette still at her lips, she rubbed her eyelid with her fingertip.

"No special reason."

"No, never," I said.

"Honest?"

"Honest. Why would I want to kill you?"

"Oh, I guess you're right," she said. "I thought for a second there that maybe it wouldn't be so bad to get murdered by someone. Like when I'm sound asleep."

"I'm afraid I'm not the killer type."

"Oh?"

"As far as I know."

She laughed. She put her cigarette out, drank down the rest of her tea, then lit up again.

"I'm going to live to be twenty-five," she said, "then die."

July, eight years later, she was dead at twenty-six.

PART TWO

JULY, EIGHT YEARS LATER

2

Sixteen Steps

I waited for the compressed-air hiss of the elevator doors shutting behind me before closing my eyes. Then, gathering up the pieces of my mind, I started off on the sixteen steps down the hall to my apartment door. Eyes closed, exactly sixteen steps. No more, no less. My head blank from the whiskey, my mouth reeking from cigarettes.

Drunk as I get, I can walk those sixteen steps straight as a ruled line. The fruit of many years of pointless self-discipline. Whenever drunk, I'd throw back my shoulders, straighten my spine, hold my head up, and draw a deep lungful of the cool morning air in the concrete hallway. Then I'd close my eyes and walk sixteen steps straight through the whiskey fog.

Within the bounds of that sixteen-step world, I bear the title of "Most Courteous of Drunks." A simple achievement. One has only to accept the fact of being drunk at face value.

No ifs, ands, or buts. Only the statement "I am drunk," plain and simple.

That's all it takes for me to become the Most Courteous Drunk. The Earliest to Rise, the Last Boxcar over the Bridge.

Five, six, seven, . . .

* * *

Stopping on the eighth step, I opened my eyes and took a deep breath. A slight humming in my ears. Like a sea breeze whistling through a rusty wire screen. Come to think of it, when was the last time I was at the beach?

Let's see. July 24, 6:30 A.M. Ideal time of year for the beach, ideal time of day. The beach still unspoiled by people. Seabird tracks scattered about the surf's edge like pine needles after a brisk wind.

The beach, hmm . . .

I began walking again. Forget the beach. All that's ages past.

On the sixteenth step, I halted, opened my eyes, and found myself planted square in front of my doorknob, as always. Taking two days' worth of newspapers and two envelopes from the mailbox, I tucked the lot under my arm. Then I fished my keys out of the recesses of my pocket and leaned forward, forehead against the icy iron door. From somewhere behind my ears, a click. Me, a wad of cotton soaked through with alcohol. With only a modicum of control of my senses.

Just great.

The door maybe one-third open, I slid my body in, shutting the door behind me. The entryway was dead silent. More silent than it ought to be.

That's when I noticed the red pumps at my feet. Red pumps I've seen before. Parked in between my mud-caked tennis shoes and a pair of cheap beach sandals, like some out-of-season Christmas present. A silence hovered about them, fine as dust.

She was slumped over the kitchen table, forehead on her arms, profile hidden by straight black hair. A patch of untanned white neckline showed between the strands of hair, through the open sleeve of her print dress—one I'd never seen before—a glimpse of a brassiere strap.

I removed my jacket, undid my black tie, took off my watch, with not a flinch from her the whole while. Looking at her back called up memories. Memories of times before I'd met her.

"Well then," I spoke up in a voice not quite my own, the sound piped in.

As expected, there was no reply. She could have been asleep, could have been crying, could have been dead.

I sat down opposite her and rubbed my eyes. A short ray of sunlight divided the table, me in light, her in shadow. Colorless shadow. A withered potted geranium sat on the table. Outside, someone was watering down the street. Splash on the pavement, smell of wet asphalt.

"Want some coffee?"

No reply.

So I got up and went over to grind coffee for two cups. It occurred to me after I ground the coffee that what I really wanted was ice tea. I'm forever realizing things too late.

The transistor radio played a succession of innocuous pop songs. A perfect morning sound track. The world had barely changed in ten years. Only the singers and song titles. And my age.

The water came to a boil. I shut off the gas, let the water cool thirty seconds, poured it over the coffee. The grounds absorbed all they could and slowly swelled, filling the room with aroma.

"Been here since last night?" I asked, kettle in hand.

An ever so slight nod of her head.

"You've been waiting all this time?"

No answer.

The room had steamed up from the boiling water and strong sun. I shut the window and switched on the air conditioner, then set the two mugs of coffee on the table.

"Drink," I said, reclaiming my own voice.

Silence.

"Be better if you drank something."

It was thirty seconds before she raised her head slowly, evenly, and gazed absently at the potted plant. A few fine strands of hair lay plastered against her dampened cheeks, an aura of wetness about her.

"Don't mind me," she said. "I didn't mean to cry."

I held out a box of tissues to her. She quietly blew her nose, then brushed the hair from her cheek.

"Actually, I planned on being gone by the time you returned. I didn't want to see you."

"But you changed your mind, I see."

"Not at all. I didn't have anywhere else I wanted to go. But I'm going now, don't worry."

"Well, have some coffee anyway."

I tuned in to the radio traffic report as I sipped my coffee and slit open the two pieces of mail. One was an announcement from a furniture store where everything was twenty percent off. The second was a letter from someone I didn't want to think about, much less read a letter from. I crumpled them up and tossed them into the wastebasket, then nibbled on leftover cheese crackers. She cupped her hands around the coffee cup as if to warm herself and fixed her eyes on me, her lip lightly riding the rim of the mug.

"There's salad in the fridge," she said.

"Salad?"

"Tomatoes and string beans. There wasn't anything else. The cucumbers had gone bad, so I threw them out."

"Oh."

I went to the refrigerator and took out the blue Okinawa glass salad bowl and sprinkled on the last drops from the bottle of dressing. The tomatoes and string beans were but chilled shadows. Tasteless shadows. Nor was there any taste to the coffee or crackers. Maybe because of the morning sun? The light of morning decomposes everything. I gave up on the coffee midway, dug a bent cigarette out of my pocket, and lit up with matches that I'd never seen before. The tip of the cigarette crackled dryly as its lavender smoke formed a tracery in the morning light.

"I went to a funeral. When it was over, I went to Shinjuku, by myself."

The cat appeared out of nowhere, yawned at length, then sprang into her lap. She scratched him behind the ears.

"You don't need to explain anything to me," she said. "I'm out of the picture already."

"I'm not explaining. I'm just making conversation."

She shrugged and pushed her brassiere strap back inside her dress. Her face had no expression, like a photograph of a sunken city on the ocean floor.

"An acquaintance of sorts from years back. No one you knew."

"Oh really?"

The cat gave his legs a good stretch, topped it off with a puff of a breath.

I glanced at the burning tip of the cigarette in my mouth.

"How did this acquaintance die?"

"Hit by a truck. Thirteen bones fractured."

"Female?"

"Uh-huh."

The seven o'clock news and traffic report came to an end, and light rock returned to the airwaves. She set her coffee back down and looked me in the face.

"Tell me, if I died, would you go out drinking like that?"

"The funeral had nothing to do with my drinking. Only the first one or two rounds, if that."

A new day was beginning. Another hot one. A cluster of skyscrapers glared through the window.

"How about something cool to drink?"

She shook her head.

I got a can of cola out of the refrigerator and downed it in one go.

"She was the kind of girl who'd sleep with anyone." What an obituary: the deceased was the kind of girl who would sleep with anyone.

"Why are you telling me this?"

Why indeed? I had no idea.

"Very well," she picked up where I trailed off, "she was the kind of girl who'd sleep with anyone, right?"

"Right."

"But not with you, right?"

There was an edge to her voice. I glanced up from the salad bowl.

"You think not?"

"Somehow, no," she said quietly. "You, you're not the type."

"What type?"

"I don't know, there's something about you. Say there's an hourglass: the sand's about to run out. Someone like you can always be counted on to turn the thing over."

"That so?"

She pursed her lips, then relaxed.

"I came to get the rest of my things. My winter coat, hats, things I left behind. I packed them up in boxes. When you have time, could you take them to the parcel service?"

"I can drop them by."

She shook her head. "That's all right. I don't want you to come. You understand, don't you?"

Of course I did. I talk too much, without thinking.

"You have the address?"

"Yes."

"That's all that's left to do. Sorry for staying so long."

"And the paperwork, was that it?"

"Uh-huh. All done."

"I can't believe it's that easy. I thought there'd be a lot more to it."

"People who don't know anything about it all think so, but it really is simple. Once it's over and done with." Saying that, she went back to scratching the cat's head. "Get divorced twice, and you're a veteran."

The cat did a back stretch, eyes closed, then quickly nestled his head into the crook of her arm. I tossed the coffee mugs and salad bowl into the sink, then swept up the cracker crumbs with a bill. My eyes were throbbing from the glare of the sun.

"I made out a list of details. Where papers are filed, trash days, things like that. Anything you can't figure out, give me a call."

"Thanks."

"Had you wanted children?" she suddenly asked.

"Nah, can't say I ever wanted kids."

"I wondered about that for a while there. But seeing how it ended up like this, I guess it was just as well. Or maybe if we'd had a child it wouldn't have come to this, what do you think?"

"There're lots of couples with kids who get divorced."

"You're probably right," she said, toying with my lighter. "I still love you. But I guess that's not the point now, is it? I know that well enough myself."

3

The Slip

Once she was gone, I downed another cola, then took a hot shower and shaved. I was down to the bottom on just about everything—soap, shampoo, shaving cream.

I stepped out of the shower and dried my hair, rubbed on body lotion, cleaned my ears. Then to the kitchen to heat up the last of the coffee. Only to discover: no one sitting at the opposite side of the table. Staring at that chair where no one sat, I felt like a tiny child in a De Chirico painting, left behind all alone in a foreign country. Of course, a tiny child I was not. I decided I wouldn't think about it and took my time with my coffee and cigarette.

For not having slept in twenty-four hours, I felt surprisingly awake. My body was hazed to the core, but my mind kept swimming swiftly around through the convoluted waterways of my consciousness, like a restless aquatic organism.

The vacant chair in front of me made me think of an American novel I'd read a while back. After the wife walks out, the husband keeps her slip draped over the chair. It made sense, now that I thought about it. True, it wouldn't really help things, but it beat having that dying geranium staring at me. Besides, probably even the cat would feel more comfortable having her things around.

I checked the bedroom, opening all of her drawers, all empty. Only a moth-eaten scarf, three coat hangers, and a packet of mothballs. Her cosmetics, toiletries, and curlers, her toothbrush, hair dryer, assortment of pills, boots, sandals, slippers, hat boxes, accessories, handbags, shoulder bags, suitcases, purses, her ever-tidy stock of underwear, stockings, and socks, letters, everything with the least womanly scent was gone. She probably even wiped off her fingerprints. A third of the books and records was gone too—anything she'd bought herself or I'd given her.

From the photo albums, every single print of her had been peeled away. Shots of the both of us together had been cut, the parts with her neatly trimmed away, leaving my image behind. Photos of me alone or of mountains and rivers and deer and cats were left intact. Three albums rendered into a revised past. It was as if I'd been alone at birth, alone all my days, and would continue alone.

A slip! She could have at least left a slip!

It was her choice, and her choice was to leave not a single trace. I could either accept it or, as I imagined was her intention, I could talk myself into believing that she never existed all along. If she never existed, then neither did her slip.

I doused the ashtray, thought more about her slip, then gave up and hit the sack.

A month had passed since I agreed to the divorce and she moved out. A non-month. Unfocused and unfelt, a lukewarm protoplasm of a month.

Nothing changed from day to day, not one thing. I woke up at seven, made toast and coffee, headed out to work, ate dinner out, had one or two drinks, went home, read in bed for an hour, turned off the lights, and slept. Saturdays and Sundays, instead of work, I was out killing time from morning on, making the rounds of movie theaters. Then I had dinner and a couple of drinks, read, and went to sleep, alone. So it went: I passed through the month the way people X out days on a calendar, one after the other.

In one sense, her disappearance was due to circumstances

beyond my control. What's done is done, that sort of thing. How we got on the last four years was of no consequence. Any more than the photos peeled out of the albums.

Nor did it matter that she'd been sleeping with a friend of mine for a long time and one day upped and moved in with him. All this was within the realm of possibility. Such things happened often enough, so how could I think her leaving me was anything out of the ordinary? The long and the short of it was, it was up to her.

"The long and the short of it is, it's up to you," I said.

It was a Sunday afternoon, as I dawdled with a pull-ring from a beer can, that she came out with it. Said she wanted a divorce.

"Either way is fine with you then?" she asked, releasing her words slowly.

"No, either way is not fine with me," I said. "I'm only saying it's up to you."

"If you want to know the truth, I don't want to leave you," she said after a moment.

"All right, then don't leave me," I said.

"But I'm going nowhere staying with you."

She wouldn't say any more, but I knew what she meant. I would be thirty in few months; she would be twenty-six. And if you considered the vastness of the rest of our lives, the foundations we'd laid barely scraped zero. All we'd done our four years together was to eat through our savings.

Mostly my fault, I guess. Probably I never should have gotten married. At least never to her.

In the beginning, she thought she was the one unfit for society and made me out to be the socially functioning one. In our respective roles, we got along relatively well. Yet no sooner had we thought we'd reached a lasting arrangement than something crumbled. The tiniest hint of something, but it was never to be recovered. We had been walking ever so peacefully down a long blind alley. That was our end.

To her, I was already lost. Even if she still loved me, it didn't matter. We'd gotten too used to each other's role. She understood it instinctively; I knew it from experience. There was no hope.

So it was that she and her slip vanished forever. Some things are forgotten, some things disappear, some things die. But all in all, this was hardly what you could call a tragedy.

July 24, 8:25 A.M.

I checked the numerals of the digital clock, closed my eyes, and fell asleep.

PART THREE

SEPTEMBER, TWO MONTHS LATER

4

The Whale's Penis and the Woman with Three Occupations

To sleep with a woman: it can seem of the utmost importance in your mind, or then again it can seem like nothing much at all. Which only goes to say that there's sex as therapy (self-therapy, that is) and there's sex as pastime.

There's sex for self-improvement start to finish and there's sex for killing time straight through; sex that is therapeutic at first only to end up as nothing-better-to-do, and vice versa. Our human sex life—how shall I put it?—differs fundamentally from the sex life of the whale.

We are not whales—and this constitutes one great theme underscoring our sex life.

When I was a kid, there was an aquarium thirty minutes by bicycle from where I lived. A chill aquarium-like silence always pervaded the place, with only an occasional splash to be heard. I could almost feel the Creature from the Black Lagoon breathing in some dim corner.

Schools of tuna circled 'round and 'round the enormous pool. Sturgeon plied their own narrow watercourse, piranha set their razor-sharp teeth into chunks of meat, and electric eels sputtered and sparked like shorted-out lightbulbs.

The aquarium was filled with countless other fish as well, all with different names and scales and fins. I couldn't figure out why on earth there had to be so many kinds of fish.

There were, of course, no whales in the aquarium. One whale would have been too big, even if you knocked out all the walls and made the entire aquarium into one tank. Instead, the aquarium kept a whale penis on display. As a token, if you will.

So it was that my most impressionable years of boyhood were spent gazing at not a whale but a whale's penis. Whenever I tired of strolling through the chill aisles of the aquarium, I'd steal off to my place on the bench in the hushed, high-ceilinged stillness of the exhibition room and spend hours on end there contemplating this whale's penis.

At times it would remind me of a tiny shriveled palm tree; at other times, a giant ear of corn. In fact, if not for the plaque—WHALE GENITAL: MALE—no one would have taken it to be a whale's penis. More likely an artifact unearthed from the Central Asian desert than a product of the Antarctic Ocean. It bore no resemblance to my penis, nor to any penis I'd ever seen. What was worse, the severed penis exuded a singular, somehow unspeakable aura of sadness.

It came back to me, that giant whale's penis, after having intercourse with a girl for the very first time. What twists of fate, what torturous circumnavigations, had brought it to that cavernous exhibition room. My heart ached, thinking about it. I felt as if I didn't have a hope in the world. But I was only seventeen and clearly too young to give up on everything. It was then and there I came to the realization I have borne in mind ever since.

Which is, that I am not a whale.

In bed now with my new girlfriend, running my fingers through her hair, I thought about whales for the longest time.

In the aquarium of my memory, it is always late autumn. The glass of the tanks is cold. I'm wearing a heavy sweater. Through the large picture window of the exhibition room, the sea is dark as lead, the countless whitecaps reminiscent of lace collars on girls' dresses.

"What're you thinking about?" she asked.

"Something long ago," I said.

She was twenty-one, with an attractive slender body and a pair of the most bewitching, perfectly formed ears. She was a part-time proofreader for a small publishing house, a commercial model specializing in ear shots, and a call girl in a discreet intimate-friends-only club. Which of the three she considered her main occupation, I had no idea. Neither did she.

Nonetheless, sizing up her essential attributes, I would have to say her natural gifts ran to ear modeling. She agreed. Which was well and good until you considered how extremely limited are the opportunities for a commercial ear model, how abysmal the status and pay. To your typical P.R. man or makeup artist or cameraman, she was just an "earholder," someone with ears. Her mind and body, apart from the ears, were completely out of the picture, disregarded, nonexistent.

"But you know, that's not the real me," she'd say. "I am my ears, my ears are me."

Neither her proofreader self nor her call girl self ever, not for one second, showed her ears to others.

"That's because they're not really me," she explained.

The office of her call girl club, registered as a "talent club" for appearances, was located in Akasaka and run by a gray-haired Englishwoman whom everyone called Mrs. X. She'd been living in Japan for thirty years, spoke fluent Japanese, and read most of the basic Chinese characters.

Mrs. X had opened an English-language tutorial school for women not five hundred yards from the call girl office and used the place to scout promising faces for the latter. Conversely, several of the call girls were also going to her English school. At reduced tuition, of course.

Mrs. X called all her call girls "dear." Soft as a spring afternoon, her "dears."

"Make sure to wear frilly undies, dear. And no pantyhose." Or "You take your tea with cream, don't you, dear?" She had a firm understanding of her market. Her clientele were wealthy businessmen in their forties and fifties. Two-thirds foreigners, the rest Japanese. Mrs. X expressed a dislike for politicians, old men, perverts, and the poor.

A dozen long-stemmed beauties she kept on call, but out of the whole bouquet my new girlfriend was the least attractive bloom. As a callgirl, she seemed no more than ordinary. In fact, with her ears hidden, she was plain. I couldn't figure out how Mrs. X had singled her out. Maybe she'd detected in her plainness some special glimmer, or maybe she thought one plain girl would be an asset. Either way, Mrs. X's sights had been right on target, and my girlfriend quickly had a number of regular customers. She wore ordinary clothes, ordinary makeup, ordinary underwear, and an ordinary scent as she'd head out to the Hilton or Okura or Prince to sleep with one or two men a week, thereby making enough to live on for a month.

Half the other nights she slept with me for free. The other half I have no idea how she spent.

Her life as a part-time proofreader for the publishing house was more normal. Three days a week she'd commute to Kanda, to the third floor of a small office building, and from nine to five she'd proofread, make tea, run downstairs (no elevator in the building) and buy erasers. She'd be the one sent out, not because anyone held anything against her, but because she was the only unmarried woman in the company. Like a chameleon, she would change with place and circumstance, able, at will, to summon or control that glimmer of hers.

I first became acquainted with her (or rather, her ears) right after I broke up with my wife. It was the beginning of August. I was doing a subcontracted copywriting job for a computer software company, which brought me face-to-face, so to speak, with her ears.

The director of the advertising firm placed a campaign proposal and three large black-and-white photos on my desk, telling me to prepare three head copy options for them within the week. All three photos were giant close-ups of an ear.

An ear?

"Why an ear?" I asked.

"Who knows? What's the difference? An ear it is. You've got a week to think about ears."

So for one whole week I ear-gazed. I taped the three giant ears to the wall in front of my desk, and all day, while smoking cigarettes, drinking coffee, clipping my nails, I immersed myself in those ears.

The job I finished in a week, but the ear shots stayed taped up on my wall. Partly it was too much trouble to take them down, partly I'd grown accustomed to those ears. But the real reason I didn't take the photos down was that those ears had me in their thrall. They were the dream image of an ear. The quintessence, the paragon of ears. Never had any enlarged part of the human body (genitals included, of course) held such strong attraction for me. They were like some great whirlpool of fate sucking me in.

One astonishingly bold curve cut clear across the picture plane, others curled into delicate filigrees of subtle shadow, while still others traced, like an ancient mural, the legends of a past age. But the supple flesh of the earlobe surpassed them all, transcending all beauty and desire.

A few days later, I rang up the photographer for the name and number of those ears.

"What's this now?" asked the photographer.

"Just curious, that's all. They're such striking ears."

"Well, I guess as far as the ears go, okay, but the girl herself is nothing special. If it's a young piece you want, I can introduce you to this bathing-suit model I shot the other day."

I refused, took down the name and number of the ears, thanked him, and hung up.

Two o'clock, six o'clock, ten o'clock, I kept trying her number, but got no answer. Apparently she was going about her own life.

It was ten the next morning before I finally got ahold of her. I introduced myself briefly, then added that I had to talk to her about some business related to the advertisement and could she see clear to having dinner with me.

"But I was told that the job was finished," she said.

"The job is finished," I said.

She seemed a bit taken aback, but didn't inquire further. We set a date for the following evening.

I called for a reservation at the fanciest French restaurant I knew. On Aoyama Boulevard. Then I got out a brand-new shirt, took my time selecting a tie, and put on a jacket I'd only worn twice before.

True to the photographer's warning, the girl was nothing special. Plain clothes, plain looks. She seemed like a member of the chorus of a second-rate women's college. But that was beside the point as far as I was concerned. What disappointed me was that she hid her ears under a straight fall of hair.

"You're hiding your ears," said I, nonchalantly.

"Yes," said she, nonchalantly.

We had arrived ahead of schedule and were the first dinner customers at the restaurant. The lights were dimmed, a waiter came around with a long match to light the red taper on our table, and the maître d'hôtel cast fishy eyes over the napkins and dinnerware to be sure all was in place. The herringbone lay of the oak floorboards gleamed to a high polish, and the waiter walked about with a click of his heels. His shoes looked loads more expensive than mine. Fresh bud roses in vases, and modern oils, originals, on white walls.

I glanced over the wine list and chose a crisp white wine, and for hors d'oeuvres *pâté de canard, terrine de dorade,* and *foie de baudroie à crème fraiche*. After an intensive study of the menu she ordered *potage tortue, salade verte,* and *mousse de sole,* while I ordered *potage d'oursin, roti de veau avec garnie persil,* and a *salade de tomate*. There went half a month's salary.

"What a lovely place," she said. "Do you come here often?"

"Only occasionally on business," I answered. "The truth of the matter is, I don't usually go to restaurants when I'm alone. Mostly I go to bars where I eat and drink whatever they've got. Easier that way. No unnecessary decisions."

"And what do you usually eat at a bar?"

"All sorts of things. Omelettes and sandwiches often enough."

"Omelettes and sandwiches," she repeated. "You eat omelettes and sandwiches every day at bars?"

"Not every day. I cook for myself every three days or so."

"So you eat omelettes and sandwiches two days out of three."

"I guess so," I said.

"Why omelettes and sandwiches?"

"A halfway decent bar can make a pretty good omelette and sandwich."

"Hmm," she said. "Pretty strange."

"Not at all."

I couldn't figure how to get out of that, so I sat there quietly admiring the ashes in the ashtray.

She turned on the juice. "Let's talk business."

"As I told you yesterday, the job is finished. No problems. So I have nothing to say."

She fished a slender clove cigarette out of her handbag, lit up with the restaurant matches, and gave me a look that said "So?"

I was about to speak when the maître d'hôtel advanced on our table. He showed me the wine label, all smiles as if showing me a photo of his only son. I nodded. He unscrewed the cork with a pleasant pop, then poured out a small mouthful in my glass. It tasted like the price of the entire dinner.

The maître d'hôtel withdrew and in his place appeared a waiter who set out the three hors d'oeuvres and a small plate before each of us. When the waiter departed, leaving us alone again, I blurted out, "I had to see your ears."

Speaking not a word, she proceeded to help herself to the *pâté* and *foie de baudroie*. She took a sip of wine.

"Sorry to have imposed," I hedged.

She smiled ever so slightly. "Fine French cuisine is no imposition at all."

"Does it bother you to have your ears discussed?"

"Not really. It depends on the angle of discussion." She shook her head as she lifted her fork to her mouth. "Tell me straight, because that's my favorite angle."

We silently sipped our wine and continued our meal.

"I turn a corner," I offered, "just as someone ahead of me turns the next corner. I can't see what that person looks like. All I can make out is a flash of white coattails. But the whiteness of the coattails is indelibly etched in my consciousness. Ever get that feeling?"

"I suppose so."

"Well, that's the feeling I get from your ears."

Again, we ate in silence. I poured wine for her, then for myself.

"It's not the scene that comes into your head," she asked, "but the feeling, right?"

"Right."

"Ever have that feeling before?"

I gave it some thought, then shook my head. "No, I guess not."

"Which means it's all on account of my ears."

"I couldn't swear to it. There's no way I could be that sure. I've never heard of the shape of someone's ears arousing anyone this way."

"I know someone who sneezed every time he saw Farah Fawcett's nose. There's a big psychological element to sneezing, you know. Once cause and effect link up, there's no escape."

"I'm no expert on Farah Fawcett's nose," I said, taking a sip of wine. Then I forgot what I was about to say.

"That's not quite what you meant, is it?" she said.

"No, not quite," I said. "The feeling I get is terribly unfocused, yet very solid." I demonstrated, holding my hands a yard apart, then compressing the span to two inches. "I'm not explaining this well, I'm afraid."

"A concentrated phenomenon based on vague motives."

"Exactly," I said. "You're seven times smarter than I am."

"I take correspondence courses."

"Correspondence courses?"

"That's right, psychology by mail."

We split the last of the *pâté*. Now I was completely lost.

"You still haven't gotten it? The relationship between my ears and your feelings?"

"In a word, no," said I. "That is, I have no firm grasp on whether your ears appeal to me directly, or whether something else in you appeals to me through your ears."

She placed both her hands on the table and shook her head gently. "Is this feeling of yours of the good variety or the bad variety?"

"Neither. Or both. I can't tell."

She pinioned her wineglass between her palms and looked me straight in the face. "It seems you need more study in the means of expressing emotions."

"Can't say I'm too good at describing them either," I said.

At that she smiled. "Never mind. I think I have a good idea of what you mean."

"Well then, what should I do?"

She said nothing for the longest while. She seemed to be thinking of something else entirely. Five dishes lay empty on the table, a constellation of five extinct planets.

"Listen," she ended the silence, "I think we ought to become friends. That is, of course, if it's all right with you."

"Of course it's all right with me," I said.

"And I mean very close friends," she said.

I nodded.

So it was we became very close friends. Not thirty minutes after we'd first met.

"As a close friend, there're a couple things I want to ask you," I said.

"Go right ahead."

"First of all, why is it you don't show your ears? Second, have your ears ever exerted any special power over anyone besides me?"

Without a word, she trained her eyes on her hands resting on the table.

"Some, yes," she said quietly.

"Some?"

"Sure. But to put it another way, I'm more accustomed to the self who doesn't show her ears."

"Which is to say that the you when you show your ears is different from the you when you don't show your ears."

"Right enough."

Two waiters cleared away our dishes and brought the soup.

"Would you mind telling me about the you who shows her ears."

"That's so long ago I doubt I can tell it very well. The truth is, I haven't shown my ears once since I was twenty."

"But when you did that modeling job, you showed your ears, didn't you?"

"Yes," she said, "but not my real ears."

"Not your real ears?"

"Those were blocked ears."

I had two spoonfuls of soup and looked up at her.

"Tell me more about your 'blocked ears.'"

"Blocked ears are dead ears. I killed my own ears. That is, I consciously cut off the passageway. . . . Do you follow me?"

No, I didn't follow her.

"Ask me, then," she said.

"By killing your ears, do you mean you made yourself deaf?"

"No, I can hear quite fine. But even so, my ears are dead. You can probably do it too."

She set her soupspoon back down, straightened her back, raised her shoulders two inches, thrust her jaw full out, held that posture for all of ten seconds, and suddenly dropped her shoulders.

"There. My ears are dead. Now you try."

Three times I repeated the movements she'd made. Slowly, carefully, but nothing left me with the impression that my ears had died. The wine was rapidly circulating through my system.

"I do believe that my ears aren't dying properly," I said, disappointed.

She shook her head. "That's okay. If your ears don't need to die, there's nothing wrong with them not dying."

"May I ask you something else?"

"Go right ahead."

"If I add up everything you've told me, it seems to come down to this: that up to age twenty you showed your ears. Then one day you hid your ears. And from that day on, not once have you shown your ears. But at such times that you must show your ears, you block off the passageway between your ears and your consciousness. Is that correct?"

A winsome smile came to her face. "That is correct."

"What happened to your ears at age twenty?"

"Don't rush things," she said, reaching her right hand across the table, lightly touching the fingers of my left hand. "Please."

I poured out the rest of the wine into our glasses and slowly drank mine.

"First, I want to know more about you," she started.

"What about me?"

"Everything. How you were brought up, how old you are, what you do for a living, stuff like that."

"It's your ordinary story. So utterly ordinary, you'd probably doze off in the middle of it."

"I like ordinary stories."

"Mine is the kind of ordinary story no one could possibly enjoy."

"That's okay, give me ten minutes' worth."

"I was born in 1948, on December twenty-fourth, Christmas Eve. Now Christmas Eve doesn't make a very good birthday. I mean, you don't get separate birthday and Christmas presents. Everyone figures they save money that way. My sign is Capricorn and my blood type is A—a perfect combination for bank tellers and civil servants. I'm not supposed to get along well with Sagittarians and Libras and Aquarians. A boring life, don't you think?"

"I'm fascinated."

"I grew up in an ordinary little town, went to an ordinary school. I was a quiet child, but grew into a bored kid. I met this ordinary girl, had an ordinary first romance. When I was eighteen, I came to Tokyo to go to college. When I got out of college, a friend and I set up a small translation service, and somehow we scraped by. Three years ago, we branched out into P.R. newsletters and advertising-related work, and that's going fairly well. I got involved with one of the women who worked at the firm. We got married four years back and got divorced two months ago. No one reason I can put it all down to. I have an old tomcat for a pet. Smoke forty cigarettes a day. Can't seem to quit. I own three suits, six neckties, plus a collection of five hundred records that are hopelessly out of style. I've memorized all the murderers' names in every Ellery Queen mystery ever written. I own the complete A *la recherche du temps perdus*, but have only read half. I drink beer in summer, whiskey in winter."

"And two days out of three you eat omelettes and sandwiches in bars, right?"

"Uh-huh," I said.

"What an interesting life."

"It's been boring so far. It'll probably be the same from here on.

Not that that bothers me. I mean, I take what I get."

I looked at my watch. Nine minutes, twenty seconds.

"But what you've just told me isn't everything, no?"

I gazed at my hands on the table. "Of course that's not everything. There's no telling every last thing about someone's life, no matter how boring."

"May I comment?"

"Certainly."

"Whenever I meet people for the first time, I get them to talk for ten minutes. Then I size them up from the exact opposite perspective of all they've told me. Do you think that's crazy?"

"No," I said, shaking my head, "I'd guess your method works quite well."

A waiter came, set the table with new plates, onto which another waiter served the entrée, topped with sauce by still another waiter. A quick double play, shortstop to second, second to first.

"Applying this method to you, I've learned one thing," she said, putting the knife to her sole mousse. "That yours is not a boring life, nor are you one to seek a boring life. Am I off base?"

"Maybe not. Maybe my life isn't boring, maybe I don't really seek a boring life. But effectively it's the same thing. Either way I've already got what's coming. Most people, they're trying to escape from boredom, but I'm trying to get into the thick of boredom. That's why I'm not complaining when I say my life is boring. It was enough to make my wife bail out, though."

"Is that why you and your wife split up?"

"Like I said before, there's no one thing I can put it all down to. But as Nietzsche said, 'The gods furl their flags at boredom.' Or something like that."

We took our time eating. She had seconds on the sauce, and I had extra bread. Then our plates were cleared away, we had blueberry sorbet, and about the time they came out with espresso I lit up a cigarette. The smoke drifted about only a short while before it was discreetly whisked away by the noiseless ventilation system.

People had begun to take their places at other tables. A Mozart concerto played from the overhead speakers.

"I'd like to ask you more about your ears, if I may," I said.

"You want to ask whether or not my ears possess some special power?"

I nodded.

"That is something you'd have to check for yourself," she said. "If I were to tell you anything, it might not be of any interest to you. Might even cramp your style."

I nodded once more.

"For you, I'll show my ears," she said, after finishing her espresso. "But I don't know if it will really be to your benefit. You might end up regretting it."

"How's that?"

"Your boredom might not be as hard-core as you think."

"That's a chance I'll have to take," I said.

She reached out across the table and put her hand on mine. "One more thing: for the time being—say, the next few months—don't leave my side. Okay?"

"Sure."

With that, she pulled a black hairband out of her handbag. Holding it between her lips, she pulled her hair back with both hands, gave it one full twist, and swiftly tied it back.

"Well?"

I swallowed my breath and gazed at her, transfixed. My mouth went dry. From no part of me could I summon a voice. For an instant, the white plaster wall seemed to ripple. The voices of the other diners and the clinking of their dinnerware grew faint, then once again returned to normal. I heard the sound of waves, recalled the scent of a long-forgotten evening. Yet all this was but a mere fragment of the sensations passing through me in those few hundredths of a second.

"Exquisite," I managed to squeeze out. "I can't believe you're the same human being."

"See what I mean?" she said.

5

Unblocked Ears

See what I mean?" she said.

She'd become so beautiful, it defied understanding. Never had I feasted my eyes on such beauty. Beauty of a variety I'd never imagined existed. As expansive as the entire universe, yet as dense as a glacier. Unabashedly excessive, yet at the same time pared down to an essence. It transcended all concepts within the boundaries of my awareness. She was at one with her ears, gliding down the oblique face of time like a protean beam of light.

"You're extraordinary," I said, after catching my breath.

"I know," she said. "These are my ears in their unblocked state."

Several of the other customers were now turned our way, staring agape at her. The waiter who came over with more espresso couldn't pour properly. Not a soul uttered a word. Only the reels on the tape deck kept slowly spinning.

She retrieved a clove cigarette from her purse and put it to her lips. I hurriedly offered her a light with my lighter.

"I want to sleep with you," she said.

So we slept together.

6

The Further Adventures of Unblocked Ears

The manifestation of her full splendor, though, I had yet to await. For the next two or three days, she exposed her ears only intermittently, then hid those marvels of creation behind her hair again and returned to ordinariness.

To her, it was as if she'd tried taking off her coat at the beginning of March. "I guess it's still not time to show my ears," she said. "I'm not entirely comfortable with them yet."

"Really, I don't mind," I said. Even with her ears covered she wasn't bad.

She'd show me her ears on occasion; mostly on sexual occasions. Sex with her with her ears exposed was an experience I'd never known. When it was raining, the smell of the rain came through crystal clear. When birds were singing, their song was a thing of sheer clarity. I'm at a loss for words, but that's what it was like.

"You don't show your ears when you sleep with other men?" I once asked her.

"Of course not," she said. "They probably don't even know I have ears."

"What's sex like for you without your ears showing?"

"A duty. Dry and tasteless, like chewing newsprint. But that's okay. Nothing bad about fulfilling a duty, you know."

"But with your ears out it's a thousand times better, isn't it?"

"Sure."

"Then you ought to show them," I said. "No need to go out of your way to put up with such dull times."

Dead serious, she stared me and said, "You don't understand anything."

For sure, there were a lot of things I didn't understand at all.

For instance, the reason why she treated me special. I couldn't for the life of me believe I might be any better or different in any way than anyone else.

But when I told her that, she only laughed.

"It's really very simple," she said. "You sought me out. That's the biggest reason."

"And supposing somebody else had sought you out?"

"At least for the present, it's you who wants me. What's more, you're loads better than you think you are."

"So why is it I get to thinking that way?" I puzzled.

"That's because you're only half-living," she said briskly. "The other half is still untapped somewhere."

"Hmm."

"In that sense, you're not unlike me. I'm sitting on my ears, and you've got only half of you that's really living. Sure seems that way, doesn't it?"

"Even if that were the case, my remaining half couldn't possibly compare to your ears."

"Maybe not," she smiled. "You wouldn't have any idea, would you?"

And with that smile in place, she lifted back her hair and unbuttoned her blouse.

That September afternoon toward summer's end, I took the day off and was lying in bed with her, stroking her hair and thinking about the whale's penis. The sea, a dark lead-gray. A brisk wind beating against the aquarium window. The lofty ceiling, the empty exhibition room. The penis severed forever from the whale, its meaning as a whale's penis irretrievably lost.

Then I gave my wife's slip one more spin-around in my thoughts. There was no real slip. Only, stuck in my head, a vague image of a slip draped over a kitchen chair. I couldn't remember what it had meant to me. Had somebody else been living my life all this time?

"Tell me, you don't wear slips, do you?" I asked my girlfriend.

She lifted her head from my shoulder and stared at me blankly.

"I don't have any."

"Umm," I said.

"But if you think you'd have a better time if I did . . ."

"No, it's not that," I quickly interjected. "That wasn't why I was asking."

"No, really, there's no need to be shy. I'm quite used to that kind of stuff from work. I wouldn't be the least bit embarrassed."

"I'm not asking for anything," I said. "Honestly, all I need is you and your ears, nothing more."

She gave a pouting shake of her head and pressed her forehead against my shoulder. Not fifteen seconds later, she looked up again.

"Listen, an important phone call is going to come through in ten minutes."

"A phone call?" I glanced over at the bedside telephone.

"That's right, the phone's going to ring."

"You can tell?"

"I can tell."

She had herself a cigarette, head resting on my chest. A moment later, her ash fell beside my navel and she pursed her lips to blow it off. I felt her ear between my fingers. It was a wonderful sensation. My head was empty with shapeless images drifting and diffusing.

"Something about sheep," she said. "Lots of sheep and one sheep in particular."

"Sheep?"

"Uh-huh," she said, handing her half-smoked cigarette to me. I took one drag, then crushed it out in an ashtray. "And that'll be the beginning of a wild adventure."

* * *

Shortly thereafter, the telephone rang. I shot her a look, but she had dozed off on my chest. I let the phone ring four times before picking up the receiver.

It was my partner. "Could you come here right away?" he said. There was an edge to his voice. "I have a terribly urgent matter to discuss with you."

"Just how urgent is it?"

"Come in and you'll find out," said he.

"Heaven knows it's got to be about sheep," I said, letting go a trial balloon. It was something I shouldn't have said. The receiver grew cold as ice.

"How did you know?" my partner asked.

The wild sheep chase had begun.

PART FOUR

A WILD SHEEP CHASE, I

7

Before the Strange Man

There are various reasons why an individual might habitually consume large quantities of alcohol, but they all effectively boil down to the same thing.

Five years ago, my business partner was a happy drunk. Three years later, he had become a moody drunk. And by last summer, he was fumbling at the knob of the door to alcoholism. As with most habitual drinkers, he was a nice-enough, regular-if-not-exactly-sharp kind of guy when sober. Everyone thought of him as a nice-enough, regular-if-not-exactly-sharp kind of guy. He thought so too. That's why he drank. Because it seemed that with alcohol in his system, he could more fully embody this idea of being that kind of guy.

Things were fine at first. But as time went on and the quantity of alcohol increased, subtle changes occurred, and these subtle changes gradually wore into a deep rut. His regularity and nice-enoughness got ahead of him, excessively so. A typical case. Typically, however, people don't think of themselves as typical cases. And not-exactly-sharp types even less so. The attempt to regain sight of what he'd lost sent him wandering in an even thicker alcoholic fog.

Still, at least for the time being, he was a regular guy until the sun went down. And since for years now I had made a conscious effort not to meet up with him after sunset, as far as I was concerned he was regular enough. Even so, I knew full well that after sunset he became not quite regular, and he himself knew it too. As neither of us would ever broach the subject, we got along the same as always. We just weren't the friends we had once been.

While I can't say I understood him one hundred percent (even seventy percent would have been doing well), for what it was worth, he had been my only friend in college, and it wasn't easy watching him deteriorate from close up. Ultimately, I guess, that's what age does.

By the time I'd get to the office he'd already had one shot of whiskey. As long as it was one shot, he could be mister regular, but there was no telling when he'd up his regular to two. When that happened, I knew we'd have to go our separate ways.

I was standing in the gust of the air conditioner, letting my sweat dry as I sipped a cool glass of barley tea. I wasn't saying anything. He wasn't saying anything. The harsh afternoon sun spilled across the linoleum floor in hallucinatory sprays. Below, on the park's expanse of greenery, people lay on the grass sunning themselves. My partner tapped at the palm of his right hand with the tip of a ballpoint pen.

"I hear you got divorced," he started.

"That was news two weeks ago," I said, still staring out the window. I took off my sunglasses, and my eyes hurt.

"So why'd you get divorced?"

"Personal reasons."

"I know that," he said. "Never heard of a divorce for other than personal reasons."

I said nothing. Didn't we have a long-standing unspoken agreement never to touch upon each other's private affairs?

"I don't mean to pry," he said, "but she was a friend of mine too. It came as a shock. I thought you two were always so close."

"We always were close. It's not like we parted on bad terms."

My partner smirked, continuing to tap the palm of his hand with the pen. He was wearing a deep-blue shirt with a black tie, hair neatly combed, cologne. While I was in a T-shirt with Snoopy carrying a surfboard, old Levi's that had been washed colorless, and dirty tennis shoes. To anyone else, he clearly was the regular one.

"You remember when she and the two of us worked together?"

"I remember very well," I said.

"Those were happy times," my partner said.

I moved away from the air conditioner, walked over to the center of the room, and dropped myself down on the plush sky-blue Swedish sofa. I extracted a filter-tip Pall Mall from the special visitors' cigarette case and lit up with the heavy tabletop lighter.

"So?" I said.

"So what I'm saying is maybe we've overextended ourselves."

"You talking about the ads and magazine work?"

My partner nodded, though it must have been hard for him to admit it. I weighed the lighter in my hand, turned the screw to adjust the flame, and felt sorry for him.

"Okay, I know what you're trying to say," I said, returning the lighter to the table, "but remember, I wasn't the one who brought in the business, and it wasn't my idea to do this work. You walked in with it. You're the one who wanted to give it a go."

"There were pressing circumstances. We had nothing . . ."

"It made money."

"Sure it made money. Let us move to a larger office and take on more staff. I got a new car, bought a condo, sent two kids to an expensive private school. Not bad for thirty years old, I suppose."

"You earned it. Nothing to be ashamed of."

"Who's ashamed?" said my partner, retrieving the ballpoint pen that had flown across his desk and taking another few pokes at the middle of his palm. "But you know, it doesn't seem real. There we were, the two of us with nothing but debts, trying to scrounge up translation work, passing out handbills down by the station."

"What's to stop us from passing out handbills now if we wanted?"

My partner looked up at me. "Hey, I'm not joking."

"Neither am I."

A silence fell between us.

"A lot of things have changed," my partner said. "The pace of our lives, our thinking. Above all, we don't even know ourselves how much we really make. A tax accountant comes in and does all that awful paperwork, with exemptions and depreciations and write-offs and what not."

"The same as everywhere else."

"I know, I know. That's what we've got to do and that's what we're doing. But it was more fun in the old days."

"*For lo the shadows of a gaol untold, Do grow about our days now many fold.*" Lines from a poem suddenly popped out of my mouth.

"How's that again?"

"Nothing, sorry. You were saying?"

"I just feel like we're engaged in some kind of exploitation."

"Exploitation?" I looked up in surprise.

There were two yards between us, and with the different heights of our seats his head rose ten inches above mine. A lithograph hung behind him. A new lithograph I'd not seen before, of a fish with wings. The fish didn't look too happy about its wings. Probably wasn't sure how to use them either.

"Exploitation?" I muttered to myself.

"Exploitation."

"And who, pray tell, is doing the exploiting?"

"Different interests, little by little."

I crossed my legs on the sky-blue sofa and fixed my gaze at the drama of his hand and ballpoint pen, now exactly at eye level.

"In any case, don't you think we've changed?" asked my partner.

"We're still the same. Not anyone or anything has changed."

"You really think so?"

"I really do. Exploitation doesn't exist. It's a fairy tale. Even you don't believe that Salvation Army trumpets can actually save the world, do you? I think you think too much."

"Well all right, maybe I do think too much," my partner said. "Last week you—I mean we—wrote the copy for that margarine ad. And it wasn't bad copy. It went over real well. But tell me, have you eaten margarine even once in the past couple years?"

"No, I hate margarine."

"Same here. That's what I mean. At the very least, in the old days we did work we believed in, and we took pride in it. There's none of that now. We're just tossing out fluff."

"Margarine is good for you. It's vegetable fat, low in cholesterol. It guards against heart problems, and lately it doesn't taste bad. It's cheap and keeps well too."

"So eat the stuff."

I sank back into the sofa, stretching out my arms and legs.

"It doesn't matter," I said. "It's the same whether we eat margarine or don't. Dull translation jobs or fraudulent copy, it's basically the same. Sure we're tossing out fluff, but tell me, where does anyone deal in words with substance? C'mon now, there's no honest work anywhere. Just like there's no honest breathing or honest pissing."

"You were more innocent in the old days."

"Maybe so," I said, crushing out a cigarette in the ashtray. "And no doubt there's an innocent town somewhere where an innocent butcher slices innocent ham. So if you think that drinking whiskey from the middle of the morning is innocent, go ahead and drink as much as you want."

The room was treated to an extended pen-on-desktop staccato solo.

"Sorry, I didn't mean to say that."

"That's okay," said my partner. "I certainly can't deny it."

The air conditioner thermostat made a funny noise. This was a terribly quiet afternoon.

"Have some confidence in yourself," I said. "Haven't we made it this far on our own? With just the two of us. The only thing that separates us from all those precious success stories is they have backers and titles."

"And to think we used to be friends," said my partner.

"We're still friends," I said. "We've come all this way together."

"I didn't want to see you get divorced."

"I know," I said. "But what do you say we start talking about sheep?"

He nodded. He placed the ballpoint pen back in its tray and rubbed his eyes.

"It was eleven o'clock this morning when the man came," my partner began.

8

Now the Strange Man

It was eleven o'clock in the morning when the man came. Now there are two types of eleven-in-the-mornings for a small-scale company like ours. That is, either absolutely busy or absolutely unbusy. Nothing in between. So at eleven A.M. we are either mindlessly working up a flurry or we are mindlessly daydreaming. In-between tasks, should there be such an animal, we set aside for the afternoon.

It was the latter sort of eleven A.M. when the man came. And a monumentally unbusy one at that. The first half of September had been insane, and then work fell flat off. Three of us took a month-delayed summer vacation, but even so the rest of the crew had been consigned to an agenda of pencil sharpening and other exciting tasks. My partner himself had stepped out to the bank to get a money draft, while someone else had repaired to the neighboring audio-equipment showroom to listen to new record releases. The secretary was left to answer the telephone as she thumbed through the "Autumn Hairstyles" pages of a women's magazine.

The man opened the door to the office without a sound, and he closed it without a sound. Not that he made any conscious effort to move quietly. It was second nature to him. So much so the secretary had no awareness whatsoever of him. The man was all the way to her desk and peering down at her before she noticed him.

"There is a matter I would like to take up with your employer," said the man. He spoke as if running a white-gloved hand over a tabletop.

What could have happened to bring him here? She looked up at the man. His eyes were too piercing for a business client, his attire too fastidious for a tax inspector, his air too intellectual for a policeman. Yet she could think of nothing else he could be. This man, a refined piece of bad news now hovering over her, had materialized out of nowhere.

"I'm afraid he's stepped out at the moment," she said, slapping her magazine shut. "He said he'd be back in another thirty minutes."

"I'll wait," pronounced the man without a moment's hesitation. A foregone conclusion, it seemed.

She wondered whether to ask his name. She decided against it and simply conducted him to the reception area. The man took a seat on the sky-blue sofa, crossed his legs, peered up at the electric wall clock directly before him, and froze in position. He moved not an iota. When she brought him a glass of barley tea a bit later, he was in the exact same pose.

"Right where you're sitting now," my partner said. "He sat there staring at the clock in the same position for a full thirty minutes."

I looked at the sofa where I was sitting, then looked up at the wall clock, then I looked back at my partner.

Despite the unusually hot late-September weather outside, the man was rather formally dressed. Impeccably. His white shirt cuffs protruded precisely two-thirds of an inch from the sleeves of his well-tailored black suit. His subtly toned striped tie, accented with a hint of asymmetry, was positioned with the utmost care. His black shoes were buffed to a fine gloss.

Mid-thirties to forty in age, five foot ten plus in height, trimmed of every last ounce of fat, slender hands without telltale wrinkles.

His long fingers suggested nothing so much as a troop of animals that had retained deep primal memories despite long years of training and control. His fingernails were meticulously manicured, a clean, perfect arc at the end of each fingertip. Truly beautiful hands, if somehow unsettling. They bespoke a high degree of specialization in some rarefied field—but what that field might be was anyone's guess.

His face was even harder to figure. It was a straightforward face, but expressionless, a blank slate. His nose and eyes were angular, as if scored with a paper knife in afterthought, his lips bloodless and thin. He was lightly tanned, though clearly not from the pleasures of the beach or the tennis court. That tan could only have been the result of some unknown sun shining in some unknown sky.

The thirty minutes passed very slowly. Coldly, solidly, rigidly. By the time my partner returned from the bank, the atmosphere in the room had grown noticeably heavy. You might even say everything in the room seemed practically nailed down to the floor.

"Of course, it only seemed that way," said my partner.

"Of course," said I.

The lone secretary was worn out from nervousness. Bewildered, my partner went over to the reception area and introduced himself as the manager. Only then did the man unfreeze, whereupon he pulled a thin cigarette out of his pocket, lit it, and with a pained expression blew out a puff of smoke. The atmosphere lightened ever so slightly.

"We don't have much time, so let's keep this short," said the man in a hush. Out of his wallet he flicked a name card sharp enough to cut your fingers with and placed it on the table. The name card was hermetically laminated, unnaturally white, and printed with tiny, intensely black type. No title or affiliation, no address, no telephone number. Only the name. It was enough to hurt your eyes just looking at it. My partner turned it over, saw that the back was entirely blank, glanced at the front side again, then looked back at the man.

"You are familiar with the party's name, I trust?" said the man.

"I am."

The man advanced his chin a few hundredths of an inch and nodded curtly. His line of vision did not shift in the least. "Burn it, please."

"Burn it?" My partner stared dumbfounded at the man.

"That name card. Burn it. Now," the man spoke sharply.

My partner hurriedly picked up the tabletop lighter and set fire to a corner of the name card. He held it by its edge until half of it had burned, then laid it in the large crystal ashtray. The two of them watched it as it burned. By the time the name card was white ash, the room was shrouded in a ponderous silence such as follows a massacre.

"I come here bearing the total authority of that party," said the man, breaking the silence at length. "Which is to say that everything I say from this point on represents that party's total volition and wishes."

"Wishes . . . ," mouthed my partner.

" 'To wish,' an elegant word to express a basic position toward a specified objective. Of course," said the man, "there are other methods of expressing the same thing. You understand, do you not?"

My partner did a quick mental translation. "I understand."

"Notwithstanding, this is neither a conceptual issue nor a political deal; this is strictly a business proposition." *Bizness*, the man enunciated, which marked him as a foreign-born Japanese; most Japanese Japanese will say *biji*ness.

"You are a *biz*nessman and I am a *biz*nessman," he went on. "Realistically, there should be nothing between us to discuss but *biz*ness. Let us leave discussions regarding the unrealistic to others. Are we agreed?"

"Certainly," said my partner.

"It is rather our role to take what unrealistic factors that exist and to work them into a more sophisticated form that might be grounded in the grand scheme of reality. The doings of men run to unrealities. Why is that?" the man asked, rhetorically. He fingered the green stone ring on the middle finger of his left hand. "Because it appears simpler. Added to which, there are circumstances whereby unreality contrives to create an impression that overwhelms reality. Nevertheless, business has no place in the world of unreality. In other words," the man said, continuing to finger his ring, "we are a breed whose very existence consists in the rechanneling of difficulties. Therefore, should anything I say from this point forward demand difficult labors or decisions of you, I ask your forbearance. Such is the nature of things."

My partner was utterly lost now, but he nodded anyway.

"Very well then, I shall state the wishes of the party concerned. Number one, it is wished that you cease publication of the public relations bulletin you produce for the 'P' Life Insurance Company."

"But—"

"Number two," the man interrupted, "it is wished that an interview be arranged with the person actually responsible for the production of this page."

Pulling a white envelope from his pocket, the man extracted a sheet of paper neatly folded in quarters and handed it to my partner. My partner unfolded the sheet of paper. Sure enough, it was a copy of a photograph for a P.R. bulletin that our office had done. An ordinary photograph of an idyllic Hokkaido landscape—clouds and mountains and grassy pastures and sheep, superimposed with lines of an undistinguished pastoral verse. That was all.

"While our wishes are herewith two, as regards the first of these, it is less a wish than a fait accompli. To be more precise, a decision has already been reached in accordance with our wishes. Should you have any doubts, please call the public relations head of the life insurance company."

"I see," said my partner.

"Nonetheless, we can easily imagine that for a company the size of yours, damages incurred by inconvenience such as this could be sizable. Fortunately, we are in a position—as you are no doubt aware—to wield no small degree of influence in this arena. Therefore, upon compliance with our second wish, granted that the person responsible gives us a report complete to our satisfaction, we are prepared to recompense you fully for your loss. Probably more than recompense, I would think."

Silence prevailed.

"If you should fail to comply with our wishes," said the man, "you will have no occupation in this or any other field, and henceforth, the world will hold no place for you, ever."

Again silence.

"Have you any questions?"

"So, uh, it's the photo that's the problem?" my partner stammered.

"Yes," said the man, choosing his words carefully, as if sorting through options on an outstretched palm. "Such is indeed the case. However, I am not at liberty to discuss the matter any further with you. I have not that authority."

"I will phone the man you want to see. He should be here by three o'clock," said my partner.

"Excellent," said the man, glancing at his wristwatch. "I shall send a car here for him at four o'clock. Now this is important: you must speak of this to absolutely no one. Is that understood?"

Whereupon the two of them parted in a most *biz*nesslike manner.

9

"The Boss"

That's the size of it," said my partner.

"I can't make head or tail of it," said I, an unlit cigarette at my lips. "First of all, I have no idea who the person on the name card is. Second, I can't imagine why he would get so upset about a photo of sheep. And last, I don't understand how he could put a stop to a publication of ours."

"The person on the name card is a major right-wing figure. His name and face are almost never publicized, so he's not widely known, but you're probably the only one in our line of work who doesn't know who he is."

"Dumb to the world, that's me," was my feeble excuse.

"He's right wing, but not the so-called right wing. Or you could say, not even right wing."

"You're losing me."

"The truth of the matter is no one knows what he thinks. He has no writings to his name, doesn't make speeches in public. He never gives interviews, is never photographed. It's not even certain he's alive. Five years back, a magazine reporter got a scoop implicating him in some shady investment deals, but the story never saw the light of day."

"Been doing your homework, I see."

"I knew the reporter personally."

I picked up the lighter and lit my cigarette. "What's the reporter doing nowadays?"

"Got transferred to administration. Files forms morning to night. Mass media is a surprisingly small world, and he made a fine example. Like a skull posted at the entrance to an African village."

"Gotcha," I said.

"But we do know something of the man's prewar background. He was born in Hokkaido in 1913, came to Tokyo after graduating from normal school, changed jobs repeatedly, and drifted to the right. He was imprisoned once, I believe. Upon his release, he was sent to Manchuria, where he fell in with the upper echelons of the Kanto Army and became party to some plot. Not much is known about the organization behind it, but he suddenly becomes a mysterious figure around this time. Rumor has it he was dealing in drugs, which may well have been true. He plundered his way all over the Chinese mainland only to board a destroyer two weeks before the Soviet troops arrived, beating a quick retreat back to Japan. In his booty—a huge, nearly inexhaustible stash of gold and silver."

"He had, you might say, uncanny timing," I threw in.

"For a fact. Our man had a real knack for seizing the moment. He'd learned instinctively when to go on the attack and when to withdraw. Plus his eyes were always trained on the right thing. Even when he was incarcerated by the Occupation forces as a Class A war criminal, his trial was cut short midway and never reconvened. For reasons of health, ostensibly, but the facts get a little fuzzy here. More likely, a deal was worked out with the Americans, what with MacArthur looking toward the Chinese mainland."

My partner pulled another ballpoint pen out of the pencil tray and twirled it between his fingers.

"When he was released fi. m Sugamo Prison, he took half his stash and put an entire faction of the conservative party on his payroll. The other half went to buying up the advertising industry. Note that this was back when advertising wasn't anything but cheap handbills."

"The gift of foresight. But weren't there claims about concealment of funds?"

"Nothing of the kind. Remember he'd bought out an entire faction of the conservatives."

"Ah."

"In any case, he used his money to corner the market on both politics *and* advertising, setting up a power base that thrives to this day. He never surfaces because he doesn't need to. So long as he keeps a grip on certain centers of political authority and on the core sectors of the public relations industry, there's nothing he can't do. Do you have any idea what it means to hold down advertising?"

"I guess not."

"To hold down advertising is to have nearly the entire publishing and broadcasting industries under your thumb. There's not a branch of publishing or broadcasting that doesn't depend in some way on advertising. It'd be like an aquarium without water. Why, ninety-five percent of the information that reaches you has already been preselected and paid for."

"There's something I still don't understand," I said. "I follow you as far as our man having the information industries in the palm of his hand, but how does that extend to his putting the clamps on a life insurance company's P.R. bulletin? That didn't even pass through the hands of any major rep. That was a direct contract."

My partner coughed, then drank down the last of his now-lukewarm barley tea. "Stocks. They're his principle source of revenue. Manipulating the market, forcing hands, takeovers, the works. His newsboys gather all the necessary information, and he picks and chooses according to his fancy. Only a minuscule slice of what really goes on ever hits the wires. All the other news is set aside for the Boss. No overt pressuring, of course, but things do get awfully close to blackmail at times. And if blackmail doesn't work, he sends word around to his politicos to go prime a few pumps."

"Every company's got to have a weak point or two."

"Every company's got a secret it doesn't want exploded right in the middle of the annual shareholders' meeting. In most cases, they'll listen to the word handed down. In sum, the Boss sits squarely on top of a trilateral power base of politicians, information services, and the stock market. So as you can probably surmise, it's as easy for him to rub out one P.R. bulletin and put us out of business as it is to shell a hardboiled egg."

"Hmm, then tell me why should such a major fixture get so heated up over one landscape photo of Hokkaido?"

"A very good question," said my partner. "I was just about to ask you the same thing."

I could only shrug.

"So tell me, how did you know all this had to do with sheep?" my partner asked. "Is something funny going on behind my back?"

"Nameless elves out in the woods have been busy at the spinning wheel."

"Care to run that by me again?

"Sixth sense."

"Give me a break," my partner sighed. "Well anyway, let me fill you in on the latest two developments. Just to snoop around a bit, I phoned up that ex-reporter at the monthly. Word has it that the Boss is down for the count with a brain hemorrhage, but it hasn't been officially confirmed yet. The other piece of news concerns the man who came in here. He turns out to be the Boss's personal secretary, his number two, the guy he entrusts with actually running the organization. Japanese-American, Stanford graduate, been working for the Boss for twelve years. He's something of a mystery man himself. Undoubtedly got a head on his shoulders. That's about all I could find out."

"Thanks," I said, meaning it.

"You're welcome," said my partner without even glancing my way.

Any way you looked at it, when my partner wasn't drinking he was far more of a regular guy than I was. He was more innocent and more considerate and more organized in his thinking. But sooner or later he'd get himself drunk. Not a comforting thought: that my betters could fall to pieces before me.

As soon as my partner left the room, I pulled the whiskey bottle out of his drawer and had myself a drink.

10

Counting Sheep

We can, if we so choose, wander aimlessly over the continent of the arbitrary. Rootless as some winged seed blown about on a serendipitous spring breeze.

Nonetheless, we can in the same breath deny that there is any such thing as coincidence. What's done is done, what's yet to be is clearly yet to be, and so on. In other words, sandwiched as we are between the "everything" that is behind us and the "zero" beyond us, ours is a ephemeral existence in which there is neither coincidence nor possibility.

In actual practice, however, distinctions between the two interpretations amount to precious little. A state of affairs (as with most face-offs between interpretations) not unlike calling the same food by two different names.

So much for metaphors.

My placing a photo of sheep in the life insurance company's P.R. bulletin can be seen from one perspective, (a), as coincidence, but from another perspective, (b), as no coincidence at all.

(a) I was looking for a suitable photo for the P.R. bulletin. By coincidence, I happened to have a photo of sheep in my drawer. I decided to use that photograph. An innocent photograph in an innocent world.

(b) The photo of the sheep in my desk drawer had been waiting for me all this time. If not for use in that bulletin, then for something else at some later date.

Come to think of it, these formulas apply across the board to everything I've experienced thus far in life. With a little practice, I'm sure I'd be able to conduct, (a), a life with my right hand and, (b), a life with my left. Not that it matters much. It's like doughnut holes. Whether you take a doughnut hole as blank space or as an entity unto itself is a purely metaphysical question and does not affect the taste of the doughnut one bit.

Sitting on the sofa drinking whiskey, blown on softly by the air conditioner like a dandelion seed wafted along on a pleasant breeze, I stared at the electric wall clock. As long as I stared at the clock, at least the world remained in motion. Not a very consequential world, but in motion nonetheless. And as long as I knew the world was still in motion, I knew I existed. Not a very consequential existence, but an existence nonetheless. It struck me as wanting that someone should confirm his own existence only by the hands of an electric wall clock. There had to be a more cognitive means of confirmation. But try as I might, nothing less facile came to mind.

I gave up and had another sip of whiskey. A burning sensation passed through my throat, traveled down the wall of my esophagus and into the pit of my stomach. Outside the window, a bright blue summer sky and billowing white clouds. A beautiful if secondhand sky showing telltale signs of wear. I took another sip of whiskey to toast the brand-new sky it once was. Not bad Scotch. Not a bad sky either, once you got used to it. A jumbo jet traversed the sky from left to right like some gleaming beetle.

I had polished off my second whiskey when it came to me: what the hell was I doing here?

What the hell was I thinking about?

Sheep.

I got up from the sofa, picked up the copy of the photo from my partner's desk, and returned to the sofa. For twenty seconds, I stared at it, sucking on the whiskey-tinged ice cubes, racking my brain to figure out what was going on in it.

The photo showed a flock of sheep on a grassy meadow. On one edge, the meadow adjoined a birch wood. Huge birch trees of the kind you find up in Hokkaido, not the puny stunted variety that flank the entrance to your neighborhood dentist's office. These were birches that four bears could have sharpened their claws on simultaneously. Given the foliage, the season was probably spring. Snow lingered on the mountain peaks in the background, in the folds of the mountainside as well. April or May. When the ground is slushy with melting snow. The sky was blue (or rather what I took for blue from the monochrome photo-gray—it could have been salmon pink for all I knew), with light white clouds drawn across the mountaintops. All things considered, the flock of sheep could only be taken for a flock of sheep, the birch wood only for a birch wood, the white clouds only for white clouds. Simply that and nothing more.

I tossed the photograph on the table, smoked a cigarette, and yawned. Then picking the photo up again, I tried counting the sheep. The meadow was so vast, the sheep scattered in patches like picnickers, that it was hard to tell whether those white specks off in the distance were sheep or just white specks. And the closer I looked, the harder it was to tell whether the white specks were actually white specks or my eyes playing tricks with me, until finally I could be sure of nothing. I took a ballpoint pen in hand and marked everything I could be sure was a sheep. The count came to thirty-two. Thirty-two sheep. A perfectly straightforward photograph. Nothing unusual about the composition, nothing particular in the way of style.

Yet there was something there. Something funny. I suppose I sensed it the first time I saw the photo three months before, and now the feeling was back.

I rolled over on the sofa and, holding the photo above my head, I went through the count once more.

Thirty-three.

Thirty-three?

I shut my eyes and shook my head. My mind was a blank. I tried counting sheep one last time, then drifted into a deep two-whiskey-afternoon sleep. The last thing I remember thinking about was my girlfriend's ears.

11

The Limo and Its Driver

The car came at four, as promised. Exactly on the dot, like a cuckoo clock. The secretary shook me awake from my deep slumber. Whereupon I went to the washroom and splashed water on my face. My drowsiness wasn't budging in the least. I yawned three times in the elevator on the way down. Yawns you could have built a lawsuit on. But who was there to do the suing? Who was there to be sued but myself?

Looming there in front of the entrance to our building was a giant submarine of a limousine. An impoverished family could have lived under the hood of that car, it was so big. The windows were opaque blue, reflective glass so you couldn't see in. The body was an awesome black, with not a smudge, not on the bumper, not on the hubcaps.

Standing alertly by the limo was a middle-aged chauffeur wearing a spotless white shirt and orange tie. A real chauffeur. I had but to approach him, and without a word he opened the car door. His eyes followed me until I was properly seated, then he closed the door. He climbed into the driver's seat and closed the door after himself. All without any more sound than flipping over a playing card. And sitting in this limo, compared to my fifteen-year-old

Volkswagen Beetle I'd bought off a friend, was as quiet as sitting at the bottom of a lake wearing earplugs.

The car interior was fitted out to the hilt. You might expect this in a limousine, but while the taste of most so-called luxury accessories is questionable, there was nothing questionable here. In the middle of my sofa-like seat was a chic push-button telephone, next to which were arranged a silver cigarette case, a lighter, an ashtray. Molded into the back of the driver's seat was a small folding desk. The air conditioning was unobtrusive and natural, the carpeting sumptuous.

Before I knew it, the limo was in motion, like a washtub gliding over a sea of mercury. The sum of money sunk into this baby must have been staggering.

"Shall I put on some music?" asked the chauffeur.

"Something relaxing, maybe."

"Very good, sir."

The chauffeur reached down below his seat, selected a cassette tape, and touched a switch in the dashboard. A peaceful cello sonata seemed to flow out of nowhere. An unobjectionable score, unobjectionable fidelity.

"They always send you to meet people in this car?" I asked.

"That is correct," answered the chauffeur cautiously. "Lately, that is all I do."

"I see."

"Originally this limousine was reserved exclusively for the Boss," said the chauffeur shortly after, his previous reserve wearing off. "However, his condition being what it is this spring, he does not venture out much. Yet what point could there be to letting this car sit there? As I am sure you realize, an automobile must be driven regularly or its performance drops off."

"Of course," I said. Apparently, then, it was no organizational secret that the Boss was in ill health. I took a cigarette out of the cigarette case, examined it, held it up to my nose. A specially made plain-cut cigarette without a brand, an aroma akin to that of Russian tobacco. I debated whether to smoke it or slip it into my pocket, but in the end merely put it back. Engraved in the center of the lighter and cigarette case was an intricately patterned emblem. A sheep emblem.

A sheep?

I shook my head and closed my eyes. All this was beyond me. It seemed that ever since the sheep photo came into my life, things had begun to escape me.

"How much longer till we get there?" I asked.

"Thirty or forty minutes, depending on the traffic."

"Then maybe you could turn down the air conditioning a bit? I'd like to catch the end of an afternoon nap."

"Most certainly, sir."

The chauffeur adjusted the air conditioning, then flicked a switch on the dashboard. A thick panel of glass slid up, sealing the passenger compartment off from the driver's seat. I was enveloped in near total silence, save for the quiet strains of Bach, but by this point, hardly anything surprised me. I buried my forehead into the backseat and dozed off.

I dreamed about a dairy cow. Rather nice and small this cow, the type that looked like she'd been through a lot. We passed each other on a big bridge. It was a pleasant spring afternoon. The cow was carrying an old electric fan in one hoof, and I asked whether she wouldn't sell it to me cheap.

"I don't have much money," I said. Really, I didn't.

"Well then," said the cow, "I might trade it to you for a pair of pliers."

Not a bad deal. So the cow and I went home together, and I turned the house upside down looking for the pliers. But they were nowhere to be found.

"Odd," I said, "they were here just yesterday."

I had just brought a chair over so I could get up and look on top of the cabinet when the chauffeur tapped me on the shoulder. "We're here," he said succinctly.

The car door opened and the waning light of a summer afternoon fell across my face. Thousands of cicadas were singing at a high pitch like the winding of a clockspring. There was the rich smell of earth.

I got out of the limo, stretched, and took a deep breath. I prayed that there wasn't some kind of symbolism to the dream.

12

Wherefore the Worm Universe

There are symbolic dreams—dreams that symbolize some reality. Then there are symbolic realities—realities that symbolize a dream. Symbols are what you might call the honorary town councillors of the worm universe. In the worm universe, there is nothing unusual about a dairy cow seeking a pair of pliers. A cow is bound to get her pliers sometime. It has nothing to do with me.

Yet the fact that the cow chose me to obtain her pliers changes everything. This plunges me into a whole universe of alternative considerations. And in this universe of alternative considerations, the major problem is that everything becomes protracted and complex. I ask the cow, "Why do you want pliers?" And the cow answers, "I'm really hungry." So I ask, "Why do you need pliers if you're hungry?" The cow answers, "To attach them to branches of the peach tree." I ask, "Why a peach tree?" To which the cow replies, "Well, that's why I traded away my fan, isn't it?" And so on and so forth. The thing is never resolved, I begin to resent the cow, and the cow begins to resent me. That's a worm's eye view of its universe. The only way to get out of that worm universe is to dream another symbolic dream.

The place where that enormous four-wheeled vehicle transported me this September afternoon was surely the epicenter of the worm universe. In other words, my prayer had been denied.

I took a look around me and held my breath. Here was the stuff of breath taking.

The limo was parked on a high hill. Behind us was the gravel road which we'd come on, trailing away in an all-too-picturesque course of twists and turns to the front gate off in the distance. Probably, at a leisurely pace, a solid fifteen minutes' walk away. Lining either side of the road stood cedars and mercury-vapor lights, stationed like pencil holders at equal intervals. Clinging to each cedar trunk were innumerable cicadas screeching feverishly, as if the end of the world were at hand.

Each row of cedars bordered on neatly mowed turf, which sloped down in banks dotted with azaleas and hydrangeas and other plants beyond my powers of identification. A flock of starlings rushed, en masse, left and right across the lawn, like the aimless migration of a sand dune.

Stone steps led down both sides of the hill: the steps to the left descended to a Japanese garden with a stone lantern and a pond, the steps to the right opened onto a small golf course. At the edge of the golf course was a gazebo the color of rum raisin, and across from it stood a classical Greek statue in stone. Beyond was an enormous garage where a different chauffeur was hosing down a different limousine. I couldn't tell the make, but it wasn't a used Volkswagen.

I folded my arms and took another look around me. An impeccable garden vista, to be sure, but oh, what a sight.

"And where is the mailbox?" I asked impertinently. I mean somebody had to go to fetch the paper every morning and evening.

"The mailbox is by the back gate," said the chauffeur. A sudden revelation. Of course there had to be a back gate.

Having concluded my viewing of the grounds, I turned straight ahead and found myself facing a massive, towering structure.

It was—how shall I put it?—a painfully solitary building. Let me explain. Say we have a concept. It goes without saying that there will be slight exceptions to that norm. Now, over time these exceptions spread like stains until finally they form a separate concept. To which other exceptions crop up. It was that kind of building, some ancient life-form that had evolved blindly, toward who knows what end.

In its first incarnation, it seems to have been a Meiji-era Western-style manor. A high-ceilinged portico offered entrance to a two-story cream-colored house. The windows tall and double-hung in the true old style, the paint redone time and again. The roof was, as expected, copper-shingled, and the rain gutters as solid as a Roman aqueduct. A fine house in itself, exuding a period charm.

But then some joker of an architect came along to attach another wing of the same style and color scheme onto the right side of the original structure. The intention wasn't bad, but the effect was unpalatable. Like serving sherbet and broccoli on the same silver platter.

This unhappy combination stood untouched for several decades until someone added a stone tower off to one side. At the pinnacle of this tower was affixed a decorative lightning rod. A mistake. Lightning was meant to strike the building and burn it down.

Now a walkway covered by a solemn roof linked the tower directly to yet another wing. This wing was a separate entity once again, though it at least carried through a unified theme. The "mutual opposition of ideologies," shall we call it. It bespoke a certain pathos, rather like the mule who, placed between two identical buckets of fodder, dies of starvation trying to decide which to eat first.

To the left of the original structure, no less antithetical to the multiple elements already there, sprawled a traditional one-story Japanese-style villa. With marvelous hallways planked straight out like bowling lanes, surrounded with hedges and well-trained pines.

This triple-feature-plus-coming-attractions mélange of a house perched atop the hill was not a common sight. Had it been someone's grand scheme constructed over many years in an effort to shake off a stupor or chase away sleep, then it was an admirable success. Needless to say, an unlikely supposition. The monstrosity stood simply for money, piles of it, to which a long line of second-rate talents, era after era, had availed themselves.

I must have been staring at this apparition a while before I noticed the chauffeur next to me, looking at his watch. A pose he looked somehow accustomed to. He'd probably stood in that same spot with any number of persons he'd driven there. All of whom had gawked at the surroundings in exactly the same way.

"View all you care to, sir. Please do take your time," he said. "We still have eight minutes free."

"It sure is big," I said, for want of anything less inappropriate to say.

"Ninety-six thousand six-hundred seventy-one square feet," said the chauffeur.

"Wouldn't surprise me if you had an active volcano in the place," I laughed, trying to inject some levity. But the joke didn't register. No one joked here.

Thus passed eight minutes.

I was conducted through the entryway to a large Western-style room on the immediate right. The ceiling, framed with elaborately carved moldings, was extraordinarily high. There was a handsome antique sofa and tea table, and on the wall a still life, the epitome of realism. Apples and a flower vase and a knife. Maybe the idea was to crack open the apples with the vase, then peel them with the knife. Seeds and cores could go in the vase.

The windows were appointed with thick curtains over lace curtains, pulled to the side with sashes of the same material. Through the opening between the curtains, a relatively sedate section of the gardens could be seen. The oak flooring was polished to a fine luster. A carpet, with a full pile despite its faded colors, covered half the floor.

Not a bad room. Not a bad room at all.

An elderly maid in kimono entered the room, set down a glass of grape juice, and left without a word. The door closed with a click. Then everything was dead quiet.

On the tea table were a silver cigarette case and lighter and ashtray identical to what was in the limo. Engraved with the same sheep emblem. I pulled one of my own filter tips out of my pocket, lit it with the silver lighter, and blew a puff of smoke up at the high ceiling. Then I took a sip of grape juice.

Ten minutes later, the door opened and in walked a tall man in a black suit. The man offered no "Welcome" or "Sorry to keep you waiting." I didn't say anything either. He took a seat opposite me, cocked his head slightly, and looked me over.

Time was surely passing.

PART FIVE

LETTERS FROM THE RAT AND ASSORTED REMINISCENCES

13

The Rat's First Letter
(Postmarked December 21st, One Year Ago)

So how's everything?

Seems like an awful long time since I saw you last. How many years is it now? What year was it?

I think I've gradually lost my sense of time. It's like there's this impossible flat blackbird flapping about over my head and I can't count above three. You'll have to excuse me, but why don't you do the counting?

I skipped town without telling anybody and maybe you had your share of troubles because of it. Or maybe you were upset at me for leaving without a word to you. You know, I meant to set things straight with you any number of times, but I just couldn't. I wrote a lot of letters and tore them all up. It should've been obvious, but there was no way I could explain to others what I couldn't even explain to myself.

I guess.

I've never been good at writing letters. Everything comes out backwards. I use exactly the wrong words. If that isn't bad enough, writing letters makes me more confused. And because I have no sense of humor, I get all discouraged with myself.

Generally, people who are good at writing letters have no need to write letters. They've got plenty of life to lead inside their own context. This, of course, is only my opinion. Maybe it's impossible to live out a life in context.

It's terribly cold now and my hands are numb. It's like they aren't my own hands. My brains, they aren't like my own brains either. Right now it's snowing. Snow like flakes of someone else's brains. And it'll pile up deeper and deeper like someone else's brains too. (What is this bullshit all about anyway?)

Other than the cold, though, I'm doing fine. How about you? I won't tell you my address, but don't take it personally. It's not like I'm trying to hide anything from you. I want you to know that. This is, you see, a delicate question for me. It's just this feeling I've got that, if I told you my address, in that instant something inside me would change. I can't put it very well.

It seems to me, though, that you always understand very well what I can't say very well. Trouble is I end up being even worse at saying things well. It's got to be an inborn fault.

Naturally everyone's got faults.

My biggest fault is that the faults I was born with grow bigger each year. It's like I was raising chickens inside me. The chickens lay eggs and the eggs hatch into other chickens, which then lay eggs. Is this any way to live a life? What with all these faults I've got going, I have to wonder. Sure, I get by. But in the end, that's not the question, is it?

In any case, I've decided I'm not giving you my address. I'm sure things'll be better that way. For me and for you.

Probably we'd have been better off born in nineteenth-century Russia. I'd have been Prince So-and-so and you Count Such-and-such. We'd go hunting together, fight, be rivals in love, have our metaphysical complaints, drink beer watching the sunset from the shores of the Black Sea. In our later years, the two of us would be implicated in the Something-or-other Rebellion and exiled to Siberia, where we'd die. Brilliant, don't you think? Me, if I'd been born in the nineteenth century, I'm sure I could have written better novels. Maybe not your Dostoyevsky, but a known second-rate novelist. And what would you have been doing? Maybe you'd only have been

Count Such-and-such straight through. That wouldn't be so bad, just being Count Such-and-such. That'd be nice and nineteenth century.

But well, enough of this. To return to the twentieth century.

Let me tell you about the towns I've seen.

Not the town where I was born, but different other towns.

There really are a lot of different other towns in the world. Each with its own specific features, incomprehensible things that attract me. Which is why I've passed through my share of towns these past few years.

Wherever I end up, I just get off at, and there's a small rotary where a map of the town is posted and a street of shops. That much is the same everywhere. Even the dogs look the same. First thing I do is a quick once-around the place before heading to a real estate agent to see about cheap room and board. Sure I'm an outsider and nobody in a small town will trust me right off, but as you know I can be decent enough if I put half a mind to it. Give me fifteen minutes, and I can generally get on good terms with most people. That much accomplished, I've found out where I can fit in and all sorts of information about the town.

Next, I look for work. This also begins with getting on good terms with a lot of different people. I'm sure this'd be a comedown for someone like you (and believe me, I've seen enough comedowns to last me) because you know you're only going to stick around for four months anyway. But there's nothing hard about getting on good terms with people. You find the local watering hole where all the kids hang out (every town has one—it's like the town navel), you become a regular customer, meet people, get an introduction for some work. Of course, you come up with some likely name and life story. So that by now I've got a string of names and identities like you wouldn't believe. At times I forget what I was like originally.

In the work department, I've done all kinds of jobs. Most have been boring, but still I enjoy the work. Most often it's been at a gasoline station. Next is tending some rinky-dink bar. I've minded shop at bookstores, even worked at a radio station. I've hired out as a day laborer. Been a cosmetics salesman. I had quite a reputation as a salesman, let me tell you. And I've slept with my share of women.

Sleeping with women each time with a different name and identity isn't half bad.

You get the picture, in all its variations.

So now I'm twenty-nine, turning thirty in another nine months.

I still don't know whether I'm cut out for this kind of life or not. I don't know if there's something universal about wanting to be a drifter. But as somebody once wrote somewhere, you need one of three things for a long life of wandering—a religious temperament, or an artistic temperament, or a psychic temperament. If you have one but only on the short side, an extended drifter's existence is out of the question. In my case, I can't see myself with any of them. In a pinch, I might say . . . no, better not.

Otherwise, I might end up opening the wrong door some day, only to find I can't back out. Whatever, if the door's been opened, I better make a go of it. I mean I can't keep buying my kicks for the rest of my life, can I?

That's about the size of it.

Like I said at the beginning (or did I?), when I think of you, I get a little uneasy. Because you probably remember me from when I was a comparatively regular guy.

Your friend,
The Rat

P.S.: I enclose a novel I wrote. It doesn't mean anything to me anymore, so do whatever you want with it. I'm sending this special delivery to make sure it reaches you by December 24. Hope it gets there on time.

Anyway, Happy Birthday.

And by the way, Merry Christmas.

The Rat's package was shoved all crumpled into my apartment mailbox on December 29. Attached was a forwarding slip. It had been sent to my previous address. There'd been no way to tell him I'd moved.

Four pages of light-brown paper packed solid with writing. I read the letter through three times before I brought out the envelope to check the blurred postmark. It was a place I'd never heard of. I got the atlas down from my bookshelf and looked the place up.

The Rat's words had reached me from a small town on the northern tip of Honshu, smack in the middle of Aomori Prefecture. According to my book of train schedules, about an hour from the city of Aomori. Five trains stopped every day, two in the morning, one at noon, two in the evening.

I'd been to Aomori several times in December. Frigid. The traffic signals freeze.

I showed the letter to my wife, wife at the time, that is. All she could say was "poor guy." What she probably meant was *you poor guys*. Hell, it makes no difference now.

I tossed the novel, around two hundred pages, into my desk drawer without bothering to read the title. I don't know why, I just didn't feel like reading it. The letter was enough.

I pulled a chair up in front of the heater and smoked three cigarettes.

The Rat's next letter came in May the following year.

14

The Rat's Second Letter (Postmarked May, This Year)

Last letter I think maybe I was a little too chatty. Even so, I've forgotten completely what I said.

I changed addresses again. Some place totally different from any place I've been up to now. It's really quiet here. Maybe a little too quiet.

In a sense, I've reached what is for me a final destination. I feel like I've come to where I was meant to come. What's more, I feel I've had to swim against the current to get here. But that's nothing I can pass judgment on.

What lousy writing! It's so vague you probably have no idea what I'm talking about. Or maybe you think I'm reading too much meaning into my fate. If that's the case, then the blame is all mine.

I want you to know that the more I try to explain to you what's going on with me, the more I start to digress like this. Still, I'm in good shape. Maybe better shape than I've ever been.

Let me put things more concretely.

Hereabouts, as I said earlier, it's incredibly quiet. There's nothing to do around here, so I read books (I've got enough books here to last me a decade) or listen to FM music or to records (got a whole lot here too). It's been ten years since I listened to so much music. To my surprise, the Rolling Stones and Beach Boys are still going strong. Time really is one big continuous cloth, no? We habitually cut out pieces of time to fit us, so we tend to fool ourselves into thinking that time is our size, but it really goes on and on.

Here, there is nothing my size. There's nobody around here to make himself the measure of everything, to praise or condemn others for their size.

Time keeps on flowing unchanged like a clear river too. Sometimes just being here I feel my slate has been cleaned, and I'm all the way back to my primal state. For example, if I catch sight of a car, it takes me a few seconds before I realize it's a car. Sure, I must have some kind of fundamental awareness that it's a car, but it doesn't quite get across to my immediate waking consciousness. These experiences have been happening to me more and more lately. Maybe it's because for a long time now I've been living by myself.

The nearest town is an hour and a half away by car. No, it's not even a town. Imagine your smallest town, then reduce it to a skeleton. I doubt you can picture it. I guess you'd have to call it a town anyway. You can buy clothes and groceries and gasoline. And if you get an urge to see other human beings, they're there to be seen.

All winter long the roads are frozen and almost no cars come through. Off the roads, it's damp, so the ground is frosted over like sherbet. When there's snowfall, it's impossible to tell what's road and what's not. It's a landscape that might as well be the end of the world.

I came here at the beginning of March. Driving through the thick of it, chains on the tires of the jeep. Just like being exiled to Siberia. But now it's May and the snow has all melted. From April on, the mountains were rumbling with snowslides. Ever hear a snowslide? Right after a snowslide comes the most perfect silence. Complete, total silence. You lose almost all sense of where you are. It's that quiet.

Sealed off in the mountains all this time, I haven't slept with a woman for the last three months. Which isn't bad, as far as that goes. All the same, if I stayed up here like this much longer, I know I'd lose all interest in people, and that's not something I want to do. So I'm thinking that when the weather gets a little warmer I'll stretch my legs and find myself a woman. I don't want to brag, but finding women has never been much of a problem for me. So long as I don't care—and staying here is living proof that I don't care—then sex appeal's easy, not a problem. It's not a big deal for me to put the moves on. The problem is, I myself am not at ease with this ability of mine. That is to say, when things get to a certain point, I lose track of where I myself stop and where my sex appeal begins. It's like where does Olivier stop and Othello begin? So midway when I find I'm not getting a return on all I'm putting into the situation, I toss everything overboard. Which makes problems for everyone all the way around. My whole life up to now has been nothing but one big repetition of this after another.

But this time I can be grateful (really, I am) that I don't have anything to throw overboard. A great feeling. The only thing I could possibly throw overboard would be myself. Not such a bad idea, throwing myself overboard. No, this is getting to sound pathetic. The idea itself, though, isn't pathetic in the least. I'm not feeling sorry for myself. It only sounds that way when I write it down.

Moan and groan.

What the hell was I talking about?

Women, that's right.

Each woman has a drawer marked "beautiful," stuffed full of all sorts of meaningless junk. That's my specialty. I pull out those pieces of junk one by one, dust them off, and find some kind of meaning in them. That's all that sex appeal really is, I think. But so what? What's that good for? There's nowhere to go from there short of stopping being myself.

So now I'm thinking about sex pure and simple. If I focus purely on sex, there's no need to get all bent out of shape whether I'm feeling sorry for myself or not.

It's like drinking beer on the shores of the Black Sea.

I just went back over what I've written so far. A few inconsistencies here and there, but pretty honest writing by my standards. All the more so because it's boring.

I don't even seem to be writing this letter to you. Probably the postbox is as far as my thinking goes. But don't get on my case for that. It's an hour and a half by jeep to the nearest postbox.

From here on, this letter is addressed to you.

I've got two favors to ask of you. Neither is in the particularly urgent category, so whenever you get around to taking care of them is fine. I'd really appreciate it. Three months ago I probably couldn't have brought myself to ask anything of you. But now I can. That's progress, I guess.

The first is a sort of sentimental request. Meaning it has to do with "the past." Five years ago when I skipped town, I was in such a confused hurry, I forgot to say goodbye to a number of people. Specifically, you and J and this woman you don't know. I guess I could probably see you again to tell you goodbye face-to-face, but with the other two I know I'll never have the chance. So if you're ever back there, can you say goodbye to them for me.

I know it's a selfish request. I ought to write them myself. But honestly, I'd rather have you go back there and see them for me. I know my feelings will get across better that way. I'm including her address and phone number separately. If she's moved or married by now, then it's okay, you don't have to see her. Leave things at that. But if she's still at the same address, give her my best.

And be sure to give J my best too. Have a beer for me.

That's one.

The other favor is maybe a bit odd.

I'm enclosing a photo. A picture of sheep. I'd like you to put it somewhere, I don't care where, but someplace people can see it. I realize I'm making this request out of the blue, but I've got no one else I can ask. I'll let you have every last ounce of my sex appeal if you do me this favor. I can't tell you the reason why, though. This photo is important to me. Sometime, at some later date, I'll explain everything to you.

I'm enclosing a check. Use it for whatever expenses you have. There's no need for you to have to worry about money. I'm hard put even to find a way to use money here, and anyway at the moment it's about the extent of what I can do for you.

Make sure you don't forget to have a beer for me.

Your friend,
The Rat

I found the letter in my mailbox as I was leaving my apartment and read it at my desk at the office.

The postmark was obliterated beyond legibility. I tore open the flap. Inside the envelope was a check for one hundred thousand yen, a piece of paper with a woman's name and address, and a black-and-white photograph of sheep. The letter was written on the same pale-green stationery as before and the check was drawn on a bank in Sapporo. Which would mean that the Rat had crossed further north to Hokkaido.

The bit about snowslides didn't register with me, but it did strike me, as the Rat himself had said, as an honest letter. Besides, nobody sends a check for one hundred thousand yen as a joke. I opened my desk drawer and tossed in the whole lot, envelope and all.

Maybe it was because my marriage was falling apart at the time, but spring that year had no joy for me. My wife hadn't come home in four days. Her toothbrush by the washbasin was caked and cracked like a fossil. The milk in the refrigerator smelled sour, and the cat was always hungry. A lazy spring sun poured in on this state of affairs. At least sunlight is always free.

A long, drawn-out dead-end street—probably just what she meant.

15

The Song Is Over

It was June before I returned to the town.

I cooked up some reason to take three days off and took the Bullet Train early one Tuesday. A white short-sleeved sports shirt, green cotton pants worn through at the knees, white tennis shoes, no luggage. I'd even forgotten to shave after getting up that morning. It was the first time I'd put on tennis shoes in ages and the heels were worn through crooked. I'd been walking off-center without knowing it.

Boarding a long-distance train without any luggage gave me a feeling of exhilaration. It was as if while out taking a leisurely stroll, I was suddenly like a dive-bomber caught in a space-time warp. In which there is nothing: no dentist's appointments, no pending issues in desk drawers, no inextricably complicated human involvements, no favors demanded. I'd left that behind, temporarily. All I had with me were my tennis shoes with their misshapen rubber soles. They held fast to my feet like vague memories of another space-time. But that hardly mattered. Nothing that some canned beer and dried-out ham sandwiches couldn't put out of mind.

It had been four years. Four years ago, the return home had been to take care of paperwork related to the family registry when I got married. When I thought back on it, what a pointless trip! It was all paperwork, no matter what anybody else thought. In the end it came down to that. What's over for one person isn't over for another. Simple as that. Beyond, the path goes in two different directions.

From that point on there was no hometown for me. Nowhere to return to. What a relief! No one to want me, no one to want anything from me.

I had a second can of beer and caught thirty minutes of shut-eye. When I woke up, that initial carefree sense of release was gone. The train moved on, and as it did, the sky turned a rain-gray. Beneath which stretched the same boring scenery. No matter how much speed we put on, there was no escaping boredom. On the contrary, the faster the speed, the more headway into boredom. Ah, the nature of boredom.

Next to me sat a business type in his mid-twenties, engrossed in a newspaper, hardly moving the whole time. Navy-blue summer suit, not a wrinkle. Starched white shirt, just back from the cleaners. Shiny black shoes.

I looked up at the ceiling of the car and puffed on a cigarette. I made mental lists of all the songs the Beatles ever recorded. Seventy-three titles before I ran out. I forget how many Paul McCartney numbers I remembered. I stared out the window awhile, then shifted my eyes back to the ceiling.

Here I was, back in town. Time passing me by. A whole decade since living here. One big blank. Not one thing of value had I gotten out of it, not one meaningful thing had I done. Boredom was all there was.

How were things before? Surely there had to have been something positive. Had there been anything that really moved me, anything that really moved anyone? Maybe, but it was all gone now. Lost, perhaps meant to be lost. Nothing I can do about it, got to let it go.

At least I was still around. If the only good Indian is a dead Indian, it was my fate to go on living.

What for?

To tell tales to a stone wall?

Really, now.

* * *

"Why stay in a hotel?" J asked, wrinkling up his face as he handed me a matchbook. "You've got a home, haven't you? Why not stay there?"

"It's not my home anymore," I said.

J didn't say anything to that.

With three plates of snacks lined up in front of me, I drank half my beer, then pulled out the Rat's letters and handed them to J. He wiped his hands on a towel, read the two letters through quickly before going over them again carefully, word by word.

"Hmm, alive and kicking, is he?"

"He's alive, all right," I said, taking another sip of beer. "But you know, before I do anything else, I've got to shave. You have a razor and some shaving cream you could lend me?"

"I do," said J, bringing out a travel kit from behind the counter. "You can use the washroom, but there's no hot water."

"Cold water's fine," I said. "As long as there's no drunk woman sprawled out on the floor. Makes it hard to shave."

J's Bar had completely changed.

The old J's Bar had been a dank place in the basement of an old building by the highway. On summer nights with the air conditioner going, a fine mist would form. After a long bout of drinking, even your shirt would be damp.

J's real name was some unpronounceable Chinese polysyllable. The nickname J was given to him by some GIs on the base where he worked after the war. His real name was soon forgotten.

In 1954, J quit his job on the base and opened a small bar. The very first J's Bar. The bar proved quite successful. A large part of the clientele was from the air force officer candidate school, and the atmosphere wasn't bad. After the bar got its start, J got married, but five years later his wife died. J never talked about the cause of her death.

In 1963, as the Vietnam War was beginning to go great guns, J sold the bar and moved far away to my hometown. There he opened the second J's Bar.

He had a cat, smoked a pack of cigarettes a day, never touched a drop of alcohol. That's the sum of everything I know about J.

Up until the time I met the Rat, I always went to J's Bar alone. I'd sip a beer slowly, smoke cigarettes, and feed coins into the jukebox. This was when J's Bar was usually empty, so I'd sit at the counter talking about all kinds of things with J, though about what exactly I don't remember. What could a shy seventeen-year-old high school student and a Chinese widower have to talk about?

When I turned eighteen and left town, the Rat came along and took my place at the bar drinking beer. Five years ago, when the Rat left town, there was no one to take his place. Six months later, when the road was widened, J had to change shops again, and the second J's Bar was relegated to legend.

The third J's Bar was a quarter of a mile away, by the river. It wasn't much bigger than the old place, but it was on the third floor of a new four-story building with an elevator. Taking an elevator to J's Bar made me feel like I had the address wrong. The same with looking out over the lights of town from the counter.

This new place had big windows facing west and south, out onto the line of hills and the area where the ocean used to be. The oceanfront had been filled in a few years back, and the whole mile there was packed with gravestone rows of tall buildings.

"Used to be water over there," I said.

"Right," said J.

"Went swimming there a lot."

"Yeah," said J, bringing a generic lighter up to the cigarette at his lips, "they bulldoze the hills to put up houses, haul the dirt to the sea for landfill, then go and build there too. And they think it's all fine and proper."

I drank my beer. The ceiling speakers were playing the latest Boz Scaggs hit. There wasn't a jukebox in sight. Almost all the customers in the place were university student couples, neatly dressed and politely sipping their highballs. No girls on the verge of passing out drunk, no hot fights brewing. You could tell that when they went home, they put on pajamas, brushed their teeth, and went straight to bed. There was nothing wrong with that. Nice and neat is fine and dandy. There's nothing in a bar or in the world at large that says things have to be a certain way.

J kept his eyes on me the whole while.

"So, everything's different and you feel out of place?"

"Not really," I said. "It's just that the chaos has changed shape. The giraffe and the bear have traded hats, and the bear's switched scarves with the zebra."

"Same as ever," J laughed.

"Times have changed," I said. "A lot of things have changed. But the bottom line is, that's fine. Everyone trades places. No complaints."

J didn't say anything.

I had myself another beer, J had another cigarette.

"How's your life going?" asked J.

"Not bad."

"How's the wife?"

"Don't really know. You know how things are between two people. There are times when I think everything's working out fine and times I don't. Maybe that's what marriage is all about."

"Well maybe," said J, scratching the tip of his nose with his little finger. "I forget what married life is like. It's been so long."

"How's the cat?"

"Died four years ago. Right after you got married. Something intestinal. . . . But really, it had a good, long life. Lived twelve years. That's longer than my wife was with me. Twelve years isn't a bad little life, is it?"

"Guess not."

"There's this animal cemetery up on the hill, so I buried it there. Overlooking the tall buildings. Anywhere around here those buildings are all you can see. Not that it makes much difference to a cat."

"Sad?"

"Sure. But not as sad as if a person had died. Does that sound funny?"

I shook my head.

J set to making some fancy cocktail and a Caesar salad for a customer. Meanwhile, I played with a Scandinavian puzzle on the counter. You were supposed to put together this picture of three butterflies midair over a field of clover, all inside a glass case. I gave up after ten minutes and put the thing aside.

"No kids?" J came back over to ask. "You're getting on the right age to have kids, you know."

"Don't want kids."

"Oh?"

"I mean, someone like me, I wouldn't know what to do if I had kids."

J chuckled and poured more beer into my glass. "You're always thinking too far ahead."

"No, that's not it. What I mean is, I don't really know if it's the right thing to do, making new life. Kids grow up, generations take their place. What does it all come to? More hills bulldozed and more oceanfront filled in? Faster cars and more cats run over? Who needs it?"

"That's only the dark side of things. Good things happen too, good people can make things worthwhile."

"Yeah? Name three," I said.

J gave it a thought, then laughed. "That's for your chidren's generation to decide, not you. Your generation . . ."

"Is already over and done with?"

"In a sense," said J.

"The song is over. But the melody lingers on."

"You always had a way of putting things."

"Just showing off," I said.

At nine o'clock, J's Bar was starting to get crowded, so I said good night to J and left. My face still tingled in the spots where I'd shaved, having only cold water. Maybe because I'd splashed on vodka lime instead of after-shave. J claimed it was just as effective, but now my whole face smelled like vodka.

The night was unexpectedly warm, though the sky was its usual heavy overcast. A moist breeze was blowing in slow and easy from the south. Same as it used to. A sea scent mingled with a hint of rain. Insects calling from the clumps of grass along the river. Everything brimming with a languid nostalgia. It seemed that it would rain any minute. When it did, it came in so fine a drizzle that you couldn't tell if it was raining or not, but I got completely drenched anyway.

I could just make out the river flowing in the white light of the mercury-vapor street lamp. The water was as clear as ever. It came straight out of the hills with nothing to pollute it along the way. The river had silted up with the small rocks and gravel washed down from the hills, creating little falls here and there. Beneath each fall, a deep pool had formed where small fish gathered.

During dry spells, the whole river used to dry up into a sandy bed, leaving only a faintly damp white trail. Years ago, on my walks, I'd trace that trail upstream, searching for where the river had gone.

The road by the river had been one of my favorites. I could walk at the same speed as the river. I could feel it breathing. It was alive. More than anything, it was the river we had to thank for creating the town. For grinding down the hills over how many hundreds of thousands of years, for hauling the dirt, filling the sea, and making the trees grow. The town belonged to the river from the very beginning, and it would always be that way.

Because this was the rainy season, the river flowed uninterrupted to the sea. The trees planted along the banks were fragrant with new leaves. There was a greenness in the air. Couples strolled arm in arm, old folks walked their dogs, high school kids hung around their motorbikes, smoking cigarettes. Your typical early summer evening.

I stopped into a liquor store, bought two cans of beer, and carried them in a paper bag down to the sea. Where the river met the sea, it turned into an inlet, or rather into a half-filled-in canal. Here was the only untouched stretch of oceanfront left, fifty yards of it. There was even something of the old beach. Small waves rolled in, leaving smooth pieces of driftwood. On the concrete jetty, bits of old nails and spray-paint graffiti remained.

Fifty yards of honest-to-goodness shoreline. If you overlooked the fact that it was hemmed in by thirty-foot-high concrete walls. And that the walls kept going straight out for several miles, channeling the sea narrowly in between. And that tall buildings lined either side. Fifty yards of sea. The rest was history.

I left the river and walked east along what had been the coastline road. Bewilderingly enough, the old jetty was still there. Now a jetty without an ocean is an odd creature indeed. I stopped at the exact spot where I used to park to look at the sea, went over to sit down on the jetty, and drank a beer. What a view! Instead of ocean, a vast expanse of reclaimed land and housing developments met my eyes. Faceless blocks of apartments, the miserable foundations of an attempt to build a neighborhood.

Asphalt roads threaded through the building complexes, here a parking lot, there a bus terminal. A gasoline station and a large park and a wonderful community center. Everything brand new, everything unnatural. On one side, the piles of soil hauled down from the hills for landfill loomed harsh and gray next to the areas which, not a part of the grand scheme, had been overtaken by quick-rooting weeds. On the other side, stupid little transplanted trees and plots of grass tried their artificial best to blend in.

Sickening.

But what was there to say? Already it was a whole new game played by new rules. No one could stop it now.

I polished off my two beers and hurled the empty cans across the reclaimed land, toward where the sea used to be. I watched them disappear into the sea of windblown weeds. Then I smoked a cigarette.

I was taking my last drag when I saw a man, flashlight in hand, heading my way. Fortyish, gray shirt, gray trousers, and a gray cap. Probably a security guard for the area.

"You just threw something, didn't you?" said the man.

"Yeah, I threw something."

"What did you throw?"

"Round, metallic, lidded objects."

The security guard put on a sour face. "Why'd you throw them?"

"No particular reason. Been throwing things from twelve years back. At times, I've thrown half a dozen things at once and nobody said a word."

"That was back then," said the security guard. "This is city property now and it's against the law to discard rubbish on city property."

I swallowed. For a moment something inside me trembled, then stopped. "The real problem here," I said, "is that what you say makes sense."

"It's the law," he said.

I sighed and took the pack of cigarettes out of my pocket.

"So what should I do?"

"Well, I can't ask you go pick them up. It's too dark and it's about to rain. So do me a favor and don't throw things again."

"I won't," I said. "Good night."

"Good night," said the security guard as he walked away.

I stretched out on the jetty and looked up at the sky. As the man said, it was starting to rain. I smoked another cigarette and thought over the encounter with the guard. Ten years ago I would have come on tougher. Well, maybe not. What difference would it make anyway?

I went back to the riverside road, and by the time I'd managed to catch a taxi the rain was coming down in a drizzle. To the hotel, I said.

"Here on a trip?" asked the old driver.

"Uh-huh."

"First time in these parts?"

"Second time," I said.

16

She Drinks Her Salty Dog, Talking about the Sound of the Waves

"I have a letter for you," I said.

"For me?" she said.

The connection was bad, so we practically had to shout, which was not very conducive to communicating delicate shades of feeling. It was like talking on a windswept hill through upturned collars.

"Actually, the letter's addressed to me, but somehow it seems to be meant more for you."

"It does, does it?"

"Yes, it does," I said. As soon as I'd said it, I knew this whole idiotic conversation was going nowhere fast.

She said nothing for a moment. Meanwhile, the connection cleared up.

"I have no idea what went on between you and the Rat. But he did ask me to see you, and that's why I'm calling. Besides, I think it'd be better if you read his letters."

"And that's why you came out all the way from Tokyo?"

"That's right."

She coughed, excused herself, then said, "Because he's your friend?"

"I suppose."

"Why do you suppose he didn't write to me directly?"

She did have a point.

"I don't know," I said, honestly.

"I don't know either. I mean, I thought everything was over. Or isn't it?"

I had no idea and I told her so. I lay back on the hotel bed, phone receiver in hand, and looked at the ceiling. I could be lying on the ocean floor counting fish, I thought. How many would I have to count before I could say I was done?

"It was five years ago when he disappeared. I was twenty-seven at the time," she said, distant voice sounding like an echo from the bottom of a well. "A lot of things can change in five years."

"True," I said.

"And really, even if nothing had changed, I wouldn't see it that way. I wouldn't want to admit it. I wouldn't be able to show my face anywhere. So as far as I'm concerned, everything's completely changed."

"I think I understand," I said.

A brief pause hovered between us.

It was she who broke the silence. "When was the last time you saw him?" she asked.

"Spring, five years ago, right before he upped and left."

"And did he tell you anything? I mean about why he was leaving town . . . ?"

"Nope."

"So he left you with no warning either?"

"That's right."

"And what did you think? At the time, I mean."

"About him up and leaving like that?"

"Yeah."

I got up from the bed and leaned against the wall. "Well, for sure I thought he'd give up and come back after six months. He never struck me as the stick-with-it type."

"But he didn't come back."

"No, he didn't."

There was a slight hesitation on her end of the line.

"Where is it you're staying now?" she asked.

I told her the name of the hotel.

"I'll meet you there tomorrow at five. The coffee lounge on the eighth floor all right?"

"Fine," I said. "I'll be wearing a white sports shirt and green cotton slacks. I've got short hair and . . ."

"I've got the picture," she said, cheerfully cutting me off. Then she hung up.

I replaced the receiver. What did she mean, she got the picture? *I* didn't get the picture, but then again, there are lots of things I don't know anything about. Age certainly hasn't conferred any smarts on me. Character maybe, but mediocrity is a constant, as one Russian writer put it. Russians have a way with aphorisms. They probably spend all winter thinking them up.

I took a shower, washed my rain-soaked hair, and with the towel wrapped around my waist, I watched an old American submarine movie on television. The creaking plot had the captain and first officer constantly at each other's throat. The submarine was a fossil, and one guy had claustrophobia. But all that didn't stop everything from working out well in the end. It was an everything-works-out-in-the-end-so-maybe-war's-not-so-bad-after-all sort of film. One of these days they'll be making a film where the whole human race gets wiped out in a nuclear war, but everything works out in the end.

I switched off the television, climbed into bed, and was asleep in ten seconds.

The drizzle still hadn't let up by five o'clock the next evening. The rain had been preceded by four or five days of crisp, clear early summer skies, fooling people into thinking the rainy season was over. From the eighth-floor window, every square inch of ground looked dark and damp, and a traffic jam stretched for several miles on the eastbound lanes of the elevated expressway.

As I stared out long and hard, things began to melt in the rain. In fact, everything in town was melting. The breakwater, the cranes, the rows of buildings, the figures beneath their black umbrellas, everything. Even the greenery was flowing down from the hills. Yet when I shut my eyes for a few seconds and opened them again, the town was back the way it had been. Six cranes loomed in the dark haze, trains headed east as if their engines had just restarted, flocks of umbrellas dodged back and forth across the streets of shops, the green hills soaked up their fill of June rain.

In a sunken area in the middle of the coffee lounge, a woman wearing a bright pink dress sat at a cerulean blue grand piano playing quintessential hotel-coffee-lounge numbers filled with arpeggios and syncopation. Not bad actually, though not an echo lingered in the air beyond the last note of each number.

It was past five o'clock and she hadn't arrived. Since I had nothing better to do, I had a second cup of coffee and watched the piano player. She was about twenty, her shoulder-length hair immaculately coiffed like whipped cream atop a cake. The coif swayed merrily, left and right, to the rhythm, bouncing back to center when the song ended. Then the next number would begin.

She reminded me of a girl I used to know in the third grade, when I was taking piano lessons. The same age, the same class. We sometimes had to play duets together. But her name and face, entirely forgotten. All I remember about her are her tiny pale hands and pretty hair and fluffy dress.

It's disturbing to realize this. Have I stripped her of her hands and hair and dress? Is the rest of her still living unattached somewhere else? Of course, this can't be. The world goes on without me. People cross streets through no intervention on my part, sharpen pencils, move fifty yards a minute west to east, fill coffee lounges with music that's refined into nothingness.

The "world"—the word always makes me think of a tortoise and elephants tirelessly supporting a gigantic disc. The elephants have no knowledge of the tortoise's role, the tortoise unable to see what the elephants are doing. And neither is the least aware of the world on their backs.

"Sorry to keep you waiting," a woman's voice from behind me said. "Work ran late, and I just couldn't get free."

"No problem. I didn't have anything to do today anyway."

She dropped her keys down on the table and ordered an orange juice without bothering to look at the menu. Her age was not easy to tell. If she hadn't mentioned it to me over the phone, I probably would not have known. If she had said she was thirty-three, she would have looked thirty-three to me. If she'd said twenty-seven, then she'd have looked twenty-seven. At face value.

Her taste in clothes was nicely succinct. Ample white cotton slacks, an orange-and-yellow checkered blouse, sleeves rolled up to the elbows, and a leather shoulder bag. None of them new, but all well cared for. She wore no rings or necklace or bracelet or earrings. Her bangs were short and brushed casually to the side.

The tiny wrinkles at the corners of her eyes might have been there from birth rather than acquired with age. Only her slender, fair neckline, visible from the button open at her collar, and the backs of her hands hinted at her age. People start aging from early, very early, on. Gradually it spreads over their entire body like a stain that cannot be wiped away.

"What sort of work?" I ventured to ask.

"Drafting work at an architectural office. I've been there for a long time now."

The conversation trailed off. I slowly took out a cigarette and lit up. The piano player stopped playing, brought the lid down, and retired somewhere for her break. I envied her.

"How long have you been friends with him?" she asked.

"Eleven years, I guess. And you?"

"Two months, ten days," she answered right off. "From the time I first met him to the time he disappeared. Two months and ten days. I remember because I keep a diary."

The orange juice came and my empty coffee cup was spirited away.

"I waited three months after he disappeared. December, January, February. The coldest time of the year. Maybe it was a cold winter that year?"

"I don't recall," I said, though the cold of winter five years ago now seemed like yesterday's weather.

"Have you ever waited for a woman like that?"

"No," I said.

"You concentrate on waiting for someone and after a certain time it hardly matters what happens anymore. It could be five years or ten years or one month. It's all the same."

I nodded.

She drank half her orange juice.

"It was that way when I was first married," she said. "I was always the one who waited, until I got tired of waiting, and in the end I didn't care. Married at twenty-one, divorced at twenty-two. Then I came here."

"It was the same with my wife."

"What was?"

"Married at twenty-one, divorced at twenty-two."

She studied my face awhile. Then stirred her orange juice with her swizzle stick. I'd spoken unnecessarily, it seemed.

"When you're young, it's hard getting married then getting divorced right away," she said. "The thing is you're looking for something two-dimensional and not quite real. It never lasts. But you can't expect something unreal to last anyway, can you?"

"I suppose not."

"In the five years between my divorce and when I met him, I was all alone in this town. Living a life that was, well, rather unreal. I hardly knew anyone, rarely went out, had no romance. I'd get up in the morning, go to the office, draft plans, stop by the supermarket on the way home to shop, and eat dinner at home alone. I'd listen to FM radio, read, write in my diary, wash my stockings in the bath. My apartment's near the ocean, so there's always the sound of the surf. It was cold and lonely."

She finished the rest of her orange juice.

"It seems I'm boring you."

I shook my head.

Past six. The lights in the lounge dimmed for cocktail hour. The lights of town began to blink on. Red lights lit up on the cranes. Fine needles of rain became visible through the gathering dusk.

"Care for a drink?" I asked.

"What do you call vodka with grapefruit juice?"

"A salty dog."

I called the waiter and ordered a salty dog and a Cutty Sark on the rocks.

"Where were we?"

"Your cold and lonely life."

"Well, if you really want to know, it hasn't been all that cold and lonely," she said. "Just the sound of the waves is. That alone puts a chill on things. When I moved in, the superintendent said I'd get used to it soon enough, but I still haven't."

"The ocean's no longer there."

She smiled softly. A hint of movement came to the wrinkles at the corner of her eyes. "True. As you say, the ocean's no longer there. But even so, I swear I can sometimes still hear the waves. It's probably imprinted into my ears over the years."

"Then the Rat appeared."

"Yes. Although I never called him that."

"What did you call him?"

"By his name. Like everybody else."

Come to think it, "The Rat" did sound a bit childish, even for a nickname. "Hmm," I said.

They brought our drinks. She took a sip of her salty dog, then wiped the salt from her lips with the napkin. The napkin came away with the slightest trace of lipstick. Then she folded the lipstick-blushed napkin deftly and laid it down.

"He was so . . . more than unreal. Do you know what I mean?"

"I think so."

"I guess it took someone as unreal as him to break through my own unreality. It struck me the very first time I met him. That's why I liked him. Or maybe I only thought so after I got to like him. It amounts to the same thing either way."

The piano player returned from her break and began to play themes from old film scores. Perfect: the wrong background music for the wrong scene.

"I sometimes think maybe, in the end, I was only using him. And maybe he sensed it all along. What do you think?"

"I wouldn't know," I said. "That's between you and him."

She said nothing.

After a full twenty seconds of silence, I realized she'd run out of things to say. I downed the last of my whiskey and retrieved the Rat's letters from my pocket, placing them in the center of the table. Where they sat for a while.

"Do I have to read them here?"

"Please take them home and read them. If you don't want to read them, then do whatever you want with them."

She nodded. She put the letters in her bag, which she fastened with a snap of the clasp. I lit up a second cigarette and ordered another whiskey. The second whiskey is always my favorite. From the third on, it no longer has any taste. It's just something to pour into your stomach.

"You came all the way from Tokyo for this reason?" she asked.

"Pretty much so."

"You're very kind."

"I've never thought about it that way. A matter of habit. If the tables were turned, I'm sure he'd do the same for me."

"Have you ever asked something like this of him?"

I shook my head. "No, but we go back a long time imposing our unrealities on each other. Whether we've managed to take care of things realistically or not is another question."

"Maybe nobody really can."

"Maybe not."

She smiled and got up, whisking away the bill. "Let me take care of this. I was forty minutes late, after all."

"If you're sure, then by all means," I said. "But one more thing, I was wondering if I could ask you a question."

"Certainly."

"Over the phone you said you could picture how I looked."

"I meant there was something I could sense about you."

"And that was enough for you to spot me right away?"

"I could tell in no time at all."

The rain kept falling at the same rate. From my hotel window, through the neon signs of the building next door, a hundred thousand strands of rain sped earthward through a green glow. If I looked down, the rain seemed to pour straight into one fixed point on the ground.

I plopped down on the bed and smoked a couple cigarettes, then called the front desk to make a reservation for a train the following morning. There was nothing left for me to do in town.

The rain kept falling until midnight.

PART SIX

A WILD SHEEP CHASE, II

17

The Strange Man's Strange Tale

The black-suited secretary took his chair and looked at me without saying a word. He didn't seem to be sizing me up, nor did his eyes betray any disdain, nor was his a pointed stare to bore right through me. Neither cool nor hot, not even in the mid-range. That gaze held no hint of any emotion known to me. The man was simply looking at me. He might have been looking at the wall behind me, but as I was situated in front of it, the end result was that the man was looking at me.

The man picked up the cigarette case from the table, opened the lid and withdrew a plain-cut cigarette, flicked the tip a few times with his fingernail, lit up with the tabletop lighter, and blew out the smoke at an oblique angle. Then he returned the lighter to the table and crossed his legs. His gaze did not waver one blink the whole time.

This was the same man my partner had told me about. He was overdressed, his fingers overly graceful. If not for the sharp curve of his eyelids and the glass-bead chill of his pupils, I would surely have thought him homosexual. Not with those eyes, though. So what did he look like? He didn't resemble any sort, anything.

If you took a good look at his eyes, they were an arresting color. Dark brown with the faintest touch of blue, the hue of the left eye, moreover, different from the right. Each seemed to focus on a wholly different subject.

His fingers pursued scant movements on his lap. Hauntingly, as if separated from his hand, they moved toward me. Tense, compelling, nerve-racking, beautiful fingers. Slowly reaching across the table to crush out the cigarette not one-third smoked. I watched the ice melt in the glass, clear ice water mixing with the grape juice. An unequally variegated mix.

The room was utterly silent. Now there is the silence you encounter on entering a grand manor. And there is the silence that comes of too few people in too big a space. But this was a different quality of silence altogether. A ponderous, oppressive silence. A silence reminiscent, though it took me a while to put my finger on it, of the silence that hangs around a terminal patient. A silence pregnant with the presentiment of death. The air faintly musty and ominous.

"Everyone dies," said the man softly with downcast eyes. He seemed to have an uncanny purchase on the drift of my thoughts. "All of us, whosoever, must die sometime."

Having said that, the man fell again into a weighty silence. There was only the frantic buzzing of the cicadas outdoors. Bodies scraping out their last dying fury against the ending season.

"Let me be as frank as possible with you," the man spoke up. His speech had the ring of a direct translation from a formulaic text. His choice of phrase and grammar was correct enough, but there was no feeling in his words.

"Speaking frankly and speaking the truth are two different things entirely. Honesty is to truth as prow is to stern. Honesty appears first and truth appears last. The interval between varies in direct proportion to the size of ship. With anything of size, truth takes a long time in coming. Sometimes it only manifests itself posthumously. Therefore, should I impart you with no truth at this juncture, that is through no fault of mine. Nor yours."

How was one to respond to this? He acknowledged my silence and continued to speak.

"You're probably wondering why I called you all this way here. It was to set the ship in forward motion. You and I shall move it forward. By discussing matters in all honesty, we shall proceed one step at a time closer to the truth." At that point, he coughed and glanced over at my hand resting on the arm of the sofa. "But enough of these abstractions, let us begin with real concerns. The issue here is the newsletter you produced. I believe you have been told this much."

"I have."

The man nodded. Then after a moment's pause, continued, "I'm sure all this came as quite a surprise to you. Anyone would be unhappy about having the product of his hard labors destroyed. All the more if it's a vital link in his livelihood. It may mean a very real loss of no mean size. Isn't that right?"

"That it is," I said.

"I would like to have you tell me about such real losses."

"In our line of work, real losses are part of business. It's not like clients never suddenly reject what's been produced. But for a small operation like ours, it can be a threat to our existence. So in order to prevent that, we honor the client's views one hundred percent. In extreme cases, this means checking through an entire bulletin line by line together with the client. That way we avoid all risks. It's not easy work, but that's the lot of the lone wolf."

"Everyone has to start somewhere," sympathized the man. "Be that as it may, am I to interpret from what you say that your company has incurred a severe financial setback as a result of the cessation of your bulletin?"

"Yes, I guess you could say that. It was already printed and bound, so we have to pay for the paper and printing within the month. There're also writers' fees for articles we farmed out. In monetary terms that comes to about five million yen, and if worse comes to worse we'll have to borrow money to pay it off. Furthermore, it's been only a year since we went overboard investing in our office facilities."

"I know," said the man.

"Then there is the question of our ongoing contract with the client. Our position is very weak, and once there's been trouble with an advertising agency, clients avoid you. We were under a one-year contract with the life insurance company, and if that's scrapped because of this, then effectively our company is sunk. We're small and without connections, but we've got a good reputation that's spread by word of mouth. If one bad word gets out, we're done for."

Even after I'd finished, the man stared at me without comment. Then he spoke up. "You speak most honestly. Moreover, what you tell me conforms to our investigations. I commend you on that. What if I were to offer unconditional payment for those canceled insurance company bulletins and inform you that your present contract would continue to be valid?"

"There would be nothing more to tell. We'd go back to our boring everyday affairs, left wondering what this was all about."

"And with a premium on top of that? I have but to write one word on the back of a name card and you would have your work cut out for you for the next ten years. And none of those measly handbills either."

"A deal, in other words."

"A friendly transaction. I out of my own goodwill have done your partner the favor of informing him that the P.R. bulletin has ceased publication. And should you show me your goodwill, I would favor you with a further display of goodwill. Do you think you could do that? My favor could prove quite beneficial. Certainly you don't expect to go on working with a dull-witted alcoholic forever."

"We're friends," I said.

There ensued a brief silence, a pebble sent plunging down a fathomless well. It took thirty seconds for the pebble to hit bottom.

"As you wish," said the man. "That is your affair. I went over your vita in some detail. You have an interesting history. Now people can generally be classified into two groups: the mediocre realists and the mediocre dreamers. You clearly belong to the latter. Your fate is and will always be the fate of a dreamer."

"I'll remember that," I said.

The man nodded. I drank half the watered-down grape juice.

"Very well, then, let us proceed to particulars," said the man. "Particulars about sheep."

The man changed positions to pull a large black-and-white photograph out of an envelope, setting it on the table before me.

The slightest breath of reality seemed to filter into the room.

"This is the photograph you used in your bulletin."

For a direct blowup of the photograph without using the negative, the image was surprisingly clear. Probably some special technology.

"As far as we know, the photo is one you personally came upon and then used in the bulletin. Is that not so?"

"That is correct."

"According to our investigations, the photograph was taken within the last six months by a total amateur. The camera, a cheap pocket-size model. It was not you who took the photograph. You have a Nikon SLR and take better pictures. And you haven't been to Hokkaido in the past five years. Correct?"

"You tell me," I said.

The man cleared his throat, then fell silent. This was a definitive silence, one you could judge the qualities of other silences by. "Anyway, what we want is a few pieces of information: namely, where and from whom did you receive that photograph, and what was your intention in using such a poor image in that bulletin?"

"I'm afraid I'm not at liberty to say," I tossed out the words with a cool that impressed even myself. "Journalists rightfully do not reveal their sources."

The man stared me in the eyes and stroked his lips with the middle finger of his right hand. Several passes, then he returned his hand to his lap. The silence continued for a while. I couldn't help thinking what perfect timing it would be if at that instant a cuckoo started to sing. But, of course, no cuckoo was to be heard. Cuckoos don't sing in the evenings.

"You are a fine one," said the man. "You know, if I felt like it, I could stop all work from coming your way. That would put an end to your claims of journalism. Supposing, of course, that your miserable pamphlets and handbills qualify as journalism."

I thought it over. Why is it that cuckoos don't sing at nightfall?

"What's more, there are ways to make people like you talk."

"I suppose there are," I said, "but they take time and I wouldn't talk until the last minute. Even if I did talk, I wouldn't spill everything. You'd have no way of knowing how much is everything. Or am I mistaken?"

Everything was a bluff, but it made sense the way things were going. The uncertainty of the silence that followed showed I had earned myself a few points.

"It is most amusing talking with you," said the man. "Your dreamer's scenario is delightfully pathetic. Ah well, let us talk about something else."

The man pulled a magnifying glass out of his pocket and set it on the table.

"Please examine the photograph as much as you care to."

I picked up the photo with my left hand and the magnifying glass with my right, and inspected the photo methodically. Some sheep were facing this way, some were facing in other directions, some were absorbed in eating grass. A scene that suggested a dull class reunion. I spot-checked each sheep one by one, looked at the lay of the grass, at the birch wood in the background, the mountains behind that, the wispy clouds in the sky. There was not one thing unusual. I looked up from the photo and magnifying glass.

"Did you notice anything out of the ordinary?"

"Not at all," I said.

The man showed no visible sign of disappointment.

"I seem to recall that you majored in biology at university," the man said. "How much do you know about sheep?"

"Practically nothing. I did mostly useless specialist stuff."

"Tell me what you know."

"A cloven-hoofed, herbivorous social animal. Introduced to Japan in the early Meiji era, I believe. Used as a source of wool and meat. That's about it."

"Very good," said the man. "Although I should like to make one small correction: sheep were not introduced to Japan in the early Meiji era, but during the Ansei reign. Prior to that, however, it is as you say: there were no sheep in Japan. True, there is some argument that they were brought over from China during the Heian period, but even if that were the case, they had long since died off in the interim. So up until Meiji, few Japanese had ever seen a sheep or understood what one was. In spite of its relatively popular standing as one of the twelve zodiacal animals of the ancient Chinese calendar, nobody knew with any accuracy what kind of animal it was. That is to say, it might as well have been an imaginary creature on the order of a dragon or phoenix. In fact, pictures of sheep drawn by pre-Meiji Japanese look like wholly fabricated monstrosities. One might say they had about as much knowledge of their subject as H. G. Wells had about Martians.

"Even today, Japanese know precious little about sheep. Which is to say that sheep as an animal have no historical connection with the daily life of the Japanese. Sheep were imported at the state level from America, raised briefly, then promptly ignored. That's your sheep. After the war, when importation of wool and mutton from Australia and New Zealand was liberalized, the merits of sheep raising in Japan plummeted to zero. A tragic animal, do you not think? Here, then, is the very image of modern Japan.

"But of course I do not mean to lecture you on the vainglory of modern Japan. The points I wish to impress upon you are two: one, that prior to the end of the late feudal period there probably was not one sheep in all of Japan; and two, that once imported, sheep were subjected to rigorous government checks. And what do these two things mean?"

The question wasn't rhetorical; it was addressed to me. "That every variety of sheep in Japan is fully accounted for," I stated.

"Precisely. To which I might add that breeding is as much a point with sheep as it is with racehorses, making it a simple matter to trace their genealogy several generations. In other words, here we have a thoroughly regulated animal. Crossbreeding with other strains can be easily checked. There is no smuggling. No one is curious enough to go to all the trouble to import sheep. By way of varieties, there are in Japan the Southdown, Spanish Merino, Cotswold, Chinese, Shropshire, Corriedale, Cheviot, Romanovsky, Ostofresian, Border Leicester, Romney Marsh, Lincoln, Dorset Horn, Suffolk, and that's about all. With this in mind," said the man, "I would like to have you take another look at the photograph."

Once again I took photo and magnifying glass in my hands.

"Be sure to look carefully at the third sheep from the right in the front row."

I brought the magnifying glass to bear upon the third sheep

from the right in the front row. A quick look at the sheep next to it, then back to the third sheep from the right.

"And what can you tell now?" asked the man.

"It's a different breed, isn't it?" I said.

"That it is. Aside from that particular sheep, all the others are ordinary Suffolks. Only that one sheep differs. It is far more stocky than the Suffolk, and the fleece is of another color. Nor is the face black. Something about it strikes one as howsoever more powerful. I showed this photograph to a sheep specialist, and he concluded that this sheep did not exist in Japan. Nor probably anywhere else in the world. So what you are looking at now is a sheep that by all rights should not exist."

I grabbed the magnifying glass and looked once more at the third sheep from the right. On close examination, there, in the middle of its back, appeared to be a light coffee stain of a mark. Hazy and indistinct, it could have been a scratch on the film. Maybe my eyes were playing tricks again. Or maybe somebody actually did spill coffee on that sheep's back.

"There's this faint stain on its back."

"That is no stain," said the man. "That is a star-shaped birthmark. Compare it with this."

The man pulled a single-page photocopy out of the envelope and handed it over directly to me. It was a copy of a picture of a sheep. Drawn apparently in heavy pencil, with black finger smudges all over the rest of the page. Infantile, yet there was something about it that commanded your attention. The details were drawn with great care. Moreover, the sheep in the photograph and the sheep in the drawing were without a doubt the same sheep. The star-shaped birthmark *was* the stain.

"Now look at this," said the man, taking a lighter from his pocket and handing it to me. It was a specially made, heavy, solid silver Dupont, engraved with the same sheep emblem I'd seen in the limo. Sure enough, the star-shaped birthmark was there on the sheep's back, plain as day.

My head began to ache.

18

The Strange Man's Strange Tale Goes On

Just a while ago, I made reference to your mediocrity," said the man. "This was by no means a criticism of you. Or to put it more simply, it is because the world itself is so mediocre that you are mediocre as such. Do you not agree?"

"Excuse me?"

"The world is mediocre. About that there is no mistake. Well then, has the world been mediocre since time immemorial? No. In the beginning, the world was chaos, and chaos is not mediocre. The mediocratization began when people separated the means of production from daily life. For when Karl Marx posited the proletariat, he thereby cemented their mediocrity. And precisely because of this, Stalinism forms a direct link with Marxism. I affirm Marx. He was one of those rare geniuses whose memory extended back to primal chaos. And by the same token, I have high regard for Dostoyevsky. Nonetheless, I do not hold with Marxism. It is far too mediocre."

The man forced back a low sound in the back of his throat.

"I am, right now, speaking with extreme honesty. I mean this as a gesture of gratitude for your previous honesty. Furthermore, I will agree to clarify whatever so-called honest doubts you might have. But know that by the time I am through talking, the options left open to you will have become extremely limited. Please understand this in advance. Quite simply, you are raising the stakes. Are we agreed?"

"What choice have I?" I said.

"Right now, an old man lies dying within this estate," he began. "The cause is clear. It is a giant blood cyst in his brain. A cyst big enough to distort the very shape of his brain. How much do you know about neurology?"

"Next to nothing."

"To put it simply then, it is a blood bomb. A blockage of circulation causing an irregular swelling. Like a snake that has swallowed a golf ball. If it explodes, the brain will cease to function. Yet an operation is out of the question. The slightest stimulus might cause it to explode. Realistically speaking, we can only wait and watch him die. He might die in another week, or it might be another month. No one can say."

The man pursed his lips and let out a slow breath.

"There is nothing odd about him dying. He is an old man, his ailment pinpointed. What is odd is that he has lived this long."

I hadn't the foggiest notion what he was trying to say.

"The fact is, there would have been nothing amiss had he died thirty-two years ago," the man continued. "Or even forty-two years ago. That blood cyst was first discovered by U.S. Army doctors conducting health examinations on Class A war criminals. This was back in the autumn of 1946, before the Tokyo War Crimes Tribunal. The doctor who discovered it was rather alarmed when he saw the X rays. To have such an enormous cyst in one's brain and still be alive—and more active than the average person at that—challenged all medical common sense. He was transferred from Sugamo to the then-army hospital, St. Luke's, for special tests.

"The tests went on for a year, though ultimately they learned nothing. Only that his death would come as no surprise to anyone, since the fact that he was alive at all was a total mystery. Still he showed no signs of disability thereafter; he kept on living with singular vitality. All brain activities were, moreover, exceedingly normal. They were at a loss for explanations. A dead end. Here was a man who theoretically should have been dead, yet was alive and walking about.

"Certainly they shed light on a number of specific symptoms. He had three-day headaches that came and went on a forty-day cycle. By his own account, these headaches began in 1936, which they conjectured was around the time his blood cyst first appeared. His headaches were so intolerable that he required painkillers. In short, narcotics. The narcotics eased the pain all right, but they also resulted in hallucinations. Highly compressed hallucinations. Only he himself knows what exactly he experienced, but it seems they were far from pleasant. The U.S. Army still retains the detailed accounts of these hallucinatory experiences. The doctors apparently made meticulous observations. I obtained these by special means and have read them through several times, and in spite of their clinical language they describe a rather grueling series of events. I doubt there are many who could take such regular punishment as those hallucinatory experiences.

"No one has any idea why these hallucinations occurred. Perhaps the cyst gave off some periodic energy and the headaches were the body's reaction. So that when that reactive buffer was removed, the energy directly stimulated specific parts of the brain, resulting in hallucinations. Of course, this is only one hypothesis, but it is a hypothesis that interested the Americans. Enough that they initiated thorough tests. Top-secret tests by Intelligence. Even now it is not clear why American Intelligence should have jumped into investigations of one man's blood cyst; however, we can imagine several possibilities.

"As the first possibility, might they not have conducted certain more delicate interrogations under the cover of medical tests? To wit, the securing of spying routes and opium routes on the Chinese mainland. Remember, Chiang Kai-shek's eventual defeat meant the loss of the Chinese connection for the U.S. But needless to say, these inquiries could not be made public. In fact, after this series of tests, the Boss was released without having to stand trial. It is conceivable that an arrangement was made behind the scenes. An exchange of information for freedom, shall we say.

"The second possibility was to lay bare an interrelationship between his marked eccentricity as the leader of the right wing and the blood cyst. I will go more into this with you later, but it is a more bemusing turn of thought. Though I doubt they ever learned anything. Did they really imagine they could uncover something of that order when the more basic fact of his living remained a mystery? Short of an autopsy, there was no way they would find anything out. Here, then, another dead end.

"The third possibility concerns brainwashing. The idea being that, perhaps, by sending one predetermined set of stimulus waves into the brain they might elicit a particular reaction. They were doing that kind of experimentation in those days. It has come to light that there was, in fact, such a brainwashing research group at the time.

"It is not clear which of these three lines of thought represented the main Intelligence directive. Nor is it clear whether their efforts, shall we call them, bore any fruit. Everything is buried in history. The only ones who know the facts are a handful of the U.S. Army elite at the time and the Boss himself. So far, the Boss has never spoken a word about this to anyone, myself included, and it is doubtful he ever will."

When he finished talking, the man cleared his throat. I had lost all track of how much time had passed since entering the room.

"In the winter of 1932, the Boss was imprisoned on charges of complicity in a plot to assassinate a key figure. His imprisonment lasted until June 1936. The official prison records and medical register still exist, and he on occasion has touched upon the subject. These glimpses tell us this: that for virtually the entire length of his stay in prison, the Boss suffered from severe insomnia. Or perhaps it was more than simple insomnia. This was insomnia raised to an exceedingly dangerous level. For three days, four days at a time, sometimes close to a week, he would not close his eyes once. In those days, the police forced confessions out of political criminals by depriving them of sleep. So the Boss must have undergone especially punishing interrogations, implicated as he was with the resistance to the Imperial rule and the controlling faction. If the prisoner tried to sleep, they would throw water on him or beat him with bamboo sticks or shine strong lights on him, anything to dash the sleeping patterns to pieces. Most humans break down if such a regimen is kept up for several months. Their sleeping mind is effectively destroyed. They die or they go crazy or they become extreme insomniacs. The Boss went the last route. It was the spring of 1936 before he had completely recovered from his insomnia. That is, around the same time as the blood cyst appeared. What do you make of that?"

"Extreme lack of sleep for some reason disrupted the flow of blood in his brain, thereby creating the cyst, is that it?"

"That would seem the most plausible, commonsense hypothesis. And since a nonprofessional can think that far, you can be sure that it occurred to the U.S. Army doctors as well. Still, that explanation alone is not quite adequate. There is something missing here. I cannot help thinking that the phenomenon of the blood cyst was the secondary manifestation of a more significant factor. Consider, for example, that among the several other people known to have had such blood cysts, not one displayed the same symptoms. Nor, furthermore, does the explanation offer sufficient reason why the Boss went on living."

Undoubtedly, there was a logic to what the man was saying.

"One more curious fact about the blood cyst. Starting from the spring of 1936, the Boss was proverbially born again, a new man. Up to that point the Boss had been, in a word, a mediocre right-wing activist. Born the third son of a poor farming household in Hokkaido, he left home when he was twelve and went to Korea, but he found no place there either so he returned to his homeland and joined a right-wing group. An angry young man, it seems, who was forever brandishing his samurai sword. Very probably he could barely read. Yet by the summer of 1936, when he was released from prison, he had risen to the top, in every sense of the word, of the right wing. He had charisma, a solid ideology, powers of speech making to command a passionate response, political savvy, decisiveness, and above all the ability to steer society by using the weaknesses of the masses for leverage."

The man took a breath and cleared his throat again.

"Of course, as a right-wing thinker his theories and conception of the world were rather silly. Still, that scarcely mattered. The real question was how far he could organize his ranks behind them. Look at the way that Hitler took half-baked notions of *lebens-*

raum and racial superiority and organized them on the national level. The Boss, however, did not take that path. The path he chose was more covert—a shadow path. Never out in the open, his was to be a presence that manipulated society from behind the scenes. And for that reason, in 1937 he headed over to the Chinese mainland. But even so—well, let us leave it at that. To return to the cyst, what I mean to say is that the period in which the cyst appeared coincided precisely with the period in which he underwent a miraculous self-transformation."

"In your hypothesis," I said, "there was no causal relationship between the cyst and the self-transformation; instead the two were governed in parallel by some mysterious overriding factor."

"You catch on quickly," said the man. "Precise and to the point."

The man removed a second cigarette from the tabletop case and flicked it with his fingernail before putting it to his lips. He did not light it. "Let us take things in order," he said.

A weighty silence ensued.

"We built a kingdom," the man began again. "A powerful underground kingdom. We pulled everything into the picture. Politics, finance, mass communications, the bureaucracy, culture, all sorts of things you would never dream of. We even subsumed elements that were hostile to us. From the establishment to the anti-establishment, everything. Very few if any of them even noticed they had been co-opted. In other words, we had ourselves a tremendously sophisticated organization. All of which the Boss built single-handedly after the war. It is as if the Boss commandeered the hull of a giant ship of state. If he pulls out the plug, the ship goes down. Passengers and all, lost at sea, and surely before anyone becomes aware of that fact."

At that the man lit his cigarette.

"Nonetheless, this organization has its limits. Namely, the king's death. When the king dies, the kingdom crumbles. The kingdom, you see, was built and maintained on this one man's genius. Which in my estimation is to say it was built and sustained by that mysterious factor. If the Boss dies, it means the end of everything, inasmuch as our organization was not a bureaucracy, but a perfectly tuned machine with one mind at its apex. Herein is the strength and weakness of our organization. Or rather, was. The death of the Boss will sooner or later bring a splintering of the organization, and like a Valhalla consumed by flames, it will plunge into a sea of mediocrity. There is no one to take over after the Boss. The organization will fall apart—a magnificent palace razed to make way for a public housing complex. A world of uniformity and certainty. Though perhaps you would think it fitting and proper. Fair allotment and all that. But think about it. The whole of Japan, leveled of mountains, coastlines or lakes, sprawling with uniform rows of public housing. Would that be the right thing?"

"I wouldn't know," I said. "I don't even know if the question itself makes sense."

"An intelligent answer," said the man, folding his fingers together on his lap. The tips of the fingers tapped out a slow rhythm. "All this talk of public housing is, as you know, merely for the sake of argument. More precisely, our organization can be divided into two elements. The part that moves ahead and the part that drives it ahead. Naturally, there are other parts managing other functions. Still, roughly divided, our organization is made up of these two parts. The other parts hardly amount to anything. The part at the forefront is the Will, and the part that backs up the forefront is the Gains. When people talk about the Boss, they make an issue only out of his Gains. And after the Boss dies, it will be only his Gains that people will clamor for a share of. Nobody wants the Will, because no one understands it. Herein we see the true meaning of what can and cannot be shared. The Will cannot be shared. It is either passed on in toto, or lost in toto."

The man's fingers kept drumming out that same slow rhythm on his lap. Other than that, everything about him had remained unchanged from the beginning. Same stare, same cold pupils, same smooth, expressionless face. That face had stayed turned toward me at the exact same angle the whole time.

"What is this Will?" I asked.

"A concept that governs time, governs space, and governs possibility."

"I don't follow."

"Of course. Few can. Only the Boss had a virtually instinctual understanding of it. One might even go so far as to say he negated self-cognition, thereupon realizing in its place something entirely revolutionary. To put it in simple terms for you, his was a revolution of labor incorporating capital and capital incorporating labor."

"A fantasy."

"Quite the contrary. It is cognition that is the fantasy," the man cut in. "Granted, everything I tell you now is mere words. Arrange them and rearrange them as I might, I will never be able to explain to you the form of Will the Boss possesses. My explanation would only show the correlation between myself and that Will by means of a correlation on the verbal level. The negation of cognition thus correlates to the negation of language. For when those two pillars of Western humanism, individual cognition and evolutionary continuity, lose their meaning, language loses meaning. Existence ceases for the individuum as we know it, and all becomes chaos. You cease to be a unique entity unto yourself, but exist simply as chaos. And not just the chaos that is you; your chaos is also my chaos. To wit, existence is communication, and communication, existence."

All of a sudden the room grew cold, and I had the inexplicable feeling that a nice warm bed had been readied for me there off to one side. Someone was beckoning me under the covers.

An illusion, of course. It was still September. Outside, countless thousands of cicadas were screeching away.

"The expansion of consciousness your generation underwent or at least sought to undergo at the end of the sixties ended in complete and utter failure because it was still rooted in the individual. That is, the attempt to expand consciousness alone, without any quantitative or qualitative change in the individual, was ultimately doomed. This is what I mean by mediocrity. How can I make you understand this? Not that I particularly expect you to understand. I am merely endeavoring to speak honestly.

"About that picture I handed you earlier," said the man. "It is a copy of a picture from the U.S. Army hospital medical records. It is dated July 27, 1946. The picture was drawn by the Boss himself at the request of the doctors. As one link in the process of documenting his hallucinatory experiences. In fact, according to the medical records, this sheep appeared with remarkably high frequency in the Boss's hallucinations. To put it in numerical terms, sheep figured in approximately eighty percent of his hallucinations, or in four out of five hallucinations. And not just any sheep. It was this chestnut-colored sheep with the star on its back.

"So it was that the Boss came to use this sheep, that is engraved on the lighter, as his own personal crest from 1936 on. I believe you will have noticed that this sheep is one and the same as the sheep in the medical records. Which is again the same as the one in your photograph. Most curious, do you not think?"

"Mere coincidence," I tossed out. I had meant to sound cool, but it didn't quite come off.

"There is more," the man continued. "The Boss was an avid collector of all available reference materials on sheep, domestic and foreign. Once a week he reviewed at length clippings concerning sheep gleaned from every newspaper and magazine published that week in Japan. I always lent him a hand in this. The Boss was emphatic about his sheep clippings. It was as if he were looking for some one thing. And ever since the Boss took ill, I've continued this effort on a personal level. I have actually taken an interest in this pursuit. Who knows what might come to light? That is how you came into the picture. You and your sheep. Any way one looks at it, this is no coincidence."

I balanced the lighter in my hand. It had an excellent feel to it. Not too heavy, not too light. To think that there was such perfect heft in the world.

"And why do you suppose the Boss was so intent on finding that sheep? Any ideas?"

"None whatsoever," I said. "It would be quicker to ask the Boss."

"If I could ask him, I would. The Boss has been in a coma for two weeks now. Very probably he will never regain consciousness. And if the Boss dies, the mystery of the sheep with the star on its back will be buried with him forever. I, for one, am not about to stand by and let that happen. Not for reasons of my own personal loss, but for the greater good of all."

I cocked open the lid of the lighter, struck the flint to light the flame, then closed the lid.

"I am sure you think that all I am saying is a load of nonsense. And perhaps it is. It might well turn out to *be* total nonsense. But just consider, this may be the sum total of all that is left to us. The Boss will die. That one Will shall die. Then everything around that Will shall perish. All that shall remain will be what can be counted in numbers. Nothing else will be left. That is why I want to find that sheep."

He closed his eyes a few seconds for the first time, saying nothing for a moment. Then: "If I might offer my hypothesis—a hypothesis and nothing more, forget I ever said a thing if it does nothing for you—I cannot help but feel that our sheep here formed the basic mold of the Boss's Will."

"Sounds like animal crackers," I said.

The man ignored my comment.

"Very probably the sheep found its way into the Boss. That would have been in 1936. And for the next forty years or so, the sheep remained lodged in the Boss. There inside, it must have found a pasture, a birch forest. Like the one in that photograph. What think you?"

"An extremely interesting hypothesis," I said.

"It is special sheep. A v-e-r-y special sheep. I want to find it and for that I will need your help."

"And what do you plan to do with it once you find it?"

"Nothing at all. There is probably nothing I could do. The scale of things is far too vast for me to do much of anything. My only wish is to see it all out at last with my own eyes. And if that sheep should wish anything, I shall do all in my power to comply. Once the Boss dies, my life will have lost almost all meaning anyway."

At that he fell silent. I too was silent. Only the the cicadas kept at it. They and the trees in the garden rustling their leaves in the near-dusk breeze. The house itself was agonizingly quiet. As if spores of death were drifting about in some unpreventable contagion. I tried to picture the pasture in the Boss's head. A pasture forlorn and forsaken, the grass withered, the sheep all gone.

"I will ask you one more time: tell me by what route you obtained the photograph," the man said.

"I cannot say," I said.

The man heaved a sigh. "I have attempted to talk to you

honestly. Therefore I had hoped that you would talk to me honestly as well."

"I am not in a position to talk. If I were to talk, it might pose problems for the person who provided it."

"Which is to say," interposed the man, "that you have some reasonable grounds to believe that some problems might come to this person in connection with the sheep."

"No grounds whatsoever. I'm playing my hunches. There's got to be a catch. I've felt that the whole time I've been talking to you. Like there's a hook somewhere. Call it sixth sense."

"And therefore you cannot speak."

"Correct," I said. Giving the situation further thought, I went on: "I'm something of an authority on troublemaking. I can claim to be second to none in the ways and means of creating problems for others. I live my life trying my best to avoid things ever coming to that. Which ultimately only creates more problems. It's all the same. That's the way things go down. Yet, no matter that I know it's all the same, it doesn't change anything. Nothing gets that way from the start. It's only a pretext."

"I am not sure I follow you."

"What I am saying is, mediocrity takes many forms."

I put a cigarette to my lips, lit it with the lighter in my hand, and took a puff. I felt ever so slightly more at ease.

"You do not have to speak if you do not want to," said the man. "Instead, I will send you out in search of the sheep. These are our final terms. If within two months from now you succeed in finding the sheep, we are prepared to reward you however you would care to request. But if you should fail to find it, it will be the end of you and your company. Agreed?"

"Do I have any choice?" I asked. "And what if no such sheep with a star on its back ever existed in the first place?"

"It is still the same. For you and for me, there is only whether you find the sheep or not. There are no in-betweens. I am sorry to have to put it this way, but as I have already said, we are taking you up on your proposition. You hold the ball, you had better run for the goal. Even if there turns out not to have been any goal."

"So that's how it stands?"

The man took a fat envelope out of his pocket and placed it

before me. "Use this for expenses. If you run out, give us a call. There is more where this came from. Any questions?"

"No questions, but one comment."

"Which is?"

"This all has got to be, patently, the most unbelievable, the most ridiculous story I have ever heard. Somehow coming from your mouth, it has the ring of truth, but I doubt anyone would believe me if I told them what happened today."

Almost imperceptibly, the man curled his lip. He conceivably could have been smiling. "From tomorrow, you're on the case. As I said, you have two months from today."

"It's a tough job. Two months might not be enough. I mean you're asking me to seek out one sheep from the entire countryside."

The man stared me straight in the face and said nothing. Making me feel like an empty pool. A filthy, cracked, empty pool that might never see another year's use. He looked at me a full thirty seconds without blinking. Then slowly he opened his mouth.

"It is time for you to be going," he said.

It sure seemed that way.

19

The Limo and Its Driver, Again

"Will you be returning to your office? Or to somewhere else?" the chauffeur asked. It was the same chauffeur from the trip out, but his manner seemed a bit more personable now. Guess he took to people easily.

I gave my arms and legs a full stretch on the roomy backseat and considered where I should go. I had no intention of returning to the office. Technically I was still on leave, and I wasn't about to try to explain all this to my partner. I wasn't about to go straight home either. Right now I needed a good dose of regular people walking on two legs in a regular way in a regular place.

"Shinjuku Station, west exit," I said.

Traffic was jammed solid in the direction of Shinjuku. Evening rush hour, among other things. Past a certain point the cars seemed practically glued in place, motionless. Every so often a wave would pass through the cars, budging them forward a few inches. I thought about the rotational speed of the earth. How many miles an hour was this road surface whirling through space? I did a quick calculation in my head and came up with a figure that could have been no faster than the Spinning Teacup at a carnival. There're many things we don't really know. It's an illusion that we know anything at all. If a group of aliens were to stop me and ask, "Say, bud, how many miles an hour does the earth spin at the equator?" I'd be in a fix. Hell, I don't even know why Wednesday follows Tuesday. I'd be an intergalactic joke.

I've read *And Quiet Flows the Don* and *The Brothers Karamazov* three times through. I've even read *Ideologie Germanica* once. I can even recite the value of *pi* to sixteen places. Would I still be a joke? Probably. They'd laugh their alien heads off.

"Would you care to listen to some music, sir?" asked the chauffeur.

"Good idea," I said.

And at that a Chopin ballade filled the car. I got the feeling I was in a dressing room at a wedding reception.

"Say," I asked the chauffeur, "you know the value of *pi*?"

"You mean that 3.14 whatzit?"

"That's the one. How many decimal places do you know?"

"I know it to thirty-two places," the driver tossed out. "Beyond that, well . . ."

"Thirty-two places?"

"There's a trick to it, but yes. Why do you ask?"

"Oh, nothing really," I said, crestfallen. "Never mind."

So we listened to Chopin as the limousine inched forward ten yards. People in cars and buses around us glared at our monster vehicle. None too comfortable, being the object of so much attention, even with the opaque windows.

"Awful traffic," I said.

"That it is, but sure as dawn follows night, it's got to let up sometime."

"Fair enough, but doesn't it get on your nerves?"

"Certainly. I get irritated, I get upset. Especially when I'm in a hurry. But I see it all as part of our training. To get irritated is to lose our way in life."

"That sounds like a religious interpretation of a traffic jam if there ever was one."

"I'm a Christian. I don't go to church, but I've always been a Christian."

"Is that so? Don't you see any contradiction between being a Christian and being the chauffeur for a major right-wing figure?"

"The Boss is an honorable man. After the Lord, the most godly person I've ever met."

"You've met God?"

"Certainly. I telephone Him every night."

"Excuse me?" I stammered. Things were starting to jumble up in my head again. "If everyone called God, wouldn't the lines be busy all the time? Like directory assistance right around noon."

"No problem there. God is your simultaneous presence. So even if a million people were to telephone Him at once, He'd be able to speak with everyone simultaneously."

"I'm no expert, but is that an orthodox interpretation? I mean, theologically speaking."

"I'm something of a radical. That's why I don't go to church."

"I see," I said.

The limousine advanced fifty yards. I put a cigarette to my lips and was about to light up when I saw I'd been holding the lighter in my hand the whole time. Without realizing it, I'd walked off with the sheep-engraved silver Dupont. It felt molded to my palm as naturally as if I'd been born with it. The balance and feel couldn't have been better. After a few seconds' thought, I decided it was mine. Who's going to miss a lighter or two? I opened and closed the lid a few times, lit up, and put the lighter in my pocket. By way of compensation, I slipped my Bic disposable into the pocket of the door.

"The Boss gave me it a few years ago," said the chauffeur out of nowhere.

"Gave you what?"

"God's telephone number."

I let out a groan so loud it drowned out everything else. Either I was going crazy or they were all looney toons.

"He told just you, alone, in secret?"

"Yes. Just me, in secret. He's a fine gentleman. Would you care to get to know Him?"

"If possible," I said.

"Well, then, it's Tokyo 9-4-5- . . ."

"Just a second," I said, pulling out my notebook and pen. "But do you really think it's all right, telling me like this?"

"Sure, it's all right. I don't go telling just anyone. And you seem like a good person."

"Well, thank you," I said. "But what should I talk to God about? I'm not Christian or anything."

"No problem there. All you have to do is to speak honestly about whatever concerns you or troubles you. No matter how trivial you might think it is. God never gets bored and never laughs at you."

"Thanks. I'll give him a call."

"That's the spirit," said the chauffeur.

Traffic began to flow smoothly as the Shinjuku skyscrapers came into view. We didn't speak the rest of the way there.

20

Summer's End, Autumn's Beginning

By the time the limousine reached its destination, a pale lavender dusk had spread over the city. A brisk wind blew between the buildings bearing tidings of summer's end, rustling the skirts of women on their way home from work.

I went to the top of a high-rise hotel, entered the spacious bar, and ordered a Heineken. It took ten minutes for the beer to come. Meanwhile, I planted an elbow on the armrest of my chair, rested my head on my hand, and shut my eyes. Nothing came to mind. With my eyes closed, I could hear hundreds of elves sweeping out my head with their tiny brooms. They kept sweeping and sweeping. It never occurred to any of them to use a dustpan.

When the beer finally arrived, I downed it in two gulps. Then I ate the whole dish of peanuts that came with it. The sweeping had all but stopped.

I went over to the telephone booth by the register and tried calling my girlfriend, her with the gorgeous ears. But she wasn't at her place and she wasn't at mine. She'd probably stepped out to eat. She never ate at home.

Next I tried my ex-wife. I reconsidered and hung up after the second ring. I didn't have anything to say to her after all, and I didn't want to come off like a jerk.

After them, there was no one to call. Smack in the middle of a city with a million people out roaming the streets, and no one to talk to. I gave up, pocketed the ten-yen coin, and exited the booth. Then I put in an order with a passing waiter for two more Heinekens.

And so the day came to an end. I could hardly have spent a more pointless day. The last day of summer, and what good had it been? Outside, an early autumn darkness had come over everything. Strings of tiny yellow street lamps threaded everywhere below. Seen from up here, they looked ready to be trampled on.

The beer came. I polished off the one, then dumped the dish of peanuts into the palm of my hand and proceeded to eat them, bit by bit. Four middle-aged women, finished with swimming lessons at the hotel pool, sat at the next table chatting over colorful tropical cocktails. A waiter stood by, rigidly upright, crooking his neck to yawn. Another waiter explained the menu to a middle-aged American couple. After the peanuts, I moved on to my third Heineken. After it was gone, I didn't know what to do with my hands.

I fished the envelope out of the hip pocket of my Levi's, tore open the seal, and started to count the stack of ten-thousand-yen notes. It looked more like a deck of cards than a bound packet of new bills. Halfway through, my fingers began to tire. At ninety-six, an elderly waiter came to clear away my empty bottles, asking whether to bring another. I nodded as I continued counting. He seemed totally uninterested in what I was doing.

There were one hundred and fifty bills. I stuck them back into the envelope and shoved it back into my hip pocket just as the new beer came. Again I ate the whole dish of peanuts, and only then did it occur to me that I was hungry. But why was I so hungry? I'd only eaten one slice of fruitcake since morning.

I called the waiter, ordered a cheese and cucumber sandwich. Hold the chips, double the pickles. Might they have nail clippers? Of course, they did. Hotel bars truly have everything you could ever want. One place even had a French-Japanese dictionary when I needed it.

I took my time with this beer, took a long look at the night scenery, took my time trimming my nails over the ashtray. I looked back at the scenery, then I filed my nails. And so on into the night. I'm well on the way to veteran class when it comes to killing time in the city.

A built-in ceiling speaker called my name. At first it didn't sound like my name. Only a few seconds after the announcement was over did it sink in that I'd heard the special characteristics of my name, and only gradually then did it come to me that my name was my name.

The waiter brought a cordless transceiver-phone over to the table.

"There has been a small change in plans," said the voice I knew from somewhere. "The Boss's condition has taken a sudden turn for the worse. There is not much time left, I fear. So we are curtailing your time limit."

"To how long?"

"One month. We cannot wait any longer. If after one month you have not found that sheep, you are finished. You will have nowhere to go back to."

One month. I thought it over. But my head was beyond dealing with concepts of time. One month, two months, was there any real difference? And who had any idea, any standard, of how much time it should take to find one sheep in the first place? "How did you know to find me here?" I asked.

"We are on top of most things," said the man.

"Except the whereabouts of one sheep," I said.

"Exactly," said the man. "Anyway, get on it, you waste too much time. You should take good account of where you now stand. You have only yourself to blame for driving yourself into that corner."

He had a point. I used the first ten-thousand yen note out of the envelope to pay the check. Down on the ground, people were still walking about on two legs, but the sight no longer gave me much relief.

21

One in Five Thousand

Returning to my apartment from the hotel bar, I found three pieces of mail together with the evening paper in my mailbox. A balance statement from my bank, an invitation to what promised to be a dud of a party, and a direct-mail flyer from a used-car dealership. The copy read: "BRIGHTEN UP YOUR LIFE—MOVE UP TO A CLASSY CAR." Thanks, but no thanks. I put all three envelopes together and tore them in half.

I took some juice out of the refrigerator and sat down at the kitchen table with it. On the table was a note from my girlfriend: "Gone out to eat. Back by 9:30." The digital clock on the table read 9:30. I watched it flip over to 9:31, then to 9:32.

When I got bored with watching the clock, I got out of my clothes, took a shower, and washed my hair. There were four types of shampoo and three types of hair rinse in the bathroom. Every time she went to the supermarket, she stocked up on something. Step into the bathroom and there was bound to be a new item. I counted four kinds of shaving cream and five tubes of toothpaste. Quite an inventory. Out of the shower, I changed into jogging shorts and a T-shirt. Gone was the grime of one bizarre day. At last I felt refreshed.

At 10:20 she returned with a shopping bag from the supermarket. In the bag were three scrub brushes, one box of paperclips, and a well-chilled six-pack of canned beer. So I had another beer.

"It was about sheep," I said.

"Didn't I tell you?" she said.

I took some sausages out of the refrigerator, browned them in a frying pan, and served them up for us to eat. I ate three and she ate two. A cool breeze blew in through the kitchen window.

I told her about what happened at the office, told her about the limo ride, the estate, the steely-eyed secretary, the blood cyst, and the heavyset sheep with the star on its back. I was talking forever. By the time I'd finished talking, it was eleven o'clock.

All that said and done, she didn't seem taken aback in the least. She'd cleaned her ears the whole time she listened, yawning occasionally.

"So when do you leave?"

"Leave?"

"You have to find the sheep, don't you?"

I looked up at her, the pull-ring of my second beer still on my finger. "I'm not going anywhere," I said.

"But you'll be in a lot of trouble if you don't."

"No special trouble. I was planning on quitting the company anyway. I'll always be able to find enough work to get by, no matter who interferes. They're not about to kill me. Really!"

She pulled a new cotton swab out of the box and fingered it awhile. "But it's actually quite simple. All you have to do is find one sheep, right? It'll be fun."

"Nobody's going to find anything. Hokkaido's a whole lot bigger than you think. And sheep—there've got to be hundreds of thousands of them. How are you going to search out one single sheep? It's impossible. Even if the sheep's got a star marked on its back."

"Make that five thousand sheep."

"Five thousand?"

"The number of sheep in Hokkaido. In 1947, there were two hundred seventy thousand sheep in Hokkaido, but now there are only five thousand."

"How is it you know something like that?"

"After you left, I went to the library and checked it out."

I heaved a sigh. "You know everything, don't you?"

"Not really. There's lot more that I don't know."

I snorted, then opened the second beer and split it between us.

"In any case, there are only five thousand sheep in Hokkaido. According to government surveys. How about it? Aren't you even a little relieved?"

"It's all the same," I said. "Five thousand sheep, two hundred seventy thousand sheep, it's not going to make much difference. The problem is still finding one lone sheep in that vast landscape. On top of which, we haven't a lead to go on."

"It's not true we don't have a lead. First, there's the photograph, then there's your friend up there, right? You're bound to find out something one way or another."

"Both are awfully vague as leads go. The landscape in the photograph is absolutely too ordinary, and you can't even read the postmark on the Rat's letter!"

She drank her beer. I drank my beer.

"Don't you like sheep?" she asked.

"I like sheep well enough."

I was starting to get confused again.

"Besides," I went on, "I've already made up my mind. Not to go, I mean." I meant to convince myself, but the words didn't come out right.

"How about some coffee?"

"Good idea," I said.

She cleared away the beer cans and glasses and put the kettle on. Then while waiting for the water to boil, she listened to a cassette in the other room. Johnny Rivers singing "Midnight Special" followed by "Roll Over Beethoven." Then "Secret Agent Man." When the kettle whistled, she made the coffee, singing along with "Johnny B. Goode." The whole while I read the evening paper. A charming domestic scene. If not for the matter of the sheep, I might have been very happy.

As the tape wound on, we drank our coffee and nibbled on a few crackers in silence. I went back to the evening paper. When I finished it, I began reading it again. Here a coup d'état, there a film actor dying, elsewhere a cat who does tricks—nothing much that related to me. It didn't matter to Johnny Rivers, who kept right on singing. When the tape ended, I folded up the paper and looked over at her.

"I can't figure it out. You're probably right that it's better to do something than nothing. Even if it's futile in the end, at least we looked for the sheep. On the other hand, I don't like being ordered and threatened and pushed around."

"To a greater or lesser extent, everybody's always being ordered and threatened and pushed around. There may not be anything better we could hope for."

"Maybe not," I said, after a moment's pause.

She said nothing and started to clean her ears again. From time to time, her fleshy earlobes showed through the long strands of hair.

"It's beautiful right now in Hokkaido. Not many tourists, nice weather. What's more, the sheep'll all be out and about. The ideal season."

"I guess."

"If," she began, crunching on the last cracker, "if you wanted to take me along, I'd surely be a help."

"Why are you so stuck on this sheep hunt?"

"Because I'd like to see that sheep myself."

"But why should I go breaking my back over this one lousy sheep? And then drag you into this mess on top of it?"

"I don't mind. Your mess is my mess," she said, with a cute little smile. "I've got this thing about you."

"Thanks."

"That's all you can say?"

I pushed the newspaper over to a corner of the table. The slight breeze coming in through the window wafted my cigarette smoke off somewhere.

"To be honest, there's something about this whole business that doesn't sit right with me. There's a hook somewhere."

"Like what?"

"Like everything but everything," I said. "The whole thing's so damn stupid, yet everything has a painful clarity to it, and the picture all fits together perfectly. Not a good feeling at all."

She paused a second, picked up a rubber band from the table, and started playing with it.

"But isn't that friend of yours already up to his neck in trouble? If not, why would he have gone out of his way to send you that photo?"

She had me there. I'd laid all my cards out on the table, and she'd trumped every one of them. She'd seen straight through me.

"I really think it has to be done. We'll find that sheep, you'll see," she said, grinning.

She finished her ear-cleaning ritual and wrapped up the cotton swabs in a tissue to throw away. Then she picked up a rubber band and tied her hair back behind her ears.

"Let's go to bed," she said.

22

Sunday Afternoon Picnic

I woke up at nine in an empty bed. No note. Only her handkerchief and underwear drying by the washbasin. Probably gone out to eat, I guessed, then to her place.

I got orange juice out of the refrigerator and popped three-day-old bread into the toaster. It tasted like wall plaster.

Through the kitchen window I could see the neighbor's oleander. Far off, someone was practicing piano. It sounded like tripping down an up escalator. On a telephone pole, three plump pigeons burbled mindlessly away. Something had to be on their mind to be going on like that, maybe the pain from corns on their feet, who knows? From the pigeons' point of view, probably it was I who looked mindless.

As I stuffed the second piece of toast down my gullet, the pigeons disappeared, leaving only the telephone pole and the oleander.

It was Sunday morning. The newspaper's weekend section included a color photo of a horse jumping a hedge. Astride the horse, an ill-complexioned rider in a black cap casting a baleful glare at the next page, which featured a lengthy description of what to do and what not to do in orchid cultivation. There were hundreds of varieties of orchids, each with a history of its own.

Royalty had been known to die for the sake of orchids. Orchids had an ineffable aura of fatalism. And on the article went. To all things, philosophy and fate.

Now that I'd made up my mind to go off in search of the sheep, I was charged up and raring to go. It was the first time I'd felt like this since I'd crossed the great divide of my twentieth year. I piled the dishes into the sink, gave the cat his breakfast, then dialed the number of the man in the black suit. After six rings he answered.

"I hope I didn't wake you," I said.

"Hardly the question. I rise quite early," he said. "What is it?"

"Which newspaper do you read?"

"Eight papers, national and local. The locals do not arrive until evening, though."

"And you read them all?"

"It is part of my work," said the man patiently. "What of it?"

"Do you read the Sunday pages?

"Of necessity, yes," he said.

"Did you see the photo of the horse in the weekend section?"

"Yes, I saw the horse photo," said the man.

"Don't the horse and rider seem to be thinking of two totally different things?"

Through the receiver, a silence stole into the room. There wasn't a breath to be heard. It was a silence strong enough to make your ears hurt.

"This is what you called me about?" asked the man.

"No, just small talk. Nothing wrong with a little topic of conversation, is there?"

"We have other topics of conversation. For instance, sheep." He cleared his throat. "You will have to excuse me, but I am not as free with my time as you. Might you simply get on with your concern as quickly as possible?"

"That's the problem," I said. "Simply put, from tomorrow I'm thinking of going off in search of that sheep. I thought it over a lot, but in the end that's what I decided. Still, I can only see myself doing it at my own pace. When I talk, I will talk as I like. I mean I have the right to make small talk if I want. I don't like having my every move watched and I don't like being pushed around by nameless people. There, I've said my piece."

"You obviously do not know where you stand."

"Nor do you know where you stand. Now listen, I thought it over last night. And it struck me. What have I got to feel threatened about? Next to nothing. I broke up with my wife, I plan to quit my job today, my apartment is rented, and I have no furnishings worth worrying about. By way of holdings, I've got maybe two million yen in savings, a used car, and a cat who's getting on in years. My clothes are all out of fashion, and my records are ancient. I've made no name for myself, have no social credibility, no sex appeal, no talent. I'm not so young anymore, and I'm always saying dumb things that I later regret. In a word, to borrow your turn of phrase, I am an utterly mediocre person. What have I got to lose? If you can think of anything, clue me in, why don't you?"

A brief silence ensued. In that interval, I picked the lint from a shirt button and with a ballpoint pen drew thirteen stars on a memo pad.

"Everybody has some one thing they do not want to lose," began the man. "You included. And we are professionals at finding out that very thing. Humans by necessity must have a midway point between their desires and their pride. Just as all objects must have a center of gravity. This is something we can pinpoint. Only when it is gone do people realize it even existed." Pause. "But I am getting ahead of myself. All this comes later. For the present, let me say that I do not turn an uncomprehending ear toward your speech. I shall take your demands into account. You can do as you like. For one month, is that clear?"

"Clear enough," I said.

"Well then, cheers," said the man.

At that, the phone clicked off. It left a bad aftertaste, the click of the receiver. In order to kill that aftertaste, I did thirty push-ups and twenty sit-ups, then washed the dishes, three days' worth. It almost had me feeling good again. A pleasant September Sunday after all. Summer had faded to a distant memory almost beyond recall.

I put on a clean shirt, a pair of Levi's without a ketchup stain, and a matching pair of socks. I brushed my hair. Even so, I couldn't bring back the Sunday-morning feeling I used to get when I was seventeen. So what else was new? Guess I've put on my share of years.

Next, I took my near-scrap Volkswagen out of the apartment-house parking lot, headed to the supermarket, and bought a dozen cans of cat food, a bag of kitty litter, a travel razor set, and underwear. At the doughnut shop, I sat at the counter and washed down a cinnamon doughnut with some tasteless coffee. The wall directly in front of the counter was mirrored, giving me an unobstructed view of myself. I sat there looking at my face, half-eaten doughnut still in hand. It made me wonder how other people saw me. Not that I had any way of knowing, of course. I finished off the doughnut and left.

There was a travel agency near the train station, where I booked two seats on a flight to Sapporo the following day. Then into the station arcade for a canvas shoulder bag and a rain hat. Each time I peeled another ten-thousand-yen note from the wad of bills in my pocket. The wad showed no sign of going down no matter how many bills I used. Only I showed signs of wear. There's that kind of money in the world. It aggravates you to have it, makes you miserable to spend it, and you hate yourself when it's gone. And when you hate yourself, you feel like spending money. Except there's no money left. And no hope.

I sat down on a bench in front of the station and smoked two cigarettes, deciding not to think about the money. The station plaza was filled with families and young couples out for a Sunday morning. Casually taking it all in, I thought of my ex-wife's parting remark that maybe we ought to have had children. To be sure, at my age it wouldn't have been unreasonable to have kids, but me a father? Good grief. What kid would want to have anyone like me for a father?

I smoked another cigarette before pushing through the crowd, each arm around a shopping bag, to the supermarket parking lot. While having the car serviced, I popped into a bookstore to buy three paperbacks. There went another two ten-thousand-yen notes. My pockets were stuffed with loose change.

When I got back to the apartment, I dumped all the change into a glass bowl and splashed cold water on my face. It had been forever since I'd gotten up, but when I looked at the clock, it was still before noon.

At three in the afternoon, my girlfriend returned. She was wearing a checkered shirt with mustard-colored slacks and intensely dark sunglasses. She had a large canvas bag like mine slung over her shoulder.

"I came packed and ready to go," she said, patting the bulging bag. "Will it be a long trip?"

"I wouldn't be surprised."

She stretched out on the sofa by the window, stared off at the ceiling with her sunglasses still on, and smoked a clove cigarette. I fetched an ashtray and went over to sit beside her. I stroked her hair. The cat appeared and jumped up on the sofa, putting his chin and forepaws over her ankles. When she'd had enough of her smoke, she transplanted what remained of the cigarette to my lips.

"Happy to be going on a trip?" I asked.

"Uh-huh, very happy. Especially because I'm going with you."

"You know, if we don't find that sheep, we won't have any place to come back to. We might end up traveling the rest of our lives."

"Like your friend?"

"I guess. In a way, we're all in the same boat. The only difference is that he's escaping out of his own choice and I'm being ricocheted about."

I ground out the cigarette in the ashtray. The cat raised his head and yawned, then resumed his position.

"Finished with your packing?" she asked.

"No, haven't begun. But I don't have too much to pack. A couple changes of clothes, soap, towel. You really don't need that whole bag yourself. If you need anything, you can buy it there. We've got more than enough money."

"I like it this way," she said, again with that cute little smile of hers. "I don't feel like I'm traveling unless I'm lugging a huge bag."

"You've got to be kidding. . . ."

A piercing bird call shot in through the open window, a call I'd never heard before. A new season's new bird.

A beam of afternoon sun landed on her cheek. I lazily watched a white cloud move from one edge of the window to the other. We stayed like that for the longest time.

"Is anything wrong?" she asked.

"I don't know how to put it, but I just can't get it through my head that here and now is really here and now. Or that I am really me. It doesn't quite hit home. It's always been this way. Only much later on does it ever come together. For the last ten years, it's been like this."

"Ten years?"

"There's been no end to it. That's all."

She laughed as she picked up the cat and let it down onto the floor. "Shall we?"

We made love on the sofa. A period piece of a sofa I'd bought at a junk store. Put your face up against it and you get the scent of history. Her supple body blended in with that scent. Gentle and warm like a vague recollection. I brushed her hair aside with my fingers and kissed her ear. The earth trembled. From that point on, time began to flow like a tranquil breeze.

I undid all the buttons of her shirt and cupped her breasts while I appreciated her body.

"Feeling really alive now," she said.

"You?"

"Mmm, my body, my whole self."

"I'm right with you," I said. "Truly alive."

How amazingly quiet, I thought. Not a sound anywhere around. Everybody but the two of us probably gone off somewhere to celebrate the first Sunday of autumn.

"You know, I really love this," she whispered.

"Mmm."

"It seems like we're having a picnic, it's so lovely."

"A picnic?"

"Yeah."

I wrapped both hands around her back and held her tight. Then I nuzzled my way through her bangs to kiss her ear again.

"It's been a long ten years for you?" she asked, down low by my ear.

"Long enough," I said. "A long, long time. Practically endless, not that I've managed to get anything over and done with."

She raised her head a tiny bit from the sofa armrest and smiled.

A smile I'd seen somewhere before, but for the life of me I couldn't place where or on whom. Women with their clothes off have a frightening similarity. Always throws me for a loop.

"Let's go look for the sheep," she said, eyes closed. "Once we get to looking for that sheep, things'll fall into place."

I looked into her face a while, then I gazed at both her ears. A soft afternoon glow enveloped her body as in an old still life.

23

Limited but Tenacious Thinking

At six o'clock, she got dressed, brushed her hair, brushed her teeth, and sprayed on her eau de cologne. I sat on the sofa reading *The Adventures of Sherlock Holmes.* The story began: "My colleague Watson is limited in his thinking to rather narrow confines, but possesses the utmost tenacity." Not a bad lead-in sentence.

"I'll be late tonight, so don't wait up for me," she said.

"Work?"

"Afraid so. I actually should have had today off, but those are the breaks. They pushed it on me because I'm taking off from tomorrow."

She went out, then after a moment or two the door opened.

"Say, what're you going to do about the cat while we're gone?" she asked.

"Oops, completely slipped my mind. But don't worry, I'll take care of it."

I brought out milk and cheese snacks for the cat. His teeth were so weak, he had a hard time with the cheese.

There wasn't a thing that looked particularly edible for me in the refrigerator, so I opened up a beer and watched television. Nothing newsworthy on the news either. On Sunday evenings like this, it's always some zoo scene. I watched the rundown of giraffes and elephants and pandas, then switched off the set and picked up the telephone.

"It's about my cat," I told the man.

"Your cat?"

"Yes, I have a cat."

"So?"

"So unless I can leave the cat with someone, I can't go anywhere."

"There are any number of kennels to be had thereabouts."

"He's old and frail. A month in a cage would do him in for sure."

I could hear fingernails drumming on a tabletop. "So?"

"I'd like you to take care of him. You've got a huge garden, surely you could take care of one cat."

"Out of the question. The Boss hates cats, and the garden is there to attract birds. One cat and there go all the birds."

"The Boss is unconscious, and the cat has no strength to chase down birds."

"Very well, then. I will send a driver for the cat tomorrow morning at ten o'clock."

"I'll provide the cat food and kitty litter. He only eats this one brand, so if you run out, please buy more of the same."

"Perhaps you would be so kind as to tell these details to the driver. As I believe I told you before, I am a busy man."

"I'd like to keep communications to one channel. It makes it clear where the responsibility lies."

"Responsibility?"

"In other words, say the cat dies while I'm gone, you'd get nothing out of me, even if I did find the sheep."

"Hmm," said the man. "Fair enough. You are somewhat off base, but you do quite well for an amateur. I shall write this down, so please speak slowly."

"Don't feed him fatty meat. He throws it all up. His teeth are bad, so no hard foods. In the morning, he gets milk and canned cat food, in the evening a handful of dried fish or meat or cheese snacks. Also please change his litter box daily. He doesn't like it dirty. He often gets diarrhea, but if it doesn't go away after two days the vet will have some medicine to give him."

Having gotten that far, I strained to hear the scrawl of a ballpoint pen on the other end of the line.

"He's starting to get lice in his ears," I continued, "so once a day you should give his ears a cleaning with a cotton swab and a little olive oil. He dislikes it and fights it, so be careful not to rupture the eardrum. Also, if you're worried he might claw the furniture, trim his claws once a week. Regular nail clippers are fine. I'm pretty sure he doesn't have fleas, but just in case it might be wise to give him a flea bath every so often. You can get flea shampoo at any pet shop. After his bath, you should dry him off with a towel and give him a good brushing, then last of all a once-over with a hair dryer. Otherwise he'll catch cold."

Scribble scribble scribble. "Anything else?"

"That's about it."

The man read back the items from his notepad. A memo well taken.

"Is that it?"

"Just fine."

"Well then," said the man. And the phone cut off.

It was already dark out. I slipped some change, my cigarettes, and a lighter into my pocket, put on my tennis shoes, and stepped outside. At my neighborhood dive, I drank a beer while listening to the latest Brothers Johnson record. I ate my chicken cutlet while listening to a Bill Withers record. I had some coffee while listening to Maynard Ferguson's "Star Wars." After all that, I felt as if I'd hardly eaten anything.

They cleared away my coffee cup and I put three ten-yen coins into the pink public phone and rang up my partner. His eldest son, who was still in grammar school, answered.

"Good day," I said.

"It's 'good evening,'" he corrected. I looked at my watch. Of course, he was right.

After a bit, my partner came to the phone.

"How'd it go?" he asked.

"Is it all right to talk now? I'm not catching you in the middle of eating?"

"We're in the middle of eating, but it's okay. Wasn't much of a meal, and anyway your story's got to be more interesting."

I related snatches of the conversation with the man in the black suit. Then I talked about the huge limo and the dying Boss. I didn't touch on the sheep. He wouldn't have believed it, and already this was too long and involved. Which naturally made everything more confusing than ever.

"I can't begin to follow you," said my partner.

"This is all confidential, you understand. If it gets out, it could mean a lot of trouble for you. I mean, with your family and all. . . ." I trailed off, picturing his high-class four-bedroom condominium, his wife with high blood pressure, his two cheeky sons. "I mean, that's how it is."

"I see."

"In any case, I have to be going on a trip from tomorrow. A long trip, I expect. One month, two months, three months, I really don't know. Maybe I'll never come back to Tokyo."

"Er . . . umm."

"So I want you to take over things at the company. I'm pulling out. I don't want to cause you any trouble. My work is pretty much done, and for all its being a co-venture, you hold down the important part. I'm only half playing there."

"But I need you there to take care of all the details."

"Consolidate your battle line, and go back to how it used to be. Cancel all advertising and editing work. Turn it back into a translation office. Like you were saying the other day yourself. Keep one secretary and get rid of the rest of the part-timers. You don't need them anymore. Nobody's going to complain if you give them two months' severance. As for the office, you can move to a smaller place. The income will go down, sure, but so will the outlay. And minus my take, yours'll increase, so in actual terms you won't be hurting. You won't have to worry about exploiting anyone so much, and taxes will be less of a problem. It'd be ideal for you."

"No go," he said, after some silence. "It won't work, I know it won't work."

"It'll be fine, I tell you. I've been through it all with you, so I know, no problem."

"It went well because we went into it together," he said. "Nothing I've tried to do by myself has ever come off."

"Now listen. I'm not talking about expanding business. I'm telling you to consolidate. The pre-industrial-revolution translation business we used to do. You and one secretary, plus five or six free-lancers you can farm out work to. There's no reason why you can't do fine."

There was a click as the last ten-yen coin dropped into the machine. I fed the phone another three coins.

"I'm not you," he said. "You can make it on your own. Not me. Things don't go anywhere unless I have someone to complain to or bounce ideas off of."

I put my hand over the receiver and sighed. The same old royal run around. Black goat eats white goat's letter unread, white goat eats black goat's letter . . .

"Hello, hello?" said my partner.

"I'm listening," I said.

On the other end of the line, I could hear his two kids fighting over which television channel to watch. "Think of your kids," I said. Not exactly fair, but I didn't have another card to play. "You can't afford to be sniveling. If you call it quits, it's all over for everybody. If you wanted to strike out against the world, you don't go having children. Straighten up, square away the business, stop drinking."

He fell silent for a long time. The waitress brought me an ashtray. I gestured with my hand for another beer.

"You've got me pinned," he came back. "I'll do my best. I have no confidence it'll go, but . . ."

I filled my glass with beer and took a sip. "It'll go fine. Think of six years ago. No money or connections, but everything came through, didn't it?" I said.

"Like I said, you have no idea how secure I felt because we started the thing together," said my partner.

"I'll be calling in again."

"Umm."

"Thanks for everything. All this time, it's been great," I said.

"Once you're finished with what you've got to do and come back to Tokyo, let's do some business together again."

"Sure thing."

I hung up.

Both he and I knew the probability of my returning to the job.

Work together six years and that much you understand.

I took my beer back to the table.

With the job out of the picture, I felt a surge of relief. Slowly but surely I was making things simpler. I'd lost my hometown, lost my teens, lost my wife, in another three months I'd lose my twenties. What'd be left of me when I got to be sixty, I couldn't imagine. There's no thinking about these things. There's no telling even what's going to happen a month from now.

I headed home and crawled into bed with my *Sherlock Holmes*. Lights out at eleven and I was fast asleep. I didn't wake once before morning.

24

One for the Kipper

At ten in the morning, that ridiculous submarine of an automobile was waiting outside my apartment building. From my third-story window, the limo looked more like an upside-down metal cookie cutter than a submarine. You could make a gigantic cookie that would take three hundred kids two weeks to eat. She and I sat on the windowsill looking down at the car.

The sky was appallingly clear. A sky from a prewar expressionist movie. Utterly cloudless, like a monumental eye with its eyelid cut off. A helicopter flying high off in the distance looked minuscule.

I locked all the windows, switched off the refrigerator, and checked the gas cock. The laundry brought in, bed covered with spread, ashtrays rinsed out, and an absurd number of medicinal items put in proper order by the washbasin. The rent paid two months in advance, the newspaper canceled. I looked back from the doorway into the lifeless apartment. For a moment, I thought about the four years of married life spent there, thought about the kids my wife and I never had.

The elevator door opened, and she called to me. I shut the steel door.

The chauffeur was intently polishing the windshield with a dry cloth as he waited for us. The car, not one single mark anywhere, gleamed in the sun to a burning, unearthly brilliance. The slightest touch of the hand and you'd get burned.

"Good morning," said the chauffeur. The very same religious chauffeur from two days ago.

"Good morning," said I.

"Good morning," said my girlfriend.

She held the cat. I carried the cat food and bag of kitty litter.

"Fabulous weather, isn't it?" said the chauffeur, looking up at the sky. "It's—how can I put it?—crystal clear."

I nodded.

"When it gets this clear, God's messages must have no trouble getting through at all," I offered.

"Nothing of the kind," said the chauffeur with a grin. "There are messages already in all things. In the flowers, in the rocks, in the clouds . . ."

"And cars?"

"In cars too."

"But cars are made by factories." Typical me.

"Whosoever makes it, God's will is worked into it."

"As in ear lice?" Her contribution.

"As in the very air," corrected the chauffeur.

"Well then, I suppose that cars made in Saudi Arabia have Allah in them."

"They don't produce cars in Saudi Arabia."

"Really?" Again me.

"Really."

"Then what about cars produced in America for export to Saudi Arabia? What god's in them?" queried my girlfriend.

A difficult question.

"Say now, we have to tell him about the cat," I launched a lifeboat.

"Cute cat, eh?" said the chauffeur, also relieved.

The cat was anything but cute. Rather, he weighed in at the opposite end of the scale, his fur was scruffy like an old, threadbare carpet, the tip of his tail was bent at a sixty-degree angle, his teeth were yellowed, his right eye oozed pus from a wound three years before so that by now he could hardly see. It was doubtful that he could distinguish between a tennis shoe and a potato. The pads of his feet were shriveled-up corns, his ears were infested with ear lice, and from sheer age he farted at least twenty times a day. He'd been a fine young tom the day my wife found him under a park bench and brought him home, but in the last few years he'd rapidly gone downhill. Like a bowling ball rolling toward the gutter. Also, he didn't have a name. I had no idea whether not having a name reduced or contributed to the cat's tragedy.

"Nice kitty-kitty," said the chauffeur, hand not outstretched. "What's his name?"

"He doesn't have a name."

"So what do you call the fella?"

"I don't call it," I said. "It's just there."

"But he's not a lump just sitting there. He moves about by his own will, no? Seems mighty strange that something that moves by its own will doesn't have a name."

"Herring swim around of their own will, but nobody gives them names."

"Well, first of all, there's no emotional bond between herring and people, and besides, they wouldn't know their name if they heard it."

"Which is to say that animals that not only move by their own will and share feelings with people but also possess sight and hearing qualify as deserving of names then?"

"There, you got it." The chauffeur nodded repeatedly, satisfied. "How about it? What say I go ahead and give the little guy a name?"

"Don't mind in the least. But what name?"

"How about 'Kipper'? I mean you were treating him like a herring after all."

"Not bad," I said.

"You see?" said the chauffeur.

"What do you think?" I asked my girlfriend.

"Not bad," she said. "It's like being witness to the creation of heaven and earth."

"Let there be Kipper," I said.

"C'mere, Kipper," said the chauffeur, picking up the cat. The cat got frightened, bit the chauffeur's thumb, then farted.

* * *

The chauffeur took us to the airport. The cat rode quietly up front next to the driver. Farting from to time to time. The driver kept opening the window, so we knew. Meanwhile, I cranked out instructions to the chauffeur about the cat. How to clean his ears, stores that sold litter-box deodorant, the amount of food to give him, things like that.

"Don't worry," said the chauffeur. "I'll take good care of him. I'm his godfather, you know."

The roads were surprisingly empty. The car raced to the airport like a salmon shooting upstream to spawn.

"Why do boats have names, but not airplanes?" I asked the chauffeur. "Why just Flight 971 or Flight 326, and not the *Bellflower* or the *Daisy*?"

"Probably because there're more planes than boats. Mass production."

"I wonder. Lots of boats are mass-produced, and they may outnumber planes."

"Still . . . ," said the chauffeur, then nothing for a few seconds. "Realistically speaking, nobody's going to put names on each and every city bus."

"I think it'd be wonderful if each city bus had a name," said my girlfriend.

"But wouldn't that lead to passengers choosing the buses they want to ride? To go from Shinjuku to Sendagaya, say, they'd ride the *Antelope* but not the *Mule*."

"How about it?" I asked my girlfriend.

"For sure, I'd think twice about riding the *Mule*," she said.

"But hey, think about the poor driver of the *Mule*," the chauffeur spoke up for drivers everywhere. "The *Mule*'s driver isn't to blame."

"Well put," said I.

"Maybe," said she, "but I'd still ride the *Antelope*."

"Well there you are," said the chauffeur. "That's just how it'd be. Names on ships are familiar from times before mass production. In principle, it amounts to the same thing as naming horses. So that airplanes treated like horses are actually given names too. There's the *Spirit of St. Louis* and the *Enola Gay*. We're looking at a full-fledged conscious identification."

"Which is to say that life is the basic concept here."

"Exactly."

"And that purpose, as such, is but a secondary element in naming."

"Exactly. For purpose alone, numbers are enough. Witness the treatment of the Jews at Auschwitz."

"Fine so far," I said. "So let's just say that the basis of naming is this act of conscious identification with living things. Why then do train stations and parks and baseball stadiums have names, if they're not living?"

"Why? Because it'd be chaos if stations didn't have names."

"No, we're not talking on the purposive level. I'd like you to explain it to me in principle."

The chauffeur gave this serious thought. He failed to notice that the traffic light had turned green. The camper van behind us honked its horn to the overture to the *The Magnificent Seven*.

"Because they're not interchangeable, I suppose. For instance, there's only one Shinjuku Station and you can't just replace it with Shibuya Station. This non-interchangeability is to say that they're not mass-produced. Are we clear on these two points?"

"Sure would be fun to have Shinjuku Station in Ekoda, though," said my girlfriend.

"If Shinjuku Station were in Ekoda, it would be Ekoda Station," countered the chauffeur.

"But it'd still have the Odakyu Line attached," she said.

"Back to the original line of discussion," I said. "If stations were interchangeable, what would that mean? If, for instance, all national railway stations were mass-produced fold-up type buildings and Shinjuku Station and Tokyo Station were absolutely interchangeable?"

"Simple enough. If it's in Shinjuku, it'd be Shinjuku Station; if it's in Tokyo, it'd be Tokyo Station."

"So what we're talking about here is not the name of a physical object, but the name of a function. A role. Isn't that purpose?"

The chauffeur fell silent. Only this time he didn't stay silent for very long.

"You know what I think?" said the chauffeur. "I think maybe we ought to cast a warmer eye on the subject."

"Meaning?"

"I mean towns and parks and streets and stations and ball fields and movie theaters all have names, right? They are all given names in compensation for their fixity on the earth."

A new theory.

"Well," said I, "suppose I utterly obliterated my consciousness and became totally fixed, would I merit a fancy name?"

The chauffeur glanced at my face in the rearview mirror. A suspicious look, as if I were laying some trap. "Fixed?"

"Say I froze in place, or something. Like Sleeping Beauty."

"But you already have a name."

"Right you are," I said. "I nearly forgot."

We received our boarding passes at the airport check-in counter and said goodbye to the chauffeur. He would have waited to see us off, but as there was an hour and a half before departure time, he capitulated and left.

"A real character, that one," she said.

"There's a place I know with no one but people like that," I said. "The cows there go around looking for pliers."

"Sounds like 'Home on the Pampas.'"

"Maybe so," I said.

We went into the airport restaurant and had an early lunch. Shrimp au gratin for me, spaghetti for her. I watched the 747s and Tristars take flight and swoop down to earth with a gravity that seemed fated. Meanwhile, she dubiously inspected each strand of spaghetti she ate.

"I thought that they always served meals on planes," she said, disgruntled.

"Nope," I said, waiting for the hot lump of gratin in my mouth to cool down, then gulping down some water. No taste but hot. "Meals only on international flights. They give you something to eat on longer domestic routes. Not exactly what you'd call a special treat, though."

"And movies?"

"No way. C'mon, it's only an hour to Sapporo."

"Then they give you nothing."

"Nothing at all. You sit in your seat, read your book, and arrive at your destination. Same as by bus."

"But no traffic lights."

"No traffic lights."

"Just great," she said with a sigh. She put down her fork, leaving half the spaghetti untouched.

"The thing is you get there faster. It takes twelve hours if you go by train."

"And where does the extra time go?"

I also gave up halfway through my meal and ordered two coffees. "Extra time?"

"You said planes save you over ten hours. So where does all that time go?"

"Time doesn't go anywhere. It only adds up. We can use those ten hours as we like, in Tokyo or in Sapporo. With ten hours we could see four movies, eat two meals, whatever. Right?"

"But what if I don't want to go to the movies or eat?"

"That's your problem. It's no fault of time."

She bit her lip as we looked out at the squat bodies of the 747s on the tarmac. 747s always remind me of a fat, ugly old lady in the neighborhood where I used to live. Huge sagging breasts, swollen legs, dried-up neckline. The airport, a likely gathering place for the old ladies. Dozens of them, coming and going, one after the other. The pilots and stewardesses, strutting back and forth in the lobby with heads held high, seemed quaintly planar, like little girls' cardboard cut-outs. I couldn't help thinking how it wasn't like the DC-7 and Friendship-7 days, but maybe it was.

"Well," she went on, "does time expand?"

"No, time does not expand," I answered. I had spoken, but why didn't it sound like my voice? I coughed and drank my coffee. "Time does not expand."

"But time is actually increasing, isn't it? You yourself said that time adds up."

"That's only because the time needed for transit has decreased. The sum total of time doesn't change. It's only that you can see more movies."

"If you wanted to see movies," she added.

As soon as we arrived in Sapporo, we actually did see a double feature.

PART SEVEN

THE DOLPHIN HOTEL AFFAIR

25

Transit Completed at Movie Theater; On to the Dolphin Hotel

The entire flight, she sat by the window and looked down at the scenery. I sat next to her reading my *Adventures of Sherlock Holmes*. Not a single cloud in the sky the whole time, the airplane riding on its shadow over the earth. Or more accurately, since we were in the plane, our shadows figured as well inside the shadow of the airplane skimming over mountain and field. Which would mean we too were imprinted into the earth.

"I really liked that guy," she said after drinking her orange juice.

"That guy who?"

"The chauffeur."

"Hmm," I said, "I liked him too."

"And what a great name, 'Kipper.' "

"For sure. A great name. The cat might be better off with him than he ever was with me."

"Not 'the cat,' 'Kipper.' "

"Right. 'Kipper.' "

"Why didn't you give the cat a name all this time?"

"Why indeed," I puzzled. Then I lit up a cigarette with the sheep-engraved lighter. "I think I just don't like names. Basically, I can't see what's wrong with calling me 'me' or you 'you' or us 'us' or them 'them.' "

"Hmm," she said. "I do like the word 'we,' though. It has an Ice Age ring to it."

"Ice Age?"

"Like 'We go south' or 'We hunt mammoth' or . . ."

When we stepped outside at Chitose Airport, the air was chillier than we'd expected. I pulled a denim shirt over my T-shirt, she a knit vest over her shirt. Autumn had come over this land one whole month ahead of Tokyo.

"We weren't supposed to run into an Ice Age, were we?" she asked on the bus to Sapporo. "You hunting mammoths, me raising children."

"Sounds positively inviting," I said.

She soon fell asleep, leaving me gazing through the bus windows at the endless procession of deep forest on both sides of the road.

We hit a coffee shop first thing on arriving in the city.

"Right off, let's set our prime directives," I said. "We'll have to divide up. That is, I go after the scene in the photograph. You go after the sheep. That way we save time."

"Very pragmatic."

"If things go well," I amended. "In any case, you can cover the major former sheep ranches of Hokkaido and study up on sheep breeds. You can probably find what you need at a government office or the local library."

"I like libraries," she said.

"I'm glad."

"Do I start right away?"

I looked at my watch. Three-thirty. "Nah, it's already getting late. Let's start tomorrow. Today we'll take it easy, find a place to stay, have dinner, take a bath, and get some sleep."

"I wouldn't mind seeing a movie," she said.

"A movie?"

"What with all that time we saved by flying."

"Good point," I said. So we popped into the first movie theater that caught our eye.

* * *

What we ended up seeing was a crime-occult double feature. There was hardly a soul in the place. It'd been ages since I'd been in a theater that empty. I counted the people in the audience to pass the time. Eight, including ourselves. There were more characters in the films.

The films were exemplars of the dreadful. The sort of films where you feel like turning around and walking out the instant the title comes on after the roaring MGM lion. Amazing that films like that exist.

The first was the occult feature. The devil, who lives in the dripping, dank cellar of the town church and manipulates things through the weak preacher, takes over the town. The real question, though, was why the devil wanted to take over the town to begin with. All it was was a miserable nothing of a few blocks surrounded by cornfields.

Nonetheless, the devil had this terrible obsession with the town and grew furious that one last little girl refused to fall under his spell. When the devil got mad, his body shook like quivering green jelly. Admittedly, there was something endearing about that rage.

In front of us a middle-aged man was snoring away like a fog horn. To the extreme right there was some heavy petting in progress. Behind, someone let out a huge fart. Huge enough to stop the middle-aged man's snoring for a moment. A pair of high school girls giggled.

By reflex, I thought of Kipper. And it was only when I did that it came to me that we'd really left Tokyo and were now in Sapporo.

Funny about that.

Amid these thoughts I fell asleep. In my dreams, I encountered that green devil, but he wasn't endearing in the least. He remained silent and I just observed his machinations.

Meanwhile, the film ended, the lights came on, and I woke up. Each member of the audience yawned as if in predetermined order. I went to the snack bar and bought ice cream for us. It was hard as a rock, probably left over from last summer.

"You slept through the whole thing?"

"Uh-huh," I said. "How was it?"

"Pretty interesting. In the end, the whole town explodes."

"Wow."

The movie theater was deathly quiet. Or rather everything around us was deathly quiet. Not a common occurrence.

"Say," she said, "doesn't it seem like your body's in a state of transit or something?"

Now that she mentioned it, it actually did.

She held my hand. "Let's just stay like this. I'm worried."

"Okay."

"Unless we stay like this, we might get transported somewhere else. Someplace crazy."

As the theater interior grew dark again and the coming attractions began, I brushed her hair aside and kissed her ear. "It's all right. Don't worry."

"You're probably right," she said softly. "I guess we should have ridden in transportation with names after all."

For the next hour and a half, from the beginning to the end of the film, we stayed in a state of quiet transport in the darkness. Her head resting on my shoulder the whole time. My shoulder became warm and damp from her breath.

We came out of the movie theater and strolled the twilit streets, my arm around her shoulder. We felt closer than ever before. The commotion of passersby was comforting; faint stars were shining through in the sky.

"Are we really in the right city, the two of us?" she asked.

I looked up at the sky. The polestar was in the right position, but somehow it looked like a fake polestar. Too big, too bright.

"I wonder," I said.

"I feel like something's out of place," she said.

"That's what it's like, coming to a new city. Your body can't quite get used to it."

"But after a while you do get used to it, don't you?"

"After two or three days, you'll be fine," I said.

When we tired of walking, we went into the first restaurant we saw, drank draft beer, and ordered some salmon and potatoes. We'd walked in willy-nilly off the street and gotten lucky. The beer really hit the spot, and the food was actually good.

"Well then," I said after coffee, "what say we settle on a place to stay?"

"I've already got an image of a place," she said.

"Like what?"

"Never mind. Get a list of hotels and read off the names in order."

I asked a waiter to bring over the yellow pages and started reading the names listed in the "Hotels, Inns" section. After forty names, she stopped me.

"That's the one."

"Which one?"

"The last one you read."

"Dolphin Hotel," I said.

"That's where we're staying."

"Never heard of it."

"But I can't see us staying at any other hotel."

I returned the phone book, then called the Dolphin Hotel. A man with an indistinct voice answered, indicating they had double and single rooms available. And did they have other types of rooms besides doubles and singles? No. Doubles and singles were all. Confused, I reserved a double. The price: forty percent less than what I'd expected.

The Dolphin Hotel was located three blocks west and one block south of the movie theater we'd gone to. A small place, totally undistinguished. Its undistinguishedness was metaphysical. No neon sign, no large signboard, not even a real entryway. The glass front door, which resembled an employees' kitchen entrance, had next to it only a copper plate engraved with DOLPHIN HOTEL. Not even a picture of a dolphin.

The building was five stories tall, but it might as well have been a giant matchbox stood on end. It wasn't particularly old; still it was strikingly run-down. Most likely it was run-down when it was built.

This was our Dolphin Hotel.

Yet she apparently fell in love with the place the moment she set eyes on it.

"Not a bad hotel, eh?" she said.

"Not bad?" I tossed back her words.

"Cozy, no frills."

"No frills," I repeated. "By frills, I'm sure you mean clean sheets or a sink that doesn't leak or an air conditioner that works or reasonably soft toilet paper or fresh soap or curtains that prevent sunstroke."

"You always look at the dark side of things," she laughed. "Anyway, we didn't come here as tourists."

On opening the door, I found the lobby bigger than expected. In the middle of it was a set of parlor furniture and a large color TV; there was a quiz show on. Not a soul was in sight.

Large potted ornamentals sat on both sides of the front door, their leaves faded, nearly brown. I stood there taking everything in. The lobby was actually a lot less spacious than it had initially seemed. It appeared large because there were so few pieces of furniture. The parlor set, a grandfather clock, and a mirror. Nothing else.

I walked over and checked out the clock and mirror. Both were commemorative presents of some event or another. The clock was seven minutes off; the mirror made my head crooked on my body.

The parlor set was about as run-down as the hotel itself. The carpet was an unappealing orange, the sort of orange you'd get by leaving a choicely sunburnt weaving out in the rain for a week, then throwing it into the cellar until it mildewed. This was an orange from the early days of Technicolor.

On closer inspection, a balding middle-aged man lay, stretched out like a dried fish, asleep on the parlor set chaise longue. At first, I thought he was dead, but his nose twitched. There were the indentations of eyeglasses on the bridge of his nose, but no glasses anywhere. Which would mean that he hadn't fallen asleep while watching television. It didn't make sense.

I stood at the front desk and peeked over the counter. Nobody there. She rang the bell. It chimed across the expanse of lobby.

We waited thirty seconds and got no response. The man on the chaise longue didn't stir.

She rang the bell again.

Now the man on the chaise longue grunted. A self-accusing grunt. Then he opened his eyes and looked us over vacantly.

She gave the bell a third, serious ring.

The man sprang up and dashed across the lobby. He edged by me and went behind the counter. He was the desk clerk.

"Terrible of me," he said. "Really terrible of me. Fell asleep waiting for you."

"Sorry to wake you," I said.

"Not at all," said the desk clerk. He brought out a registration card and a ballpoint pen. He was missing the tips of the little and middle fingers on his left hand.

I wrote my name on the card but had second thoughts and crumpled it up and stuffed it in my pocket. I took another card and wrote a fake name and a fake address. An ordinary name and address, but not bad for a spur-of-the-moment name and address. I put down my occupation as real estate.

The desk clerk picked up his thick celluloid-rimmed glasses from beside the telephone and peered intently at the registration card.

"Suginami, Tokyo, . . . 29 years old, realtor."

I took a tissue from my pocket and wiped the ink from my fingers.

"Here on business?" asked the clerk.

"Uh, sort of," I said.

"How many nights?"

"One month," I said.

"One month?" He gave me a blank-white-sheet-of-drawing-paper look. "You'll be staying here one whole month?"

"Is there something wrong with that?"

"No, uh, nothing wrong, but well, we like to settle up payment three days at a time."

I set my satchel on the floor, counted out twenty ten-thousand-yen notes, and laid them on the counter.

"There's more if that runs out," I said.

The clerk scooped up the bills with the three fingers of his left hand and counted them with his right. Then he made out a receipt. "Would there be anything special you might care to see in the way of a room?"

"A corner room away from the elevator, if possible."

The clerk turned around and squinted at the keyboard. After

much ado, he chose room 406. The keyboard was almost entirely full. A real success story, the Dolphin Hotel.

There was no such thing as a bellboy, so we carried our bags to the elevator. As she said, no frills. The elevator shook like a large dog with lung disease.

"For an extended stay, there's nothing like your small, basic hotel."

"Your small, basic hotel"—not a bad turn of phrase. Like something from the travel pages of a women's fashion magazine: "After a long trip, your small, basic hotel is just the thing."

Nonetheless, the first thing I did upon opening the door to our small, basic hotel room was to grab a slipper to smash a cockroach that was creeping along the window frame. Then I picked up two pubic hairs lying by the foot of the bed and disposed of them in the trash. A new experience for me, seeing a cockroach in Hokkaido. Meanwhile, she ran the bath to temperature. And believe me, it was one noisy faucet.

"I tell you, we should've stayed in a better hotel," I opened the bathroom door and yelled in her direction. "We've got more than enough money."

"It's not a question of money. Our sheep hunt begins here. No argument, it had to be here."

I stretched out on the bed and smoked a cigarette, switched on the television and ran through all the channels, then turned it off. The only thing decent was the reception. Presently, the bathwater stopped and her clothes came flying out, followed by the sound of the hand shower.

Parting the window curtains, I looked out across the way onto a sordid menagerie of buildings every bit as incomprehensible as our Dolphin Hotel. Each one a dingy ash gray and reeking of piss just by their looks. Although it was already nine o'clock, I could see people in the few lit windows, busily working away. I couldn't tell what line of work it was, but none of them looked terribly happy. Of course, to their eyes, I probably looked a bit forlorn too.

I drew the curtains shut and returned to the bed, rolled over on the hard-as-asphalt starched sheets, and thought about my ex-wife. I thought about the man she was living with now. I knew almost everything there was to know about him. He'd been my friend, after all, so why shouldn't I know? Twenty-seven years old. A not very well-known jazz guitarist, but regular enough as not very well-known jazz guitarists go. Not a bad guy. No style, though. One year he'd drift between Kenny Burrell and B.B. King, another year between Larry Coryell and Jim Hall.

Why she'd up and choose him after me, I couldn't figure. Granted, you can pick out certain characteristics among individuals. Yet the only thing he had over me was that he could play guitar, and the only thing I had over him was that I could wash dishes. Most guitarists can't wash dishes. Ruin their fingers and there goes everything.

Then I found myself thinking about sex with her. By default, I tried to calculate the number of times we'd had sex in our four years of married life. An approximate count at best, and admittedly, what would be the point of an approximate count? I should have kept a diary. Or at least made some mark in a notebook. That way I'd have an accurate figure. Accurate figures give things a sense of reality.

My ex-wife kept precise records about sex. Not that she kept a diary per se. She recorded in a notebook exact data about her periods from her first year on and included sex as a supplementary reference. Altogether there were eight of these notebooks, all kept in a locked drawer together with important papers and photographs. These she showed to no one. That she kept records about sex is the full extent of my knowledge. What and how much she wrote, I have no idea. And now that we're no longer together, I'll probably never know.

"If I die," she told me, "burn these notebooks. Douse them in kerosene and let them burn till ash, then bury them. I'd never forgive you if one word remained."

"But I'm the one who's been sleeping with you. I pretty much know every inch of your body. What's there to be ashamed of at this late date?"

"Body cells replace themselves every month. Even at this very moment," she said, thrusting a skinny back of her hand before my eyes. "Most everything you think you know about me is nothing more than memories."

The woman—save for the month or so prior to our divorce—

was singularly methodical in her thinking. She had an absolutely realistic grasp on her life. Which is to say that no door once closed ever opened again, nor as a rule was any door left wide open.

Now all I know about her is my memories of her. And these memories fade further and further into the distance like displaced cells. Was it all biology?

26

Enter the Sheep Professor

We woke the next morning at eight, donned our clothes, headed down in the elevator, and out to a nearby coffee shop for breakfast. No, the Dolphin Hotel had no coffee shop.

"Like I said yesterday, we'll split up," I said, passing her a copy of the sheep photo. "I'll use the mountains in the background as a handle toward searching out the place. You'll research places where they raise sheep. You know what to do. Any clue, anything, it doesn't matter how small, is fine. Anything is an improvement over scouring the entire island of Hokkaido totally blind."

"I'm fine. Leave it up to me."

"Okay, let's meet back at the hotel in the evening."

"Don't worry so much," she said, putting on sunglasses. "Finding it's going to be a piece of cake."

Of course, it was no piece of cake. Things never happen that way. I went to the Territorial Tourist Agency, did the rounds of various tourist information centers and travel agents, inquired at the Mountaineering Association. In general, I checked all the places that had anything to do with tourism and mountains. Nobody could recall ever having seen the mountains in the photograph.

"They're such ordinary-looking mountains too," they all said. "Besides, the photo shows only a small part of them."

One whole day on the pavement and that was about as close to progress as I got. That is, the realization that it'd be difficult to identify mountains with nothing to distinguish them and with only a partial view of them.

I stopped into a bookstore and bought *The Mountains of Hokkaido* and a Hokkaido atlas, then went into a café, had two ginger ales, and skimmed through my purchases. As far as mountains were concerned, there was an unbelievable number in Hokkaido, all of them about the same in color and in shape. I tried comparing the mountains in the Rat's photograph with every mountain in the book; after ten minutes, I was dizzy. It was no comfort to learn that the number of mountains in the book represented but a tiny fraction of all the mountains in Hokkaido. Complicated by the fact that a mountain viewed from one angle gave a wholly different impression than from another angle.

"Mountains are living things," wrote the author in his preface to the book. "Mountains, according to the angle of view, the season, the time of day, the beholder's frame of mind, or any one thing, can effectively change their appearance. Thus, it is essential to recognize that we can never know more than one side, one small aspect of a mountain."

"Just great," I said out loud. An impossible task. At the five o'clock bell, I went out to sit on a park bench and eat corn with the pigeons.

Her efforts at information gathering fared better than mine, but ultimately they were futile too. We compared notes of the day's trials and tribulations over a modest dinner at a restaurant behind the Dolphin Hotel.

"The Livestock Section of the Territorial Government knew next to nothing," she said. "They've stopped keeping track of sheep. It doesn't pay to raise sheep. At least not by large-scale ranching or free-range grazing."

"In a way that makes the search easier."

"Not really. Ranchers still raise sheep quite actively and even have their own union, which the authorities keep tabs on. With middle- and small-scale sheep raising, however, it's difficult to keep any accurate count going. Everyone keeps a few sheep pretty much like they do cats and dogs. For what it's worth, I took down the addresses of the thirty sheep raisers they had listings for, but the papers were four years old and people move around a lot in four years. Japan's agricultural policies change every three years just like that, you know."

"Just great," I sighed into my beer. "Seems like we've come to a dead end. There must be more than a hundred similar mountains in Hokkaido, and the state of sheep raising is a total blank."

"This is the first day. We've only just begun."

"Haven't those ears of yours gotten the message yet?"

"No message for the time being," she said, eating her simmered fish and miso soup. "That much I know. I only get despairing messages when I'm confused or feeling some mental pinch. But that's not the case now."

"The lifeline only comes when you're on the verge of drowning?"

"Right. For the moment, I'm satisfied to be going through all this with you, and as long as I'm satisfied, I get no such message. So it's up to us to find that sheep on our own."

"I don't know," I said. "In a sense, if we don't find that sheep we'll be up to our necks in it. In what, I can't say, but if those guys say they're going to get us, they're going to get us. They're pros. No matter if the Boss dies, the organization will remain and their network extends everywhere in Japan, like the sewers. They'll have our necks. Dumb as it sounds, that's the way it is."

"Sounds like *The Invaders*."

"Ridiculous, I know. But the fact is we've gotten ourselves smack in the middle of it, and by 'ourselves' I mean you and me. At the start it was only me, but by now you're in the picture too. Still feel like you're not on the verge of drowning?"

"Hey, this is just the sort of thing I love. Let me tell you, it's more fun than sleeping with strangers or flashing my ears or proofreading biographical dictionaries. This is living."

"Which is to say," I interjected, "we're not drowning so we have no rope."

"Right. It's up to us to find that sheep. Neither you nor I have left so much behind, really."

Maybe not.

We returned to the hotel and had intercourse. I like that word *intercourse.* It poses only a limited range of possibilities.

Our third and fourth days in Sapporo came and went for naught. We'd get up at eight, have breakfast, split up for the day, and when evening came we'd exchange information over supper, return to the hotel, have intercourse, and sleep.

I threw away my old tennis shoes, bought new sneakers, and went around showing the photograph to hundreds of people. She made up a long list of sheep raisers based on sources from the government offices and the library, and started phoning every one of them. The results were nil. Nobody could place the mountain, and no sheep raiser had any recollection of a sheep with a star on its back. One old man said he remembered seeing that mountain in southern Sakhalin before the war. I wasn't about to believe that the Rat had gone to Sakhalin. No way can you send a letter special delivery from Sakhalin to Tokyo.

Gradually, I was getting worn down. My sense of direction had evaporated by our fourth day. When south became opposite east, I bought a compass, but going around with a compass only made the city seem less and less real. The buildings began to look like backdrops in a photography studio, the people walking the streets like cardboard cutouts. The sun rose from one side of a featureless land, shot up in a cannonball arc across the sky, then set on the other side.

The fifth, then the sixth day passed. October laid heavy on the town. The sun was warm enough but the wind grew brisk, and by late in the day I'd have to put on a thin cotton windbreaker. The streets of Sapporo were wide and depressingly straight. Up until then, I'd had no idea how much walking around in a city of nothing but straight lines can tire you out.

I drank seven cups of coffee a day, took a leak every other hour. And slowly lost my appetite.

"Why don't you put an ad in the papers?" she proposed. "You know, 'Friends want to get in touch with you' or something."

"Not a bad idea," I said. It didn't matter if we came up empty-handed; it had to beat doing nothing.

So I placed a three-line notice in the morning editions of four newspapers for the following day.

Attention: Rat
Get in touch. Urgent!
Dolphin Hotel, Room 406

For the next two days, I waited by the phone. The day of the ad there were three calls. One was a call from a local citizen.

"What's this 'Rat'?"

"The nickname of a friend," I answered.

He hung up, satisfied.

Another was a prank call.

"Squeak, squeak," came a voice from the other end of the line. "Squeak, squeak."

I hung up. Cities are damn strange places.

The third was from a woman with a reedy voice.

"Everybody always calls me Rat," she said. A voice in which you could almost hear the telephone lines swaying in the distant breeze.

"Thank you for taking the trouble to call. However, the Rat I'm looking for is a man," I explained.

"I kind of thought so," she said. "But in any case, since I'm a Rat too, I thought I might as well give you a call."

"Really, thank you very much."

"Not at all. Have you found your friend?"

"Not yet," I said, "unfortunately."

"If only it'd been me you were looking for . . . but no, it wasn't me."

"That's the way it goes. Sorry."

She fell silent. Meanwhile, I scratched my nose with my little finger.

"Really, I just wanted to talk to you," she came back.

"With me?"

"I don't quite know how to put it, but I fought the urge ever since I came across your ad in the morning paper. I didn't mean to bother you . . ."

"So all that about your being called Rat was a made-up story."

"That's right," she said. "Nobody ever calls me Rat. I don't even have any friends. That's why I wanted to call you so badly."

I heaved a sigh. "Well, uh, thanks anyway."

"Forgive me. Are you from Hokkaido?"

"I'm from Tokyo," I said.

"Then you're up here looking for a friend who's also from Tokyo?"

"That's correct."

"How old is this friend?"

"Just turned thirty."

"And you?"

"About the same."

"Single?"

"Yes."

"I'm twenty-two. I suppose things get better as time goes on."

"Well," I said, "who knows? Some things get better, some don't."

"It'd be nice if we could get together and discuss things over dinner."

"You'll have to excuse me, but I've got to stay here and wait for a call."

"Oh, yes," she said. "Sorry about everything."

"Anyway, thanks for calling."

I hung up.

Clever, very clever. A call girl, maybe, looking for some business. True, she might really have been just a lonely girl. Either way it was the same. I still had zero leads.

The following day there was only one call, from a mentally disturbed man. "A rat you say? Leave it to me." He talked for fifteen minutes about fending off rats in a Siberian camp. An interesting tale, but no lead.

While waiting for the telephone to ring, I sat in the half-sprung chair by the window and spent the day watching the work conditions on the third floor office across the street. Stare as I might all day long, I couldn't figure out what the company did. The company had ten employees, and people were constantly running in and out like in a basketball game. Someone would hand someone papers, someone would stamp these, then another someone would stuff them into an envelope and rush out the door. During the lunch break, a big-breasted secretary poured tea for everyone. In the afternoon, several people had coffee delivered. Which made me want to drink some too, so I asked the desk clerk to take messages while I went out to a coffee shop. I bought two bottles of beer on the way back. When I resumed my seat at the window, there were only four people left in the office. The big-breasted secretary was joking with a junior employee. I drank a beer and watched the office activities, but mainly her.

The more I looked at her breasts, the more unusually large they seemed. She must have been strapped into a brassiere with cables from the Golden Gate Bridge. Several of the junior staff seemed to have designs on her. Their sex drive came across two panes of glass and the street in between. It's a funny thing sensing someone else's sex drive. After a while, you get to mistaking it for your own.

At five o'clock, she changed into a red dress and went home. I closed the curtain and watched a Bugs Bunny rerun on television. So went the eighth day at the Dolphin Hotel.

"Just great," said I. This "just great" business was becoming a habit. "One-third of the month gone and we still haven't gotten anywhere."

"So it would seem," said she. "I wonder how Kipper's getting on?"

After supper, we rested on the vile orange sofa in the Dolphin Hotel lobby. No one else around except our three-fingered clerk. He was keeping busy, up on a ladder changing a light bulb, cleaning the windows, folding newspapers. There may have been other guests in the place; perhaps they were all in their rooms like mummies kept out of the light of day.

"How's business?" the desk clerk asked timidly as he watered the potted plants.

"Nothing much to speak of," I said.

"Seems you placed an ad in the papers."

"That I did," I said. "I'm trying to track down this one person on some land inheritance."

"Inheritance?"

"Yes. Trouble is the inheritor's disappeared, whereabouts unknown."

"Do tell. Sounds like interesting work."

"Not really."

"I don't know, there's something of *Moby Dick* about it."

"*Moby Dick?*"

"Sure. The thrill of hunting something down."

"A mammoth, for example?" said my girlfriend.

"Sure. It's all related," said the clerk. "Actually, I named this place the Dolphin Hotel because of a scene with dolphins in *Moby Dick*."

"Oh-ho," said I. "But if that's the case, wouldn't it have been better to name it the Whale Hotel?"

"Whales don't have quite the image," he admitted with some regret.

"The Dolphin Hotel's a lovely name," said my girlfriend.

"Thank you very much," smiled the clerk. "Incidentally, having you here for this extended stay strikes me as most auspicious, and I'd like to offer you some wine as a token of my thanks."

"Delighted," she said.

"Much obliged," I said.

He went into a back room and emerged after a moment with a chilled bottle of white wine and three glasses.

"A toast. I'm still on the job, so just a sip for me."

We drank our wine. Not a particularly fine wine, but a light, dry, pleasant sort of wine. Even the glasses were swell.

"You a *Moby Dick* fan?" I thought to ask.

"You could say that. I always wanted to go to sea ever since I was a child."

"And that's why you're in the hotel business today?" she asked.

"That's why I'm missing fingers," he said. "Actually, they got mangled in a winch unloading cargo from a freighter."

"How horrible!" she exclaimed.

"Everything went black at the time. But life's a fickle thing. Somehow or other, I ended up owning this hotel here. Not much of a hotel, but I've done all right by it. Ten years I've had it."

Which would mean he wasn't the desk clerk, but the owner.

"I couldn't imagine a finer hotel," she encouraged.

"Thank you very much," said the owner, refilling our wine glasses.

"For only ten years, the building has taken on quite a lot of, well, character," I ventured forth unabashedly.

"Yes, it was built right after the war. I count myself most fortunate that I could buy it so cheaply."

"What was it used for before it was a hotel?"

"It went by the name of the Hokkaido Ovine Hall. Housed all sorts of papers and resources concerning . . ."

"Ovine?" I said.

"Sheep," he said.

"The building was the property of the Hokkaido Ovine Association, that is, up until ten years ago. What with the decline in sheep raising in the territory, the Hall was closed," he said, sipping his wine. "Actually, the acting director at the time was my own father. He couldn't abide the thought of his beloved Ovine Hall shutting down, and so on the pretext of preserving the sheep resources he talked the Association into selling him the land and the buildiing at a good price. Hence, to this day the whole second floor of the building is a sheep reference room. Of course, being resource materials, most of the stuff is old and useless. The dotings of an old man. The rest of the place is mine for the hotel business.

"Some coincidence," I said.

"Coincidence?"

"If the truth be known, the person we're looking for has something to do with sheep. And the only lead we've got is this one photograph of sheep that he sent."

"You don't say," he said. "I'd like to have a look at it if I might."

I pulled out the sheep photo that I'd sandwiched between the pages of my notebook and handed it to him. He picked up his glasses from the counter and studied the photo.

"I do seem to have some recollection of this," he said.

"A recollection?"

"For certain." So saying, he took the ladder from where he'd left it under the light and leaned it up against the opposite wall.

He brought down a framed picture. Then he wiped off the dust and handed the picture to us.

"Is this not the same scenery?"

The frame itself was plenty old, but the photo in it was even older, discolored too. And yes, there were sheep in it. Altogether maybe sixty head. Fence, birch grove, mountains. The birch grove was different in shape from the one in the Rat's photograph, but the mountains in the background were the same mountains. Even the composition of the photograph was the same.

"Just great," I said to her. "All this time we've been passing right under this photograph."

"That's why I told you it had to be the Dolphin Hotel," she blurted out.

"Well then," I asked the man, "exactly where is this place?"

"Don't rightly know," he said. "The photograph's been hanging in that spot since Ovine Hall days."

"Hmph," I grunted.

"But there's a way to find out."

"Like what?"

"Ask my father. He's got a room upstairs where he spends his days. He hardly ever comes out, he's so wrapped up in his sheep materials. I haven't set eyes on him for half a month now. I just leave his meals in front of his door, and the tray's empty thirty minutes later, so I know he's alive."

"Would your father be able to tell us where the place in the photograph is?"

"Probably. As I said before, he was the former director of Ovine Hall, and anyway he knows all there is to know about sheep. Everyone calls him the Sheep Professor."

"The Sheep Professor," I said.

27

The Sheep Professor Eats All, Tells All

According to his Dolphin Hotel–owner son, the Sheep Professor had by no means had a happy life.

"Father was born in Sendai in 1905, the eldest son of a landholding family," the son explained. "I'll go by the Western calendar, if that's all right with you."

"As you please."

"They weren't independently wealthy, but they lived on their own land. An old family previously vested with a fief from the local castle lord. Even yielded a respected agriculturalist toward the end of the Edo period.

"The Sheep Professor excelled in scholastics from early on, a child wonder known to everyone in Sendai. And not just schooling. He surpassed everyone at the violin and in middle school even performed a Beethoven sonata for the Emperor during his visit to the area. The Emperor gave him a gold watch.

"The family tried to push him in the direction of law, but the Sheep Professor flatly refused. 'I have no interest in law,' said the young Sheep Professor.

" 'Then go ahead with your music,' said his father. 'There ought to be at least one musician in the family.'

"'I have no interest in music either,' replied the Sheep Professor.

"There was a brief pause.

"'Well then,' his father spoke up, 'what path is it you want to take?'

"'I am interested in agriculture. I want to learn agricultural administration.'

"'Very well,' said his father a second later. What else could he say? The Sheep Professor was considerate and earnest, the sort of youth who once he said something would stick by his word. His own father couldn't get a word in edgewise.

"The following year, as per his wishes, the Sheep Professor matriculated at the Agriculture Faculty of Tokyo Imperial University. His child-wonder love of studies showed no sign of abating even there. Everyone, including his professors, was watching him. Scholastically he excelled as always, and he enjoyed tremendous popularity. He was, in a nutshell, one of your chosen few. Untainted by dissipation, reading every spare moment. If he tired of reading, he'd play his violin in the university courtyard, his gold watch ever in the pocket of his school uniform.

"He graduated at the top of his class and entered the Ministry of Agriculture and Forestry as one of the elite. His senior thesis was, simply stated, a unified scheme of large-scale agriculturalization for Japan, Korea, and Taiwan, which some decried as slightly too idealistic. It was, nonetheless, the talk of the time.

"After two years in the Ministry, the Sheep Professor went to the Korean peninsula to conduct research in rice cultivation. His report, published as *A Study on Rice Cropping on the Korean Peninsula*, was adopted by the government.

"In 1934, the Sheep Professor was called back to Tokyo and was introduced to a young army officer. For the big, imminent North China campaign, the Sheep Professor was asked to establish a self-sufficiency program based on sheep. This was to be the Sheep Professor's first encounter with sheep. The Sheep Professor concentrated on developing a general framework for ovine productivity in Japan, Manchuria, and Mongolia. The following spring, he embarked on a site-observation tour.

"The spring of 1935 passed uneventfully. The events happened in July. Setting out on horseback, unaccompanied, on his observation tour, the Sheep Professor disappeared. Whereabouts unknown.

"Three days, four days passed. Still no Professor. The army search team combed the terrain desperately, but he was nowhere to be found. Perhaps he had been attacked by wolves or abducted by tribesmen. Then at dusk a week later, just as everyone had given up hope, one utterly disheveled Sheep Professor wandered back into camp. His face was haggard, with cuts in several places, but his eyes retained their gleam. His horse was gone, his watch was gone. His explanation, which everyone seemed willing to accept, was that he'd lost his way and his horse fell injured.

"Not one month later, a bizarre rumor began to spread through the government offices. Word had gotten out that he enjoyed a 'special relationship' with sheep. What this 'special relationship' meant, no one knew. Whereupon his superior summoned him to his office and conducted an interrogation to set the record straight. Rumors are not to be tolerated in colonial societies.

" 'Did you in truth experience a special relationship with sheep?' queried his superior.

" 'I did,' answered the Sheep Professor.

"The interrogation went something like this:

Q: By this special relationship, do you mean you engaged in sexual relations with sheep?
A: No, that is not the case.
Q: Please explain.
A: It was a mental relationship.
Q: That is not an explanation.
A: It is difficult to find the right words, sir, but perhaps spiritual communion comes close.
Q: You would tell me you had spiritual communion with sheep?
A: That is correct.
Q: Are you telling me that during the week of your disappearance you had spiritual communion with sheep?

A: That is correct.
Q: Do you not think that is sufficient reason for dismissal from your offices?
A: It is my office to study sheep, sir.
Q: Spiritual communion is not a recognized course of study. Henceforth, I would ask that you amend your ways. Consider your graduation with honors from the Agriculture Faculty of Tokyo Imperial University, your brilliant work record upon entering the Ministry. There are great expectations of you as the standard-bearer of agricultural administration for tomorrow's East Asia.
A: I understand.
Q: Then forget about this spiritual communion nonsense. Sheep are livestock. Simply livestock.
A: It is impossible for me to forget.
Q: You will have to explain the circumstances.
A: The reason, sir, is that there is a sheep inside me.
Q: That is not an explanation.
A: Further explanation is impossible.

"February 1936. The Sheep Professor is ordered home to Japan. After undergoing numerous similar interrogations, he is transferred in the spring to the Ministry Reference Collection. There he catalogues reference materials and organizes bookshelves. In other words, he has been purged from the core elite of the East Asian agricultural administration.

" 'The sheep has now gone from inside me,' the Sheep Professor told a close friend at the time. 'But it used to be there inside.'

"1937. Sheep Professor retires from the Ministry of Agriculture and Forestry and, availing himself of a Ministry loan under the Japan-Manchuria Sheep Scheme, which used to be in his charge, moves to Hokkaido and becomes a shepherd. 56 head of sheep.

"1939. Sheep Professor marries. 128 head of sheep.

"1942. Eldest son born (present owner-operator of the Dolphin Hotel). 181 head of sheep.

"1946. American Occupation Forces appropriate Sheep Professor's sheep ranch as a training camp. 62 head of sheep.

"1947. Sheep Professor enters employ of Hokkaido Ovine Association.

"1949. Wife dies of bronchitis.

"1950. Sheep Professor assumes directorship of Hokkaido Ovine Association.

"1960. Eldest son loses fingers at Port of Otaru.

"1967. Hokkaido Ovine Hall closes.

"1968. Dolphin Hotel opens.

"1978. Young real estate agent inquires about sheep photograph."

Me, in other words.

"Just great," I said.

"By all means, I would like to meet your father," I said.

"I have no objection to your meeting him, but since my father dislikes me, you'll have to excuse me if I ask you to go alone," said the son of the Sheep Professor.

"Dislikes you?"

"Because I lost two fingers and am balding."

"I see," I said. "An eccentric man, your father."

"As his son, it's not for me to say, but yes, an eccentric man indeed. A completely changed man since he encountered sheep. Extremely difficult, sometimes even cruel. Deep down in his heart he's kind. If you heard him play his violin, you'd know that. Sheep hurt my father, and through my father, sheep have also hurt me."

"You love your father, don't you?" said my girlfriend.

"Yes, that I do. I love him very much," said the Dolphin Hotel owner, "but he dislikes me. He never once held me since the day I was born. Never once had a kind word for me. And since I lost my fingers and started going bald, he's done nothing but ridicule me."

"I'm sure he doesn't mean to ridicule you," she said.

"I can't believe that he would either," I said.

"You're too kind," said the hotel man.

"Shall we go and try to see him directly, then?" I asked.

"I don't know," said the hotel man. "Though I'm sure he'll see you if you're careful about two things. One is to state clearly that you wish to inquire about sheep."

"And the other?"

"Don't say that I told you about him."

"Fair enough," I said.

We thanked the Sheep Professor's son and headed up the stairs. The air at the top of the stairs was chilly and damp. The lights were dim, scarcely revealing the dust drifts in the corners of the hallway. The whole place smelled indistinctly of old papers and old body odors. We walked down the long hallway, as per the son's instructions, and knocked on the ancient door at the end. An old plastic plaque affixed to the door read DIRECTOR'S OFFICE. No answer. I knocked again. Again, no answer. At the third knock, there was a groan, and then the response—"Don't bother me. Go away."

"We've come to ask a few things about sheep, if we might."

"Eat shit!" yelled the Sheep Professor from inside. A mighty healthy voice for seventy-three.

"We really have to talk with you," I shouted through the door.

"Don't give me this you-want-to-talk-about-sheep crap," said the Sheep Professor.

"But it's something that probably ought to be discussed," I coaxed. "It's about a sheep that disappeared in 1936."

There was a brief silence, then the door flew open. Before us stood the Sheep Professor.

The Sheep Professor had long hair, white as snow. His eyebrows were also white, hanging down over his eyes like icicles. He stood five foot ten. A self-possessed figure. Sturdy-boned. His nose thrust out from his face at a challenging angle, like a ski jump.

His body odor permeated the entire room. No, I would hesitate to call it body odor. Beyond a certain point, it ceased to be body odor and blended into time, merged with the light. What had probably once been a large space was so packed with old books and papers you could hardly see the floor. Almost all the publications were scholarly tomes written in foreign languages. Without exception, all were covered with stains. On the right, against the wall, was a filthy bed, and before the window a huge mahogany desk and revolving chair. The desktop was in relative order, papers neatly stacked and surmounted by a paperweight in the shape of a sheep. The room was dark, the only illumination coming from a dust-covered lamp's sixty-watt bulb.

The Sheep Professor was wearing a gray shirt, black cardigan, and herringbone trousers that had all but lost their shape. In the light of the room, his gray shirt and black cardigan could have passed for a white shirt and gray cardigan. Maybe those had been the original colors, hard to say.

The Sheep Professor sat behind his desk, motioning with his finger for us to sit down on the bed. We made our way over, straddling books as if crossing a minefield, and sat down. The bed was so palpably grimy I was afraid my Levi's would stick to the sheets. The Sheep Professor folded his fingers on top of his desk and stared at us intently. His fingers were thick with black hair right up to his knuckles. The blackness in stark contrast to the brilliant white of his head.

Suddenly, the Sheep Professor picked up the telephone and shouted into the receiver: "Bring me my supper, quick!"

"Well now," said the Professor. "You say you have come to discuss a sheep that disappeared in 1936?"

"That's right," I said.

"Hmm," he said. Then abruptly, with great volume, he blew his nose into a wad of paper. "Is there something you wish to tell? Or something you wish to ask?"

"Both."

"First, let me hear what you have to tell."

"We know what became of the sheep that escaped you in the spring of 1936."

The Sheep Professor snorted. "Are you telling me that you know I threw away everything I had for a sheep I have been trying to track down for forty-two years?"

"We are aware of that," I said.

"You could be making this up."

I pulled out the silver lighter from my pocket and placed it on his desk together with the Rat's sheep photograph. He reached out a hairy hand, picked up the lighter and photograph, and examined them at length under the lamp. Particles of silence floated about the room for the longest time. The solid double-hung window shut out the city noise; only the sputter of the old lamp punctuated the silence.

The old man, having finished his examination of the lighter and photograph, turned off the lamp with a click and rubbed his eyes with stubby fingers. As if he were trying to press two lightbulbs into his skull. When he removed his fingers, his eyes were murky red, like a rabbit's.

"Forgive me," said the Sheep Professor. "I've been surrounded by idiots for so long, I've grown distrustful of people."

"That's okay," I said.

My girlfriend smiled politely.

"Can you imagine what it's like to be left with a solitary thought when its embodiment has been pulled out from underneath you, roots and all?" asked the Professor.

"No, I can't."

"It's hell. A maze of a subterranean hell. Unmitigated by even one shaft of light or a single draft of water. That's been my life for forty-two years."

"Because of this sheep?"

"Yes, yes, yes. All because of that sheep. That sheep left me stranded in the thick of everything. In the spring of 1936."

"And it was to search for this sheep that you left the Ministry of Agriculture, am I correct?"

"Those paper pushers were all morons. They hadn't the slightest idea of the true value of things. Probably'll never catch on to the monumental significance of that sheep."

There came a knock on the door, followed by a woman's voice. "I've brought you your meal."

"Leave it," said the Sheep Professor.

The sound of the tray being set on the floor was followed by the echo of receding footsteps.

My girlfriend opened the door and brought the meal tray over to the Sheep Professor's desk. On the tray were soup, salad, a roll, and meatballs for the Professor, plus two coffees for us.

"You've eaten already?" asked the Sheep Professor.

"Yes, thank you," I said.

"What did you have?"

"Veal in wine sauce," I said.

"Shrimp, grilled," she said.

The Sheep Professor grunted. Then he ate his soup and crunched the croutons. "Excuse me if I eat while you talk. I'm hungry."

"By all means," we said.

The Sheep Professor ate his soup and we sipped our coffee. As he ate, the Professor stared headlong into his bowl.

"Would you know where the place in this photograph is?" I asked.

"I would indeed. I know it very well."

"Would you tell us?"

"Just hold on," said the Sheep Professor, setting aside his now-empty bowl. "One thing at a time. Let's start with the events of 1936. First I'll talk, then you talk."

I nodded.

The Sheep Professor began. "It was the summer of 1935 when the sheep entered me. I had lost my way during a survey of open-pasture grazing near the Manchuria-Mongolia border, when I happened across a cave. I decided to spend the night there. That night I dreamed about a sheep that asked, could it go inside me? Why not? I said. At the time, I didn't think much of it. It was a dream, after all." The old man chortled as he moved on to his salad.

"It was a breed of sheep I'd never set eyes on before. Because of my work I was acquainted with every breed of sheep in the world, but this one was unique. The horns were bent at a strange angle, the legs squat and stocky, eyes clear as spring water. The fleece was pure white, except for a brownish star on its back. There is no such sheep anywhere in the world. That's why I told the sheep it was all right to enter my body. As a sheep specialist, I was not about to let go of such a find."

"And what did it feel like to have this sheep inside your body?"

"Nothing special, really. It just felt like there was this sheep inside me. I felt it in the morning. I woke up and there was this sheep inside. A perfectly natural feeling."

"Do you experience headaches?"

"Never once since the day I was born."

The Sheep Professor went at his meatballs, glazing them in sauce before shoveling them into his mouth with gusto. "In parts of Northern China and Mongol territory, it's not uncommon to hear of sheep entering people's bodies. Among the locals, it's believed that a sheep entering the body is a blessing from the gods. For instance, in one book published in the Yuan dynasty it's written that a 'star-bearing white sheep' entered the body of Genghis Khan. Interesting, don't you think?"

"Quite."

"The sheep that enters a body is thought to be immortal. And so too the person who hosts the sheep is thought to become immortal. However, should the sheep escape, the immortality goes. It's all up to the sheep. If the sheep likes its host, it'll stay for decades. If not—zip!—it's gone. People abandoned by sheep are called the 'sheepless.' In other words, people like me."

Chomp, chomp.

"Ever since that sheep entered my body, I began reading on ethnological studies and folklore related to sheep. I went around interviewing locals and checking old writings. Pretty soon talk went around that I'd been entered by a sheep, and word got back to my commanding officer. My commanding officer didn't take kindly to it. I was labeled 'mentally unfit' and promptly shipped home to Japan. Your typical 'colony case.'"

Having polished off three meatballs, the Sheep Professor moved on to the roll.

"The basic flaw of modern Japan is that we've learned absolutely nothing from our contact with other Asian peoples. The same goes for our dealings with sheep. Sheep raising in Japan has failed precisely because we've viewed sheep merely as a source of wool and meat. The daily-life level is missing from our thinking. We minimize the time factor to maximize the results. It's like that with everything. In other words, we don't have our feet on solid ground. It's not without reason that we lost the war."

"That sheep came with you to Japan, I take it," I said, returning to the subject.

"Yes," said the Sheep Professor. "I returned by ship from

Pusan. The sheep came with me."

"And what on earth do you suppose the sheep's purpose was?"

"I don't know," the Sheep Professor spat out. "The sheep didn't tell me anything. But the beast did have one major purpose. That much I do know. A monumental plan to transform humanity and the human world."

"One sheep planned to do all that?"

The Sheep Professor nodded as he popped the last morsel of his roll into his mouth and brushed the crumbs from his hands. "Nothing so alarming. Consider Genghis Khan."

"You have a point," I said. "But why now? Why Japan?"

"My guess is that I woke the sheep up. It probably would've gone on sleeping in that cave for hundreds of years. And stupid me, I had to go and wake it up."

"It's not your fault," I said.

"No," said the Professor, "it is my fault. I should have caught on a long time ago. I would have had a hand to play. But it took me a long time to catch on. And by the time I did, the sheep had already run off."

The Sheep Professor grew silent. He rubbed his icicled white brow with his fingers. It was as if the weight of forty-two years had infiltrated the furthest reaches of his body.

"One morning I awoke and the sheep was gone. It was then that I understood what it meant to be 'sheepless.' Sheer hell. The sheep goes away leaving only an idea. But without the sheep there is no expelling that idea. That is what it is to be 'sheepless.'"

Again the Sheep Professor blew his nose on a wad of paper. "Now it's your turn to talk."

I began with the route the sheep took after it left the Sheep Professor. How the sheep had entered the body of a rightist youth in prison. How as soon as this youth got out of prison he became a major right-wing figure. How he then crossed over to the Chinese continent and built up an intelligence network and a fortune in the process. How he'd been marked a Class A war criminal, but how he was released in exchange for his intelligence network on the continent. And how, utilizing the fortune he brought back from China, he'd laid claim to the whole underside of postwar politics, economics, information, etc., etc.

"I've heard of this man," the Sheep Professor said bitterly. "Somehow the sheep has an uncanny sense of the most competent targets."

"Only this spring, the sheep left his body. The man himself is in a coma, on the verge of death. Up until now, it seems that a brain dysfunction covered for the sheep."

"Such bliss. Better that the 'sheepless' be without this shell of half-consciousness."

"Why do you suppose the sheep left his body—after all this time building up a huge organization?"

The Sheep Professor let out a deep sigh. "You still don't understand? It's the same with that man as it was with me. He outlived his usefulness. People have their limits, and the sheep has no use for people who've reached their limit. My guess is that he did not fully comprehend all that the sheep had cut out for him. His role was to build a huge organization, and once that was complete, he was tossed. Just as the sheep used me as a means of transport."

"So what has the sheep been up to since?"

The Sheep Professor picked up the photograph from the desk and gave it a flick of his fingers. "It has roamed all over Japan to search out a new host. To the sheep, that would probably mean a new person to put on top of the organization by one scheme or another."

"And what is the sheep seeking?"

"As I said before, I can't express that in words with any precision. What the sheep seeks is the embodiment of sheep thought."

"Is that good?"

"To the sheep's thinking, of course it's good."

"And to yours?"

"I don't know," said the old man. "I really don't know. Ever since the sheep departed, I can't tell how much is really me and how much the shadow of the sheep."

"A while ago, you said something about having a hand to play. What would that be?"

"I have no intention of telling you that." The Sheep Professor shook his head.

Once again, silence shrouded the room. Outside, a hard rain began to fall. The first rain since we'd arrived in Sapporo.

"One last thing: could you tell us where the place in the photograph is?" I asked.

"The homestead where I lived for nine years. I raised sheep there. Appropriated right after the war by the American Forces, and when they repatriated the place to me I sold it to some rich man as a vacation home with pasture. Ought to still be the same owner."

"And would he still be raising sheep?"

"I don't know. But from the photograph it sure looks as if he's raising sheep. Whatever, it's a good remove from any settlements. Not another house in sight. The roads are blocked in the winter. I'm sure the owner uses the place only two, maybe three months a year. It's nice and quiet there."

"Does anyone look after the place when the owner's not there?"

"I doubt if anyone stays there over the winter. Other than myself, I can't imagine any other human staying there the winter through. You can pay the municipal shepherds in the town at the foot of the hills to look after the sheep. The roof of the house is sloped so that the snow naturally slides off onto the ground, and no worry about burglars. Even if somebody did steal something up there, it'd be a pain to get it to town. It's staggering, the amount of snow that falls there."

"So is anyone there now?"

"Hmm. Maybe not now. The snow's going to start soon and bears'll be roaming around for food before they go into hibernation. You're not planning to head up there?"

"Probably will have to. We have no other real lead."

The Sheep Professor sat for a while with his mouth shut. Tomato sauce from the meatballs at the corner of his mouth.

"You should probably know that prior to you one other person came here asking about the homestead. Around February it was. Age and appearance, well, kind of like you. He said he was interested in the photograph in the hotel lobby. I was pretty bored at the time, so I told him this and that. He said he was looking for material for a novel he was writing."

Out of my pocket I pulled a snapshot of the Rat and me together. It was taken in the summer eight years before, in J's Bar. I was in profile, smoking a cigarette, the Rat was looking at the camera, signaling thumbs up. Both of us were young and tan.

"This one's you, eh?" said the Sheep Professor, holding the snapshot under the lamp. "Younger than now."

"You're right."

"The other one's that man. He looked older than in this photo and had a moustache, but it was him."

"A moustache?"

"A neat little moustache and the rest stubble."

I tried to picture the Rat with a moustache, but couldn't quite see it.

The Sheep Professor drew us a detailed map to the homestead. You had to change trains near Asahikawa to a branch line and travel three hours to get to the town at the foot of the hills. From there it was three hours by car to the homestead.

"Thank you kindly for everything," I said.

"If you really want to know the truth, I think the fewer people that get involved with that sheep the better. I'm a prime example. There's not a soul the happier for having tangled with it. The values of one lone individual cannot bear up before the presence of that sheep. But well, I guess you've got your reasons."

"That I do."

"Be careful now," said the Sheep Professor. "And place the dishes by the door if you would."

28

Farewell to the Dolphin Hotel

We took one day to ready for our departure.

We got mountaineering supplies and portable rations at a sporting-goods store, and bought heavy fishermen's knit sweaters and woolen socks at a department store. At a bookstore, we bought a 1:50,000-scale map of the area we were headed for and a tome on the local history. We also settled on some rugged spiked boots and padded thermal underwear.

"All these layers do absolutely nothing for my line of work," she said.

"When you're out in the snow, you won't have time to think about that," I said.

"You planning to stay until the heavy snows?"

"Can't tell. But I do know it'll already be starting by the end of October. Better to be prepared. No telling what to expect."

We hauled our purchases back to the hotel and stuffed them into a large backpack, then we gathered together all the extra items we'd brought from Tokyo and left them with the Dolphin Hotel man. As a matter of fact, almost everything she'd brought in her bag was extra. A cosmetics set, five books and six cassettes, one paper bag full of stockings and underwear, T-shirts and shorts, a travel alarm clock, a sketchbook and set of twenty-four colored pencils, stationery and envelopes, bath towel, mini first-aid kit, hair dryer, cotton swabs.

"But why are you bringing your dress and high-heels with us?"

"What am I supposed to do if we go to a party?" she pleaded.

"What makes you think there's going to be a party?"

There was no reasoning with her. She managed to fit her dress, neatly folded, and high heels into our backpack along with our pared-down effects. For cosmetics, she switched to a travel compact she picked up at a nearby shop.

The hotel owner accepted the luggage graciously. I settled the bill up through the following day and told him we'd be back in a week or two.

"Was my father of any help?" he asked worriedly.

I said that he'd helped enormously.

"I sometimes wish I could go off in search of something," he declared, "but before getting even that far, I myself wouldn't have the slightest idea what to search for. Now my father, he's someone who been searching for something all his life. He's still searching today. Ever since I was a little boy, my father's told me about the white sheep that came to him in his dreams. So I always thought that's what life is like. An ongoing search."

The lobby of the Dolphin Hotel was hushed as ever. An elderly maid was going up and down the stairs with a mop.

"My father's seventy-three now and still no sheep. I don't know if the thing even exists. Still, I can't help think that it hasn't been such a bad life for him. I want to see my father happy now more than ever, but he just belittles me and won't listen to a word I say. That's because I have no purpose in life."

"But you have the Dolphin Hotel," my girlfriend said sweetly.

"Besides, your father's stepped down from his sheep searching," I added. "We've taken up the rest."

The hotel owner smiled.

"If that's so, there's nothing more for me to say. We two ought to get on very happily."

"I sure hope so," I said.

Later, when we were alone, she asked me, "Do you really think those two deserve each other?"

"They've been together this long . . . They'll be all right. At least after forty-two years, we're on the track of the same sheep."

"I like those two."

"I like them too."

We finished our packing and had intercourse, then went out and saw a movie. In the movie there were a lot of men and women having intercourse too. Nothing wrong with watching others having intercourse, after all.

PART EIGHT

A WILD SHEEP CHASE, III

29

The Birth, Rise, and Fall of Junitaki Township

It was an early morning train we took from Sapporo to Asahikawa. I opened a beer as I settled down to the voluminous, slip-cased *Authoritative History of Junitaki Township*. Junitaki was the township in which the Sheep Professor's homestead was located. Reading up on its history probably had no practical value, but it couldn't hurt.

The author was born in 1940 in Junitaki and, after graduating from the literature department of Hokkaido University, was active as a local historian, or so the cover copy said. For being so active, he had only one book to his name. Published in May 1970. First edition, probably the only edition.

According to the author, the first settlers arrived in what today is Junitaki early in the summer of 1881. Eighteen persons total, all poor dirt farmers from Tsugaru, meager farm tools, clothes, bedding, cook pots, and knives being the sum of their possessions.

They passed through an Ainu village near Sapporo, and with the little money they had, they engaged a lean, dark-eyed Ainu youth as a guide. The youth's name in Ainu translated into "Full Moon on the Wane" (suggesting a tendency toward manic depression, the author hypothesized).

Perhaps the youth was not cut out to be a guide; still, he proved far better than he might have at first appeared. Hardly understanding any Japanese, he led these eighteen grim, suspicious farmers north, up along the Ishikari River. He had a clean picture in mind where to go to find fertile land.

On the fourth day, the entourage arrived at this destination. Endowed with vast waters, the whole landscape was alive with beautiful flowers.

"Here is good," said the youth. "Few wild animals, fertile soil, plenty of salmon."

"Nothing doing," said the leader of the farmers. "We want farther in."

The youth understood the farmers to believe they'd find better land the farther in they went. Fine. If that's what they want, off into the interior.

So the entourage continued their march north for another two days. There the youth found a rise where, if the soil was not exactly as rich as the earlier spot, at least there was no fear of flooding.

"How about it?" asked the youth. "Here is also good."

The farmers shook their heads.

This scene repeated itself any number of times until finally they arrived at the site of present-day Asahikawa. Seven days and one hundred miles from Sapporo.

"What about here?" asked the youth, more uncertain than ever.

"No go," answered the farmers.

"But from here, we climb mountains," said the youth.

"We don't mind," said the farmers gleefully.

And so they crossed the Shiogari Pass.

Needless to say, there was a reason why the farmers had passed up the rich bottomland and insisted on going deep into the wilderness. The fact was, they were on the lam. They had skipped town, walking out on sizable debts, and wanted to get as far away from civilization as possible.

Of course, the Ainu youth had no way of knowing this. And so naturally his initial surprise at the farmers' rejection of fertile farmland soon turned to bewilderment, distress, and loss of self-confidence.

Nevertheless, the youth's character was sufficiently complex that by the time the entourage crossed the Shiogari Pass, he had given himself over to his incomprehensible fate, leading them northward, ever northward. He took pains to choose the most rough trails, the most perilous bogs, to please his patrons.

Four days north of the Shiogari Pass, the entourage came on to a west-flowing river. By consensus, it was decided they should head east.

This tack sent them up horrible trails through horrible terrain. They fought through seas of brush bamboo, hacked their way across fields of shoulder-high grass a half-day at a time, waded through mud up to their chests, squirmed up crags, anything to get farther east. At night, they spread their tarps over the riverbank and kept an ear out for the howling of wolves while they slept. Their arms, scraped raw from the bush bamboo, were beset at every turn by gnats and mosquitoes that would burrow into their ears to suck blood.

Five days east, they found their way blocked by mountains and could go no further. What lay beyond was not fit for human settlement, the youth declared. Upon hearing this, the farmers halted in their tracks. This was July 8, 1881, 150 miles overland from Sapporo.

First thing, they surveyed the lay of the land, tested the water, checked the soil. It was reasonably good farmland. Then they divided the land among the group and erected a communal log cabin in the center.

The Ainu youth came upon a band of Ainu hunters passing through the area. "What is this area called?" he asked them.

"Do you really think this asshole of a terrain even deserves a name?" they replied.

So for the time being, this frontier was without a name. As another dwelling (or at least another dwelling that desired human contact) did not exist for forty miles, the settlement had no need for a name. In fact, when in 1889 an official census taker from the Territorial Government pressed the group for a name, the settlers remained steadfastly indifferent. Sickle and hoe in hand, they met in the communal hut and decided against naming the settlement. The official was literally up a creek. All he could do was to count the falls in the nearby river, twelve, and report the name of Junitaki-buraku, or Twelve Falls Settlement, to the Territorial Government. From then on, the settlement bore the formal appellation Junitaki-buraku (and later, Junitaki-mura, Twelve Falls Village).

The area fanned a sixty-degree arc between two mountains and was cut down the middle by a deep river gorge. An asshole of a terrain for sure. The ground was covered with brush bamboo while huge evergreens spread their roots far and wide. Wolves and elk and bears and muskrats and birds competed in the wilderness for the meager food available. Everywhere flies and mosquitoes swarmed.

"You all really want to live here?" asked the Ainu youth.

"You bet," replied the farmers.

It is not obvious why the Ainu youth, instead of returning to his own home, chose to stay on with the settlers. Perhaps he was curious, hypothesized the author (who loved to hypothesize). Whatever the case, if he had not remained, it's doubtful the settlers could have made it through the winter. The youth taught the settlers how to root for winter vegetables, how to survive the snow, how to fish in the frozen river, how to lay traps for the wolves, how to escape the attention of bears before hibernation, how to determine the weather from the direction of the wind, how to prevent chilblains, how to roast bush bamboo roots for food, how to fell evergreen trees in a set direction. Soon, everyone came to recognize the youth's value, and the youth himself regained his confidence. He eventually took a Japanese name and married the daughter of one of the settlers, with whom he had three children. No more "Full Moon on the Wane."

Yet, even with the practical knowledge of the Ainu youth, the settlers' lot was miserable. By August, each family had built its own hut, which being a hurriedly thrown together affair of split logs did next to nothing to keep out the winter wind. It was not uncommon to awaken and find a foot of snow by one's pillow. Most families had but one set of bedding besides, so the menfolk typically had to sleep curled up by the fire. When their store of food was used up, the settlers went out in search of fish and whatever shriveled-up wild plants they could find deep beneath the snow. It was an especially cold winter. No one died, however. There was no fighting, no tears. Their strength was their inbred poverty.

Spring came. Two children were born and the settlers' number rose to twenty-one. Two hours before giving birth the mothers were working in the fields, and the morning after giving birth they were working in the fields.

The group planted corn and potatoes. The men felled trees and burned the roots to clear more land. New life came over the face of the earth, young plants bore fruit, but just when the settlers were sighing with relief, they were beset by swarm after swarm of locusts.

The locusts swept in over the mountains. At first, they looked like a giant black cloud. Then there came a rumbling. No one had any idea what was about to overtake them. Only the Ainu youth knew. He ordered the men to build fires in their fields. Dousing their last piece of furniture in their last drop of oil, the men burned everything they could lay their hands on. The womenfolk banged pots with pestles. They did everything in their power, but everything was not enough. Hundreds of thousands of locusts swooped down on their crops and laid them to waste. Nothing was left in their wake.

When the locusts departed, the youth went out into the fields and wept. Not one of the settlers shed a tear. They gathered up the dead locusts and burned them, and as soon as they were in ashes, the settlers continued to clear land.

They went back to eating fish and wild vegetables all through the next winter. In spring, another three children were born. People planted the fields. In summer, they were visited by locusts again. And again all the crops were chewed down to the roots. This time, however, the Ainu youth did not weep.

The onslaught of the locusts finally stopped the third year. A long spell of rain had gotten to the locust eggs. But the excessive rain damaged the crops. The following year saw an unusual infestation of beetles, and the summer after that was unusually cold.

Having read that far, I shut the book, opened another beer, and pulled a box lunch of salmon roe out of my pack.

She sat across from me with folded arms, fast asleep. The autumn morning sun, slanting in through the train window, spread a thin blanket of light over her lap. A tiny moth blew in from somewhere and fluttered about like a scrap of paper. The moth ended up on her breast and stayed there before flying off again. Once the moth had flown off, she looked the slightest bit older.

I smoked a cigarette, then resumed reading the *Authoritative History of Junitaki Township.*

By the sixth year, the settlement was at last holding its own. The crops were bearing, the cabins refurbished, and everyone had adjusted to life in a cold climate. Sawed-board houses took their place among the log cabins, hearths were built, lamps hung. People loaded up a boat with what little they had in the way of extra produce and dried fish and elk antlers, traveled two days to market in the nearest town, and bought salt and clothing and oil in exchange. Some learned how to make charcoal from the timber felled in clearing fields. A number of similar settlements sprang up downstream and trade was established.

As groundbreaking continued, it became apparent that the settlement was sorely short of hands, so the group convened the village council, and after two days decided to call in reinforcements from the old hometown. The question of the reneged loans arose, but from replies to inquiries carefully couched in their letters home, they learned that their creditors had long since given up on trying to collect. The eldest of the settlers then sent off notes to their old buddies, asking that they join the settlers in working the new land. In 1889, the census was conducted, the same year the settlement was officially named.

The following year, six new families, comprising nineteen new settlers, came to the settlement. They were greeted with upgraded log cabins. A tearful reunion was had by all. The new residents were given land, and with the help of the first settlers they planted crops and built their own houses.

By 1893, four more new families had arrived with sixteen people. By 1897, seven more new families had arrived with twenty-four people.

The number of settlers rose steadily. The communal hut was expanded into a more formal meeting hall, and next to it they built a small shrine. The settlement officially became a village. From Junitaki-buraku to Junitaki-mura. The postman began to make appearances, however infrequently. And while millet was the main diet of the villagers, they now occasionally mixed in real white rice.

Of course, they were not without their share of misfortune. Officials came through to levy taxies and enforce military service. The Ainu youth, by now in his mid-thirties, was particularly upset by these developments. He could not understand why such things as taxes and military service were at all necessary.

"It seems to me things were better off like they used to be," he said.

Even so, the village kept on developing.

In 1903, they discovered higher ground near the village suitable for grazing, and the village set up a communal sheep pasture. An official from the Territorial Government instructed them in building fences, supplying irrigation, and constructing livestock shelter. Next, prison labor was called in to lay a road along the river, and as time went on, flocks of sheep, bought cheap from the government, were being herded up the road. The farmers had not the slightest idea why the government was being so generous. Well, why not? they thought. After so hard a struggle, this was welcome relief.

Of course, the government was not being generous for nothing, giving them these sheep. Prodded by the military's goal of self-sufficiency in thermal wool for the upcoming campaign on the continent, the government had ordered the Ministry of Agriculture and Business to increase efforts in sheep raising, and the Ministry had forced these plans on the Territorial Government. The Russo-Japanese War was drawing near.

In all the village, it was again the Ainu man, no longer a youth, who showed the greatest interest in sheep. He learned methods of sheep raising from the territorial official and took on the responsibility of the village pasture. There is no knowing exactly why he became so devoted to the sheep. It may have been the complexities of life brought on by a village population suddenly growing by leaps and bounds.

The pasture became home to thirty-six head of Southdowns and twenty-one head of Shropshires in addition to two Border collies. The Ainu man became an able shepherd, and with each passing year the number of sheep and dogs increased. He came to love his sheep and his dogs with all his heart. The officials were most satisfied. Puppies were farmed out as top sheepdogs to similar sheep farms established nearby.

When the Russo-Japanese War broke out, five village youths were conscripted and sent to the front line in China. Two were killed and one lost his left arm when an enemy grenade exploded in a skirmish over a small hill. When the fighting ended three days later, the other two gathered up the scattered bones of their fellow village youths. All had been sons of first- and second-wave settlers. One of the dead was the eldest son of the Ainu youth-turned-shepherd. He died wearing an army-issue wool overcoat.

"Why send boys off to war in a foreign land?" the Ainu shepherd went around asking people. By then he was forty-five.

Nobody would answer him. The Ainu shepherd broke off from the village and stayed out at the pasture, spending his waking and sleeping hours with the sheep. His wife had died from bronchitis five years earlier, and his two remaining daughters had both married. For his services in minding the sheep, the village provided him with scant wages and food.

After losing his son, the Ainu shepherd grew embittered. He died at age sixty-two. One winter morning, the boy who was his helper found him sprawled out dead on the floor of the sheephouse. Frozen. Two sorry-eyed grandpuppies of the original two Border collies whined at his side. The sheep, oblivious, were grazing away at the hay in their enclosure. The low grinding rhythm of sheep teeth sounded like a chorus of castanets.

The history of Junitaki went on, but history for the Ainu youth ended there. I got up to go to the john and piss two beers' worth. When I returned to my seat, she was awake and gazing distractedly out the window. Rice fields stretched far and wide. Occasionally there'd be a silo. Rivers drew near, then retreated. I smoked a cigarette, taking in the scenery together with her profile taking in the scenery. She spoke not a word. Once I finished my cigarette, I went back to the book. The shadow of a steel bridge flashed across the page.

After the unhappy tale of the Ainu youth who became a shepherd, got old, and died, the remaining history was rather boring fare. An outbreak of sheep bloat claimed ten head, severe cold dealt a temporary blow to crops, but other than that everything went smoothly with the village. In the Taisho era it was incorporated as a township and newly renamed Junitaki-cho. Junitaki-cho did well, building more facilities, a primary school, a town hall, a postal service outpost. By this time, the settling of Hokkaido was nearly complete.

With arable land reaching its limit, several young men left Junitaki-cho to seek their fortune in the new worlds of Manchuria and Sakhalin. In 1937, the Sheep Professor made his appearance in town.

Read the history: "Ministry of Agriculture and Forestry technical administrator much recognized for his studies in Korea and Manchuria, Dr. ______ (aged 32) took leave of his post due to special circumstances and established his own sheep ranch in a mountain valley north of Junitaki-cho."

Nothing else about him was written.

The author himself seemed to have gotten bored by the events of the thirties on, his reportage becoming spotty and fragmentary. Even the writing style faltered, losing the clarity of his discussion of the Ainu youth.

I skipped the thirty-one years between 1938 and 1965 and jumped to the section entitled "Junitaki Today." Of course, the book's "today" being 1970, it was hardly today's "today." Still, writing the history of one town obviously imposed the necessity of bringing it up to a "today." And even if such a today soon ceases to be today, no one can deny that it is in fact a today. For if a today ceased to be today, history could not exist as history.

According to my *Authoritative History of Junitaki Township*, in

1965 the population had dropped to 15,000, a decrease of 6,000 from ten years prior, due almost entirely to a decline in farming. The unusually high rate of agrarian disenfranchisement came about in reaction, it stated, to changes within the national infrastructure in a period of rapid industrial growth, as well as to the peculiar nature of cold-climate farming in Hokkaido.

What became of their abandoned farmlands? They were reforested. The land that their forefathers had sweated blood clearing, the descendants now planted with trees. Ironic how that worked.

Which was to say that the primary industry in Junitaki today was forestry and lumber milling. The town now boasted several small mills where they made television cabinets, vanities, and tourist-trade figurines of bears and Ainus. The former communal hut was converted into the Pioneer Museum, where the farming tools and eating utensils from early settlement days were kept on display. There were also keepsakes of the village youths who had died in the Russo-Japanese War. Also a lunch box bearing the teeth marks of a brown bear. And even the letter to the old hometown inquiring about the debt collectors.

But if the truth be known, Junitaki today was a dreadfully dull town. The townsfolk, when they came home from work, watched an average of four hours of television before going to bed each night. Balloting ran high, but it was never any surprise who won the election. The town slogan was "Bountiful Humanity in Bountiful Nature." Or so the sign in front of the station read.

I closed the book, yawned, and fell asleep.

30

The Further Decline of Junitaki and Its Sheep

We caught the connecting train in Asahikawa and headed north over the Shiogari Pass, traveling by largely the same route the Ainu youth and the eighteen dirt farmers had taken a century before.

The autumn sun shone brilliantly though the last vestiges of virgin forest and the blazing red leaves of the rowan ash. The air was still and clear. So much so just looking at the scenery made your eyes hurt.

The train was empty at first, but midway a whole carload of commuting high school students piled in and we were plunged into their commotion, their shouting and dandruff and body odors and incomprehensible conversations and sexual urges with no outlet. This went on for thirty minutes until they disappeared all at the same station. Once again, the train was empty, with not a voice to be heard.

We split a chocolate bar between us and munched on it as the scenery paraded before our eyes. A tranquil light spilled over the ground. Everything seemed so far away, as if we were looking through the wrong end of a telescope. She whistled snatches of *Johnny B. Goode*. This may have been the longest we two had ever not spoken.

* * *

It was afternoon when we got off the train. Standing on the platform, I took a deep breath and gave myself a good stretch. The air was so fresh I felt as if my lungs were going to collapse. The sun on my arms was warm and sensuous, even as the air was three or four degrees cooler than in Sapporo.

A row of old brick warehouses lined the tracks, and alongside these was a pyramid stack of logs three yards long, soaked and dark from the rain of the previous night. After the train we'd come on pulled out of the station, there was no one in sight, only a flowerbed of marigolds that were swaying in the cool breeze.

From the platform, we could see a typical small-scale regional city. Complete with main street, modest department store, bus terminal, tourist information center. A singularly dull town, if first impressions were any indication.

"This is our destination?" she asked.

"No, not here. We've got another train ride from here. Our destination is a much, much smaller town than this."

I yawned and took another deep breath.

"This is our transit point. Here's where the first settlers turned eastward."

"First settlers?"

In the time before our connecting train arrived, we sat down in front of the heater in the waiting room, and I related snippets of the history of Junitaki-cho. The chronology got a bit confused, so I used a page from my notebook to make a simplified timeline based on the summary at the back of the *Authoritative History*. On the left side of the page, I listed dates and developments in the history of Junitaki-cho and on the right the major events in the history of Japan in the same period. A fairly respectable chronological table.

For example, in 1905 Port Arthur fell and the Ainu youth's son was killed in the war. And if my memory served me correctly, that was also the year the Sheep Professor was born. Incrementally, history linked up.

"Looking at things this way," she said, comparing the left and right sides of the chronology, "we Japanese seem to live from war to war."

"Sure seems that way," I said.

"How did things ever get like this?"

"It's complicated. I can't really say. Not just like that."

"Humph."

The waiting room, like most waiting rooms, was deserted and unremarkable. The benches were miserably uncomfortable, the ashtrays swollen with waterlogged cigarette butts, the air stale. On the walls were travel posters and most-wanted lists. The only other people there were an old man wearing a camel-hair sweater and a mother with her four-year-old son. The old man sat glued in position, poring through a literary magazine. He turned the pages as slowly as if he were peeling away adhesive tape. Fifteen minutes from one page to the next. The mother and child looked like a couple whose marriage was on the rocks.

"What it comes down to is that everyone's poor, but we want to believe that if things work out, we'll be through with poverty."

"Like the people in Junitaki-cho."

"Exactly. That's why they worked themselves to death to break new ground. Even so, most of the settlers died poor."

"How come?"

"It's the territory. Hokkaido's cold country, every few years there's a killer frost. If their crops die, there's no food to eat, no income to buy oil. They can't even buy next year's seeds. So they put their land in hock and borrow money at high interest. But no agriculture in any region is productive enough to pay off that interest, and in the end the land is taken away from them. That's what reduces many farmers to tenant farming."

I flipped through the pages of my *Authoritative History* and read to her: "By 1930, the number of self-employed farmers had fallen to 46 percent of the population of Junitaki-cho. They had been dealt a double blow, a depressed market compounded by a killer frost."

"So after all their struggles to clear a new land for themselves to farm, they only got deeper in debt," she concluded.

As there were still forty minutes before our train, she decided to take a walk around town by herself. I stayed behind in the waiting room, had a Coke, and took up where I'd left off in another book I'd been reading. I was soon bored with it and put it away. I could not concentrate. My head was full of Junitaki-cho sheep chomping up all the print I could feed them. I closed my eyes and sighed. A passing freight train sounded its whistle.

A few minutes before departure time, she returned with a bag of apples. We ate them for lunch, then boarded the train.

The train had surely seen better days. Weak portions of the floorboards were buckled and worn. Walking the aisle was enough to make you sway from side to side. The seat coverings had lost their pile and the cushions were like month-old bread. An air of doom, mixed with toilet and kerosene smells, filled the car. I spent ten minutes trying to raise a window to let in some fresh air, but no sooner did I get it open than some fine sand blew in and I had to spend an equal amount of time closing the window.

The train had two cars. There was a total of fifteen passengers, lumped together by the common bonds of disinterest and ennui. The old man in the camel-hair sweater was still reading his magazine. At his reading speed, the issue may have gotten to be three months old. One heavy middle-aged lady was training her gaze at a distant point in space outside, as if a critic listening to a Scriabin sonata.

The children were quiet too. They sat still and stared out the window. Occasionally, someone coughed with a dry rasp that sounded like a mummy tapped on the head with a pair of tongs.

Each time the train pulled into a station, someone got off. Whenever someone got off, the conductor also got off to collect the ticket, then the conductor would get back on. The conductor was so totally without expression he could have pulled off a bank robbery without covering his face. No new passengers ever got on.

Outside, the river stretched forever, muddy brown from the rains. Glinting in the autumn sun, it looked like a spillway of café au lait. An improved road along the river popped in and out of view, and infrequently there'd be a huge truck hurtling westward with a load of lumber. On the whole, though, the road seemed practically unused. Roadside billboards relayed their sponsors' messages to no one, nowhere. I warded off boredom by looking at each new billboard, noting the sharp, urban appeal. A terrifically tanned girl in a bikini pursed her lips over a Coke, a middle-aged character actor wrinkled his brow at a tilted glass of Scotch, a diver's watch lavishly splashed with water, a model in the midst of a slick, sophisticated interior, doing her nails. The new pioneers of advertising were carving a mean streak deep into the country.

After two hours and forty minutes, we reached Junitaki-cho, the final stop. Somewhere along the line we had dozed off, apparently missing the station announcement. The diesel engine had squeezed out its last breath, and everything went silent. I woke with a start, the silence tingling on my skin. When I looked around, no other passengers were on board.

I brought our bags down from the rack, roused her with a couple of taps on the shoulder, and we got off. The wind that whisked the length of the platform was already tinged with a late-autumn chill. The dark shadows of the hills crept across the ground like fatal stains. Directly beyond the streets the two ranges of hills on either side of the town seemed to meet, neatly enfolding the town like two cupped hands protecting a match flame from the wind. The hills towered above the narrow station platform.

We stood there, rather at a loss, gazing at the scene for a few minutes.

"Where's the Sheep Professor's old homestead?" she asked.

"Up in the mountains. Three hours from here by car."

"Do we head straight out?"

"No," I said. "If we set out right now, it'll be the middle of the night before we got there. Let's stay here overnight and get a fresh start in the morning."

In front of the station was a small rotary, which was empty. No one milling about. No taxis picking up or letting off customers. Just, in the middle, a bird-shaped fountain with no water in it. The bird looked vacantly up at the sky with an open mouth and nothing to say. Around the fountain was planted a circular bank of marigolds. One glance told you the town was far more run-down than it had been a decade ago. Almost no one was out on the streets, and the few that were seemed to share the distracted run-down expression of a town on the wane.

To the left of the rotary were a half dozen old warehouses, from the days of shipping by rail. Of old-fashioned brick construction, they had high-pitched roofs and steel doors that had been painted countless times, only to have been abandoned in the end. Huge crows perched in rows along the roof ridges, silently surveying the town. Next came an empty lot under a thicket of weeds that could make you break out in hives up to your shoulder, in the center of which were the remains of two old cars left out to the elements. Both cars were missing tires, their guts ripped out from beneath pried hoods.

The GUIDE TO THE TOWN, posted next to the deserted rotary, was so weathered you could barely make it out. The only discernible words were JUNITAKI-CHO and NORTHERN LIMIT OF LARGE-SCALE RICE FARMING.

Directly in front of the rotary was a small street lined with shops. A street not unlike such streets anywhere in Japan except that the road was absurdly wide, giving the town an impression of even greater sparseness, and chill. On either side of the road was a line of rowan ashes, in brilliant foliage but somehow no less chill. It was a chill that infused every living thing, without regard for human fortune. The listless day-to-day goings-on of the town residents—everything—were engulfed in that chill.

I hiked my backpack up onto my shoulders and walked to the end of the five-hundred-yard-long commercial district, looking for a place to stay. There was no inn of any kind. A third of the shops had their shutters pulled down. A half-torn sign in front of a watch shop banged about in the wind.

Where the street of shops cut off abruptly, there was a large parking lot, again overgrown with weeds. In it were a cream-colored Honda Fairlady and a sports car, a red Toyota Celica. Both brand new. What a picture they made, their mint condition smack in the middle of a deadbeat town.

Beyond the shops, the road ambled down a slope to the river, where it split left and right at a T. Along this road were small one-story wood-frame houses, with dust-gray trees that thrust brambled limbs up into the sky. I don't know what it was, but every tree had the most eccentric array of branches. Each house had, at its front door, identical large fuel tanks with matching milk-delivery boxes. And on every rooftop stood unimaginably tall television antennae. These silver feelers groped about in the air, in defiance of the mountains that formed a backdrop to the town.

"But there's no inn," she said worriedly.

"Not to worry. Every town has got to have an inn."

We retraced our steps back to the station and asked the two attendants there where we could find one. Aged far enough apart to have been parent and child, they were obviously bored silly and explained the whereabouts of the lodgings in distressingly thorough detail.

"There are two inns," said the elder attendant. "One is on the expensive side, the other is fairly cheap. The expensive one is where we put up important officials from the Territorial Government and hold special banquets."

"The food is not bad at all there," said the younger attendant.

"The other is where traveling businessmen or young folk or, well, where regular people stay. The looks of it might put you off, but it's not unsanitary or anything. The bath is something else."

"Though the walls are thin," said the younger.

Whereupon the two them launched into debate over the thinness of the walls.

"We'll go for the expensive one," I said. No reason to economize. There was the envelope, still stuffed with money.

The younger attendant tore a sheet off a memo pad and drew a precise map of the way to the inn.

"Thank you," I said. "I guess you don't get as many people coming through here as you did ten years ago."

"No, that's for sure," said the elder. "Now there's only one lumber mill and no other industry to speak of. The bottom's fallen out of agriculture. The population's gone way down too."

"Hell, there aren't enough students to form proper classes at the school anymore," added the younger.

"What's the population?"

"They say it's around seven thousand, but really it's got to be less than that. More like five thousand, I'd guess," the younger said.

"Take this spur line, boy, before they shut us down, which may be any day. Come what may, we're the third deepest in the red of any line in the country," the elder said with finality.

I was surprised to hear that there were train lines more run-down than this one. We thanked them and left.

The inn was down the slope and to the right of the street of shops, three hundred yards along the river. An old inn, nice enough, with a glimmer of the charm it must have had in the heyday of the town. Facing the river, it had a well-cared-for garden. In one corner of the garden, a shepherd puppy buried its nose in a food dish, eating an early evening meal.

"Mountaineering is it?" asked the maid who showed us to our room.

"Mountaineering it is," I answered simply.

There were only two rooms upstairs. Each a spacious layout, and if you stepped out into the corridor, you had a view of the same café-au-lait river we'd seen from the train.

My girlfriend wanted to take a bath, so I went to check out the Town Hall. Town Hall was located on a desolate street two blocks west of the street of shops, yet the building was far newer and in much better shape than I'd expected.

I walked up to the Livestock Section in Town Hall, introduced myself with a magazine namecard from two years before when I'd posed as a free-lance writer, and broke into a spiel about needing to ask a few questions about sheep raising, if they didn't mind. It was pretty farfetched that a women's weekly magazine would have need for a piece on sheep, but the livestock officer bought the line immediately and conducted me into his office.

"At present, we have two-hundred-some sheep in the township, all Suffolks. That is to say, meat sheep. The meat is parceled out to nearby inns and restaurants, and enjoys considerable favor."

I pulled out my notebook and jotted down appropriate notes. No doubt this poor man would be buying the women's magazine for the next several issues. Which, admittedly, made me feel embarrassed.

"A cooking article, I assume?" he stopped to ask once he'd detailed the current state of sheep raising.

"Well, of course that's part of it," I said. "But more than that, we're looking to paint a total picture of sheep."

"A total picture?"

"You know, their character, habits, that sort of thing."

"Oh," said my informant.

I closed my notebook and drank the tea that had been served. "We'd heard there was an old sheep ranch up in the hills somewhere."

"Yes, there is. It was appropriated by the U.S. Army after the war and is no longer in use. For about ten years after the Americans returned it, a rich man from somewhere used the place for a villa, but it's so far out of the way that he finally stopped going up there. The house is as good as abandoned now. Which is why the ranch is on loan to the town. We ought to buy it and turn the place into a tourist ranch, but I'm afraid the finances of this township aren't up to it. First, we'd have to improve the road . . ."

"On loan?"

"In the summer, our municipal sheep farm takes about fifty head up into the mountains. There isn't enough grass in the municipal pasture and it's quite fine pastureland up there, as pastures go. When the weather starts turning bad around the latter half of September, the sheep are brought back down."

"Would you happen to know when it is that the sheep are up there?"

"It varies from year to year, but generally speaking it's from the beginning of May to the latter half of September."

"And how many men take the sheep up there?"

"One man. The same man's been doing it these ten years."

"Would it be possible to meet this man?"

The official placed a call to the municipal sheep farm.

"If you go there now, you can meet him," he said. "Shall we drive there?"

I declined politely at first, but I soon learned that I couldn't otherwise get to the sheep farm. There were no taxis or car rentals in town, and on foot it would have taken an hour and a half.

The livestock officer drove a small sedan. He passed our inn and headed west, taking a long concrete bridge to cross over a cold marshy area, then climbing up a mountain slope. Tires spun over the gravel.

"Coming from Tokyo, you probably think this is a ghost town."

I said something noncommittal.

"The truth is we are dying. We'll hold on as long as we have the railway, but if that goes we'll be dead for sure. It's a curious thing, a town dying. A person dying I can understand. But a whole town dying . . ."

"What will happen if the town dies?"

"What *will* happen? Nobody knows. They'll all just run away before that, not wanting to know. If the population falls below one thousand—which is well within the realm of possibility—we'll pretty much be out of a job, and we might be the ones who have to run out on everything."

I offered him a cigarette and gave him a light with the sheep-engraved Dupont lighter.

"There's plenty of good jobs in Sapporo. I've got an uncle who runs a printing company there, and he needs more hands. Work comes from the school system, so business is steady. Really, moving there would be the best thing. At least it'd beat monitoring shipments of sheep and cattle way out here."

"Probably," I said.

"But when it comes to actually packing up and leaving, I can't bring myself to do it. Can you see what I mean? If the town's really going to die, then the urge to stay on and see the town to its end wins out."

"Were you born here in this town?" I asked.

"Yes," he said, but did not go on. A melancholy-hued sun had already sunk a third of the way behind the hills.

Two poles stood at the entrance to the sheep farm and between them hung a sign: JUNITAKI-CHO MUNICIPAL SHEEP FARM. The road passed under the sign and led up a slope, disappearing into the dense autumn foliage.

"Beyond the woods there's the sheep house and behind that the caretaker's quarters. What shall we do about you getting back to town?"

"It's downhill. I can manage on foot. Thanks for everything."

The car pulled out of view, and I walked between the poles and up the slope. The last rays of the sun added an orange tinge to the already golden maple leaves. The trees were tall, patches of sunlight filtering down through the boughs and shimmering on the gravel road.

Emerging from the woods, I came upon a narrow building on the face of the hill, and with it the smell of livestock. The sheep house was roofed in red corrogated iron, pierced in three places by ventilation stacks.

There was a doghouse at the entrance to the house. No sooner had I seen it than a small Border collie came out on a tether and barked two or three times. It was a sleepy-eyed old dog with no threat in its bark. When I rubbed its neck, it calmed right down. Yellow plastic bowls of food and water were placed in front of the doghouse. As soon as I released my hand, the dog went back in the doghouse, satisfied, aligned its paws with the portal, and lay down on the floor.

The interior of the sheep house was dim. No one was around. A wide concrete walkway led down the middle, and to either side were the sheep pens. Along the walkway were gutters for draining off the sheep piss and wash water. Here and there windows cut through the wood-paneled walls, revealing the jaggedness of the hills. The evening sun cast red over the sheep on the right side, plunging the sheep on the left side into a murky blue shadow.

The instant I entered the sheep house, all two hundred sheep turned in my direction. Half the sheep stood, the other half lay on the hay spread over their pen floors. Their eyes were an unnatural blue, looking like tiny wellsprings flowing from the sides of their faces. They shone like glass eyes which reflected light from straight on. They all stared at me. Not one budged. A few continued munching away on the grass in their mouth, but there was no other sound. A few, their heads protruding from their pens, had stopped drinking water and had frozen in place, fixing their eyes on me. They seemed to think as a group. Had my standing in the entrance momentarily interrupted their unified thinking? Everything stopped, all judgment on hold. It took a move by me to restart their mental processes. In their eight separate pens, they began to move. The ewes gathered around the seed ram in the female pen; in the males-only pens, the rams vied for dominant position. Only a few curious ones stayed at the fence staring at me.

Attached to the long, level black ears that stuck out from the sides of their face were plastic chips. Some sheep had blue chips, some yellow chips, some red chips. They also had colored markings on their backs.

I walked on tiptoe so as not to alarm them. Feigning disinterest, I approached one pen and extended my hand to touch the head of a young ram. It flinched but did not move away. Tense, wide-eyed, rigid. Perhaps he would be the gauge of my intrusion. The other sheep glared at us.

Suffolk sheep are peculiar to begin with. They're completely black, yet their fleece is white. Their ears are large and stick flat out like moth wings, and their luminous blue eyes and long bony noses make them seem foreign. These Suffolks neither rejected nor accepted my presence, regarding me more as a temporary manifestation. Several pissed with a tinkling flourish. The piss flowed across the floor, under their feet, into the gutter.

I exited the sheep house, petting the Border collie again and taking a deep breath.

The sun had set behind the mountains. A pale violet gloom spread over the slant of the hills like ink dispersing in water. I circled around the back of the sheep house, crossed a wooden bridge over a stream, and headed toward the caretaker's quarters. A cozy little one-story affair, dwarfed by a huge attached barn that stored hay and farm tools.

The caretaker was next to the barn, stacking plastic bags of disinfectant beside a yard-wide by yard-deep concrete trough. As I approached, he glanced up once, then returned to the task at hand, unaffected by my presence. Not until I was in front of him did he stop and wipe his face with the towel around his neck.

"Tomorrow's the day for disinfecting the sheep," he said, pulling out a crushed pack of cigarettes and lighting up. "This here's where we pour the liquid disinfectant and make the sheep swim from end to end. Otherwise, being indoors, they get all kinds of bugs over the winter."

"You do all this by yourself?"

"You kidding? I got two helpers. Them and me and the dog. The dog does most of the work, though. The sheep trust the dog. He ain't no sheepdog if the sheep don't trust him."

The man was a couple inches shorter than me, solidly built. He was in his late forties, with closed-cropped hair, stiff and straight as a hairbrush. He pulled his rubber gloves off as if he were peeling off a layer of skin. Whacking himself on his pants, he stood with his hands in his patch pockets. He was more than a caretaker of sheep; he was rather like a drill sergeant at a military school.

"So you've come to ask something, eh?"

"Yes, I have."

"Well, do your askin'."

"You've been in this line of work a long time?"

"Ten years," he said. "If that's a long time, I don't know, but I do know my sheep. Before that I was in the Self-Defense Forces."

He threw his hand towel around his neck and looked up at the sky.

"You stay here through the winter?"

"Well, uh," he coughed, "I guess so. No other place for me to go. Besides, there's a lot of busywork to take care of over the winter. We get near to six feet of snow in these parts. It piles up and if the roof caves in, you got yourself some flat sheep. Plus I feed them, clean out the sheep house, and this and that."

"When summer comes around, you take half of them up into the mountains?"

"That's right."

"How difficult is it walking so many sheep?"

"Easy. That's what people used to do all the time. It's only in recent years you got sheep keepers, not sheep herders. Used to be they'd keep them on the move the whole year 'round. In Spain in the seventeen hundreds, they had roads all over the country no one but shepherds could use, not even the King."

The man spat phlegm onto the ground, rubbing it into the dirt with his shoe.

"Anyway, as long as they're not frightened, sheep are very cooperative creatures. They'll just follow the dog without asking any questions."

I took out the Rat's sheep photograph and handed it to the caretaker. "This is the place in the photo, right?"

"Sure is," said the man. "No doubt about it: they're our sheep too."

"What about this one?" I pointed with my ballpoint pen to the stocky sheep with the star on its back.

The man squinted at the photograph a second. "No, that's not one of ours. Sure is strange, though. There's no way it could've gotten in there. The whole place is fenced in with wire, and I check each animal morning and night. The dog would notice if a strange one got in. The sheep would raise a fuss too. But you know, never in my life have I ever seen this breed of sheep."

"Did anything strange happen this year when you were up in the mountains with the sheep?"

"Nothing at all," he said. "It was peaceful as could be."

"And you were up there alone all summer?"

"No, I wasn't alone. Every other day staffers came up from town, and then there'd be some official observers too. Once a week I went down to town, and a replacement looked after the sheep. Need to stock up on provisions and things."

"Then you weren't holed up there alone the whole time?"

"No. Summer lasts as long as the snow doesn't get too deep, and it's only an hour and a half to the ranch by jeep. Hardly more than a little stroll. Of course, once it snows and cars can't get through, you're stuck up there the whole winter."

"So nobody's up on the mountain now?"

"Nobody but the owner of the villa."

"The owner of the villa? But I heard that the place hasn't been used in ages."

The caretaker flicked his cigarette to the ground and stepped on it. "It *hasn't* been used in ages. But it is now. If you had half a mind to, no reason why you couldn't live there. I put in a little upkeep on the house myself. The electricity and gas and phone are all working. Not one pane of glass is broken."

"The man from Town Hall said nobody was up there."

"There's lots of stuff those guys don't know. I've gotten work on the side from the owner all along, never spilled a word to anyone. He told me to keep it quiet."

The man wanted another cigarette, but his pack was empty. I offered him my half-smoked pack of Larks, folding against it a ten-thousand-yen note. The man considered the gratuity for a second, then put one cigarette to his lips and pocketed everything else. "Much obliged," he said.

"So when did the owner show up?"

"Spring. Wasn't yet spring thaw, so it must've been March. It was maybe five years since he'd been up here. Don't rightly know why he came after all this time, but well, that's the owner's business and none of mine. He told me not to tell a soul. He must have had his reasons. In any case, he's been up there ever since. I buy him his food and fuel in secret and deliver it by jeep a little at a time. With all he's got, he could hold out for a year, easy."

"He wouldn't happen to be about my age, with a moustache, would he?"

"Uh-huh," said the caretaker. "That's the guy."

"Just great," I said. There was no need to show him the photograph.

31

Night in Junitaki

Negotiations with the caretaker went smoothly with supplementary monetary lubrication. The caretaker was to pick us up at the inn at eight in the morning, then drive us up to the sheep farm on the mountain.

"Disinfecting sheep can wait until afternoon, I figure," said the caretaker. A hard-line realist.

"There's one other thing that bothers me," he said. "The ground's going to be soft from yesterday's rain, and there's one place the car might not be able to get through. So I might have to ask you to walk from that point. Not through any fault of mine."

"That's okay," I said.

Walking back down the hill, I suddenly recalled that the Rat's father had a vacation villa in Hokkaido. Come to think of it, the Rat had said so a number of times years back. Up in the mountains, big pasture, old two-story house. I always remember important details long afterward. It should have struck me the moment I got the Rat's letter. If I'd thought of it first, there'd have been any number of ways to follow up on it.

Annoyed with myself, I trudged back to town down a mountain road that was growing darker and darker. In the hour and a half I walked, I encountered only three vehicles. Two were large diesel trucks loaded down with lumber, one a small tractor. All three were heading downhill, but no one called out to offer me a ride. So much the better as far as I was concerned.

It was past seven by the time I reached the inn, and the night was already pitch black. My body was chilled to the core. The shepherd puppy stuck its nose out of the doghouse and whined in my direction.

She was wearing jeans and my crew-neck sweater, totally absorbed in a computer game in the recreation room near the entrance of the inn. Apparently a remodeled old parlor, the room still boasted a magnificent fireplace. A real wood-burning fireplace. In addition, there were four computer games and two pinball tables; the pinball tables were old Spanish cheapies, models you'd never be able to find anywhere.

"I'm starved," she said.

I placed our order for dinner and took a quick bath. Drying off, I weighed myself, the first time in a long while. One hundred thirty-two pounds, same as ten years ago. The extra inch I put on around the middle had been neatly trimmed away over the last week.

When I got back to the room, dinner was laid out.

32

An Unlucky Bend in the Road

The morning was hazy and cool. I sympathized with those sheep. Swimming though the cold disinfectant on a day like this could be brutal. Maybe sheep don't feel cold? Maybe they don't feel anything.

Hokkaido's short autumn season was drawing to a close. The thick gray clouds in the north were intimations of the snows to come. Flying from September Tokyo to October Hokkaido, I'd lost my autumn. There'd been the beginning and the end, but none of the heart of autumn.

I woke at six and washed my face. I sat alone in the corridor, looking out the window until breakfast was ready. The waters of the river had subsided somewhat since the day before and were now running clear. Rice fields spread out on the opposite bank, where irregular morning breezes traced random waves through the ripened, tall grassiness, as far as the eye could see. A tractor crossed the concrete bridge, heading toward the hills, its puttering engine faintly audible in the wind. Three crows flew out of the now-golden birch woods. Making a full circle above the river and landing on a railing of the building. Perched there, the crows acted the perfect bystanders from an avant-garde drama. Soon tiring of even that role, however, the crows flew off one by one and disappeared upstream.

The sheep caretaker's old jeep was parked outside the inn at eight o'clock sharp. The jeep had a box-shaped roof, apparently a surplus job if the Self-Defense Forces issue number legible on the front fender was any indication.

"You know, there's something funny going on," the caretaker said as soon as he saw me. "I tried to telephone ahead up on the mountain, but I couldn't get through."

She and I climbed into the backseat. It smelled of gasoline. "When was the last time you tried calling?" I asked.

"Well, around the twentieth of last month, I guess. I haven't gotten in touch once since then. Call generally comes in from him whenever there's something he needs. A shopping list or something."

"Did you get the phone to ring?"

"Not even a busy signal. Must be a line down somewhere. Not unlikely if there's been a big snow."

"But there hasn't been any snow."

The caretaker looked up at the roof of the jeep and rolled his head around to crack his neck. "Then we'll just have to go take a look, won't we?"

I nodded. The gasoline fumes were starting to get to me.

We crossed the concrete bridge and started up the hill by the same road I'd taken yesterday. Passing the Municipal Sheep Farm, all three of us turned to look at the two poles with the sign over the entrance. The farm was stillness itself. I could picture the sheep: each staring off into its own silent space with limpid blue eyes.

"You leave the disinfecting to the afternoon?"

"Yeah, well, no real hurry or nothin'. So long's it gets done before it snows."

"When does it start to snow?"

"Wouldn't be surprised if it snowed next week," said the caretaker. With one hand on the steering wheel, he looked down and coughed. "It'll be into November before it gets to piling up, though. Ever know a winter in these parts?"

"No," I said.

"Well, once it starts to collect, it piles up nonstop as if a dam's burst through. By then, there's nothin' you can do but crawl indoors and hang your head. People were never meant to live in these parts in the first place."

"But you've been living here all this time."

"That's because I like sheep. Sheep are good-natured creatures. They even remember people by their face. A year looking after sheep is over before you know it, and then it starts to add up. In the autumn they mate, spring they lamb, summer they graze. When the lambs get big, in the autumn they're mating. 'Round and 'round. It all repeats itself. The sheep change every year, it's only me getting older. And the older I get, the less I want to live in town again."

"What do sheep do over the winter?" asked my girlfriend.

His hands still on the steering wheel, the caretaker turned around and gazed at her, practically drinking in her face, as if he hadn't noticed her before. The road was paved and straight and there wasn't another car in sight; even so, I broke into a nervous sweat.

"They stay put indoors all winter long," said the caretaker, at last turning his eyes back to the road.

"Don't they get bored?"

"Do you get so bored with your own life?"

"I can't really say."

"Well, the same with sheep," said the caretaker. "They don't think about stuff like that, and it wouldn't do 'em any good if they did. They just pass the winter eating hay, pissing, getting into spats, thinking about the babies in their bellies."

The hills grew steeper and steeper, and the road started to curve into switchbacks. Pastoral scenery gradually gave way to sheer walls of dark primal forest on both sides of the road. Occasionally, there'd be an opening to a glimpse of the flatlands below.

"Under snow, we wouldn't be getting through here," said the caretaker. "Not that there's any need to."

"Aren't there any ski areas or mountaineering courses?" I asked.

"Not here, nothing. And that's why there're no tourists. Which is why the town's going nowhere fast. Up until the early sixties, the town was fairly active as a model for cold-zone agriculture. But ever since the rice surplus, everybody's lost interest in farming in an icebox. Stands to reason."

"What happened to the lumber mills?"

"Weren't enough hands to go around, so they moved to more convenient places. You can still find small mills in a few towns today, but not many. Now, trees cut here in the mountains pass right through town and are taken to Nayori and Asahikawa. That's why the roads are in top shape while the town's going to pieces. A large truck with snow tires'll get through most any snowblock."

Unconsciously, I brought a cigarette to my lips, but before lighting up I remembered the gasoline fumes and returned it to the pack. So I sucked on a lemon drop instead. The result: the uncommon taste of lemon gasoline.

"Do sheep quarrel?" asked my girlfriend.

"You bet they quarrel," said the caretaker. "It's the same with any animal that goes around in groups. Each and every sheep has a pecking order in the sheep society. If there's fifty sheep in a pen, then there's number one sheep right down to number fifty sheep. And each one knows exactly where it belongs."

"Amazing," she said.

"It makes managing 'em that much easier for me too. You pull on number one sheep, and the rest just follow along, no questions asked."

"But if they all know their place, why should they fight?"

"Say one sheep gets hurt and loses its strength, its position becomes unstable. So the sheep under it get feisty and try for better position. When that happens, they're at it for three days."

"Poor things."

"Well, it all evens out. The sheep that gets the boot, when it was young, gave some other sheep the boot, after all. And when it all comes down to the butcher block, there's no number one or number fifty. Just one happy barbecue."

"Humph," she said.

"But the real pitiful one is the stud ram. You know all about sheep harems, don't you?"

"No, I don't," I said.

"When you're raising sheep, the most important thing you got to keep an eye on is mating. So you keep 'em separate, the males with the males, the females with the females. Then you throw one male into the pen with the females. Generally, it's the strongest number one male. In other words, you're serving up the best seed. After a month, when all the business is done, this stud ram gets returned to the males-only pen. But during the time the stud's been busy, the other males have worked out a new pecking order. And thanks to all that servicing, the stud is down to half his weight and there's no way he can win a fight. So all the other males gang up on him. Now there's a sad story."

"How do sheep fight?"

"They bump heads. Sheep foreheads are hard as steel and all hollow inside."

She said nothing, but seemed to be deep in thought. Probably trying to picture angry sheep beating their heads together.

After thirty minutes' drive, the paved surface suddenly disappeared, and the road narrowed to half its width. From both sides, dark primal forests rushed in like giant waves at our jeep. The temperature dropped.

The road was terrible. It bounced the jeep around like a seismographic needle, agitating the gasoline in the plastic tank at our feet. The gas made ominous sounds, as if someone's brains were sloshing about, ready to come flying out of their skull. Was I nervous about it? You bet.

The road went on like this for twenty or thirty minutes. I couldn't steady myself even to read my watch. The whole while nobody said a word. I held tight to the belt attached to the seat, as she clung to my right arm. The caretaker concentrated on holding on to the steering wheel.

"Left," the caretaker suddenly spoke up. Not knowing what to expect, I turned to see a wall in the dark forest torn wide open, the ground falling away. The valley was vast, and the view was spectacular. But without a hint of warmth. The rock face was sheer, stripped of every bit of life. You could smell its menacing breath.

Back straight ahead on the road a slick, conical mountain now appeared. At the tip, a tremendous force had twisted the cone out of shape.

Hands tight on the steering wheel, the caretaker jutted his chin forward in the direction of the cove.

"We're headed 'round the other side of that."

The strong wind that climbed the right slope from the valley sent the thick foliage sweeping upward, lightly spraying sand against the windows.

At some point near the top of the cone, the switchbacks came to an end, the slope on the right changing into volcanic crags, then eventually into a steep stone face. Squeezed on a narrow ledge chiseled into a featureless expanse of rock, the jeep crept along.

Suddenly, the weather took a turn for the worse. The blue-tinged patches of light-gray sky wearied of their fickle subtleties and turned dark, mixing in an uneven sooty black. Imparting a grim cast to the mountains.

In this caldron of a mountain, the winds whirled around, wheezing and moaning awfully. I wiped the sweat from my brow. Under my sweater, I was all cold sweat too.

The caretaker pursed his lips with each cut of the wheel, pulling right, right again. Then he leaned forward as if straining to hear something, slowing the jeep gradually until, where the road widened slightly, he stepped on the brake. He turned off the engine, and we sat, delivered into the midst of a frozen silence. There was only the wind taking its survey of the land.

The caretaker rested both hands on the wheel. A half hour seemed to pass before he got out of the jeep and tapped the ground with the sole of his work shoe. I climbed out of the jeep after him and stood beside him, looking down at the road surface.

"No good," said the caretaker. "It rained a lot harder than I thought."

The road did not seem all that damp to me. On the contrary, it looked hard-packed and dry.

"The core is damp," he explained. "It fools everyone. Things are different in these parts."

"Different?"

Instead of answering, he took a cigarette out of his pocket and lit up. "How about taking a short walk with me?"

We walked two hundred yards to the next bend. I could feel the nasty chill. I zipped my windbreaker all the way up and turned my collar, but the cold insisted.

Right where the road began to curve, the caretaker stopped. Facing the cliff on the right, cigarette still at his lips, he grimaced. Water, a light clayey brown, was trickling out of the middle of the cliff, flowing down the rock, and slowly crossing the road. I swiped my finger across the rock face. It was more porous than it seemed, the surface crumbling at the slightest touch.

"This here's one hell of a curve," said the caretaker. "The surface is loose, but that's not all. It's, well, bad luck. Even the sheep are afraid of it."

The caretaker coughed and tossed his cigarette to the ground. "I hate to do this to you, but I don't want to chance it."

I nodded.

"Think you can walk it the rest of the way?"

"Walking isn't the question. It's the vibrations from our walking that make me nervous."

The caretaker gave one more good hard stamp of his shoe. A split second later came a dull, depressing retort. "It's okay for walking."

We returned to the jeep.

"It's about another three miles from here," said the caretaker. "Even with the woman, you'll get there in an hour and a half. One straight road, not much of a rise. Sorry I can't take you the whole way."

"That's all right. Thanks for everything."

"You thinking to stay up there?"

"I don't know. I might be back down tomorrow. It might take a week. Depends on how things go."

He put another cigarette to his lips, but this time before he could even light up he started coughing. "You better watch out, though. The way things look, it'll probably be an early snow. And once the snow sets in, you're not gettin' out."

"I'll keep an eye out," I said.

"There's a mailbox by the front door. The key's wedged in the bottom. If nobody's there, use that."

We unloaded the jeep under the lead-gray skies. I took my windbreaker off and slipped on a heavy mountaineering parka. I was still cold.

With great difficulty, the caretaker managed to turn the jeep around, bumping into the cliff repeatedly. Each time he hit the cliff, it would crumble. Finally, he succeeded in turning completely around, honked his horn, and waved. I waved back. The jeep swung around the bend and was gone.

We were totally alone. As if we'd been dropped off at the edge of the world.

We set our backpacks on the ground and stood there saying nothing, trying to get our bearings. Below us a slender ribbon of silver river wound its way through the valley, both banks covered in dense green forest. Across the valley broke waves of low, autumn-tinged hills and beyond that a hazy view of the flatlands. Thin columns of smoke rose from the fields where rice straw was being burned after the harvest. A breathtaking panorama, but it made me feel no better. Everything seemed so remote, so . . . alien.

The sky was weighed down with a moist, uniform gray—clouds that seemed, as one, to blanket all light. Below, lumps of dense black cloud matter blew by, almost within touching distance. The clouds raced eastward from the direction of the Asian continent, cutting across the Japan Sea to Hokkaido on their way to the Sea of Okhotsk with remarkable speed. It all contributed to making us aware of the the utter precariousness of where we stood. One passing gust and this whole crumbling curve plastered against the cliff could easily drag us to the bottom of the abyss.

"Let's get moving," I said, shouldering my monster backpack. Something awful, whether rain or sleet, was in the air, and I wanted to be near someplace with a roof. I sure didn't want to get drenched out here in the cold.

We hoofed it away from that "dead man's curve" on the double. The caretaker was right: the place was bad luck. There was a feeling of doom that first came over my body, then went on to strike a warning signal in my head. The sort of feeling you get when you're crossing a river and all of a sudden you sink your feet into mud of a different temperature.

In just the three hundred yards we walked, the sound of our

footsteps on the road surface went through any number of changes. Time and again, spring-fed rivulets snaked across our path.

Even after we cleared the curve, we did not slow down, trying to create as much distance from the spot as we could. Only after thirty minutes did we relax as the cliff eased back into a less precipitous slope and trees came into view.

Having made it this far, we had no problem with the rest of the way. The road flattened out, and the mountains lost their sharp ridges. Gradually, we were in the midst of a peaceful highland scene.

In another thirty minutes, the cone was completely behind us, and we came onto a plateau surrounded by mountains that looked like cutouts. It was as if the top half of a gigantic volcano had collapsed. A sea of birch trees in their autumn foliage stretched forever. Among the birches were brilliantly hued shrubs and undergrowth, here and there a toppled birch, brown and rotting.

"Seems like a nice enough place," said my girlfriend.

After that curve, it looked like a nice place indeed.

The road led us straight up through this sea of birches. It was barely wide enough for a jeep and absolutely straight. Not one bend, no steep slopes. If you looked ahead, everything was sucked into one point. Even the black clouds passed directly over that point.

And it was quiet. The sound of the wind itself was swallowed by the grand expanse of forest. The air was split by the cry of a fat blackbird. Once the bird was out of sight, the silence flowed back in, a viscous fluid filling every opening. The leaves that had fallen on the road were saturated from the rain of two days before. The road seemed endless, like the birch forest around it. The low clouds, which had been terrifying only a short while before, now seemed surreal through the woods.

After another fifteen minutes, we came to a clear stream. There was a sturdy birch-trunk bridge with handrails, and nearby, a small clearing. We set down our packs, went down to the stream, and helped ourselves to a drink. It was the best-tasting water I'd ever had. Cold enough to redden my hands, and sweet, with a scant trace of earth.

The clouds kept on their appointed course, but unaccountably the weather was bearing up. She adjusted the laces of her mountain shoes, I sat back on the handrail and smoked a cigarette. Downstream, I could hear a waterfall. Not a very big waterfall from the sound of it. A playful breeze blew in from the left, sending a ripple through the piles of leaves and scattering them.

I finished my cigarette and ground it out with my shoe, only to find another butt right next to my foot. I picked it up. A flattened Seven Stars. Not wet, so it had been from after the rains. Which meant either yesterday or today.

I tried to recall what brand of cigarette the Rat smoked. But I couldn't remember if he even smoked. I gave up and tossed the cigarette butt into the stream. The current whisked it off downstream in an instant.

"What is it?" she asked.

"I found a fresh cigarette butt, so somebody must have been sitting here having a smoke like me not too long ago."

"Your friend?"

"I wish I could say."

She sat herself down next to me and pulled back her hair, giving me the first view of her ears in a long time. The sound of the waterfall grew faint, then came back.

"You still like my ears?" she asked.

I smiled and quickly reached out my hand to touch them.

"You know I do," I said.

After yet another fifteen minutes, the road suddenly came abruptly to an end, just as the sea of birches suddenly stopped. Before us was a vast lake of a pasture.

Posts set at five-yard intervals surrounded the pasture. Wire connecting them, old, rusty wire. We had, it seemed, found our way to the sheep pasture. I pushed open the well-worn double gate and entered. The grass was soft, the soil dark and moist.

Black clouds were passing over the pasture. In the direction of their flight, a tall, jagged line of mountains. The angle was different, to be sure, but there was no mistaking: these were the same mountains in the Rat's photograph. I didn't need to pull out the photograph to check.

Still, it was unsettling seeing with my very own eyes a scene I had by now seen hundreds of times in a photograph. The depth of the actual place seemed artificial. Less my being there than the sense that the scene had been temporarily thrown together in order to match the photograph.

I leaned on the gate and heaved a sigh. This was it, what we'd been searching for. And whatever meaning that search might have had, we'd found it.

"We made it, eh?" she said, touching my arm.

"We made it," I said. Nothing more to say.

Straight on across the pasture stood an old American-style two-story wood-frame house. The house that the Sheep Professor had built forty years before and the Rat's father had then bought. Nothing was nearby to compare it to, so from a distance it was difficult to tell how big it was. It was, in any case, squat and expressionless. Painted white, beneath the overcast skies it looked a foreboding gray. From the middle of the mustard-, almost rust-colored gabled roof a rectangular brick chimney protruded. Instead of a fence around the house, there was a stand of evergreens which protected it from the elements. The place seemed curiously uninhabited. An odd house the more I looked at it. It wasn't particularly inhospitable or cold, nor built in any unusual way, nor even much in disrepair. It was just . . . odd. As if a great creature had grown old without being able to express its feelings. Not that it didn't know how to express them, but rather that it didn't know what to express.

The smell of rain was suddenly everywhere. Time to get moving. We made a beeline across the pasture for the house. The clouds blowing in from the west were no longer gentle passing puffs; big threatening rain clouds were on the approach.

The pasture was huge. No matter how fast we walked, we seemed to make no progress. I couldn't get any feeling for the distance. Come to think of it, this was the first level ground we'd walked on, so even things far off seemed within reach.

A flock of birds crossed the course of the clouds on their way north.

When, after hours it seemed, we finally made it to the house, the patter of rain had already started. Up close, the house was bigger and older than it had appeared from a distance. The white paint was blistered and peeling, the flakes on the ground long since brown from the rain. At this point, you'd have to strip off all the dead layers of paint before you could think about putting on a new coat. The prospect of painting such a house—why was I even thinking of this?—made me wince. A house where no one lives goes to pieces, and this house, without a doubt, was on its way there.

The trees, in contrast to the ailing house, were thriving, enveloping it like the treehouse in *The Swiss Family Robinson*. Long untrimmed, their branches spread wildly.

With the road up the mountain so tortuous, what a feat it must have been for the Sheep Professor to build this house. Hauling the lumber, doing all the work, sinking his entire savings into it, no doubt. To think that this same Sheep Professor was now holed up in a dark room at the Dolphin Hotel! You couldn't ask for a better (or worse) personification of an unrewarded life.

I stood in the cold rain staring up at the house. Even up close, it showed no signs of habitation. Layers of fine sand had accumulated on the wooden shutters of the high, narrow double-hung windows. Rain had fixed the sand into configurations onto which another layer of sand had been blown, to be fixed in place by yet new rain.

In the middle of the front door at eye level was a four-inch-square windowpane covered on the inside with a cloth. The brass doorknob had been blasted with sand too, and grit crumbled off to the touch. The knob was as loose as an old molar, yet the door wouldn't open. Made of three planks of oak, it was sturdier than it looked. I knocked loudly on it a couple of times for the hell of it. As expected, no answer. All I did was hurt my hand. The boughs of the huge pin oak swayed in a gust of wind, producing a virtual sandslide.

As the caretaker had said, the key was in the bottom of the mailbox. An old-fashioned brass key, tarnished white where hands had touched it.

"Don't you think they're a little careless leaving the key like that?" asked my girlfriend.

"Know any burglars who'd come all this way, steal something, and haul it back down?"

The key fit the keyhole remarkably well. I turned it, there was a loud click, and the bolt unlocked.

It was dim, unnaturally dim. The shutters had been drawn for a long time, and it took a while for my eyes to adjust. There was gloom everywhere.

The room was large. Large, quiet, and smelling like an old barn. A smell I remembered from childhood. Old furniture and cast-off carpets. We closed the door behind us, shutting the sound of the wind out entirely.

"Hello?" I shouted. "Anybody home?"

Of course not. It was clear no one was there. Only the presence of a grandfather clock ticking away beside the fireplace.

For a brief instant, I felt a sense of vertigo. There in the darkness, time turned on its head. Moments overlapped. Memories crumbled. Then it was over. I opened my eyes and everything fell back into place. Before my eyes was a plain gray space, nothing more.

"Are you all right?" she asked worriedly.

"I'm all right," I said. "Let's check upstairs."

While she searched for a light switch, I checked the grandfather clock. It was the kind that had three weights you wound up on chains. Although all three had hit bottom, the clock was eking out its last increments of motion. Given the length of the chains, it would have taken about a week for the weights to hit bottom. Which meant that sometime during the week someone had been here to wind the clock.

I wound the three weights up to the top, then sat down on the sofa and stretched out my legs. An old prewar sofa, but quite comfortable. Not too soft, not too hard, and smelling like the palm of your hand.

A click, and the lights came on. She emerged from the kitchen, sat on the chaise, and lit up a clove cigarette. I lit up one myself.

I'd learned to like them from her.

"Seems your friend was planning to spend the winter here," she said. "There's a whole winter's worth of fuel and food in the kitchen. A regular supermarket."

"But no sign of him."

"What about upstairs?"

We climbed the stairs next to the kitchen. They careened off at an angle halfway up. Emerging onto the second floor, we seemed to have entered a different atmospheric layer.

There were three bedrooms on the second floor. One big room to the left of a hallway and two smaller rooms to the right. Each room had a bare minimum of furniture, each room on the gloomy side. The big room had twin beds and a dresser. The beds were stripped down to their frames. Time was dead in the air.

Only in the farther small bedroom was there any lingering scent of human occupation. The bed was neatly made, the pillow with a slight indentation, and a pair of blue pajamas was folded at the head of the bed. An old-model lamp sat on the side table next to an overturned book. A Conrad novel.

Beside the bed was a heavy oak chest of drawers. In it an inventory of men's sweaters, shirts, slacks, socks, and underwear. The sweaters and slacks were well worn, invariably frayed somewhere, but good clothes. I could swear I'd seen some of them before. They were the Rat's, all right. Shirts with a fifteen-inch neck, slacks with a twenty-nine-inch waist.

Next to the window were an old table and chair of a singularly simple design you don't see often anymore. In the desk drawer, a cheap fountain pen, three boxes of ink cartridges, and a letter set, the stationery unused. In the second drawer, a half-used supply of cough drops and various and sundry small items. The third drawer, empty. No diary, no notebook, nothing. He'd done away with all extras. Everything was squared away. Too much. I ran my finger over the desktop, and it came up white with dust. Not a whole lot of dust. Maybe a week's worth.

I lifted up the double-hung window and pushed open the shutters. Low black clouds were swooping in. The wind had gathered strength, and you could almost see it cavorting through the pasture like a wild animal. Beyond that were the birches and beyond them the mountains. It was the exact same vista as in the photograph. Except there were no sheep.

We went back downstairs and sat on the sofa. The grandfather clock gave a command chime performance, then struck twelve times. We were silent until the last note was swallowed into the air.

"What do we do now?" she asked.

"We wait. What else?" I said. "The Rat was here a week ago. His things are still here. He's got to come back."

"But if the snow sets in before that, we'll be here all winter and our time will run out."

True enough.

"Don't your ears tell you anything?"

"They're out of commission. If I open my ears, I get a headache."

"Well, then, I guess we stretch out and wait for the Rat," I said.

Which was to say we'd run out of options.

While she went into the kitchen and made coffee, I took a quick once-around the big living room, inspecting it corner to corner. The fireplace, a real working fireplace set in the middle of the main wall, was clean and ready for use. But it had not been used recently. A few oak leaves, having gotten in through the chimney, sat in the hearth. A large kerosene heater stood nearby. The fuel gauge read full.

Next to the fireplace was a built-in glass-paneled bookcase completely filled with old books. I pulled out a few volumes and leafed through them. All were prewar editions, almost none of any value. Geography and science and history and philosophy and politics. Utterly useless, the lot of them, except maybe as documents of an intellectual's required reading forty years ago. There were postwar editions too, of similar worth. Only *Plutarch's Lives* and *Selected Greek Tragedies* and a handful of novels had managed to survive the erosion of years. This was a first for me: never before had I set eyes on so grand a collection of useless tomes.

To the side of the bookcase was a display shelf, likewise built-in, and on it a stereo hi-fi—bookshelf speakers, amplifier, turntable—

the kind popular in the mid-sixties. Some two hundred old records, every one scratched beyond reckoning, but at least not worthless. The musical taste was not as eroded as the ideology. I switched on the vacuum-tube amplifier, picked a record at random, and lowered the needle. Nat King Cole's *South of the Border*. All at once the room felt transported back to the 1950s.

The wall opposite had four six-foot double-hung windows, equidistantly spaced. You could see the rain coming down in torrents now. A gray rain, which obscured the line of mountains in the distance.

The room was wood-floored, with an eight-by-twelve-foot carpet in the middle, on which were arranged a set of drawing-room furniture and a floor lamp. A dining table stood in one corner of the room, covered with dust.

The vacant aftermath of a room.

A door, set inconspicuously into the wall, opened into a fair-sized trunk room. It was stacked high and tight with surplus furniture, carpets, dishes, a set of golf clubs, a guitar, a mattress, overcoats, mountaineering boots, old magazines. Even junior high school exam reference books and a radio-controlled airplane. Mostly products of the fifties and sixties.

The house kept its own time, like the old-fashioned grandfather clock in the living room. People who happened by raised the weights, and as long as the weights were wound, the clock continued ticking away. But with people gone and the weights unattended, whole chunks of time were left to collect in deposits of faded life on the floor.

I took a few old screen magazines back to the living room. The photo feature of one was *The Alamo*. John Wayne's directorial debut with the all-out support of John Ford. I want to make a grand epic that lingers in the hearts of all Americans, John Wayne said. He looked corny as hell in a beaver cap.

My girlfriend appeared with coffee, and we faced each other as we drank. Drops of rain tapped intermittently on the windows. The time passed slowly as chill infiltrated the room. The yellow glow of the light bulbs drifted about the room like pollen.

"Tired?" she asked.

"I guess," I said, gazing absently out the window. "We've been running around searching like crazy all this time, and now we've ground to a halt. Can't quite get used to it. After all we did to find the scene in the photograph, there's no Rat and no sheep."

"Get some sleep. I'll make dinner."

She brought a blanket down from upstairs and covered me. Then she readied the kerosene heater, placed a cigarette between my lips, and lit it for me.

"Show a little spirit. Everything's going to be fine."

"Thanks," I said.

At that, she disappeared into the kitchen.

All alone, my body felt heavy. I took two puffs of the cigarette, put it out, pulled the blanket up to my neck, and shut my eyes. It only took a few seconds before I fell asleep.

33

She Leaves the Mountain; Hunger Strikes

The clock struck six and I woke up on the sofa. The lights were out, the room enveloped in dense evening gloom. Everything from the core of my being to the tips of my fingers was numb. Darkness had spread over my skin like ink.

The rain had let up, and nightbirds sang through the window glass. The flames of the heater cast faint, undulating, elongated shadows on the white walls of the room. I got up and switched on the floor lamp, walked into the kitchen, and drank two glasses of cold water. A pot of stew, still warm, was on the stove. An ashtray held two clove cigarettes, crushed out.

Immediately, instinctively, I knew she was gone.

I stood there, hands on the cooktop, and tried to sort out my thoughts.

She was no longer here, that much was certain. No argument or guesswork about it. She was, in fact, not here. The vacated atmosphere of the house was final, undeniable. It was a feeling I had known well in the couple of months between the time my wife left me and the time I met my girlfriend.

I went upstairs to check. I opened the closet doors. No sign of her. Her shoulder bag and down jacket had vanished. So had her boots in the vestibule. Without a doubt, she was gone. I looked in all the places where she might have left a note, but there was nothing. She was probably already down the mountain.

I could not accept the fact of her disappearance. I was barely awake, but even if I were totally lucid, this—and everything that was happening to me—was far beyond my realm of comprehension. There was almost nothing one could do except let things take their course.

Sitting on the sofa, I felt a sudden hunger. And not an ordinary hunger either.

I went from the kitchen into the provisions cellar and uncorked a bottle of red wine. Overchilled but drinkable. Returning to the kitchen, I cut a few slices of bread, then peeled an apple. As I waited for the stew to heat, I had three glasses of wine.

When the stew was ready, I moved to the living-room table and ate dinner listening to the Percy Faith Orchestra playing "Perfidia." After dinner, I drank the coffee left in the pot, and with a deck of cards that was sitting on the mantel I dealt myself a hand of solitaire. A game invented and fashionable in nineteenth-century England, later popular for its simple rules. A mathematician once calculated the success rate of solitaire as one in twenty-five. I gave it three tries—without success, of course. I cleared away the cards and dishes. Then I finished off the rest the wine.

Night had come. I closed the shutters and lay down on the sofa to listen to scratchy old records.

When would the Rat show?

Assuming he'd be back. After all, he'd stocked up on a winter's supply of fuel and provisions.

But that was assuming. The Rat might have given up on the place and returned to town. Or maybe he'd taken up with some woman. Practically anything was possible.

Which could mean that I was in a fine mess. My one-month time limit, now exactly half over, would soon be past. No Rat, no sheep, just the man in the black suit dragging me into his Götterdämmerung. Even though I was nobody, he'd do it. I had no doubt about it.

In the city, the second week of October is a most urbane time of year. If all this hadn't happened, I'd be eating omelettes and drinking whiskey now. A beautiful time in a beautiful season, in the evening as the rains lifted, chunks of ice and a solid-wood bar top, time flowing slowly, easily, like a gentle stream.

Turning all this over in my mind, I started to imagine another me somewhere, sitting in a bar, nursing a whiskey, without a care in the world. The more I thought about it, the more that other me became the real me, making this me here not real at all.

I shook my head clear.

Outside, night birds kept up a low cooing.

I went upstairs and made the bed in the small room that the Rat hadn't been using. Mattress and sheets and blankets were all neatly stacked in the closet by the stairs.

The furniture was exactly the same as in the Rat's room. Bedside table and desk and chair and lamp. Old-fashioned, but products of an age when things were made to be strong and functional. Without frills.

Predictably, the view from the window at the head of the bed looked out over the pasture. The rain had stopped, and the thick cloud cover was beginning to break. There was a lovely half-moon that illuminated the pasture now and again. A searchlight sweeping over what might as well have been the ocean floor.

Crawling under the covers, still in my clothes, I gazed at the scene that soon dissolved, soon reappeared. A faded image of my girlfriend rounding the unlucky bend in the road, heading alone down the mountain, came to mind. Then that disappeared, to be replaced by the flock of sheep and the Rat taking their photograph. Again the moon hid behind a cloud, and when it re-emerged, even they had gone.

I read my *Sherlock Holmes* by lamplight.

34

A Find in the Garage; Thoughts in the Middle of the Pasture

Birds of a kind I'd never seen before clung like Christmas ornaments to the pin oaks by the front door, chirping away. The world shone moistly in the morning light.

I made toast in a primitive toaster, the type where you turn the slices of bread by hand. I coated a frying pan with butter, fried a couple eggs sunnyside-up, drank two glasses of grape juice. I was feeling lonely without her, but the fact that I could feel lonely at all was consolation. Loneliness wasn't such a bad feeling. It was like the stillness of the pin oak after the little birds had flown off.

I washed the dishes, then rinsed the egg yolk from my mouth and brushed my teeth for a full five minutes. After lengthy deliberations, I decided to shave. There was an almost new can of shaving cream and a Gillette razor at the washbasin. Toothbrush and toothpaste, soap, lotion, even cologne. Ten hand towels, each a different color, lay neatly folded on the shelf. Not a spot on mirror or washbasin. True to methodical Rat-form.

The same was pretty much true of the lavatory and the bathroom. The grouting between the tiles had been scrubbed with brush and cleanser. It was gleaming white, a work of art. The box sachet in the lavatory gave off the fragance of a gin-with-lime you'd get at a fancy bar.

I went into the living room to smoke my morning cigarette. I had three packs of Larks left in my backpack. When those were gone, it'd be no smoking for me. I lit up a second cigarette and thought about what it'd be like without smokes. The morning sun felt wonderful, and sitting on the sofa, which molded itself to my body, was pure luxury. Before I knew it, a whole hour had passed. The clock struck a lazy nine o'clock.

I began to understand why the Rat had put the house in such order, scrubbed between the tiles, ironed his shirts, and shaved, though surely he had no one to meet. Unless you kept moving up here, you'd lose all sense of time.

I got up from the sofa, folded my arms, and walked once around the room, but I couldn't see anything that needed doing. The Rat had cleaned anything that was cleanable. He'd even brushed the soot from the ceiling.

I decided instead to go for a walk. It was spectacular weather. The sky was feathered with a few white brushstroke clouds, the air filled with the songs of birds.

In back of the house was a large garage. A cigarette butt lay on the ground in front of the old double doors. Seven Stars. This time, the cigarette butt turned out to be rather old. The paper had come apart, exposing the filter.

Ashtrays. I had seen only one in the house, and it had shown no trace of use. The Rat didn't smoke! I rolled the filter around in the palm of my hand, then threw it back onto the ground.

I undid the heavy bolt and opened the garage doors to find a huge interior. The sunlight slanted in through the cracks in the siding, creating a series of parallel lines on the dark soil. There was the smell of dirt and gasoline.

An old Toyota Land Cruiser sat there. Not a speck of mud on the body or tires. The gas tank was almost full. I felt under the dash where the Rat always hid his keys. As expected, the key was there. I inserted it in the ignition and gave it a turn. Right away the engine was purring. It was the same Rat, always good at tuning his automobiles. I cut the engine, put the key back, then looked around the driver's seat. There was nothing noteworthy—road maps, a towel, half a bar of chocolate. In the backseat, unusually dirty for the Rat, was a roll of wire and a large pair of pliers. I opened the rear door and swept the debris into my hand, holding it up to the sunlight leaking in through a knothole in the siding. Cushion stuffing. Or sheep wool. I pulled a tissue out of my pocket, wrapped up the debris, and put it in my breast pocket.

I couldn't understand why the Rat hadn't taken the car. The fact that the car was in the garage meant that he had walked down the mountain or that he hadn't gone down at all. Neither made sense. Up to three days ago the cliff road would have been easy to drive. Would he abandon the house to camp out up here?

Puzzled, I shut the garage doors and walked out into the pasture. There was no reasonable explanation possible from such unreasonable circumstances.

As the sun rose higher in the sky, steam rose from the pasture. The mountains seemed to mist over, and the smell of grass was overwhelming.

I walked through the damp grass to the middle of the pasture. There lay a discarded old tire, the rubber white and cracked. I sat down on it and surveyed my surroundings. From here the house looked like a white rock jutting out from the shoreline.

In this solitary state, the memory of the ocean swim meets I used to participate in when I was a kid came to me. On distance swims between two islands, I would sometimes stop mid-course to look around. To find myself equidistant between two points gave me the funniest feeling. To think that back on dry land people were going about business as usual was pretty peculiar too. Unsettling, that society could go on perfectly well without me.

I sat there for fifteen minutes before ambling back to the house. I sat down on the living-room sofa and continued reading my *Sherlock Holmes*.

At two o'clock, the Sheep Man came.

35

The Sheep Man Cometh

As the clock struck two, there came a knocking on the door. Two times at first, a two-breath pause, then three times.

It took me a while to recognize it as knocking. That anyone should knock on the door hadn't occurred to me. The Rat wouldn't knock, it was his house. The caretaker might knock, but he certainly wouldn't wait for a reply before walking in. Maybe my girlfriend—no, more likely she'd steal in through the kitchen door and help herself to a cup of coffee. She wasn't the type to knock.

I opened the door, and standing there, two yards away, was the Sheep Man. Showing markedly little interest in either the open door or myself who opened it. Carefully inspecting the mailbox as if it were a rare, exotic specimen. The Sheep Man was barely taller than the mailbox. Four foot ten at most. Slouched over and bowlegged besides.

There were, moreover, six inches between the doorsill, where I stood, and ground level, where he stood, so it was as if I were looking down at him from a bus window. As if ignoring his decisive shortcomings, he continued his scrutiny of the mailbox.

"CanIcomein?" the Sheep Man said rapid-fire, facing sideways the whole while. His tone was angry.

"Please do," I said.

hal.

He crouched down and gingerly untied the laces of his mountaineering boots. They were caked with a sweet-roll-thick crust of mud. The Sheep Man picked up his boots with both hands and, with practiced technique, whacked them solidly together. A shower of hardened mud fell to the ground. Then demonstrating consummate knowledge of the lay of the house, he put slippers on and padded over to the sofa and sat down.

Just great, I thought.

The Sheep Man wore a full sheepskin pulled over his head. The arms and legs were fake and patched on, but his stocky body fit the costume perfectly. The hood was also fake, but the two horns that curled from his crown were absolutely real. Two flat ears, probably wire-reinforced, stuck out level from either side of the hood. The leather mask that covered the upper half of his face, his matching gloves, and socks, all were black. There was a zipper from neck to crotch.

On his chest was a pocket, also zippered, from which he extracted his cigarettes and matches. The Sheep Man put a Seven Stars to his mouth, lit up, and let out a long sigh. I fetched the washed ashtray from the kitchen.

"Iwannadrink," said the Sheep Man. I duly went into the kitchen and got a half-bottle of Four Roses and two glasses with ice.

He poured whiskey over the ice, I did the same, we drank without a toast. As he drank, the Sheep Man mumbled to himself. His pug nose was big for his body, and with each breath he took, his nostrils flared dramatically. The two eyes that peered through the mask darted restlessly around the room.

When the Sheep Man finished his whiskey, he seemed more at ease. He put out his cigarette and with both hands rubbed his eyes under his mask.

"Woolgetsinmyeyes," said the Sheep Man.

I didn't know how to respond and said nothing.

"Youcamehereyesterdayafternooneh?" said the Sheep Man, rubbing his eyes some more. "Beenwatchingyouthewholetime."

The Sheep Man stopped to pour a slug of whiskey over the half-melted ice and downed it one gulp.

"Andthewomanleftalonethisafternoon."

"You watched that too, did you?"

"Watchedher?Wedroveheraway."

"Drove her away?"

"Surestuckourheadthroughthekitchendoorsaidyoubettergoho me."

"Why?"

That threw the Sheep Man into a pout. "Why?" was obviously not the way to phrase a question to him, but before I could say anything else, his eyes slowly took on a different gleam.

"ShewentbacktotheDolphinHotel," said the Sheep Man.

"Did she say so?"

"Didn'tsaynothing.ButwheresheisistheDolphinHotel."

"How do you know that?"

Again the Sheep Man refused to speak. He put both hands on his knees and glared at the glass on the table.

"But she did go back to the Dolphin Hotel?" I said.

"UhhuhtheDolphinHotel'sanicehotel.Smellslikesheep," said the Sheep Man.

Silence again.

On closer inspection, I could see that the Sheep Man's fleece was filthy, the wool stiff with oil.

"Did she say anything by way of a message when she left?"

"Nope," the Sheep Man said, shaking his head. "Shedidn'tsay anythingandwedidn'task."

"When you told her she'd better leave, she upped and left without a word?"

"Right. Wetoldhershe'dbetterleavebecauseshewaswantingtole ave."

"She came up here because she wanted to."

"Wrong!" screamed the Sheep Man. "Shewantedtogetoutbut sheherselfwasconfused.That'swhywechasedherhome.Youconfus edher." The Sheep Man stood up and slammed his right hand down flat on the table. His whiskey glass slid two inches.

The Sheep Man froze in that pose until gradually his eyes lost their zeal and he collapsed back into the sofa, out of steam.

"Youconfusedthatwoman," the Sheep Man said, this time more calmly. "Notaverynicethingatall.Youdon'tknowathing.All youthinkaboutisyourself."

"You're telling me she shouldn't have come here?"

"That'sright.Shewasn'tmeanttocomehere.Youdon'tthinkabou tanythingbutyourself."

I sat there speechless, lapping my whiskey.

"Butstillwhat'sdoneisdone.Anywayit'soverforher."

"Over?"

"You'llneverseethatwomanagain."

"Because I only thought about myself?"

"That'sright.Becauseyouthoughtonlyaboutyourself.Justdeser ts."

The Sheep Man stood up and went to a window, forced up the window frame with one hand, and took a breath of the fresh air. No mean show of strength.

"Gottaopenwindowsonnicedayslikethis," said the Sheep Man. Then the Sheep Man did a quick half-turn around the room and stopped before the bookcase, peering over the spines of the books with folded arms. Sprouting from the rear end of his costume was a tiny tail. In this position, he looked like a sheep standing up on its two hind legs.

"I'm looking for a friend of mine," I ventured.

"Areyou?" said the Sheep Man, back to me in total disinterest.

"He was living here. Up to a week ago."

"Wouldn'tknow."

The Sheep Man stood in front of the fireplace shuffling the cards from the mantel.

"I'm also looking for a sheep with a star mark on its back," I pressed on.

"Haven'tseenit," said the Sheep Man.

But it was obvious that the Sheep Man knew something about the Rat and the sheep. His lack of concern was too affected. The timing of his response too pat, his tone false.

I changed tactics. Pretending I'd given up, I yawned, taking up my book from the table and flipping through the pages. A slightly vexed Sheep Man returned to the sofa and quietly eyed me reading the book.

"Readingbooksfun?" asked the Sheep Man.

"Hmm," I responded.

The Sheep Man bided his time. I kept reading to spite him.

"Sorryforshouting," said the Sheep Man in a low voice. "So

metimesit'slikethesheepinmeandthehumaninmeareatoddssoIgetlikethat.Didn'tmeananythingbyit.Andbesidesyoucomeonsayingthingstothreatenus."

"That's okay," I said.

"Toobadyou'llneverseethatwomanagain.Butit'snotourfault."

"Hmm."

I took the three packs of Larks out of my backpack and gave them to the Sheep Man. The Sheep Man was taken aback.

"Thanks.Neverhadthisbrand.Butdon'tyou needthem?"

"I quit smoking," I said.

"Yesthat'swise," the Sheep Man nodded in all seriousness. "They'rereallybadforyou."

He filed the cigarette packs away carefully in a pocket on his arm. The fleece buckled out in a rectangular lump.

"I've absolutely got to see my friend. I've come a long, long way here to see him."

The Sheep Man nodded.

"The same goes for that sheep."

The Sheep Man nodded.

"But you don't know anything about them, I take it?"

The Sheep Man shook his head forlornly. His fake ears flapped up and down. This time his denial was much weaker than before.

"It'saniceplacehere," the Sheep Man changed the subject. "Beautifulscenerygoodcleanair.You'regonnalikeithere."

"Yeah, it's a nice place," I said.

"It'sevennicerinthewinter.Nothingbutsnowallaround,everythingfrozenup.Alltheanimalssleepingnohumanfolk."

"You stay here all winter?"

"Uhhuh."

I didn't ask anything else. The Sheep Man was just like an animal. Approach him and he'd retreat, move away and he'd come closer. As long as I wasn't going anywhere, there was no hurry. I could take my time.

With his left hand the Sheep Man pulled at the fingers of his black right glove, one after the other. After a number of tugs, the glove slipped off, revealing a flaking blackened hand. Small but fleshy, an old burn scar from the base of his thumb to midway around the back of his hand.

The Sheep Man stared at the back of his hand, then turned it over to look at the palm. Exactly the way the Rat used to do, that gesture. But no way was this Sheep Man the Rat. There was a difference in height of eight inches between them.

"Yougonnastayhere?" asked the Sheep Man.

"No, as soon as I find either my friend or the sheep, I'm leaving. That's all I came for."

"Winter'snicehere," repeated the Sheep Man. "Sparklingwh ite.Everythingallfrozen."

The Sheep Man snickered to himself, flaring those enormous nostrils. Dingy teeth peered out from his mouth, the two front teeth missing. There was something uneven to the rhythm of the Sheep Man's thoughts, which seemed to have the whole room expanding and contracting.

"Gottabe going," the Sheep Man said suddenly. "Thanksfor thesmokes."

I nodded.

"Hopeyoufindyourfriendandthatsheepbeforetoolong."

"Hmm," I said. "Let me know if you hear of anything."

The Sheep Man hemmed and hawed, ill at ease. "Umwellyes surething."

I fought back the urge to laugh. The Sheep Man was one lame liar.

He put his glove back on and stood up to go. "I'llbeback.Can'tsa yhowmanydaysfromnowbutI'llbeback." Then his eyes clouded. "Noimpositionisit?"

"You kidding?" I threw in a quick shake of the head. "By all means, I'd love to see you again."

"WellI'llbeback," said the Sheep Man, then slammed the door behind him. He almost caught his tail, but it slipped through safe and sound.

Through a space in the shutters, I watched the Sheep Man stand staring at that peeling whitewashed mailbox, exactly as he had when he first appeared. Then wriggling a bit to adjust the costume better to his body, he took off fleetfoot across the pasture toward the woods in the east. His level ears were like a diving board of a swimming pool. In the growing distance, the Sheep Man became a fuzzy white dot, finally merging into the white of the birches.

Even after the Sheep Man disappeared from view, I kept staring at the pasture and birch woods. Had the Sheep Man been an illusion?

Yet here were a bottle of whiskey and Seven Stars butts left on the table, and there on the sofa were a few strands of wool. I compared them with the wool from the backseat of the Land Cruiser. Identical.

As a way to focus my thoughts, I went into the kitchen to fix some Salisbury steak. I minced up an onion and browned it in the frying pan. Meanwhile, I defrosted a chunk of beef from the freezer, then ground it with a medium blade. The kitchen was what you might call compact, but even so it had more than your typical run of utensils and seasonings.

If they'd only pave the road here, you could open a mountain-chalet-style restaurant. Wouldn't be bad, windows wide open, a view of the flocks, blue sky. Families could let their kids play with the sheep, lovers could stroll in the birch woods. A success for sure.

The Rat could run it, I could cook. The Sheep Man could be good for something too. His costume would be perfect up here in the mountains. Then for a practical, down-to-earth touch, the caretaker could join us; you need one practical person. The dog too. Even the Sheep Professor could drop in.

Scrambling eggs with a wooden spatula, I tossed these ideas around in my head.

But my beautiful-eared girlfriend—was she lost to me forever? The thought depressed me, though what the Sheep Man said was probably right. I should have come here on my own. I should not have . . . I shook my head. Then I took up where I'd left off with the restaurant.

Now, if we could get J to come up here. He would be central to the scheme . . .

While waiting for the onions to cool, I sat down by the window and gazed back out at the pasture.

36

The Winds' Own Private Thoroughfare

Three uneventful days passed. Not one thing happened. The Sheep Man didn't show. I fixed meals, ate them, read my book, and when the sun went down, I drank whiskey and went to sleep.

The morning air of the pasture turned steadily cooler. Day by day, the bright golden leaves of the birches turned more spotted as the first winds of winter slipped between the withered branches and across the highlands toward the southeast. Stopping in the center of the pasture, I could hear the winds clearly. No turning back, they pronounced. The brief autumn was gone.

Without exercise and without smoking, I had quickly gained six pounds. So I started to get up at six and jog a crescent halfway around the pasture. That took off a couple of pounds. It was tough not smoking, but with no store around for twenty miles, what was one to do? Each time I felt like smoking, I thought about her and her ears. Compared to everything I'd lost this far, losing smoking was trivial. And indeed it was.

With all this free time, I cooked up a storm. I made a roast beef. I defrosted a salmon and marinated it. I searched the pasture for edible vegetables and simmered my findings with bonito flakes and soy sauce. I made simple cabbage pickles. I prepared a number of snacks in case the Sheep Man showed up for a drink. The Sheep Man, however, never came.

Most of the afternoons I would pass looking out at the pasture. I soon began seeing things. A figure emerging from the birch woods and running straight in my direction. Usually it was the Sheep Man, but sometimes it was the Rat, sometimes my girlfriend. Other times it was the sheep with the star on its back.

In the end, though, nobody ever materialized. Only the winds blowing across the pasture. It was as if the pasture were the winds' own private thoroughfare. The winds raced across the pasture, never looking back, on missions of utmost urgency.

On the seventh day after my arrival on the mountain, the first snow fell. The winds had been unusually calm from morning, the skies overcast with dense lead-gray clouds. After my morning run and shower, as I settled down to coffee and records, the snow started. A hard snow. It struck the windowpanes with a battery of dull thuds. The wind had picked up, driving the snow down at a thirty-degree angle. Rather like the slanting lines of some department-store wrapping-paper pattern. Soon the storm intensified and everything outside was awash in white. The entire mountain range and woods were obscured. This was no pitiful snow as sometimes falls in Tokyo. This was the real thing, an honest-to-goodness north-country snow. A snow to blanket everything and freeze deep into the heart of the earth.

The snow was blinding. I drew the curtain and curled up to read by the heater. The record ended, the needle lifted, and all was silence. The sort of silence that follows in the wake of the death of all living things. I set down my book and for no particular reason felt the urge to walk through the house. From the living room into the kitchen, checking the storeroom, bath and cellar, upstairs to open the doors of each room. There was no one, of course. Only silence which rolled like oil into every corner. Only silence which changed ever so slightly from room to room.

I was all alone. Probably more alone than I'd been in all my life.

I'd been dying for a smoke the past two days, but as there were no cigarettes, I'd been drinking whiskey straight. One winter like this and I'd end up an alcoholic. Not that there was enough liquor around to do the trick, though. Three bottles of whiskey, one bottle of brandy, twelve cases of canned beer, and no more. Obviously, the same thought had occurred to the Rat.

Was my partner, my former partner, that is, still hitting the bottle? Had he managed to put the company in order, turn it back into a small translation firm, as I suggested? Maybe he'd done exactly that. But could he really make a go of it without me, as he worried? Our time together was up. Six years together, and now back to square one.

The snow let up by early afternoon. Abruptly, just as it had begun. The thick clouds tore off in places as grand columns of sunlight thrust down to play in the pasture. It was magnificent.

The hard snow lay sprinkled on the ground like candy. Solidified into pellets as if to defy melting away. Yet by the time the clock struck three, the snow had all but melted. The ground was thoroughly wet, the twilight sun enfolding the pasture in a soft light. The birds sang as if set free.

After dinner, I borrowed two books from the Rat's room, *Bread Baking* and the Conrad novel, then made myself comfortable on the living-room sofa. One-third of the way into the novel, I came across a four-inch-square newspaper clipping the Rat had been using for a bookmark. No date, but from the color of the paper it must have been recent. It was local news, a symposium on aging and society to be held at a Sapporo hotel, a rally at a train station near Asahikawa, a lecture on the Middle East crisis. Nothing to grab the Rat's interest, or mine. On the reverse, classified ads. I yawned, shut the book, went to heat up the leftover coffee.

I suddenly realized that this was the first time, in what now seemed like years, that I had seen a newspaper, and that I'd been left behind an entire week from the goings-on of the world. No radio or television, no newspapers, no magazines. A nuclear missile could have destroyed Tokyo, an epidemic could have swept the world, Martians could have occupied Australia, I wouldn't have known. Of course, the Land Cruiser in the garage had a radio, but I discovered that I had no pressing desire to go listen after all. If something could take place without my knowing, it was just as well. I had no real need to know. I, in any case, had plenty on my mind already.

Something gnawed at me. Something that had passed before my eyes but which I'd been too dense to notice. All the same, on an unconscious level, it had registered. I deposited my coffee cup in the sink and returned to the living room. I took another look at the newspaper clipping. There it was on the reverse:

Attention: Rat
Get in touch. Urgent!
Dolphin Hotel, Room 406

I put the clipping back in the book and sank into the sofa.

So the Rat knew I was looking for him. Question: how had he found the item? By accident, when he'd come down off the mountain? Or maybe he'd been searching for something through several weeks' worth of papers?

And why didn't he contact me? Had I already checked out of the Dolphin Hotel by the time he came across it? Had his telephone line already gone dead?

No. The Rat could have gotten in touch if he wanted to, he just didn't want to. Because I was at the Dolphin Hotel, he figured I'd find my way up here, so that if he wanted to see me, he had only to wait, or at least leave me a note.

What it boiled down to was this: for some reason the Rat didn't want to face me. Even so, he wasn't rejecting me. If he didn't want me here, he could have shut me out any number of ways. It was his house, after all.

Grappling with these two propositions, I watched the second hand sweep slowly around the face of the clock. After one full circumgyration, my reasoning had made no progress. I couldn't figure out what lay at the center of all this.

The Sheep Man knew something. That much was certain. Someone who had monitored my arrival on the scene was sure to know about the Rat's living here for six months.

In fact, the Sheep Man's behavior seemed to reflect the Rat's will. The Sheep Man had driven my girlfriend down off the mountain, leaving me here alone. His showing up was undoubtedly a front. Something funny was going on. You could read it everywhere. Something was about to happen.

I turned out the lights and went upstairs, climbed into bed, and looked out at the moon and pasture. Stars peeked through a tear in the clouds. I opened the window and smelled the night air. Among the rustling leaves I could hear a call in the distance. A strange cry, neither bird nor beast.

I woke and went for my run in the pasture, showered, and ate breakfast. A morning like the others. The sky was overcast like the day before, but the temperature had risen a bit. Not much chance of snow.

Into jeans and a sweater and a jacket over that, then tennis shoes, and I was off across the pasture. Heading for the woods to the east where I'd seen the Sheep Man disappear, I made my way into the thicket. There was no real path to speak of, no sign of human life. Occasionally, there'd be an old birch toppled over.

The forest floor was flat, except for a long, yard-wide trough, like a dried-up streambed or an abandoned trench. The trough wound its way through the woods for miles. Sometimes sunken deep, sometimes shallow, ankle-deep in dead leaves.

The ditch gave on to a ridge trail, both sides of which sloped down to dry hollows. Plump birds shuffled across the path through the leaves, losing themselves in the undergrowth. Here and there, brush azaleas blazed bright red.

I walked around for an hour and lost all sense of direction. At this rate, I was hardly going to find the Sheep Man. I roamed the bottom of one dry hollow until I heard the sound of water. I sought out the river, then followed it downstream. If my memory served me correctly, there had to be a waterfall and near it, the road we'd walked up.

After another ten minutes, I came across the waterfall. Splashing as it struck the rocks in the gorge below, lapping into frozen pools. There was no sign of fish, though a few fallen leaves traced slow circles on the surface of the pools. I crossed from rock to rock, made my way down below the falls, then crawled up the slippery opposite bank. I had reached the road.

Seated on the edge of a bridge, watching me, was the Sheep Man. A big sailcloth bag of firewood was slung over his shoulder.

"Wanderaroundtoomuchyou'llbebearbait," said the Sheep

Man. "There'sboundtobeoneaboutinthesepartsyouknow.Yesterdayafternoonlfoundtraces.Ifyouhavetowalkaroundyououghttoputabellonyourhiplikeus."

The Sheep Man shook a little bell fastened to his hip with a safety pin.

"I've been looking for you," I said after catching my breath.

"Iknow," said the Sheep Man. "I'veseenyousearching."

"Well then, why didn't you call out?"

"You'retheonewhowantedtosearchmeout. So I held back."

The Sheep Man took a cigarette out of his pocket and smoked it with great pleasure. I sat down next to him.

"You live around here?"

"Hmm," said the Sheep Man. "Butdon'ttellanybody.Nobodyknows."

"But my friend knows all about you."

Silence.

"And if you're friends with my friend, that makes us friends, no?"

"Iguessso," said the Sheep Man cautiously. "Iguessitprobably does."

"And if you're my friend, you wouldn't lie to me, would you? Think about it."

"Errno," answered one perplexed Sheep Man. He licked his parched lips. "Ican'ttellyouI'mrealsorryIcan'ttellyouIcan't.I'mnotsupposedto."

"Someone's put it to you to keep quiet?"

The Sheep Man clammed up. The wind whistled through the barren trees.

"Nobody's around to hear," I whispered.

The Sheep Man looked me in the eye. "Youdon'tknowathing aboutourwaysheredoyou?"

"No, I don't."

"Welllistenthisisnoordinaryplacewegothere.Thatmuchyoushouldknow."

"But just the other day you told me this was such nice country."

"Forusyes," said the Sheep Man, "Forusthisistheonlyplacetolive.Ifwewerechasedoutofherewe'dhavenoplacetogo."

At that, the Sheep Man shut up. He would not say another word on the subject. I looked at his sailcloth bag filled with firewood.

"That your heating for the winter?"

The Sheep Man nodded silently.

"But I didn't see any smoke."

"Nofireyet.Nottillthesnowsetsin.Butevenafteritsnowsyouwou ldn'tbeabletoseethesmokefromourfire.Wegotaspecialwayofbuil dingfires." He grinned, self-satisfied.

"So when will the snow begin to pile up around here?"

The Sheep Man looked up at the sky, then looked at me. "Thesnow'llcomeearlythisyear.Maybeanothertendays."

"In another ten days the road will freeze over?"

"Probably.Nobodycomingupandnobodygoingdown.Wonderf ultimeofyear."

"And you've been living here how long?"

"Longtime," said the Sheep Man. "Reallongtime."

"What do you eat?"

"TubersshootsnutsbirdswhateverlittlefishandcrabsIcancatch."

"Don't you get cold?"

"Winter'ssupposedtobecold."

"If you need something, I'd be glad to share whatever I've got."

"ThanksbutI'mfinejustnow."

The Sheep Man suddenly stood up and started walking off in the direction of the pasture. So I got up to follow him.

"Why'd you take to hiding out up here?"

"You'dlaughifItoldyou," said the Sheep Man.

"No, I wouldn't laugh, I swear," I said. I couldn't imagine what there'd be to laugh about.

"Youwon'ttellanyone?"

"I won't tell anyone."

"Ididn'twanttogoofftowar."

For the next few minutes, we walked on without a word between us.

"War with whom?" I asked.

"Dunno," coughed out the Sheep Man. "ButIdidn'twanttogo.

Anywaythat'swhyI'masheep.Asheepwhostayswherehebelongsup here."

"You from Junitaki-cho?"

"Uhhuhbutdon'ttellanyone."

"I won't," I said. "You don't like the town?"

"Thetowndownthere?"

"Yeah."

"Don'tlikeitatall.Toofullofsoldiers," the Sheep Man coughed again. "Whereyoufrom?"

"Tokyo."

"Heardaboutthewar?"

"Nope."

At that the Sheep Man seemed to lose all interest in me. He remained silent until we reached the entrance to the pasture.

"Care to stop by the house?" I asked the Sheep Man.

"Gottalayinwintersupplies," he said. "Realbusy.Maybenextti me."

"I'd like to see my friend," I said. "I've got something I have to see him about next week."

The Sheep Man shook his head forlornly. His ears flapped. "SorrybutlikeIsaidbeforeit'snotuptous."

"Well, then, pass the word on if you can."

"Hmm," said the Sheep Man.

"Thanks a lot," I said. I turned to leave.

"Ifyougooutwalking," the Sheep Man called out as he departed, "makesureyoudon'tforgetthebell."

I headed straight back for the house as the Sheep Man disappeared into the woods to the east, the same as before. A winter-dark wordless green pasture stretched between us.

That afternoon I baked bread. The Rat's *Bread Baking* proved to be a thoughtfully written cookbook. On the cover was written: "If you can read, then you can bake bread." It was no exaggeration. The smell of bread filled the house, making it warm all over. For a fledgling effort, it didn't taste too bad either. There was plenty of flour and yeast in the kitchen, enough for bread the whole winter long, if it turned out I had to stay. And more rice and spaghetti than I cared to think about.

That evening, I had bread and salad and ham and eggs, with canned peaches for dessert.

The next morning I cooked rice and made a pilaf of canned salmon and seaweed and mushrooms.

For lunch, it was cheesecake from the freezer and strong milk tea.

At snacktime, I treated myself to hazelnut ice cream topped with Cointreau.

In the evening, broiled chicken and a can of Campbell's soup.

I was putting on weight again.

Early in the afternoon of the ninth day, as I was looking through the bookcase, I noticed one volume that seemed like it may have been read recently. It was the only one without dust on it, its spine protruding a bit farther out than the rest.

I pulled it out and sat on the chaise longue to flip through it. *The Heritage of Pan-Asianism*. A wartime edition. The paper was cheap and gave off a stink when I turned the pages. The contents, as expected from a wartime publication, terribly one-sided. Real boring too; stuff to yawn over every three pages. On some pages, words had been crossed out. There was not a single line on the February 26th Incident.

Tucked into the book, toward the end, was a sheet of white notepaper. After the yellowing pages, that white sheet came as some kind of miracle. It marked, on the right page, an addendum to the book. A list of names, birthdates, and permanent residences of all the so-called Pan-Asianists famous and unknown. I scanned the list from top to bottom, and there around the middle was the Boss. The very same "sheeped" Boss in whose name I had been brought here. His permanent residence, Hokkaido—Junitaki-cho.

In a daze, I set the book down in my lap. Words did not even form in my head. It was as if someone, or something, had given me a solid whack from behind.

How could I not have figured it out? It should have occurred to me first thing. The moment I learned that the Boss was from a poor farming background in Hokkaido I should have checked up on it. No matter how skillfully the Boss had managed to rub out his past, there would have been some way to search out the facts. That black-suited secretary would surely have looked it up for me.

Well no, maybe not.

I shook my head.

No way he wouldn't have looked that up himself. The man was not so careless. He would have checked every possible angle, complicated or not. Just as he had done his homework on me.

So he already knew everything.

That was indisputable. And yet, he had gone to great lengths to convince me, or rather to blackmail me, in order to get me up here. Why? If it was something that needed doing, surely he was in a better position to do it and to do a crack job of it. And if I were for some reason to be a pawn, why wouldn't he have told me the name of the place from the beginning?

As I sorted through my confusion, I started to get mad. More and more, this had turned into one grotesque comedy of mishaps, and I didn't think it was funny. How much did the Rat know? And while we're at it, how much did the man in the black suit know? Here I was, smack in the center of everything without a clue. At every turn, I'd been way off base, way off the mark. Of course, you could probably say the same thing about my whole life. In that sense, I suppose I had no one to blame. All the same, what gave them the right to treat me like this? I'd been used, I'd been beaten, I'd been wrung dry.

I was ready to get the hell off the mountain, but somehow that offered no satisfaction. I had gotten in too deep. I wanted to scream, I wanted to cry, but for what? Long, long before this moment, there had to have been something worth crying about.

I went into the kitchen and got the bottle of whiskey. I could think of nothing to do but drink.

37

Things the Mirror Shows, Things the Mirror Doesn't

The morning of the tenth day, I decided to forget everything. I had already forgotten what I was supposed to forget.

In the middle of my morning run, it began to snow again. This time an opaque snow, a sticky, wet sleet edging toward ice flakes. Unlike the first loose snow, this one was nasty. It stuck to the body. I cut short my run, returned to the house, and drew a bath. While the bath was coming to temperature, I plunked myself down in front of the heater, but still I couldn't get warm. A damp chill had seeped into me. I couldn't bend my fingers and my ears burned and felt brittle, as if they would drop off any second. All over, my skin felt like cheap pulp paper.

A thirty-minute soak in the tub and hot tea with brandy finally brought my body back to normal, although for the next two hours I suffered from intermittent chills. So this was winter on the mountain.

The snow kept falling straight through until evening, covering the entire pasture in white. The snow let up just as night cloaked the world in darkness, and once again a profound hush drifted in like mist. A hush I could do nothing to deny. I put the record player on automatic repeat and listened to *White Christmas* twenty-six times.

* * *

The snow did not stick for long. As the Sheep Man had predicted, the ground would not freeze for a while yet. The following day, my eleventh, was bright and clear. The prodigal sun bided its time, leaving the pasture a patchwork of snow, which gleamed in the sunlight. The snow that had collected on the roof's gables came sliding down in would-be icebergs that broke up on the ground with an unnerving thud. Melting snow dripped outside the windows. Everything sparkled. Each droplet clinging to each tip of every oak leaf shone.

I dug my hands into my pockets and stood by the window, gazing out. There things unfolded entirely apart from me. Unrelated to my existence—unrelated to anybody's existence—everything came to pass. The snow fell, the snow melted.

I decided to do some housecleaning, accompanied by the sounds of snow dripping and tumbling. Holed up as I was on account of the snow, my body needed to do something; besides, wasn't I a guest in someone else's house? I have never been one to object to cleaning and cooking.

Still, cleaning a large house proved a lot harder work than I had imagined. Jogging ten miles was easy in comparison. I dusted every nook and cranny, then went around with the large vacuum cleaner to suck up the dust. I damp-mopped the wood floors, then got down on my hands and knees to wax them. It left me half out of breath, but thanks to having quit smoking, the other half of my breath managed to hold its own. None of that terrible rasping and catching in my throat.

I went into the kitchen for a glass of cold grape juice and finished straightening up what remained in one bout of cleaning before noon. I threw open the shutters, and the newly waxed floors glittered. There was a wonderful, nostalgic melding of the rich earthy scent of the country and the smell of the wax.

I washed out the rags I'd used to wax the floors, then put a pot of water on to boil. For the spaghetti, into which I mixed cod roe, plenty of butter, white wine, and soy sauce. A great lunch, complete with a woodpecker calling from the nearby woods.

I made short work of the spaghetti, washed up the dishes, then returned to the chores. I scrubbed the bathtub and washbasin, cleaned the toilet, polished the furniture. Thanks to the Rat, nothing was very dirty to begin with; a spray of furniture polish was about all that was needed. Next I pulled out a long hose and rinsed down the windows and shutters. With that, the whole house freshened up. After I washed the windows, my cleaning was done. I spent the remaining two hours before evening listening to records.

As I headed up to the Rat's room to borrow another book, I noticed the full-length mirror at the foot of the stairs. I'd overlooked it, and it was filthy. I wiped it down with a cloth, but no amount of wiping or glass cleaner would do the trick. I couldn't understand why the Rat would let this one mirror stay so dirty. I hauled over a bucket of warm water and worked on the mirror with a nylon scrub, cutting through the hardened grease. There was enough grime on the mirror to turn the bucket water black.

The crafted wooden frame told me it was an antique, probably worth a pretty sum, so I was careful not to work too enthusiastically.

The mirror reflected my image from head to toe, without warping, almost pristinely. I stood there and looked at myself. Nothing new. I was me, with my usual nothing-special expression. My image was unnecessarily sharp, however. I wasn't seeing my mirror-flat mirror-image. It wasn't myself I was seeing; on the contrary, it was as if I were the reflection of the mirror and this flat-me-of-an-image were seeing the real me. I brought my right hand up in front of my face and wiped my mouth. The me through the looking glass went through the same motions. But maybe it was only me copying what the me in the mirror had done. I couldn't be certain I'd wiped my mouth out of my own free will.

I filed the word "free will" away in my head and pinched my ear with my left hand. The me in the mirror did exactly the same. Apparently he had filed the word "free will" away in his head the same as I had.

I gave up and left the mirror. He also left the mirror.

On the twelfth day, snow fell for the third time. It was snowing before I woke up. An awfully silent snow, this one neither hard nor sticky wet. Pirouetting down slowly from the sky, melting before it amounted to anything. The kind of tranquil snow that makes you close your eyes, gently.

I pulled the old guitar out of the trunk room and, after tuning it with great difficulty, tried my hand at some old tunes. I practiced along with Benny Goodman's *Air Mail Special,* and soon it was noontime. I made a sandwich of thick slices of ham on my homemade, already rock-hard bread, and opened a can of beer. After thirty minutes more of guitar practice, who should show up but the Sheep Man.

"IfIbotheryouI'llleave," said the Sheep Man through the open front door.

"No, not at all. I was getting kind of bored anyway," I said, setting the guitar on the floor.

The Sheep Man whacked the mud off his boots the same as before, then came in. His body seemed to have filled out his thick sheep costume. He sat in the sofa opposite me, hand on the armrest and snuggled into position.

"It's not going to stick yet?" I asked.

"Notyet," answered the Sheep Man. "There'ssnowthatsticks andsnowthatdoesn't.Thisisnonsticksnow."

"Hmm."

"Thestickingsnowcomesnextweek."

"Care for a beer?"

"Thanks.ButI'dreallyratherhaveabrandy."

I went to the kitchen, got him his brandy and me a beer, and carried it all back into the living room together with a cheese sandwich.

"Youwereplayingguitar," said the Sheep Man with interest. "Welikemusictoo.Can'tplayanyinstrumentthough."

"Neither can I. Haven't played in close to ten years."

"That'sokayawplaysomethingforme."

I didn't want to dampen the Sheep Man's spirits, so I played through the melody of *Airmail Special,* tacked on one chorus and an ad lib, then lost count of the bars and threw in the towel.

"You'regood," said the Sheep Man in all seriousness. "Proba blyloadsoffuntoplayaninstrumenteh?"

"If you're good. But if you want to get good, you have to train your ears. And when you've trained your ears, you get depressed at your own playing."

"Nahc'monreally?" said the Sheep Man.

The Sheep Man took dainty little sips from his brandy snifter, while I drank my beer from the can.

"Iwasn'tabletopassonyourmessage," said the Sheep Man.

I nodded.

"That'sallIcametosay."

I glanced over at the calendar on the wall. Only three more days until the time limit, the date marked in red. But what did that mean anymore?

"Things have changed," I spoke up. "I'm very, very angry. Never in my entire life have I been angry like this."

The Sheep Man sat there, snifter in hand, and said nothing.

I picked up the guitar by the neck and smashed its back against the bricks of the fireplace. With the crash came a loud, cacophonous twang of strings. The Sheep Man flew out of the sofa, his ears trembling.

"I've got a right to be angry," I said, addressing this fact rather to my own attention. Well, I did have the right to be angry.

"IfeelbadthatIcouldn'tcomeacrossforyou.Butyoumustunderstand.Wereallydolikeyou."

The two of us stood there. We looked at the snow. The snow was fluffy, like stuffing spilling out of a torn cloud.

I went into the kitchen for another beer. Each time I walked past the stairs, there was the mirror. The other me had apparently gone for another beer too. We looked each other in the face and sighed. Living in two separate worlds, we still thought about the same things. Just like Groucho and Harpo in *Duck Soup*.

Behind me the living room was reflected in the mirror. Or else it was his living room behind him. The living room behind me and the living room behind him were the same living room. Same sofa, same carpet, same clock and painting and bookcase, every last thing the same. Not particularly uncomfortable as living rooms go, if not in the finest taste. Yet something was different. Or maybe it was simply that I felt that something was different.

I grabbed another blue Löwenbrau and on the way back to the living room, can in hand, I looked once more at the living room in the mirror, then looked over at the living room. The Sheep Man was on the sofa, lazily gazing out at the snow.

I checked the Sheep Man in the mirror. But there wasn't any Sheep Man in the mirror! There was nobody in the living room at all, only an empty sofa. In the mirror world, I was alone. Terror shot through my spine.

"Youlookpale," said the Sheep Man.

I plopped down on the sofa and, saying nothing, pulled the ring off the beer can and took a sip.

"Probablycaughtcold.Winterinthesepartscangettoyouifyou're notusedtoit.Air'sdamptoo.Youshouldgettobedearlytoday."

"Nope," I said. "Today I'm not going to sleep. I'm going to wait up for my friend here."

"Youknowhe'scomingtoday?"

"I know," I said. "He'll be here tonight by ten o'clock."

The Sheep Man looked up at me. The eyes peering through his mask had literally no expression.

"Tonight I'll pack, tomorrow I'll be gone. If you see him, tell him that. I don't think it'll be necessary, though."

The Sheep Man nodded comprehendingly. "Surewillbelonely whenyougo.Can'tbehelpedthoughIguess.BythewaycanIhavethat cheesesandwich?"

"Sure."

The Sheep Man wrapped the sandwich in a paper napkin, slipped it into his pocket, then put on his gloves.

"Hopewemeetagain," said the Sheep Man as he was leaving.

"We will," I said.

The Sheep Man left across the pasture to the east. Eventually, the veil of snow took him in. Afterward all was silent.

I poured an inch of brandy into the Sheep Man's snifter and downed it in one swallow. My throat burned, and gradually my stomach burned, but after thirty seconds my body stopped trembling. Only the ticking of the grandfather clock pounding inside my head.

Probably I did need to get some sleep.

I fetched a blanket from upstairs and slept on the sofa. I felt totally exhausted, like a child who'd been wandering around in the woods for three days. I closed my eyes and the next instant I was asleep.

I had a terrifying dream. A dream too terrifying to recall.

38

And So Time Passes

Darkness crept in through my ear like oil. Someone was trying to break up the frozen globe of the earth with a massive hammer. The hammer struck the earth precisely eight times. But the earth failed to break up. It only cracked a little.

Eight o'clock, eight at night.

I woke with a shake of the head. My body was numb, my head ached. Had someone put me in a cocktail shaker with cracked ice and like a madman shaken me up?

There's nothing worse than waking up in total darkness. It's like having to go back and live life all over from the beginning. When I first opened my eyes, it was as if I were living someone else's life. After an extremely long time, this began to match up with my own life. A curious overlap this, my own life as someone else's. It was improbable that such a person as myself could even be living.

I went to the kitchen sink and splashed water on my face, then drank down a couple of glasses quickly. The water was cold as ice, but still my face was burning hot. I sat back down on the sofa amid the darkness and silence and began gradually to gather up the pieces of my life. I couldn't manage to grasp too much, but at least it was my life. Slowly I returned to myself. It's hard to explain what it is to get there, and it'd undoubtedly try your interest.

I had the feeling that someone was watching me, but I didn't pay it any mind. It's a feeling you get when you're all alone in a big room.

I thought about cells. Like my ex-wife had said, ultimately every last cell of you is lost. Lost even to yourself. I pressed the palm of my hand against my cheek. The face my hand felt in the dark wasn't my own, I didn't think. It was the face of another that had taken the shape of my face. But I couldn't remember the details. Everything—names, sensations, places—dissolved and was swallowed into the darkness.

In the dark the clock struck eight-thirty. The snow had stopped, but thick clouds still covered the sky. No light anywhere. For a long time, I lay buried in the sofa, fingers in my mouth. I couldn't see my hand. The heater was off, so the room was cold. Curled up under the blanket, I stared blankly out. I was crouching in the bottom of a deep well.

Time. Particles of darkness configured mysterious patterns on my retina. Patterns that degenerated without a sound, only to be replaced by new patterns. Darkness but darkness alone was shifting, like mercury in motionless space.

I put a stop to my thoughts and let time pass. Let time carry me along. Carry me to where a new darkness was configuring yet newer patterns.

The clock struck nine. As the ninth chime faded away, silence slipped in to fill its place.

"May I say my piece?" said the Rat.

"Fine by me," said I.

39

Dwellers in Darkness

Fine by me," said I.

"I came an hour earlier than the appointed time," said the Rat apologetically.

"That's okay. As you can see, I wasn't doing anything."

The Rat laughed quietly. He was behind me. Almost as if we were back-to-back.

"Seems like the old days," said the Rat.

"I guess we can never get down to a good honest talk unless we've got time on our hands," I said.

"It sure seems that way." The Rat smiled.

Even in absolute lacquer-black darkness, seated back-to-back, I could tell he was smiling. You can tell a lot just by the tiniest change in the air. We used to be friends. So long ago, though I could hardly remember when.

"Didn't someone once say, 'A friend to kill time is a friend sublime'?"

"That was you who said that, no?"

"Sixth sense, sharp as ever. Right you are."

I sighed. "But this time around, with all this happening, my sixth sense has been way off. So far off it's embarrassing. And despite the number of hints you all have been giving me."

"Can't be helped. You did better than most."

We fell silent. The Rat seemed to be looking at his hand.

"I really made you go through a lot, didn't I?" said the Rat. "I was a real pain. But it was the only way. There wasn't another soul I could depend on. Like I wrote in those letters."

"That's what I want to ask you about. Because I can't accept everything just like that."

"Of course not," said the Rat, "not without my setting the record straight. But before that, let's have a beer."

The Rat stopped me before I could stand up.

"I'll get it," said the Rat. "This is my house, after all."

I heard the Rat walk his regular path to the kitchen in total darkness and take an armful of beer out of the refrigerator, me opening and closing my eyes the whole while. The darkness of the room was only a bit different in hue from the darkness of my eyes shut.

The Rat returned with his beer, which he set on the table. I felt around for a can, removed the pull ring, and drank half.

"It hardly seems like beer if you can't see it," I said.

"You have to forgive me, but it has to be dark."

We said nothing while we drank.

"Well then," said the Rat, clearing his throat. I set my empty back on the table and kept still, wrapped in my blanket. I waited for him to start talking, but no words followed. All I could hear was the Rat shaking his can to check how much was left. Old habit of his.

"Well then," said the Rat a second time. Then downing the last of his beer in one chug, he set the can back on the table with a dry clank. "First of all, let's begin with why I came here. Is that all right?"

I didn't answer. The Rat continued to speak.

"My father bought this place when I was five. Just why he went out of his way to buy property up here I don't know. Probably he got a good deal through some American military route. As you can see, the place is terribly inconvenient to get to and, aside from summer, the road is useless once the snow sets in. The Occupation Forces had planned on improving the road and using the place for a radar station or something, but the time and expense involved apparently changed their mind. And with the town being so poor, they can't afford to do anything about the road. It wouldn't help them to upgrade the road either. Which all makes this property a losing proposition, long since forgotten."

"How about the Sheep Professor? Wouldn't he be thinking to come back home here?"

"The Sheep Professor is living in his memories. He's got nowhere to go home to."

"Maybe not."

"Have some more beer," said the Rat.

"Fine for now," I said. With the heater off, I was nearly frozen through. The Rat opened another can and drank by himself.

"My father took a liking to this property, carried out some road improvements on his own, fixed up the house. He put a lot of money into it, I believe. Thanks to which, if you had a car, you could lead a fairly good life here, at least during the summer. Heat, flush toilet, shower, telephone, emergency electrical generator. How on earth the Sheep Professor lived here before that, I don't know."

The Rat made a noise that was neither belch nor sigh.

"Until I was fifteen, we came here every summer. My folks, my sister and me, and the maid who did the chores. When I think of it, those were probably the best years of my life. We leased the pasture to the town—still do, in fact—so when summer rolled around, the place was full of the town's sheep. Sheep up to your ears. That's why my memories of summer are always tied up with sheep.

"After that, the family almost never came up here. We got another vacation house closer to home for one thing, and my sister got married for another. I wasn't counting myself in the family much anymore, my father's company was going through hard times, and well, all sorts of things were going on. Whatever, the property was abandoned. The last time I came up here was eleven years ago. And that time I came alone. By myself for a month."

The Rat lingered for a second, as if he were remembering.

"Were you sad?" I asked.

"Me, sad? You got to be kidding. If it was possible, I would have stayed on up here. But no way that could have happened. It's my father's house, after all. You wouldn't have caught me doing my old man the service."

"But what about now?"

"The same goes," said the Rat. "I got to say that this was the last place I wanted to come back to. Yet when I came across the photograph of this place in the Dolphin Hotel, I wanted to see it one more time. For sentimental reasons. Even you get that way at times, don't you?"

"Yeah," I said. There was my shoreline that got filled in.

"That's when I heard the Sheep Professor's story. About the dream sheep with a star on its back. You know about that, I take it?"

"Indeed I do."

"So to put it simply," said the Rat, "I heard that story and hurried up here wanting to spend the whole winter. I couldn't shake the urge. Father or not, it didn't matter to me anymore. I pulled together my kit and came up. Like I was being drawn up here."

"That's when you ran into the sheep?"

"That's right," said the Rat.

"What happened after that is difficult to talk about," said the Rat.

The Rat took his second empty can and squeezed a dent into it.

"Maybe you could ask me questions? You already know pretty much what there is to know, right?"

"Okay, but if it makes no difference to you, let's not start at the beginning."

"Fire away."

"You're already dead, aren't you?"

I don't know how long it took the Rat to reply. Could have been a few seconds, could have been . . . It was a long silence. My mouth was all dry inside.

"That's right," said the Rat finally. "I'm dead."

40

The Rat Who Wound the Clock

I hanged myself from a beam in the kitchen," said the Rat. "The Sheep Man buried me next to the garage. Dying itself wasn't all that painful, if you worry about that sort of thing. But really, that hardly matters."

"When?"

"A week before you got here."

"You wound the clock then, didn't you?"

The Rat laughed. "Damn, if that's not a mystery. I mean the very, very last thing I did in my thirty-year life was to wind a clock. Now why should anyone who's about to die wind a clock? Makes no sense."

The Rat stopped speaking, and everything was still, except for the ticking of the clock. The snow absorbed all other sound. We were like two castaways in outer space.

"What if . . ."

"Stop it," the Rat cut me short. "There are no more ifs. You know that, right?"

I shook my head. No, I didn't.

"If you had come here a week earlier, I still would have died. Maybe we could've met under warmer, brighter circumstances. But it's all the same. I would have had to die. Otherwise things would have only gotten harder. And I guess I didn't want to bear that kind of hardship."

"So why did you have to die?"

There was the sound of his rubbing the palms of his hands together.

"I don't want to talk too much about that. It would only turn into a self-acquittal. And there's nothing more inappropriate than a dead man coming to his own defense, don't you think?"

"But if you don't tell me, I'll never know."

"Have some more beer."

"I'm cold," I said.

"It's not that cold."

With trembling hands, I opened another beer and drank a sip. And with the drink in me, it really didn't seem as cold.

"Okay, if you promise not to tell this to anyone."

"Even if I did tell someone, who'd believe me?"

"You got me there," said the Rat with a chuckle. "I doubt anyone would believe it. It's so crazy."

The clock struck nine-thirty.

"Mind if I stop the clock?" asked the Rat. "It makes such a racket."

"Help yourself. It's your clock."

The Rat stood up, opened the door to the grandfather clock, and grabbed the pendulum. All sound, all time, vanished.

"What happened was this," said the Rat. "I died with the sheep in me. I waited until the sheep was fast asleep, then I tied a rope over the beam in the kitchen and hanged myself. There wasn't enough time for the sucker to escape."

"Did you have to go that far?"

"Yes, I had to go that far. If I waited, the sheep would have controlled me absolutely. It was my last chance."

The Rat rubbed his palms together again. "I wanted to meet you when I was myself, with everything squared away. My own self with my own memories and my own weaknesses. That's why I sent you that photograph as a kind of code. If by some accident it steered you this way, I thought I would be saved in the end."

"And have you been saved?"

"Yeah, I've been saved all right," said the Rat, quietly.

* * *

"The key point here is weakness," said the Rat. "Everything begins from there. Can you understand what I'm getting at?"

"People are weak."

"As a general rule," said the Rat, snapping his fingers a couple of times. "But line up all the generalities you like and you still won't get anywhere. What I'm talking about now is a very individual thing. Weakness is something that rots in the body. Like gangrene. I've felt that ever since I was a teenager. That's why I was always on edge. There's this something inside you that's rotting away and you feel it all along. Can you understand what that's like?"

I sat silent, wrapped up in the blanket.

"Probably not," the Rat continued. "There isn't that side to you. But, well, anyway, that's weakness. It's the same as a hereditary disease, weakness. No matter how much you understand it, there's nothing you can do to cure yourself. It's not going to go away with a clap of the hand. It just keeps getting worse and worse."

"Weakness toward what?"

"Everything. Moral weakness, weakness of consciousness, then there's the weakness of existence itself."

I laughed. This time the laugh came off. "You start talking like that and there's not a human alive who isn't weak."

"Enough generalities. Like I said before. Of course, it goes without saying that everybody has his weaknesses. But real weakness is as rare as real strength. You don't know the weakness that is ceaselessly dragging you under into darkness. You don't know that such a thing actually exists in the world. Your generalities don't cover everything, you know."

I could say nothing.

"That's why I left town. I didn't want others to see me sinking any lower. Traveling around alone in unknown territory, at least I wouldn't cause problems for anyone. And ultimately . . . ," the Rat trailed off for a bit.

"Ultimately, because of this weakness, I couldn't escape the specter of the sheep. There was nothing I myself could do about it. Probably even if you had shown up at the time, I wouldn't have been able to do anything about it. Even if I'd made up my mind to go down from the mountain, it would have been the same. I probably still would have come back up in the end. That's what weakness is."

"What did the sheep want of you?"

"Everything. The whole lock, stock, and barrel. My body, my memory, my weakness, my contradictions . . . That's the sort of stuff the sheep really goes for. The bastard's got all sorts of feelers. It sticks them down your ears and nose like straws and sucks you dry. Gives me the creeps even now."

"And for what in return?"

"Things far too good for the likes of me. Not that the sheep got around to showing me anything in real form. All I ever saw was one tiny slice of the pie. And . . ."

The Rat trailed off again.

"And it was enough to draw me in. More than I'd care to confess. It's not something I can explain in words. It's like, well, like a blast furnace that smelts down everything it touches. A thing of such beauty, it drives you out of your mind. But it's hair-raising evil. Give your body over to it and everything goes. Consciousness, values, emotions, pain, everything. Gone. What it comes closest to is a dynamo manifesting the vital force at the root of all life in one solitary point of the universe."

"Yet you were able to reject it."

"Yes. Everything was buried along with my body. There remains only one last thing to do in order to see it buried forever."

"One last thing?"

"One last thing. And that I have to ask you to do. But let's not talk about it now."

We both took sips of beer. I was warming up.

"The blood cyst works kind of like a whip, doesn't it?" I asked. "For the sheep to manipulate the host."

"Exactly. Once that forms, there's no escaping the sheep."

"So what on earth was the Boss after, doing what he was doing?"

"He went mad. He probably couldn't take the heat of that blast furnace. The sheep used him to build up a supreme power base. That's why the sheep entered him. He was, in a word, disposable.

The man was zero as a thinker, after all."

"So when the Boss died, you were earmarked to take over that power base."

"I'm afraid so."

"And what lay ahead after that?"

"A realm of total conceptual anarchy. A scheme in which all opposites would be resolved into unity. With me and the sheep at the center."

"So why did you reject it?"

Time trailed off into death. And over this dead time, a silent snow was falling.

"I guess I felt attached to my weakness. My pain and suffering too. Summer light, the smell of a breeze, the sound of cicadas—if I like these things, why should I apologize. The same with having a beer with you . . ." The Rat swallowed his words. "I don't know why."

What could I say.

"Somehow or other, we have created two completely different entities out of the same ingredients," said the Rat. "Do you believe the world is getting better?"

"Better or worse, who can tell?"

The Rat laughed. "I swear, in the kingdom of generalities, you could be *imperius rex*."

"Sheeplessly."

"You bet, sheeplessly." The Rat threw back his third beer in one chug, then clunked the empty can down on the floor.

"You'd better be heading down the mountain as soon as you can. Before you get snowed in. You don't want to spend the whole winter here. Another four, maybe five days, the snow'll start to collect, and listen, it's a real trick traveling down frozen mountain roads."

"And what will you do from now on?"

The Rat let go a good, jolly laugh from off in the dark. "For me there is no 'from now on'. I just fade away over the winter. How long it takes depends on how long this one winter is. I don't know. But one winter is one winter. I'm glad I got to see you. A brighter, warmer place would have been nicer, of course."

"J sends his regards."

"Give him my regards, too, would you?"

"I also saw her."

"How was she?"

"All right. Still working for the same firm."

"Then she's not married?"

"No. She wanted to hear directly from you whether it was over or not."

"It's over," said the Rat, "as you know. Even if I was unable to end it on my own, the fact is it's over. My life had no meaning. Of course, to borrow upon your venerable generalities, this is to say that everyone's life has no meaning. Am I right?"

"So be it," I said. "Just two last questions."

"Okay."

"First, about our Sheep Man."

"The Sheep Man's a good guy."

"But the Sheep Man, the one who came visiting here, was you, right?"

The Rat rolled his neck around to crack it a couple of times. "Right. I took his form. So you could tell, could you?"

"Midway on," I said. "Up until then, though, I had no idea."

"To be absolutely honest, you surprised me, breaking the guitar. It was the first time I'd seen you so angry, and what's more, that was the first guitar I ever bought. A cheapie, but still . . ."

"Sorry about that. I was only trying to shake you up enough to show yourself."

"That's all right. Come tomorrow, everything'll be gone anyway," said the Rat dryly. "So now your other question is about your girlfriend, right?"

"Right."

The Rat said nothing for a long while. I could hear him rub his palms together and sigh. "I didn't want to deal with her. She was an extra factor I hadn't counted on."

"An extra factor?

"Uh-huh. I meant this to be an in-group party. But she stumbled into the middle of it. We should never have allowed her to get mixed up in this. As you know very well, the girl's got amazing powers. Still, she wasn't meant to come here. The place is far beyond even her powers."

"What happened to her?"

"She's okay. Perfectly well," said the Rat. "Only there's nothing that you'd find attractive in her anymore. Sad, but that's how it is."

"How's that?"

"It's gone. Evaporated. Whatever it was she had, it's not there anymore."

I couldn't bring myself to say anything.

"I know how you must feel," continued the Rat. "But sooner or later, it was bound to disappear. Me and you, these girls with their certain somethings, we've all got to go sometime."

I thought about his words.

"I better be going," said the Rat. "It's getting on time. But we'll meet again, I just know it."

"Sure thing," I said.

"Preferably somewhere brighter, maybe in summer," said the Rat. "But for now, one last request. Tomorrow morning at nine, I want you to set the grandfather clock, then connect the cords behind the clock. Connect the green cord to the green cord and the red cord to the red cord. Then at nine-thirty I want you to get the hell out of here and go down the mountain. I've got a rendezvous with a fellow at twelve o'clock sharp. Got it?"

"Good as done."

"Glad I got to see you."

A moment's pause came between us.

"Goodbye," said the Rat.

"See you," said I.

Still snug in the blanket, I closed my eyes and listened. The Rat's shoes scuffed across the floor, the door opened. Freezing cold air entered the room. Not a breeze, but a slow-spreading, sinking chill.

The Rat stood in the open doorway for a moment. He seemed to be staring at something, not the scenery outside, not the room interior, not me, some completely other thing. The doorknob or the tip of his shoe, something. Then, as if closing the door of time, the door swung shut with a click.

Afterward all was silent. There was nothing else left but silence.

41

Green Cords and Red Cords; Frozen Seagulls

After the Rat disappeared, an unbearable cold spread throughout the house. I tried to throw up, but nothing would come, only gasps of stale breath.

I went upstairs, took off my sweater, and burrowed under the covers. I was swept by alternating waves of chills and fever. With each wave the room would swell and contract. My blanket and underwear were soaked in sweat, which congealed into a cold, constricting skin.

"Wind the clock at nine," someone whispers in my ear. "Green cord to green cord . . . red cord to red cord . . . get the hell out by nine-thirty."

"Don'tworry," says the Sheep Man. "It'llgofine."

"The cells replace themselves," says my ex-wife. She is holding a white lace slip in her right hand.

My head rocks.

Red cord to red cord . . . green cord to green cord . . .

"You don't understand a thing, do you?" accuses my girlfriend.

No, I don't understand a thing.

There comes the sound of waves. Heavy winter waves. A lead-gray sea specked with whitecaps. Frozen seagulls.

I am in the airtight exhibition room of the aquarium. Row upon row of whales' penises on display. It's hot and stuffy. Someone better open a window.

Someone opens a window. Shivering cold. Seagull cries, sharp piercing voices ripping at my flesh.

"Remember the name of your cat?"

"Kipper," I reply.

"No, it's not Kipper," the chauffeur says. "The name's already changed. Names change all the time. I bet you can't even remember your own name."

Shivering cold. And seagulls, far too many seagulls.

"Mediocrity walks a long, hard path," says the man in the black suit. "Green cord via red cord, red cord via green cord."

"Heardanythingaboutthewar?" asks the Sheep Man.

The Benny Goodman Orchestra strikes up "Airmail Special." Charlie Christian takes a long solo. He is wearing a soft cream-colored hat.

42

Return Visit to the Unlucky Bend

Birds were singing.

Sunlight spilled in stripes across the bed from between the shutter slats. My watch lying on the floor read 7:35. My blanket and shirt were as wet as if they'd been soaked in a bucket of water.

My head was still fuzzy, but the fever had gone. Outside, the world was a snowswept landscape. The pasture gleamed positively silver in the new morning light. My face was pale, my cheeks stripped of their flesh overnight. I coated my entire face with three times the necessary amount of shaving cream, and I proceeded to shave methodically. Then I went and pissed out a bucket and a half.

I was so exhausted from the piss that I collapsed on the chaise longue for fifteen minutes. The birds kept on singing. The snow had begun to melt and drip from the eaves. Occasionally in the background there'd be a sharp creaking.

It was almost on eight-thirty by the time I got up. I drank two glasses of grape juice, ate a whole apple. Then I picked out a bottle of wine, a large Hershey bar, and two more apples from the cellar.

I packed my things. The room took on a forlorn air. Everything was coming to an end.

Checking with my watch, at nine o'clock I wound up the three weights of the grandfather clock. Then I slid the heavy timepiece around and connected the four cords behind. Green cord to green cord, red cord to red cord.

The cords come out of four holes drilled in the back. One pair above, one pair below. The cords were secured with twists of the same wire I'd seen in the jeep. I pushed the grandfather clock back in place, then went to the mirror and bid farewell to myself.

"Hope all goes well," I said.

"Hope all goes well," the other I said.

I crossed the middle of the pasture the same way as I had come. The snow crunched beneath my feet. The pasture looked like a silver volcanic lake. Not a footprint anywhere. Only mine which, when I turned around, led back in a trail to the house. My tracks meandered all over the place. It's not easy to walk in a straight line.

From this far off, the house looked almost like a living thing. Cramped and hunched over, it twisted to shake the snow down from its gabled roof. A block of snow slid off the roof and dashed to the ground with a thud.

I kept walking across the pasture. On through the endless birch woods, across the bridge, around the base of the conical peak, onto the unlucky bend in the road.

Miraculously, the snow on the curve had not frozen to the road. No matter, I was sure that as carefully as I stepped, I would get dragged to the bottom of that sheer drop. It was an effort just to keep walking until I cleared that curved ledge clinging to the crumbling cliff face. My armpits were soaked with sweat. A regular childhood nightmare.

Off to the right were the flatlands. They too were covered in snow, the Junitaki River glistening right down the middle. I thought I could hear a steam whistle in the distance. It was marvelous, actually.

I took a breath and hitched up my backpack, then set off down the gentle slope. At the next bend was a brand-new jeep. In front of the jeep, the Boss's black-suited secretary.

43

The Twelve-O'clock Rendezvous

"I have been waiting for you," said the man in the black suit. "Albeit only for twenty minutes."

"How'd you know?"

"The place? Or the time?

"The time," I said, setting down my backpack.

"How do you think I got to be the Boss's secretary? Diligence? IQ? Tact? No. I am the Boss's secretary because of my special capacities. Sixth sense. I believe that's what you would call it."

He was wearing a beige down jacket over ski pants and green Ray-Ban glasses.

"We used to have many things in common, the Boss and I. Things that reached beyond rationality and logic and morality."

"Used to?"

"The Boss died a week ago. We had a beautiful funeral. All Tokyo is turned upside down now, trying to decide a successor. The whole mediocre lot of them running around like fools."

I sighed. The man took a silver cigarette case out of his jacket pocket, removed a plain-cut cigarette, and lit up.

"Smoke?"

"No thanks," I said.

"But I must say you did your stuff. Much more than I expected.

Honestly, you surprised me. At first, I thought I might have to help you along and give you hints when you got stuck. Which makes your coming across the Sheep Professor an even greater stroke of genius. I almost wish you would consider working for me."

"So I take it you knew about this place here from the very beginning?"

"Naturally. Come now, who do you think I am?"

"May I ask you something, then?"

"Certainly," said the man, in top spirits. "But keep it short."

"Why didn't you tell me right from the start?"

"I wanted you to come all this way spontaneously of your own free will. And I wanted you to lure him out of his lair."

"Lair?"

"His mental lair. When a person becomes sheeped, he is temporarily dazed out of his mind and goes into retreat. As with, say, shell shock. It was your role to coax him out of that state. Yet in order for him to trust you, you had to be a blank slate, as it were. Simple enough, is it not?"

"Quite."

"Lay out the seeds and everything is simple. Constructing the program was the hard part. Computers can't account for human error, after all. So much for handiwork. Ah, but it is a pleasure second to none, seeing one's painstakingly constructed program move along exactly according to plan."

I shrugged.

"Well then," the man continued, "our wild sheep chase is drawing to a close. Thanks to my calculations and your innocence. I've got him right where I want him. True?"

"So it would seem," I said. "He's waiting for you up there. Says you've got a rendezvous at twelve o'clock sharp."

The man and I glanced at our watches simultaneously. Ten-forty.

"I had better be going," the man said. "Must not keep him waiting. You may ride down in the jeep, if you wish. Oh yes, here is your recompense."

The man reached into his pocket and handed me a check. I pocketed it without looking at it.

"Should you not examine it?"

"I don't believe there's any need."

The man laughed, visibly amused. "It has been a pleasure to do business with you. And by the way, I dissolved your partner's company. Regrettable. It had such promise too. There is a bright future for the advertising industry. You should go into it on your own."

"You must be crazy," I said.

"We shall meet again, I expect," said the man. And he set off on foot around the curve toward the highlands.

"Kipper's doing fine," said the chauffeur, as he drove the jeep down. "Gotten nice and fat."

I took the seat next to the chauffeur. He was a different person than the man who drove that monster of a limo. He told me in considerable detail about the Boss's funeral and about his Kipper-sitting, but I hardly heard a word.

It was eleven-thirty when the jeep pulled up in front of the station. The town was dead still. Except for an old man shoveling away the snow from the rotary and a gangly dog sitting nearby wagging its tail.

"Thanks," I told the chauffeur.

"Don't mention it," he said. "By the way, have you tried God's telephone number?"

"No, I haven't had time."

"Since the Boss died, I can't get through. What do you suppose happened?"

"Probably just busy," I suggested.

"Maybe so," said the chauffeur. "Well now, take care."

"Goodbye," I said.

There was a train leaving at twelve o'clock sharp. Not a soul on the platform. On board only four passengers, including myself. Even so, it was a relief to see people after so long. One way or another, I'd made it back to the land of the living. No matter how boring or mediocre a world it might be, this was it.

The departure bell sounded as I chewed on my chocolate bar. Then, as the ringing stopped and the train clanked into readiness, there came the sound of a distant explosion. I lifted the window all the way open and stuck my head out. Ten seconds later there was a second explosion. The train started moving. After three minutes, in the direction of the conical peak, a column of black smoke was slowly rising.

I stared at it until the train cut a curve to the right and the smoke was out of sight.

EPILOGUE

It's all over," said the Sheep Professor, "all over."

"Over and done."

"I suppose I should thank you."

"Now that I've lost practically everything."

"No, you haven't," the Sheep Professor shook his head. "You've got your life."

"As you say," I said.

The Sheep Professor threw himself facedown on his desk, sobbing, as I left the room. I had robbed him of his obsession, woeful though it had been, and whether I was right to have done it, I was never more unsure.

"She departed for somewhere," said the proprietor of the Dolphin Hotel. "She made no mention of any destination. You don't look very well."

"I'm fine," I said.

I picked up the bags and checked into the same room as before. With the same view of the same unfathomable company. The woman with the big breasts was nowhere to be seen. Two young male employees worked at their desks, smoking. One was reading lists of figures, one was drawing a broken-line graph with a ruler on a huge sheet of paper. Maybe it was because the big-breasted woman wasn't there, but the office seemed like a wholly different place. Only the fact that I couldn't figure out what kind of company it was remained the same. At six o'clock, all employees exited, and the building grew dark.

I turned on the television and watched the news. There was no report of any explosion on any mountain. But wait, did that explosion happen yesterday? What on earth had I done for one whole day? Where had I been? My brain throbbed.

Well, one day had passed in any case.

In just this way, one day at a time, I learned to distance myself from "memory." Until that day in the uncertain future when a distant voice calls from out of the lacquer blackness.

I switched off the television and toppled over onto the bed with my shoes still on. All alone, I stared up at the stain-blotched ceiling. Reminders of persons long dead and forgotten.

The room changed colors to the pulse of neon lights. My watch ticked away by my ear. I undid the band and tossed it onto the floor. Traffic sounds came in soft chorus, layer upon layer. I tried to sleep, but without success. Who can sleep with such inexpressibleness?

I donned a sweater and headed out to town, stepping into the first discotheque I happened upon. I had three whiskeys-on-the-rocks while taking in the non-stop soul music. That helped give me a sense of the normal. And getting back to normal was everything. Everybody was counting on me to be normal.

Returning to the Dolphin Hotel, I found the three-fingered proprietor sitting on the chaise longue, watching the late night news.

"I'll be leaving tomorrow morning at nine," I said.

"Back to Tokyo, is it?"

"No," I said. "I have one place to stop off before that. Wake me at eight, please."

"Okay," he said.

"Thanks for everything."

"Don't mention it." Then the proprietor let out a sigh. "Father refuses to eat. At this rate, he'll die."

"He took a great blow."

"I know," said the proprietor sadly. "Not that my father ever tells me anything."

"Give it time."

The following day I took a plane to Tokyo-Haneda, then flew off again. The sea was shining when I arrived at my destination.

J was peeling potatoes the same as ever. A young female part-timer was filling flower vases and wiping off the tables. Hokkaido had lost its autumn, but autumn still held on here. Through the windows of J's Bar, the hills were in beautiful color.

I sat at the counter and had a beer before the bar opened. Cracking peanuts with one hand.

"It's hard to come by peanuts that crack so nice and crisp," said J.

"Oh?" I said, nibbling away.

"So tell me, no vacation still?"

"I quit."

"Quit?"

"It's a long story."

J finished peeling the potatoes, then dumped them into a large colander to rinse. "What will you do from here on?"

"Don't know. I've got some severance money coming, plus my half of the sale of the business. Not much really. And then there's this."

I pulled the check out of my pocket and passed it over to J, amount unseen. J looked at it and shook his head.

"This is unbelievable money, unbelievable."

"You said it."

"But it's a long story, right?"

I laughed. "Let me leave it with you. Put it in the shop safe."

"Where would I have a safe here?"

"How about the cash register?"

"I'll put it in my safe-deposit box at the bank," said J worriedly. "But what do you plan to do with it?"

"Say, J, it took a lot of money to move to this new location didn't it?"

"That it did."

"Loans?"

"Real big ones."

"Will that check pay off those loans?"

"With change to spare. But . . ."

"How about it? What say you take on the Rat and me as co-partners? No worry about dividends or interest. A partnership in name is fine."

"But I couldn't do that."

"Sure you could. All you got to do in return is take in the Rat and me whenever one of us gets into a fix."

"That's no different than what I've done all along."

Beer glass in hand, I looked J in the face. "I know. But that's how I want it."

J laughed and shoved the check into his pocket. "I still remember the very first time you got drunk. How many years ago was that now?"

"Thirteen."

"Already?"

J talked about old times the next half hour, something he rarely did. Customers began to filter in, and I got up to leave.

"But you only just got here," said J.

"The well-mannered child doesn't overstay," said I.

"Did you see the Rat?"

I took a deep breath, both hands on the counter. "I saw him all right."

"That a long story too?"

"A longer story than you've ever heard in your whole life."

"Can't you give me the highlights?"

"Highlights wouldn't mean anything."

"Was he well?"

"Fine. He wished he could see you."

"Do you suppose I'll get to see him sometime?"

"You'll get to see him. He's a co-partner, after all. That's money the Rat and I earned."

"Well then, I'm glad."

I stepped down from the barstool and took a whiff of the old place.

"Oh, and as I'm a co-partner, how about a pinball machine and jukebox?"

"I'll have them here by your next visit," said J.

I walked along the river to its mouth. I sat down on the last fifty yards of beach, and I cried. I never cried so much in my life.

I brushed the sand from my trousers and got up, as if I had somewhere to go.

The day had all but ended. I could hear the sound of waves as I started to walk.

Dance Dance Dance

1

I often dream about the Dolphin Hotel.

In these dreams, I'm there, implicated in some kind of ongoing circumstance. All indications are that I *belong* to this dream continuity.

The Dolphin Hotel is distorted, much too narrow. It seems more like a long, covered bridge. A bridge stretching endlessly through time. And there I am, in the middle of it. Someone else is there too, crying.

The hotel envelops me. I can feel its pulse, its heat. In dreams, I am part of the hotel.

I wake up, but where? I don't just think this, I actually voice the question to myself: "Where am I?" As if I didn't know: I'm here. In my life. A feature of the world that is my existence. Not that I particularly recall ever having approved these matters, this condition, this state of affairs in which I feature. There might be a woman sleeping next to me. More often, I'm alone. Just me and the expressway that runs right next to my apartment and, bedside, a glass (five millimeters of whiskey still in it) and the malicious—no, make that indifferent—dusty morning light. Sometimes it's raining. If it is, I'll just stay in bed. And if there's whiskey still left in the glass, I'll drink it. And I'll look at the raindrops dripping from the eaves, and I'll think about the Dolphin Hotel. Maybe I'll stretch, nice and slow. Enough for me to be sure I'm myself and not part of something else. Yet I'll remember the feel of the dream. So much that I swear I can reach out and touch it, and the whole of that *something* that includes me will move. If I strain my ears, I can hear the slow, cautious sequence of play take place, like droplets in an intricate water puzzle falling, step upon step, one after the other. I listen carefully. That's when I hear someone softly, almost imperceptibly, weeping. A sobbing from somewhere in the darkness. Someone is crying for me.

The Dolphin Hotel is a real hotel. It actually exists in a so-so section of Sapporo. Once, a few years back, I spent a week there. No, let me get that straight. How many years ago was it? Four. Or more precisely, four and a half. I was still in my twenties. I checked into the Dolphin Hotel with a woman I was living with. She'd chosen the place. *This is where we're staying,* was what she said. If it hadn't been for her, I doubt I'd ever have set foot in the place.

It was a tiny dump of a hotel. In the whole time we were there, I don't know if we saw another paying customer. There were a couple of characters milling around the lobby, but who knows if they were staying there? A few keys were always missing from the board behind the front desk, so I guess there were other hotel guests. Though not too many. I mean, really, you hang out a hotel sign somewhere in a major city, put a phone number in the business listings, it stands to reason you're not going to go entirely without customers. But granting there were other customers besides ourselves, they were awfully quiet. We never heard a sound from them, hardly saw a sign of their presence—with the exception of the arrangement of the keys on the board that changed slightly each day. Were they like shadows creeping along the walls of the corridors, holding their breath? Occasionally we'd hear the dull rattling of the elevator, but when it stopped the oppressive silence bore down once more.

A mysterious hotel.

What it reminded me of was a biological dead end. A genetic retrogression. A freak accident of nature that stranded some organism up the wrong path without a way back. Evolutionary vector eliminated, orphaned life-form left cowering behind the curtain of history, in The Land That Time Forgot. And through no fault of anyone. No one to blame, no one to save it.

The hotel should never have been built where it was. That was the first mistake, and everything got worse from there. Like a button on a shirt buttoned wrong, every attempt to correct things led to yet another fine—not to say elegant—mess. No detail seemed right. Look at anything in the place and you'd find yourself tilting your head a few degrees. Not enough to cause you any real harm, nor enough to seem particularly odd. Who knows? You might get used to this slant on things (but if you did, you'd never be able to view the world again without holding your head out of true).

That was the Dolphin Hotel. *Normalness,* it lacked. Confusion piled on confusion until the saturation point was reached, destined in the not-too-distant future to be swallowed in the vortex of time. Anyone could recognize that at a glance. A pathetic place, woebegone as a three-legged black dog drenched in December rain. Sad hotels existed everywhere, to be sure, but the Dolphin was in a class of its own. The Dolphin Hotel was conceptually sorry. The Dolphin Hotel was tragic.

It goes without saying, then, that aside from those poor, unsuspecting souls who happened upon it, no one would willingly choose to stay there.

A far cry from its name (to me, the "Dolphin" sobriquet suggested a pristine white-sugar candy of a resort hotel on the Aegean Sea), if not for the sign hung out front, you'd never have known the building was a hotel. Even with the sign and the brass plaque at the entrance, it scarcely looked the part. What it really resembled was a museum. A peculiar kind of museum where persons with peculiar curiosities might steal away to see peculiar items on display.

Which actually was not far from the truth. The hotel was indeed part museum. But I ask, would anyone want to stay in such a hotel? In a lodge-cum-reliquary, its dark corridors blocked with stuffed sheep and musty fleeces and mold-covered documents and discolored photographs? Its corners caked with unfulfilled dreams?

The furniture was faded, the tables wobbled, the locks were useless. The floorboards were scuffed, the light bulbs dim; the washstand, with ill-fitting plug, couldn't hold water. A fat maid walked the halls with elephant strides, ponderously, ominously coughing. And the sad-eyed, middle-aged owner, stationed permanently behind the front desk, had two fingers missing. The kind of a guy, by the looks of him, for whom nothing goes right. A veritable specimen of the type—dredged up from an overnight soak in thin blue ink, soul stained by misfortune, failure, defeat. You'd want to put him in a glass case and cart him to your science class: *Homo nihilsuccessus*. Almost anyone who saw the guy would, to a greater or lesser degree, feel their spirits dampen. Not a few would be angered (some folks get upset seeing miserable examples of humanity). So who would stay in that hotel?

Well, *we* stayed there. *This is where we're staying*, she'd said. And then later she disappeared. She upped and vanished. It was the Sheep Man who told me so. *Thewomanleft-alonethisafternoon,* the Sheep Man said. Somehow, the Sheep Man knew. He'd known that she had to get out. Just as I know now. Her purpose had been to lead me there. As if it were her fate. Like the Moldau flowing to the sea. Like rain.

When I started having these dreams about the Dolphin Hotel, she was the first thing that came to mind. She was seeking me out. Why else would I keep having the same dream, over and over again?

She. What was her name? The months we'd spent together, and yet I never knew. What *did* I actually know about her? She'd been in the employ of an exclusive call girl club. A club for members only; persons of less-than-impeccable standing not welcome. So she was a high-class hooker. She'd had a couple other jobs on the side. During regular business hours she was a part-time proofreader at a small publishing house; she was also an ear model. In other words, she kept busy. Naturally, she wasn't nameless. In fact I'm sure she went by a number of names. At the same time, practically speaking, she didn't have a name. Whatever she carried—which was next to nothing—bore no name. She had no train pass, no driver's license, no credit cards. She did carry a little notebook, but that was scrawled in an indecipherable code. Apparently she wanted no handle on her identity. Hookers may have names, but they inhabit a world that doesn't need to know.

I hardly knew a thing about her. Her birthplace, her real age, her birthday, her schooling and family background—zip. Precipitate as weather, she appeared from somewhere, then evaporated, leaving only memory.

But now, the memory of her is taking on renewed reality. A palpable reality. She has been calling me via that circumstance known as the Dolphin Hotel. Yes, she is seeking me once more. And only by becoming part of the Dolphin Hotel will I ever see her again. Yes, there is no doubt: it is she who is crying for me.

Gazing at the rain, I consider what it means to belong, to become part of something. To have someone cry for me. From someplace distant, so very distant. From, ultimately, a dream. No matter how far I reach out, no matter how fast I run, I'll never make it.

Why would anyone want to cry for me?

She is definitely calling me. From somewhere in the Dolphin Hotel. And apparently, somewhere in my own mind, the Dolphin Hotel is what I seek as well. To be taken into that scene, to become part of that weirdly fateful venue.

It is no easy matter to return to the Dolphin Hotel, not a simple question of ringing up for a reservation, hopping on a plane, flying to Sapporo, and mission accomplished. For the hotel is, as I've suggested, as much circumstance as place, a state of being in the guise of a hotel. To return to the Dolphin Hotel means facing up to a shadow of the past. The prospect alone depresses. It has been all I could do these four years to rid myself of that chill, dim shadow. To return to the Dolphin Hotel is to give up all I'd quietly set aside during this time. Not that what I'd achieved is anything great, mind you. However you look at it, it's pretty much the stuff of tentative convenience. Okay, I'd done my best. Through some clever juggling I'd managed to forge a connection to reality, to build a new life based on token values. Was I now supposed to give it up?

But the whole thing started there. That much was undeniable. So the story *had* to start back there.

I rolled over in bed, stared at the ceiling, and let out a deep sigh. *Oh give in,* I thought. But the idea of giving in didn't take hold. *It's out of your hands, kid. Whatever you may be thinking, you can't resist. The story's already decided.*

2

I got sent to Hokkaido on assignment. As work goes, it wasn't terribly exciting, but I wasn't in a position to choose. And anyway, with the jobs that come my way, there's generally very little difference. For better or worse, the further from the midrange of things you go, the less relative qualities matter. The same holds for wavelengths: Pass a certain point and you can hardly tell which of two adjacent notes is higher in pitch, until finally you not only can't distinguish them, you can't hear them at all.

The assignment was a piece called "Good Eating in Hakodate" for a women's magazine. A photographer and I were to visit a few restaurants. I'd write the story up, he'd supply the photos, for a total of five pages. Well, somebody's got to write these things. And the same can be said for collecting garbage and shoveling snow. It doesn't matter whether you like it or not—a job's a job.

For three and a half years, I'd been making this kind of contribution to society. Shoveling snow. You know, cultural snow.

Due to some unavoidable circumstances, I had quit an office that a friend and I were running, and for half a year I did almost nothing. I didn't feel like doing anything. The previous autumn all sorts of things had happened in my life. I got divorced. A friend died, very mysteriously. A woman ran out on me, without a word. I met a strange man, found myself caught up in some extraordinary developments. And by the time everything was over, I was overwhelmed by a stillness deeper than anything I'd known. A devastating absence hovered about my apartment. I stayed shut-in for six months. I never went out during the day, except to make the absolute minimum purchases necessary to survive. I'd venture into the city with the first gray of dawn and walk the deserted streets, and when the streets started to fill with people, I holed up back indoors to sleep.

Toward evening, I'd rise, fix something to eat, feed the cat. Then I'd sit on the floor and methodically go over the things that had happened to me, trying to make sense of them. Rearrange the order of events, list up all possible alternatives, consider the right or wrong of what I'd done. This went on until the dawn, when I'd go out and wander the streets again.

For half a year that was my daily routine. From January through June 1979. I didn't read one book. I didn't open one newspaper. I didn't watch TV, didn't listen to the radio. Never saw anyone, never talked to anyone. I hardly even drank; I wasn't in a drinking frame of mind. I had no idea what was going on in the world, who'd become famous, who'd died, nothing. It wasn't that I stubbornly resisted information, I simply had no desire to know anything. Even so, I knew things were happening. The world didn't stop. I could feel it in my skin, even sitting alone in my apartment. Though little did it compel me to show interest. It was like a silent breath of air, breezing past me.

Sitting on the floor, I'd replay the past in my head. Funny, that's all I did, day after day after day for half a year, and I never tired of it. What I'd been through seemed so vast, with so many facets. Vast but real, very real, which was why the experience persisted in towering before me, like a monument lit up at night. And the thing was, it was a monument to me. I inspected the events from every possible angle. I'd been damaged, badly, I suppose. The damage was not petty. Blood had flowed, quietly. After a while some of the anguish went away, some surfaced only later. And yet my half year indoors was not spent in convalescence. Nor in autistic denial of the external world. I simply needed time to get back on my feet.

Once on my feet, I tried not to think about where I was heading. That was another question entirely, to be thought out at a later date. The main thing was to recover my equilibrium.

I scarcely talked to the cat.

The telephone rang. I let it ring.

If someone knocked on the door, I wasn't there.

There were a few letters. A couple from my former partner, who didn't know where I was or what I was up to and was concerned. Was there anything he could do to help? His new business was going smoothly, old acquaintances had asked about me.

My ex-wife wrote, needing some practical affairs taken care of, very matter-of-fact. Then she mentioned she was getting married—to someone I didn't know, and probably never would. Which meant she'd split up with that friend of mine she'd gone off with when we divorced. Not surprising, them splitting up. The guy wasn't so great a jazz guitarist and he wasn't so great a person either. Never could understand what she saw in him—but none of my business, eh? About me, she said she wasn't worried. She was sure I'd be fine whatever it was I chose to do. She reserved her worries for the people I'd get involved with.

I read these letters over a few times, then filed them away.

And so the months passed.

Money wasn't a problem. I had saved plenty enough to live on, and I wasn't thinking about what came later. Winter was past.

And spring took hold. The scent of the wind changed. Even the darkness of night was different.

At the end of May, Kipper, my cat, died. Suddenly, without warning. I woke up one day and found him curled up on the kitchen floor, dead. He himself probably hadn't known it was happening. His body was cold and hard, like yesterday's roast chicken, sheen gone from the fur. He could hardly have claimed he had the best life. Never really loved by anyone, never seeming really to love anyone either. His eyes always had this uneasy look, like, *what now?* You don't see that look in a cat too often. But anyway, he was dead. Nothing more. Maybe that's the best thing about death.

I put his body in a Seiyu supermarket bag, placed him on the backseat of the car, and drove to the hardware store for a shovel. I turned off the highway a good ways up in the hills and found an appropriate grove of trees. A fair distance back from the road I dug a hole one meter deep and laid Kipper in his shopping bag to rest. Then I shoveled dirt on top of him. Sorry, I told the little guy, that's just how it goes. Birds were singing the whole time I was burying him. The upper registers of a flute recital.

Once the hole was filled in, I tossed the shovel into the trunk of the car, and got back on the highway. I turned the radio on as I drove home to Tokyo.

Which is when the DJ had to put on Ray Charles moaning about being *born to lose . . . and now I'm losing you.*

I felt like crying. Sometimes one little thing will do the trick. I turned the radio off and pulled into a service area. First, I washed the dirt from my hands, then went into the restaurant. I could only manage a third of a sandwich, but I put down two cups of coffee.

What was Kipper doing now? I wondered. Down there in the dark. The sound of the dirt hitting the Seiyu bag echoed in my brain. That's just how it goes, pal, for me the same as you.

I sat staring at my unfinished sandwich for an hour. Until a violet-uniformed waitress came by and nervously asked if she could clear the plate away.

That's that, I thought. So now, back to society.

3

It takes no great effort to find work in the giant anthill of an advanced capitalist society. That is, of course, so long as you're not asking the impossible.

When I still had my office, I did my share of editing and writing, and I'd gotten to know a few professionals in the field. So as I embarked on a free-lance career, there was no major retooling required. I didn't need much to live on anyway.

I pulled out my address book and made some calls. I asked if there was work available. I said I'd been laying back but was ready to take stuff on. Almost immediately jobs came my way. Though not particularly interesting jobs, mostly filler for PR newsletters and company brochures. Speaking conservatively, I'd say half the material I wrote was meaningless, of no conceivable use to anyone. A waste of pulp and ink. But I did the work, mechanically, without thinking. At first, the load wasn't much, maybe a couple hours a day. The rest of the time I'd be out walking or seeing a movie. I saw a lot of movies. For three months, I had an easy time of it. I was slowly getting back in touch.

Then, in early autumn, things began to change. Work orders increased dramatically. The phone rang nonstop, my mailbox was overflowing. I met people in the business and had lunch with them. They promised me more work.

The reason was simple. I was never choosy about the jobs I did. I was willing to do anything, I met my deadlines, I never complained, I wrote legibly. And I was thorough. Where others slacked off, I did an honest write. I was never snide, even when the pay was low. If I got a call at two-thirty in the morning asking for twenty pages of text (about, say, the advantages of non-digital clocks or the appeal of women in their forties or the most beautiful spots in Helsinki, where, needless to say, I'd never been) by six A.M., I'd have it done by five-thirty. And if they called back for a rewrite, I had it to them by six. You bet I had a good reputation.

The same as for shoveling snow.

Let it snow and I'd show you a thing or two about efficient roadwork.

And with not one speck of ambition, not one iota of expectation. My only concern was to do things systematically, from one end to the other. I sometimes wonder if this might not prove to be the bane of my life. After wasting so much pulp and ink myself, who was I to complain about waste? We live in an advanced capitalist society, after all. Waste is the name of the game, its greatest virtue. Politicians call it "refinements in domestic consumption." I call it meaningless waste. A difference of opinion. Which doesn't change the way we live. If I don't like it, I can move to Bangladesh or Sudan.

I for one am not eager to live in Bangladesh or Sudan.

So I kept working.

And soon enough, it wasn't just PR work. I got called to do bits and pieces for regular magazines. For some reason, mostly women's magazines. I started doing interviews, minor legwork reportage. But really, the work wasn't much of an improvement over PR newsletters. Due to the nature of these magazines, most of the people I had to interview were in show business. No matter what you asked them, they had only stock replies. You could predict what they'd answer before you asked the question. In the worst cases, the manager would insist on seeing the questions in advance. So I always came with everything written out. Once I asked a seventeen-year-old singer something that wasn't on the list, which caused her manager to pipe up: "That wasn't what we agreed on—she doesn't have to answer that." That was a kick. I wondered if the girl couldn't answer what month followed October without this manager by her side. Still, I did my best. Before each interview I did my homework, surveyed available sources, tried to come up with questions others wouldn't think to ask. I took pains structuring the article. Not that these efforts received any special recognition. They never got me an appreciative word. I went the extra step because, for me, it was the simplest way. Self-discipline. Giving my disused fingers and head a practical—and if at all possible, harmless—dose of overwork.

Social rehabilitation.

After that, my days were busier than ever. Not only with double or triple my regular load, but with a lot of rush jobs too. Without fail, jobs that had no takers found their way to me. My role in those circles was the junkyard at the edge of town. Anything, particularly if complicated or a pain, would get hauled to me for disposal.

By way of thanks, my savings account swelled to figures I'd never seen the likes of, though I was too busy to spend much of it. So when a guy I knew offered me a good deal, I got rid of my nothing-but-headaches car and bought his year-old Subaru Leone. Hardly any miles on it, stereo and air-conditioning. A real first for me. And I moved to an apartment in Shibuya, closer to the center of town. It was a bit noisy—the expressway passing right outside my window—but you got used to it.

I slept with a few women I met through work.

Social rehabilitation.

I had a sense about which women I ought to sleep with. And which women I'd be able to sleep with, which not. Maybe even which I shouldn't sleep with. It's an intelligence that comes with age. I also knew when to call it quits, all very nice and easy so no one got hurt. The only thing missing was those tugs on the heartstrings.

The deepest I got involved was with a woman who worked at the phone company. I met her at a New Year's party. Both of us were tipsy, we joked with each other, liked each other, and ended up back at my place. She had a good head on her shoulders and terrific legs. We went for rides in my new-used Subaru. She'd call, whenever the mood struck, and come over and spend the night. She was the only relationship with one foot in the door like that. Though both of us knew there was no place this thing could go. Still, we quietly shared something approaching a pardon from life. I knew days of peace for the first time in ages. We exchanged tenderness, talked in whispers. I cooked for her, gave her birthday presents. We'd go to jazz clubs and have cocktails. We never argued, not once. We knew exactly what we wanted in each other. And even so, it ended. One day it stopped, as if the film simply slipped off the reel.

Her departure left me emptier than I would have suspected. For a while, I stayed in again.

The problem was that I hadn't wanted her, really wanted her. I'd liked her, liked being with her. She brought me back to gentle feelings. But what it came down to was, *I never felt a need for her*. Not three days after she got out of my life, the realization hit home. That ultimately, all the time I'd been next to her, I might as well have been on the moon. The whole while I'd felt her breasts against me, I'd really wanted something else.

It took four years to get my life back on steady ground. I carefully dispatched each piece of work that came my way, and people came to feel they could depend on me. Not many, but a few, even became friendly. Though, it goes without saying, that wasn't enough. Not enough at all. Here I'd spent all this time trying to get up to speed, and I was back to where I started.

Okay, I thought, age thirty-four, square one. What do you do now?

I didn't have to think much about that one. I knew already. The answer had been floating over my head like a dark, dense cloud. All I had to do was take action, instead of putting it off and putting it off. *I had to go to the Dolphin Hotel.* That's where it all started.

I also had to find *her*. The woman who'd first guided me to the Dolphin Hotel, *she* who'd been a high-class call girl in her own covert world of night. (Under astonishing circumstances, I was to learn this nameless woman's name sometime later, but, for reasons of convenience, unorthodox as it will seem, I'll tell it to you now. Pardon me, please. It was Kiki.) Yes, Kiki held the key. I had to call her back to me. To a life with me she'd left never to return. Was it possible? Who knew, but I had to try. From then would begin a new cycle.

I packed my bags, did double time to finish up outstanding work, then canceled all the jobs I'd penciled in for the next month. I said I was leaving Tokyo on family business. A couple of editors made noises, but what could they do? I'd never let them down before, and besides I was giving them plenty of advance notice to find other ways and means. In the end, it was fine. I'd be back in a month, I told them.

Then I took a flight to Hokkaido. This was the beginning of March 1983.

Of course, the family business wasn't over in anything near a month.

4

I booked a taxi for two days, and the photographer and I raced around Hakodate in the snow checking out eateries in the city.

I'm good at researching, very systematic, very efficient. The most important thing about this sort of job is to do your homework and set up a schedule. That's the key. When it comes to gathering materials beforehand, you can't beat organizations that compile information for people in the field. Become a member and pay your dues; they'll look up almost anything for you. So if by chance you're researching eating places in Hakodate, they can dig up quite a bit. They use mainframe computer retrieval, arrange the facts in file format, print out hard copy, even deliver to your doorstep. Granted, it's not cheap, but plenty worth the time it buys.

In addition to that, I do a little walking for information myself. There are reading rooms specializing in travel materials, libraries that collect local newspapers and regional publications. From all of these sources, I pick out the promising spots, then call them up to check their business hours. This much done, I've saved a lot of trouble on site. Then I draw lines in a notebook and plan out each day's itinerary. I look at maps and mark in the routes we'll travel. Trying to reduce uncertainties to a minimum.

Once we arrive in Hakodate, the photographer and I go

around to the restaurants in order. There are about thirty. We take a couple of bites—just enough to get the taste—then casually leave the rest of the meal uneaten. Refinements in consumption. We're still undercover at this stage, so no picture taking. Only after leaving the premises do the photographer and I discuss the food and evaluate it on a scale of one to ten. If it passes, it stays on the list; if not, it's out. We generally figure on dropping at least half. Taking a parallel tack, we also check the local papers for listings of places we've missed, selecting maybe five. We go to these too, and weed out the not-so-good. Then we've got our finalists. I call them up, give the name of the magazine, tell them we'd like to do a feature on them—text with photos. All that in two days. Nights, I stay in my hotel room, laying down the basic copy.

The next day, while the photographer does quick shots of the food and table settings, I talk to the restaurant owners. Saves on time. So we can call it a wrap in three days. True, there are those in our league who take even less time. But they don't do any research. They do a handful of the more well-known spots, cruise through without eating a thing, write brief comments. It's their business, not mine. If I may be perfectly frank, I doubt that many writers take as many pains as I do at this level of reportage. It's the kind of work that can break you if you're too serious about it, or you can kick back and do almost nothing. The worst of it is, whether you're earnest or you loaf, the difference will hardly show in the finished piece. On the surface. Only in the finer points can you find any hint of the distinction.

I'm not explaining this out of pride or anything.

I just wanted you to have a rough idea of the job, the sort of expendables I deal with.

On the third night, I finish writing.

The fourth day is left free, just in case.

But since the work has been completed and we don't have anything else in the tube, we rent a car and head off for a day of cross-country skiing. That evening, the two of us settle down to drinks over a nice, simmering hot pot. One day's relaxation. I turn over my manuscript to the photographer, and that's it. My job's done, the work's in someone else's hands.

But before turning in that evening, I rang up Sapporo directory assistance for the number of the Dolphin Hotel. I didn't have to wait long. I sat up in bed and sighed. Well, at least the Dolphin Hotel hadn't gone under. Relief, I guess. Because I wouldn't have been surprised if it had, a mysterious place like that. I took a deep breath, dialed the number —and someone answered immediately. As if they'd been just waiting for it to ring. So immediately, in fact, I was taken aback.

"Hello, Dolphin Hotel!" went a cheerful voice.

It was a young woman. A woman? What's going on? I don't remember a woman being there.

It didn't figure, so I checked if the address was the same. Yes, it was exactly where the Dolphin Hotel I knew used to be. Maybe the hotel had hired someone new, the owner's niece or something. Nothing so odd about that. I told her I wanted to make a reservation.

"Thank you very much, sir," she chirped. "Please wait a moment while I transfer you to our reservations desk."

Our reservations desk? Now I was really confused. I couldn't begin to digest that one. What the hell happened to the old joint?

"Sorry to keep you waiting. This is the reservations desk. How may I help you?" This time, a young man's voice. The brisk, friendly pitch of the professional hotel man. Curiouser and curiouser.

I asked for a single room for three nights. I gave him my name and my Tokyo phone number.

"Very well, sir. That's three nights, starting from tomorrow. Your single room will be waiting for you."

I couldn't think of anything to say to that, so I thanked him and hung up, completely disoriented. Shouldn't I have asked for an explanation? Oh well, it'd all become clear once I got there. And anyway, I couldn't *not* go. I didn't have an alternative.

I asked the concierge to check the schedule for trains to Sapporo. After that, I got room service to send up a bottle of whiskey and some ice, and I stayed up watching a late-night movie on TV. A Clint Eastwood western. Clint didn't smile once, didn't sneer. I tried laughing at him, but he never broke his deadpan. The movie ended and I'd had my fill of whiskey, so I turned out the light and slept straight through the night. If I dreamed, I don't remember.

All I could see outside the window of the early morning express train was snow. It was a bright, clear day, so the glare soon got to be too much. I didn't see another passenger looking out the windows. They all knew what snow looks like.

I'd skipped breakfast, so a little before noon I made my way to the dining car. Beer and an omelet. Across from me sat a fiftyish man in a suit and tie, having beer with a ham sandwich. He looked like a mechanical engineer, and that's just what he was. He spoke to me first, telling me he serviced jets for the Self-Defense Forces. Then he filled me in on how Soviet fighters and bombers invaded our airspace, though he didn't seem particularly upset about it. He was more concerned about the economics of F4 Phantoms. How much fuel they guzzled in one scramble, a terrible waste. "If the Japanese had made them, you can bet they'd be more efficient. And at no loss to performance either! There's no reason why we couldn't build a low-cost fighter if we wanted to."

That's when I proffered my words of wisdom, that waste is the highest virtue one can achieve in advanced capitalist society. The fact that Japan bought Phantom jets from America and wasted vast quantities of fuel on scrambles put an extra spin in the global economy, and that extra spin lifted capitalism to yet greater heights. If you put an end to all the waste, mass panic would ensue and the global economy would go haywire. Waste is the fuel of contradiction, and contradiction activates the economy, and an active economy creates more waste.

Well, maybe so, the engineer admitted, but having been a wartime child who had to live under deprived conditions, he couldn't grasp what this new social structure meant. "Our generation, we're not like you young folks," he said, straining a smile. "We don't understand these complex workings of yours."

I couldn't say I exactly understood things either, but as I wasn't eager for the conversation to drag on, I kept quiet. No, I'm not used to things; I just recognize them for what they are. There's a decisive difference between those two propositions. Which is just as well, I supposed, as I finished my omelet and excused myself.

I slept for thirty minutes, and the rest of the trip I read a biography of Jack London I'd bought near the Hakodate station. Compared to the grand sweep and romance of Jack London's life, my existence seemed like a squirrel with its head against a walnut, dozing until spring. For the time being, that is. But that's how biographies are. I mean, who's going to read about the peaceful life and times of a nobody employed at the Kawasaki Municipal Library? In other words, what we seek is some kind of compensation for what we put up with.

Arriving at Sapporo, I decided to take a leisurely stroll to the hotel. It was a pleasant enough afternoon, and I was carrying only a shoulder bag.

The streets were covered in a thin layer of slush, and people trained their eyes carefully at their feet. The air was exhilarating. High school girls came bustling along, their rosy red cheeks puffing white breaths you could have written cartoon captions in. I continued my amble, taking in the sights of town. It had been four and a half years since I was in Sapporo. It seemed like much longer.

Along the way I stopped into a coffee shop. All around me normal, everyday city types were going about their normal, everyday affairs. Lovers were whispering to each other, businessmen were poring over spread sheets, college kids were planning their next ski trip and discussing the new Police album. We could have been in any city in Japan. Transplant this coffee shop scene to Yokohama or Fukuoka and nothing would seem out of place. In spite of which—or, rather, all the more because—here I was, sitting in this coffee shop, drinking my coffee, feeling a desperate loneliness. I alone was the outsider. I had no place here.

Of course, by the same token, I couldn't really say I belonged to Tokyo and its coffee shops. But I had never felt this loneliness there. I could drink my coffee, read my book, pass the time of day without any special thought, all because I was part of the regular scenery. Here I had no ties to anyone. Fact is, I'd come to reclaim myself.

I paid the check and left. Then, without further thought, I headed for the hotel.

I didn't know the way exactly and part of me worried that I might miss the place. I didn't. How could anyone have? It had been transformed into a gleaming twenty-six-story Bauhaus Modern–Art Deco symphony of glass and steel, with flags of various nations waving along the driveway, smartly uniformed doormen hailing taxis, a glass elevator shooting up to a penthouse restaurant. A bas-relief of a dolphin was set into one of the marble columns by the entrance, beneath which the inscription read:

l'Hôtel Dauphin

I stood there a good twenty seconds, mouth agape, staring up at it. Then I let out a long, deep breath that might as easily have been beamed straight to the moon. Surprise was not the word.

5

I couldn't stand around gawking at the façade forever. Whatever this building was, the address was correct, as was the name—for the most part. And anyway, I had a reservation, right? There was nothing to do but go in.

I walked up the gently sloped driveway and pushed my way through the shiny brass revolving door. The lobby was large enough to be a gymnasium, the ceiling at least two stories high. A wall of glass rose the full height, and through it cascaded a brilliant shower of sunlight. The floor space was appointed with a fleet of luxurious designer sofas, between which were stationed planters of ornamental trees. Lots of them. The overall decor focused on an oil painting—three tatami mats large—of some Hokkaido marshland. Nothing outstanding artistically, but impressive, if only for its size. At the far end of the lobby a posh coffee bar beckoned. The sort of place where you order a sandwich and they bring you four deviled ham dainties arrayed like calling cards on a silver tray with an embellishment of potato crisps and *cornichons*. Throw in a cup of coffee and you're spending enough to buy a frugal family of four a midday meal.

The lobby was crowded. Apparently a function was in progress. A group of well-dressed, middle-aged men sat on facing sofas, nodding and smiling magnanimously. Jaws thrust out, legs crossed, identically. A professional organization? Doctors or university professors? On their periphery—perhaps they were part of the same gathering—cooed a clutch of young women in formal dress, some of them in kimono, some in floor-length dresses. There were a few Westerners as well, not to mention the requisite salarymen in dark suits and harmless ties, attaché cases in hand.

In a word, business was booming at the new Dolphin Hotel.

What we had here was a hotel founded on a proper outlay of capital and now enjoying proper returns. But how the hell had this come about? Well, I could guess, of course. Having once put together a PR bulletin for a hotel chain, I knew the whole process. Before a hotel of this scale is built, someone first costs out every aspect of the venture in detail, then consultants are called in and every piece of information is input into their computers for a thorough simulation study. Everything including the wholesale price and usage volume of toilet paper is taken into account. Then students are hired to go around the city—Sapporo in this case—to do a market survey. They stop young men and women on the street and ask how many weddings they expect to attend each year. You get the picture. Little is left unchecked. All in an effort to reduce business risk.

So the Hôtel Dauphin project team had gone to great lengths over many months to draw up as precise a plan as possible. They bought the property, they assembled the staff, they pinned down flash advertising space. If money was all it took—and they were convinced they'd make that money back—there'd be no end of funds pouring in. It's big business of a big order.

Now, the only enterprises that could embark on such a big business venture were the huge conglomerates. Because even after paring away the risks, there's bound to be some hidden factor of uncertainty lurking around, which only a major player can conceivably absorb.

To be honest, this new Dolphin Hotel wasn't my kind of hotel.

Or at least, under normal circumstances, if I had to choose a place to stay, I wouldn't go for one that looked like this. The rates are too high; too much padding, too many frills. But this time the die had been cast.

I went to the front desk and gave my name, whereupon three light blue blazered young women with toothpaste-commercial smiles greeted me. This smile training surely figured into the capital outlay. With their virgin-snow white blouses and immaculate hairstyles, the receptionists were picture-perfect. Of the three, one wore glasses, which of course suited her nicely. When she stepped over to me, I actually felt a shot of relief. She was the prettiest and most immediately likable. There was something about her expression I responded to, some embodiment of hotel spirit. I half expected her to produce a tiny magic wand, like in a Disney movie, and tap out swirls of diamond dust.

But instead of a magic wand, she used a computer, swiftly typing in my name and credit card number, then verifying the details on the display screen. Then she handed me my card-key, room number 1523. I smiled as I accepted the hotel brochure from her. When had the hotel opened? I asked. Last October, she answered, almost in reflex. It was now in its fifth month of operation.

"You know," I began, donning *my* professional smile, "I seem to remember a small hotel with a similar name in this location a few years ago. Do you have any idea what became of it?"

A slight disturbance clouded her smile. Quiet ripples spread across her face, as if a beer bottle had been tossed into a sacred spring. By the time the ripples subsided, her reassumed smile was a shade less cheerful than before. I observed the changes with great interest. Would the sprite of the spring now appear to ask whether the item I disposed of had a gold or silver twist top?

"Well, now," she hedged, touching the bridge of her

glasses with her index finger. "That was before we opened our doors, so I really couldn't—"

Her words cut off. I waited for her to continue, but she didn't.

"I'm terribly sorry," she said.

"Oh," I said. Seconds went by. I found myself liking her. I wanted to touch the bridge of my glasses as well, except that I wasn't wearing any glasses. "Well, then, is there anyone you can ask?"

She held her breath a second, thinking it over. The smile vanished. It's exceedingly difficult to hold your breath and keep smiling. Just try it if you don't believe me.

"I'm terribly sorry," she said again, "but would you mind waiting a bit?" Then she retreated through a door. Thirty seconds later, she returned with a fortyish man in a black suit. A real live hotelier by the looks of him. I'd met enough of them in my line of work. They are a dubious species, with twenty-five different smiles on call for every variety of circumstance. From the cool and cordial twinge of disinterest to the measured grin of satisfaction. They wield the entire arsenal by number, like golf clubs for particular shots.

"May I help you, please," he said, sending a midrange smile my way with a polite bow of the head. When he noted my attire, however, the smile was quickly adjusted down three notches. I was wearing my fur-lined hunting jacket with a Keith Haring button pinned to the chest, an Austrian Army–issue Alps Corps fur cap, a rough-and-ready pair of hiking trousers with lots of pockets, and snow-tire treaded work boots. All fine and practical items of dress, but just a tad unsuitable for this hotel lobby. No fault of mine, only a difference in life-style.

"You had a question concerning our hotel, I believe?" he voiced most properly.

I put both hands on the counter and repeated my query.

The man cast a glance at my Mickey Mouse watch with the same clinical unease a vet might direct at a cat's sprained paw.

"Might I inquire," he regained his composure to speak, "why you wish to know about the previous hotel? If you don't mind my asking, that is?"

I explained as simply as I could: A good while back I had stayed at the old Dolphin Hotel and gotten to know the owner; now, years later, I visit and everything's completely changed. Which makes me wonder, what happened to the old guy?

The man nodded attentively.

"In all honesty, I'm not entirely clear on the details myself," he chose his words guardedly. "Nevertheless, my understanding of the history of this hotel is that our concerns purchased the property where the previous Dolphin Hotel stood and erected on the site what we now have before us. As you can see, the name was for all intents and purposes retained, but let me assure you that the management is altogether separate, with no relation whatsoever to its predecessor."

"Then why keep the name?"

"You must forgive me, I'm afraid I really don't . . ."

"And I suppose you wouldn't have any idea where I could find the former owner?"

"I *am* sorry, but no, I do not," he answered, moving on to smile number 16.

"Is there anyone else I could ask? Someone who might know?"

"Since you insist," the man began, straining his neck slightly. "We are merely employees here, and accordingly we are strictly out of touch with any goings on prior to when the current premises opened for business. So unfortunately, if someone such as yourself desires to know anything more specific, there's really very little . . ."

Certainly what he said made sense, yet something caught in the back of my mind. Something artificial, manufactured really, about the responses from both the young woman and the stiff now fielding my questions. I couldn't put my finger on anything exactly, yet I couldn't swallow the line. Do your share of interviews and you get this professional sixth sense. That tone of voice when someone's hiding something, that knowing expression of someone who's lying. No real evidence to go on. Only a hunch, that there was more here than being said.

Still, it was clear that nothing more would come from pushing them further. I thanked the man; he excused himself and withdrew. After his black suit had vanished from view, I asked the young woman about meals and room service, and she went on at length. While she spoke, I peered straight into her eyes. Beautiful eyes. I swear I almost began to see things in them. But when she met my gaze, she blushed. Which made me like her even more. Why was that? Was it that hotel spirit in her? Whatever, I thanked her, turned away, and took the elevator up to my floor.

Room 1523 proved to be quite a room. Both the bed and the bath were far too big for a single. A full complement of shampoo, conditioner, and after-shave was provided, as was a bathrobe. The refrigerator was chock-full of snacks. There was an ample writing desk, with plenty of stationery and envelopes. The closet was large, the carpet deep-piled. I took off my coat and boots and picked up the hotel brochure. Quite a production. They hadn't spared any expense on this job.

L'Hôtel Dauphin represents a wholly new development in quality city center lodgings, the brochure stated. *Complete with the latest conveniences and full twenty-four-hour services. Our guest rooms are spacious and sumptuously styled. Featuring the finest selection of products, a restful atmosphere, and a warm at-home feeling. "Professional space with a human face."*

In other words, they'd spent a lot of money, so the rates were high.

Indeed, this was a very well turned out hotel. A big shopping arcade in the basement, an indoor pool, sauna, and tanning salon. Tennis courts, a health club with training coaches and exercise equipment, conference rooms outfitted for simultaneous translation, five restaurants, three lounges, even a late-night café. Not to mention a limousine service, free work space, unlimited business supplies available to all guests. Anything you could want, they'd thought of—and then some. A rooftop heliport?

Intelligent facilities in an impeccable decor.

But what of the commercial group that owned and operated this hotel? I reread the brochure from cover to cover. Not one mention of the management. Odd, to say the least. It was unthinkable that any but the most experienced hotel chain could run a topflight operation like this, and any enterprise of such scale would be certain to stamp its name everywhere and take every opportunity to promote its full line of hotels. You stay at one Prince Hotel and the brochure lists every Prince Hotel in the whole of Japan. That's how it is.

And then there was still the question, why would a hotel of this class take on the name of a dump like the old Dolphin?

I couldn't come up with even a flake of an answer to that one.

I threw the brochure onto the table, fell back into the sofa with my feet kicked up, and looked out my fifteenth-story window. All I could see was blue sky. I felt like I was flying.

All this was fine, but I missed the old dive. There'd been a lot to see from those windows.

6

I puttered around in the hotel, seeing what there was to see. I checked out the restaurants and lounges, took a peek at the pool and sauna and health club and tennis courts, bought a couple of books in the shopping arcade. I criss-crossed the lobby, then gravitated to the game center and played a few rounds of backgammon. That alone took up the afternoon. The hotel was practically an amusement park. The world is full of ways and means to waste time.

After that, I left the hotel to have a look around the area. As I strolled through the early evening streets, the lay of the town gradually came back to me. Back when I'd stayed at the old Dolphin Hotel, I covered this area with depressing regularity, day after day. Turn here, and there was this or that. The old Dolphin hadn't had a dining room—if it had, I doubt I would have been inclined to eat there—so we, Kiki and I, would always go someplace nearby for meals. Now I felt like I was visiting an old neighborhood and was content just to wander about, taking in familiar sights.

When the sun went down, the air grew cold. The streets echoed with the wet sounds of slush underfoot. There was no wind, so walking was not at all unpleasant. It was still crisp and clear. Even the piles of exhaust-gray snow plowed up on every corner looked positively enchanting beneath the streetlights.

The area had changed markedly from the old days. Of course, those "old days" were only four years back, as I've said, so most of the places I'd frequented were more or less the same. The local atmosphere was basically the same as well, but signs of change were everywhere. Stores were boarded up, announcements of development to come tacked over. A large building was under construction. A drive-through burger stand and designer boutiques and a European auto showroom and a trendy café with an inner courtyard of *sara* trees—all kinds of new establishments had popped up one after the next, pushing aside the dingy old three-story blockhouses and cheap eateries festooned with traditional *noren* entrance curtains and the sweetshop where a cat lay napping by the stove. The odd mix of styles presented an all-too-temporary show of coexistence, like the mouth of a child with new teeth coming in. A bank had even opened a new branch, maybe a spillover of the new Dolphin Hotel capitalization. Build a hotel of that scale in a perfectly ordinary—if a bit neglected—neighborhood, and the balance is upset. The flow of people changes, the place starts to jump. Land prices go up.

Or perhaps the changes were more cumulative. That is, the upheaval hadn't been wrought by the new Dolphin Hotel alone, but was a stage in the greater infrastructural changes of the area. Some long-term urban redevelopment program, for example.

I went into a small bar I remembered, and had a few drinks and a bite to eat. The place was dirty, noisy, cheap, and good. The kind of hole-in-the-wall I always look for when I have to eat out alone. Places like this put me at ease, never make me lonely. I can talk to myself and nobody listens or cares.

After eating, I still wanted something else, so I asked for some saké. As the warm brew seeped into my system, the question came to me: What on earth am I doing up here? The Dolphin Hotel, such that I was seeking, no longer existed. It didn't matter what it was I was looking for, the place was no more. And not merely gone, it'd been replaced by this idiotic

Star Wars high-tech hotel-a-thon. I was too late. My dreams of the once-Dolphin Hotel had been nothing more than dreams of Kiki, long vanished out the door. Perhaps there *was* someone crying for me. But that too was gone. Nothing was left. What could you possibly hope to find here, kid?

You said it, I thought. Or maybe I had my mouth open and actually said it to myself. *There's nothing left here. Not one thing left for you.*

I clamped my lips tight and stared at the bottle of soy sauce on the counter.

You live by yourself for a stretch of time and you get to staring at different objects. Sometimes you talk to yourself. You take meals in crowded joints. You develop an intimate relationship with your used Subaru. You slowly but surely become a has-been.

I left the bar and headed back to the hotel. I'd walked a fair bit, but it wasn't hard finding my way back. I had only to look up to see the new Dolphin Hotel towering above everything else. Like the three wise men guided by a star to Jerusalem or Bethlehem or wherever it was, I steered straight for the main attraction.

After a bath, toweling my hair dry, I gazed out over the Sapporo cityscape. When I stayed at the old Dolphin, hadn't there been a small office building outside my window? What kind of office, I never did figure out, but it was a company and people were busy. That had been my view day after day. What ever became of that company? There'd been a nice-looking woman working there. Where was she now?

I had nothing to do, so I shuffled around the room before flicking on the TV. It was the same old nausea-inducing fare. Not even original nausea-inducing fare. It was phony, synthetic, but being synthetic, it wasn't entirely repugnant. If I didn't turn the thing off, though, I felt sure I'd be seeing the results of some real nausea.

I pulled on some clothes and went up to the lounge on the twenty-sixth floor. I sat at the bar and ordered a vodka-and-soda with lemon. One whole wall of the lounge was window, providing a sweeping panorama of Sapporo at night. A Star Wars alien city set. Otherwise, it was a comfortable, quiet place, with real crystal glasses that had a nice ring.

Besides myself, there were only three other customers. Two middle-aged men talking in a hush at a back table. Some very important matter by the look of things. A plot to assassinate Darth Vader? And sitting at a table directly to their right, a girl of twelve or thirteen, plugged in to a Walkman, sipping a drink through a straw. She was a pretty girl. Her long hair, unnaturally straight, draped silkily against the edge of the table. She tapped her fingers on the tabletop, keeping time to the rhythm she was hearing. Her long fingers made a more childlike impression than the rest of her. Not that she was trying to act like an adult. No, not disagreeable or arrogant, but aloof.

Yet, in fact, the girl wasn't looking at anything. She was completely oblivious to her surroundings. She was wearing jeans and white Converse All Stars and a sweatshirt emblazoned with GENESIS, sleeves rolled up to her elbows, and she seemed to be concentrating entirely on the music. Sometimes she'd move her lips to form fragments of lyrics.

"Lemonade," the bartender volunteered, as if to excuse the presence of a minor. "The girl's waiting for her mother."

"Hmm," I answered, noncommital. Certainly, you don't go into a hotel bar after ten at night and expect to find a young girl sitting by herself with a drink and a Walkman. But if the bartender hadn't broached the subject, I probably wouldn't have thought anything was out of the ordinary. The girl just seemed a part of the place.

I ordered another drink and made small talk with the bartender. The weather, the view, assorted topics. Then nonchalantly I dropped the line that, hey, this place sure has changed, hasn't it? To which the bartender strained a smile and admitted that, until recently, he'd been working at a hotel in Tokyo, so he scarcely knew anything about Sapporo. And at that point, a new customer walked in, terminating our fruitless conversation.

I drank a total of four vodka-and-sodas. I could have drunk any number more but decided to call it quits. The girl was still in her seat, grafted to the Walkman. Her mother hadn't shown, and the ice in her glass had melted, which she didn't seem to notice. Yet when I got up from the counter, she looked up at me for two or three seconds, and smiled. Or perhaps it was the slightest trembling of her lips. But to me, it looked like she smiled. Which—I know it sounds strange—really shook me up. I felt as if I'd been chosen. A charge shot through me; my body seemed to lift up a few centimeters.

A bit disarmed, I boarded the elevator and returned to my room. A smile from a twelve-year-old girl? How could anything so innocent have set me off so much? She could have been my daughter.

And Genesis—what a stupid name for a band.

But because the girl had that sweatshirt on, the name seemed somehow symbolic. *Genesis.*

Why do rock groups have overblown names like that?

I fell back onto the bed with my shoes still on. Closed my eyes and the young girl's image came to me. Walkman. White fingers tapping tabletop. Genesis. Melted ice.

Genesis.

With my eyes shut, I could feel the alcohol swimming around inside me. I pulled off my work boots, got out of my clothes, and crawled under the covers. I was too tired, too drunk, to feel much of anything. I waited for the woman next to me to say, "Had a bit too much, have we?" But there was no such conversation.

Genesis.

I reached out to turn out the light. Will my dreams take me to the Dolphin Hotel? I wondered in the dark.

When I awoke the next morning, I felt a hopeless emptiness. No dream, no hotel. Zilch.

My work boots lay at the foot of the bed where they'd fallen. Two tired puppies.

Outside my window the sky hung low and gray. It looked

like snow, which added to my malaise. The clock read five after seven. I punched the remote control and watched the morning news as I lay in bed. Something about an upcoming election. Fifteen minutes later I got up and went to the bathroom to wash and shave, humming the overture to *The Marriage of Figaro* as a wake-me-up. Or was it the overture to *The Magic Flute*? I racked my brain, but couldn't get it straight. I cut my chin shaving, then popped a button from my cuff getting into my shirt. The signs for the day were not good.

At breakfast, I saw the young girl I'd seen in the bar, sitting with a woman I took to be her mother. Wearing the same GENESIS sweatshirt but at least without the Walkman. She'd hardly touched her bread or scrambled eggs, seemed absolutely bored drinking her tea. Her mother was a smallish woman in her early forties. Hair pulled into a tight bun, eyebrows exactly like her daughter's, slender, refined nose, camel-colored sweater that looked like it was cashmere over a white blouse. She wore her clothes well, clothes that suit a woman accustomed to the attentions of others. There was a touching world-weariness in the way she buttered her toast.

As I passed by their table, the girl glanced up at me. Then smiled. A more definitive smile than last night's. Unmistakably, a smile.

I ate my breakfast alone and tried to think, but after that smile I couldn't focus. No matter what came to mind, the thoughts spun around uselessly. In the end, I stared at the pepper shaker and didn't think at all.

7

There was nothing for me to do. Nothing I should do, and nothing I wanted to do. I'd come all this way to the Dolphin Hotel, but the Dolphin Hotel that I wanted had vanished from the face of the earth. What to do?

I went down to the lobby, planted myself in one of the magnificent sofas, and tried to come up with a plan for the day. Should I go sightseeing? Where to? How about a movie? Nah, nothing I wanted to see. And why come all the way to Sapporo to see a movie? So, what to do?

Nothing to do.

Okay, it's the barbershop, I said to myself. I hadn't been to a barber in a month, and I was in need of a cut. Now that's making good use of free time. If you don't have anything better to do, go to the barber.

So I made tracks for the hotel barbershop, hoping that it'd be crowded and I'd have to wait my turn. But of course the place was empty, and I was in the chair immediately. An abstract painting hung on the blue-gray walls, and Jacques Rouchet's *Play Bach* lilted soft and mellow from hidden speakers. This was not like any barbershop I'd been to—you could hardly call it a barbershop. The next thing you know, they'll be playing Gregorian chants in bathhouses, Ryuichi Sakamoto in tax office waiting rooms. The guy who cut my hair was young, barely twenty. When I mentioned that there used to be a tiny hotel here that went by the same name, his response was, "That so?" He didn't know much about Sapporo either. He was cool. He was wearing a Men's Bigi designer shirt. Even so, he knew how to cut hair, so I left there pretty much satisfied.

What next?

Short of other options, I returned to my sofa in the lobby and watched the scenery. The receptionist with glasses from yesterday was behind the front desk. She seemed tense. Was my presence setting off signals in her? Unlikely. Soon the clock pushed eleven. Lunchtime. I headed out and walked around, trying to think what I was in the mood for. But I wasn't hungry, and no place caught my fancy. Lacking will, I wandered into a place for some spaghetti and salad. Then a beer. Outside, snow was still threatening, but not a flake in sight. The sky was solid, immobile. Like Gulliver's flying island of Laputa, hanging heavily over the city. Everything seemed cast in gray. Even, in retrospect, my meal—gray. Not a day for good ideas.

In the end, I caught a cab and went to a department store downtown. I bought shoes and underwear, spare batteries, a travel toothbrush, nail clippers. I bought a sandwich for a late-night snack and a small flask of brandy. I didn't need any of this stuff, I was just shopping, just killing time. I killed two hours.

Then I walked along the major avenues, looking into windows, no destination in mind, and when I tired of that, I stepped into a café and read some Jack London over coffee. And before long it was getting on to dusk. Talk about boring. Killing time is not an easy job.

Back at the hotel, I was passing by the front desk when I heard my name called. It was the receptionist with glasses. She motioned for me to go to one end of the counter, the car-rental section actually, where there was a display of pamphlets. No one was on duty here.

She twirled a pen in her fingers a second, giving me a I've-got-something-to-tell-you-but-I-don't-know-how-to-say-it look. Clearly, she wasn't used to doing this sort of thing.

"Please forgive me," she began, "but we have to pretend we're discussing a car rental." Then she shot a quick glance out of the corner of her eye toward the front desk. "Management is very strict. We're not supposed to speak privately to customers."

"All right, then," I said. "I'll ask you about car rates, and you answer with whatever you want to say. Nothing personal."

She blushed slightly. "Forgive me," she said again. "They're real sticklers for rules here."

I smiled. "Still, your glasses are very becoming."

"Excuse me?"

"You look very cute in those glasses. Very cute," I said.

She touched the frame of these glasses, then cleared her throat. The nervous type. "There's something I've been wanting to ask you," she regained her composure. "It's a private matter."

If I could have, I would have patted her on the head to comfort her, but instead I kept quiet and looked into her eyes.

"It's what we talked about last night, you know, about there having been a hotel here," she said softly, "with the same name as this one. What was that other hotel like? I mean, was it a *regular* hotel?"

I picked up a car-rental pamphlet and acted like I was studying it. "That depends on what you mean by 'regular.'"

She pinched the points of her collar and cleared her throat again. "It's . . . hard to say exactly, but was there anything strange about that hotel? I can't get it out of my mind."

Her eyes were earnest and lovely. Just as I'd remembered. She blushed again.

"I guess I don't know what you mean, but I'm sure it will take a little time to talk about and we can't very well do it here. You seem like you're pretty busy."

She looked over at the other receptionists at the front desk, then bit her lower lip slightly. After a moment's hesitation, she spoke up. "Okay, could you meet me after I get off work?"

"What time is that?"

"I finish at eight. But we can't meet near here. Hotel rules. It's got to be somewhere far away from here."

"You name the place. I don't care how far, I'll be there."

She thought a bit more, then scribbled the name of a place and drew me a map. "I'll be there at eight-thirty."

I pocketed the sheet of paper.

Now it was her turn to look at me. "I hope you don't think I'm strange. This is the first time I've done something like this. I've never broken the rules before. But this time I don't know what else to do. I'll explain everything to you later."

"No, I don't think you're strange. Don't worry," I said. "I'm not so bad a guy. I may not be the most likable person in the world, but I try not to upset people."

She twirled her pen again, not quite sure how to take that. Then she smiled vaguely and pushed up the bridge of her glasses. "Well, then, later," she said, and gave me a businesslike bow before returning to her station at the front desk. Charming, if a little insecure.

I went up to my room and pulled a beer from the refrigerator to wash down my department-store roast beef sandwich. Okay, at least we have a plan of action. We may be in low gear, but we're rolling. But where to?

I washed and shaved, brushed my teeth. Calmly, quietly, no humming. Then I gave myself a good, hard look in the mirror, the first time in ages. No major discoveries. I felt no surge of valor. It was the same old face, as always.

I left my room at half past seven and grabbed a taxi. The driver studied the map I showed him, then nodded without a word, and we were off. It was a-thousand-something-yen distance, a tiny bar in the basement of a five-story building. I was met at the door with the warm sound of an old Gerry Mulligan record.

I took a seat at the counter and listened to the solo over a nice, easy J&B-and-water. At eight-forty-five she still hadn't shown. I didn't particularly mind. The bar was plenty comfortable, and by now I was getting to be a pro at killing time. I sipped my drink, and when that was gone, I ordered another. I contemplated the ashtray.

At five past nine she made her entrance.

"I'm sorry," she said in a flurry. "Things started to get busy at the last minute, and then my replacement was late."

"Don't worry. I was fine here," I said. "I had to pass the time anyway."

At her suggestion we moved to a table toward the back. We settled down, as she removed her gloves, scarf, and coat. Underneath, she had on a dark green wool skirt and a lightweight yellow sweater—which revealed generous volumes I'm surprised I hadn't noticed before. Her earrings were demure gold pinpoints.

She ordered a Bloody Mary. And when it came, she sipped it tentatively. I took another drink of my whiskey and then she took another sip of her Bloody Mary. I nibbled on nuts.

At length, she let out a big sigh. It might have been bigger than she had intended, as she looked up at me nervously.

"Work tough?" I asked.

"Yeah," she said. "Pretty tough. I'm still not used to it. The hotel just opened so the management's always on edge about something."

She folded her hands and placed them on the table. She wore one ring, on her pinkie. An unostentatious, rather ordinary silver ring.

"About the old Dolphin Hotel . . . ," she began. "But wait, didn't I hear you were a magazine writer or something?"

"Magazine?" I said, startled. "What's this about?"

"That's just what I heard," she said.

I shut up. She bit her lip and stared at a point on the wall.

"There was some trouble once," she began again, "so the

management's very nervous about media. You know, with property being bought up and all. If too much talk about this gets in the media, the hotel could suffer. A bad image can ruin business."

"Has something been written up?"

"Once, in a weekly magazine a while ago. There were these suggestions about dirty dealings, something about calling in the *yakuza* or some right-wing thugs to put pressure on the folks who were holding out. Things like that."

"And I take it the old Dolphin Hotel was mixed up in this trouble?"

She shrugged and took another sip. "I wouldn't be surprised. Otherwise, I don't think the manager would have acted so nervous talking to you about the old hotel. I mean, it was almost like you sounded an alarm. I don't know any of the details, but I did hear once about the Dolphin name in connection with an older hotel. From someone."

"Someone?"

"One of the blackies."

"Blackies?"

"You know, the black-suit crowd."

"Check," I said. "Other than that, you haven't heard anything about the old Dolphin Hotel?"

She shook her head and fiddled with her ring. "I'm scared," she whispered. "I'm so scared I . . . I don't know what to do."

"Scared? Because of me and magazines?"

She shook her head, then pressed her lip against the rim of her glass. "No, it's not that. Magazines don't have anything to do with it. If something gets printed, what do I care? The management might get all bent out of shape, but that's not what I'm talking about. It's the whole place. The whole hotel, well, I mean, there's always something a little weird about it. Something funny . . . something . . . warped."

She stopped and was silent. I'd finished my whiskey, so I ordered another round for the both of us.

"What do you mean by 'warped'?" I tried prompting her. "Do you mean anything specific?"

"Of course I do," she said sharply. "Things have happened, but it's hard to find the words to describe it. So I never told anyone. I mean, it was really real, what I felt, but if I try to explain it in words, then it sort of starts to slip away."

"So it's like a dream that's very real?"

"But this *wasn't* a dream. You know dreams sort of fade after a while? Not this thing. No way. It's always stayed the same. It's always real, right there, before my eyes."

I didn't know what to say.

"Okay, this is what happened," she said, taking a drink of her Bloody Mary and dabbing her lips with the napkin. "It was in January. The beginning of January, right after New Year's. I was working the late shift, which I don't generally like, but on that day it was my turn. Anyway, I didn't get through until around midnight. When it's late like that, they send you home in a taxi because the trains aren't running. So after I changed clothes, I realized that I'd left my book in the staff lounge. I guess I could have waited until the next day, but the girl I was going to share the taxi with was still finishing up, so I decided to go get it. I got in the employee elevator and punched the button for the sixteenth floor, which is where the staff lounge and other staff facilities are—we take our coffee break there and go up there a lot.

"Anyway I was in the elevator and the door opened and I stepped out like always. I didn't think anything of it, I mean, who would? It's something that you do all the time, right? I stepped out like it was the most natural thing in the world. I guess I was thinking about something, I don't remember what. I think I had both hands in my pockets and I was standing there in the hallway, when I noticed that everything around me was dark. I mean, like absolutely pitch black. I turned around and the elevator door had just shut. The first thing I thought was, uh-oh, the power's gone out. But that's impossible. The hotel has this in-house emergency generator, so if there's a power failure, the generator kicks on automatically. We had these practice sessions during training, so I know. So, in principle, there's not supposed to be anything like a blackout. And if on the million-to-one chance something goes wrong with the generator, then emergency lights in the hallway are supposed to come on. So what I'm saying is, it wasn't supposed to be pitch black. I should have been seeing green lamps along the hall.

"But the whole place was completely dark. All I could see were the elevator call buttons and the red digital display that says what floor it's on. So the first thing I did was press the call buttons, but the elevator kept going down. I didn't know what to do. Then, for some reason, I decided to take a look around. I was really scared, but I was also feeling really put out.

"What I was thinking was that something was wrong with the basic functions of the hotel. Mechanically or structurally or something. And that meant more hassle from the management and no holidays and all sorts of annoying stuff. So, the more I thought about these things, the more annoyed I got. My annoyance got bigger than my fear. And that's how I decided to, you know, just have a look around. I walked two or three steps and—well, something was really strange. I mean, I couldn't hear the sound of my feet. There was no sound at all. And the floor felt funny, not like the regular carpet. It was hard. Honest. And then the air, it felt different, too. It was . . . it was moldy. Not like the hotel air at all. Our hotel is supposed to be fully air-conditioned and management is very fussy about it because it's not like ordinary air-conditioning, it's supposed to be *quality* air, not the dehumidified stuff in other hotels that dries out your nose. Our air is like natural air. So the stale, moldy air was really a shock. And it smelled like it was . . . old—you know, like when you go to visit your grandparents in the country and you open up the old family storehouse—like that. Stagnant and musty.

"I turned around and now even the elevator call buttons had gone out. I couldn't see a thing. Everything was out, completely, which was really frightening. I mean, I was entirely alone in total darkness, and it was utterly quiet. *Utterly*. There wasn't a single sound. Strange. You'd think that in a power failure, at least one person would be calling out. And this was when the hotel was almost full. You'd've thought a lot of people would be making noise. Not this time."

Our drinks arrived, and we each took sips. Then she set hers down and adjusted her glasses.

"Did you follow me so far?"

"Pretty much," I said. "You got off the elevator on the sixteenth floor. It's pitch black. It smells strange. It's too quiet. Something funny is going on."

She let out a sigh. "I don't know if it's good or bad, but I'm not especially a timid person. At least I think I'm pretty brave. I'm not the type who screams her head off when the lights go out. I get scared but I don't freak out. I figure that you ought to go check things out. So I started feeling my way blind up the hallway."

"In which direction?"

"To the right," she said, raising her right hand. "I felt my way along the wall, very slowly, and after a bit the hallway turned to the right again. And then, up ahead, I could see a faint glow. Really faint, like candlelight leaking in from far away. My first thought was that someone had found some emergency candles and lit them. I kept going, but when I got closer, I saw that the light was coming from a room with the door slightly ajar. The door was pretty strange too. I'd never seen an old door like that in the hotel before. I just stood there in front of it, not knowing what to do next. What if somebody was inside? What if somebody weird came out? What was this door doing here in the first place?

"So I knocked on the door softly, very softly. It was hardly a knock at all, but it came out sounding really loud —maybe because the hallway was dead quiet. Anyway, no response. I waited ten seconds, and during those ten seconds, I was just frozen. I hadn't the slightest idea what I was going to do. Then I heard this muffled noise. I don't know, it was like a person in heavy clothing standing up, and then there were these footsteps. Really slow, *shuffle . . . shuffle . . . shuffle . . .* , like he was wearing slippers or something. The footsteps came closer and closer to the door."

She stared off into space and was shaking her head.

"*That* was when I started to freak out. Like maybe these footsteps weren't human. I don't know how I came to that conclusion. It was just this creepy feeling I got, because human feet don't walk like that. Chills ran up my spine, I mean seriously. I ran. I didn't even look where I was going. I must have fallen once or twice, I think, because my stockings were torn. This part I don't remember very well. All I can remember is that I ran. I panicked. Like what if the elevator's dead? Thank god, when I finally got back there, the red floor-number light and call buttons were lit up and everything. The elevator was on the ground floor. I started pounding the call buttons and then the elevator started coming back up. But much slower than usual. Really, it was like this incredible slug. Like, *second . . . third . . . fourth . . .* I was praying, *c'mon, hurry up, oh come on*, but it didn't do any good. The thing took forever. It was like somebody was jamming the controls."

She let out a deep breath and sipped her drink again. Then she played with her ring a second longer.

I waited for her to continue. The music had stopped, someone was laughing.

"I could still hear those footsteps, *shuffle . . . shuffle . . . shuffle . . .* , getting closer. They just didn't stop, *shuffle . . . shuffle . . . shuffle . . .* , moving down the hall, coming toward me. I was terrified! I was more terrified than I'd ever been in my whole life. My stomach was practically squeezed up into my throat. I was sweating all over, but I was cold. I had the chills. The elevator wasn't anywhere near. *Seventh . . . eighth . . . ninth . . .* The footsteps kept coming."

She paused for twenty or thirty seconds. And once again, she gave her ring a few more turns, almost as if she were tuning a radio. A woman at the counter said something, which drew another laugh from her companion. If only they'd hurry up and put on a record.

"I can't really describe how I felt. You just have to experience it," she spoke dryly.

"Then what happened?"

"The next thing I knew, the elevator was there," she said, shrugging her shoulders. "The door opened and I could see that nice, familiar light. I fell in, literally. I was shaking all over, but I managed to push the button for the lobby. When it got there, I must've scared everyone silly. I was all pale and speechless and trembling. The manager came over and shook me, and said, 'Hey, what's wrong?' So I tried to tell him about the strange things on the sixteenth floor, but I kept running out of breath. The manager stopped me in the middle of my story and called over one of the staff boys, and all three of us went back up to the sixteenth floor. Just to check things out. But everything was perfectly normal up there. All the lights were shining away, there was no old smell, everything was the same as always, as it was supposed to be. We went to the staff lounge and asked the guy who was there if he knew anything about it, but he swore up and down he'd been awake the whole time and the power hadn't gone out. Then, just to be sure, we walked the entire sixteenth floor from one end to the other. Nothing was out of the ordinary. It was like I'd been bewitched or something.

"We went back down and the manager took me into his office. I was sure he was going to scream at me, but he didn't even get mad. He asked me to tell him what happened again in more detail. So I explained everything as clearly as I could, from the beginning, right down to those footsteps coming after me. I felt like a complete idiot. I was sure he was going to laugh at me and say I'd dreamed the whole thing up.

"But he didn't laugh or anything. Instead, he looked dead serious. Then he said: 'You're not to tell anyone about this.' He spoke very gently. 'Something must have gone wrong, but we shouldn't upset the other employees, so let's keep this completely quiet.' And let me tell you, this manager is not the type to speak gently. He's ready to fly off the handle at any second. That's when it occurred to me—that maybe I wasn't the first person this happened to."

She now sat silent.

"And you haven't heard anybody talk about something like this? Weird experiences, or strange happenings, or anything mysterious? What about rumors?"

She thought it over and shook her head. "No, not that I'm aware of. But there really is something funny about the place. The way the manager reacted when I told him what happened and all those hush-hush conversations going on all the time. I really can't explain any better, but something isn't right. It's not at all like the hotel I worked at before. Of course, that wasn't such a big hotel, so things were a little different, but this is *real* different. That hotel had its own ghost story—every hotel's probably got one—but we all could laugh at it. Here, it's not like that at all. Nobody laughs. So it's even more scary. The manager, for example, if he made a joke of it, or even if he yelled at me, it wouldn't have seemed so strange. That way, I would've thought there was just a malfunction or something."

She squinted at the glass in her hand.

"Did you go back to the sixteenth floor after that?" I asked.

"Lots of times," she said matter-of-factly. "It's still part of my workplace, so I go there when I have to, whether I like it or not. But I only go during the day. I never go there at night, I don't care what. I don't ever want to go through *that* again. That's why I won't work the night shift. I even told my boss that."

"And you've never mentioned this to anyone else?"

She shook her head quickly. "Like I already said, this is the first time. No one would've believed me anyway. I told you about it because I thought maybe you'd have a clue about this sixteenth-floor business."

"Me?"

She gazed at me abstractedly. "Well, for one thing, you

knew about the old Dolphin Hotel and you wanted to hear what happened to it. I couldn't help hoping you might know something about what I'd gone through."

"Nope, afraid not," I said, after a bit. "I'm not a specialist on the hotel. The old Dolphin was a small place, and it wasn't very popular. It was just an ordinary hotel."

Of course I didn't for a moment think the old Dolphin was just an ordinary hotel, but I didn't want to open up that can of worms.

"But this afternoon, when I asked you about the Dolphin Hotel, you said it was a long story. What did you mean by that?"

"That part of it's kind of personal," I said. "If I start in on that, it gets pretty involved. Anyway, I don't think it has anything to do with what you just told me."

She seemed disappointed. Pouting slightly, she stared down at her hands.

"Sorry I can't be of more help," I said, "especially after all the trouble you took to tell me this."

"Well, don't worry, it's not your fault. I'm still glad I could tell you about it. These sort of things, you keep them all to yourself and they really start to get to you."

"Yup, you gotta let the pressure out. If you don't, it builds up inside your head." I made an over-inflated balloon with my arms.

She nodded silently as she fiddled with her ring again, removing it from her finger, then putting it back.

"Tell me, do you even believe my story? About the sixteenth floor and all?" she whispered, not raising her eyes from her fingers.

"Of course I believe you," I said.

"Really? But it's kind of *peculiar*, don't you think?"

"That may be, but peculiar things do happen. I know that much. That's why I believe you. It all links up somewhere, I think."

She puzzled over that a minute. "Then you've had a similar experience?"

"Yeah, at least I think I have."

"Was it scary?" she asked.

"No, it wasn't like your experience," I answered. "No, what I mean is, things connect in all kinds of ways. With me . . ." But for no reason I could understand, the words died in my throat. As if someone had yanked out the telephone line. I took a sip of whiskey and tried again. "I'm sorry. I don't know how to put it. But I definitely have seen my share of unbelievable things. So I'm quite prepared to believe what you've told me. I don't think you made up the story."

She looked up and smiled. An individual smile, I thought, not the professional variety. And she relaxed. "I don't know why," she said, "but I feel better talking to you. I'm usually pretty shy. It's really hard for me to talk to people I don't know, but with you it's different."

"Maybe we have something in common," I laughed.

She didn't know what to make of that remark, and in the end didn't say anything. Instead, she sighed. Then she asked, "Feel like eating? All of a sudden, I'm starving."

I offered to take her somewhere for a real meal, but she said a snack where we were would do.

We ordered a pizza. And continued talking as we ate. About work at the hotel, about life in Sapporo. About herself. After high school, she'd gone to hotelier school for two years, then she worked at a hotel in Tokyo for two years, when she answered an ad for the new Dolphin Hotel. She was twenty-three. The move to Sapporo was good for her; her parents ran an inn near Asahikawa, about 120 kilometers away.

"It's a fairly well-known inn. They've been at it a long time," she said.

"So after doing your job here, you'll take over the family business?" I asked.

"Not necessarily," she said, pushing up the bridge of her glasses. "I haven't thought that far ahead. I just like hotel work. People coming, staying, leaving, all that. I feel comfortable there in the middle of it. It puts me at ease. After all, it's the environment I was raised in."

"So that's why," I said.

"Why what?"

"Why standing there at the front desk, you looked like you could be the spirit of the hotel."

"Spirit of the hotel?" she laughed. "What a nice thing to say! If only I really could become like that."

"I'm sure you can, if that's what you want," I smiled back.

She thought that over a while, then asked to hear my story.

"Not very interesting," I begged off, but still she wanted to hear. So I gave her a short rundown: thirty-four, divorced, writer of odd jobs, driver of used Subaru. Nothing novel.

But still she was curious about my work. So I told her about my interviews with would-be starlets, about my piece on restaurants in Hakodate.

"Sounds like fun," she said, brightening up.

"'Fun' is not the word. The writing itself is no big thing. I mean I like writing. It's even relaxing for me. But the content is a real zero. Pointless in fact."

"What do you mean?"

"I mean, for instance, you do the rounds of fifteen restaurants in one day, you eat one bite of each dish and leave the rest untouched. You think that makes sense?"

"But you couldn't very well eat everything, could you?"

"Of course not. I'd drop dead in three days if I did. And everyone would think I was an idiot. I'd get no sympathy whatsoever."

"So what choice have you got?" she said.

"I don't know. The way I see it, it's like shoveling snow. You do it because somebody's got to, not because it's fun."

"Shoveling snow, huh?" she mused.

"Well, you know, cultural snow," I said.

We drank a lot. I lost track of how much, but it was past eleven when she eyed her watch and said she had an early morning. I paid the bill and we stepped outside into flurries of snow. I offered to have my taxi drop her at her place, about ten minutes away. The snow wasn't heavy, but the road was frozen slick. She held on tight to my arm as we walked to the taxi stand. I think she was more than a little inebriated.

"You know that exposé about how the hotel got built," I asked as we made our way carefully, "do you still remember the name of the magazine? Do you remember around when the article came out?"

She knew right off. "And I'm sure it was last autumn. I didn't see the article myself, so I can't really say what it said."

We stood for five minutes in the swirling snow, waiting for a cab. She clung to my arm.

"It's been ages since I felt this relaxed," she said. The same thought occurred to me too. Maybe we really did have something in common, the two of us.

In the taxi we talked about nothing in particular. The snow and chill, her work hours, things in Tokyo. Which left me wondering what was going to happen next. One little push and I could probably sleep with her. I could feel it. Naturally I didn't know whether she wanted to sleep with me. But I understood that she wouldn't mind sleeping with me. I could tell from her eyes, how she breathed, the way she talked, even her hand movements. And of course, I knew I wouldn't mind sleeping with her. There probably wouldn't be any complications either. I'd have simply happened through and gone off. Just as she herself had said. Yet, somehow, the resolve failed me. The notion of fairness lingered somewhere in the back of my mind. She was ten years younger than me, more than a little insecure, and she'd had so much to drink she couldn't walk straight. It'd be like calling the bets with marked cards. Not fair.

Still, how much jurisdiction does fairness hold over sex? If fairness was what you wanted, your sex life would be as exciting as the algae growing in an aquarium.

The voice of reason.

The debate was still raging when the cab pulled up to her plain, reinforced-concrete apartment building and she briskly swept aside my entire dilemma. "I live with my younger sister," she said.

No further thought on the matter needed or wanted. I actually felt a bit relieved.

But as she got out, she asked if I would see her to her door. Probably no reason for concern, she apologized, but every once in a while, late at night, there'd be a strange man in the hall. I asked the driver to wait for a few minutes, then accompanied her, arm in arm, up the frozen walk. We climbed the two flights of stairs and came to her door marked 306. She opened her purse to fish around for the key. Then she smiled awkwardly and said thanks, she'd had a nice time.

As had I, I assured her.

She unlocked the door and slipped the key back into her purse. The dry snap of her purse shutting resounded down the hall. Then she looked at me directly. In her eyes it was the old geometry problem. She hesitated, couldn't decide how she wanted to say good-bye. I could see it.

Hand on the wall, I waited for her to come to some kind of decision, which didn't seem forthcoming.

"Good night," I said. "Regards to your sister."

For four or five seconds she clamped her lips tight. "The part about living with my sister," she half whispered. "It's not true. Really, I live alone."

"I know," I said.

A slow blush came over her. "How could you know?"

"Can't say why, I just did," I said.

"You're impossible, you know that?"

The driver was reading a sports newspaper when I got back to the cab. He seemed surprised when I climbed back into the taxi and asked him to take me to the Dolphin.

"You really going back?" he said with a smirk. "From the look of things, I was sure you'd be paying me and sending me on. That's the way it usually happens."

"I bet."

"When you do this job as long as I have, your intuition almost never misses."

"When you do the job that long, you're bound to miss sometime. Law of averages."

"Guess so," the cabbie answered, a bit nonplussed. "But still, kinda odd, aren'tcha pal?"

"Maybe so," I said, "maybe so."

Back in my room, I washed up before getting into bed. That was when I started to regret what I'd done—or didn't do—but soon fell fast asleep. My bouts of regret don't usually last very long.

First thing in the morning, I called down to the front desk and extended my stay for another three days. It was the off-season, so they were happy to accommodate me.

Next I bought a newspaper, headed out to a nearby Dunkin' Donuts and had two plain muffins with two large cups of coffee. You get tired of hotel breakfasts in a day. Dunkin' Donuts is just the ticket. It's cheap and you get refills on the coffee.

Then I got in a taxi and told the driver to take me to the biggest library in Sapporo. I looked up back numbers of the magazine the Dolphin Hotel article was supposed to be in and found it in the October 20th issue. I xeroxed it and took it to a nearby coffee shop to read.

The article was confusing to say the least. I had to read it several times before I understood what was going on. The reporter had tried his best to write a straightforward story, but his efforts had been no match for the complexity of the details. Talk about convolution. You had to sit down with it before the general outline emerged. The title, "Sapporo Land Dealings: Dark Hands behind Urban Redevelopment." And printed alongside, an aerial photograph of the nearly completed new Dolphin Hotel.

The long and the short of the story was this: Certain parties had bought up a large tract of land in one section of the city of Sapporo. For two years, the names of the new property holders were moved around, under the surface, in surreptitious ways. Land values grew hot for no apparent reason. With very little else to go on, the reporter started his investigation. What he turned up was this: The properties were purchased by various companies, most of which existed only on paper. The companies were fully registered, they paid taxes, but they had no offices and no employees. These paper companies were tied into still other paper companies. Whoever they were, their juggling of property ownership was truly masterful. One property bought at twenty million yen was resold at sixty million, and the next thing you knew it was sold again for two hundred million yen. If you persisted in tracing each paper company's holdings back through this maze of interconnecting fortunes, you'd find that they all ended at the same place: B INDUSTRIES, a player of some renown in real estate. Now B INDUSTRIES was a real company, with big, fashionable headquarters in the Akasaka section of Tokyo. And B INDUSTRIES happened to be, at a less-than-public level, connected to A ENTERPRISES, a massive conglomerate that encompassed railway lines, a hotel chain, a film company, food services, department stores, magazines, . . . , everything from credit agencies to damage insurance. A ENTERPRISES had a direct pipeline to certain political circles, which prompted the reporter to pursue this line of investigation further. Which is how he found out something even more interesting. The area of Sapporo that B INDUSTRIES was so busily buying up was slated for major redevelopment. Already, plans had been set in motion to build subways and to move governmental offices to the area. The greater part of the moneys for the infrastructural projects was to come from the national level. It seems that the national, prefectural, and municipal governments had worked together on the planning and agreed on a comprehensive program for the zoning and scale and budget. But when you lifted up this "cover," it was obvious that every square meter of the sites for redevelopment had been systematically bought up over the last few years. Someone was leaking information to A ENTERPRISES, and, moreover, the leak existed well before the redevelopment plans were finalized. Which also suggested that, politically speaking, the final plans had been a fait accompli probably from the very beginning.

And this is where the Dolphin Hotel entered the picture. It was the spearhead of this collusive cornering of real estate. First of all, the Dolphin Hotel secured prime real estate. Hence, A ENTERPRISES could set up offices in this new chrome-and-marble wonder as its local base of operations. The place was both a beacon and a watchtower, a visible symbol of change as well as a nerve center which could redirect the flow of people in the district. Everything was proceeding according to the most intricate plans.

That's advanced capitalism for you: The player making the maximum capital investment gets the maximum critical information in order to reap the maximum desired profit with maximum capital efficiency—and nobody bats an eye. It's just part of putting down capital these days. You demand the most return for your capital outlay. The person buying a used car will kick the tires and check under the hood, and the conglomerate putting down one hundred billion yen will check over the finer points of where that capital's going, and occasionally do a little fiddling. Fairness has got nothing to do with it. With that kind of money on the line, who's going to sit around considering abstract things like that?

Sometimes they even force hands.

For instance, suppose there's someone who doesn't want to sell. Say, a long-established shoe store. That's when the tough guys come out of the woodwork. Huge companies have their connections, and you can bet they count everyone from politicians and novelists and rock stars to out-and-out *yakuza* in their fold. So they just call on the boys with their samurai swords. The police are never too eager to deal with matters like this, especially since arrangements have already been made up at the top. It's not even corruption. That's how the system works. That's capital investment. Granted, this sort of thing isn't new to the modern age. But everything before is nothing compared to the exacting detail and sheer power and invulnerability of today's web of capitalism. And it's megacomputers that have made it all possible, with their inhuman capacity to pull every last factor and condition on the face of the earth into their net calculations. Advanced capitalism has transcended itself. Not to overstate things, financial dealings have practically become a religious activity. The new mysticism. People worship capital, adore its aura, genuflect before Porsches and Tokyo land values. Worshiping everything their shiny Porsches symbolize. It's the only stuff of myth that's left in the world.

Latter-day capitalism. Like it or not, it's the society we live in. Even the standard of right and wrong has been subdivided, made sophisticated. Within good, there's fashionable good and unfashionable good, and ditto for bad. Within fashionable good, there's formal and then there's casual; there's hip, there's cool, there's trendy, there's snobbish. Mix 'n' match. Like pulling on a Missoni sweater over Trussardi slacks and Pollini shoes, you can now enjoy hybrid styles of morality. It's the way of the world—philosophy starting to look more and more like business administration.

Although I didn't think so at the time, things were a lot simpler in 1969. All you had to do to express yourself was throw rocks at riot police. But with today's sophistication, who's in a position to throw rocks? Who's going to brave what tear gas? C'mon, that's the way it is. Everything is rigged, tied into that massive capital web, and beyond this web there's another web. Nobody's going anywhere. You throw a rock and it'll come right back at you.

The reporter had devoted a lot of energy to following the paper trail. Still, despite his outcry—or rather, all the more because of his outcry—the article curiously lacked punch. A rallying cry it wasn't. The guy just didn't seem to realize: Nothing about this was suspect. It was a *natural* state of affairs. Ordinary, the order of the day, common knowledge. Which is why nobody cared. If huge capital interests obtained information illegally and bought up property, forced a few political decisions, then clinched the deal by having *yakuza* extort a little shoe store here, maybe beat up the owner of some small-time, end-of-the-line hotel there, so what? That's life, man. The sand of the times keeps running out from under our feet. We're no longer standing where we once stood.

The reporter had done everything he could. The article was well researched, full of righteous indignation, and hopelessly untrendy.

I folded it, slipped it into my pocket, and drank another cup of coffee.

I thought about the owner of the old Dolphin. Mister Unlucky, shadowed by defeat since birth. No way he could have made the cut for this day and age.

"Untrendy!" I said out loud.

A waitress gave me a disturbed look.

I took a taxi back to the hotel.

8

From my room I rang up my ex-partner in Tokyo. Somebody I didn't know answered the phone and asked my name, then somebody else came on the line and asked my name, then finally my ex-partner came to the phone. He seemed busy. It had been close to a year since we'd spoken. Not that I'd been consciously avoiding him; I simply didn't have anything to talk to him about. I'd always liked him, and still did. But the fact was, my ex-partner was for me (and I for him) "foregone territory." Again, not that we'd pushed each other into that position. We'd just gone our own separate ways, and those two paths didn't seem to cross. No more, no less.

So how's it going? I asked him.

Well enough, he said.

I told him I was in Sapporo. He asked me if it was cold.

Yeah, it's cold, I answered.

How's work? was my next question.

Busy, his one-word response.

Not hitting the bottle too much, I hoped.

Not lately, he wasn't drinking much these days.

And was it snowing up here? His turn to ask.

Not at the moment, I kept the ball in the air.

We were almost through with our polite toss-and-catch.

"Listen," I broke in, "I've got a favor to ask." I'd done

him one a long while back. Both he and I remembered it. Otherwise, I'm not the type to go asking favors of people.

"Sure," he said with no formalities.

"You remember when we worked on that in-house newsletter for that hotel group?" I asked. "Maybe five years ago?"

"Yeah, I remember."

"Tell me, is that connection still alive?"

He gave it a moment's thought. "Can't say it's kicking, but it's alive as far as alive goes. Not impossible to warm it up if necessary."

"There was one guy who knew a lot about what was going on in the industry. I forget his name. Skinny guy, always wore this funny hat. You think you can get in contact with him?"

"I think so. What do you want to know?"

I gave him a brief rundown on the Dolphin scandal article. He took down the date the piece appeared. Then I told him about the old, tiny Dolphin that was here before the present monster Dolphin and said I'd like to know more about the following things: First, why had the new hotel kept the old Dolphin name? Second, what was the fate of the old owner? And last, were there any recent developments on the scandal front?

He jotted it all down and read it back to me over the phone.

"That's it?"

"That'll do," I said.

"Probably in a hurry, too, huh?" he asked.

"Sorry, but—"

"I'll see what I can do today. What's your number up there?"

I gave it to him.

"Talk to you later," he said and hung up.

I had a simple lunch in a café in the hotel. Then I went down to the lobby and saw that the young woman with glasses was behind the counter. I took a seat in a corner of the lobby and watched her. She was busy at work and didn't seem to notice me. Or maybe she did, but was playing cool. It didn't really matter, I guess. I liked seeing her there. As I thought to myself, I could have slept with her if I wanted to.

There are times when I need to chat myself up like that.

After I'd watched her enough, I took the elevator back to my room and read a book. The sky outside was heavy with clouds, making me feel like I was living in a poorly lit stage set. I didn't know when my ex-partner would call back, so I didn't want to go out, which left me little else to do but read. I soon finished the Jack London and started in on the Spanish Civil War.

It was a day like a slow-motion video of twilight. Uneventful, to put it mildly. The lead gray of the sky mixed ever so slowly with black, finally blending into night. Just another quality of melancholy. As if there were only two colors in the world, gray and black, shifting back and forth at regular intervals.

I dialed room service and had them send up a sandwich, which I ate a bite at a time between sips of a beer. When there's nothing to do, you do nothing slowly and intently. At seven-thirty, my ex-partner rang.

"I got ahold of the guy," he said.

"A lot of trouble?"

"Mmm, some," he said after a slight pause, making it obvious that it had been extremely difficult. "Let me run through everything with you. I suppose you could say the lid was shut pretty tight on this one. And not just shut, it was bolted down and locked away in a vault. No one had access to it. Case closed. No dirt to be dug up anymore. Seems there might have been some small irregularities in government or city hall. Nothing important, just fine tuning, as they say. Nobody knows any more than that. The Attorney's Office snooped around, but couldn't come up with anything incriminating. Lots of lines running through this one. Hot stuff. It was hard to get anything out of anyone."

"This concern of mine is personal. It won't make trouble for anyone."

"That's exactly what I told the guy."

Still holding the receiver, I reached over to the refrigerator to get another beer, and poured it into a glass.

"At the risk of sounding like your mother, a word to the wise: If you're going to pry, you're going to get hurt," my ex-partner said. "This one, it seems, is big, real big. I don't know what you've got going there, but I wouldn't get in too deep if I were you. Think of your age and standing, you ought to live out your life more peaceably. Not that I'm the best example, mind you."

"Gotcha," I said.

He coughed. I took another sip of beer.

"About the old Dolphin owner, seems the guy didn't give in until the very last, which brought him a lot of grief. Should've walked right out of there, but he just wouldn't leave. Couldn't read the big picture."

"He was that type," I said. "Very untrendy."

"He got the bad end of the business. A bunch of *yakuza* moved into the hotel and had a field day. Nothing so bad as to bother the law. They set up court in the lobby, and stared down anyone who walked into the place. You get the idea, no? Still, the guy held out for the count."

"I can see it," I said. The owner of the Dolphin Hotel was well acquainted with misery in its various forms. No small measure of misfortune was going to faze him.

"In the end, the Dolphin came out with the strangest counteroffer. Your guy told them he'd pack up shop on one condition. And you know what that was?"

"Haven't a clue," I said.

"Take a guess. Think, man, just a bit. It's the answer to one of your other questions."

"On the condition that they kept the Dolphin Hotel name. Is that it?"

"Bingo," he said. "Those were the terms, and that's what the buyers agreed to."

"But c'mon, why?"

"It's not such a bad name. 'Dolphin Hotel' sounds fair enough, as names go."

"Well, I guess," I said.

"What's more, this hotel was supposed to be the flagship for a whole new chain of hotels that A ENTERPRISES was planning. Luxury hotels, not their usual top-of-the-middle class. And they didn't have a name for it yet."

"Voilà! The Dolphin Hotel Chain."

"Right. A chain to rival the Hiltons and Hyatts of the world."

"The Dolphin Hotel Chain," I tried it out one more time. A heritage passed on, a dream unfurled. "So then what happened to the old Dolphin owner?"

"Who knows?"

I took another sip of my beer and scratched my ear with the tip of my pen.

"When he left they gave him a good chunk of money, so he could be doing almost anything. But there's no way to trace him. He was a bit player, just passing through."

"I suppose."

"And that's about it," said my ex-partner. "That's all I could find out. Nothing more. Will that do you?"

"Thanks. You've been loads of help," I said.

He cleared his throat.

"You out some dough?" I asked.

"Nah," he said. "I'll buy the guy dinner, then take him to a club in Ginza, pay his carfare home. That's not a lot, so forget about it. I can write it off as expenses anyway. Everything's deductible. Hell, my accountant tells me all the time to spend more. So don't worry about it. If you ever feel like going to a Ginza club, let me know. It'll be on me. Seeing as you've never been to any of those places."

"And what's the attraction of a Ginza club?"

"Booze, girls," he said. "Kind words from my tax accountant."

"Why don't you go with him?"

"I did, not so long ago," he said, sounding absolutely bored.

We said our good-byes and hung up.

I started to think about my ex-partner. He was the same age as me, and already he was getting a paunch. All kinds of prescription drugs in his desk. Actually concerned about who won elections. Worried about his kids' education. He was always fighting with his wife, but basically he was a real family man. He had his weaknesses to be sure, he was known to drink too much, but he was a hardworking, straightforward kind of guy. In every sense of the word.

We'd teamed up right after college and gotten on pretty well. It was a small translation business, and it gradually expanded in scale. We weren't exactly the closest of friends, but we made a fine enough partnership. We saw each other every day like that, but we never fought once. He was quiet and well-mannered, and I myself wasn't the arguing type. We had our differences, but managed to keep working together out of mutual respect. But when something unforeseen came up, we split up, perhaps at the best time too. He got started again, kept up both ends of the business, maybe better than when we were together, honestly. That is, if his client list is anything to go on. The company got bigger, he got a whole new crew. Even psychologically, he seemed a lot more secure.

More likely I was the one with problems. And I probably exerted a not-so-healthy influence over him. Which helps to explain why he was able to find his way after I left. Fawning and flattering to get the best out of his people, cracking stupid jokes with the woman who keeps the books, dutifully taking clients out to Ginza clubs no matter how dull he found it. He might have been too nervous to do that if I were still around. He was always aware of how I saw him, worried about what I would think. That was the kind of guy he was. Though, to tell the truth, I didn't pay a lot of attention to what he was doing next to me.

Good he's his own man now. In every way.

That is, by my leaving, he wasn't afraid to act his age, and he came into his own.

So where did that leave me?

At nine o'clock the phone rang. I wasn't expecting a call —nobody besides my ex-partner knew I was here—so at first the sound of the phone ringing didn't register. After four rings I picked up the receiver.

"You were watching me in the lobby today, weren't you?" It was my receptionist friend. She didn't seem angry, but then she wasn't exactly happy either. Her voice was without equivocation.

"Yes, I was," I admitted.

Silence.

"I don't like it when people watch me while I'm working. It makes me nervous and I start making mistakes. I could feel your eyes on me the whole time."

"Sorry, I won't stare at you again," I said. "I was only watching you to give myself confidence. I didn't think you'd get so nervous. From now on I'll be more careful. Where are you calling from?"

"Home," she answered. "I'm just about to take a bath and go to bed. You extended your stay, didn't you?"

"Uh-huh. Business got postponed a bit."

Another short silence.

"Do you think I'm too nervous?" she asked.

"I don't know. It's a different thing for everybody. But in any case, I promise not to stare again. I don't want to ruin your work."

She thought it over a second, then we said good night.

I hung up the phone, took a bath, and stretched out on the sofa reading until eleven-thirty. Then I dressed and stepped out into the hall. I walked it from one end to the other. It was like a maze. At the farthest recess was the staff elevator, a little hidden from view, next to the emergency staircase. If you followed the signs pointing past the guest rooms, you came to an elevator marked FREIGHT ONLY. I stood before it, noting that the elevator was stopped on the ground floor. No one seemed to be using it. From speakers in the ceiling came the strains of "Love Is Blue." Paul Mauriat.

I pressed the button. The elevator roused itself and started to ascend. The digital display registered the floors—1, 2, 3, 4, 5, 6—slowly but surely advancing, to the rhythm of the music. If someone was in the elevator, I could always plead ignorance. It was a mistake guests were probably making all the time. 11, 12, 13, 14—and rising steadily. I took one step back, dug my hands in my pockets, and waited for the doors to open.

15—the count stopped. There was a moment's pause, and not a sound, then the door slid open. The elevator was empty.

Awfully quiet, I thought to myself. A far cry from that wheezing contraption in the old hotel. I got in and pressed 16. The door shut, soundlessly, again, I felt a slight movement, and the door opened. The sixteenth floor. Bright, fully lit, with "Love Is Blue" flowing out of the ceiling. No darkness, no musty odor. For good measure, I walked the entire floor from end to end. It proved to have the exact same layout as the fifteenth. Same winding hallways, same interminable array of guest rooms, same vending machine alcove midway along, same bank of guest elevators.

The carpet was deep red, rich with soft pile. You couldn't hear your own footsteps. In fact, everything was resoundingly hushed. There was only "A Summer Place," probably by Percy Faith. After getting to the end, I turned around and walked back halfway to where the guest elevators were and took one down to the fifteenth floor. Then I went through the whole routine all over again. Staff elevator to the sixteenth floor, where there was the same, perfectly ordinary, well-lit floor as before. And it was still "A Summer Place."

I gave up and went down to the fifteenth floor again, had two sips of brandy and hit the sack.

At dawn, the black changed back to gray. It was snowing. Well now, I thought, what do I do today?

As usual, there wasn't anything to do.

I walked in the snow to Dunkin' Donuts, chewed on a couple doughnuts, and read the morning paper as I sipped my coffee. I skimmed through an article about local elections. I looked through the movie listings. Nothing I particularly wanted to see, but there was this one film featuring a former junior high school classmate of mine. A teen angst movie by the title of *Unrequited Love*, with an up-and-coming teenage actress and an up-and-coming teenage singer. I could guess the sort of role my classmate would play: handsome, young teacher with his wits about him, tall, slim, all-around athlete, girls swooning all over him. Naturally the lead girl has a crush on him. So she spends Sunday baking cookies and takes them to his apartment. But there's a boy who's got his eyes on her. Average boy, kind of shy, . . . Typical. I could see the movie without seeing it.

When this classmate of mine became an actor, I went to see his first few films, partly out of curiosity. But before long I didn't bother. Every movie was straight out of the same mold, and every role he had was basically the same: tall, handsome, athletic, clean-cut, often a student at first, then later teacher or doctor or young elite salaryman, adored by the girls around him. He had perfect teeth, a charming smile. Very suave. Though still not anything you'd want to pay money to see. Now I'm not a snob who only goes to see Fellini or Tarkovsky. No, not by any means. But this guy's films were the pits. Low-budget productions with cliché plots and mediocre dialogue, movies you could tell even the directors didn't care about.

Although, come to think of it, in real life the guy had been pretty much like the parts he played. He was nice enough, but who actually knew anything about him? We were in the same class during junior high school, and once we shared the same lab table on a science experiment. We were friendly. But even back then he was too nice to be real—just like in his movies. Girls were already falling all over him. If he talked to them, their eyes would go moist. If he lit a Bunsen burner with those graceful hands of his, it was like the opening ceremony of the Olympics. None of the girls ever noticed I was alive.

His grades were good too, always first or second in the class. Kind, sincere, friendly. It didn't matter what kind of clothes he wore, he always looked neat and clean. Even when he took a leak, there was something elegant about him. And there's hardly a male around who looks elegant when pissing. Of course, he was good at sports, active in school government. There was talk that he had a thing going with the most popular girl in the class, but no one knew for sure. All the teachers thought he was great, and on Parents' Day all the mothers would be enchanted with him too. He was just that type. Though, like I said, it was hard to know what the guy was thinking.

His life was practically right out of the movies.

Why the hell would I pay money to go see a movie like that?

I tossed the newspaper into the trash and walked back to the hotel in the snow. In the lobby, I glanced at the front desk, but my friend was nowhere to be seen. I went over to the video game corner and played a couple rounds of Pacman and Galaxy. Nerve-racking. Games like those bring out the aggression in people. But they do kill time.

After that I went back to my room and read.

The day was impossible to get a handle on. When I got tired of reading, I looked out the window at the snow. It snowed the entire day. I found it inspiring that a sky could actually snow this much. At twelve o'clock I went down to the café for lunch. Then I returned to my room and read and watched the snow.

But the day wasn't a complete loss. Around four o'clock, while I lay in bed reading, there was a knock on the door. It was my receptionist friend, standing there in glasses and light blue blazer. Without waiting for me to open the door any wider, she slipped into the room like a shadow and shut the door.

"Hotel policy. If they catch me here, I'm fired," she said quickly.

She looked around the room and sat down on the sofa, straightening the hem of her skirt at her knees. Then she breathed a sigh. "I'm on my break now," she said.

"I'm going to have a beer. Want something to drink?" I asked.

"No thanks. I don't have too much time. You've been holed up inside here all day, haven't you?"

"I didn't have anything special to do. I'm just whiling away the hours, reading and watching the snow," I said.

"What's the book?"

"It's about the Spanish Civil War. The whole history, from beginning to end. Full of innuendo." To be sure, the Spanish Civil War was rich in historical suggestion. It was a real old-fashioned war.

"Listen, don't take this wrong," she interrupted me.

"Don't take what wrong?" I asked.

Pause.

"You mean, your coming to my room?" I asked.

"Uh-huh."

I sat down on the edge of the bed, beer in hand. "Don't worry. I was surprised to see you standing at my door, but pleasantly surprised. I'm happy for some company. It's been pretty boring."

She stood up and in the middle of the room removed her blazer. She draped it over the back of a chair, carefully so it wouldn't wrinkle. Then she walked over to me at the edge of the bed and sat down, her legs neatly aligned. Without the blazer, she seemed vulnerable, defenseless. I put my arm around her and she rested her head on my shoulder. Her white blouse was pressed crisply, and she smelled nice. We stayed in this position for five minutes. Me just holding her, her just sitting there, head on my shoulder, eyes closed, breathing softly, almost as if she were asleep. Out in the street, the snow kept falling, without end, swallowing all sound.

She was tired. She needed somewhere to roost. I was the nearest tree branch. I understood. It seemed unreasonable, unfair, that a woman so young and beautiful should be so exhausted. Of course, it was neither unreasonable nor unfair. Exhaustion pays no mind to age or beauty. Like rain and earthquakes and hail and floods.

Then she raised her head, stood up, and slipped her blazer back on. She walked over to the sofa, sat down, and fiddled with the ring on her pinkie. In her uniform, she seemed stiff and distant.

I kept sitting on the edge of the bed.

"You know that weird experience you had on the sixteenth floor?" I began, "did you do anything special or was there something out of the ordinary? Like before you got into the elevator, or while you were going up?"

She cocked her head quizzically. "Hmm . . . let me think. No, I don't think so. But I can't really remember."

"There wasn't a hint of anything odd?"

"Everything was like always," she shrugged. "There was nothing unusual at all. And, really, it was a completely normal elevator ride, but when the door opened everything was pitch black. That's all."

"I see," I said. "How about dinner somewhere tonight?"

She shook her head. "I'm sorry. I've made other plans for tonight."

"How about tomorrow?"

"I have swim club tomorrow."

"Swim club?" I said, smiling. "Did you know they had swim clubs in ancient Egypt?"

"No," she said, "but I find it awfully hard to believe, don't you?"

"No, it's the truth. I learned that from some research I had to do once," I explained. A token from the department of useless facts.

She looked at her watch and got up. "Well, thanks," she said. And slid out the door, as noiselessly as when she entered. So much for my only handle on the day. It left me wondering how the ancient Egyptians filled their days, what little pleasures they enjoyed as they whiled their weary way to death. Learning to swim, wrapping mummies. And the sum accomplishment of that you call a civilization.

9/

By eleven o'clock that night I was out of things to do. I'd pretty well done everything. I'd trimmed my nails, taken a bath, cleaned my ears, even watched the news on TV. Did push-ups, sit-ups, stretched, ate dinner, finished my book. But I wasn't sleepy. I thought about checking out the staff elevator one more time, but it was too early for that. I had to wait until after midnight for the comings and goings of the employees to fall off.

In the end I decided to go up to the lounge on the twenty-sixth floor. I nursed a martini while gazing out blankly at the flecks of white swirling down through the void. I thought about the ancient Egyptians, tried to imagine what kind of lives they led. Who were the ones that joined the swim club? No doubt, it was the Pharaoh's clan, aristocrats, the upper classes. Trendy, jet-set ancient Egyptians. They probably had their own private section of the Nile or built special pools to teach their chic strokes in. Complete with handsome, likable swim instructor, like my friend the movie star, who'd say things like, "Excellent, Your Highness, only perhaps Thou might extend Thy right arm a little further for the crawl."

The sky-blue waters of the Nile, the scintillating sun (thatched cabañas and palm fronds a must), spear-bearing soldiers to beat back the crocodiles and commoners, swaying reeds, the Pharaoh's crowd. Princes, sure, but what about princesses? Did women learn to swim? Cleopatra, for instance. In her younger days looking like Jodie Foster, would she have swooned over my classmate, the swim instructor? Most likely. That's what he was there for.

Somebody ought to make a film like that. I, for one, would pay to see it.

No, the swim instructor couldn't be of poor birth. He'd be the son of the King of Israel or Assyria or somewhere like that, captured in battle and dragged back to Egypt, a slave. But he doesn't lose an iota of his good-naturedness, even if he is a slave. That's where he differs from Charlton Heston or Kirk Douglas. He flashes his brilliant white teeth in a smile and takes a leak, aristocratically. Then, standing on the banks of the Nile, he takes out a ukulele and bursts into a chorus of "Rock-a-Hula Baby." Obviously he's the only man for the part.

Then, one day, the Pharaoh and entourage happen by. The swim instructor's out scything reeds when he sees a barge capsize. Without the least hesitation, he dives into the river, swims a magnificent crawl out and rescues a little girl and races the crocodiles back to shore. All with powerful grace. As gracefully as he'd lit the Bunsen burner in science class. The Pharaoh is most impressed and thinks, that's it, I'll get this youth to teach my princes how to swim. The previous swim instructor had proven insubordinate and was thrown into the bottomless pit just the week before. Thus my classmate becomes the Royal Swim Instructor. And he's so likable everyone adores him. At night, the ladies-in-waiting anoint their bodies with oils and perfumes and hasten to his bed. The princes and princesses are all devoted to him.

Cut to a spectacle scene on the order of *The Bathing Beauty* or *The King and I*. My classmate and the princes and princesses in a grand synchronized swim routine in celebration of the Pharaoh's birthday. The Pharaoh is overjoyed, which further boosts the youth's stock. Still, he doesn't let it go to his head. He's a paragon of humility. He smiles the same as ever, and pisses elegantly. When a lady-in-waiting slips under the covers with him, he spends a full one hour on foreplay, brings her all the way to climax, then afterward strokes her hair and says, "You're the best." He's a good guy.

For a moment, I tried to picture sleeping with an Egyptian court lady, but the image wouldn't gel. The more I forced it, the more everything turned into 20th Century Fox's *Cleopatra*. Very epic. Elizabeth Taylor, Richard Burton, Rex Harrison. The "Hollywood Exotic" mode—olive-skinned, long-legged slave girls waving long-handled fans over Liz, who strikes various glamorous poses to seduce my classmate. A specialty of the Egyptian femme fatale.

But the Jodie Foster Cleopatra has fallen head-over-heels for him.

Mediocre fare, admittedly, but that's the movies.

He's pretty much gone on Jodie Cleopatra, too.

But he's not the only one who's crazy about Jodie Cleopatra. There's a dark, dark Arabian prince who's burning with passion for her. He's so in love with her that just thinking about her is enough to make him dance. The role is tailor-made for Michael Jackson. He's crossed the Arabian sands all the way to Egypt for her love. We see him dancing around the caravan camp fire, shaking a tambourine, singing "Billie Jean." His eyes gleam in the starlight. So of course there ensues a major face-off between Michael and my classmate, our swim instructor. A rivalry between lovers. . . .

I'd gotten this far when the bartender came over and said sorry, closing time. It was a quarter past twelve; I was the last customer in the lounge, glasses were already drying on towels, the bartender almost through cleaning up. Had I been tweaking this nonsense all this time? What an idiot! I signed the bill, downed the last of my martini, and walked out, shuffling my way to the elevators, hands useless in my pockets.

Still, wasn't Jodie Cleopatra obliged to marry her younger brother? My dream scenario had a life of its own. I couldn't get it out of my head. The scenes kept on coming. Her shiftless and crooked younger brother. Now who'd be good for the part? Woody Allen? Gimme a break. This isn't a comedy! We don't need a court jester cracking stupid jokes and hitting himself over the head with a plastic mallet.

We'll work on the brother later. The Pharaoh's got to go to Laurence Olivier. Always got a migraine, always pressing fingers to his temples. Throws anyone who gets on his nerves into the bottomless pit or makes them swim the Nile with the crocs. Intelligent, cruel, and high-strung. Digs out people's eyes and throws the poor souls into the desert.

Oh, the casting, the casting, and then the elevator arrived. The door opened, ever so silently. I got in and pressed 15. And went back to my Egyptian movie. Not that I really wanted to, but there was no way to stop it.

The scene changes to the desert wastelands. Unbeknownst to all, in a cave in the wilderness lives a solitary prophet-recluse, cast out of society by the Pharaoh. With his eyes gouged out, he has miraculously survived his long trek across the desert. A sheepskin shields him from the merciless sun. He dwells in total darkness, eating locusts and wild grasses. He gains inner vision and sees the future. He sees the fall of the Pharaoh, Egypt's twilight, a world shifting on its foundations.

It's the Sheep Man, I think. *The Sheep Man?*

The elevator door opened silently, and I exited without thought. The Sheep Man? In ancient Egypt? Isn't this all meaningless pastiche anyway? I reasoned these things out, standing, hands in my pockets, in total darkness.

Total darkness?

Only then did I notice the complete absence of light. Not one speck of light. As the elevator door shut behind me, I was enveloped in lacquer black darkness. I couldn't see my own hands. The Muzak was gone too. No "Love Is Blue," no "A Summer Place." And the air was chill and moldy.

I stood there alone, abandoned in utter nothingness.

10

The darkness was deathly absolute.

I could not distinguish one shape or object. I could not see my own body. I could not get any sense of anything *out there*. I was in a great black vacuum.

I was reduced to pure concept. My flesh had dissolved; my form had dissipated. I floated in space. Liberated of my corporeal being, but without dispensation to go anywhere else. I was adrift in the void. Somewhere across the fine line separating nightmare from reality.

I stood. But I could not move. My arms and legs felt paralyzed. I was at the bottom of the sea, the pressure dense, crushing, inexorable. Dead silence strained against my eardrums. The darkness was without reprieve. No mental adjustment could make it less absolute. It was impenetrable—black painted over black painted over black.

Unconsciously I groped around in my pockets. On the right was my wallet and key holder, on the left my room card-key and handkerchief and small change. All useless now. Now if I hadn't quit smoking, I'd at least be carrying a lighter or some matches. As if that would make a difference. I pulled my hands out of my pockets and reached out to touch a wall. I found one all right, alarmingly slick and chill, not exactly a wall you'd expect to find in the climate-controlled Dolphin Hotel.

Easy now. Think it through.

Okay, this is exactly what happened to my receptionist friend. I am merely retracing her steps. There is no need for alarm. She survived; I will too. Calm down; do what she did. Now, something funny is definitely going on here. Maybe it has something to do with me? With the old Dolphin Hotel? That's why I came here, isn't it? Yes. So go through the motions and finish the job.

Scared?

Damned straight.

I was scared, scared witless. I felt naked. Cast into the midst of violent particle drifts of intense black, thrashing about me like blind eels. I was overcome with my helplessness. My shirt was drenched in cold sweat, my throat felt raspy, dry.

Where the hell was I? I wasn't *here*, at l'Hôtel Dauphin, that's for sure. I had crossed a line and I had entered this world in limbo. I shut my eyes and breathed deeply.

I know it sounds ridiculous, but I found myself longing for "Love Is Blue." The sound of Muzak—any Muzak—would give me strength. I'd have settled for Richard Clayderman. Or Los Indios Tabajaras, José Feliciano, Julio Iglesias, Sergio Mendes, The Partridge Family, 1910 Fruitgum Company, Mitch Miller and chorus, Andy Williams in duet with Al Martino . . . , anything.

But enough. My mind went blank. From fear? Could fear lurk in empty space?

Michael Jackson dancing around the camp fire with his tambourine singing "Billie Jean." The camels entranced by the song.

I must be getting a little confused.

I must be getting a little confused.

Seems like an echo inside my head. An echo inside my head.

I took another deep breath, and tried to drive meaningless images from my mind.

I braced myself and turned right, arms extended. But my

legs would not move, as if they were not mine. The muscles and nerves would not respond. I was sending the signals, but nothing was happening. I was immersed in fluid darkness. I was trapped, I was immobilized.

The darkness was without end. I was being propelled toward the center of the earth. I would never resurface. Think of something else, kid. Think, or fear will take over your whole being. How about that Egyptian film scenario? Where were we? The Sheep Man enters. Move on from desert wilderness back to palace of the Pharaoh. Tinsel towers aglitter with the treasures of Africa. Nubian slaves everywhere. Dead center, the Pharaoh. Music, by Miklos Rozsa. The Pharaoh is pissed off. *Something is rotten in the state of Egypt*, he thinks. *I smell a plot in the palace. I can feel it in my bones. I must set it right.*

One foot at a time, I stepped forward, carefully. That was when it occurred to me. What my receptionist friend had been able to do. Amazing! Thrown into some crazy black hole and she's able to go check out everything for herself.

And now she's wearing her black racing swimsuit, doing her laps at the swim club. And who's there but my movie star classmate. Sure enough, she goes gaga at the sight of him. He gives her pointers on the right arm extension for the crawl. She gazes at him, her eyes aglow. And that very night, she slips into his bed. I'm crushed. I can't let this happen. She doesn't know a thing. Oh, he's nice and kind all right. He says sweet things and he gets her juices going. But that's as far as the kindness goes. That's just foreplay.

The hallway bent to the right.

Just like she said.

But she's in bed with my classmate. Gently he takes off her clothes, lavishing compliments on her about each part of her body. And he's being sincere. Great, just great. Got to hand it to the guy. But little by little the anger mounts inside me. This was wrong!

The hallway bends to the right.

I turned right, feeling my way along the wall. Far off up

ahead there was a faint light. As if filtered through layers and layers of veils.

Just like she said.

My classmate is kissing her all over. Slowly, with such finesse, from the nape of her neck to her shoulders to her breasts. Camera angle shows his face and her back. Then the camera dollies around to reveal her face. But it isn't my receptionist friend, no. It's Kiki! My high-class call-girl friend with the world's most beautiful ears, who was with me at the old Dolphin. Kiki, who disappeared without a word, without a trace. And here she is, sleeping with my classmate.

It's a real scene from a real movie. Every shot and cut according to plan. Maybe a little too planned—it looks so commonplace. They are making love in an apartment, the light shining in through the blinds. Kiki. What's she doing here? Time and space must be getting out of whack.

Time and space must be getting out of whack.

I kept walking toward the light. As my feet took the lead, the image in my head evaporated.

FADE OUT.

I proceeded along the wall. No more thinking. Concentrate on moving feet forward. Carefully, surely. The dim light ahead begins to leak and spread, from a door. But I still don't know where I am. And I can barely tell that it's a door. It isn't like anything I saw when I made the rounds earlier. On the door, a metal plate, a number engraved on it. I can't read the number. It's dark, the plate's tarnished. But, at the very least, I *know* this isn't the Dolphin Hotel. The doors are different. The air is wrong too. That smell, what is it? Like old papers. The light sways from time to time. Candlelight.

I thought about my receptionist friend again. I should have slept with her when I could have. Who knew if I'd ever return to the real world? Would I ever get another chance to see her? I was jealous of the real world and her swim club. Or maybe I wasn't jealous. Maybe it was a matter of regret, an overblown, distorted sense of regret, although maybe what it came down to, plunged in this darkness, was I was jealous. It'd been years. I'd forgotten what it felt like to be jealous. It's such a personal emotion. Maybe I was feeling jealous now. Maybe, but toward a swim club?

This is stupid.

I swallowed. It sounded like a metal baseball bat striking a barrel drum. That was saliva?

Then a strange vibration, a half sound. I had to knock. That's right, like she said. I summoned up my courage and let go with a tiny rap. Something that didn't necessarily demand to be heard. But it was a huge, booming noise. Cold and heavy as death.

I held my breath.

Silence. Just like with her. How long it lasted, I couldn't tell. It might have been five seconds, it might have been a minute. Time wasn't fixed. It wavered, stretched, shrank. Or was it me that wavered, stretched, and shrank in the silence? I was warped in the folds of time, like a reflection in a fun house mirror.

Then that sound. A rustling, amplified, like fabric. Something getting up from the floor. Then footsteps. Coming toward me. The scuffling of slippers. Something, but not human. Like she said. Something from another reality—a reality that existed *here*.

There was no escape. I did not move. Sweat streamed down my back. Yet, as the footsteps grew closer and closer, unaccountably my fears began to subside. It's all right, I said to myself. Whatever it is, it is not evil. I knew. I knew there was nothing to fear. I could let it happen.

I felt aswirl with warm secretions. I gripped the doorknob, I shut my eyes, I held my breath. You're all right, you're fine. I heard a tremendous heartbeat through the darkness. It was my own. I was enveloped in it, I was a part of it. There was nothing to fear. It was all connected.

The footsteps halted. They were beside me. *It* was beside me. My eyes were shut. *It is beginning to come together*. I knew. I knew I was connected to this place. The banks of the

Nile and the perfumed Nubian court ladies and Kiki and the Dolphin Hotel and rock 'n' roll, everything, everything, everything! An implosion of time and physical form. Old light, old sound, old voices.

"Beenwaitingforyou. Beenwaitingforages. Comeonin."

I knew who it was without opening my eyes.

11

We faced each other across a small table, talking. The table was very old, round, set with one candle in the middle. The candle had been stuck directly onto a saucer. And that was the entire inventory of furnishings in the room. There weren't any chairs. We sat on piles of books.

It was the Sheep Man's room.

Narrow and cramped. The walls and ceiling had the feeling of the old Dolphin Hotel, but it wasn't the old hotel either. At the far end of the room was a window, boarded up from inside. Boarded up a long time ago, if the rusty nails and gray dust in the cracks of the boards were any indication. The room was a rectangular box. No lights. No closet. No bath. No bed. He must've slept on the floor, wrapped in his sheep costume.

There was barely enough room to walk. The floor was littered with yellowing old books and newspapers and scrapbooks filled with clippings. Some were worm-eaten, falling apart at their bindings. All, from what I could tell, having to do with the history of sheep in Hokkaido. All, probably, from the archive at the old Dolphin Hotel. The sheep reference room, which the owner's father, the Sheep Professor, pretty much lived in. What ever became of him?

The Sheep Man looked at me across the flickering candle

flame. Behind him, his disproportionately enormous shadow played over a grimy wall.

"Beenalongtime," he spoke from behind his mask. "Let's-ussee, youthinnerorwhat?"

"Yeah, I might have lost some weight."

"Sotellus, what'stheworldoutside? Wedon'tgetmuchnews, notinhere."

I crossed my legs and shook my head. "Same as ever. Nothing worth mentioning. Everything's getting more complicated. Everything's speeding up. No, nothing's really new."

The Sheep Man nodded. "Nextwarhasn'tbegunyet, wetakeit?"

Which was the Sheep Man's last war? I wasn't sure. "Not yet," I said.

"Butsoonerorlateritwill," he voiced, uninflected, folding his mitted hands. "Youbetterwatchout. War'sgonnacome, nothreewaysaboutit. Markourwords. Can'ttrustpeople. Won'tdoanygood. They'llkillyoueverytime. They'llkilleachother. They'llkilleveryone."

The Sheep Man's fleece was dingy, the wool stiff and greasy. His mask looked bad too, like something patched together at the last minute. The poor light in the damp room didn't help and maybe my memory was wrong, but it wasn't just the costume. The Sheep Man was worn-out. Since the last time I'd seen him four years ago, he'd shrunk. His breathing came harder, more disturbing to the ears, like a stopped-up pipe.

"Thoughtyou'dgetheresooner," said the Sheep Man. "Webeenwaiting, allthistime. Meanwhile, somebodyelsecame-'round. Wethought, maybe, butwasn'tyou. Howdoyoulikethat? Justanybody, comewanderinginhere. But anyway, was-expectingyousooner."

I shrugged my shoulders. "I always thought I would come back, I guess. I knew I had to, but I didn't have it together. I dreamed about it. About the Dolphin Hotel, I mean. Dreamed about it all the time. But it took a while to make up my mind to come back."

"Triedtoputitoutofmind?"

"I guess so, yes," I said. Then I looked at my hands in the flickering candlelight. A draft was coming in from somewhere. "In the beginning I thought I should try to forget what I could forget. I wanted a life completely dissociated from this place."

"Becauseyourfrienddied?"

"Yes. Because my friend died."

"Butyoucameback," said the Sheep Man.

"Yes, I came back," I said. "I couldn't get this place out of my mind. I tried to forget things, but then something else would pop up. So it didn't matter whether I liked it or not, I sort of knew I belonged here. I didn't really know what that meant either, but I knew it anyway. In my dreams about this place, I was . . . part of everything. Someone was crying for me here. Someone wanted me. That's why I came back. What *is* this place anyway?"

The Sheep Man looked me hard in the face and shook his head. "'Fraidwedon'tknowmuch. It'srealbig, it'srealdark. All-weknow'sthisroom. Beyondhere, wedon'tknow. Butanyway, you'rehere, somust'vebeentime. Timeyoufoundyourwayhere. Wayweseeit, atleast. . . ." The Sheep Man paused to ruminate. "Maybesomebody'scryingforyou, throughthisplace. Somebodywhoknewyou, knewyou'dbeheadinghereanyway. Likeabird, comingbacktothenest. . . . Butlet'sussayitdifferent. Ifyouweren'tcomingbackhere, thisplacewouldn'texist." The Sheep Man wrung his mitts. The shadow on the wall exaggerated every gesture on a grand scale, a dark spirit poised to seize me from above.

Like a bird returning to the nest? Well, it did have that feel about it. Maybe my life had been following this unspoken course all this time.

"Sonow, yourturn," said the Sheep Man. "Tellus'bout-yourself. Thishere'syourworld. Noneedstandingonceremony. Takeyourtime. Talkallyouwant."

There in the dim light, staring at the shadow on the wall, I poured out the story of my life. It had been so long, but slowly, like melting ice, I released each circumstance. How I managed to support myself. Yet never managed to go anywhere. Never went anywhere, but aged all the same. How nothing touched me. And I touched nothing. How I'd lost track of what mattered. How I worked like a fool for things that didn't. How it didn't make a difference either way. How I was losing form. The tissues hardening, stiffening from within. Terrifying me. How I barely made the connection to this place. This place I didn't know but had this feeling that I was part of. . . . This place that maybe I knew instinctively I belonged to. . . .

The Sheep Man listened to everything without saying a word. He might even have been asleep. But when I was through talking, he opened his eyes and spoke softly. "Don'tworry. Youreallyarepartofhere, really. Alwayshavebeen, alwayswillbe. Itallstartshere, itallendshere. Thisisyourplace. It'stheknot. It'stiedtoeverything."

"Everything?"

"Everything. Thingsyoulost. Thingsyou'regonnalose. Everything. Here'swhereitalltiestogether."

I thought about this. I couldn't make any sense of it. His words were too vague, fuzzy. I had to get him to explain. But he was through talking. Did that mean explanation was impossible? He shook his woolly head silently. His sewed-on ears flapped up and down. The shadow on the wall quaked. So massively I thought the wall would collapse.

"It'llmakesense. Soonenough, it'llallmakesense. Whenthetimecomes, you'llunderstand," he assured me.

"But tell me one thing then," I said. "Why did the owner of the Dolphin Hotel insist on the name for the new hotel?"

"Hediditforyou," said the Sheep Man. "Theyhadtokeepthename, soyou'dcomeback. Otherwise, youwouldn'tbehere. Thebuildingchanges, theDolphinHotelstays. Likewesaid, it'sallhere. Webeenwaitingforyou."

I had to laugh. "For me? They called this place the Dolphin Hotel just for me?"

"Darntootin'. Thatsostrange?"

I shook my head. "No, not strange, just amazing. It's so

out-of-the-blue, it's like it's not real."

"Oh, it'sreal," said the Sheep Man softly. "RealastheDolphinHotelsigndownstairs'sreal. Howrealdoyouwant?" He tapped the tabletop with his fingers, and the flame of the candle shuddered. "Andwe'rereallyhere. Webeenwaiting. Foryou. Wemadearrangements. Wethoughtofeverything. Everything, soyoucouldreconnect, witheveryone."

I gazed into the dancing candle flame. This was too much to believe. "I don't get it. Why would you go to all the trouble? For *me*?"

"Thisisyourworld," said the Sheep Man matter-of-factly. "Don'tthinktoohardaboutit. Ifyou'reseekingit, it'shere. Theplacewasputhereforyou. Special. Andweworkedspeciallhardtogeyoubackhere. Tokeepthingsfromfallingapart. Tokeepyoufromforgetting."

"So I really am part of something here?"

"'Courseyoubelonghere. Everybody'sallinhere, together. Thisisyourworld," repeated the Sheep Man.

"So who are you? And what are you doing here?"

"WearetheSheepMan," he chortled. "Can'tyoutell? Weweartthesheepskin, andweliveinaworldhumanscan'tsee. Wewerechasedintothewoods. Longtimeago. Long, longtimeago. Canhardlyrememberwhatwewerebefore. Butsincethenwebeenkeepingoutofsight. Easytodo, ifthat'swhatyouwant. Thenwecamehere, tolookaftertheplace. It'ssomewhere, outoftheelements. Thewoodsgotwildanimals. Knowwhatwemean?"

"Sure," I said.

"Weconnectthings. That'swhatwedo. Likeaswitchboard, weconnectthings. Here'stheknot. Andwetieit. We'rethelink. Don'twantthingstogetlost, sowetietheknot. That'sourduty. Switchboardduty. Youseekforit, weconnect, yougotit. Getit?"

"Sort of," I said.

"So," resumed the Sheep Man, "sonowyouneedus. Else, youwouldn'tbehere. Youlostthings, soyou'relost. Youlostyourway. Yourconnectionscomeundone. Yougotconfused, thinkyougotnoties. Buthere'swhereitalltiestogether."

I thought about what he said. "You're probably right. As you say, I've lost and I'm lost and I'm confused. I'm not anchored to anything. Here's the only place I feel like I belong to." I broke off and stared at my hands in the candle-light. "But the other thing, the person I hear crying in my dreams, is there a connection here? I think I can feel it. You know, if I could, I think I want to pick up where I left off, years ago. That must be what I need you here for."

The Sheep Man was silent. He didn't seem to have more to say. The silence weighed heavily, as if we'd been plunged to the bottom of a very deep pit. It bore down on me, pinning my thoughts under its gravity. From time to time, the candle sputtered. The Sheep Man turned his gaze toward the flame. Still the silence continued, interminably. Then slowly, the Sheep Man raised his eyes toward me.

"We'lldowhatwecan," said the Sheep Man. "Though-we'regettingoninyears. Hopewestillgotthestuffinus, hehheh. We'lltry, butnoguarantees, nopromisesyou'regonnabe-happy." He picked at a snag in his fleece and searched for words. "Wejustcan'tsay. Inthatotherworld, mightnotbeany-placeanymore, notanywhereforyou. You'restartingtolook-prettyfixed, maybetoofixedtopryloose. You'renotsoyoung-anymore, either, yourself."

"So where does that leave me?"

"Youlostlotsofthings. Lostlotsofpreciousthings. Notany-body'sfault. Buteachtimeyoulostsomething, youdroppeda-wholestringofthingswithit. Nowwhy? Why'dyouhavetogo-anddothat?"

"I don't know."

"Hardtododifferent. Yourfate, orsomethinglikefate. Tendencies."

"Tendencies?"

"Tendencies. Yougottendencies. Soevenifyoudidevery-thingoveragain, yourwholelife, yougottendenciestodojust-whatyoudid, alloveragain."

"Yes, but where does that leave me?"

"Likewesaid, we'lldowhatwecan. Trytoreconnectyou,

towhatyouwant," said the Sheep Man. "Butwecan'tdoit-alone. Yougottaworktoo. Sitting'snotgonnadoit, thinking's-notgonnadoit."

"So what do I have to do?"

"Dance," said the Sheep Man. "Yougottadance. Aslong-asthemusicplays. Yougotta dance. Don'teventhinkwhy. Start-tothink, yourfeetstop. Yourfeetstop, wegetstuck. Wegetstuck, you'restuck. Sodon'tpayanymind, nomatterhowdumb. You-gottakeepthestep. Yougottalimberup. Yougottaloosenwhat-youbolteddown. Yougottauseallyougot. Weknowyou're tired, tiredandscared. Happenstoeveryone, okay? Justdon't-letyourfeetstop."

I looked up and gazed again at the shadow on the wall.

"Dancingiseverything," continued the Sheep Man. "Danceintip-topform. Dancesoitallkeepsspinning. Ifyoudo-that, wemightbeabletodosomethingforyou. Yougottadance. Aslongasthemusicplays."

Dance. As long as the music plays, echoed my mind.

"Hey, what is *this world* you keep talking about? You say that if I stay fixed in place, I'm going to be dragged from *that world* to *this world*, or something like that. But isn't this world meant for me? Doesn't it exist for me? So what's the problem? Didn't you say this place really exists?"

The Sheep Man shook his head. His shadow shook a hurricane. "Here'sdifferent. You'renotready, notforhere. Here's-toodark, toobig. Hardtoexplain. Likewesaid, wedon't-knowmuch. Butit'sreal, allright. Youandustalkinghere'sreal-ity. Butit'snottheonlyonereality. Lotsofrealitiesoutthere. Wejustchosethisone, because, well, wedon'tlikewar. Andwe-hadnothingtolose. Butyou, youstillgotwarmth. Sohere'stoo-cold. Nothingtoeat. Nottheplaceforyou."

No sooner had the Sheep Man mentioned the cold than I noticed the temperature in the room. I burrowed my hands in my pockets, shivering.

"Youfeelit, don'tyou?" asked the Sheep Man.

Yes, I nodded.

"Time'srunningout," warned the Sheep Man. "Themoretimepasses, thecolderitgets. Youbetterbegoing."

"Wait, one last thing. I guess you've been around all this time, except I haven't seen you. Just your shadow everywhere. You're just sort of always *there.*"

The Sheep Man traced an indefinite shape with his finger. "That'sright. We'rehalfshadow, we'reinbetween."

"But I still don't understand," I said. "Here I can see your face and body clearly. I couldn't before, but now I can. Why?"

"Youlostsomuch," he bleated softly, "thatnowyoucanseeus."

"Do you mean . . . ?" And bracing myself, I asked the big question: "Is this the world of the dead?"

"No," replied the Sheep Man. His shoulders swayed as he took a breath. "Youandus, we'reliving. Breathing. Talking."

"I don't get it."

"Dance," he said. "It'stheonlyway. Wishwecouldexplainthingsbetter. Butwetoldyouallwecould. Dance. Don'tthink. Dance. Danceyourbest, likeyourlifedependedonit. Yougottadance."

The temperature was falling. I suddenly seemed to remember this chill. A bone-piercing, damp chill. Long ago and far away. But where? My mind was paralyzed. Fixed and rigid.

Fixed and rigid.

"Youbettergo," urged the Sheep Man. "Stayhere, you'llfreeze. Butifyouneedus, we'rehere. Youknowwheretofind us."

The Sheep Man escorted me out to the bend in the hallway, dragging his feet along, *shuffle . . . shuffle . . . shuffle.* We said good-bye. No handshake, no special salutations. Just good-bye, and then we parted into the darkness. He returned to his tiny room and I continued to the elevator. I pressed the call button. When the elevator arrived, the door opened without a sound. Bright light spilled out over me into the hallway. I got in and collapsed against the wall. The door closed. I did not move.

Well . . . , I thought to myself. Well what? Nothing came after. My mind was a huge vacuum. A vacuum that went on and on endlessly nowhere. Like the Sheep Man said, I was tired and scared. And alone. And lost.

"Yougottadance," the Sheep Man said.

You gotta dance, echoed my mind.

"Gotta dance," I repeated out loud.

I pressed the button for the fifteenth floor.

When the elevator got there, "Moon River" greeted me from the ceiling speakers. The real world—where I probably could never be happy, and never get anywhere.

I glanced at my watch. Return time, three-twenty A.M.

Well now, I thought. *Well now well now well now well now well now well now . . .*, echoed my mind.

12

Back in my room, I ran a bath. I undressed, then slowly sank in. But strangely, I couldn't get warm. My body was so chilled, sitting in the hot water only made me shiver. I considered staying in the tub until I stopped shivering, but before that happened, the steam made me woozy, so I climbed out. I pressed my forehead against the window to clear my head, then poured myself a brandy which I downed in one gulp before dropping into bed. I wanted to sleep without the taint of a thought in my head, but no such luck. I lay in bed, conscious beyond control. Eventually morning came, heavy, overcast. It wasn't snowing, but clouds filled the sky, thick and seamless, turning the whole town gray. All I saw was gray. A sump of a city slushed with sunken souls.

Thinking wasn't what kept me awake. I hadn't been thinking at all. I was too tired to think. Except that one hardened corner of my head insisted on pushing my psyche into high gear. I was on edge, irritable, as if trying to read station signs from a speeding train. A station approaches. The letters blur past. You can almost read something, but you're traveling too fast. You try again, when the next station careens into view, but you fly by before you can make anything out. And then the next station . . . Backwater flags in the middle of nowhere. The train sounds its whistle. High, shrill, piercing.

This routine went on until nine, when I got out of bed. I shaved, but had to keep telling myself *I'm shaving now* to get me through. I dressed and brushed my hair and went down to the hotel restaurant. I sat at a table by the window and ordered coffee and toast. It took me an eternity to get through the toast, which tasted like lint and was gray from the sky. The sky foretold the end of the world. I drank my coffee and read and reread and reread the menu. My head was too hard. Nothing would register. The train raced on. The whistle screamed. I felt like a dried lump of toothpaste. All around me, people were devouring their breakfasts, stirring their coffee, buttering their toast, forking up their ham and eggs. Plates and cutlery *clink-clink-clinking*. A regular train yard.

I thought about the Sheep Man. He existed at this very moment. Somewhere, in a small time-space warp of this hotel. Yes, he was here. And he was trying to tell me something. But it was no good. I couldn't read it. I was speeding by too fast for the message to register. My head was too thick to make out the words. I could only read what wasn't moving: *(A) Continental Breakfast—Juice (choice of orange, grapefruit, or tomato), Toast or . . .*

Someone was talking to me. Seeking my response. But who? I looked up. It was the waiter. Immaculate in his white uniform, coffee pot in both hands, like a trophy. "Care for more coffee, sir?" he asked politely. I shook my head. He moved on and I got up to go. Leaving the train yard behind.

Back in my room, I took another bath. No shivers this time. I took a long stretch in the tub, softening my stiff joints. I got my fingers moving freely again. Yes, this was my body all right. Here I am now. Back in a real room, in a real tub. Not aboard some superexpress train. No whistle in my ears. No need to read station signs. No need to think at all.

Out of the bath, I crawled into bed. Ten-thirty. Great, just great. I half considered canning the sleep and going out for a walk, but before I could focus, sleep overtook me. The houselights went down and suddenly everything went dark. It happened quickly. I can remember the instant I fell asleep. As if a giant, gray gorilla had sneaked into the room and whacked me over the head with a sledgehammer. I was out cold.

My sleep was hard, tight. Too dark to see anything. No background Muzak. No "Moon River" or "Love Is Blue." A simple no-frills sleep. Someone asks me, "What comes after 16?" I answer, "41." The gray gorilla steps in and says, "He's out." That's right, I was asleep. All rolled up in a tight little squirrel ball inside a steel sphere. A solid steel wrecking ball, fast asleep.

Something is calling me.

A steam whistle?

No, something else, the gulls inform me.

Somebody's trying to cut open the steel ball with a blowtorch. That's the sound.

No, not that, chant the gulls. Like a Greek chorus.

It's the phone, I think.

The gulls vanish.

I reach out and grope for the bedside telephone. "Yes?" I hear myself saying. But all I hear is a dial tone. *Beeeeeeee eeeeeeee*, comes a noise from somewhere else. The doorbell! Somebody's ringing the doorbell! *Beeeeeeeeeeeeeee.*

"The doorbell," I mumbled.

Gone are the gulls. No one applauds. No "bingo," no nothing.

Beeeeeeeeeeeeeee.

I threw on a bathrobe and went to the door. Without asking who it is, I opened up.

My receptionist friend. She slipped inside and shut the door.

The back of my head was numb. Did that ape have to whack me so hard? It feels like there's a dent in my skull.

She noted my bathrobe, and her brows knitted. "Sleeping at three in the afternoon?" she said in disbelief.

"Three in the afternoon?" I repeated. It didn't make much sense even to me. "Why?" I asked myself.

"What time did you get to bed? Really!"

I tried to think. It took real effort. Nothing came.

"It's okay, don't bother," she said, shaking her head. Then she plopped down on the sofa, adjusted the frame of her glasses, and looked at me straight in the face. "You look terrible."

"Yeah, I bet I do," I said.

"You're pale and puffed up. Are you okay? Do you have a fever?"

"I'm okay. I just need some sleep. Don't worry. I'm generally pretty healthy. Are you on break?"

"Yes," she said. "I wanted to see you. I hope I'm not intruding."

"Not at all," I said, sitting down on the bed. "I'm zonked, but no, you're not intruding."

"You won't try anything funny?"

"I won't try anything funny."

"Everyone says they won't, but they all do."

"Maybe everyone does, but I don't," I said.

She thought it over and tapped her finger on her temple as if to verify the mental results. "Well, I guess probably not. You're kind of different from other people."

"Anyway, I'm too sleepy right now," I added.

She stood up and peeled off her light blue blazer, draping it over the back of the chair like the day before. This time, though, she didn't sit next to me. She walked over to the window and stood, gazing out at the sky. Maybe she was surprised to find me in such a haggard state, in only a bathrobe—but you can't have everything. I don't make my living looking great all the time.

"Listen," I spoke up. "I didn't tell you, but I think we have a few things in common."

"Oh?" she said without emotion. "For instance?"

"For instance—," I began, but right then my mental transmission stalled. I couldn't think of a thing. I couldn't get words to come. Maybe it was only a feeling. But if it was a feeling between the two of us, however slight, that at least meant something. No *for instance* or *even so*. Knowing it was enough.

"I don't know," I picked up again. "I need to put my thoughts in order. A method to the madness. First organize, then ascertain."

"Wow, that's really something," she addressed the windowpane. While her voice didn't ring entirely cynical, it didn't quite have the ring of enthusiasm either.

I got into bed, leaned back against the headboard, and observed her. That wrinkle-free white blouse. Navy blue tight skirt. Stockinged legs. Yet, even she was tinged gray, like an old photograph. Actually quite wonderful. I felt like I'd connected to something. Next thing I knew I had an erection. Not bad. Gray sky, exhaustion, hard-on at three in the afternoon.

I continued to watch her. Even when she turned around and saw me looking, I kept looking.

"Why are you staring at me like that?" she demanded.

"I'm jealous of your swim club," I said.

She shook her head, then broke into a smile. "You're a strange guy, you know?"

"Not strange," I said. "Confused. I need to put my thoughts in order."

She drew close and felt my forehead.

"Well, no fever," she said. "You should get some sleep. Pleasant dreams."

I wanted her to stay here with me. By my bedside, while I slept. But I knew that was impossible, so I didn't say anything. I watched her put on her light blue blazer and leave. And then the gray gorilla entered the room with his sledgehammer again. "That's okay, I was falling asleep anyway," I started to tell him. But the words weren't out of my mouth before another blow fell.

"What comes after 25?" somebody asks. "71," I answer. "He's out," says the gray gorilla. Surprise, surprise, I thought. Hit me that hard and I'm not going to be in a coma? Darkness overcame me once again.

13

Knots.

It was nine P.M. I was eating dinner alone, having awakened from a deep sleep at eight. I got up and was awake, about as abruptly as I'd fallen asleep. There was no middle ground between sleeping and waking. And my head seemed to be back in working order. All postcranial gray gorilla lesions had vanished. I wasn't drowsy or sluggish and I had no shivers. I remembered everything with great clarity. I had an appetite—I was ravenous. So I headed out to the local watering hole I'd gone to the first night and had a few nibbles with drinks. Drinks and grilled fish and simmered vegetables and crab and potatoes. The place was packed, thick with smoke and smells and noise, everybody and his neighbor screaming at each other.

Need to organize, I thought.

Knots? I queried myself in the midst of the chaos. I brought the words softly to my lips: You have but to seek and the Sheep Man shall connect.

Not that I completely understood what that meant. It was a bit too figurative, metaphoric. But maybe it was the sort of thing you *had* to express metaphorically. For one thing, I could hardly believe the Sheep Man had chosen to speak that way for his amusement. Maybe it was the only way.

Through that world of the Sheep Man—via his switchboard—all sorts of things were connected. Some connections led to confusion, he'd said. Because I lost track of what I wanted. So were all my ties meaningless?

I drank and stared at the ashtray in front of me.

What had become of Kiki? I'd felt her presence very strongly in dreams. It was she who'd called me here. It was she who needed me. She was the reason I'd come to the Dolphin Hotel. But I had yet to hear her voice. Her message was cut off. As if someone had pulled the plug.

Why was everything so vague?

Perhaps the lines were crossed. I had to get clear what it was she wanted from me. Enlist the help of the Sheep Man and link things up one by one. No matter how out of focus the picture, I had to unravel each strand patiently. Unravel, then bind all together. I had to recover my world.

But where to begin? Not a clue. I was flat against a high wall. Everything was mirror-slick. No place for the hand, no place to reach out and grab. I was at wit's end.

I paid my bill and left. Big flakes of snow tumbled down from the sky. It wasn't really coming down yet, but the sound of the town was different because of the snow. I walked briskly around the block to sober up. Where to begin? Where to go? I didn't know. I was rusting, badly. Alone like this, I would gradually render myself useless. Great, just great. Where to begin? My receptionist friend? She seemed nice. I did like her. I did feel a bond between us. I could sleep with her if I tried. But then what? Where would I go from there? Nowhere, probably. Just another thing to lose. *I don't know what I want.* And, if that's the case, as my ex-wife said, I'd only hurt people.

Once more around the block. Snow quietly coming down. Sticking to my coat, lingering a brief instant, then disappearing. I tried to put my thoughts in order. People walked past, puffing white breaths into the air. It was so cold the skin of my face hurt. Still, I kept going around the block, kept trying to think. My ex-wife's words stuck in my head like a curse. Worse, because it was true. I hurt everybody. If I kept going like this, I'd go on losing them too.

"Go home to the moon!" were my last girlfriend's parting words. No, not departing—*returning*. She was braving it back to the big, bad, real world.

Then along comes Kiki. Yes! Kiki's got to be the touchstone. But her message had vaporized midway.

So where to begin?

I closed my eyes and struggled for an answer. But in my head no one was at home. No Sheep Man, no gulls, no gray gorilla. I was abandoned, sitting in a vast empty chamber, alone. No one could give me the answer. I'd sit, grow old, and shrivel in that room. No dancing here. Very sad.

Why couldn't I read the station signs?

The answer was to come the following afternoon. As usual, with no prior warning, out of nowhere. Like a gorilla whack out of the gray.

14

Strangely enough—but not that strangely, I suppose—when I hit the sack at midnight, I fell asleep immediately. And I didn't wake until eight in the morning. Precisely at eight, as if I'd come full cycle. I felt rested—and hungry. So I went back to Dunkin' Donuts, and then went for a walk around town. The streets were frozen solid, feather-soft snow drifting quietly down. As ever, the sky was heavy with clouds. Not exactly weather for a carefree stroll, but getting out was good for my spirits. The cold was bracing and cleared my head. I hadn't resolved a thing, so why a simple stretch should make a difference was curious.

After an hour, I made my way back to the hotel. My receptionist friend was on duty at the front desk, together with a colleague busy with a guest. My friend was on the phone, smiling her professional smile, unconsciously twirling a pen between her fingers. I walked up and waited until she finished her call.

She shot me a look of reproach, but she didn't let it interfere with her manual-perfect professional smile. "How may I help you?" she asked politely.

I cleared my throat. "Excuse me," I began, "but I heard that two girls were tragically attacked by an alligator at the swim club last night. Do you know if there's any truth to that story?"

"Well, one never knows about these things, does one?" she replied, the fastidious artificial flower of her smile pinned in place. Her cheeks blushed slightly, her nostrils taut. "I can't say I know anything about it, sir. Excuse me, but are you certain that was the story you heard?"

"It was a huge alligator, by all accounts, the size of a Volvo station wagon. It came flying through the skylight, shattering glass everywhere, and it swallowed the two girls in one bite. Then it had half a potted palm for dessert. I was wondering if the creature was still at large. Do you think it's safe to go out?"

"Forgive me," she broke in, without a flicker of change in her expression, "but have you considered contacting the police yourself, sir? I'm sure they could provide you with the most recent developments on the case. There's a police station not far from here. You might try asking there."

"Thank you. I'll do that," I said. "May the Force be with you."

"Not at all, sir," she said coolly, adjusting her glasses.

Not long after I returned to my room, she called.

"Would you care to tell me what that was all about?" Her calm monotone scarcely disguised her anger. "You weren't going to do anything funny during business hours. Didn't I ask you that? I hate pranks like that when I'm working."

"I just had to talk to you," I said apologetically. "I wanted to hear your voice. It was a dumb joke. I'm sorry. I only wanted to say hello. I really didn't mean to bother you."

"It's very upsetting. I told you that. When I'm on duty, I get tense. So please, don't do anything like that again. You promised not to stare too."

"I wasn't staring. I was just trying to talk to you."

"Well, then, from now on, no more talking like that. *Please.*"

"I promise, I promise. No talking. No staring and no

talking. I'll be as quiet as granite. But you know, while I've got you on the line, are you free this evening? Or do you have mountain-climbing lessons tonight?"

There was the sound of a dry laugh, half of it silence, and then she hung up.

I waited for thirty minutes, but she didn't call back. I'd pissed her off. Sometimes people don't know when I'm kidding, any more than when I'm being serious. At a loss for something better to do, I went out walking again. With luck, I might run into something new. Anyway, the idea of exercise seemed more appealing than sitting and doing nothing. May the Force be with me.

I walked for an hour and succeeded only in getting cold. The snow kept coming down. At twelve-thirty I popped into a McDonald's for a cheeseburger and coke and fries. I didn't even know why. For reasons that escape me, I sometimes just find myself eating the stuff. Maybe my physical makeup's been programmed for periodic ingestion of junk food. Maybe I did "need a break today."

After McDonald's, I walked for another thirty minutes. Still no major revelations. The snow picked up. The storm was getting fierce. I zipped my coat all the way to the collar and wrapped my scarf around over my nose. Even then I was cold. And I had to take a leak. Why'd I have to go and drink a coke on a day like this? I scanned the area for a place where I could use the toilet, but the only possibility was a movie theater. A real deadbeat establishment, but they had to have a toilet. And it was probably warm in there. Why not? I had time to kill anyway. So what was playing? A domestic double bill, one of which was *Unrequited Love*, that movie starring my former classmate. Well, fancy that.

After relieving myself at length, I bought a hot coffee and took it into the theater. The place was empty, as expected, and warm. It was thirty minutes into the film, but it was hardly like walking into a complicated plot. My classmate played a tall, handsome biology teacher, the object of a young girl's adoration. Predictably, she was gaga over him, practically fainting at the sight of him. And of course, there was this other guy—who did kendo in his spare time—earnestly in love with her. Talk about an original concept. Hell, *I* could've written this movie.

Even so, I had to admit, my classmate—whose real name was Ryoichi Gotanda, not exactly the stuff for making girls swoon, so he'd been given some dashing screen pseudonym—played his role with a little bit of complexity. Not only was he handsome and nice, etc., but he also exuded traces of a troubled past. Common garden-variety wounds, to be sure—maybe he'd been a student radical or maybe he'd gotten a girl pregnant and abandoned her—but better than nothing. From time to time, the film would have these flashbacks—CUT TO ACTUAL FOOTAGE OF STUDENT TAKEOVER OF TOKYO UNIVERSITY—inserted with all the subtlety of a monkey lobbing clay against a wall.

Anyway, Gotanda played his part to the hilt. But the film was ludicrous and the director such an obvious zero talent and the script so embarrassingly infantile, with an endless succession of breathtakingly meaningless scenes and close-ups of the girl, that Gotanda was doomed from the start. No matter how much real acting he did, you couldn't bear to watch.

Then, at one point in the film, Gotanda's in bed in his apartment on a Sunday morning with some woman when the girl who's in love with him shows up with homemade cookies or something. Good grief, I *did* write this movie. Gotanda's oh-so sweet and slow and sincere in bed, close to what I'd imagined. It's very nice sex. And he probably has very nice-smelling armpits too. His hair has been mussed sensuously. He's caressing the woman's back. She's naked. The camera dollies around to zoom in on her. And suddenly I see her face—

It's Kiki!

I froze in my seat. I could hear the sound of an empty bottle rolling down the aisle. Unbelievable! This was the exact same image I'd seen in that dark corridor of the

Dolphin. Gotanda sleeping with *her*!

That's when I knew: *We were all connected.*

That's the only scene Kiki appears in. Sunday morning, in bed with Gotanda. That's it. Gotanda had gone to a bar on Saturday night, picked her up, and brought her home. Then they fuck one more time in the morning. That's when his love-smitten pupil, the girl lead, enters. He's forgotten to lock the door. That's the whole scene. Kiki has only one line. And it's a pretty awful line at that. This is how it goes:

KIKI

What was that all about?

After the girl lead runs out in shock and Gotanda's all in a daze, that's the line Kiki says.

I wasn't even sure if it was her own voice. My memories of her weren't very clear, nor were the movie theater speakers too sharp on audio fidelity. I could remember her body, though. The shape of her back, the feel of her neck, her silky breasts—yes, it was *she* all right. I sat there riveted to my seat, staring at the screen. The scene couldn't have lasted more than a couple of minutes. Kiki's in Gotanda's embrace, she flows to his caresses, she closes her eyes in a state of bliss, her lips tremble slightly. She lets out a little sigh. I can't tell whether she's acting or not—but let's suppose it's acting. This is a movie, after all. Not that I believe for a moment that Kiki could act. Which poses definite phenomenological problems.

Suppose Kiki wasn't acting, then that meant she really was coming on to Gotanda's lovemaking. But if she was acting, then that meant she wasn't the woman I knew. She didn't believe in acting. She wasn't meant to act. Either way, though, I was burning with jealousy.

First a swim club, now a stupid movie. Was I capable of getting jealous of *any*thing? Was this a good sign?

Now the girl lead opens the door. She catches sight of the two naked bodies embracing. She swallows her breath. She shuts her eyes. She turns and runs.

Gotanda is stunned. Kiki says: "What was that all about?" Close-up of Gotanda's dazed face. FADE OUT.

Aside from that cameo, Kiki appeared in no other scene. Forget the dumb plot, I was all eyes at the screen, and I know she wasn't anywhere. She was destined to be a one-night stand, witness to one fleeting scene in Gotanda's life, before vanishing forever. That was her role. The same as with me. Suddenly she's there, she sees what there is to see, then she's gone.

The movie ended. The lights came up. Music played. I remained in my seat, transfixed by the blank white screen. Was this reality? The film was over, but I didn't get it. What was Kiki doing in a movie? And together with Gotanda, no less. Absurd. I must have been mistaken. Got the wrong circuit. Got my wires crossed somewhere. How else could I explain it?

I walked around again for a while after leaving the theater. Thinking about Kiki the whole time. "What was that all about?" she whispered into my ears.

What *was* that all about?

It *had* to have been her. It *couldn't* be a mistake. She'd made the same face when I made love to her, her lips trembled like that, she'd sighed like that. That wasn't acting. No way. But this was a movie.

It didn't make sense.

The more I walked, the less I trusted my memory. Maybe the movie was a hallucination.

An hour and a half later, I went back to the same movie theater. And I watched *Unrequited Love* again from the beginning. Sunday morning, Gotanda is making love to a woman. The woman's back is to the camera. The camera dollies around. The woman's face comes into view. It's Kiki! Plain as day. Enter the girl lead. Who swallows her breath. Shuts her eyes. Runs. Gotanda, dazed and confused. KIKI: "What was that all about?" FADE OUT.

Exactly the same, down to the last detail.

I'd seen it a second time and I still didn't believe it. Not at all. There had to be something wrong here. Why would Kiki be sleeping with Gotanda?

The following day, I went to the movies again. I sat stiffly through *Unrequited Love* another time, waiting for that one scene. Antsy and impatient. At last the scene came up. Sunday morning, Gotanda is making love to a woman. The woman's back is to the camera. The camera dollies around. The woman's face comes into view. It's Kiki! Plain as day. Enter the girl lead. Who swallows her breath. Shuts her eyes. Runs. Gotanda, dazed and confused. KIKI: "What was that all about?" FADE OUT.

There in the dark, I let out a deep sigh.

Okay, okay. You win. This is real. There's no mistake. *We are connected.*

15

I sank back into my seat, folded my hands in front of my nose, and asked the old familiar: What to do?

The same question. But now I knew I really needed to think things over calm and collected. Needed to put things in order. Needed to sort through the confused connections.

Something was confused here, that was for sure. Something was amiss. Kiki and Gotanda and I were all connected, in a tangle, but why? I had to untangle us. I had to recover my own sense of reality. But maybe the connections weren't confused, maybe this was a totally unrelated, new connection. Still, I had to untangle the entangled threads. In order not to break any.

Here was a clue. I had to get moving. I couldn't stand still. I had to dance. So light on my feet that it all keeps spinning.

You gotta dance, the Sheep Man said.

Gotta dance, echoed my mind.

Time to return to Tokyo. Nothing more for me here. The Dolphin Hotel had fulfilled its purpose. Once I got back to Tokyo, I'd have a lot of knots to untie.

I bundled myself up and left the theater. Snow was falling thicker than ever, nearly obscuring my way. The entire city was as icy as a corpse, and every bit as depressing.

Back at the hotel, I rang up All Nippon Airways and

booked a flight to Tokyo that evening.

"Because of the snow, there's a good chance of delay or even cancellation," the reservation lady informed me. I didn't care. I'd made up my mind and the sooner I got back to Tokyo the better. Then I packed and went down to settle my bill. My friend with the glasses was on duty at the front desk. I asked to speak to her at the car-rental desk.

"Urgent business came up and I have to go back to Tokyo," I explained.

"Thank you very much. Please come again," she said with a professional smile. Could she have been hurt that I was giving her so little notice?

"I plan to be back soon," I said. "When I do get back, we'll go to dinner and talk things over. There's a lot I want to tell you. First I have things to straighten out in Tokyo. But when I'm done, I'm coming back. I don't know how many months it'll take, but I'm coming back. There's something—I don't know how to put it—special about this place. So sooner or later I know I'll be here again."

"Hmm," she said, rather dubiously.

"Hmm," I countered, rather positively. "I'm sure what I'm saying sounds phony."

"Not at all," she said, expressionless. "One can't be sure about things so many months down the road."

"It won't be so many months. We'll meet again. I really feel that we share something special too," I said, as sincerely as I meant it. "Don't you have that feeling?"

She tapped her pen on the countertop in lieu of a response. "And I suppose you're going to tell me you're taking the next flight out?"

"Well, uh, yes, I planned to. If they're flying, that is. But with this weather, we may not get off the ground."

"Well, if you do leave by the next plane, I have a request."

"Of course."

"There's a thirteen-year-old girl who has to get back to Tokyo. Her mother had to leave suddenly on business, and the girl's been left here in the hotel. I realize it's a terrible imposition, but could the girl possibly accompany you down to Tokyo? She's got a lot of luggage, and I'm afraid to send her off on a plane by herself."

"I don't really understand," I said. "Isn't it kind of off-the-wall for a mother to run off somewhere and leave her child behind?"

My friend shrugged. "I suppose, but she *is* off-the-wall. She's an artist, a famous photographer, and she can be quite eccentric. An idea popped into her head, and she was off and running. She completely forgot about the child. Later on, we got this call from her, about her daughter being somewhere around the hotel, and could we please put her on a flight back to Tokyo. That was it."

"Shouldn't she come and get the girl herself?"

"That's not for me to say. Besides, she's in Kathmandu on this job, and she said she'd be busy for another week. She's very famous and she's a regular guest at the hotel, so who am I to contradict her? She said that if I got her daughter to the airport, she'd be fine by herself the rest of the way. Maybe so, but really, the girl's a child, and if anything were to happen to her, it'd be our responsibility."

"Great," I said. Then the thought occurred to me. "It wouldn't happen to be a kid with long hair and rock 'n' roll sweatshirts and a Walkman, would it?"

"The very same. How did you know?"

"Fun for the whole family."

My friend snapped into action immediately. She phoned ANA and reserved a seat for the girl on my flight. She buzzed the girl and told her that someone—someone she knew—was going to take her back to Tokyo and that she should gather her things together right away. She called the bellboy and sent him up to the girl's room for the bags. She summoned the hotel limousine service. I couldn't help expressing my admiration.

"I told you I liked my job. I'm cut out for it."

"But if someone gives you a hard time, you'd rather cut out."

She tapped her pen. "That's different. I don't like being the butt of jokes."

"I didn't mean it that way. Please believe me," I said. "I was only trying to be funny. No offense intended, honest. I only joke around because I need to relax."

She pursed her lips slightly and looked me in the face. With the look of someone surveying the lowlands from a hill after the floodwaters have subsided. Then she spoke in a voice that was almost a sigh, almost a snort. "By the way, could I ask you for your business card, please? As a professional measure, of course, seeing as how I'm entrusting a young girl to your care."

"As a professional measure," I muttered and pulled out a card for her. For what it's worth, I do carry business cards. For what it's worth, at least a dozen people have told me how necessary for business they are. She eyed my card as if it were a dust rag.

"And could I ask what your name is?" I had to try.

"Next time, maybe," she said, pushing up her glasses with her middle finger. "*If* we meet again."

"Of course we will," I said.

Soft and silent as a new moon, a smile drifted across her face.

Ten minutes later the bellboy and the girl appeared in the lobby. The bellboy was lugging two huge Samsonite suitcases. Each could have held a full-grown German shepherd, standing. A bit much for a thirteen-year-old girl to haul to the airport all by herself, to be sure. She was wearing tight jeans and boots, and her sweatshirt of the day read TALKING HEADS. Over which she wore an expensive-looking fur stole. There was the same transparent sense about her as before. A beauty that was so vulnerable, so high-strung. A balance too delicate to last.

Talking Heads. Not bad, for a band name. Like something out of Kerouac.

The girl looked me over, blasé. She didn't smile. But she did raise an eyebrow, then turned to my receptionist friend with glasses.

"Don't worry, he's all right," my friend said.

"I'm not as bad as I look," I declared.

The girl looked at me again. Then she made an *oh-well-I-suppose* sort of nod.

"Really, you'll be fine," my friend went on. "The old man tells funny jokes—"

"*Old man*!" I gasped.

"He throws in a nice word from time to time," she continued, paying me no attention, "he's a real gentleman to us ladies. Besides, he's a friend of mine. So you'll be just fine."

The two of them proceeded to the limousine at the entrance of the hotel. I followed, dignity deflated, quietly behind.

The weather was terrible. The road to the airport all ice and snow. Antarctica.

"What's your name?" I asked the girl.

The girl stared at me, then shook her head briefly. *Gimme a break*. Then she slowly looked around as if searching for something, but all there was to see was the blizzard outside. "*Yuki*," she said. *Snow*.

"You can say that again."

"It's my *name*!" she hissed.

Then she pulled her Walkman out of her pocket and plugged in to her own private pop music microcosm. The rest of the way to the airport she never gave me so much as a glance.

Snow, eh? Such a charming character, so full of social grace. You'd think she'd at least offer me a stick of gum every time she helped herself to some. Not that I wanted any, but hadn't she heard of polite? It would have made me feel like I was riding in the same car with her. I sank into my seat, aging by the minute, and shut my eyes.

Only later did I learn that "Yuki" actually was her name.

I thought about when I was her age. I used to collect pop records myself. Singles. Ray Charles' "Hit the Road, Jack," Ricky Nelson's "Travelin' Man," Brenda Lee's "All Alone Am I." I owned maybe a hundred 45s. I used to listen to them day in and day out. I knew all the lyrics by heart. The things kids can memorize. Always the most meaningless, idiotic lines. Stuff about a *China doll down in old Hong Kong, waiting for my return. . . .*

Not quite Talking Heads. But okay, the times they are a-changin'.

I stationed Yuki in the waiting room and went to purchase our tickets. The flight was running an hour late, but the ticket agent warned that the chances were it'd be delayed even longer. "Please listen for the announcement," she said. "At the moment, visibility is extremely bad."

"Do you think the weather will improve?" I asked.

"That's what the forecast says, but it may take some time," she said grimly. She probably had to say the same thing two hundred times. Enough to depress anyone.

I returned to Yuki with the news. She glanced up at me with a *hmmph* sort of look, but didn't say a word.

"Who knows when we'll get on, so let's not check in yet. It might be a disaster trying to get our luggage back," I said.

A *whatever-you-say* look. Again, not a word.

"I guess there's nothing we can do but wait. No fun getting stuck at an airport for hours, though." No one could accuse me of not keeping up my end of the non-conversation. "Have you eaten?"

She nodded.

"What do you say we go to the coffee shop anyway? We could get something to drink. Whatever you want."

An *I-don't-know-about-this* look. She had a whole repertoire of expressions.

"Okay, let's go," I said, rising to my feet. And off we went, rolling her Samsonites along.

The coffee shop was crowded. All flights out of Sapporo were delayed, and everyone looked uniformly on edge. We waded through waves of irritability. I ordered a sandwich and coffee. Yuki asked for hot chocolate.

"How long were you staying at the hotel?" Well, somebody had to try to be civil.

After a moment's thought, a real live answer: "Ten days."

"And when did your mother leave?"

She looked out the window at the snow a bit, then: "Three days ago."

I felt like we were practicing a Beginning English language drill.

"So your school's been on vacation all this time?"

That did the trick. "No, my school hasn't been on vacation all this time. Don't bug me," she snapped. She retrieved her Walkman from her pocket and plugged her ears in.

I finished my coffee and read the paper. Was every female in the world out to give me a hard time? Was it just my luck or a fundamental flaw in me?

If I had a choice, I'd rather it be just my luck, I decided, folding up my newspaper and pulling out a paperback of *The Sound and the Fury*. Faulkner, and Philip K. Dick too. When besieged by groundless fatigue, there's something about them you can always relate to. That's why I always pack a novel—for times like these.

Yuki went to the restroom, came back, changed the batteries in her Walkman. Thirty minutes later the announcement came: The flight to Tokyo, Haneda Airport, was delayed four hours due to continued poor visibility. Great, just great. More agony sitting here.

Look on the bright side, I tried cheering myself up. Use the power of positive thinking. Give yourself five minutes to consider how you can turn a miserable situation to your benefit and that little light bulb is going to click on. Maybe it will, and then again maybe it won't. But something had to beat sitting and killing time in this noisy, smoke-filled hole.

I told Yuki to stay put while I went back into the lobby. I walked over to a car rental and the woman behind the counter quickly did the paperwork for a Toyota Corolla Sprinter, complete with stereo. A microbus gave me a lift to the lot, where I was handed the keys to a white car with brand-new snow tires. I drove ten minutes back to the airport and went to fetch Yuki in the coffee shop. "Let's go for a three-hour ride."

"In the middle of a blizzard? What are we going to see? And where are we going anyway?"

"Nowhere. Just around," I said. "But the car's got a stereo and you can play your music as loud as you want. Better for your ears than listening to that Walkman."

A *you-gotta-be-kidding* shake of the head this time. All the same, as I got up to go, she stood up too.

I got her suitcases into the trunk, then pointed the car out into the snow-swept no-man's-land. Yuki fished a cassette tape out of her bag, popped it into the stereo, and David Bowie was singing. Followed by Phil Collins, Jefferson Starship, Thomas Dolby, Tom Petty & the Heartbreakers, Hall & Oates, Thompson Twins, Iggy Pop, Bananarama. Typical teenage girl's stuff.

Then the Stones came on with "Goin' to a Go-Go." "I know this one," I boasted. "The Miracles did it ages ago. Smokey Robinson and the Miracles. Years ago when I was fifteen or sixteen."

"Oh," said Yuki with not a flicker of interest.

Next it was Paul McCartney and Michael Jackson singing "Say Say Say."

The wipers were going full force, batting away at the flakes. Few cars on the road. Almost none in fact. We were warm, riding around in the car, and the rock music pleasant. I even didn't mind Duran Duran. Singing along, I kept our wheels on the straight roads. We did this for ninety minutes, when she noticed the cassette I'd borrowed from the car rental.

"What's that?" she asked.

"Oldies," I said.

"Put it on."

"Can't guarantee you'll like it."

"That's okay. I can handle it. I've been listening to the same tapes for the last ten days."

No sooner had I punched the PLAY button than Sam Cooke's "Wonderful World" came on. *Don't know much about history* . . . Sam the Man, killed when I was in ninth grade. Then it was "Oh Boy," by Buddy Holly, another dead man. Airplane crash. Bobby Darin, "Beyond the Sea." He was gone, too. Elvis "Hound Dog" Presley. A drugged stiff. Everyone dead and gone. Everyone except maybe Chuck Berry with his "Sweet Little Sixteen." And me, singing along.

"You really remember the words, don't you!" Yuki said, genuinely impressed.

"Who wouldn't? I was just as crazy about rock as you are," I said. "I used to be glued to the radio every day. I spent all my allowance on records. I thought rock 'n' roll was the best thing ever created."

"And now?"

"I still listen sometimes. I like some songs. But I don't listen so carefully, and I don't memorize all the lyrics anymore. They don't move me like they used to."

"How come?"

"*How come?*"

"Yeah, *how come?* Tell me."

"Maybe it's because after all this time I think that really good songs—or really good anything—they're hard to find," I said. "Like if you listen to the radio for a whole hour, there's maybe one decent song. The rest is mass-produced garbage. But back then I never thought about it, and it was great just listening. Didn't matter what it was. I was a kid. I was in love. And when you're a kid you can relate to anything, even if it's silly. Am I making sense to you?"

"Kind of."

The Del Vikings' "Come Go with Me" came on, and I sang along on the chorus. "Are you bored?" I asked Yuki.

"Uh-uh, not so much," she answered.

"Not so much at all," I threw in.

"Now that you're not young anymore, do you still fall in love?" asked Yuki.

I had to think about that one. "Difficult question," I said finally. "You got any boy you like?"

"No," she said flatly. "But there sure are a lot of creeps out there."

"I know what you mean," I said.

"I'd rather just listen to music."

"I know what you mean."

"You do?" she said, surprised.

"Yeah, I really do," I said. "Some people say that's escapism. But that's fine by me. I live my life, you live yours. If you're clear about what you want, then you can live any way you please. I don't give a damn what people say. They can be reptile food for all I care. That's how I looked at things when I was your age and I guess that's how I look at things now. Does that mean I have arrested development? Or have I been right all these years? I'm still waiting on the answer to that one."

Jimmy Gilmer's "Sugar Shack." I whistled the riff during the refrain. A huge expanse of pure white snow spread out to the left of the road. *Just a little shack made out of wood. Espresso coffee tastes mighty good* . . . . 1964.

"You know," remarked Yuki, "anyone ever tell you you're . . . different?"

"Hmmph." My response.

"Are you married?"

"I was once."

"So you're not married now?"

"That's right."

"Why?"

"Wife walked out on me."

"Are you telling the truth?"

"Yeah, I'm telling the truth. She went to live with someone else."

"Oh."

"You can say that again," I said.

"But I think I can see how your wife must've felt."

"What do you mean?"

She shrugged her shoulders but didn't say anything. I made no effort to probe further.

"Want some gum?" she asked after a bit.

"No thanks."

By now, the two of us were chiming in on the back chorus of the Beach Boys' "Surfin' U.S.A." All the dumb parts. *Inside—outside—U.S.A.* Maybe I wasn't entirely relegated to the dustheap of "old men" after all.

The snow was starting to lighten. We headed back to the airport, turned in the keys at the car rental, checked in, and thirty minutes later were at the gate.

In the end, the plane took off five hours late. Yuki fell asleep as soon as we left the ground. She was beautiful, sleeping next to me. Finely made, exquisite, and fragile. The stewardess brought around drinks, looked over at Yuki, and smiled broadly at me. I had to smile too. I ordered a gin and tonic. And as I drank, I thought about Kiki. The scene played over and over again in my head. Kiki and Gotanda are in bed, making love. The camera pans around. And there she is. "What was that all about?" she says.

Yes, *what was that all about?*

16

After collecting our bags at Haneda, Yuki told me where she lived.

Hakone.

"That's a pretty long haul," I said. It was already past eight in the evening, and even if I got a taxi to take her, she'd be wiped out by the time she reached there. "Do you know anybody in Tokyo? A relative or a friend?"

"No one like that, but we have a place in Akasaka. It's small, but Mama uses it when she comes to town. I can stay there. Nobody's there now."

"You don't have any family? Besides your mother?"

"No," answered Yuki. "Just Mama and me."

"Hmm," I said. Unusual family situation, but what business was it of mine? "Why don't we go to my place first? Then we can eat dinner somewhere. Then afterward, I'll drive you to your Akasaka apartment. That okay with you?"

"Anything you say."

We caught a cab to my apartment in Shibuya, where I got out of my Hokkaido clothes. Leather jacket, sweater, and sneakers. Then we got in my Subaru and drove fifteen minutes to an Italian restaurant I sometimes go to. Call it an occupational skill; I do know how to locate good eating establishments.

"It's like those pigs in France," I told her, "trained to grunt when they find a truffle."

"Don't you like your work?"

"Nah. What's to enjoy? It's all pretty meaningless. I find a good restaurant. I write it up for a magazine. Go here, try this. Why bother? Why shouldn't people just go where they feel like and order what they want? Why do they need someone to tell them? What's a menu for? And then, after I write the place up, the place gets famous and the cooking and service go to hell. It always happens. Supply and demand gets all screwed up. And it was me who screwed it up. I do it one by one, nice and neat. I find what's pure and clean and see that it gets all mucked up. But that's what people call information. And when you dredge up every bit of dirt from every corner of the living environment, that's what you call enhanced information. It kind of gets to you, but that's what I do."

She eyed me from across the table, as if she were looking at some rare species in the zoo.

"But still you do it," she said.

"It's my job," I replied, then suddenly I remembered that I was with a thirteen-year-old. Great. What did I think I was doing, shooting my mouth off like that to a girl not half my age? "Let's go," I said. "It's getting late. I'll take you to your apartment."

We got in the Subaru. Yuki picked up one of my cassettes and put it on to play. Driving music. The streets were empty, so we made it to Akasaka in no time.

"Okay, point the way," I said.

"I'm not telling," Yuki answered.

"What?" I said.

"I said I'm not telling you. I don't want to go home yet."

"Hey, it's past ten," I tried reasoning with her. "It's been a long, hard day. And I'm dog-tired."

This made little impression on her. She was unbudgeable. She just sat there and stared at me, while I tried to keep my eyes on the road. There was no emotion whatsoever in her stare, but it still made me jumpy. After a while, she turned to look out the window.

"I'm not sleepy," she began. "Anyway, once you drop me off, I'll be all alone, so I want to keep driving and listening to music."

I thought it over. "All right. We drive for one hour. Then you're going home to bed. Fair?"

"Fair," said Yuki.

So we drove around Tokyo, music playing on the stereo. It's because we let ourselves do these things that the air gets polluted, the ozone layer breaks up, the noise level increases, people become irritable, and our natural resources are steadily depleted. Yuki lay her head back in her seat and gazed silently at the city night.

"Your mother's in Kathmandu now?" I asked.

"Yeah," she answered listlessly.

"So you'll be on your own until she returns?"

"We have a maid in Hakone."

"Hmm, this sort of scene happens all the time?"

"You mean Mama up and leaving me?"

"Yeah."

"All the time. Work is the only thing Mama thinks of. She doesn't mean to be mean or anything, that's just how she is. She only thinks about herself. Sometimes she forgets I'm around. Like an umbrella, you know, I just slip her mind. And then she's outa there. If she gets it into her head to go to Kathmandu, that's it, she's off. She apologizes later. But then the same thing happens the next time. She dragged me up to Hokkaido on a whim—and that was kind of fun—but she left me alone in the room all the time. She hardly ever came back to the hotel and I usually ate by myself. . . . But I'm used to it now, and I guess I don't expect anything more. She says she'll be back in a week, but maybe from Kathmandu she'll fly off to somewhere else."

"What's your mother's name?" I asked.

I'd never heard of her.

"Her professional name," she tried again, "is Amé. *Rain.*

That's why I'm Yuki. *Snow*. Dumb, huh? But that's her idea of a sense of humor."

Of course I'd heard of Amé. Who hadn't? Probably the most famous woman photographer in the country. She was famous, but she herself never appeared in media. She kept a low profile. She only accepted work that she liked. Well-known for her eccentricity. Her photos were known for the way they startled you and stuck in your mind.

"So that means your father's the novelist, Hiraku Makimura?" I said.

Yuki shrugged. "He's not such a bad person. No talent though."

Years back I'd read a couple of his early novels and a collection of short stories. Pretty good stuff. Fresh prose, fresh viewpoint. Which is what made them best-sellers. He was the darling of the literary community. He appeared on TV, was in all the magazines, expressed an opinion on the full spectrum of social phenomena. And he married an up-and-coming photographer who went by the name of Amé. That was his peak. After that, it was downhill all the way. He never wrote anything decent. His next two or three books were a joke. The critics panned them, they didn't sell.

So Makimura underwent a transformation. From naïf novelist he was suddenly avant-garde. Not that there was any change in the lack of substance. Makimura modeled his style on the French *nouvelle vague*, rhetoric for rhetoric's sake. A real horror. He managed to win over a few brain-dead critics with a weakness for such pretensions. But after two years of the same old stuff, even they got tired of him. His talent was gone, but he persisted, like a once-virile hound sniffing the tail of every bitch in the neighborhood. By that time, he and Amé had divorced. Or more to the point, Amé had written him off. At least that was how it played in the media.

Yet that wasn't the end of Hiraku Makimura. Early in the seventies, he broke into the new field of travel writing as a self-styled adventurer. Good-bye avant-garde, time for action and adventure. He visited exotic and forbidden destinations in far corners of the globe. He ate raw seal meat with the Eskimos, lived with the pygmies, infiltrated guerrilla camps high in the Andes. He cast aspersions on armchair literarians and library shut-ins. Which wasn't so bad at first, but after ten years, the pose wore thin. After all, we're no longer living in the age of Livingstone and Amundsen. The adventures didn't have the stuff they used to, but Makimura's prose was pompous as ever.

And the thing of it was, they'd ceased to be real adventures. By now he was dragging around whole entourages, coordinators and editors and cameramen. Sometimes TV would get into the act and there'd be a dozen crew members and sponsors tagging along. Things got to be staged, more and more. Before long, everyone had his number.

Not such a bad person perhaps. But like his daughter said, no talent.

Nothing more was said about Yuki's father. She obviously didn't want to talk about the guy. I was sorry I brought him up.

We kept quiet and listened to the music. Me at the wheel, eyes on the lights of the blue BMW in front of us. Yuki tapped her boot along with Solomon Burke and watched the passing scenery.

"I like this car," Yuki spoke up after a while. "What is it?"

"A Subaru," I said. "I got it used from a friend. Not many people look twice at it."

"I don't know much about cars, but I like the way it feels."

"It's probably because I shower it with warmth and affection."

"So that makes it nice and friendly?"

"Harmonics," I explained.

"What?"

"The car and I are pals. We help each other out. I enter its space, and I give off good vibes. Which creates a nice atmosphere. The car picks up on that. Which makes me feel good, and it makes the car feel good too."

"A machine can feel good?"

"You didn't know that? Don't ask me how, though. Machines can get happy, but they can get angry too. I have no logical explanation for it. I just know from experience."

"You mean, machines are like humans?"

I shook my head. "No, not like humans. With machines, the feeling is, well, more finite. It doesn't go any further. With humans, it's different. The feeling is always changing. Like if you love somebody, the love is always shifting or wavering. It's always questioning or inflating or disappearing or denying or hurting. And the thing is, you can't do anything about it, you can't control it. With my Subaru, it's not so complicated."

Yuki gave that some thought. "But that didn't get through to your wife? Didn't she know how you felt?" she asked.

"I guess not," I said. "Or maybe she had a different perspective on the matter. So in the end, she split. Probably going to live with another man was easier than adjusting her perspective."

"So you didn't get along like with your Subaru?"

"You said it." Of all the things to be talking about to a thirteen-year-old.

"And what about me?" Yuki suddenly asked.

"What about you? I hardly know you."

I could feel her staring at me again. Much more of this and pretty soon she'd bore a hole in my left cheek. I gave in. "Okay, of all the women I've gone out with, you're probably the cutest," I said, eyes glued on the road. "No, not probably. Without question, absolutely, the cutest. If I were fifteen, I'd fall in love with you just like that. But I'm thirty-four, and I don't fall in love so easily. I don't want to get hurt anymore. So it's safer with the Subaru. All right?"

Yuki gave me a blank look. "Pretty weird," was all she could say.

Which made me feel like the dregs of humanity. The girl probably didn't mean anything by it, but she packed a punch.

At eleven-fifteen we were back in Akasaka.

Yuki kept her part of the bargain and told me how to get to the apartment. It was a smallish redbrick condo on a quiet back street near Nogi Shrine. I pulled up to the building and killed the engine.

"About the money and all," she said before opening the door, "the plane and the dinner and everything—"

"The plane fare can wait until your mother gets back. The rest is on me. Don't worry about it. I don't go dutch on dates."

Yuki shrugged and said nothing, then got out and dropped her wad of gum into a convenient potted plant.

Thank you very much. You're quite welcome. I bandied with myself. Then I took a business card out of my wallet. "Give this to your mother when she returns. And in the meanwhile, if you need anything, you can call me at this number. Let me know if I can help out."

She snapped up the card, glared at it a second, then buried it in her coat pocket.

I pulled her overweight suitcases out of the car, and we took the elevator to the fourth floor. Yuki unlocked the door, and I brought the suitcases in. It was a dinette-kitchen-bedroom-bath studio. Practically brand-new, spick-and-span as a showroom, complete with neatly arrayed furniture and appliances, all tasteful and expensive and without sign of use. The apartment had the unlived-in charm of a glossy magazine spread. Very chic, very unreal.

"Mama hardly ever uses this place," Yuki declared, as she watched me scan the place. "She has a studio nearby, and she usually stays there when she's in Tokyo. She sleeps there, and she eats there. She only comes here between jobs."

"I see," I said. Busy woman.

Yuki hung up her fur coat and turned on the heater. Then she brought out a pack of Virginia Slims and lit up with a cool flick of the wrist. I couldn't say I thought much of a thirteen-year-old smoking. Yet there was something positively attractive about that pencil-thin filter poised on her sharp knife-cut lips, her long lashes luxuriating on the updraft. Picture perfect. I held my peace. If I were fifteen years old, I really would have fallen for her. As fatefully as the snow on the roof comes tumbling down in spring. I would have lost my head and been terribly unhappy. It took me back years. Made me feel helpless, a teenage boy pining away again for a girl who could almost have been Yuki.

"Want some coffee?"

I shook my head. "Thanks, but it's late. I'm heading home."

Yuki deposited her cigarette in an ashtray and showed me to the door.

"Mind the cigarette and heater before you turn in."

"Yes, Dad," she replied.

Back in my own apartment at last, I collapsed on the sofa with a beer. I glanced through my mail. Nothing but business and bills. File under: later. I was dead, didn't want to do anything. Still, I was on edge, too pumped up with adrenaline to sleep. What a day!

How long had I stayed in Sapporo? The images jumbled together in my head, crowding into my sleep time. The sky had been a seamless gray. Implicating events and dates. Date with receptionist with glasses. Call to ex-partner for background on Dolphin Hotel. Talk with Sheep Man. Movie showing Gotanda and Kiki. Beach Boys, thirteen-year-old girl, and me. Tokyo. So how many days altogether?

You tell me.

Tomorrow, I told myself. *It can wait.*

I went into the kitchen and poured myself a whiskey. Straight, neat, and otherwise unadulterated. Plus some crackers. A bit damp, like my head, but they'd have to do. I put on an old favorite of the Modernaires singing Tommy Dorsey numbers. Nice and low. A bit out-of-date, like my head. A bit scratchy, but not enough to bother anyone. A perfection of sorts. That didn't go anywhere. Like my head.

What was that all about? Kiki repeated in my brain.

The camera pans around. Gotanda's able fingers sail gently down her back. Seeking for that long-lost sea passage.

What was going on here? I was thoroughly confused. Gone was my self-confidence. Love and used Subarus were two different things. Weren't they? I was jealous of Gotanda's fingers. Had Yuki put out her cigarette? Had she turned off the heater? *Yes, Dad.* You said it. No confidence at all. Was I doomed to rot, muttering away to myself like this in this elephants' graveyard of advanced capitalist society?

Leave it to tomorrow. Everything.

I brushed my teeth, changed into my pajamas, then polished off the last of the whiskey in my glass. The moment I got into bed, the phone rang. At first I just stared at the thing ringing there in the middle of the room, and finally I picked it up.

"I turned off the heater," Yuki began. "Put out my cigarette. Everything's okay. Sleep easier now?"

"Yes, thank you," I replied.

"Nighty-night then," she said.

"Good night," I said.

"Hey," Yuki started, then paused, "you saw that guy in the sheepskin up at the Sapporo hotel, didn't you?"

I sat down on the bed, holding the telephone to my chest as if keeping a cracked ostrich egg warm.

"You can't fool me. I know you saw him. I knew that right away."

"You saw the Sheep Man?" I blurted out.

"Mmm," Yuki skirted the question, then clicked her tongue. "But we can talk about that later. Next time, huh? We'll have a long talk. I'm beat right now."

And she hung up, just like that. *Click.*

I had a pain in my temples. I went to the kitchen and poured myself another whiskey. I was trembling all over. A roller coaster was rumbling under me. *It's all connected*, the Sheep Man had said.

Connected.

All sorts of strange connections were starting to come together.

17

I leaned up against the sink in the kitchen and downed the whiskey. What should I do? How could Yuki have known about the Sheep Man? Should I ring her back? But I really was exhausted. It'd been one long day. Maybe I should wait for her to call. Did I know her phone number?

I climbed into bed and stared at the phone. I had a feeling that Yuki might call. If not Yuki, somebody else. At times like this, the telephone becomes a time bomb. Nobody knows when it's going to go off. But it's ticking away with possibility. And if you consider the telephone as an object, it has this truly weird form. Ordinarily, you never notice it, but if you stare at it long enough, the sheer oddity of its form hits home. The phone either looks like it's dying to say something, or else it's resenting that it's trapped inside its form. Pure idea vested within a clunky body. That's the telephone.

Now the phone company. All those lines coming together. Lines stretching all the way from this very room. Connecting me, in principle, to anyone and everyone. I could even call Anchorage if I wanted. Or the Dolphin Hotel, for that matter, or my ex-wife. Countless possibilities. And all tied together through the phone company switchboard. Computer-processed these days of course. Converted into strings of digits, then transmitted via telephone wires to underground cable or undersea tunnel or communications satellite, ultimately finding its way to us. A gigantic computer-controlled network.

But no matter how advanced the system, no matter how precise, unless we have the will to communicate, there's no connection. And even supposing the will is there, there are times like now when we don't know the other party's number. Or even if we know the number, we misdial. We are an imperfect and unrepentant species. But suppose we clear those hurdles, suppose I manage to get through to Yuki, she could always say, "I don't want to talk now. Bye." *Click!* End of conversation, before it ever began. Talk about one-way communication.

Actually, the telephone looked rather irritated.

It—or let's call it a "she"—seemed pissed off at being less than pure idea. Angered at the uncertain and imperfect grounds upon which volitional communication must necessarily base itself. So very imperfect, so utterly arbitrary, so wholly passive.

I propped myself up on my pillow and watched the telephone fume. A perfectly pointless exercise. *It's not my fault*, the phone seemed to be telling me. Well, that's communication. Imperfect, arbitrary, passive. The lament of the not-quite-pure idea. But I'm not to blame either. The phone probably tells this to all the boys. It's just that being part of these quarters of mine makes her—it—all the more irritable. Which makes me feel responsible. As if I'm aiding and abetting all the imperfection.

Take my ex-wife, for example. She'd just sit there and, without a word, put me in my place. I'd loved her. We'd had some really good times. Traveled together. Made love hundreds of times. Laughed a lot. But sometimes, she'd give me the silent treatment. Usually at night, subtle, but unrelenting. As punishment for my imperfection, my arbitrariness and passiveness.

I knew what was eating her. We got along well, but what she was after, the image in her mind, was somewhere else, not where I was. She wanted a kind of autonomy of communication. A scene where the hero—whose name was "Communication"—led the masses to a bright, bloodless revolution, spotless white flags waving. So that perfection could swallow imperfection and make it whole. To me, love is a pure idea forged in flesh, awkwardly maybe, but it had to connect to somewhere, despite twists and turns of underground cable. An all-too-imperfect thing. Sometimes the lines get crossed. Or you get a wrong number. But that's nobody's fault. It'll always be like that, so long as we exist in this physical form. As a matter of principle.

I explained it to her. Over and over again.

Then one day she left.

Or else I'd magnified that imperfection, and helped her out the door.

I looked at the telephone and replayed scenes of me getting it on with my wife. For the three months before she left, she hadn't wanted to sleep with me once. Because she was sleeping with the other guy. At the time, I didn't have the least idea.

"Sorry dear, but why don't you go sleep with someone else? I won't be mad," she'd said. And I thought she was joking. But she was serious. I told her I didn't want to sleep with another woman, which was true. But she wanted me to, she said. Then we could think things over from there.

In the end, I didn't sleep with anyone. I'm not a prude, but I don't go sleeping with women just to think things over. I sleep with someone because I want to.

Not long after that, she walked out on me. But say I had gone and slept with someone like she wanted me to, would that have kept her from leaving? Did she really believe that that would've put our communication on even slightly more autonomous grounds? Ridiculous.

Already past midnight, but the drone of the expressway showed no sign of letting up. Every now and then a motorcycle would blast by. The soundproof glass dampened the noise, but not much. It was right out there, up against my life, oppressing me. Circumscribing me to this one patch of ground.

I grew tired of looking at the phone and closed my eyes.

And as soon as I did, the surrender I must have been waiting for silently filled the void. Very deftly and ever so quick. Sleep came over me.

After breakfast, I thumbed through my address book for the number of a guy in talent management I'd met when I needed to interview young stars. It was ten in the morning when I rang him up, so naturally he was still asleep. That's showbiz. I apologized, then told him I had to find Gotanda. He moaned and groaned, but eventually came across with the goods. The number for Gotanda's agency, a midsize entertainment production firm.

I called up and got his manager on the line. I said I was a magazine writer and wanted to talk with Gotanda. Was I doing a piece on him? Not exactly, this was personal. How personal? Well, I happened to be a junior high school classmate of his, and this was urgent. Fine, he'd pass the message on. No, I had to talk to Gotanda directly. Me and how many others?

"But this is very important," I insisted. "So if you'd be so kind as to put us in touch, I'm sure I can return the favor on a professional level."

The manager considered my proposition. Of course it was a lie. I didn't have any strings to pull. My whole claim to editorial sway consisted of going out and doing the interview I was assigned to do. A glorified gofer. But the manager didn't know that.

"And you're sure this isn't coverage?" he said. "Because all media have to go through me. Out front and official."

No, this was one-hundred-percent personal.

The guy asked for my number. "Junior high school classmate, eh?" he said with a sigh. "He'll call tonight or tomorrow. *If* he feels like it."

"Of course," I said.

The guy yawned and hung up. Couldn't blame him. It was only ten-thirty.

Before noon I drove to Aoyama to do my shopping at the fancy-schmancy Kinokuniya supermarket. Parking my Subaru among the Saabs and Mercedes in the lot, I almost felt as if I were exposing myself, the twin of this narrow-shouldered old chassis of mine. Still, I admit it: I enjoy shopping at Kinokuniya. You may not believe this, but the lettuce you buy there lasts longer than lettuce anywhere else. Don't ask me why. Maybe they round up the lettuce after they close for the day and give them special training. It wouldn't surprise me. This is advanced capitalism, after all.

At home, there were no messages on my answering machine. No one had called. I put away the vegetables to the "Theme from *Shaft*" on the radio. *Who's that man? Shaft! Right on!*

Then I went to see *Unrequited Love* yet again. That made four times. I couldn't *not* see it. I concentrated on the critical scene, trying to catch every detail.

Nothing had changed. It was Sunday morning. Everything bathed in peaceful Sunday light. Window blinds drawn. A woman's bare back. A man's caressing fingers. Le Corbusier print on wall. Bottle of Cutty Sark on table at side of bed. Two glasses, ashtray, pack of Seven Stars. Stereo equipment. Flower vase. Daisies. Peeled-off clothes on floor. Bookshelf. The camera pans. It's Kiki. I shut my eyes involuntarily. Then I open them. Gotanda is embracing her. Gently, softly. "No way," I say. Out loud. A young kid four seats away shoots me a look. The girl lead comes into frame. Hair in a ponytail. Yachting windbreaker and jeans. Red Adidases. She's holding a container of cookies. She walks right in, then dashes out. Gotanda is dumbfounded. He sits up in bed, squinting into the light, following the girl with his eyes. Kiki rests a hand on his shoulder, her words drenched with world-weariness. "What was that all about?"

After I left the theater, I walked around the streets of Shibuya.

I walked, through the swarming crowds of school kids, as Gotanda's slender, well-mannered fingers played over her back in my mind. I walked to Harajuku. Then to Sendagaya past the stadium, across Aoyama Boulevard toward the cemetery and over to the Nezu Museum. I passed Café Figaro and then Kinokuniya and then the Jintan Building back toward Shibuya Station. A bit of a hike. It was getting late. From the top of the hill, I could see the neon signs coming on as the dark-suited masses of salarymen crossed the intersection like instinct-blinded salmon. When I got back to my apartment, the red message lamp on my answering machine was blinking. I switched on the room lights, took off my coat, and pulled a beer out of the fridge. I sat down on my bed, took a sip, and pushed PLAY.

"Well, been a long time." It was Gotanda.

18

"Well, been a long time."

Gotanda's voice came through bright and clear. Not too fast, not too slow. Not too loud, not too soft. Not tense, not inordinately relaxed. A perfect voice. I knew it was Gotanda in a second. It's not the sort of voice you forget once you've heard it. Any more than his smiling face, his sparkling white teeth, his finely sculpted nose. Actually, I'd never paid any attention to Gotanda's voice before, couldn't really recall it either, but obviously it'd stuck subconsciously to the inside of my skull, and it came back to me immediately, as vivid as the tolling of a bell on a still night. Amazing.

"I'm going to be at home tonight, so call. I don't go to bed until morning anyway," he said, then enunciated his telephone number, twice. "Be talking to you."

From the exchange, his place couldn't have been so far from here. I wrote the number down, then carefully dialed. At the sixth ring, an answering machine kicked on. A woman's voice saying, "I'm out right now, but if you'd care to leave a message." I left my name and the time and said that I'd be in all evening. Complicated world we live in. I hung up and was in the kitchen when the phone rang.

It was Yuki. What was I up to? My response: Chewing

on a stalk of celery and having a beer. Hers: Yuck. Mine: It's not so bad. She wasn't old enough to know things could be a lot worse.

"So where are you calling from?" I asked.

"Akasaka," she said. "How about going for a drive?"

"Sorry, I can't today," I said. "I'm waiting for an important business call. How about another time? But first I got a question. When we talked yesterday, you said you'd seen a man in a sheep suit? Can you tell me more about that? I need to know."

"How about another time?" she said, then slammed the phone down.

I munched on the celery and thought about what to have for dinner. Spaghetti.

First slice two cloves of garlic and brown in olive oil. Tilt the frying pan on its side just so, to pool the oil, and cook over a low flame. Toss in dried red peppers, fry together but remove before oil gets too spicy. Touch-and-go. Then cut thin slices of ham into strips and sauté until crisp. Last, add to al dente spaghetti, toss, sprinkle with chopped parsley. Serve with salad of fresh mozzarella and tomatoes.

Okay, let's do it.

The water for the spaghetti was just about to boil when the telephone rang. I turned off the gas and went to pick up the phone.

It was Gotanda. "He–ey, long time. Takes me back. How're you doing?"

"All right, I guess."

"So what's up? My manager said you had something urgent. Hope we don't have to dissect a frog again," he laughed.

"No, nothing like that. I know this call is out of the blue, but I just needed to ask you something. Sorry, I know you're busy. Anyway, this may sound kind of strange, but—"

"Listen, are you busy right now?" Gotanda interrupted.

"No, not at all. I had some time on my hands, so I was about to fix dinner."

"Perfect. How about a meal? I was just thinking about looking for a dinner partner. You know how it is. Nothing tastes good when you eat alone."

"Sure, but I didn't mean to . . . I mean, I called so suddenly and—"

"No problem. We all get hungry whether we like it or not, and a man's got to eat. I'm not forcing myself to eat on your account. So let's go have a good meal somewhere and talk about old times. Haven't seen you in ages. I really want to see you. I hope I'm not imposing. Or am I?"

"C'mon, I'm the one who wanted to talk to you."

"Well, then, I'll swing by and pick you up. Where are you?"

I told him where my apartment building was.

"Not so far from here. Maybe twenty minutes. So get yourself ready to go. I don't know about you, but I'm starving."

I'd hop to it, I said, and hung up. Old times?

What old times could Gotanda possibly have to talk about? We weren't especially close back then. He was the bright boy of the class, I was a nobody. It was some kind of miracle that he even remembered who I was.

I shaved and put on the classiest items in my wardrobe: an orange striped shirt and Calvin Klein tweed jacket, an Armani knit tie (a birthday present from a former girlfriend), just-washed jeans, and brand-new Yamaha tennis shoes. Not that he'd ever think this was classy. I'd never eaten with a movie star before. What was one supposed to wear anyway?

Twenty minutes later on the dot, my doorbell rang. It was Gotanda's chauffeur, who politely informed me that Gotanda was downstairs. In a metallic silver Mercedes the size and shape of a motorboat. The glass was also silvered so you couldn't see in. The chauffeur opened the door with a smart, professional snap of the wrist and I got in. And there was Gotanda.

"Who–oa, been a while, eh?" he flashed me his smile. He didn't shake my hand, and I guess I was glad.

"Yeah, it has, hasn't it?" I said.

He wore a dark blue windbreaker over a V-neck sweater and faded cream corduroy slacks. Old Asics jogging shoes. Impeccable. Perfectly ordinary clothes, but the way he wore them was perfect. He gave my outfit a once-over and offered, "*Trés chic.*"

"Thanks," I said.

"Just like a movie star." No irony, just kidding. We both laughed. Which let us relax.

I sized up the interior of the car.

"Not bad, eh?" he said. "The agency lets me use it whenever I want. Complete with driver. This way there're no accidents, no drunken driving. Safety first. They're happy, I'm happy."

"Makes sense," I said.

"But if it were up to me, I would never drive this baby. I don't like cars this big."

"Porsche?"

"Maserati."

"I like cars even smaller," I said.

"Civic?"

"Subaru."

"Subaru," he repeated, nodding. "You know, the first car I ever bought was a Subaru. With the money I made on my first picture, I bought a used Subaru. Boy, I loved that car. I used to drive it to the studio when I had my second supporting role. And someone got on my case right away. *Kid, if you want to be a star, you can't drive a Subaru.* What a business. So I traded it in. But it was a great car. Dependable. Cheap. Really terrific."

"Yeah, I like mine too."

"So why do you think I drive a Maserati?"

"I haven't the foggiest."

"I have this expense account I got to use up," he said with a tilt of his eyebrow. "My manager keeps telling me, spend more, more. I'm never using it up fast enough. So I went and bought an expensive car. One high-priced automobile can write off a big chunk of earnings. It makes everybody happy."

Good grief. Didn't anyone have anything else on their mind but expense account deductions?

"I'm really hungry," he said, running his hand through his hair. "I feel like a nice, thick steak. Are you up for something like that?"

"Whatever you say."

He gave directions to the driver, and we were off. Gotanda looked at me and smiled. "Don't mean to get too personal," he said, "but since you were fixing a meal for yourself, I take it you're single."

"Correct," I said. "Married and divorced."

"Just like me," he said. "Married and divorced. Paying alimony?"

"Nope."

"Nothing?"

"Nothing. She didn't want a thing."

"You lucky bastard," he said, grinning. "I don't pay alimony either, but the marriage broke me. I suppose you heard about my divorce?"

"Vaguely."

It'd been in all the magazines. His marriage four or five years ago to a well-known actress, then the divorce a couple years later. But as usual, who knew the real story? The rumor was that her family didn't like him—not so unusual a thing—and that she had this cordon of relatives who muscled in on every move she made, public and private. Gotanda himself was more the spoiled, rich-kid type, used to the luxury of living life at his own pace. So there was bound to be trouble.

"Funny, isn't it? One minute we're doing a science experiment together, the next thing you know we're both divorced. Funny," he forced a smile, then lightly rubbed his eyes. "Tell me, how come you split up?"

"Simple. One day the wife up and walked out on me."

"Just like that?"

"Yup. No warning, not a word. I didn't have a clue. I thought she'd gone out to do the shopping or something, but she never came back. I made dinner and I waited. Morning came and still no sign of her. A week passed, a month passed. Then the divorce papers came."

He took it all in, then he sighed. "I hope you don't mind my saying this, but I think you got a better deal than I did."

"How's that?"

"With me, the wife didn't leave. I got thrown out. Literally. One day, I was thrown out on my ear." He gazed out through the silvered glass. "And the worst part about it was, she planned the whole thing. Every last detail. When I wasn't around, she changed the registration on everything we owned. I never noticed a thing. I trusted her. I handed everything over to her accountant—my official seal, my IDs, stock certificates, bankbooks, everything. They said they needed it for taxes. Great, I'm terrible at that stuff, so I was happy for them to do it. But the guy was working for her relatives. And before I knew it, there wasn't a thing to my name left. They stripped me to the bone. And then they kicked me out. A real education, let me tell you," he forced another smile. "Made me grow up real fast."

"Everybody has to grow up."

"You're right there. I used to think the years would go by in order, that you get older one year at a time," said Gotanda, peering into my face. "But it's not like that. It happens overnight."

The place we went to was a steak house in a remote corner of Roppongi. Expensive, by the looks of it. When the Mercedes pulled up to the door, the doorman and maître d' and staff came out to greet us. We were conducted to a secluded booth in the back. Everyone in the place was very fashionable, but Gotanda in his corduroys and jogging shoes was the sharpest dresser in the place. His nonchalance oozed style. As soon as we entered, everyone's eyes were on him. They stared for two seconds, no longer, as if it were some unwritten law of etiquette.

We sat down and ordered two scotch-and-waters. Gotanda proposed the toast: "To our ex-wives."

"I know it sounds stupid," he said, "but I still love her. She treated me like dirt and I still love her. I can't get her out of my mind, I can't get interested in other women."

I stared at the extremely elegant ice cubes in the crystal tumblers.

"What about you?" he asked.

"You mean how do I feel about my ex-wife? I don't know. I didn't want her to go. But she left all right. Who was in the wrong? I don't know. It sure doesn't matter now. I'm used to it, though I suppose 'used to it' is about the best I can do."

"I hope I'm not touching a sore spot?"

"No, not really," I said. "Fact is fact, you can't run away from it. You can't really call it painful, you don't really know what to call it."

He snapped his fingers. "That's true. You really can't pin it down. It's like the gravity's changed on you. You can't even call what you're feeling pain."

The waiter came and took our orders. Steak, both medium rare, and salad and another round of scotch.

"Oh yeah, wasn't there something you wanted to talk to me about? Let's get that out of the way first. Before we get too plastered."

"It's kind of a strange story," I began.

He floated me one of his pleasant smiles. Well-practiced, but still, without malice.

"I like strange stories," he said.

"Well, here goes. The other day I went to see the movie you have out."

"*Unrequited?*" he said with a grimace, his voice dropping to a whisper. "Terrible picture. Terrible director, terrible script, it's always like that. Everybody involved with the thing wishes they could forget it."

"I saw it four times," I said.

His eyes widened, as if he were peering into the cosmic void. "I'd be willing to bet there's not a human alive in this galaxy who's sat through that movie four times."

"Someone I knew was in the film," I said. "Besides you, I mean."

Gotanda pressed an index finger into his temple and squinted. "Who?"

"The girl you were sleeping with on the Sunday morning."

He took a sip of whiskey. "Oh yeah," he said, nodding. "Kiki."

"Kiki," I repeated.

Kiki. Kiki. Kiki.

"That was the name I know her by anyway. In the film world, she went by Kiki. No last name, that was it."

Which is how, finally, I learned *her* name.

"And can you get in touch with her?" I asked.

"Afraid not."

"Why not?"

"Let's take it from the top. First of all, Kiki wasn't a professional actress. Actors, famous or not, all belong to some production company. So you get in contact with them through their agents. Most of them live next to their phones, waiting for the call, you know. But not Kiki. She didn't belong to any production group I knew of. She just happened through that one time."

"Then how did she land that part?"

"I recommended her," he said dryly. "I asked her if she wanted to be in a picture, and I introduced her to the director."

"What for?"

He took a sip of whiskey. "The girl had—maybe not talent exactly—she had the makings of . . . presence. She had *something*. She wasn't really beautiful. She wasn't a born actress. But you got the feeling that if she ever got on film, she could pull the whole frame into focus. And that's talent, you know. So I asked the director to put her in the picture. And she *made* that scene. Everyone thought she was great. I don't mean to brag, but that scene was the best thing in the movie. It was real. Didn't you think so?"

"Yeah, I did," I had to agree. "Very real."

"So I thought the girl would go into movies. She could've cut the ice. But then she disappeared. Vanished. Like smoke, like morning dew."

"Vanished?"

"Like literally. Maybe a month ago. I'd been telling everyone she was exactly what we needed for this new part, and she was set. All the girl had to do was to show up, and it was hers. I even called her up the day before to remind her. But she never showed. That was the last time we ever talked."

He raised a finger to call over the waiter and ordered two more scotches.

"One question, though it's none of my business," Gotanda said. "Did you ever sleep with her?"

"Uh-huh."

"So then, well, if I were to say, supposing I slept with her too, would that bother you?"

"Not especially," I said.

"Good," said Gotanda, relieved. "I'm a terrible liar. So I'll come right out with it. We slept together a few times. She was a good kid. A little mixed-up maybe, but really a good person. She should've become an actress. Could've done some good things. Too bad."

"And you really don't know where to contact her? Or what her real name is?"

"Afraid not. I don't know of any way to find her. Nobody knows. 'Kiki' is all there is to go on."

"Weren't there any pay slips in the film company accounting department?" I asked. "They've got to put your real name and address on those things. For the tax office and all."

"Don't you think I checked? Not a clue. She didn't bother

to pick up her pay. No money accepted, so no record, nothing."

"She didn't pick up her pay?"

"Don't ask me why," said Gotanda, well into his third drink. "The girl's a mystery. Maybe she wanted to keep her name and address a secret. Who knows? But whatever, now we have three things in common. Science lab in junior high. Divorce. And Kiki."

Presently our steaks and salads arrived. Beautiful steaks. Magazine-perfect medium rare. Gotanda dug in with gusto. His table manners were less than finishing-school polished, but he did have a casual ease that made him an ideal dining companion. Everything he ate looked appetizing. He was charming. He had a grace you don't encounter every day. A woman would be snowed.

"So tell me, where did you meet Kiki?" I asked, cutting into my steak.

"Let's see, where was it?" he thought out loud. "Oh yeah, I called for a girl and she showed up. You know what I mean, there are these numbers you call. Right?"

"Uh-huh."

"After my divorce, for a while there I would call up and these girls would come and spend the night. No fuss, no muss. I wasn't up for an amateur and if I was sleeping with someone in the industry it'd be splashed all over the magazines. So that's the companionship I had. They weren't cheap, but they kept quiet about it. Absolutely confidential. A guy at the agency gave me an introduction to this club, and all the girls were nice and easy. Professional, but without the attitude. They enjoy themselves too."

He brought a forkful of steak to his mouth and slowly savored the juiciness.

"Mmm, not bad," he said.

"Not bad at all," I seconded. "This is a great place."

"Great, but you get tired of it six times a month."

"You come here six times a month?"

"Well, I'm used to the place. I can walk right in and no

one bats an eye. The employees don't whisper. They're used to famous people, so they don't stare. No one coming to ask for your autograph when you've got your mouth full. It's hard to relax and eat in other places. Really."

"Rough life," I kidded. "Plus you can't slack off on that expense account."

"You said it! So where were we?"

"Up to the part about call girls."

"Oh right," said Gotanda, wiping his mouth with his napkin. "So, one time I call for the usual girl. But she's not available. Instead, they send these two other girls. I get to choose, because I'm such a special customer. Well, one of the girls was Kiki. It was tough to decide, so I slept with both of them."

"Hmm," I said.

"That bother you?"

"If I were still in high school, maybe. But not now, no."

"I never did anything like that in high school, that's for sure," chuckled Gotanda. "But anyway, I slept with both of them. It was a funny combination. I mean, one girl was absolutely gorgeous. I'm talking stunning. Some expensive work on that body, let me tell you. Every square millimeter of her dripping with money. In my business you run into plenty of beautiful women, and this girl was no slouch. She had a nice personality, intelligent too. And then there was Kiki. Not a real beauty. Pretty enough, but no pizzazz, not like the typical club girl. She was more, well, . . ."

"Ordinary?" I offered.

"Yeah, ordinary. Regular clothes, hardly any makeup, not a super conversationalist either. She didn't seem to care a lot about what people thought of her. No one you'd give a second look. And the strange thing about her was, somehow she was more attractive, she interested me more. After the three of us got it on, we were sitting on the floor, drinking and listening to music and talking. I hadn't enjoyed myself like that in ages. Not since college. I felt so relaxed with them that the three of us got together a few more times after that."

"When was this?"

"This was about six months after I got divorced, so that makes maybe a year and a half ago," he said. "We had this threesome five or six times. I never slept with Kiki alone. I wonder why. I really should have."

"Yeah, why not?"

He set his knife and fork down on his plate, then pressed at his temple again. Seemed to be a mannerism of his. And a charming one too.

"Maybe I was scared," Gotanda said.

"What do you mean?"

"Scared to be alone with her," he said, picking up his cutlery. "There was something challenging about her, almost threatening. At least that was the feeling I got. No, not exactly threatening."

"Sort of suggestive? Or leading?"

"Yeah, maybe. I can't really say. But whatever it was, I got only a hint of it. I never got the full frontal effect. So anyway, I never felt like sleeping with just her. Despite the fact that she attracted me more. Does this make any sense to you?"

"I guess."

"Somehow, if I'd slept with Kiki, just the two of us, I wouldn't have been able to relax. I'd have wanted to go a lot deeper with her. Don't ask me why. But that wasn't what I was after. I only wanted to sleep with girls as a kind of release. Even though I really did like Kiki."

We ate in silence for a moment or two.

"When Kiki didn't show for the audition, I rang up her club," Gotanda went on, as if he'd just remembered. "I specifically asked for her, but she wasn't there. They told me they didn't know where she was. True, she could've told them to say that if I called. Who knows? But in any case, she evaporated, just like that."

The waiter cleared the table and asked if we wanted coffee.

"No, but I'd like another drink," said Gotanda. "How about you?"

"I'm in your hands."

And so we were brought our fourth round.

"What do you think I did today?" Gotanda asked out of nowhere.

I told him I had no idea.

"I assisted a dentist, all afternoon. Background study for a role. Right now I'm doing this series where I play a dentist. Ryoko Nakano's an optometrist, and we have clinics in the same neighborhood. We've known each other since childhood, but something's always conspiring to keep us apart. Pretty harmless stuff. But, well, TV dramas are all the same. You ever seen it?"

"No, can't say I have," I said. "I don't watch TV. Except the news. And I only watch it twice a week."

"Smart," said Gotanda. "It's a stupid program anyway. If I wasn't in it, I wouldn't watch it myself. But it's a popular show. The ratings are pretty high. You know how the public loves this kind of stuff. And you wouldn't believe the mail I get every week. Dentists writing in, complaining about how such-and-such a procedure wasn't rendered right or the treatment for such-and-such a toothache should have been something else. And then there are these jokers who say they never saw such a poor excuse for a show. Well, if you don't like it, don't watch."

"Nobody's forcing them to."

"The funny thing is, I always get stuck playing a doctor or a teacher or somebody wholesome and respectable like that. I've played more doctor roles than I can count. The only thing I haven't been is a proctologist! Imagine how much fun that would be! But I've been a vet and a gynecologist and of course I've been a teacher of every curriculum in the book. I've even taught home economics. What do you make of all this?"

"Well, obviously, you radiate trust," I laughed.

"Yes, a fatal flaw," Gotanda laughed back. "Once, I played

this crooked used-car salesman. A bullshit artist with one glass eye. Boy, I had fun with that. The role had some bite to it, and I wasn't bad either. But no way. The letters came pouring in. It was too mean a role for the noble likes of me. Somebody even threatened to boycott the sponsor! Toothpaste, if I remember correctly. So my character got scratched in the middle of the season. Written right out. A pretty important part, killed by natural selection. And ever since then, it's been doctors and teachers, doctors and teachers."

"Complicated life."

"Or a truly simple one," he laughed again. "Anyway, today I was doing time as a dental assistant, studying technique. I've been doing this for a while now, and I swear, I can probably do a simple procedure myself. The dentist—the real live dentist—even praised the way I handle the tools. I have this gauze mask on, and none of the patients knows it's me. But still, they all relax when I talk to them."

"Can't stop radiating that trust, can you?"

"Yup, that's what I'm beginning to think. Matter of fact, *I* get to feeling so relaxed I wonder if I wasn't cut out to be a *real* dentist or a doctor or a teacher or something. I could've done that, you know. Maybe I'd be happier doing something like that."

"You're not happy now?"

"Don't know," said Gotanda, finger in the middle of his forehead this time. "It's this trust business I'm such a pro at. I don't know whether *I* trust myself. Everybody else trusts me, sure, but, really, I'm nothing but this image. A push of the button and—*brrp!*—I'm gone. Right?"

"Hmm."

"If I really was a doctor or a teacher, no one could switch me off. I'm always there."

"True, but even with acting, you always have to be there."

"Sometimes I just get tired," said Gotanda. "I get headaches, and I just lose track. I mean, it's like which is me and which the role? Where's the line between me and my shadow."

"Everybody feels that way, not just you."

"I know that. Everybody loses track of themselves. Only in me, the slant is too strong. It's, well, fatal. I've always been this way, since I don't know when. To be honest, I was always envious of you."

"Of me?" I was incredulous. "Why the hell would *you* be envious of *me*?"

"I don't know, you always seemed to get along just fine doing your own thing. Didn't matter what others thought, you didn't really care. You did what you wanted, how you wanted. You were solid." He raised his glass and looked through it. "I, on the other hand, was the eternal golden boy. I never did anything wrong, I got the best grades, I won elections, I was a star athlete. Girls liked me. And teachers and parents *believed* in me. How do things like this happen? I never really understood what was going on, but you sort of get into a groove, you know. You probably can't even imagine what I'm talking about."

No, not really, I told him.

"After junior high, I went to this school that was big in soccer. We almost made it to the nationals. So it was like an extension of junior high. I kept on being *good*. I had a girlfriend. She was gorgeous. Used to come cheer for me at the soccer matches. That's how we met. But we didn't go all the way, as we used to say. We only fooled around. We'd go to her place when her folks weren't home and we'd fool around. We'd have dates at the library. High school days right out of NHK Teen Playhouse."

Gotanda took a sip of whiskey.

"Things changed a bit in college. There was all this campus unrest, the United Student Front. I got put in a leading role again. And I played the role all right. I did everything. Put up barricades, slept around, smoked dope, listened to Deep Purple. The riot squad broke in and we got dragged off to jail. After that, there wasn't much for us to do.

"That was when the girl I was living with talked me into doing underground theater. So I tried out, partly as a joke, but gradually it got interesting. I was this beginner, and I lucked into a couple decent roles. Pretty soon I realized I had a talent for that kind of thing. I'd have this role and I could actually make it work. After a couple years, people started to know who I was. Even if I was a real mess in those days. I drank a lot, slept around all the time. But that's how everyone was.

"One day a guy from the movies came around and asked if I'd ever considered acting on-screen. Of course I was interested, so I tried out and I landed a bit part. It wasn't a bad part—I was this sensitive young man—and that led to something else. There was even talk of TV. Things got busy, and I had to quit the theater group. I was sorry to leave but, you know how it is, you think, there's a big, wide world out there, gotta move on. And, well, you know the rest. I'm a doctor and a teacher and I hustle antacid lozenges and instant coffee in between. Real big, wide world, eh?"

Gotanda sighed. A charming sigh, but a sigh no less.

"Life straight out of a painting, don't you think?"

"Not such a bad painting, though," I said.

"You got a point. I haven't had it bad. But when I think back on my life, it's like I didn't make one choice. Sometimes I wake up in the middle of the night and it scares me. Where's the first-person 'I'? Where's the beef? My whole life is playing one role after another. Who's been playing the lead in my life?"

I didn't say anything.

"I guess I'm running off at the mouth."

"Doesn't bother me," I told him. "If you want to talk, you ought to talk. I won't spread it around."

"I'm not worried about that," said Gotanda, looking me in the eye. "Not worried in the least. There's something about you—I don't know what it is—somehow I know I can trust you. I trust you from the word go. But it's hard to be open with people. I could talk—well, maybe I could—to my ex-wife. For a while there, until everyone around us screwed up the works, we really understood and loved each other. If it was just the two of us, things might have worked out. But she was too insecure. She needed her family too much, couldn't get out from under them. So that's when I . . . No, I'm getting ahead of myself. That's a whole other story. What I want to know is, is all this talk a drag?"

Nope, I said, not a drag at all.

After that he talked about our science lab unit. How he was always uptight, having to see to it that the experiment came out right, having to explain things to the slow girl. How, again, he envied my puttering along at my own pace. I, however, could scarcely recall what we'd done in science class. So I was at a total loss what there'd been to envy. All I remember was that Gotanda was good with his hands. Setting up the microscope, things like that. Meanwhile, I could relax precisely because he tended to all the hard tasks.

I didn't say that to him. I just listened.

At some point, a well-appointed man in his forties came up to our table and tapped Gotanda on the shoulder. They exchanged greetings and talked show business. The fellow glanced at me, pegged me immediately as a nobody, and continued his conversation. I was invisible.

When the fellow left, after a promise of lunch and golf, Gotanda fretted one eyebrow a few millimeters, raised two fingers to gesture for a waiter, and asked for the check. Which he signed, with no ceremony whatsoever.

"It's all expenses," he said. "It's not money, it's expenses."

19

Then we rode in the Mercedes to a bar down a back street in Azabu. We took seats at one end of the counter and had a few more drinks. Gotanda could hold his liquor; he didn't show the least sign of inebriation, not in his color or his speech. He went on talking. About the inanity of the TV stations. About the lamebrained directors. About the no-talents who made you want to throw up. About the so-called critics on news shows. He was a good storyteller. He was funny, and he was incisive.

He wanted to hear about me. What sorts of turns my life had taken. So I proceeded to relate snippets of the saga. The office I set up with a friend and then quit, the personal life, the free-lance life, the money, the time, . . . Taken in gloss, an altogether sedate, almost still life. It hardly seemed to be my own story.

The bar began to fill up, making conversation difficult. People were ogling Gotanda's famous face. "Let's get out of here. Come over to my place," he said, rising to his feet. "It's close by. And empty. And there's drink."

His condo proved to be a mere two or three turns of the Mercedes away. He gave the driver the rest of the night off, and we went in. Impressive, with two elevators, one requiring a special key.

"The agency bought me this place when I got thrown out

of my house," he said. "They couldn't have their star actor broke and living in a dump. Bad for the image. Of course, I pay rent. On a formal level, I lease the place from the office. And the rent gets deducted from expenses. Perfect symmetry."

It was a penthouse condo, with a spacious living room and two bedrooms and a veranda with a view of Tokyo Tower. Several Persian rugs on the hardwood floor. Ample sofa, not too hard, not too soft. Large potted plants, post-modern Italian lighting. Very little in the way of decorator frills. Only a few Ming dynasty plates on the sideboard, *GQ* and architectural journals on the coffee table. And not a speck of dust. Obviously he had a maid too.

"Nice place," I said with understatement.

"You leave things to an interior designer and it ends up looking like this. Something you want to photograph, not live in. I have to knock on the walls to make sure they're not props. Antiseptic, no scent of life."

"Well, you've got to spread your scent around."

"The problem is, I haven't got one," he voiced expressionlessly.

He put a record on a Bang & Olufsen turntable and lowered the cartridge. The speakers were old-favorite JBL P88s, the music an old Bob Cooper LP. "What'll you have?" he asked.

"Whatever you're drinking," I said.

He disappeared into the kitchen and returned with vodka and soda and ice and sliced lemons. As the cool, clean West Coast jazz filtered through this glorified bachelor pad, I couldn't help thinking, antiseptic or not, the place was comfortable. I sprawled on the sofa, drink in hand, and felt utterly relaxed.

"So out of all the possibilities, here I am," Gotanda addressed the ceiling light, drink in hand also. "I could have been a doctor. In college I got my teaching credentials. But this is how I end up, with this life-style. Funny. The cards were laid out in front of me, I could have picked any one. I could've done all right whatever I chose. Not a doubt in my mind. All the more reason not to make a choice."

"I never even got to see the cards," I said in all honesty. Which elicited a laugh from Gotanda. He probably thought I was joking.

He refilled our glasses, squeezed a lemon, and tossed the rind into the trash. "Even my marriage was by default, almost. We were in the same film and went on location together. We got friendly and went on drives. Then after the filming was over, we dated a couple of times. Everyone thought what a nice couple we made, so we thought, yeah, what a nice couple we make, let's get married. Now I don't know if you realize it, but the film industry's a small world. It's like living in a tenement at one end of a back alley. Not only do you see everybody's dirty laundry, but once rumors start, you can't stop 'em. All the same, I did like her, truly. She was the best thing I ever laid hands on. That really came home to me after we got married. I tried to make it last, but it was no go. The second I make a conscious choice, I chase the thing away. But if I'm on the receiving end, if it's not me that's making the decision, it seems like I can't lose."

I didn't say anything.

"I'm not looking on the dark side," he said. "I still love her. Maybe that's the problem. I still think of her. How it might have been if we both had given up acting and settled down to a quiet life. Wouldn't need a condo that looked like this. Wouldn't need a Maserati. None of that. Only a decent job and our own little place. Kids. After work I'd stop somewhere for a beer and let off steam. Then home to the wife. A Civic or Subaru on installment. That's the life. That would be everything I needed—if she was there. But it's not going to happen. She wanted something different. And her family —don't get me started on them. Anyway, I guess some things just don't work out. But you know what? I slept with her last month."

"With your former wife?"

"Yup. Do you think that's normal?"

"I don't think it's abnormal," I said.

"She came here, I couldn't figure out what for. She rings up, wants to drop by. Of course, I say. So we're drinking, the two of us, just like old times, and we end up in bed together. It was great. She told me she still liked me and I told her how I wished we could start all over again. But she didn't say anything to that. She just listened and smiled. I started going on about having a normal life, a regular home, like I was telling you now. And she listened and smiled, but she wasn't really listening. She didn't hear a word of it. It was like talking to a wall. Futile. She was feeling lonely and wanted to be with someone. I happened to be available. Not a nice thing to say about yourself, but it's true. She's a world apart from somebody like you or me. For her, loneliness is something you have others remove for you. And once it's gone, everything's okay. Doesn't go any further. I can't live that way."

The record finished. He raised the cartridge and stood thinking in silence for a moment.

"What do you think about calling in some girls?" he asked.

"Fine by me. Whatever you want," I said.

"You never bought a woman?" he asked.

Never, I told him.

"How come?"

"Never occurred to me," I said, honestly.

Gotanda shrugged his shoulders. "Well tonight, I think you should. Play along with me, okay?" he said. "I'll ask for the girl who came with Kiki. She might know something about her."

"I leave it up to you," I said. "But don't tell me you can write it off as expenses."

He laughed as he refilled his glass. "You won't believe it, but I can. There's a whole system. This place has this front as a party service, so they can make out these very legitimate receipts. Sex as 'business gifts and entertainment.' Amazing, huh?"

"Advanced capitalism," I said.

While waiting for the girls to arrive, Kiki and her fabulous ears came to mind. I asked Gotanda if he'd ever seen them.

"Her ears?" he said, puzzled. "No, I don't think so. Or if I did, I don't remember. What about her ears?"

Oh, nothing, I told him.

It was past twelve when the girls arrived. One was Gotanda's stunningly beautiful companion to Kiki. And really, she was stunning. The sort of woman who'd linger in your memory even if she never spoke a word to you. Not glitter and glamour, but refinement. Under her coat she wore a green cashmere sweater and an ordinary wool skirt. Simple earrings, no other adornment. Very well-bred university girl.

The other woman wore glasses and a soft-colored dress. She wasn't beautiful like her companion. She was more what you would call appealing and fresh. With long legs and slender arms, and tan as if she'd spent the last week on the beach in Guam. Her hair was short and neatly pinned up. She wore silver bangles that played on her wrists with her brisk movements, her flesh trim and taut, like a sleek carnivore.

Memories of high school came to mind. These two distinct types were to be found in any class. The elegant beauty and the quick-witted mink. It was like being at a reunion. Especially with Gotanda there, so relaxed and effervescent. He seemed to have slept with both of them before, so it was all, "Hey there, how's it going?" Gotanda introduced me as a former schoolmate, now a writer. Both smiled warmly, fine-we're-all-friends-here smiles.

We sat on the floor with brandy-and-sodas, Joe Jackson and the Alan Parsons Project playing in the background. Gotanda put on his dentist act for the girl with the glasses. Then he whispered something to her and she giggled. Then the Beauty was leaning on my shoulder and holding my hand. Her scent was lovely. She was every man's, every boy's dream. The high school girl you'd always wanted, now come back years later. *I always liked you though I didn't know how to tell you at the time. Why didn't you try to reach me?* I put my arm around her, and she gently closed her eyes, seeking out my ear with the tip of her nose. She kissed me lightly on the neck, breathing softly. Then I noticed that Gotanda and his girl weren't around. Why didn't I turn the lights down a bit? my coed cooed. I got up and switched off the overhead lights, leaving only a low table lamp on. Bob Dylan was droning *it's all over now, baby blue.*

"Undress me nice and slow," she whispered into my ear. So I took off first her sweater, then her skirt, then her blouse and stockings. Out of reflex I almost started to fold her things, but then realized that in this scene there was no need to do that. She in turn undressed me. Armani tie, Levi's, T-shirt.

She stood before me in scanty bra and panties. "Well, what do you think?" she asked with a smile.

"Super," I said. She had a beautiful body. Full, brimming with life, clean and sexy.

"*How* super?" she wanted to know. "If you tell me better, I'll do you the best ever."

"It's like old times. Takes me back to high school." I was being honest.

She squinted curiously, then smiled. "Unique, I'll say that."

"Did I say something wrong?"

"Not at all," she said. Then she came over next to me and did things nobody in my thirty-four years had ever done for me. Delicate, yet daring, things you wouldn't think of so readily. But somebody obviously had. The tension slipped out of my body as I closed my eyes, giving myself over to the flow of sensations. This was utterly different from any sex I'd known before.

"Not bad, huh?" she said, whispering again.

"Not bad," I agreed.

It put my mind at ease, like the best music, released the pockets of tension from my being, sent my temporal senses into limbo. Instead, there was a quiet intimacy, a blending of time and space, a perfect self-contained form of communication. And to think it was tax deductible! "Not bad," I said again. What was Dylan going on about now? "A Hard Rain's A-Gonna Fall." She snuggled into the crook of my arm. What a world, where you can sleep with gorgeous women while listening to Bob Dylan and then write off the whole works! Unthinkable in the sixties.

It's all just images, I found myself thinking. Pull out the plug and it'll all go away. A 3-D sex scene. Complete with eau de cologne, soft touchie-feelies, hot breath.

I followed the expected course, I came, then we took a shower. We returned to the living room, wrapped in oversized towels, to listen to Dire Straits and sip some brandy.

She asked me about my work, what kind of things I wrote. I explained briefly and she said, how uninteresting. Well, it depends, I told her. What I did was shovel cultural snow. To which she responded that her work was to shovel sensual snow. I had to laugh. But wouldn't I like to shovel some more snow, right about now? And so we rolled over on the carpet and made love again, this time very simply, very slowly. And she knew just how to please me. Uncanny.

Later, both lying full-length in Gotanda's luxurious tub, I asked her about Kiki.

"Kiki?" she said. "Now there's a name I haven't heard in a while. You know Kiki?"

She pursed her lips like a child and tried to think. "She's not anywhere now. She just disappeared, all of a sudden. We were pretty close too. Sometimes we'd go out shopping or drinking together. Then, without warning, she was gone. A month, maybe two months ago. But that's not so unusual. You don't need to hand in a formal resignation in this line of work. If you want to quit, you quit. You don't have to tell anyone. I'm sorry she left. We were friends, but that's how it goes. We're not girl scouts, after all," she said, stroking my thighs and cock with her long graceful fingers. "Have you slept with Kiki?"

"There was a time we lived together. Four years ago."

"Four years ago?" she said with a smile. "That's ancient history. Four years ago, I was still in high school."

"Hmm." I let it pass. "You know of any way I could get to see Kiki?"

"Pretty difficult, I'd say. I honestly don't have any idea where she went. It's like I told you, she just up and left. Practically vanished into a blank wall. Haven't a clue how you'd go about looking for her. So, you still got a thing for her?"

I stretched out in the tub and looked up at the ceiling. Was I still in love with Kiki?

"I don't know. But that's almost beside the point now. I just have to see her. Something's been telling me Kiki wants to see me. I keep dreaming about her."

"Strange," she said, looking me in the eye. "I sometimes dream about Kiki, too."

"What sort of dreams?"

She didn't reply. She only smiled and said she'd like another drink. She rested against my chest and I threw my arm around her naked shoulder. Gotanda and his girl showed no sign of emerging from the bedroom. Asleep, I supposed.

"I know you won't believe me," she then said, "but I like being with you like this. I enjoy it, no business, no acting. It's the truth."

"I believe you," I said. "I'm enjoying myself, too. I feel really relaxed. It's like a class reunion."

"Unique, again," she giggled.

"About Kiki," I pressed on, "isn't there anyone who'd know? Her real name, her address, that sort of thing?"

She shook her head slowly. "We almost never talk about those things. Why else would we bother with these names?

She was Kiki. I'm Mei, the other girl's Mami. Everyone's four letters or less. It's our cover. Private life is out-of-bounds. We don't know and we don't ask. Manners, you know. We're all real friendly and we go out together sometimes. But it's not really us. We don't actually know each other. Mei, Kiki. These names don't have real lives. We're all image. Signs tacked up in empty air. That's why we respect each other's illusions. Does that make sense?"

"Perfect sense," I said.

"Some of our customers take pity on us. But we don't do this just for the money. Me, for example, I do it 'cause it's fun. And because the club is strictly for members only, we don't have to worry about crazies, and everyone wants to have fun with us. After all, we're all in this made-up world together."

"Shoveling snow for the fun of it," I threw in.

"Right, shoveling snow for fun," she laughed. Then putting her lips to my chest, "Sometimes even snowball fights."

"Mei." I said her name over again. "I once knew a girl whose name really was Mei. She worked as a receptionist at the dentist's next to my office. From a farming family up in Hokkaido. Skinny, dark. Everyone called her Mei the Goat Girl."

"Mei the Goat Girl," she repeated. "And your name?"

"Winnie the Pooh," I said.

"Our own little fairy tale."

I drew her to me and kissed her. It was a heady kiss, a nostalgic kiss. Then we drank our umpteenth brandy-and-soda, and snuggled together while listening to the Police. Soon Mei had drifted off to sleep, no longer the beautiful dream woman, but only an ordinary, brittle young girl. A class reunion. The clock read four o'clock and everything was still. Mei the Goat Girl and Winnie the Pooh. Images. Deductible fairy tales. What a day! Connections that almost connected but didn't. Follow the string until it snaps. I'd met Gotanda after all these years, even come to like him, really.

Through him I'd met Mei the Goat Girl. We made love. Which was wonderful. Shoveled sensual snow. But none of it led anywhere.

I made some coffee, and at half past six the others woke up. Mei had on a bathrobe. Mami came in wearing a paisley pajama top and Gotanda the bottom. I was in my jeans and T-shirt. We all took seats at the dining table and passed around the toast and marmalade. The FM station was playing "Baroque for You." A Henry Purcell pastoral.

"Morning at camp," I said.

Cuck–koo, sang Mei.

At seven-thirty Gotanda called a taxi for the girls. Mei kissed me good-bye. "If you find Kiki, give her my best," I said. I handed her my card and asked her to call if she learned anything.

"Hope we can meet again and shovel some more snow," she winked.

"Shovel snow?" Gotanda asked.

Gotanda and I sat down to another cup of coffee. It was like a commercial. A quiet morning, sun rising, Tokyo Tower gleaming in the distance. *Tokyo begins its mornings with Nescafé.*

Time for normal people to be starting their day. Not for us though. Like it or not, we two were excluded.

"Find out anything about Kiki?" asked Gotanda.

I shook my head. "Only that she'd disappeared. Just like you said. No leads, not a clue. Mei didn't even know her real name."

"I'll ask around the film company," he said. "Maybe somebody knows something."

He pouted slightly and pressed at his temple with the handle of his coffee spoon. He sure was good at it.

"But tell me, what do you plan to do if you find her?" he

asked. "Try to win her back? Or is it just for old times?"

I told him I didn't know. I hadn't thought that far.

Gotanda saw me home in his spotless brown Maserati.

"Mind if I call you again soon?" he said. "It really was terrific seeing you. Don't know anyone else I can talk to like we did. That is, if it's okay by you."

"Of course," I said. And I thanked him again for the steak and drinks and girls and . . .

He gave a quiet shake of his head. Without a word, I understood everything he meant to say.

20

The next few days passed uneventfully. The phone rang, but the whole time I kept the answering machine on and didn't bother picking up. Nice to know that my services were still in demand, though. I cooked meals, went into Shibuya, and saw *Unrequited Love* every day. It was spring break, so the theater was always packed with high school students. It was like an animal house. I wanted to burn the place down.

Now that I knew what to look for, I was able to find Kiki's name, in fine type, in the opening credits.

Then after her scene, I'd leave the theater and walk my usual course. From Harajuku to the Jingu Stadium, Aoyama Cemetery, Omotesando, past the Jintan Building, back to Shibuya. Sometimes I'd stop for a coffee along the way. Spring had surely come, bringing its familiar smells. The earth persisted in its measured orbit of the sun. I always find it a cosmic mystery that spring knows when to follow winter. And how is it that spring always brings out the same smells? Year after year, however subtle, exactly identical.

The town was plastered with election posters. Ugly and repugnant. Trucks were making the rounds, blaring out speeches by politicians. So loud you couldn't tell what they were saying. Noise.

I walked and I thought about Kiki. And before long I

noticed I'd regained my stride, a lift had come back to my step. My awareness of things around me had sharpened. I was moving forward intently, one step at a time. I had focus, a goal. Which somehow, quite naturally, lightened my step, almost gave me soft-shoe footwork. This was a good sign. *Dance.* Keep in step, light but steady. Freshen up, maintain the rhythm, keep things going. I had to pay careful attention where this was leading me to next. Had to make sure I stayed in *this world.*

The last four or five days of March passed in this way. On the surface, there was no progression at all. I'd do the shopping, make meals in the kitchen, see *Unrequited*, go for long walks. I'd play back the answering machine when I got home—inevitably calls about work. At night, I'd read and drink alone. Every day was a repeat of the day before.

Drinking alone at night, I fixated on sex with Mei the Goat Girl. Shoveling snow. An oddly isolated memory, unconnected to anything. Not to Gotanda, not to Kiki. But ever so real. Down to the smallest details, in some sense even more vivid than waking reality, though ultimately unconnected. I liked it that way. A self-bound meeting of souls. Two persons joined together respecting their illusions and images. That fine-we're-all-friends-here smile. Morning at camp. *Cuck–koo.*

I tried to picture Kiki and Gotanda sleeping together. Did she give him the same ultra-sexy service as Mei gave me? Were all the girls at the club drilled in such professional know-how? Or was Mei strictly her own technician? I had no idea, and I couldn't very well ask Gotanda. All the time Kiki was living with me, she was, if anything, rather passive about sex. Sure, she warmed up and responded, but she never made the first move, never had demands of her own. Not that I ever had any complaints. She was wonderful when she relaxed. Her soft inviting body, quiet easy breath, hot vagina. No, I had no complaints. I just couldn't picture her delivering professional favors to anyone—to Gotanda, for instance. Maybe I lacked the imagination.

How do prostitutes keep their private sex separate from their professional sex? Before Mei, I'd never slept with a call girl. I'd slept with Kiki. And Kiki was a call girl. But I didn't sleep with Kiki the call girl, I slept with Kiki. And conversely I'd slept with Mei the call girl, but not Mei. There probably was nothing to gain from correlating these two circumstances. That would only make matters more complicated. And anyway, where does sex stop being a thing of the mind? Where does technique begin? How far does the real thing go, how much is acting? Was sufficient foreplay a spiritual concern? Did Kiki actually enjoy sex with me? Was she really acting in the movie? Were Gotanda's graceful fingers sliding down her back turning her on?

Caught in the cross hair of the real and the imaginary.

Take Gotanda. His doctor persona was all image. Yet he looked more like a real doctor than any doctor I knew. All the dependability and trust he projected.

What was *my* image? Did I even have one?

Dance, the Sheep Man said. *Dance in tip-top form.Dance so it all keeps spinning.*

Did that mean I would then have an image? And if I did, would people be impressed? Well, more than they'd be impressed by my real self, I bet.

When I awoke the following morning, it was April. As delicately rendered as a passage from Truman Capote, fleeting, fragile, beautiful. April, made famous by T.S. Eliot and Count Basie.

I went to Kinokuniya for some overpriced groceries and well-trained vegetables. Then I picked up two 6-packs of beer and three bottles of bargain wine.

When I got back home, there was a message from Yuki, her voice totally disinterested. She said she'd call again around twelve. Then she slammed down the receiver. A common phrasing in her body language.

I dripped some coffee, then sat down with a mug and the

latest 87th Precinct adventure, something I've failed to quit for ten years now. Then a little past noon, the phone rang.

"How's it going?" It was Yuki.

"Okay."

"What are you doing?" she asked.

"Thinking about lunch. Smoked salmon with pedigreed lettuce and razor-sharp slices of onion that have been soaked in ice water, brushed with horseradish and mustard, served on French butter rolls baked in the hot ovens of Kinokuniya. A sandwich made in heaven!"

"It sounds okay."

"It's not okay. It's nothing less than uplifting. And if you don't believe me, you can ask your local bee. You could also ask your friendly clover. They'll tell you—it really is great."

"What's this bee and clover stuff? What're you talking about?"

"Figure of speech."

"You know," said Yuki, "you ought to try growing up. I'm only thirteen, but even so I sometimes think you're kind of dumb."

"You mean I should become more conventional? Is that what you're telling me? Is that what growing up means?"

"I want to go for a drive," she ignored my question. "How about tonight?"

"I think I'm free," I said.

"Well, then, be here at five in Akasaka. You remember how to get here, don't you?"

"Yeah, but don't tell me you've been alone all this time?"

"Uh-huh. Nothing's happening in Hakone. I mean, the place is on top of a mountain. Who wants to go there to be alone? More fun in town."

"What about your mother? She hasn't returned?"

"Not that I know of. I can't keep track of her. I'm not *her* mother, you know. She hasn't called or anything, so maybe she's still in Kathmandu."

"What about money?"

"I'm okay for money. I've got a cash card that I pinched

from her purse. One less card, she'll never notice. I mean, if I don't look out for myself, I'll die. Mama's such a space cadet, as you know."

My turn to ignore her. "You been eating healthy?"

"I'm eating. What did you think? I'd die if I didn't."

"That's not what I asked. I said, are you eating *healthy*?"

Yuki coughed. "Let's see. First there was Kentucky Fried Chicken, then McDonald's, then Dairy Queen, . . . And what else?"

"I'll be there at five," I said. "We'll go somewhere decent to eat. You can't survive on the garbage you've been putting down. An adolescent girl needs nourishment. You're at a very delicate time of life, you know. Bad diet, bad periods."

"You're an idiot," she muttered.

"Now, if it's not too much to ask, would you give me your phone number?"

"Why?"

"Because one-way communication isn't fair. You know my number, I don't know yours. You call me when you feel like it, I can't call you. It's one-sided. Besides, suppose something came up suddenly, I wouldn't be able to reach you."

She paused, muttered some more, then gave me her number.

"But don't think you can change plans anytime you feel like it," said Yuki. "Mama's so good at it already, you wouldn't stand a chance."

"I promise. I won't change plans. Cross my heart and hope to die. You can ask the cabbage moth, you can ask the alfalfa. There's not a human alive who keeps promises better than me. But sometimes the unexpected happens. It's a big, complicated world, you know. And if it happens, don't you think it'd be nice if I could get through to you? Got it?"

"Unforeseeable circumstances," she said.

"Out of the clear blue sky."

"Nice if they didn't happen," said Yuki.

"Nice if they didn't," I echoed.

But of course they did.

21

They showed up a little past three in the afternoon.

I was in the shower when the doorbell started ringing. By the time I got there, it was on ring number eight. I opened up, and there stood two men.

One in his forties, one in his thirties. The older guy was tall, with a scar on his nose. A little too well-tanned for this time of the year, a deep, tried-and-true bronze of a fisherman, not the precious color you get from the beach or ski slope. He had stiff hair, obscenely large hands, and a gray overcoat. The younger guy was short with longish hair and narrow, intense eyes. A generation ago he might have been called bookish. The fellow at the literary journal meeting who ran his hands through his hair as he declared, "Mishima's our man." He had on a dark blue trench coat. Both guys in regulation black shoes, cheap and worn-out. The sort you wouldn't glance at twice if you saw them lying by the side of the road. Nor were the fellas the type you'd go out of your way to make friends with.

Without a word of introduction, Bookish flashed his police ID. Just like in the movies. I'd never actually seen a police ID before, but one look convinced me it was the real thing. It fit with the worn-out shoes. Something in the way he pulled it out of his pocket, he could have been selling his literary journal door-to-door.

"Akasaka precinct," Bookish announced, and asked if I was who I was.

Uh-huh.

Fisherman stood by silently, both hands in the pockets of his overcoat, nonchalantly propping the door open with his foot. Just like in the movies. Great!

Bookish filed away his ID, then gave me the once-over. Me in bathrobe and wet hair.

"We need you to come down to headquarters for questioning," said Bookish.

"Questioning? About what?"

"Everything in due time," he said. "We have formal procedures to follow for this sort of thing, so why don't we get going right away."

"Huh? Okay, but mind if I get into some clothes?"

"Certainly," said Bookish flatly, without the slightest change of expression. If Gotanda played a cop, he'd do a better job. That's reality for you.

The fellas waited in the doorway while I got some clothes on and turned off switches. Then I stepped into my blue topsiders, which the two cops stared at as if they were the trendiest thing on the market.

A patrol car was parked near the entrance to my building, a uniformed cop behind the wheel. Fisherman got into the backseat, then me, then Bookish. Again, like in the movies. Bookish pulled the door shut and the car took off.

The streets were congested, but did they turn on the siren? No, they made like we were going for a ride in a taxi. Sans meter. We spent more time stopped in traffic than moving, which gave everybody in all the cars and on the street plenty of opportunity to stare at me. No one uttered a word. Fisherman looked straight ahead, arms folded. Bookish looked out the window, grimacing like he was laboring over a literary exercise. The school of dark-and-stormy metaphors. *Spring as concept raged in upon us, a somber tide of longing. Its advent roused the passions of those nameless multitudes fallen between the cracks of the city, sweeping them noiselessly toward the quicksands of futility.*

I wanted to erase the whole passage from my head. What the hell was "spring as concept"? Just where were these "quicksands of futility"? I was sorry I started the whole dumb train of thought.

Shibuya was full of mindless junior high students dressed like clowns, same as ever. No passions, no quicksand.

At police headquarters, I was taken to an interrogation room upstairs. Barely three meters square with one tiny window. Table, two steel office chairs, two vinyl-covered stools, clock on the wall. That was it. On the table, a telephone, a pen, ashtray, stack of folders. No vase with flowers. The gumshoes entered the room and offered me one of the steel office chairs. Fisherman sat down opposite me, Bookish stood off to the side, notepad open. Lots of silent communication.

"So what'd you do last night?" Fisherman finally got going after a lengthy wait. Those were the first words I'd heard out of his mouth.

Last night? What was I doing? I could hardly think last night was any different from any other night. Sad but true. I told them I'd have to think about it.

"Listen," Fisherman said, coughing, "legal rigmarole takes a long time to spit out. We're asking you a simple question: From last evening until this morning what did you do? Not so hard, is it? No harm in answering, is there?"

"I told you, I have to think about it," I said.

"You can't remember without thinking? This was yesterday. We're not asking about last August, which maybe you don't remember either," Fisherman sneered.

Like I told you before, I was about to say, then I reconsidered. I doubted they would understand a temporary memory loss. They'd probably think I had some screws loose.

"We'll wait," said Fisherman. "Take all the time you need." He pulled a pack of cigarettes from his jacket pocket and lit up with a Bic. "Smoke?"

"No thanks," I said. According to *Brutus* magazine,

today's new urbanite doesn't smoke. Apparently these two guys didn't know about this, Fisherman with his Seven Stars, Bookish with his plain Hopes, chain-smoking.

"We'll give you five minutes," said Bookish, very deadpan. "After that you will tell us something simple, such as, where you were last night and what you were doing there."

"Don't rush the guy. He's an intellectual," Fisherman said to Bookish. "According to his file here, this isn't his first time talking to the law. University activist, obstruction of public offices. We have his prints. Files sent to the prosecutor's office. He's used to our gentle questioning. Steel-reinforced will, it says here. He doesn't seem to like the police very well. You know, I bet he knows all about his rights, as provided for in the constitution. You think he'll be calling for his lawyer next?"

"But he came downtown with us of his own volition and we merely asked him a simple question," Bookish said to Fisherman. "I haven't heard any talk of arrest, have you? I don't think there's any reason for him to call his lawyer, do you? Wouldn't make sense."

"Well, if you ask me, I think it's more than an open-and-shut case of hating cops. The gentleman has a negative psychological reaction to anything that resembles authority. He'd rather suffer than cooperate," Fisherman went on.

"But if he doesn't answer our questions, what can we do but wait until he answers. As soon as he answers, he can go home. No lawyer's going to come running down here just because we asked him what he was doing last night. Lawyers are busy people. An intellectual understands that."

"Well, I suppose," said Fisherman. "If the gentleman can grasp that principle, then we can save each other a lot of time. We're busy, he's busy. No point in wasting valuable time when we could be thinking deep thoughts. It gets tiresome. We don't want to wear ourselves out unnecessarily."

The duo kept up their comic routine for the allotted five minutes.

"Well, it looks like time's up," Fisherman smiled. "How

about it? Did you remember anything?"

I hadn't. True, I hadn't been trying very hard. Current situation aside, the fact was, I couldn't remember a thing. The block wouldn't budge. "First of all, I'd like to know what's going on," I spoke up. "Unless you tell me what's going on, I'm not saying a thing. I don't want to say anything that may prove inopportune. Besides, it's common courtesy to explain the circumstances before asking questions. It's a breach of good manners."

"He doesn't want to say anything that may prove *inopportune*," Bookish mocked me. "Where is our *common courtesy*? We don't want to have a—what did he call it?—*breach of good manners*."

"I told you the gentleman was an intellectual," said Fisherman. "He looks at everything slanted. He hates cops. He subscribes to *Asahi Shimbun* and reads *Sekai*."

"I do not subscribe to newspapers and I do not read *Sekai*," I broke in. Had to put my foot down somewhere. "And as long as you don't tell me why I'm here, I'm not going to feel a lot like talking. If you want to keep insulting me, go ahead. I've got as much time to sit around shooting the breeze as you guys do."

The two detectives looked at each other.

Fisherman: "Are you telling us that if we're polite and explain these circumstances to you, you'll cooperate and give us some answers?"

Me: "Probably."

Bookish, folding his arms and glancing high up the wall: "The guy's got a sense of humor."

Fisherman rubbed the horizontal scar on his nose. Probably a knife gash, and fairly deep, judging from how it tugged at the surrounding flesh. "Listen," he got serious. "We're busy, and this isn't a game. We all want to finish up and go home in time to eat dinner with the family. We don't have anything against you, and we got no axes to grind. So if you'll just tell us what you did last night, there'll be no more demands. If you got a clear conscience, what's the grief in telling us? Or is it you got guilty feelings about something?"

I stared at the ashtray.

Bookish snapped his notepad shut and slipped it into his pocket. For thirty seconds, no one said a word. During which time, Fisherman lit up another Seven Stars.

"Steel-reinforced will," said Fisherman.

"Want to call the Committee on Human Rights?" asked Bookish.

"Please," Fisherman and his partner were at it again, "this is not a human rights issue. This is the duty of the citizen. It's written, right here in your favorite *Statutes of Law*, that citizens are obliged to cooperate to the fullest extent with police investigations. So what do you have against us officers of the law? We're good enough to ask for directions when you're lost, we're good enough to call if a robber breaks into your home, but we're not good enough to cooperate with just a little bit. So let's try this again. Where were you last night and what were you doing?"

"I want to know what's going on," I repeated.

Bookish blew his nose with a loud honk. Fisherman took a plastic ruler out of the desk drawer and whacked it against the palm of his hand.

"Listen, guy," pronounced Bookish, tossing a soiled tissue into the trash, "you do realize that your position is becoming worse and worse?"

"This is not the sixties, you know. You can't keep carrying on with this antiestablishment bullshit," said Fisherman, disgruntled. "Those days are over. You and me, we're hemmed in up to here in society. There's no such thing as establishment and antiestablishment anymore. That's passé. It's all the same big-time. The system's got everything sewed up. If you don't like it, you can sit tight and wait for an earthquake. You can go dig a hole. But getting sassy with us won't get you or us anywhere. It's a dead grind. You understand?"

"Okay, we're beat. And maybe we've not shown you proper respect. If that's the case, I'm sorry. I apologize."

Bookish's turn again, notepad open again. "We've been working on another job and hardly even slept since yesterday. I haven't seen my kids in five days. And although you have no respect for me, I'm a public servant. I try to keep society safe. So when you refuse to answer a simple question, you can bet it rubs us the wrong way. And when I say things are looking worse for you, it's because the more tired we get, the worse our temper gets. An easy job ends up being not so easy after all. Of course you got rights, the law's on your side, but sometimes the law takes a long time to kick in and so it gets put in the hands of us poor suckers on duty. You get my drift?"

"Don't misunderstand, we're not threatening you," Fisherman interjected. "He was just giving you a friendly warning. He doesn't want anything bad to happen to you."

I kept my mouth shut and looked at the ashtray. A plain old dirty glass ashtray without markings. How many decades had it sat here on this desk?

Fisherman kept slapping his hands with the ruler. "Very well," he gave in. "I'll explain the circumstances. It's not the procedure we follow when asking questions, but since we want your respect, we'll try things your way."

He picked up a folder, removed an envelope and produced three large photographs. Black-and-white site photos, without much in the way of artistry. That much was clear at a glance. The first photo showed a naked woman lying facedown on a bed. Long legs, tight ass, hair fanned out from the neck up. Her thighs were parted just enough to reveal what was between them. Her arms flung out to the sides. She could have been sleeping.

The second photo was more graphic. She was turned over, her pubic area, breasts, face exposed. Her legs and arms arranged stiffly at attention. Her eyes open wide, glassy, her mouth contorted out of shape. The woman was not sleeping. The woman was dead.

The woman was Mei.

The third photo was a close-up of Mei's face. Mei. No

longer beautiful. Cold, ice cold. Chafe marks around her neck.

My mouth went dry, I couldn't swallow. My palms itched. Mei. So full of life and sex. Now cold, dead.

I stopped myself from shaking my head, from showing any reaction. I knew the two guys were watching my every move. I restacked the three photos and casually handed them back to Fisherman. I tried to look unaffected.

"Do you know this woman?" asked Fisherman.

"No." I could've said yes, of course, but then I would've had to tell them about Gotanda, who was my link to Mei, and his life would be ruined if this got out to the media. True, he might have been the one who coughed up my name. But I didn't know that. I'd have to risk it. *They* weren't about to bring up Gotanda's name.

"Take another look," Fisherman said slowly. "This is extremely important, so do look again carefully before you answer. Have you ever seen this woman before? Don't bother lying to us. We're not babes in the woods. We catch you lying, you'll *really* be in trouble. Understand?"

I took a lengthy look at the three photographs. I didn't want to look at all, but that would have given me away.

"I don't know her," I said. "But she's dead, right?"

"Dead," Bookish repeated after me. "Very dead. Extremely dead. Completely dead. As you can see for yourself. This fox is naked and dead. Once a very fine specimen, but now that she's dead it cuts no ice. She's dead, like all dead people. You let her decay, her skin starts to crack and shrivel, the rot oozes out. And the stink! And the bugs. Ever see that?"

Never, I said.

"Well, we've seen it plenty. It gets to where you can't even tell that it was a woman. It's dead meat. Rotten steak. And once the smell gets in your nose, you don't think of food, let me tell you. It's a smell you never forget. True, if you let things go for a long, long, long time, then all you got are bones. No smell. Everything's all dried up. White, beautiful, clean bones. Needless to say, this lady didn't make it that far. And she wasn't rotting either. Just dead. Just stiff. You could tell she had to be some piece when she was warm. But seeing her like this, I didn't even twitch.

"Somebody killed this woman. She had the right to live. She was barely twenty. Somebody strangled her with a stocking. Not a very quick way to go. It's painful and it takes time. You know you're going to die. You're thinking why do I have to die like this? You want to go on living. But you can feel the oxygen drying up. Your head goes foggy. You piss. You lose the feeling in your legs. You die slow. Not a nice way to die. We'd like to catch the son of a bitch who killed this gorgeous young thing. And I think you're going to help us.

"Yesterday at noon, the lady reserved a double room in a luxury hotel in Akasaka. At five P.M., she checked in, alone," Fisherman recounted the facts. "She told the desk her husband would show up later. Phony name, phony telephone number. At six P.M., she called room service for dinner for one. She was alone at the time. At seven P.M., the empty tray was put out in the hall. The DO NOT DISTURB sign was hanging on the door. Checkout time was twelve noon. When the lady didn't check out, the front desk called her room at twelve-thirty. No answer. The DO NOT DISTURB sign was still on the door. There was no response. When hotel security unlocked the door, the lady was naked and dead, exactly as you see in this first photograph. No one saw the lady's 'husband.' The hotel has a restaurant on the top floor, so there's a lot of people going in and out. Very popular place to rendezvous."

"There was no identification in her handbag," said Bookish. "No driver's license, address book, credit cards, no bank card. No initials on her clothing. Besides cosmetics, birth-control pills, and thirty thousand yen, the only item in her possession, tucked, almost hidden, in her wallet, was a business card. *Your* business card."

"You're going to say you really don't know her?" Fisherman tried again.

I shook my head. I wanted to give these guys all the cooperation I could. I really did. I wanted to see her killer caught as much as anyone. But I had the living to think about.

"Well, then, now that you know the circumstances, why don't you tell us where you were last night and what you were doing," Bookish drummed on.

My memory came rushing back. "At six o'clock I ate supper at home by myself, then I read and had a couple of drinks, then before midnight I went to bed."

"Did you see anyone?" asked Fisherman.

"I didn't see anyone. I was alone the entire time."

"Any phone calls to anyone? Anyone call you?"

I told them I didn't take any calls. "A little before nine, one came in on the machine. When I played it back, it was work-related."

"Why keep the answering machine on, if you're at home?"

"I'm on a break. I don't want to have to talk business."

They asked for the name of the caller, and I told them.

"So you ate dinner alone, and you read all evening?"

"After washing the dishes, yes."

"What was the book?"

"You may not believe it, but it was Kafka. *The Trial.*"

Kafka. *The Trial.* Bookish made note.

"Then, you read until twelve," Fisherman kept going. "And drank."

"First beer was around sundown. Later brandy."

"How much did you drink?"

"Two cans of beer, and then I guess a quarter of a bottle of brandy. Oh, and I also ate some canned peaches."

Fisherman took everything down. *Also ate canned peaches.* "Anything else?"

I tried, but it really had been a night without qualities. I'd quietly read my book, while somewhere off in the still of the night Mei was strangled with a stocking. I told them there was nothing else.

"I'd advise you to try harder," said Bookish with a cough.

"You realize what a vulnerable position you're in, don't you?"

"Listen, I didn't do anything, so how can I be in a vulnerable position? I work free-lance, so I hand my business card out all over the place. I don't know how this girl got ahold of my card. Just because she had it on her doesn't mean I killed her."

"People don't carry around business cards that don't mean anything to them in the safest corner of their wallets," Fisherman said. "We have two hypotheses. One, the lady arranged to meet one of your business associates in the hotel and that person killed her. Then the guy dumped something into her bag to throw us off the track. Except the card, that single card, was wedged too deep in her wallet for that. Hypothesis number two, the lady was a professional lady of the night. A prostitute. A high-class prostitute. The kind that fulfills her duties at luxury hotels. The kind that doesn't carry any identification on her person. But for some reason the john kills her. He doesn't take any money, so it's possible he's a psycho, a nut case. Those are our angles. What do you think?"

I cocked my head to the side and kept silent.

"Your business card is the central piece of evidence in this case," said Fisherman leadingly, rapping his pen on the desk.

"A business card is just a piece of paper with a name printed on it," I said. "It's not evidence. It doesn't prove anything."

"Not yet it doesn't." He kept rapping on the desk. "The Criminal ID boys are going over the room for traces. There's an autopsy going on right now. By tomorrow we'll know a lot more. So you know what? You're going to wait with us. Meanwhile, be a good idea if you start remembering more details. It might take all night. Take your time, you'll be surprised at what you can remember. Why don't we start from the beginning? What did you do when you woke up in the morning?"

I looked at the clock on the wall. Ten past five. I suddenly remembered my date with Yuki.

"I need to call somebody first, okay?" I said to Fisherman. "I was supposed to meet someone at five. It was important."

"A girl?" questioned Fisherman.

"Right."

He held out the phone to me.

"You're going to tell me that something came up and you can't come," Yuki said immediately, beating me to the punch.

"Something unforeseen. Really," I explained. "I'm sorry, it's not my fault. I've been hauled down to the Akasaka police station for questioning. It'll take too long to tell you about it now, but it looks like they're going to hold onto me for a while."

"Police? What'd you do?"

"I didn't do anything. There was a murder, and the cops wanted to talk to me. That's all."

"What a drag," Yuki remarked, unmoved.

"I'll say."

"You didn't kill anyone, did you?"

"Of course I didn't kill anyone. I'm a bungler, not a murderer. They're just asking about, you know, circumstances. But I'm sorry I'm going to let you down. I'll make it up to you."

"What a drag," said Yuki, then slammed down the receiver in her inimitable fashion.

I passed the phone back to Fisherman. They had been straining to listen in, but didn't seem to come away with much. If they knew it was a thirteen-year-old girl, you can be sure their opinion of me wouldn't have shot up.

They had me go over the fine points of my movements all day yesterday. They wrote everything I said down. Where I'd gone, what I ate. I gave them the full rundown on the *konnyaku* yam stew I'd eaten for dinner. I explained how I shaved the bonito flakes. They didn't think I was being humorous at all. They just wrote everything down. The pages were mounting fast.

At half past six they sent out for food—salty, greasy, tasteless, terrible—which we all ate with relish. Then we had some lukewarm tea, while they smoked. Then we got back to questions and answers.

At what time had I changed into pajamas? From what page to what page of *The Trial* had I read? I tried to tell them what the story was about, but they didn't show much interest.

At eight o'clock I had to take a leak. Which they let me do alone, happily. I breathed deeply. Not the ideal place to breathe deeply, but at least I could breathe. Poor Mei.

When I got back, Bookish wanted to know about my solitary telephone caller that evening. Who was he? What did he want? What was my relationship with him? Why didn't I call him back? Why was I taking a break from work? Didn't I need to work for a living? Did I declare my taxes?

My question, which I didn't ask, was: Did they actually think all this was helpful? Maybe they *had* read Kafka. Were they trying to wear me down so that I'd let the truth escape? Well, they'd succeeded. I was so exhausted, so depressed, I was answering everything they asked with a straight face. I was under the mistaken impression that I'd get out of here quicker that way.

By eleven, they hadn't stopped. And they showed no sign of stopping. They'd been able to take turns, leave the room and take a nap while the other kept at me. I hadn't had that luxury. Instead, they offered me coffee. Instant coffee, with sugar and white powder mixed in.

At eleven-thirty I made my declaration: I was tired and wasn't going to answer any more questions.

"Aww, c'mon, *pul-eeze*," Bookish said lamely, drumming his fingers on the table. "Listen, we're going as fast as we can, but this investigation is very important. We have a dead lady on our hands, so I'm afraid you're going to have to stick it out."

"I find it hard to believe these questions have any importance at all," I said.

"Petty details serve their purpose. You'd be surprised how many cases are solved by petty details. What looks like petty isn't always petty, especially when it comes to homicide. Murder isn't petty. Sorry, but why don't you just hang around a while. To be perfectly frank, if we felt like it, we could designate you a prime witness and you'd be stuck here as long as we liked. But that would take a lot of paperwork. Bogs everything down. That's why we're being nice, asking you to go through this with us nice and easy. If you cooperate, we won't have to get rough."

"If you're sleepy, there's a bunk downstairs," Fisherman said. "Catch a few hours of shut-eye, you might remember something."

Okay, a few hours sleep would be nice. Anywhere was better than this smoke-filled hole.

Fisherman walked me down a dark corridor, down an even darker stairwell, to another corridor. This was not boding well. Indeed, the bunk room was a holding tank.

"Nice place, but can I get something with a better view?"

"All due apologies. It's our only model," said Fisherman without expression.

"No way. I'm going home. I'll be back tomorrow."

"Don't worry, we're not locking you in," said Fisherman. "A cell is just a room if you don't lock the door."

I was too tired to argue. I gave up. I stumbled in and fell onto the hard cot. Damp mattress, cheap blanket, smell of piss. Love it.

"It won't be locked," Fisherman repeated as he shut the door with a cold, solid *thunk*.

I sighed and pulled the blanket over me. Someone somewhere was snoring loudly. It seemed to come from far off, but it could've been in the next cell. Very disturbing.

But Mei, Mei! You were on my mind last night. I don't know if you were alive at the time, but you were on my mind. I was slowly taking off your clothes, and then we were making love. It was our little class reunion. I was so relaxed, I thought someone had loosened the main screw of this world. But now, Mei, there's nothing I can do for you. Not a damned thing. I'm sorry. We lead such tenuous lives. I don't want Gotanda to get caught up in a scandal. I don't want to ruin his image. He wouldn't get work after that. Trashy work in a trashy world of trashy images. But he trusted me, as a friend. So it's a matter of honor. But Mei, my little Goat Girl Mei, we did have a good time together. It was so wonderful. Like a fairy tale. It's no comfort to you, Mei, but I'll never forget you. Shoveling snow until dawn. Holding you tight in that world of images, making love on deductible expenses. Winnie the Pooh and Mei the Goat Girl. Strangling is a horrible way to die. And you didn't want to die, I know. But there's nothing I can do for you now. I don't know what's right or wrong. I'm doing all I can. This is how I live. It's the system. I bite my lip and do what I got to. Good night, Mei, my little Goat Girl. At least you'll never have to wake again. Never have to die again.

Good night, I voiced the words.

Good night, echoed my mind.

Cuck–koo, sang Mei.

22

The next day wasn't much different than the previous. In the morning the three of us reassembled in the interrogation room over a silent breakfast of coffee and bread. Then Bookish loaned me an electric razor, which was not exactly sharp. Since I hadn't planned ahead and brought my toothbrush, I gargled as best I could.

Then the questioning started. Stupid, petty legal torture. This went on at a snail's pace until noon.

"Well, I guess that about does it," said Fisherman, laying his pen down on the desk.

As if by prior agreement, the two detectives sighed simultaneously. So I sighed too. They were obviously stalling for time, but obviously they couldn't keep me here forever. One business card in a dead woman's wallet does not constitute sufficient cause for detention. Even if I didn't have an alibi. They'd have to strap me down—at least until the fingerprinting and autopsy yielded a more plausible suspect.

"Well," said Fisherman, pounding the small of his back as he stretched. "About time for lunch."

"As you seem to have finished your questions, I'll be going home," I told them.

"I'm afraid that's not possible," Fisherman said with fake hesitation.

"And why not?" I asked.

"We need to have you sign the statement you've made."

"I'll sign, I'll sign."

"But first, read over the document to verify that the contents are accurate. Word by word. It's extremely important you know what you're signing your name to."

So I read those forty-odd sheets of official police transcriptions. Two hundred years from now, I couldn't help but think, they might be of some value in reconstructing our era. Pathologically detailed, faultlessly accurate. A real boon to research. The daily habits of an average, thirty-four-year-old, single male. A child of his times. The whole exercise of reading it through in this police interrogation room was depressing. But read it I did, from beginning to end. Now I could go home. I straightened the stack of papers and said that everything looked in order.

Playing with his pen, Fisherman glanced over at Bookish. Bookish pulled a single cigarette from his box of Hope Regulars on top of the radiator, lit up and grimaced into the smoke. I had an awful feeling.

"It's not that simple," Bookish spoke in that slow professional tone reserved for elucidating matters to the unordained. "You see, the statement's got to be in your own hand."

"In my own *hand*?"

"Yes, you have to copy everything over. In your own handwriting. Otherwise, it's not legally valid."

I looked at the stack of pages. I didn't have the strength to be angry. I wanted to be angry, I wanted to fly into a rage, I wanted to pound on the desk and scream, *You jerks have no right to do this!* I wanted to stand up and walk out of there. And strictly speaking, I knew they had no right to stop me. Yes, but I was too tired. Too tired to say a word, too tired to protest. If I wasn't going to protest, I'd be better off doing what I was told. Faster and easier. *I'm wimping out*, I confessed to myself. *I'm worn out and I'm wimping out.* Used to be, they'd have to tie me down. But then again, their junk food and cigarette smoke and razor that chewed up my face wouldn't have gotten to me either. I was getting weak in my old age.

"No way," I surprised myself by saying. "I'm going home. I have the right to go home. You can't stop me."

Bookish sputtered something indecipherable. Fisherman stared up at the ceiling and rapped his pen on the desk. *Tap-tap-tap, tap, tap-tap, tap-tap, tap.*

"You're making things difficult," said Fisherman succinctly. "But very well. If that's the way it's going to be, we'll get a summons. And we'll forcibly hold you here for investigation. Next time won't be such a picnic. We don't mind that, you know. It'll be easier for us to do our job that way too. Isn't that right?" he tossed the question over to Bookish.

"Yes sir, that's going to be even easier in the long run. That's what we should've done earlier. Let's get a summons," he declared.

"As you like," I said. "But I'm free until the summons is issued. If and when the summons comes through, you know where to find me. Otherwise, I don't care. I'm outa here."

"We can place a temporary hold on your person until the summons is issued."

I almost asked them to show me where it said that in *Statutes of Law*, but now I *really* didn't have the energy. I knew they were bluffing, but it didn't matter.

"I give up. I'll write out my statement. But I need to make a phone call first."

Fisherman passed me the telephone. I dialed Yuki's number.

"I'm still at the police station," I said. "It looks like this'll take all night. So I guess I won't make it over today either. Sorry."

"You're still in the clink?"

"A real drag." This time I beat her to the punch.

"That's not fair," she came back. There's a lot of descriptive terms out there.

"What have you been doing?"

"Nothing special," she said. "Just lying around, listening to music, reading magazines, eating cake. You know."

The two detectives tried to listen in again.

"I'll call you as soon as I get out of here."

"*If* you get out of there," said Yuki flatly.

"Well, okay then, lunchtime," announced Fisherman, soon as I hung up.

Lunch was *soba*, cold buckwheat noodles. Overcooked and falling apart. Hospital food, practically a liquid diet. An aura of incurable illness hovered over it. Still, the two of them wolfed the stuff down, and I followed suit. To wash down the starch, Bookish brought in more of his famous lukewarm tea.

The afternoon passed as slowly as a silted-up river. The ticking of the clock was the only sound in the room. A telephone rang in the next room. I did nothing but write and write and write and write. Meanwhile the two detectives took turns resting. Sometimes they'd go out into the corridor and whisper.

I kept the pen moving. *At six-fifteen I decided to make dinner, first taking the yam cake out of the refrigerator . . .*

By evening I'd copied twenty pages. Wielding a pen for hours on end is hard work. Definitely not recommended. Your wrist starts to go limp, you get scribe's elbow. The middle finger of your hand begins to throb. Drift off in your thoughts for a second and you get the word wrong. Then you have to draw a line through it and thumbprint your mistake. It could drive a person batty. It was driving *me* batty.

For dinner, we had generic take-out food again. I hardly ate. The tea was still sloshing around in my gut. I felt woozy, lost the sense of who I was. I went to the toilet and looked in the mirror. I could barely recognize myself.

"Any findings yet?" I asked Fisherman. "Fingerprints or traces or autopsy results?"

"Not yet," he said. "These things take time."

I kept at it until ten. I had five more pages to go, but I'd reached my limit. I couldn't write another word and I told them so. Fisherman conducted me to the tank and I dozed right off.

In the morning, it was the same electric razor, coffee, and bread. The five pages took two hours. Then I signed and thumbprinted each sheet. Then Bookish checked the whole lot.

"Am I free to go now?" I asked hopefully.

"If you answer a few more questions, yes, you can go," said Bookish.

I heaved a sigh. "Then you're going to have me do more paperwork, right?"

"Of course," answered Bookish. "This is officialdom. Paperwork is everything. Without the paper and your prints, it doesn't exist."

I pressed my fingers into my temples. It felt as if some loose object were lodged inside. As if something had found its way into my head and ballooned up to where it was impossible to remove.

"This won't take too long. Be over before you know it."

More mindless answers to more mindless questions. Then Fisherman called Bookish out into the corridor. The two stood whispering for I don't know how long. I leaned back in my chair and studied the patterns of mildew on the ceiling. The blackened patches could have been photographs of pubic hair on dead bodies. Spreading down along the cracks in the wall like a connect-the-dots picture. Mildew, cultured in the body odor of the poor fools ground down in this room the last several decades. From a systematic effort to undermine a person's beliefs, dignity, and sense of right and wrong. From psychological coercion that fed on human insecurity and left no visible scars. Where far removed from sunlight and stuffed with bad food, you sweat uncontrollably. Mildew.

I placed both hands on the desk and closed my eyes,

thinking of the snow falling in Sapporo. The Dolphin Hotel and my receptionist friend with glasses. How was she getting along? Standing behind the counter, flashing that professional smile of hers? I wanted to call her up this very second. Tell her some stupid joke. But I didn't even know her name. *I didn't even know her name.*

She sure was cute. Especially when she was working hard. Imbued with that indefinable hotel spirit. She loved her work. Not me. I never once enjoyed mine. I do good work, but I have never *loved* my work. Away from her work, she was vulnerable, uncertain, fragile. I could have slept with her if I'd felt like it. But I didn't.

I want to talk to her again.

Before someone killed her too.

Before she disappeared.

23

The two detectives came back into the room to find me still lost in the mildew. They both stood.

"You can go home now," Fisherman told me, expressionless. "Thanks for your cooperation."

"No more questions. You're done," Bookish added his comments.

"Circumstances have changed," Fisherman said. "We can't keep you here any longer. You're free to go. Thank you again."

I got up from my chair and pulled on my jacket, which reeked of cigarette smoke. I didn't have a clue what had happened, but I was happy to get the hell out of there. Bookish accompanied me to the entrance.

"Listen, we knew you were clean last night," he said. "We got the results from the coroner and the lab. You were clean. Absolutely clean. But you're hiding something. You're biting your tongue. You're not so hard to read. That's why we figured we'd hold you, until you spit it out. You know who that woman is. You just don't want to tell us. For some reason. You know, that's not playing ball. We're not going to forget that."

"Forgive me, but I don't know what you're talking about," I said.

"We might call you in again," he said, digging into his cuticle with a matchstick. "And if we do, you can be sure we'll work you over good. We'll be so on top of things that lawyer of yours won't be able to do a damn thing."

"Lawyer?" I asked, all innocence.

But by then he'd disappeared into the building. I grabbed a taxi back home.

I ran a bath and took a nice, long soak. I brushed my teeth, washed my face, shaved. I couldn't get rid of the smoke on me. What a hole that place was!

Refreshed, I boiled some cauliflower, which I ate along with a beer. I put on Arthur Prysock backed by the Count Basie Orchestra. An unabashedly gorgeous record. Bought sixteen years before. Once upon a time.

After that I slept. Just enough sleep to say I'd been somewhere and back, maybe thirty minutes. When I woke up, it was one in the afternoon. Still time in the day. I packed my gear, threw it into the Subaru, and drove to the Sendagaya Pool. After an hour's swim I was almost feeling human again. And I was hungry.

I called Yuki. When I reported that I'd been released, she gave me a cool *that's nice.* As for food, she'd eaten only two cream puffs all day, sticking to her junk-ridden regimen. If I came over now, though, she'd be ready and waiting, and probably pleased.

I tooled the Subaru through the outer gardens of Meiji Shrine, down the tree-lined avenue before the art museum, and turned at Aoyama-Itchome for Nogi Shrine. Every day was getting more and more like spring. During the two days I'd spent inside the Akasaka police station, the breeze had become more placid, the leaves greener, the sunlight fuller and softer. Even the noises of the city sounded as pleasant as Art Farmer's flügelhorn. All was right with the world and I was hungry. The pressure lodged behind my temples had magically vanished.

Yuki was wearing a David Bowie sweatshirt under a brown leather jacket. Her canvas shoulder bag was a patchwork of Stray Cats and Steely Dan and Culture Club buttons. Strange combination, but who was I to say?

"Have fun with the cops?" asked Yuki.

"Just awful," I said. "Ranks up there with Boy George's singing."

"Oh," she remarked, unimpressed with my cleverness.

"Remind me to buy you an Elvis button for your collection," I said, pointing at her bag.

"What a nerd," she said. Such a rich vocabulary.

We went to a restaurant where we each had a roast beef sandwich on whole wheat and a salad. I made her drink a glass of wholesome milk too. I skipped the milk for myself, got coffee instead. The meat was tender and alive with horseradish. Very satisfying. *This* was a meal.

"Well then, where to from here?" I asked Yuki.

"Tsujido," she said without hesitation.

"Okay by me," I said. "To Tsujido we shall go. But what's there to see in Tsujido?"

"Papa lives there," said Yuki. "He says he wants to meet you."

"Me?"

"Yeah, you. Don't worry, he's not such a bad guy."

I sipped my second cup of coffee. "You know, I never said he was a bad guy. Anyway, why would he want to meet me? You told him about me?"

"Sure. I phoned him and told him how you'd helped me get back from Hokkaido and how you got picked up by the cops and might never come out. So Papa had one of his lawyer friends make inquiries about you. He's got all kinds of connections. He's real practical that way."

"I see," I said. "So that's what it was."

"He can be handy sometimes."

"I'll say."

"Papa said that the police had no right to hold you there like that. If you didn't want to stay there, you were free to go. Legally, that is."

"I knew that myself," I said.

"Why didn't you just go home then? Just up and say, I'm going. *Sayonara.*"

"That's a difficult question," I said after some moments' thought. "Maybe I was punishing myself."

"Not normal," she said, propping up her chin.

It was late in the afternoon and the roads to Tsujido were empty. Yuki had brought a bagful of tapes with her. A complete travel selection, from Bob Marley's "Exodus" to Styx's "Mister Roboto." Some were interesting, some not. Which was pretty much all you could say about the scenery on the way. It all sped past. Yuki sank into her seat silently listening to the music. She tried on the pair of sunglasses I'd left on the dashboard, and at one point she lit up a Virginia Slim. I concentrated on driving. Methodically shifting gears, eyes fixed on the road ahead, carefully checking each traffic sign.

I was jealous of Yuki. Here she was, thirteen years old, and everything, including misery, looked, if not wonderful, at least new. Music and places and people. So different from me. True, I'd been in her place before, but the world was a simpler place then. You got what you worked for, words meant something, things had beauty. But I *wasn't* happy. I was an impossible kid at an impossible age. I wanted to be alone, felt good being alone, but never had the chance. I was locked in these two frames, home and school. I had this crush on a girl, which I didn't know what to do about. I didn't know what love meant. I was awkward and introverted. I wanted to rebel against my teachers and parents, but I didn't know how. Whatever I did, I bungled. I was the exact opposite of Gotanda.

Even so, there were times that I saw freshness and beauty. I could smell the air, and I really loved rock 'n' roll. Tears were warm, and girls were beautiful, like dreams. I liked movie theaters, the darkness and intimacy, and I liked the deep, sad summer nights.

"Hey," I said to Yuki. "Could you tell about that man in

the sheepskin? Where did you meet him? And how did you know I'd met him too?"

She looked at me, placing the sunglasses back on the dashboard, then shrugged. "Okay, but first, will you answer something for me?"

"I guess so," I agreed.

Yuki hummed along with a hangover-heavy Phil Collins song for a moment, then picked up the sunglasses again and played with them. "Do you remember what you said after we got back from Hokkaido? That I was the prettiest girl you ever dated?"

"Uh-huh."

"Did you mean that? Or were you just trying to make me like you? Tell me honestly."

"Honestly, it's the truth," I said.

"How many girls have you dated, up to now?"

"I haven't counted."

"Two hundred?"

"Oh, come on," I laughed. "I'm not that kind of a guy. I may play the field, but my field's not that big. I'd say fifteen, max."

"That few?"

I nodded. This gave her something to puzzle over.

"Fifteen, huh?"

"Around there," I said. "Twenty on the outside."

"Twenty, huh?" sighed a disappointed Yuki. "But out of all of them, I'm the prettiest?"

"Yes, you are the prettiest," I said.

"You never liked the beautiful type?" she asked, lighting up her second Virginia Slim. I spotted a policeman at the intersection ahead, grabbed the cigarette out of her hand, and flung it out the window.

"I dated some pretty girls," I went on. "But none of them was as pretty as you. I mean that. You probably will take this wrong, but you're pretty in a different way. Nothing like most girls. But please, no smoking in the car, okay? You'll stink it up. And I don't want cops poking their nose in.

Besides, don't you know that girls who smoke too much when they're young get irregular periods?"

"Gimme a break," she cried.

"Now tell me about the guy in the sheepskin," I said.

"The Sheep Man?"

"How do you know that was his name?"

"You said it over the phone. *The Sheep Man.*"

"Did I?"

"Uh-huh."

We were stopped at an intersection, waiting for the light to change. Traffic, as we neared Tsujido, had picked up, and the light had to change twice before we could move on.

"So about the Sheep Man. Where did you see him?"

Yuki shrugged. "I never saw him. He just came into my head, when I saw you," she said, winding a strand of her fine straight hair around her finger. "I just had this feeling. About a guy dressed in a sheepskin. Like a hunch. Whenever I ran into you at the hotel, I had this . . . feeling. So I brought it up. That was it."

I tried to make sense of that. I had to think, had to wrack my brains.

"What do you mean by *like a hunch*?" I pressed her. "You mean you didn't really see him? Or you only caught a *glimpse* of him?"

"I don't know how to put it," she said. "It wasn't like I saw him with my own eyes. It was more this feeling that *someone* had seen him, even though he was invisible. I couldn't see anything, but inside, the feeling I had had a kind of shape. Not a definite shape. Something like a shape. If I had to show it to someone, they probably wouldn't know what it was. It could only make sense to me. I'm not explaining this very well. Am I coming through at all?"

"Vaguely."

Yuki raised her eyebrows and nibbled at the frame of my sunglasses.

"Let me go over this again," I tried. "You sensed something in me, some kind of feeling, or ideation—"

"Ideation?"

"A very strong thought. And it was attached to me and you visualized it, like you do in a dream. You mean something like that?"

"Yeah, something kind of like that. A strong thought, but not only that. There was some *thing* behind it. Something powerful. Like energy that was creating the thinking. I could just feel that it was out there. They were like vibes that I could see. But not like a dream. Like an *empty dream*. That's it, an empty dream. Nobody's there, so you don't see anybody. You know, like when you turn the contrast on the TV real low and the brightness way up. You can't see a thing. But there's an image in the picture, and if you squint real hard, you can *feel* what the image is. You know what I mean?"

"Uh-huh."

"Anyway, I could sort of see this man in a sheepskin. He didn't seem evil or anything like that. Maybe he wasn't even a man. But the thing is, he wasn't bad. I don't know how to put it. You can't see it, but it's like a heat rubbing, you know it's something, like a form without a shape." She clicked her tongue. "Sorry, awful explanation."

"You're explaining just fine."

"Really?"

"Really," I said.

We continued our drive along the sea. Beside a pine grove, I pulled the car over and suggested we go for a short walk. The afternoon was pleasant, hardly any wind, the surf gentle. Just a rippling sheet of tiny waves drawing in toward shore. Perfect peaceful periodicity. The surfers had all given up and were sitting around on the beach in their wet suits, smoking. The white smoke trail from burning trash rose nearly straight up into the blue, and off to the left drifted the island of Enoshima, faint and miragelike. A large black dog trotted across the breakers from right to left. In the distance fishing boats dotted the deeper waters, while noiseless white clouds of sea gulls swirled above them. Spring had come even to the sea.

Yuki and I strolled the path along the shore, passing joggers and high school girls on bicycles going the other way. We ambled in the direction of Fujisawa, then we sat down on the sand and looked out to sea.

"Do you often have experiences like that?" I asked.

"Sometimes," said Yuki. "Rarely, actually. I get these feelings from very few people. And I try to avoid them if I can. If I get a feeling, I try not to think about it, I try to close it off. That way I don't have to feel it so deep. It's like if you close your eyes, you don't have to see what's in front of you. You know something's there, like with a scary part in the movies, but you don't have to see it if you shut your eyes and keep them shut until the scary part is over."

"But why should you close yourself up?"

"Because it's horrible to see it," she said. "When I was small, I didn't close up. At school, if I felt something, I just came right out and told everybody about it. But then, it made everyone sick. If someone was going to get hurt, I'd say, so-and-so is going to get hurt, and sure enough, she would. That happened over and over again, until everyone started treating me like a weird spook. That's what they called me. 'Spook.' That was the kind of reputation I had. It was terrible. So ever since then, I decided not to say anything. And now if I feel like I'm going to feel anything, I just close myself up."

"But with me you didn't close up."

She shrugged. "It was an accident. There wasn't any warning. Really, suddenly, the image just popped up. The very first time I saw you. I was listening to music . . . Duran Duran or David Bowie or somebody . . . and I wasn't on guard. I was relaxed. That's why I like music."

"Then you're kind of clairvoyant?" I asked. "Like when, say, you knew beforehand that a classmate was going to get hurt."

"Maybe. But kind of different. When something's going to happen, there's this atmosphere that gives me the feeling it's going to happen. I know it sounds funny, for instance, with someone who's going to get injured on the high bar, there's this carelessness or this overconfidence that's in the air, almost like waves. People who are sensitive can pick up these waves. They're like pockets in the air, maybe even solid pockets in the air. You can tell that there's danger. That's when those empty dreams pop up. And when they do . . . Well, that's what they are. They aren't like premonitions. They're more unfocused. But they appear and I can see them but I'm not talking about them anymore. I don't want people calling me a spook. I just keep my mouth shut. I might see that that person over there is maybe going to get burned. And maybe he does get burned. But he can't blame me. Isn't that horrible? I hate myself for it. That's why I close up. If I close myself, I don't hate myself."

She scooped up sand and sifted it through her fingers.

"Is there really a Sheep Man?" she asked.

"Yes, there really is," I said. "There's a place in that hotel where he lives. A whole other hotel in that hotel. You can't see it most of the time. But it's there. That's where the Sheep Man lives, and all sorts of things connect to me through there. The Sheep Man is kind of like my caretaker, kind of like a switchboard operator. If he weren't around, I wouldn't be able to connect anymore."

"Huh? Connect?"

"Yeah, when I'm in search of something, when I want to connect, he's the one who does it."

"I don't get it."

I scooped up some sand and let it run through my fingers too.

"I still don't really understand it myself. But that's how the Sheep Man explained it to me."

"You mean, the Sheep Man's been there from way back?"

"Uh-huh, for ages. Since I was a kid. But I didn't realize he had the form of the Sheep Man until not so long ago.

Why is he around? I don't know. Maybe I needed him. Maybe because as you get older, things fall apart, so something needs to help hold things together. Put the brakes a little on entropy, you know. But how do I know? The more I think about it, the stranger it seems. Stupid even."

"You ever tell anybody else about it?"

"No. If I did, who would believe me? Who would understand what the hell I was talking about? And anyway, I can't explain it very well. You're the first person I've told."

"I've never talked to anybody about this thing I have either. Mama and Papa know about it a little, but we never discussed it or anything. After what happened in school, I just clamped up about it."

"Well, I guess I'm glad we had this talk," I said.

"Welcome to the Spook Club," said Yuki.

"I haven't gone to school since last summer vacation," Yuki told me as we strolled back to the car. "It's not because I don't like to study. I just hate the place. I can't stand it. It makes me sick, physically sick. I was puking every day and every time I puked, they'd gang up on me some more. Even the teachers were picking on me."

"Why would anyone want to pick on someone as pretty as you?"

"Kids just like to pick on other kids. And if your parents are famous, it can be even worse. Sometimes they treat you special, but with me, they treat me like trash. Anyway, I have trouble getting along with people to begin with. I'm always tense because I might have to close myself up any moment, you know. So I developed this nervous twitch, which makes me look like a duck, and they tease me about that. Kids can be really mean. You wouldn't believe how mean . . ."

"It's all right," I said, grabbing for Yuki's hand and holding it. "Forget about them. If you don't feel like going to school, don't. Don't force yourself. School can be a real nightmare. I know. You have these brown-nosing idiots for classmates and these teachers who act like they own the world. Eighty percent of them are deadbeats or sadists, or both. Plus all those ridiculous rules. The whole system's designed to crush you, and so the goodie-goodies with no imagination get good grades. I bet that hasn't changed a bit."

"Was it like that for you too?"

"Of course. I could talk a blue streak about how idiotic school is."

"But junior high school is compulsory."

"That's for other people to worry about, not you. It's not compulsory to go someplace where you're miserable. Not at all. You have rights too, you know."

"And then what do I do after that? Is it always going to be like this?"

"Things sure seemed that way when I was thirteen," I said. "But that's not how it happens. Things can work out. And if they don't, well, you can deal with that when the time comes. Get a little older, you'll fall in love. You'll buy brassieres. The whole way you look at the world will change."

"Boy, are you a dolt!" she turned to me and shook her head in disbelief. "For your information, thirteen-year-old girls already wear bras. You're half a century behind, I swear!"

"I'm only thirty-four," I reminded her.

"Fifty years," said Yuki. "Time flies when you're a dolt."

And at that, she walked to the car ahead of me.

24

By the time we reached Yuki's father's house near the beach, it was dusk. The house was big and old, the property thick with trees. The area exuded the old charm of a Shonan resort villa. In the grace of the spring evening all was still. Cherry trees were beginning to fill out with buds, a prelude to the magnolias. A masterful orchestration of colors and scents whose change day to day reflected the sweep of the seasons. To think there were still places like this.

The Makimura villa was circumscribed by a high wooden fence, the gate surmounted by a small, traditional gabled roof. Only the nameplate was new. We rang the doorbell and soon a tall youth in his mid-twenties came to let us in. With short-cropped hair and a pleasant smile, he was clean-cut and amiable—not unlike Gotanda but without the refinement. Apparently Yuki had met him several times before. Leading us around to the back of the house, he introduced himself as Makimura's assistant.

"I act as his chauffeur, deliver his manuscripts, research, caddy, accompany him overseas, whatever," he explained eagerly. "I am what in times past was known as a gentleman's valet."

"Ah," I said.

I felt sure Yuki was about to come out with something

rude, but to my surprise she said nothing. Apparently she could be discreet if she wanted to.

Makimura was practicing his golf swing in the backyard. A green net had been stretched between the trunks of two pines. The famous writer was trying to hit the target in the center with little white balls. When his club sliced through the air, you'd hear this *whoosh*. One of my least favorite sounds. Asthmatic and hollow. Though it was pure prejudice that I should feel that way. I hated golf.

Makimura set down his club and wiped his forehead with a towel. "Good to see you," he said to Yuki, who pretended not to have heard. Averting her eyes, she fished a stick of gum from the pocket of her jacket and began to chew with loud *crack*s. Then she wadded up the wrapper and tossed it into a potted plant.

"How about a hello at least?" Makimura tried again.

"Hello," Yuki sneered, plunging her hands into her pockets and wandering off.

"Boy, bring us some beer," Makimura called out rather curtly.

"Yes sir," the manservant answered in a clear voice and hurried into the house. Makimura coughed and spat, wiped his forehead again. Then ignoring my presence for the time being, he squinted at the target on the green net and concentrated. I concerned myself idly with the moss-covered rocks.

The whole scene seemed artificial—and more than a little absurd. There wasn't anything specific that seemed odd. It was more the sense that I had happened upon the stage of an elaborate parody. The author and his valet—except that Gotanda could have played either role better and with more sophistication and appeal.

"Yuki tells me you've been looking after her," said the famous man.

"It wasn't anything special," I said. "I merely got her onto a flight coming back from Hokkaido. More important, though, let me thank you for the help with the police."

"Uh, oh that? No, not at all. Glad to be able to return a

favor. It's so rare that my daughter asks me for anything. I was very happy to help. I hate the police. I had a run-in with them at the Diet way back in the sixties when Michiko Kanba was killed. Back in those times—"

At that he bent over from the waist and gripped his golf club, tapping its head on his foot. He turned to look me in the face, then glanced down at my feet and up at my face again.

"—when a man knew what was right and what wasn't right," said Hiraku Makimura.

I nodded without much conviction.

"You play golf?"

"I'm afraid not," I said.

"You dislike golf?"

"I don't like it or dislike it. I've never played."

He laughed. "There's no such thing as not liking or disliking golf. People who've never played golf hate golf. That's the way it is. So be honest with me."

"Okay, I don't like golf," I said.

"Why not?"

"I guess it strikes me as silly. The overblown gear, the cute carts, the flags and the pompous clothes and shoes. The look in the eyes, the way ears prick up when you crouch down to read the turf. Little things like that bother me."

"The way ears prick up?"

"Just something I've observed. It doesn't mean anything. But there's something about golf that doesn't sit well with me," I answered, summing up.

Makimura stared at me blankly.

"Is there something wrong with you, son?"

"Not at all," I said. "I'm perfectly normal. I guess my jokes aren't very funny."

Before long, the manservant brought out beer on a tray with two glasses. He set the tray down, poured for us, then quickly disappeared.

"Cheers," said Makimura, raising his glass.

"Cheers," I said, doing the same.

I couldn't quite place Makimura's age, but he had to be at least in his mid-forties. He wasn't tall, but his solid frame made him seem like a large man. Broad-chested, thick arms and neck. His neck was thick. If it were trimmer, he could have passed for a sportsman, as opposed to someone with years of dissipated living. I remembered photos of a young, slender Makimura with a piercing gaze. He hadn't been particularly handsome, but he had presence, which he still had. How many years ago had it been? Fifteen? Sixteen? Today, his hair was short, peppered with gray. He was well-tanned and wore a wine-red Lacoste shirt, which couldn't be buttoned around the neck.

"I hear you are a writer," said Makimura.

"Not a real writer," I said. "I produce fill on demand. Negligible stuff, based on how many words they need. Somebody's got to do it, and I figure it might as well be me. I'll spare you my spiel about shoveling snow."

"Shoveling snow, huh?" repeated Makimura, glancing over at the golf clubs he'd set aside. "Clever notion."

"Pleased you think so," I said.

"Well, you like writing?"

"I can't say I like or dislike it. I'm proficient at it, or should I say efficient? I've got the knack, the know-how, the stance, the punch, all that. I don't mind that aspect."

"Uh-huh."

"If the level of the job is low enough, it's very simple anyway."

"Hmm," he mused, pausing several seconds. "You think up that phrase, 'shoveling snow'?"

"I did," I said.

"Mind if I use it somewhere? It's an interesting expression."

"Go right ahead. I didn't take out a copyright on it."

"It's exactly the way I feel sometimes," said Makimura, fingering his earlobe. "That it doesn't amount to a hill of beans. It didn't used to be that way. The world was smaller, you could get a handle on things, you knew—or thought you knew—what you were doing. You knew what people wanted. The media wasn't this huge, vast thing."

He drained his glass, then poured us two more glasses. I declined, said I was driving, but he ignored me.

"But not now. There's no justice. No one cares. People do whatever they have to do to survive. Shoveling snow. Just like you say," he said, eyeing the green net stretched between the tree trunks. Thirty or forty white golf balls lay on the grass.

Makimura seemed to be thinking of what to say next. That took time. Not that it concerned him, he was used to people waiting on his every word. I decided to do the same. He kept pulling at his earlobe.

"My daughter's taken to you," Makimura began again, finally. "And she doesn't take to just anyone. Or rather, she doesn't take to almost everyone. She hardly says a word to me. She doesn't say much to her mother either, but at least she respects her. She's got no respect for me. None whatsoever. She thinks I'm a fool. She hasn't got any friends. She doesn't go to school, she just stays in her room alone, listening to that noise she calls music. She's got problems with people. But for some reason, you, she takes to you. I don't know why."

"Me either."

"Maybe you're a kindred spirit?"

"Maybe."

"Tell me, what do you think of Yuki?"

This was starting to feel like a job interview. "Yuki's thirteen, a terrible age," I answered straightforwardly. "And from what I can see, her home environment's a disaster. No one looks after her. No one takes responsibility for her. No one talks to her. She's lonely and she's hurt. She's got two famous parents. She's too beautiful for her own good. And she's acutely sensitive to everything around her. That's a pretty heavy burden for a thirteen-year-old girl to bear."

"And no one's giving her proper attention."

"That's what I think."

He heaved a long sigh. He let go of his ear and stared at his fingers. "I think you're right, absolutely right. But *I* can't do a thing about it. When her mother and I divorced, I signed papers that said I would lay off Yuki. I can't get around that. I wasn't the most faithful husband at the time, so I wasn't in any position to contest it. In fact, I'm supposed to get Amé's permission even before seeing Yuki like this. And the other thing is, like I said before, Yuki doesn't have a whole lot of respect for me. So I'm in a double bind. But I'd do anything for her if I could."

He turned his gaze back toward the green net. Evening was gathering, darker and deeper.

"Still, things can't continue the way they've been going," I said. "You know that her mother flew off to Kathmandu and it was three days before she remembered that Yuki was still in that hotel in Hokkaido? Three days! And after I brought Yuki back to Tokyo, she stayed in that apartment and didn't go anywhere for days. As far as I know, all she did was listen to rock and eat junk food. I hate to sound wholesome and middle-class, but this isn't healthy."

"I'm not arguing. What you say is one hundred percent correct," said Makimura. "No, make that two hundred percent. That's why I wanted to talk to you. Why I had you come all the way down here."

I had an ominous feeling. The horses were dead. The Indians had stopped beating their drums. It was too quiet. I scratched my temple.

"I was wondering," he began cautiously, "if you wouldn't like to look after Yuki. Nothing formal or anything like that. Just two or three hours a day. Spend time with her, make sure she's all right and eating reasonable meals. That's all. I'll pay you for your time. You can think of it as tutoring without having to teach. I don't know how much you make, but I can guarantee you something close to that. The rest of the time you can do as you like. That's not such a bad deal, is it? I've already talked to her mother about it. She's in Hawaii now, and she agreed that it was a good idea. Even if it doesn't look that way, she has Yuki's best interests at heart, really. She's just . . . different. She's brilliant, but sometimes her head's off in the stratosphere. She forgets about people and things around her. She even has trouble with arithmetic."

"Right," I said, smiling without much conviction, "but what Yuki needs more than anything else is a parent's love—you know, completely unconditional love. I'm not her parent and I can't give her that. She also needs friends her own age. Which leads me to another thing: I'm a man, and I'm too old. A thirteen-year-old girl is already a woman in some ways. Yuki's very pretty and emotionally unstable. Are you going to put a girl like that in the care of some guy out of nowhere? What do you know about me? I was just hauled in by the cops in connection with a homicide. What if I was the murderer?"

"Are you the killer?"

"Of course not."

"Well, then what's the problem? I trust you. If you say you're not the killer, then you're not the killer."

"But why trust me?"

"You don't seem the killer type. You don't seem the statutory rapist type either. Those things are pretty clear," said Makimura. "Plus Yuki's the key here, and I trust Yuki's instincts. Sometimes, as a matter of fact, her instincts are too acute for comfort. She's like a medium. There've been times when I could tell she was seeing something I couldn't. Know what I mean?"

"Kind of," I said.

"She gets it from her mother. It's her eccentric side. Her mother focused all of it on her art. That way, people call it talent. But Yuki hasn't got any place to direct that side of her, not yet anyway. It's just overflowing, with no place to go. Like water spilling out of a bucket. I'm not like either of them. I'm not eccentric. Which is why neither of them gives me the time of day. When we were living together, it got so I didn't want to see another woman's face. I don't know if you can imagine what it was like, living with Amé and Yuki. Rain and snow. Amé's private joke! Frigging weather report. They wore me out completely. Of course I love them both. I still talk to Amé now and then. But I don't ever want to live with her again. That was hell. I may have had talent once, but living like that sapped me dry. That's the truth. But even so, I haven't done badly, I must say. Shoveling snow, huh? I like that. But we're getting off track—what were we talking about?"

"About whether you should trust me."

"That's right. I trust Yuki's intuition. Yuki trusts you. Therefore I trust you. And you can trust me. I'm not such a bad person. I may write crap, but I can be trusted," he said, spitting again. "Well, how about it? Will you look after Yuki? What you've said about the role of the parent isn't lost on me. I agree entirely. But the kid is, well, exceptional. And as you can see, she'll barely talk to me. You're the only one I can depend on."

I peered down into the foam of the beer in my glass. What was I supposed to do? Strange family. Three misfits and Boy Friday. Space Family Robinson.

"I don't mind seeing Yuki that often," I said, "but I can't, I won't, do it every day. I have my own life to look after, and I don't like seeing people out of obligation. I'll see her when I feel like it. I don't need your money, I don't want your money. I'm not hard up and the money I spend with Yuki won't be any different than the money I spend with friends. I like Yuki a lot and I enjoy seeing her, but I don't want the responsibility. Do you read me? Because whatever happens with Yuki, the responsibility ultimately comes back to you."

Makimura nodded several times. The rolls of flesh beneath his ears quivered. Golf wasn't going to trim away that fat. That called for a whole change of life. But that was beyond him. If he'd been capable, he'd have changed long ago.

"I understand what you're saying, son, and it makes a lot of sense," he said. "I'm not trying to push any responsibility onto you. No need to assume responsibility at all. I just don't have any other options, so I bow to your judgment. This isn't about responsibility. And the money we can think about when the time comes. I'm a man who always pays his debts. Just remember that. I leave it to you. You do as you like. If you need money, you get in touch with me or Amé. Neither of us is short in that department. So don't be a stranger."

I didn't say a word.

"I'd say you're one stubborn young man," Makimura added.

"I'm not stubborn. I just work according to my system."

"Your system," he said. Then he fingered his earlobe again. "Your system may be beside the point these days. It went out with handmade vacuum tube amplifiers. Instead of wasting all your time trying to build your own, you ought to buy a brand-new transistor job. It's cheaper and it sounds better. And if it breaks down they come fix it in no time. When it gets old, you can trade it in. Your system may not be so watertight anymore, son. It might've been worth something once upon a time. But not now. Nowadays money talks. It's whatever money will buy. You can buy off the rack and piece it all together. It's simple. It's not so bad. Get stuck on your system and you'll be left behind. You can't cut tight turns and you get in everybody's way."

"Advanced capitalist society."

"You got it," said Makimura. Then he fell silent.

Nearby a dog was baying neurotically. Someone was fumbling through a Mozart piano sonata. Makimura sat down on the back porch with his beer, thinking.

Darkness was swallowing the whole scene. Things were losing their shapes and melting together. Suddenly there was Gotanda, his graceful fingers stroking Kiki's bare back; there were the snow-swept streets of Sapporo, *Cuck–koo* from Mei the Goat Girl, the flatfoot rapping the plastic ruler in the palm of his hand, the Sheep Man at the end of a dark corridor, . . . all fusing and blending. I must be tired, I thought. But I wasn't. It was only the essence of things leaching away, then swirling into chaos. And I was looking down on it as if it were some cosmic sphere. A piano played, a dog barked, someone was saying something. Someone was speaking to me.

"Say, son—." It was Makimura.

I glanced up at him.

"You know something about that murdered woman, don't you?" he was saying. "The newspapers say they still don't know who she is, and the only lead is a business card in her wallet. They were supposed to be questioning that party, but your name didn't come out. According to my lawyer, you pulled one over on them. You said you didn't know anything, but that's not to say you don't, am I right?"

"What makes you think that?"

"I just do," he said, picking up a golf club and holding it straight out like a sword. "The more I listened to you talk, the more it kind of grew on me. You fuss over tiny details, but you're awful generous with big things. There's a pattern that builds up. I figure you know more than you say, maybe you're covering for somebody. You're an interesting character. Almost like Yuki that way. You have a hard time just surviving. This time you came through okay, but the next time you may not be so lucky. Remember, the police aren't so nice. I've got no beef with your system—I actually have respect for it—but you could get hurt, sticking to your guns like that. Times have changed. You got to adapt."

"I'm not sticking to my guns," I said. "It's more like just a dance. Something the body remembers. It's a habit. The music plays, the body moves. It almost doesn't matter what else is happening. If too many things get in my head, I might end up blowing my steps. I'm clumsy, not trendy."

Hiraku Makimura glared at his golf club in silence.

"You're odd, you know?" he said. "You remind me of something."

"Same here." Picasso's *Dutch Vase and Three Bearded Knights*?

"I like you, son. I trust you as a person. I'm sorry that I have to ask you to look out for Yuki. But I'll make it up to you someday. I always repay favors. Like I said before."

"I heard."

25

At seven o'clock, Yuki came sauntering back. She'd been walking on the beach. Would she like dinner, then? Not hungry, she said. She wanted to go home.

"Well, drop by whenever you feel in the mood," said her father. "This month I'll be in Japan straight through." Then he turned to me and thanked me for making the long trip, apologizing for not being able to be more hospitable.

Boy Friday saw us out. As we turned the corner from the backyard, I spied a four-wheel-drive Jeep Cherokee, a Honda 750cc, and an off-road mountain bike parked in a corner of the grounds.

"Heavy-duty living, eh?" I commented to Friday.

"Well, it's not namby-pamby," Friday responded after a moment. "Mr. Makimura doesn't live in an ivory tower. He's into action, he lives for adventure."

"A bozo," Yuki mumbled.

Both Friday and I pretended not to have heard her.

No sooner had we gotten into the Subaru than Yuki said she was famished. I pulled into a Hungry Tiger along the coast road and we ordered steaks.

"What did you talk about?" she asked me over dessert.

There was no reason to hide anything, so I gave her a general recap.

"Figures," she sneered. "Just the sort of thing he'd dream up. What'd you tell him?"

"I said I wasn't cut out for an arrangement like that. It wouldn't be bad, us getting together and hanging out, whenever we wanted to. That could be fun, but no formal arrangement. You know, I may be an old man next to you, but we still have plenty to talk about, don't you think?"

She shrugged.

"If you didn't feel like seeing me, you could just say so. People shouldn't feel obligated to see each other. See me when you feel like it. We could tell each other things we can't say to anyone else, share secrets. Or no?"

She seemed to hesitate, then nodded, "Umm."

"You shouldn't let the stuff build up inside. It gets to a point where you can't keep it under control. You got to let off the pressure or it'll explode. *Bang!* Know what I mean? Life is hard enough. Holding down the fort all by your lonesome is tough. And it's tough for me too. But the two of us, I think maybe we can understand each other. We can talk pretty honestly."

She nodded.

"I can't force you. But if you want to talk, just call up. This has nothing to do with what your father and I discussed. And try not to think of me as a big brother or something. We're friends. I think we can be good for each other."

Yuki didn't respond. She finished off her dessert and gulped down a glass of water. Then she peered over at the heavyset family stuffing their jowls at the next table. Mother and father and daughter and baby brother. All wonderfully rotund.

I planted my elbows on the table and drank my coffee, watching Yuki watch them. She was truly a beautiful girl. I could feel a small polished stone sinking through the darkest waters of my heart. All those deep convoluted channels and passageways, and yet she managed to toss her pebble right down to the bottom of it all. If I were fifteen, I'd have been a goner for sure, I thought for the twentieth time.

How could her classmates be so rotten? Was her beauty too much to be around everyday? Too pointed? Too intense? Too aloof? Did she make them afraid of her?

Well, she certainly wasn't cool like Gotanda. Gotanda had this remarkable awareness of the effect he had on others, and he held it in reserve. He controlled it. He never lorded it over people, never scared them off. And even when his presence had inflated to star proportions, he could smile and joke about it. It was his nature. That way everyone around him could smile along and think, *Now there's one nice guy*. And Gotanda really was a nice guy. But Yuki was different. Yuki was not nice.

She didn't have it in her to keep tabs on everyone else's emotions and then to fit her own emotions in without stomping on people. It was all she could do to keep on top of herself. As a result, she hurt others, which only hurt herself. A hard life. A little too hard for a thirteen-year-old. Hard even for an adult.

I couldn't begin to predict what the girl would do from here on. Maybe she'd find a way to express herself, like her mother did, and make her way in art. Maybe she'd channel her powers into something positive. I couldn't swear to it, but like her father, I could sense an aura, a talent, in her. She was extraordinary.

Then again, she might become a perfectly normal eighteen-year-old. It wouldn't be the first time.

Humans achieve their peak in different ways. But whoever you are, once you're over the summit, it's downhill all the way. Nothing anyone can do about it. And the worst of it is, you never know where that peak is. You think you're still going strong, when suddenly you've crossed the great divide. No one can tell. Some people peak at twelve, then lead rather uneventful lives from then on. Some carry on until they die; some die at their peak. Poets and composers have lived like furies, pushing themselves to such a pitch they're gone by thirty. Then there are those like Picasso, who kept breaking ground until well past eighty.

And what about me?

My peak? Would I even have one? I hardly had had anything you could call a life. A few ripples. Some rises and falls. But that's it. Almost nothing. Nothing born of nothing. I'd loved and been loved, but I had nothing to show. It was a singularly plain, featureless landscape. I felt like I was in a video game. A surrogate Pacman, crunching blindly through a labyrinth of dotted lines. The only certainty was my death.

No promises you're gonna be happy, the Sheep Man had said. *So you gotta dance. Dance so it all keeps spinning.*

I gave up and closed my eyes.

When I opened them again, Yuki was sitting across the table from me.

"You okay?" she said, concerned. "You looked like you blew a fuse. Did I say something wrong?"

I smiled. "No, it wasn't anything you said."

"You just thought of something unpleasant?"

"No, I just thought that you're too beautiful."

Yuki looked at me with her father's blank stare. Then silently she shook her head.

Yuki paid for dinner. Her father had given her lots of money, she informed me. She took the check over to the register, peeled a ten-thousand-yen note from a wad of five or six, handed it over to the cashier, then scooped up the change without even looking at it.

"Papa thinks that all he has to do is fork over money and everything's cool," she said, piqued. "He's real dim. But that's why I can treat you today. Makes us even, kind of, right? You're always treating me, so fair's fair."

"Thank you," I said. "But you know, all this goes against classic date etiquette."

"Huh?"

"On a dinner date, even if the girl is paying for it, she doesn't run up to the register with the bill. She lets the guy do it, then pays him back, or she gives him the money ahead of time. That's the way to do it. Males are very sensitive creatures. Of course, I'm not such a macho guy, so I don't care. But you ought to know that there are lots of sensitive fellows out there who really do care."

"Gross!" she said. "I'll never go out with guys like that."

"It's, well, just an angle on things," I said, easing the Subaru out of the parking space. "People fall in love without reason, without even wanting to. You can't predict it. That's love. When you get to the age that you wear a brassiere, you'll understand."

"I told you, dummy. I already have one!" she screamed and pounded me on the shoulder.

I almost plowed the car into a dumpster, and had to stop. "I was only kidding," I said. "It was a stupid joke, but you ought to give your laugh muscles some practice anyway."

"Hmmph," she pouted.

"Hmmph," I echoed.

"It was stupid, that's for sure," she said.

"It was stupid, that's for sure," I said.

"Stop it!" she cried.

I was tempted not to, but didn't, and pulled the car out of the lot.

"One thing, Yuki, and this is not a joke. Don't hit people while they're driving," I said. "You could get us killed. So date etiquette lesson number two: *Don't die. Go on living.*"

On the way back, Yuki hardly said a word to me. She melted into her seat, and appeared to be thinking. Though it was hard to tell if she was asleep or awake. She wasn't listening to her tapes. So I put on Coltrane's *Ballads* that I'd brought along. She didn't utter a word, barely noticed anything was on. I hummed along with the solos.

The road was a bore. I concentrated on the taillights of the cars ahead. When we got onto the expressway, Yuki sat up and started chewing gum. Then she lit a cigarette. Three, four puffs and out the window it went. I was going to say something if she lit up a second, but she didn't. She could tell what was on my mind.

As I pulled up in front of the Akasaka condo, I announced, "Here we are, Princess."

Whereupon she balled up her wad of gum in its wrapper and placed it on the dashboard. Then she sluggishly opened the car door, got out, and started walking. Didn't say goodbye, didn't shut the door, didn't look back. Okay, a difficult age, I thought. She seemed like a character out of Gotanda's movies. The sensitive, complex girl. No doubt, Gotanda could have played my part loads better than I did. And probably Yuki would be head over heels in love with him. It wouldn't make a movie otherwise. Good grief, I can't stop thinking about Gotanda! I reached across her seat and pulled the door shut. *Slam!* Then I listened to Freddie Hubbard's "Red Clay" on the way home.

After waking the next morning, I went to the train station. Before nine and Shibuya was swarming with commuters. Yet despite the spring air, you could count the number of smiles on one hand. I bought two papers at the kiosk, went to Dunkin' Donuts, and read the news over coffee. Opening ceremonies for Tokyo Disneyland, fighting between Vietnam and Cambodia, Tokyo mayoral election, violence in the schools. Not one line about a beautiful young woman strangled in an Akasaka hotel. What's one homicide compared to the opening of a Disney theme park anyway? It's just one more thing to forget.

I checked the movie listings and saw that *Unrequited Love* had finished its run. Which brought Gotanda to mind again. I had to let him know about Mei.

I tried calling him from the pink phone in Dunkin' Donuts. Naturally he was out, so I left a message on his machine: urgent. Then I tossed the newspapers in the trash and headed home. Walking back, I tried to imagine why on earth Vietnam and Cambodia, two communist countries, should be fighting. Complicated world.

It was my day for catching up on things.

There were tons of things I had to do. Very practical matters. I put on my practical-minded best and attacked things head-on.

I took shirts to the cleaners and picked some up. I stopped by the bank, got some cash from the ATM, paid my phone and gas bills, paid my rent. I had new heels put on my shoes. I bought batteries for the alarm clock. I returned home and straightened up the place while listening to FEN. I scrubbed the bathtub. I cleaned the refrigerator, the stove, the fan, the floors, the windows. I bagged the garbage. I changed the sheets. I ran the vacuum cleaner. I was wiping the blinds, singing along to Styx's "Mister Roboto," when the phone rang at two.

It was Gotanda.

"Can you meet me? I can't talk over the phone," I said.

"Sure. But how urgent is it? I'm right in the middle of a shoot right now. Can it wait two or three days?"

"I don't think it can. Someone's been killed," I said. "Someone we both know and the cops are on the move."

Silence came over the line. An eloquent silence as only Gotanda could deliver. Smart, cool, and intelligent. I could almost hear his mental gears whirring at high speed. "Okay, how about tonight? It'll have to be pretty late. That okay?"

"Fine."

"I'll call you around one or two. Sorry, but I won't have one free minute before that."

"No problem. I'll be up."

We hung up and I replayed the entire conversation in my mind.

Someone's been killed. Someone we both know and the cops are on the move.

A regular mob flick. Involve Gotanda and everything becomes a scene from the movies. Little by little reality retreated from view. Made me feel like I was playing a scripted role. Gotanda in dark glasses, trench coat collar turned up, leaning against his Maserati. Charming. A radial tire commercial. I shook the image off and returned to my blinds.

At five, I walked to Harajuku and wandered through the teenybopper stalls along Takeshita Street. There was plenty of stuff inscribed with Kiss and Iron Maiden and AC/DC and Motorhead and Michael Jackson and Prince, but Elvis? No. Finally, after visiting several stores, I found what I was looking for: a badge that read ELVIS THE KING.

Then to Tsuruoka's for tempura and beer. The sun went down, the hours passed. My Pacman kept crunching away at the dotted lines. I was making no progress. Getting closer to nothing. Even as the lines seemed to be multiplying. But lines to Kiki were nowhere to be seen. I'd been sent off on detours. Energies expended on sideshows, never on the main event. Where the hell was the main event? *Was* there a main event?

Free until after midnight, I went to see Paul Newman in *The Verdict*. Not a bad movie, but I kept losing myself in thought and losing track of the story. I was expecting Kiki's naked back to appear on screen at any moment. Kiki, Kiki, what did you want from me?

The end credits came on and I left the theater, hardly having any grasp of the plot. I walked, stepped into a bar, and had a couple vodka gimlets. I got back home at ten and read, waiting for Gotanda to call.

I eventually tossed my book aside and lay back in bed. I thought about Kipper. Dead and buried, quiet in the quiet ground.

The next thing I knew the room was flooded with silence.

Waves of helplessness washed over me. I needed to rouse myself. I closed my eyes and counted from one to ten in Spanish, ending in a loud *finito* and a clap of the hands. My own spell to conquer helplessness. One of the many skills I'd acquired living alone. Without these tricks I may not have survived.

26

It was twelve-thirty when Gotanda called.

"Things have been crazy. Sorry about the late hour, but could I ask you to drive to my place this time?"

No problem, I told him, and I was on my way.

He came down immediately after I rang the doorbell. To my surprise, he *really* had a trench coat on. Which did suit him. No dark glasses though, just a pair of normal glasses, which gave him the look of an intellectual.

"Again, sorry this had to be so late," Gotanda said as we greeted each other. "What a day it's been. Incredibly busy. And I have to go to Yokohama after this. A shoot first thing in the morning, so they booked me a room."

"Why don't I drive you there?" I offered. "We'd have more time to talk, and it'd save you some time too."

"Great, if you're sure you don't mind."

Not at all, I assured him, and he quickly got his things together.

"Nice car," he said as we settled into the Subaru. "Honest, it's got a nice feel to it."

"We have an understanding."

"Uh-huh," he said, nodding as if he understood.

I slid a Beach Boys tape into the stereo and we were on our way. As soon as we got on the expressway to Yokohama, it began to drizzle. I turned on the wipers, then stopped them, then turned them on again. It was a very fine spring rain.

"What do you remember about junior high?" Gotanda asked out of nowhere.

"That I was a hopeless nobody," I answered.

"Anything else?"

I thought a second. "You're going to think I'm nuts, but I remember you lighting Bunsen burners in science class.

"What?"

"It was just, I don't know, so perfect. You made lighting the flame seem like a great moment in the history of mankind."

"Well of course it was," he laughed. "But, okay, I get what you mean. Believe me, it was never my intention to show anybody up. Even though I guess I did look like a prima donna. Ever since I was a kid, people were always watching me. Why? I don't know. Naturally I knew it was happening, and it made me into a little performer. It just stuck with me. I was always acting. So when I actually became an actor, it was a relief. I didn't have to be embarrassed about it," he said, placing one palm atop the other on his lap and gazing down at them. "I hope I wasn't a total shit, or was I?"

"Nah," I said. "But that's not what I meant at all. I only wanted to say you lighted that burner with style. I'd almost like to see you do it again sometime."

He laughed and wiped his glasses. With style, of course. "Anytime," he said. "I'll be waiting with the burner and matches."

"I'll bring a pillow in case I swoon," I added.

We laughed some more. Then Gotanda put his glasses back on and turned the stereo down slightly. "Shall we get on with our talk, about that dead person?"

"It was Mei," I said flat out, peering out beyond the wipers. "She's been murdered. Her body was found in a hotel in Akasaka, strangled with a stocking. Killer unknown."

Gotanda faced me abruptly. It took him three or four seconds to grasp what I had said, then his face wrenched in realization. Like a window frame twisting in a big quake. I glanced over at him out of the corner of my eye. He seemed to be in shock.

"When was she killed?" he asked finally.

I gave him the details, and he was quiet again, as if to set his feelings in order.

"That's horrible," he finally said, shaking his head. "Horrible. Why? Why would anyone kill Mei? She was such a good kid. It's just—" He shook his head again.

"A good kid, yes," I said. "Right out of a fairy tale."

He sighed deeply, his face suddenly aged with fatigue. Until this moment he had managed to contain an unbearable strain within himself. Yet, even fatigue was becoming to him, serving as a rather distinguished accent on his life. Unfair to say, I suppose, hurt and tired as he was. Whatever he touched, even pain, seemed to turn to refinement.

"The three of us used to talk until dawn," Gotanda spoke, his voice barely a whisper. "Me and Mei and Kiki. Maybe it was right out of a fairy tale, but where do you even find a fairy tale these days? Man, those times were wonderful."

I stared at the road ahead, Gotanda stared at the dashboard. I turned the wipers on and off. The stereo played on, low, the Beach Boys and sun and surf and dune buggies.

"How did you know she'd been killed?" Gotanda asked.

"The police hauled me in," I explained. "I'd given Mei my business card, and she had it deep in her wallet. Matter of fact, it was the only thing on her with any kind of name. So they picked me up for questioning. Wanted to know how I knew her. A couple of tough, dumb flatfoots. But I lied. I told them I'd never seen her before."

"Why'd you lie?"

"Why? You were the one introduced us, buying those two girls that night, right? What do you think would've happened if I'd blabbed? Have you lost your thinking gear?"

"Forgive me," he said. "I'm a little confused. Stupid."

"The cops didn't believe me at all. They could smell the lies. They put me through the wringer for three days. A thorough job, careful not to infringe on the law. They never touched me, bodily, that is. But it was hard. I'm getting old, I'm not what I used to be. They pretended they didn't have a place for me to sleep and threw me in the tank. Technically, I wasn't in the tank because they didn't lock the door. It was no picnic, let me tell you. You think you're losing your mind."

"Know what you mean. I was held for two weeks once. Not pleasant. I didn't get to see the sun the whole time. I thought I'd never get out. It gets to you, how they ride you. They know how to break you," he said, staring at his fingernails. "But three days and you didn't talk?"

"What do you think? Of course not. If I started in midway with 'Well, actually—,' it'd be all over. Once you take a line, you've got to stick by it to the end."

Gotanda's face twisted again. "Forgive me. Introducing you to Mei and getting you caught up in this mess."

"No reason for you to apologize," I said. "I thoroughly enjoyed myself with her. That was then. This is something else. It's not your fault she's dead."

"No, it's not, but still you had to lie to the cops for me. You got dragged into the middle of it. *That* was my fault. Because I was involved."

I turned to give him a good hard look and then went straight to the heart of the matter. "*That* isn't a problem. Don't worry about it. No need to apologize. You got your stake and I respect it, fully. The bigger problem is, they weren't able to identify her. She's got relatives, hasn't she? We want to catch the psycho who killed her, don't we? I would have told them everything if I could. That's what's eating me. Mei didn't deserve to die that way. At the least, she should have a name."

Gotanda closed his eyes for so long I almost thought he'd gone to sleep. The Beach Boys had finished their serenade. I pushed the EJECT button. Everything went dead silent. There was only the drone of the tires on the wet asphalt.

"I'll call the police," Gotanda intoned as he opened his eyes. "An anonymous phone call. And I'll name the club she was working for. That way they can get on with their investigation."

"Genius," I said. "You've got a good head on your shoulders. Why didn't I think of it? But suppose the police put the screws to the club. They'll find out that a few days before she was killed, you had Mei sent to your place. Bingo, they've got you downtown. What's the point of me keeping my mouth shut for three days?"

"You're right. You got me. I *am* confused."

"When you're confused," I said, "the best thing to do is sit tight and wait for the coast to clear. It's only a matter of time. A woman got strangled to death in a hotel. It happens. People forget about it. No reason to feel guilty. Just lie low and keep quiet. You start acting smart now, you'll only make things worse."

Maybe I was being hard on him. My tone a little too cold, my words too harsh, but hell, I was in this pretty deep too. I apologized. "Sorry," I said. "I didn't mean to light into you like that. I couldn't lift a finger to help the girl. That's all, it's not your fault."

"But it is my fault," he insisted.

Silence was growing oppressive, so I put on another tape. Ben E. King's "Spanish Harlem." We said nothing more until we reached Yokohama, an unspoken bond between us. I wanted to pat him on the back and say it's okay, it's all over and done with. But a person had died. She was cold, alone, and nameless. That fact weighed more heavily than I could bear.

"Who do you think killed her?" asked Gotanda much later.

"Who knows?" I said. "In that line of work, you get all types. Anything can happen."

"But the club is real careful about screening the clients. It's so organized, they should be able to find the guy easily."

"You'd think so, but it could be anybody else too. Whatever, she made a mistake, and it turned out to be fatal. It happens, I guess," I said. "She lived in this world of images that was safe and pure. But there are rules even in that world. Somebody breaks the rules and the fantasy's kaput."

"It doesn't make sense," said Gotanda. "Why would such a beautiful, intelligent girl want to become a hooker? Why? She could've had a good life, a decent job. She could've modeled, she could've married a rich guy. How come a hooker? Okay, the money's good, but she didn't seem all that interested in money. You think she really wanted this fairy tale?"

"Maybe," I answered. "Like me, like you. Like everybody. Only everybody goes about it different. That's why you never know what's going to happen."

When we pulled up to the New Grand Hotel in Yokohama, Gotanda suggested I stay over too. "I'm sure we can get you a room. We'll call up room service and knock back some drinks. I don't think I can sleep right away."

I shook my head, no. "I'll take a rain check on those drinks. I'm pretty worn out. I'll just go home and collapse."

"You sure?" he said. "Well, thanks for driving me down here. I feel like I haven't said a responsible thing all day."

"You're tired too," I said. "But listen, with someone who's dead, there's no rush to make amends. She'll be dead for a long time. Let's think things over when we're in better spirits. You hear what I'm saying? She's dead. Extremely, irrevocably dead. Feel guilt, feel whatever you like, she's not coming back."

Gotanda nodded. "I hear you."

"Good night," I said.

"Thanks again," he said.

"Light a Bunsen burner for me next time, and we'll call it even."

He smiled as he got out of the car. "Strange to say, but you're the only friend I have who'd say that. Not another soul. We meet after twenty years, and the thing you chose to remember!"

At that he was off. He turned up the collar of his trench coat and headed through the spring drizzle into the New Grand. Almost like *Casablanca*. The beginning of a beautiful friendship . . .

The rain kept coming down, steadily, evenly. Soft and gentle, drawing new green shoots up into the spring night. *Extremely, irrevocably dead,* I said aloud.

I should have stayed overnight and drunk with Gotanda, it occurred to me. Gotanda and I had four things in common. One, we'd been in the same science lab unit. Two, we were both divorced. Three, we'd both slept with Kiki. And four, we'd both slept with Mei. Now Mei was dead. *Extremely, irrevocably.* Worth a drink together. Why didn't I stay and keep him company? I had time on my hands, I had nothing planned for tomorrow. What prevented me? Maybe, somehow, I didn't want it to seem like a scene from a movie. Poor guy. He was just so unbearably charming. And it wasn't his fault. Probably.

When I got back to my Shibuya apartment, I poured myself a whiskey and watched the cars on the expressway through the blinds.

27

A week passed. Spring made solid advances, never once retreated. A world away from March. The cherries bloomed and the blossoms scattered in the evening showers. Elections came and went, a new school year started. Bjorn Borg retired. Michael Jackson was number one in the charts the whole time. The dead stayed dead.

It was a succession of aimless days. I went swimming twice. I went to the barber. I bought newspapers, never saw an article about Mei. Maybe they couldn't identify her.

On Tuesday and Thursday Yuki and I went out to eat. On Monday we went for a drive with the music playing. I enjoyed these times. We shared one thing. We had time to waste.

When I didn't see her, Yuki stayed indoors during the day, afraid that truant officers might nab her. Her mother had yet to return.

"Why don't we go to Disneyland then?" I asked.

"I don't want to go," she sneered. "I hate those places."

"You hate all that gooey Mickey Mouse kid stuff, I take it?"

"Of course I hate it," she said.

"But it's not good for you to stay indoors all the time," I said.

"So why don't we go to Hawaii?" she said.

"What? Hawaii?"

"Mama phoned up and asked if I wanted to come to Hawaii. That's where she is right now, taking pictures. She leaves me alone all this time and then suddenly she gets worried about me. She can't come home yet, and since I'm not going to school anyway, she said to get on a plane and come see her. Hawaii's not such a bad idea, yeah? Mama said she'd pay your way. I mean, I can't go alone, right? Let's go, please. Just for one week. It'll be fun."

I laughed. "What exactly is the difference between Disneyland and Hawaii?"

"No truant officers in Hawaii."

"Well, you got a point there."

"Then you'll go?"

I thought it over, and the more I thought about it the more I liked it. Getting out of Tokyo *had* to be a good idea. I'd reached a dead end here. My head was stuck. I was in a funk. And Mei was extremely, irrevocably dead.

I'd been to Hawaii once. For one day only. I was going to Los Angeles on business and the plane had engine trouble, so we set down in Hawaii overnight. I bought a pair of sunglasses and swim trunks in the hotel and spent the day on the beach. A great day. No, Hawaii was not such a bad idea.

Swim, drink fruit drinks, get a tan, and relax. I might even have a good time. Then I could reset my sights and get on with whatever I had to do.

"Okay, let's go," I said.

"Goody!" Yuki squealed. "Let's go buy the tickets."

But before doing that, I made a call to Hiraku Makimura and explained the offer that was on the table.

He was immediately positive. "Might do you some good too, son. You need to stretch your legs," he said, "take a break from all that shoveling you do. It'd also put you out of harm's way with the police. That mess isn't cleared up yet, is it? They're bound to knock on your door again."

"Maybe so," I said.

"Go. And don't worry about money," he said. Any discussions you had with this guy always turned to money. "Go for as long as you like."

"I figure on a week at the most. I still have a pile of things to get back to."

"As you like," Makimura said. "When are you going? Probably the sooner the better. That's how it is with vacations. Go when the mood strikes. That's the trick. You hardly need to take anything with you anyway. I tell you what—we'll get you tickets for the day after tomorrow. How's that?"

"Fine, but I can buy my own ticket."

"Details, details, always fussing. This is in my line of work. I know how to get the best seats for the cheapest price. Let me do this. Each to his own abilities. Don't say anything. I don't want to hear your-system-this your-system-that. I'll take care of the hotel too. Two rooms. What do you think—you want something with a kitchenette?"

"Well, I like to be able to cook my own sometimes, but it's—"

"I know just the place. I stayed there once myself. Near the beach, quiet, clean."

"But I—"

"Just leave it all to me, okay? I'll get the word to Amé. You just go to Honolulu with Yuki, lie on the beach and have a good time. Her mother's going to be busy anyway. When she's working, daughter or whoever doesn't exist. So don't worry. Just make sure Yuki eats well. And, oh yes, you got a visa?"

"Yes, but—"

"Good. Day after tomorrow, son. Don't forget your passport. Whatever you need, get it there. You're not going to Siberia. Siberia was rough, let me tell you. Horrible place. Afghanistan wasn't much better either. Compared to them, Hawaii's like Disneyland. And you're there in no time. Fall asleep with your mouth open and you're there. By the way, son, you speak English?"

"In normal conversation I—"

"Good," he said. "Perfect in fact. There's nothing more to say. Nakamura will meet you with the tickets tomorrow. He'll also bring the money I owe you for Yuki's flight down from Hokkaido."

"Who's Nakamura?"

"My assistant. The young man who lives with me."

Boy Friday.

"Any other questions?" asked Makimura. "You know, I like you, son. Hawaii. Wonderful place. Wonderful smells. A playground. Relax. No snow to shovel over there. I'll see you whenever you get back."

Then he hung up.

The famous writer.

When I reported to Yuki that all systems were go, she squealed again.

"Can you get ready by yourself? Pack your swimsuit and whatever you need?"

"It's only Hawaii," she said patronizingly. "It's like going to the beach at Oiso. We're not going to Kathmandu, you know."

The next day I ran errands: to the bank for cash, to the bookstore for a few paperbacks, to the cleaners for my shirts. At three o'clock, I met Boy Friday at a coffee shop in Shibuya, where he handed me a thick envelope of cash, two first-class open tickets to Hawaii, two packets of American Express travelers cheques, and a map to the hotel in Honolulu.

"It's all been arranged. Just give them your name when you get there," Nakamura said. "The reservation's for two weeks, but it can be changed for shorter or longer. Don't forget to sign the travelers cheques when you get home. Use them as you please. It's all on expense account. That's the word from Mr. Makimura."

"Everything's on expense account?" I couldn't believe it.

"Maybe not everything, but as long as you get receipts, it should be fine. That's my job. Please get receipts for whatever you spend," he laughed good-naturedly.

I promised I would.

"Take care of yourselves and have a good trip," he said.

"Thanks," I said.

At nightfall I rummaged through the refrigerator and made dinner.

Then I quickly threw together some things for the trip. Was I forgetting anything?

Nothing I could think of.

Going to Hawaii's no big deal. You need to take a lot more stuff going to Hokkaido.

I parked my travel bag on the floor and laid out what I'd wear the next day. Nothing more to do, I took a bath, then drank a beer while watching the news. No news to speak of, except for a not-too-promising weather forecast. Great, we'll be in Hawaii. I lay in bed and had another beer. And I thought of Mei. Extremely, irrevocably dead Mei. She was in a very cold place now. Unidentified. Without customers. Without Dire Straits or Bob Dylan. Tomorrow Yuki and I were going to Hawaii, on someone else's expense account. Was this any way to run a world?

I tried to shake Mei's image from my head.

I tried to think about my receptionist friend at the Dolphin Hotel. The one with the glasses, the one whose name I didn't know. For some reason the last couple of days I'd been wishing I could talk to her. I'd even dreamed about her. But how could I even ring her up? What was I supposed to say—"Hello, I'd like to talk to the receptionist with glasses at the front desk"? They'd probably think I was some joker. A hotel is serious business.

There had to be a way. Where there's a will, et cetera.

I rang up Yuki and set a time to meet the next day. Then asked if by chance she knew the name of the receptionist in

Sapporo, the one who'd entrusted her to me, the very one with the glasses.

"I think so," she said, "because it was an odd name. I'm sure I wrote it in my diary. I don't remember it, but I could check."

"Would you, right now?" I asked.

"I'm watching TV."

"Forgive me, but it's urgent. Very urgent."

She grumbled, but fetched her diary. "It's Miss Yumiyoshi," she said.

"Yumiyoshi?" I repeated.

"I told you it was an odd name. Sounds Okinawan, doesn't it?"

"No, they don't have names like that in Okinawa."

"Well, anyway, that's her name. Yu-mi-yo-shi," Yuki pronounced. "Okay? Can I watch TV now?"

"What are you watching?"

She hung up without responding.

Next I rang up the Dolphin Hotel and asked to speak to my receptionist friend by name. I didn't know how far this would go, but the operator connected us and Miss Yumiyoshi even remembered me. I hadn't been written off entirely.

"I'm working," she spoke in a low voice, cool and clean. "I'll call you later."

"Fine then, later," I said.

While waiting for her call back, I rang up Gotanda and was just leaving a message that I was going to Hawaii when he came on the line.

"Sounds great. I'm envious," he said. "Wish I could go too."

"Why not? What's stopping you?" I asked.

"Not as easy as you think. It looks like I'm loaded, but I'm so deep in debt you wouldn't believe."

"Oh?"

"The divorce, the loans. You think I do all these ridiculous commercials for fun? I can write off expenses, but I can't pay off my debts. Tell me you don't think that's odd."

"You owe that much?"

"I owe a lot," he said. "I'm not even sure how much. Not as smart as I look, am I? Money gives me the creeps. The way I was brought up. Vulgar to think about it, you know. Didn't your mother ever tell you that? All I had to do was work hard, live modestly, look at the big picture. Good advice—for then maybe. Whoever heard of living modestly these days? Whoever heard of the big picture? What my mother never told me was where the tax accountant fit in. Maybe my mother never heard about debts and deductions. Well, I got plenty of both. Which means I gotta work and I can't go to Hawaii with you. Sorry, once you get me going I can't stop."

"That's okay, I don't mind," I said.

"Anyway, it's my problem, not yours. We'll go together the next time, okay? I'm going to miss you. Take care of yourself."

"It's just Hawaii," I laughed. "I'll be back in a week."

"Still. Give me a call when you get back, will you?"

"Sure thing," I said.

"And while you're lying on the beach at Waikiki, think of me. Playing dentist to pay my debts."

Miss Yumiyoshi called a little before ten. She was back at her apartment. Ah yes—simple building, simple stairs, simple door. Her nervous smile. It all came back so poignantly. I closed my eyes, and the snowflakes danced silently in the depths of the night. I almost felt like I was in love.

"How did you know my name?" was the first thing she asked.

"Don't worry. I didn't do anything I shouldn't have. Didn't pay anyone off. Didn't tap your phone. Didn't work anybody over until they talked." I explained that Yuki had told me.

"I see," she said. "How did it go with her, by the way? Did you get her to Tokyo safe and sound?"

"Safe and sound," I said. "I got her to her front door. In fact I still see her now and then. She's fine. Odd, but fine."

"Kind of like you," said Yumiyoshi matter-of-factly. She spoke as if she were relating the most commonly known fact in the world. Monkeys like bananas, it doesn't rain much in the Sahara. "Tell me, why did you want to keep me in the dark about your name?" I asked.

"I didn't mean to, honest. I meant to tell you the next time we met," she said. "If you have an unusual name, you tend to be careful about it."

"I checked the telephone directory. Did you know that there are only two Yumiyoshis in all of Tokyo?"

"I know," she said. "I used to live in Tokyo, remember? I used to check the telephone book all the time. Wherever I went, I checked the phone book. There's one Yumiyoshi in Kyoto. Anyway, what did you want?"

"Nothing special," I said. "I'm going on a trip from tomorrow. And I wanted to hear your voice before I left. That's all. Sometimes I miss your voice."

She didn't respond, and in her silence I could hear the slight cross talk of a woman speaking, as if at the end of a long corridor. Quiet yet crisp, strangely charged electricity, with what I took to be a tone of bitterness. There were pained breaks and jags in her voice.

"You know how I told you about the sixteenth floor in total darkness?" Yumiyoshi spoke up.

"Uh-huh," I said.

"Actually, it happened again," she said.

It was my turn not to respond.

"Are you still there?" she asked.

"I'm here," I said. "Go on."

"First, you have to tell me the truth. Did you *honestly* believe what I told you that time? Or were you just humoring me?"

"I *honestly* believed you," I said. "I didn't have the

chance to tell you, but the very same thing happened to me. I took the elevator, stepped out into total darkness. I experienced the very same thing. So I believe you, I believe you."

"You went there?"

"I'll give you the whole story next time. I still don't know how to put it into words. Lots of things I don't understand. So you see, I really do need to talk to you again. But never mind that, tell me what happened to you. That's much more important."

Silence. The cross talk had died.

"Well, about ten days ago," Yumiyoshi began, "I was riding in the elevator down to the parking garage. It was around eight at night. The elevator went down, the door opened, and suddenly I was in that place again. Exactly like before. It wasn't in the middle of the night, and it wasn't on the sixteenth floor. But it was the same thing. Totally dark, moldy, kind of dank. The smell and the air were exactly the same. This time, I didn't go looking around. I stood still and waited for the elevator to come back. I ended up waiting a long time, I don't know how long. When the elevator finally got there, I got in and left. That was it."

"Did you tell anyone about it?" I asked.

"You think I'm crazy?" she said. "After the way they reacted the last time? Not on your life."

"Yeah, better not tell a soul."

"But what am I supposed to do? Whenever I get into an elevator now, I'm scared that I'm going to end up in darkness. And in a hotel like this, you have to ride the elevators a lot. What am I going to do? I can't talk to anybody but you about this."

"So why didn't you call sooner?" I asked.

"I did, several times," her voice hushed to a whisper. "But you were never in."

"But my machine was on, wasn't it?"

"I hate those things. They make me nervous."

"Fair enough. Well, let me tell you what I know about what's going on. There's nothing evil about that darkness. It doesn't harbor any ill will, so there's no need to feel threatened. But there *is* someone who lives there. This guy heard your footsteps, but he's someone who'd never do you any harm. He'd never hurt a fly. So I think that if you find yourself in that darkness again, you should just shut your eyes, get back in the elevator, and leave. Okay?"

Yumiyoshi chewed silently on my words. "May I say what I honestly think?"

"Of course."

"I don't understand you," she said. "I don't understand you at all. When I think about you, I realize I don't know a thing about you, really."

"Hmm. I've told you already how old I am. But I guess for someone my age, I've got a lot of undefined territory. I've left too many loose ends hanging. So now, I'm trying to tie up as many of those loose ends as I can. If I manage to do that, maybe then I can explain things a little more clearly. Maybe then we can understand each other better."

"We can only hope," she said with third-person detachment. She sounded like a TV anchorwoman. *We can only hope. Next on the news . . .*

I told her I was going to Hawaii.

"Oh," she remarked, unmoved. End of conversation. We said good-bye and hung up. I drank a shot of whiskey, turned out the light, and went to sleep.

28

Next on the news. I lay on the beach at Fort DeRussy looking up at the high blue sky and palm fronds and sea gulls and did my newscaster spiel. Yuki was next to me. I lay face up on my beach mat, she lay on her belly with her eyes shut. Next to her a huge Sanyo radio-cassette deck was playing Eric Clapton's latest. Yuki wore an olive-green bikini and was covered head-to-toe with coconut oil. She looked sleek and shiny as a slim, young dolphin. A burly Samoan trudged by carrying a surfboard, while a deep-brown lifeguard surveyed the goings-on from his watchtower, his gold chain flashing. The whole town smelled of flowers and fruit and suntan oil.

Next on the news.

Stuff happened, people appeared, scenes changed. Not very long ago I was wandering around, nearly blind, in a Sapporo blizzard. Now I was lolling on the beach at Waikiki, gazing up at the blue. One thing led to another. Connect the dots. Dance to the music and here's where it gets you. *Was I dancing my best?* I checked back over my steps in order. Not so bad. Not sublime, but not so bad. Put me back in the same position and I'd make the same moves. That's what you call a system. Or tendencies. Anyway my feet were in motion. I was keeping in step.

And now I was in Honolulu. Break time.

Break time. I hadn't meant to say it aloud, but apparently I did. Yuki rolled over and squinted at me suspiciously.

"What've you been thinking about?" she said hoarsely.

"Nothing much," I said.

"Not that I care, but would you mind not talking to yourself so loud that I can hear? Couldn't you do it when you're alone?"

"Sorry, I'll keep quiet."

Yuki gave me a restive look.

"You act like an old geezer who's not used to being around people," said Yuki, then rolled over away from me.

We'd taken a taxi from the airport to the hotel, changed into T-shirts and shorts, and the first thing we did was to go buy that big portable radio-cassette deck. It was what Yuki wanted.

"A real blaster," as she said to the clerk.

Other than a few tapes, she needed nothing else. Just the blaster, which she took with her whenever we went to the beach. Or rather, that was my role. Native porter. B'wana memsahib with blaster in tow.

The hotel, courtesy of Makimura, was just fine. A certain unstylishness of furniture and decor notwithstanding (though who went to Hawaii in search of chic?), the accommodations were exceedingly comfortable. Convenient to the beach. Tenth-floor tranquillity, with view of the horizon. Sea-view terrace for sunbathing. Kitchenette spacious, clean, outfitted with every appliance from microwave to dishwasher. Yuki had the room next door, a little smaller than mine.

We stocked up on beer and California wine and fruit and juice, plus sandwich fixings. Things we could take to the beach.

And then we spent whole days on the beach, hardly talking. Turning our bodies over, now front, now back, soaking up the rays. Sea breezes rustled the palms. I'd doze off, only to be roused by the voices of passersby, which made me wonder where I was. Hawaii, it'd take me a few moments to realize. Hawaii. Sweat and suntan oil ran down my cheek. A range of sounds ebbed and flowed with the waves, mingling with my heartbeat. My heart had taken its place in the grand workings of the world.

My springs loosened. I relaxed. *Break time.*

Yuki's features underwent a remarkable change from the moment we touched down and that sweet, warm Hawaiian air hit her. She closed her eyes, took a deep breath, then looked at me. Tension seemed to fall off her. No more defensiveness, no irritation. Her gestures, the way she ran her hands through her hair, the way she wadded up her chewing gum, the way she shrugged, . . . She eased up, she slowed down.

With her tiny bikini, dark sunglasses, and hair tied tight atop her head, it was hard to tell Yuki's age. Her body was still a child's body, but she had a kind of poise far more grown-up than her years. Her slender limbs showed strength. She seemed to have entered her most dynamic phase of growth. She was becoming an adult.

We rubbed oil on each other. It was the first time anyone ever told me I had a "big back." Yuki, though, was so ticklish she couldn't stay still. It made me smile. Her small white ears and the nape of her neck, how like a *girl's* neck it was. How different from a mature woman's neck. Though don't ask me what I mean by that.

"It's better to tan slow at first," Yuki told me with authority. "First you tan in the shade, then out in direct sun, then back in the shade. That way you don't get burned. If you blister, it leaves ugly scars."

"Shade, sun, shade," I intoned dutifully as I oiled her back.

And so I spent our first afternoon in Hawaii lying in the shade of a palm tree listening to an FM station. From time to time I'd go in the water or go to a bar at the beach for an ice-cold piña colada. Yuki didn't swim a single stroke. She aimed to relax, she said. She had a hot dog and pineapple juice.

The sun, which seemed huge, sank into the ocean, and the sky turned brilliant shades of red and yellow and orange. We lay and watched the sky tint the sails of the sunset-cruise catamarans. Yuki could hardly be budged.

"Let's go," I urged. "The sun's gone down and I'm hungry. Let's go get a fat, juicy, charcoal-broiled hamburger."

Yuki nodded, sort of, but didn't get up. As if she were loath to forfeit what little time that remained. I rolled up the beach mats and picked up the blaster.

"Don't worry. There's still tomorrow. And after tomorrow, there's the day after tomorrow," I said.

She looked up at me with a hint of a smile. And when I held out my hand, she grabbed it and pulled herself up.

29

The following morning, Yuki said she wanted to go see her mother. She didn't know where she was, but she had her phone number. So I rang up, exchanged greetings, and got directions. Amé had rented a small cottage near Makaha, about forty-five minutes out of Honolulu.

We rented a Mitsubishi Lancer, turned the radio up loud, rolled down the windows, and were on our way. Everywhere we passed was filled with light and surf and the scent of flowers.

"Does your mother live alone?" I asked Yuki.

"Are you kidding?" Yuki curled her lip. "No way the old lady could get by in a foreign country on her own. She's the most impractical person you ever met. If she didn't have someone looking after her, she'd get lost. How much you want to bet she's got a boyfriend out there? Probably young and handsome. Just like Papa's."

"Huh?"

"Remember, at Papa's place, that pretty gay boy who lives with him? He's *so–o* clean."

"Gay?"

"Didn't you think so?"

"No, I didn't think anything."

"You're dense, you know that! You could tell just by looking at him," said Yuki. "I don't know if Papa's gay too, but that boy sure is. Absolutely, two hundred percent gay."

Roxy Music came on the radio and Yuki turned the volume up full blast.

"Anyway, Mama's weakness is for poets. Young poets, failed poets, any kind of poets. She makes them recite to her while she's developing film. That's her idea of a good time. Kind of nerdy if you ask me. Papa should've been a poet, but he couldn't write a poem if he got showered with flowers out of the clear blue sky."

What a family! Rough-and-tumble writer father with gay Boy Friday, genius photographer mother with poet boyfriends, and spiritual medium daughter with . . . Wait a minute. Was I supposed to be fitting into this psychedelic extended family? I remembered Boy Friday's friendly, attractive smile. Maybe, just maybe, he was saying, *Welcome to the club.* Hold it right there. This gig with the family is strictly temporary. Understand? A short R&R before I go back to shoveling. At which point I won't have time for the likes of this craziness. At which point I go my own way. I like things less involved.

Following Amé's instructions, I turned right off the highway before Makaha and headed toward the hills. Houses with roofs half-ready to blow off in the next hurricane lined either side of the road, growing fewer and fewer until we reached the gate of a private resort community. The gatekeeper let us in at the mention of Amé's name.

Inside the grounds spread a vast, well-kept lawn. Gardeners transported themselves in golf carts, as they diligently attended to turf and trees. Yellow-billed birds fluttered about. Yuki's mother's place was beyond a swimming pool, trees, a further expanse of hill and lawn.

The cottage was tropical modern, surrounded by a mix of trees in fruit. We rang the doorbell. The drowsy, dry ring of the wind chime mingled pleasantly with strains of Vivaldi coming from the wide-open windows. After a few seconds the door opened, and we were met by a tall, well-tanned white man. He was solidly built, mustachioed, and wore a faded aloha shirt, jogging pants, and rubber thongs. He seemed to be about my age, decent-looking, if not exactly handsome, and a bit too tough to be a poet, though surely the world's got to have tough poets too. His most distinguished feature was the entire lack of a left arm from the shoulder down.

He looked at me, he looked at Yuki, he looked back at me, he cocked his jaw ever so slightly and smiled. "Hello," he greeted us quietly, then switched to Japanese, "*Konnichiwa.*" He shook our hands, and said come on in. His Japanese was flawless.

"Amé's developing pictures right now. She'll be another ten minutes," he said. "Sorry for the wait. Let me introduce myself. I'm Dick. Dick North. I live here with Amé."

Dick showed us into the spacious living room. The room had large windows and a ceiling fan, like something out of a Somerset Maugham novel. Polynesian folkcrafts decorated the walls. He sat us on the sizable sofa, then he brought out two Primos and a coke. Dick and I drank our beers, but Yuki didn't touch her drink.

She stared out the window and said nothing. Between the fruit trees you could see the shimmering sea. Out on the horizon floated one lone cloud, the shape of a pithecanthropus skull. Stubbornly unmoving, a permanent fixture of the seascape. Bleached perfectly white, outlined sharp against the sky. Birds warbled as they darted past. Vivaldi crescendoed to a finish, whereupon Dick got up to slip the record back in its jacket and onto a rack. He was amazingly dexterous with his one arm.

"Where did you pick up such excellent Japanese?" I asked him for lack of anything else to say.

Dick raised an eyebrow and smiled. "I lived in Japan for ten years," he said, very slowly. "I first went there during the War—the Vietnam War. I liked it, and when I got out, I went to Sophia University. I studied Japanese poetry, haiku and tanka, which I translate now. It's not easy, but since I'm a poet myself, it's all for a good cause."

"I would imagine so," I said politely. Not young, not especially handsome, but a poet. One out of three.

"Strange, you know," he spoke as if resuming his train of thought, "you never hear of any one-armed poets. You hear of one-armed painters, one-armed pianists. Even one-armed pitchers. Why no one-armed poets?"

True enough.

"Let me know if you think of one," said Dick.

I shook my head. I wasn't versed in poets in general, even the two-armed variety.

"There are a number of one-armed surfers," he continued. "They paddle with their feet. And they do all right too. I surf a little."

Yuki stood up and knocked about the room. She pulled down records from the rack, but apparently finding nothing to her liking, she frowned. With no music, the surroundings were so quiet they could lull you into drowsiness. In the distance there was the occasional rumble of a lawn mower, someone's voice, the ring of a wind chime, birds singing.

"Quiet here," I remarked.

Dick North peered down thoughtfully into the palm of his one hand.

"Yes. Silence. That's the most important thing. Especially for people in Amé's line of work. In my work too, silence is essential. I can't handle hustle and bustle. Noise, didn't you find Honolulu noisy?"

I didn't especially, but I agreed so as to move the conversation along. Yuki was again looking out the window with her *what-a-drag* sneer in place.

"I'd rather live on Kauai. Really, a wonderful place. Quieter, fewer people. Oahu's not the kind of place I like to live in. Too touristy, too many cars, too much crime. But Amé has to stay here for her work. She goes into Honolulu two or three times a week for equipment and supplies. Also, of course, it's easier to do business and to meet people here.

She's been taking photos of fishermen and gardeners and farmers and cooks and road workers, you name it. She's a fantastic photographer."

I'd never looked that carefully at Amé's photographic works, but again, for convenience sake, I agreed. Yuki made an indistinct toot through her nose.

He asked me what sort of work I did.

A free-lance writer, I told him. He seemed to show interest, thinking probably I was a kindred spirit. He asked me what sort of things I wrote.

Whatever, I write to order. Like shoveling snow, I said, trying the line now on him.

Shoveling snow, he repeated gravely. He didn't seem to understand. I was about to explain when Amé came into the room.

Amé was dressed in a denim shirt and white shorts. She wore no makeup and her hair was unkempt, as if she'd just woken up. Even so, she was exceedingly attractive, exuding the dignity and presence that impressed me about her at the Dolphin Hotel. The moment she walked into the room, she drew everyone's attention to her. Instantaneously, without explanation, without show.

And without a word of greeting, she walked over to Yuki, mussed her hair lovingly, then pressed the tip of her nose to the girl's temple. Yuki clearly didn't enjoy this, but she put up with it. She shook her head briskly, which got her hair more or less back into place, then cast a cool eye at a vase on a shelf. This was not the utter contempt she showed her father, however. Here, she was displaying her awkwardness, composing herself.

There was some unspoken communication going on between mother and daughter. There was no "How are you?" or "You doing okay?" Just the mussing of hair and the touch of the nose. Then Amé came over and sat down next to me, pulled out a pack of Salems and lit up. The poet ferreted out an ashtray and placed it ceremoniously on the table. Amé deposited the matchstick in it, exhaled a puff of smoke, wrinkled up her nose, then put her cigarette to rest.

"Sorry. I couldn't get away from my work," she began. "You know how it is with pictures. Impossible to stop midway."

The poet brought Amé a beer and a glass, and poured for her.

"How long are you going to be in Hawaii?" Amé turned to me and asked.

"About a week," I said. "We don't have a fixed schedule. I'm on a break right now, but I'm going to have to get back to work one of these days."

"You should stay as long as you can. It's nice here."

"Yes, I'm sure it's nice here," I responded, but her mind was already somewhere else.

"Have you eaten?" she then asked.

"I had a sandwich along the way," I answered, "but not Yuki."

"What are we doing for lunch?" she directed her question toward the poet.

"I seem to remember us fixing spaghetti an hour ago," he spoke slowly and deliberately. "An hour ago would have been twelve-fifteen, so that probably would qualify as what we did for lunch."

"Is that right?" she commented vaguely.

"Yes, indeed," said the poet, smiling in my direction. "When Amé gets wrapped up in her work, she loses all track of everything. She forgets whether she's eaten or not, what she'd been doing where. Her mind goes blank from concentrating so intensely."

I smiled politely. But intense concentration? This seemed more in the realm of psychopathology.

Amé eyed her beer glass absently for a while before picking it up. "That may be so, but I'm still hungry. After all, we didn't eat any breakfast," she said. "Or did we?"

"Let me relate the facts as I remember them. At seven-thirty this morning you had a fairly large breakfast of grapefruit and toast and yogurt," Dick recounted. "In fact, you were rather enthusiastic about it, saying how a good breakfast is one of the pleasures in life."

"Did I?" said Amé, scratching the side of her nose. She stared off into space thinking it over, like a scene out of Hitchcock. Reality recedes until you can't tell who's sane and who's not.

"Well, it doesn't matter. I'm incredibly hungry," she said. "You don't mind if I've already eaten, do you?"

"No, I don't mind," laughed her poet lover. "It's your stomach, not mine. And if you want to eat, I say you should eat as much as you want. Appetite's a good thing. It's always that way with you. When your work's going well, you get an appetite. Shall I fix you a sandwich?"

"Thanks. And could you get me another beer?"

"Certainly," he said, disappearing into the kitchen.

"And you, have you had lunch?" Amé asked me.

"I had a sandwich en route," I repeated.

"Yuki?"

No, was Yuki's terse reply.

"Dick and I met in Tokyo," Amé spoke to me as she crossed her legs. But she could have as well been explaining things to Yuki. "He's the one who suggested I go to Kathmandu. He said it would inspire me. Kathmandu was wonderful, really. Dick lost his arm in Vietnam. It was a land mine. A 'Bouncing Betty,' the ones that fly up into the air and explode. *Boom!* The guy next to him stepped on it and Dick lost his arm. Dick's a poet. He speaks good Japanese too, don't you think? We stayed in Kathmandu a while, then we came here to Hawaii. After Kathmandu, we wanted somewhere warm. That's when Dick found this place. The cottage belongs to a friend of his. I use the guest bathroom as a darkroom. Nice place, don't you think?"

Then she exhaled deeply, as if she'd said all there was to say. She stretched and was quiet. The afternoon silence deepened, particles of light flickered like dust, drifting freely in all directions. The white pithecanthropus skull cloud still floated above the horizon. Obstinate as ever. Amé's Salem lay burning in the ashtray, hardly touched.

How did Dick manage to make sandwiches with just one arm? I found myself wondering. How did he slice the bread? How did he keep the bread in place? Was it a matter of meter and rhyme?

When the poet emerged bearing a tray of beautiful ham sandwiches, well-made, well-cut, there was no end to my admiration. Then he opened a beer and poured it for Amé.

"Thanks, Dick," she said, then turned to me. "Dick's a great cook."

"If there were a cooking competition for one-armed poets, I'd win hands down," he said with a wink. And then he was back in the kitchen, making coffee. Despite his lack of an arm, Dick was far from helpless.

Amé offered me a sandwich. It was delicious, and somehow lyrical in composition. Dick's coffee was good too.

"It's no problem, you with Yuki, just the two of you?" Amé picked up the conversation again.

"Excuse me?"

"I'm talking about the music, of course. That rock stuff. It doesn't give you a headache?"

"No, not especially," I said.

"I can't listen to that stuff for more than thirty seconds before I get a splitting headache. Being with Yuki is fine, but the music is intolerable," she said, screwing her index finger into her temple. "The kinds of music I can put up with are very limited. Some baroque, certain kinds of jazz. Ethnic music. Sounds that put you at ease. That's what I like. I also like poetry. Harmony and peace."

She lit up another cigarette, took one puff, then set it down in the ashtray. I was sure she would forget about it too, and she did. Amazing that she hadn't set the house on fire. I was beginning to understand what Hiraku Makimura meant about Amé's wearing him down. Amé didn't give anything. She only took. She consumed those around her to sustain herself. And those around her always gave. Her talent was manifested in a powerful gravitational pull. She believed it was her privilege, her right. *Harmony and peace*. In order for her to have that, she had everyone waiting on her hand and foot.

Not that it made any difference to me, I wanted to shout. I was here on vacation. I had my own life, even if it was doing you-know-what. Let all this weirdness reach its natural level. But maybe it didn't matter what I thought? I was a member of the supporting cast.

Amé finished her sandwich and walked over to Yuki, slowly running her fingers through the girl's hair again. Yuki stared at the coffee cups on the table, expressionless. "Beautiful hair," said Amé. "The hair I always wanted. So shiny and silky straight. My hair's so unmanageable. Isn't that right, Princess?" Again she touched the tip of her nose to Yuki's temple.

Dick cleared away the dishes. Then he put on some Mozart chamber music. He asked me if I wanted another beer, but I told him I'd already had enough.

"Dick, I'd like to discuss some family matters with Yuki," Amé spoke with a snap in her voice. "Mother and daughter talk. Why don't you show this gentleman the beach? We should be about an hour."

"Sure," the poet answered, rising to his feet. He gave Amé a loving peck on the forehead, donned a white canvas hat and green Ray-Bans. "See you in an hour. Have a nice chat." Then he took me by the arm and led me out. "We've got a great beach here," he said.

Yuki shrugged and gave me a blank look. Amé was about to light up another Salem. Leaving the women on their own, we stepped out into the afternoon sun.

As I drove the Lancer down to the beach, Dick mentioned that with a prosthetic arm, driving would be no problem.

Still, he preferred not to wear one. "It's unnatural," he explained. "I wouldn't feel at ease. It might be more convenient having one, but I'd be so self-conscious with it. It wouldn't be me. I'm trying to train myself to live one-armed. I'm limited in what I can do, but I do okay."

"How do you slice bread?"

"Bread?" He thought it over a second, as if he didn't know what I was talking about. Then it dawned on him. "Oh, slicing bread? Why sure, that's a reasonable question. It's not so hard. I use one hand, of course, but I don't hold the knife the usual way. I'd be useless if I did that. The trick is to keep the bread in place with your fingers while you move the blade. Like this."

Dick demonstrated with his hand, but for the life of me I couldn't imagine how it would actually work. Yet I'd seen his handiwork. His slices were cleaner than most people with two hands could cut.

"Works perfectly well," he declared with a smile. "Most things I can manage with one hand. I can't clap, but I can do push-ups. Chin-ups too. It takes practice, but it's not impossible. How did you think I sliced bread?"

"I don't know, maybe with your feet?"

That drew a laugh from him. "Clever," he said. "I'll have to write a poem about that. The one-armed poet making sandwiches with his feet. Very clever."

I didn't know whether to agree or not.

A little ways down the coast highway, we pulled over and bought a six-pack, then walked to a deserted area of the beach. We lay down and drank beer after beer, but it was so hot the beer didn't seem to go to my head.

The beach was very un-Hawaiian. Unsightly scrub bushes, uneven sands, somehow rocky, but at least it was off the tourist track. A few pickup trucks were parked nearby, local families hanging out, veteran surfers doing their stuff. The pithecanthropus cloud was still pinned in place, sea gulls going around like washing-machine suds.

We talked in spurts. Dick had nothing but awe and respect for Amé. She was a true artist, he repeated several times. When he spoke about her, his Japanese trailed off into English. He said he couldn't express his feelings in Japanese.

"Since meeting her, my own thinking about poetry has changed. Her photographs—how can I put it?—strip poetry bare. I mean, here we are, choosing our words, braiding strands to cut a figure. But with her photos it's immediate, the embodiment. Out of thin air, out of light, in the gap between moments, she grabs things just like that. She gives physical presence to the depths of the human psyche. Do you know what I mean?"

Kind of, I allowed.

"Sometimes it frightens me, looking at her photos. My whole being is thrown into question. It's that overwhelming. She's a genius. Not like me and not like you . . . Forgive me, that's awfully presumptuous of me. I don't even know a thing about you."

I shook my head. "That's okay, I understand what you're saying."

"Genius is rare. I'm not talking about talent, or even first-rate talent. With genius, you're lucky just to encounter it, to see it right there before your eyes. And yet—," he paused, opening his hand up in a gesture of helplessness. "And yet, in some sense, the experience can be pretty upsetting. Sometimes it's like a needle piercing straight through my ego."

I gazed out at the ocean as I listened. The surf was rough, the waves breaking hard. I buried my fingers in the hot sand, scooped some up and let it drizzle down. Over and over again. Meanwhile, the surfers caught the waves they'd been waiting for and paddled back out.

"But you know," Dick went on, "even with my ego sacrificed, her talent attracts me. It makes me love her even more. Sometimes I think I've been drawn into a whirlpool. I already have a wife—she's Japanese too—and we have a child. I love them, I love them very much. Even now I love them. But from the first time I met Amé, I was drawn right in to her. I couldn't resist her. And I knew it was happening. I knew it wasn't going to come my way again, not in this life. That's when I decided—if I go with her, there'll come a time that I'll regret it. But if I don't go with her, I'll be losing the key to my existence. Have you ever felt that way about something?"

Never, I told him.

"Odd," Dick continued. "I'd struggled so hard to have a quiet, stable life. A wife and kid, a small house, my own work. I didn't make a lot of money, but the work was worth doing. I was writing and translating, and it was a good life, I thought. I'd lost my arm in the war, and that was pretty traumatic, but I worked hard at getting my head together and I found some peace and I was doing all right. Life was all right. And then—" He lifted his palm in a broad flat sweep. "In an instant it was lost. Just like that. I have no place to go. I have no home in Japan anymore, I have no home in America. I've been away too long."

I wanted to offer him some words of comfort, but didn't know what to say. I continued scooping up sand and letting it fall. Dick stood up, walked over to a bush and took a leak, then walked slowly back.

"Confession time," he said, then smiled. "I wanted to tell someone. What do you think?"

What was I supposed to think? We weren't kids. You choose who you sleep with, and whirlpool or tornado or sandstorm, you make a go of what you choose. This Dick made a good impression on me. I respected him for all the difficulties he overcame with only one arm. But this difficulty probably cut deeper.

"I'm afraid I'm not an artist," I said. "So I can't really understand what it means to have an artistically inspiring relationship. It's beyond me. I'm sorry."

Dick seemed saddened by my response and looked out to sea. I shut my eyes. And the next thing I knew, I was waking up. I'd dozed off. Maybe the beer after all. The heat made my head feel light. My watch read half past two. I shook my head from side to side and sat up. Dick was playing with a dog at the edge of the surf. I felt bad. I hoped I hadn't offended him.

But what was I supposed to have said?

Was I cold? Of course I could appreciate his feelings. One arm or two, poet or not, it's a tough world. We all have to live with our problems. But weren't we adults? Hadn't we come this far already? At the very least, you don't go asking impossible questions of someone you've just met. That wasn't courteous.

Cold.

Dick rang the doorbell when we got back, and Yuki opened the door with a totally unamused look on her face. Amé was seated on the sofa, cigarette at her lips, eyes peering off into space as if she were in Zen meditation. Dick walked over and planted a kiss on her forehead.

"Finished talking?" he asked.

"Mmm," she said, cigarette still in her mouth. Affirmative, I assumed.

"We had a nice relaxing time on the beach, looked off the edge of the earth, and caught some rays," Dick reported.

"We have to be going," said Yuki flatly.

My thoughts exactly. Time we were getting back to the real world of tourist-town Honolulu.

Amé stood up. "Well, come visit again. I'd like to see you," she said, giving her daughter a tweak on the cheek.

I thanked Dick for his hospitality and had just helped Yuki into the car when Amé hooked me by the elbow. "I have something to tell you," she said. She led me to a small playground a bit up the road. Leaning against the jungle gym, she put a cigarette to her mouth and seemed almost bothered that she'd have to strike a match to light it.

"You're a decent fellow, I can tell," she began earnestly. "So I know I can ask a favor of you. I want you to bring the child here as often as you can. I don't have to tell you that I love her. She's my child. I want to see more of her. Understand? I want to talk with her. I want to become friends with her. I think we can become friends, good friends, even before being parent and child. So while she's here, I want to talk with her a lot."

Amé gave me a meaningful look.

I couldn't think of an appropriate reply. But I had to say something. "That's between you and her."

"Of course," she said.

"So if she wants to see you, certainly, I'll be happy to bring her around," I said. "Or if you, as her parent, tell me to bring her here, I'll do that. One way or the other. But other than that, I have no say in this. Friends don't need the intervention of a third party. Friendship's a voluntary thing. At least that's the way I know it."

Amé pondered over what I'd said.

I got started again: "You say you want to be her friend. That's very good. But before being Yuki's friend, you're her mother, whether you like it or not. Yuki's thirteen. She *needs* a mother. She needs someone who will love her and hold her and be with her. I know I'm way out of line shooting my mouth off like this. But Yuki doesn't need a part-time friend; she needs a situation that accepts her one hundred percent. *That's* what she needs first."

"You don't understand," said Amé.

"Exactly. I don't understand," I said. "But let's get this straight. Yuki's still a child and she's been hurt. Someone needs to protect her. It's a lot of trouble, but somebody's got to do it. That's responsibility. Can't you understand that?"

"I'm not asking you to bring her here every day," she said. "Just when she wants to come. I'll be calling regularly too. Because I don't want to lose that child. The way things are going, she's going to move away from me as she grows up. I understand that, so what I want are psychological ties. I want a bond. I know I probably haven't been a great mother. But I have so much to do before being a mother.

There's nothing I can do about it. The child knows that. That's why what I want is a relationship beyond mother and daughter. Maybe you could call it blood friends."

On the drive back, we listened to the radio. We didn't talk. Occasionally I'd whistle, but otherwise silence prevailed. Yuki gazed out the window, face turned away from me. For fifteen minutes. But I knew something was coming. I told myself, very plainly: You'd better stop the car somewhere.

So that's what I did. I pulled over into a beach parking lot. I asked Yuki how she was feeling. I asked her if she wanted something to drink. Yuki said nothing.

Two girls wearing identical swimsuits walked slowly under the palms, across my field of vision, stepping like cats balancing on a fence. Their swimsuits were a skimpy patchwork of tiny handkerchiefs that any gust of wind might easily blow away. The whole scene had this wild, too-real unreality of a suppressed dream.

I looked up at the sky. A mother wants to make friends with her daughter. The daughter wants a mother more than a friend. Ships passing in broad daylight. Mother has a boyfriend. A homeless, one-armed poet. Father also has a boyfriend. A gay Boy Friday. What does the daughter have?

Ten minutes later it began. Soft sobs at first, but then the dam burst. Her hands neatly folded in her lap, her nose buried in my shoulder, her slim body trembling. *Cry, go ahead and cry. If I were in your position I'd cry too. You better believe I'd cry.*

I put my arm around her. And she cried. She cried until my shirt sleeve was sopping. She cried and cried and cried.

Two policemen in sunglasses crossed the parking lot flashing revolvers. A German shepherd wandered by, panting in the heat. Palm trees swayed. A huge Samoan climbed out of a pickup truck and walked his girlfriend to the beach. The radio was playing.

"Don't ever call me Princess again," she said, head still resting in my shoulder.

"Did I do that?" I asked.

"Yes, you did."

"I don't remember."

"Driving back from Tsujido, that night. Don't say it again."

"I won't. I promise I won't. I swear on Boy George and Duran Duran. Never, never, never again."

"That's what Mama always calls me. *Princess.*"

"I won't call you that again."

"Mama, she's always hurting me. She's just got no idea. And yet she loves me. I know she does."

"Yes, she does."

"So what am I supposed to do?"

"The only thing you can. Grow up."

"I don't want to."

"No other way," I said. "Everyone does, like it or not. People get older. That's how they deal with it. They deal with it till the day they die. It's always been this way. Always will be. It's not just you."

She looked up at me, her face streaked with tears. "Don't you believe in comforting people?"

"I *was* comforting you."

She brushed my arm from her shoulder and took a tissue from her bag. "There's something really abnormal about you, you know," she said.

We went back to the hotel. We swam. We showered. We went to the supermarket and bought fixings for dinner. We grilled the steak with onions and soy sauce, we tossed a salad, we had miso soup with tofu and scallions. A pleasant supper. Yuki even had half a glass of California wine.

"You're not such a bad cook," Yuki said.

"No, not true. I just put my heart into it. That's the difference. It's a question of attitude. If you really work at something, you can do it, up to a point. If you really work at being happy, you can do it, up to a point."

"But anything more than that, you can't."

"Anything more than that is luck," I said.

"You really know how to depress people, don't you? Is that what you call being adult?"

We washed the dishes, then went out walking on Kalakaua Avenue as the lights were blinking on. We critiqued the merchandise of different offbeat shops, eyed the outfits of the passersby, took a rest stop at the crowded Royal Hawaiian Hotel garden bar. I got my requisite piña colada; Yuki asked for fruit punch. I thought of Dick North and how he would hate the noisy city night. I didn't mind it so much myself.

"What do you think of my mother?" Yuki asked when our drinks arrived.

"Honestly, I don't know what to think," I said after a moment. "It takes me a while to consider everything and pass judgment. Afraid I'm not very bright."

"But she did get you a little mad, right?"

"Oh yeah?"

"It was all over your face," said Yuki.

"Maybe so," I said, taking a sip and looking out on the night sea. "I guess I did get a little annoyed."

"At what?"

"At the total lack of responsibility of the people who should be looking after you. But what's the use? Who am I to get mad? As if it does any good."

Yuki nibbled at a pretzel from a dish on the table. "I guess nobody knows what to do. They want to do something, but they don't know how."

"Nobody seems to know how."

"And you do?"

"I'm waiting for hints to take shape, then I'll know what action to take."

Yuki fingered the neck of her T-shirt. "I don't get it," she said.

"All you have to do is wait," I explained. "Sit tight and wait for the right moment. Not try to change anything by force, just watch the drift of things. Make an effort to cast a fair eye on everything. If you do that, you just naturally know what to do. But everyone's always too busy. They're too talented, their schedules are too full. They're too interested in themselves to think about what's fair."

Yuki planted an elbow on the table, then swept the pretzel crumbs from the tablecloth. A retired couple in matching aloha shirt and muumuu at the next table sipped out of a big, brash tropical drink. They looked so happy. In the torch-lit courtyard, a woman was playing the electric piano. Her singing was less than wonderful, but two or three pairs of hands clapped when her vocal stylings were over. And then Yuki grabbed my piña colada and took a quick sip.

"Yum," she exclaimed.

"Two votes yum," I said. "Motion passed."

Yuki stared at me. "What is *with* you? I can't figure you out. One minute you're Mister Cool, the next you're bonkers from the toes up."

"If you're sane, that means you're off your rocker. So don't worry about it," I replied, then ordered another piña colada from a frighteningly cheerful waitress. She wiggled off, trotted back with the drink, then vanished leaving behind a mile-wide Cheshire grin.

"Okay, so what am I supposed to do?" said Yuki.

"Your mother wants to see more of you," I said. "I don't know any more than that. She's not my family, and she's as unusual as they come. As I understand her, she wants to get out of the rut of a mother-daughter relationship and become friends with you."

"Making friends isn't so easy."

"Agreed," I said. "Two votes not so easy."

With both elbows now on the table, Yuki gave me a dubious look.

"And what do you think? About Mama's way of thinking."

"What I think doesn't matter. The question is, what do you think? You could think it's wishful thinking on her part. Or you could think it's a constructive stance worth considering. It all depends on you. But don't make any rush decisions. You should take your time thinking it over."

Yuki propped her chin up on her hands. There was a loud guffaw from the counter. The pianist launched into "Blue Hawaii." Heavy breathing to a tinkling of high notes. *The night is young and so are we. . . .*

"We're not doing so well right now," said Yuki. "Before going to Sapporo was the worst. She was on my case about not going to school. It was real messy. We hardly spoke to each other. I never wanted to see her. That dragged on and on. But then Mama doesn't think like normal people do. She says whatever comes into her head and then she forgets it right after she's said it. She's serious when she says it, but after that she might as well have never said a thing. And then out of nowhere, she wants to play mother again. That's what really pisses me off."

"But—," I tried to interrupt.

"But she *is* interesting. She isn't like anybody else in the world. She may be the pits as a mother and she's really screwed me up, but she *is* interesting. Not like Papa. I don't really know what to think, though. Now she says she wants to be friends. She's so . . . overwhelming, so powerful, and I'm just a kid. Anyone can see that, right? But *no–o*, not her. Mama says she wants to be friends, but the harder she tries, the more it hurts me. That's how it was in Sapporo. She tried to get close to me, she actually tried. So I started to get closer to her. I tried, honest. But her head's always so full of stuff, she just spaces out. And the next thing I know, she's gone." Yuki sent her half-nibbled pretzel out over the sand. "Now if that's not loopy, what is? I like Mama. I guess I like her. And I guess I wouldn't mind if we were friends. I just don't want to have everything dumped back on me again like that. I hate that."

"Everything you say is right," I said. "Completely understandable."

"Not for Mama. She wouldn't understand if you spelled it all out for her."

"No, I don't think so either."

The next day dawned with another glorious Hawaiian sunrise. We ate breakfast, then went to the beach in front of the Sheraton. We rented boards and tried to surf. Yuki enjoyed herself so much that afterward we went to a surf shop near the Ala Moana Shopping Center and bought two used boards. The salesclerk asked if we were brother and sister. I said yes. I was glad we didn't look like father and daughter.

At two o'clock we were back on the beach, lazing. Sunbathing, swimming, napping, listening to the radio and tuning out, thumbing through paperbacks, people-watching, listening to the wind in the palms. The sun slowly traveled its prescribed path. When it went down, we returned to our rooms, showered, ate some spaghetti and salad, then we went to see a Spielberg movie. After the movie we took a walk and ended up at the Halekulani poolside bar, where I had a piña colada again and Yuki her usual fruit punch.

A dance band was playing "Frenesi." An elderly clarinetist took a long solo, reminiscent of Artie Shaw, while a dozen retired couples in silks and satins danced around the pool, faces illuminated by the rippling blue light from below. A hallucinatory vision. After how many years, these people had finally made it to Hawaii. They glided gracefully, their steps learned and true. The men moved with their backs straight, chins tucked in, the women with their evening dresses swirling, drawing cheek-to-cheek as the band played "Moon Glow."

"I'm getting sleepy again," said Yuki. But this time, she walked back alone. Progress.

Returning to my room, I opened a bottle of wine and watched Clint Eastwood's *Hang 'Em High* on the tube. By the time I was on my third glass, I was so sleepy I gave up on the whole thing and got ready to knock off. It'd been another perfect Hawaiian day.

And it wasn't over yet.

Five minutes after I'd crawled into bed, the doorbell rang. A little before midnight. Terrific. What did Yuki want now? I got myself decent and got to the door as the bell sounded another time. I flung the door open—only to find that it wasn't Yuki at all. It was an attractive young woman.

"Hi," said the attractive young woman.

"Hi," I said back.

"My name is June," she said with a slight accent. She seemed to be Southeast Asian, maybe Thai or Filipino or Vietnamese. Petite and dark, big eyes. Wearing a sleek dress of some lustrous pink material. Her purse and shoes were pink too. Tied on her left wrist was a large pink ribbon. Gift-wrapped. She placed a hand on the door and smiled.

"Hi, June," I said.

"I come in?" she asked, pointing behind me.

"Just a minute. You must have the wrong party. Which room do you want?"

"Umm, wait second," she said and pulled a piece of paper from her purse. "Mmm, Mistah . . ." She showed me the note.

"That's me."

"No mistake?"

"No mistake. But not so fast," I said. "I'm the fellow you want, but I don't know who you are. What's going on?"

"I come in first? Here people listen. People think strange things. Everything relax, no problem. No gun, no holdup. Okay?"

True, we'd wake Yuki up if we continued talking in the corridor. I let June in.

I asked her if she wanted something to drink. She'd have what I'd have. I mixed two gin-and-tonics, which I placed on the low table between us. She boldly crossed her legs as she brought the drink to her lips. Beautiful legs.

"Okay, June, why are you here and what do you want?"

"I come make you happy," she said naturally.

"Who told you to come?"

She shrugged. "Gentleman friend who not want say. He already pay. He pay from Japan. He pay for you. Understand?"

Makimura. It had to be Makimura. The way that man's mind worked! What a world! Everyone wanting to buy me women.

"He pay for all night. So we can enjoy. I very good," June said, lifting her legs to remove her pink high heels. She then lay down on the floor, very provocatively.

"I'm sorry, but I can't go through with this," I interrupted her.

"Why? You gay?"

"No, I'm not gay. It's a difference of opinion between me and the gentleman who paid for you. I'm afraid I can't accept, June."

"But I get money. I cannot pay back. He care whether we fuck or not fuck? I don't call overseas and say, 'Yessir, we fuck three times.'"

I sighed.

"Let's do it," she said simply. "It feel good."

I didn't know what to think. One foot in dreamland after a long day, then someone you don't know shows up and says "Let's fuck." Good grief.

"We drink one more gin tonic, okay?"

I agreed somehow. June fixed our drinks, then switched the radio on. "*Saiko!*" June said, throwing in some Japanese for effect, relaxing as if she were at home. "Great." Then sipping her drink, she leaned against me. "Don't think too much," she said, reading my mind. "I very good. I know very much. Don't try do nothing, I do everything. Gentleman in Japan out of picture. Now just you and me."

June ran her fingers across my chest. My resolve was weakening steadily. This was beginning to seem quite easy. If I could just live with the fact that Makimura had bought me a prostitute. But it was only sex. Erection, insertion, ejaculation, that's all folks.

"Okay," I said, "Let's do it."

"Thatta boy!" exclaimed June, downing her gin-and-tonic.

"But tonight I'm very tired. So no special stunts."

"I do everything. But you do two things."

"Which are?"

"Turn off light, untie ribbon."

Done. We headed into the bedroom. June had her dress off in a flash, then set about undressing me. She may not have been Mei, but she was skilled at her job and she took pride in her skills. She was fingers and tongue all over me. She got me hard and then she made me come to the beat of Foreigner on the radio. The night had just begun.

"Was that good?"

"V–very," I panted.

We treated ourselves to another round of drinks.

Suddenly I had a thought. "June, last month you wouldn't have had a 'Mei' here, would you?"

"Funny man!" June burst out laughing. "I like jokes. And next month she is July, right?"

I tried to tell her that it wasn't a joke, but it didn't do any good. So I shut up. And when I did, June did another professional job on me. I didn't have to do a thing, exactly like she said. I just lay there.

She was as fast and efficient as a service station attendant. You pull up and hand over the keys. She takes care of everything else: fill up the tank, wash and wax, check the oil, empty the ashes. Could you call it sex? Well, whatever it was, we kept at it until past two when we finally ran out of gas and conked out. It was already light out when we awoke. We'd left the radio on. June was curled up naked next to me, her pink dress and pink shoes and pink ribbon lying on the floor.

"Hey, get up," I said, trying to rouse her. "You've got to get out of here. There's a little girl coming over for breakfast."

"Okay, okay," she muttered, grabbing up her bag and walking naked into the bathroom to brush her teeth and comb her hair.

When she was ready to leave, she tossed her lipstick into her bag and closed it with a snap. "So when I come next?"

"Next?"

"I get money for three nights. We fuck last night, we fuck two more nights. Maybe you want different girl? I no mind. Men like sleep with lots girls."

"No, you're who I want, of course," I said, at a loss for what else to say. Three nights? Did Makimura want me milked dry?

"You very nice. You no regret. I do wild next time. Okay? You count on me. Night after tomorrow, okay? I have free night. I do whole works."

"Okay," I told her, handing her ten dollars for carfare.

"Thank you, you very nice. Bye-bye."

I cleaned the place up before Yuki arrived, got rid of all the telltale signs, including the pink ribbon. But the moment Yuki stepped into the room a stern expression came over her face. She knew right away. I pretended not to notice her demeanor, whistling as I prepared the coffee and toast and brought them to the table.

She didn't say a word through breakfast, refused to respond to my attempts at conversation.

Finally she placed both hands on the table and glared at me. "You had a woman here last night, didn't you?" she said.

"You really pick up on things, don't you?" I tried to make light of the situation.

"Who was she? Some girl you picked up somewhere?"

"Oh c'mon. I'm not that good. She came here of her own doing."

"Don't lie to me! Nothing happens like that."

"I'm not lying, I promise. The woman really did come here on her own," I said. I tried to explain: The woman suddenly showed up and turned out to be a gift from her father. Maybe it was his idea of giving me a good time, or maybe he was worried and figured if I was sexually sated, I'd stay out of his daughter's bed.

"That's exactly the kind of garbage he'd pull," said Yuki, resigned but angry. "Why does he always operate on the lowest level? He never understands anything, anything important. Mama's screwy, but Papa's head is on ass backwards."

"Yeah, he's totally off the mark."

"So then why'd you let her in? That woman."

"I didn't know what was coming off. I had to talk with her."

"But don't tell me you . . ."

"It wasn't so simple, I—"

"You didn't!" Yuki flew into a huff. Then, at a loss for what to say, she blushed.

"Well, yes. It's a long story. But the truth of the matter is, I couldn't say no."

She closed her eyes and pressed her hands to her cheeks. "I don't believe this!" Yuki screamed, her voice breaking. "I can't believe you'd do such a thing!"

"Of course, I refused at first," I tried to defend myself. "But in the end—what can I say?—I gave in. It wasn't just the woman, though of course it was the woman. It was your father and your mother and the way they have this influence on everybody they meet. So I figured what the hell. Also, the woman didn't seem like such a bad deal."

"I can't believe you're saying this!" Yuki cried. "You let Papa buy a woman for you? And you think nothing of it? That's so shameless, that's wrong. How could you?"

She had a point.

"You have a point," I said.

"That's really, really shameless."

"I admit it. It's really, really shameless."

We repaired to the beach and surfed until noon. During which time Yuki didn't speak a single word to me. When I asked if she wanted to have lunch, she nodded. Did she want to eat back at the hotel? She shook her head. Did she want to eat out? She nodded. After a bit more nonverbal conversation, we settled for hot dogs, sitting out on the grass by Fort DeRussy. Three hours and still not a peep out of her.

So I said, "Next time I'll just say no."

She removed her sunglasses and stared at me as if I were a rip in the sky. For a full thirty seconds. Then she brushed back her bangs. "Next time?!" she enunciated, incredulous. "What do you mean, *next time*?"

So I did my best to explain how her father had prepaid for two more nights. Yuki pounded the ground with her fist. "I don't *believe* this. This is really barfbag."

"I don't mean to upset you, Yuki, but think of it this way. Your father is at least showing concern. I mean, I am a male of the species and you are a young, very pretty female."

"Really and truly barfbag," Yuki screamed, holding back tears. She stormed off back to the hotel and I didn't see her until evening.

30

Hawaii.

The next few days were bliss. A respite of peace. When June showed up for my next installment, I begged a fever and turned her down politely. She was very gracious. She got a mechanical pencil from her bag and jotted down her number on a notepad. I could call when I felt up to it. Then she said good-bye and left, swinging her hips off into the sunset.

I took Yuki to her mother's a few more times. I took walks with Dick North on the beach, I swam in their pool. Dick could swim amazingly well. Having just one arm hardly seemed to make a difference. Yuki and her mother talked by themselves, about what I had no idea. Yuki never told me and I never asked.

On one occasion Dick recited some Robert Frost to me. My understanding of English wasn't good enough, but Dick's delivery alone conveyed the poetry, which flowed with rhythm and feeling. I also got to see some of Amé's photos, still wet from the developing. Pictures of Hawaiian faces. Ordinary portraits, but in her hands the subjects came alive with honest island vitality and grace. There was an earthiness, a chilling brutality, a sexiness. Powerful, yet unassuming. Yes, Amé had talent. *Not like me and not like you*, as Dick had said.

Dick looked after Amé in much the same way I looked after Yuki. Though he, of course, was far more thorough. He cleaned house, washed clothes, cooked meals, did the shopping. He recited poetry, told jokes, put out her cigarettes, kept her supplied with Tampax (I once accompanied him shopping), made sure she brushed her teeth, filed her photos, prepared a typewritten catalogue of all her works. All single-handedly. I didn't know where the poor guy found the time to do his own creative work. Though who was I to talk? I was having my trip paid by Yuki's father, with a call girl thrown in on top.

On days when we didn't visit Yuki's mother, we surfed, swam, lolled about on the beach, went shopping, drove around the island. Evenings, we went for strolls, saw movies, had piña coladas and fruit drinks. I had plenty of time to cook meals if I felt like it. We relaxed and got beautifully tanned, down to our fingertips. Yuki bought a new Hawaiian-print bikini at a boutique in the Hilton, and in it she looked like a real local girl. She got quite good at surfing and could catch waves that were beyond me. She listened to the Rolling Stones. Whenever I left her side on the beach, guys moved in, trying to strike up a conversation with her. But Yuki didn't speak a word of English, so she had no trouble ignoring them. They'd be shuffling off, disgruntled, when I got back.

"Do guys really desire girls so much?" Yuki asked.

"Yeah. Depends on the individual of course, but generally I guess you could say that men desire women. You know about sex, don't you?"

"I know enough," said Yuki dryly.

"Well, men have this physical desire to sleep with women," I explained. "It's a natural thing. The preservation of the species—"

"I don't care about the preservation of the species. I don't want to know about science and hygiene. I want to know about *sex drive*. How does that work?"

"Okay, suppose you were a bird," I said, "and flying was something you really enjoyed and made you feel good. But there were certain circumstances that, except on rare occasions, kept you from flying. I don't know, let's say, lousy weather conditions, the direction of the wind, the season, things like that. But the more you couldn't fly, the more you wanted to fly and your energy built up inside you and made you irritable. You felt bottled up or something like that. You got annoyed, maybe even angry. You get me?"

"I get you," she said. "I always feel that way."

"Well, that's your sex drive."

"So when was the last time you flew? That is, before Papa bought that prostitute for you?"

"The end of last month."

"Was it good?"

I nodded.

"Is it always good?"

"No, not always," I said. "Bring two imperfect beings together and things don't always go right. You're flying along nice and easy, and suddenly there's this enormous tree in front of you that you didn't see before, and *cr–rash*."

Yuki mulled this over. Imagining, perhaps, a bird flying high, its peripheral vision completely missing the danger straight ahead. Was this a bad explanation or what? Was she going to take things the wrong way? Aww, what the hell, she'd find out for herself soon enough.

"The chance of things going right gradually improves with age," I continued my explanation. "You get the knack of things, and you learn to read the weather and wind. On the other side of the coin, sex drive decreases with age. That's just how it goes."

"Pathetic," said Yuki.

"Yes, pathetic."

Hawaii.

Just how many days had I been in the Islands? The concept of time had vanished from my head. Today comes after yesterday, tomorrow comes after today. The sun comes up, the sun goes down; the moon rises, the moon sets; tide comes in, tide goes out.

I pulled out my appointment book and checked the calendar. We'd been in Hawaii for ten days! It was approaching the end of April. Wasn't I going to stay for one week? Or was it one month? Days of surfing and piña coladas. Not bad as far as that went.

But how did I get to this spot? It started with me looking for Kiki, except that I didn't know that was her name at the time. I'd retraced my steps to Sapporo, and ever since, there'd been one weird character after another. And now, look at me, lying in the shade of a coconut palm, tropical drink in hand, listening to Kalapana.

What happened along the way? Mei was murdered. The police hauled me in. Whatever happened with Mei's case? Did the cops find out who she was? What about Gotanda? How was he doing? The last time I saw him he looked awful, tired and run-down. And then we left everything half-assed up in the air.

Pretty soon I had to be getting back to Japan. But it was so hard to take the first step in that direction. Hawaii had been the first real release from tension in ages—for both Yuki and me—and boy, had we needed it. Day after day I was thinking about almost nothing. Just swimming and lying in the sun getting tan, driving around the island listening to the Stones and Bruce Springsteen, walking moonlit beaches, drinking in hotel bars.

I knew this couldn't go on forever. But I couldn't get myself moving. And I couldn't bear to see Yuki get all uptight again. It was a perfect excuse.

Two weeks passed.

One day toward dusk, Yuki and I motored our way through downtown Honolulu. Traffic was bad, but we were in no hurry, content to drive around and take in all the roadside attractions. Porno theaters, thrift shops, Chinese grocers, Vietnamese clothing stores, used book and record shops, old men playing go, guys with blurry eyes standing on street corners. Funny town, Honolulu. Full of cheap, good, interesting places to eat. But not a place for a girl to walk alone.

Right outside the downtown area, toward the harbor, the city blocks became sparser, less inviting. There were office buildings and warehouses and coffee shops missing letters from their signs, and the buses were full of people going home from work.

That's when Yuki said she wanted to see *E.T.* again.

Okay, after dinner, I said.

Then she said what a great movie it was and how she wished I was more like E.T. and then she touched my forehead with her index finger.

"Don't do that," I said. "It'll never heal."

That drew a chuckle from her.

And that's when it happened.

When something connected up inside my head with a loud *clink*. Something happened, though I didn't know then what it was.

It was enough to make me slam on the brakes, though. The Camaro behind us honked bitterly and showered me with abuses as it pulled around us. I had seen something, and something connected. Just there now, something very important.

"What's the matter?" Yuki said, or so I thought she said.

I may not have heard a thing. Because I was deep in thought at that moment. I was deep in thought thinking that I'd just seen *her*. *Kiki*. I'd just seen Kiki—in downtown Honolulu! She was here! Why? It was definitely her. I'd driven past, close enough to have reached out and touched her. She was walking in the opposite direction, right beside the car.

"Listen, close all the windows and lock all the doors. Don't set a foot outside. And don't open up for anyone. I'll be right back," I said, leaping out of the car.

"Hey, wait! Don't leave me here!"

But I was already running down the sidewalk, bumping into people, pushing them out of my way. I didn't have time to be polite. I had to catch up with her. I had to stop her, I had to talk to her, I had found her! I ran for two blocks, I ran for three blocks. And then, way up ahead, I spotted her, in a blue dress with a white bag swinging at her side in the early evening light. She was heading back toward the hustle and bustle of town. I followed, reaching the main drag, where the sidewalk traffic got thicker. A woman three times the size of Yuki couldn't seem to get out of my way. But I kept going, trying to catch up. As Kiki kept walking. Not fast, not slow, at normal speed. But not turning around to look behind her, not glancing to the side, not stopping to board a bus, just walking straight ahead. You'd think I'd be right up with her any second now, but the distance between us never seemed to close.

The next thing I knew she turned a corner to the left. Naturally I followed suit. It was a narrow street, lined on both sides with nondescript, old office buildings. There was no sign of her anywhere. Out of breath, I came to a standstill. What is this? How could she disappear on me again? But Kiki hadn't disappeared. She'd just been hidden from view by a large delivery truck, because there she was again, walking at the same clip on the far sidewalk.

"Kiki!" I yelled.

She heard me, apparently. She shot a glance back in my direction. There was still some distance between us, it was dusk, and the streetlights weren't on yet, but it was Kiki all right. I was sure of it. I *knew* it was her. And she knew who was calling her. She even smiled.

But she didn't stop. She'd simply glanced over her shoulder at me. She didn't slacken her pace. She kept on walking and then entered a building. By the time I got there, it was too late. No one was in the foyer, and the elevator door was just shutting. It was an old elevator, the kind with a clock-like dial that told you what floor it was on. I took the time to breathe, eyes glued to the dial. Eight. She'd gotten off on eight. I pressed the button, then impulsively decided to take the stairs instead.

The whole building seemed to be empty, dead quiet. The gummy slap of my rubber soles on the linoleum steps resounded hollow through the dusty stairwell.

The eighth floor wasn't any different. Not a soul in sight. I looked left and right and saw nothing to suggest life. I walked down the hall and read the signs on each of the seven or eight doors. A trading company, a law office, a dentist, . . . None in business, the signs old and smudged. Nondescript offices on a nondescript floor of a nondescript building on a nondescript street. I went back and reexamined the signs on the doors. Nothing seemed to connect to Kiki; nothing made sense. I strained my ears, but the building was as quiet as a ruins.

Then came the sound. A clicking of heels, high heels. Echoing eerily off the ceilings, bearing a weight . . . the dry weight of old memories. All of a sudden, I was wandering through the labyrinthine viscera of a large organism. Long-dead, cracked, eroded. By something beyond reality, beyond human rationality, I had slipped through a fault in time and entered this . . . thing.

The clicking heels continued to echo, so loudly, so deeply, that it was difficult to determine which direction they were coming from. But listening carefully, I traced the steps to the distant end of a corridor that turned to the right. I moved quickly, quietly, to the door farthest. Those steps, the clicking of the heels, grew murky, remote, but they were there, beyond the door. An unmarked door. Which was unnerving. When I'd checked a minute before, each door had a sign.

Was this a dream? No, not with such continuity. All the details followed in perfect order. I'm in downtown Honolulu, I chased Kiki here. Something's gone whacky, but it's real.

I knocked.

The footsteps stopped, the last echo sucked up midair. Silence filled the vacuum.

For thirty seconds I waited. Nothing. I tried the doorknob. And with a low, grating grumble, the door opened inward. Into a room that was dark, tinged with the somber blue of the waning of the day. There was a faint smell of floor wax. The room was empty, with the exception of old newspapers scattered on the floor.

Footsteps again. Exactly four footsteps, then silence.

The sound seemed to emerge from somewhere even farther. I walked toward the window and discovered another door set off to the side. It opened onto a stairwell that went up. I gripped the cold metal handrail, tested my footing, then slowly climbed into what became total black darkness. The stairs rose at a steep pitch. I imagined I could hear sounds above. The stairs ended. I groped for a light switch; there wasn't any. Instead, my hand found another door.

It opened into what I sensed to be a sizable space, perhaps an attic. There was not the total darkness of the stairwell, but it was still not light enough to see. Faint refractions from the glow of the streetlights below stole in through a skylight. I held on to the doorknob.

"Kiki!" I shouted.

There was no response.

I stood still, waiting, not knowing what to do. Time evaporated. I peered into the darkness, ears alert. Slowly, uncertainly, the light filtering into the room seemed to increase. The moon? The lights of the city? I proceeded cautiously into the center of the space.

"Kiki!" I called out again.

No response.

I turned slowly around, straining to see what I could. Odd pieces of furniture were arranged in the corners of the room. Gray silhouettes that might be a sofa, chairs, a table, a chest. Peculiar, very peculiar. The stage had been set as if by centrifuge, surreal, but real. I mean, the furniture looked *real.*

On the sofa was a white object. A sheet? Or the white bag Kiki'd been carrying? I walked closer and discovered that it was something quite different.

The something was bones.

Two human skeletons were seated side by side on the sofa. Two complete skeletons, one larger, one smaller, sitting exactly as they might have when they were alive. The larger skeleton rested one arm on the back of the sofa. The smaller one had both hands placed neatly on its lap. It was as if they'd died instantly, before they knew what hit them, their flesh having fallen away, their position intact. They almost seemed to be smiling. Smiling, and incredibly white.

I felt no fear. Why, I don't have the slightest idea, but I was quite calm. Everything in this room was so still, the bones clean and quiet. These two skeletons were extremely, irrevocably dead. There was nothing to fear.

I walked slowly around the room. There were six skeletons in all. Except for one, all were whole. All sat in natural positions. One man (at least from the size, I imagined it was a man) had his line of vision fixed on a television. Another was bent over a table still set with dishes, the food now dust. Yet another, the only skeleton in an imperfect state, lay in bed. Its left arm was missing from the shoulder.

I squeezed my eyes shut.

What on earth was this? Kiki, what are you trying to show me?

Again, I heard footsteps. Coming from another room, but in which direction? It seemed to have no location at all. As far as I could see, this room was a dead end. There was no other way out. The footsteps persisted, then vanished. The silence that lingered then was so dense it was suffocating. I wiped the sweat from my face with the palm of my hand. Kiki had disappeared again.

I exited through the door I'd entered from. One last glance: the six skeletons glowing faintly in the deep blue gloom. They almost seemed ready to get up and move about once I was gone. They'd switch on the TV, help themselves to hot food. I closed the door quietly, so as not to disturb them, then went back downstairs to the empty office. It was as before, not a soul around, old newspapers scattered on the floor.

I went over to the window and looked down. The streetlights glowed brightly; the same trucks and vans were parked in the narrow thoroughfare. The sun had completely set. Nobody in sight.

But lying on the dust-covered windowsill, I noticed a scrap of paper, the size of a business card. I picked it up and studied it carefully. There was a phone number on it. The paper was fresh, the ink unfaded. Curious. I slipped it in my pocket and went out into the corridor.

I was trying to find the building superintendent to ask about the office, when I remembered Yuki, stranded in the car, in a seedy section of town. How long had I left her there? Twenty minutes? An hour? The sky was sliding into night.

Yuki was dazed, her face buried into the seat, the radio on, when I got back to the car. I tapped on the window, and she unlocked the door.

"Sorry," I said solemnly.

"All kinds of weird people came. They yelled and they banged on the windshield and rocked the car," she said, almost numb. "I was scared out of my mind."

"I'm very sorry."

She looked me in the face. Then her eyes turned to ice. The pupils lost their color, the slightest tremor raced over her features like the surface of a lake rippled by a fallen leaf. Her lips formed unspoken words. *Where on earth did you go?*

"I don't know," my voice issued from somewhere and blurred out into the distance like those echoing footsteps. I pulled a handkerchief from my pocket and slowly wiped the sweat from my brow. "I don't know."

Yuki squinted and reached out to touch my cheek. Her

fingertips were soft and smooth. She sniffed the air around me, her tiny nostrils swelling slightly. She gave me another long look. "You *saw* something, didn't you?"

I nodded.

"But you can't say what. You can't put it into words. Can't explain, not to anyone. But I can see it." She leaned over and grazed her cheek against mine. "Poor thing," she said.

"How come?" I asked, laughing. There was no reason to laugh, but I couldn't not laugh. "All things considered, I'm the most ordinary guy you could hope to find. So why do these weird things keep happening to me?"

"Yeah, why?" said Yuki. "Don't look at me. I'm just a kid. You're the adult here."

"True enough."

"But I understand how you feel."

"I don't."

"At times like this, adults need a drink."

We went to the Halekulani bar. The one indoors, not the one by the pool. I ordered a martini this time, and Yuki got a lemon soda. We were the only customers in the place. The balding pianist, with a Rachmaninoff scowl, was at the concert grand running through old standards—"Stardust," "But Not for Me," "Moonlight in Vermont." Flawlessly, with lackluster. Then he finished off with a very serious Chopin prelude. Yuki clapped for this, and the pianist forced a smile.

On my third martini, I shut my eyes and that room came to mind again. The sort of scene where you wake up drenched in sweat, relieved that it was just a dream. But it hadn't been a dream. I knew it and so did Yuki. She knew I'd *seen* something. Those six skeletons. What did they mean? Who were they? Was that one-armed skeleton supposed to be Dick North?

What was Kiki trying to tell me?

I remembered the scrap of paper in my pocket, the scrap

of paper I'd found on the windowsill. I went to the phone and dialed the number. No answer. Only endless ringing, like plumb bobs hanging in bottomless oblivion. I returned to my bar stool and sighed. "I'm thinking about going back to Japan tomorrow. If I can get a seat, that is," I said. "I've been here a little too long. It's been great, but time to go back. I've got things I got to clear up back home."

Yuki nodded, as if she'd known this all along. "It's okay, don't worry about me. Go back if you think you should."

"What are you going to do? Stay here? Or do you want to go back with me?"

Yuki shrugged her shoulders. "I think I'll go stay with Mama for a while. I don't think she'd mind. I'm not in the mood to go back yet."

I finished up the last of my martini.

"We'll do this then: I'll drive you out to Makaha tomorrow. That way I get to see your mother one more time. And then I'll head off to the airport."

That night we had our last dinner together at a seafood restaurant near Aloha Tower. Yuki didn't talk much, and neither did I. I was sure I would drift off at any moment, mouth full of fried oysters, to join those skeletons in the attic.

Yuki gave me meaningful glances throughout the meal. After we were done, she said, "You better go home to bed. You look terrible."

Back in my room I poured myself some wine and turned on the television. The Yankees vs. the Orioles. I had no desire to watch baseball, but I left the game on anyway. It was a link to reality.

The wine had its effect. I got sleepy. And then I remembered the slip of paper in my pocket and tried the number again. No answer again. I let the telephone ring fifteen times. I glared at the tube to see Winfield step into the batter's box, when something occurred to me.

What was it? My eyes were fixed on the screen.

Something resembled something. Something was connected to something.

Nah, unlikely. But what the hell, check it out. I took the slip of paper and went to get the notepad where June had written her phone number. I compared the two numbers.

Good grief. They were the same.

Everything, everything, was linking up. Except I didn't have a clue what it meant.

The next morning I rang up JAL and booked a flight for the afternoon. I paid our bills, and Yuki and I were on our way to Makaha. For once, the sky was overcast. A squall was brewing on the horizon.

"Sounds like there's a Pacman crunching away at your heart," said Yuki. "*Bip-bip-bip-bip-bip-bip-bip-bip.*"

"I don't understand."

"Something's eating you."

I thought about that as I drove on. "Every so often I glimpse this shadow of death," I began. "It's a very dense shadow. As if death was very close, enveloping me, holding me down by the ankles. Any minute now it could happen. But it doesn't scare me. Because it's never my death. It's always someone else's. Still, each time someone dies it wears *me* down. How come?"

Yuki shrugged.

"Death is always beside me, I don't know why. And given the slightest opening, it shows itself."

"Maybe that's your key. Maybe death's your connection to the world," Yuki said.

"What a depressing thought," I said.

Dick North seemed sincerely sad to see me leave. Not that we had a great deal in common, but we did enjoy a certain ease with each other. And I respected him for the poetry he brought to practical concerns. We shook hands. As we did, the one-armed skeleton came to mind. Could that really be this man?

"Dick, do you ever think about death? How you might die?" I asked him, as we sat around one last time.

He smiled. "I thought about death a lot during the War. There was death all around, so many ways you could get killed. But lately, no, I don't have time to worry about what I don't have control over. I'm busier in peace than in war," he laughed. "What makes you ask?"

No reason, I told him.

"I'll think about it. We'll talk about it next time we meet," he said.

Then Amé asked me to take a walk with her, and we strolled along a jogging path.

"Thanks for everything," said Amé. "Really, I mean it. I'm not very good at saying these things. But—umm—well, I mean it. You've really helped smooth things out. Yuki and I have been able to talk. We've gotten closer. And now she's come to stay with me."

"Isn't that nice," I said. I couldn't think of anything less banal to say. Of course Amé barely heard me.

"The child seems to have calmed down considerably since she met you. She's not so irritable and nervous. I don't know what it is, but you certainly have a way with her. What do you have in common with her?"

I assured her I didn't know.

What did I think ought to be done about Yuki's schooling?

"If she doesn't want to go to school, then maybe you should think of an alternative," I said. "Sometimes it's bad to force school on a kid, especially a kid like Yuki who's extra sensitive and attracts more attention than she likes. A tutor might be a good idea. I think it's pretty clear Yuki isn't cut out for all this cramming for entrance exams and all the silly competition and peer pressure and rules and extracurricular activities. Some people can do pretty well without it. I'm being idealistic, I know, but the important thing is that Yuki finds her talent and has a chance to cultivate it. Maybe she'll decide to go back to school. That would be okay too, if that's her decision."

"You're right, I suppose," Amé said after a moment's thought. "I'm not much of a group person, never kept up with school either, so I guess I understand what you're saying."

"If you understand, then there shouldn't be anything to think about. Where's the problem?"

She swiveled her head, going from side to side, popping her neck bones.

"There is no problem. I mean, the only problem is, I don't have unshakable confidence in myself as a mother. So I don't have it in me to stand up for her like that. If you lack confidence, you give in. Deep down, you worry that the idea of not going to school is socially wrong."

Socially wrong? "I can't make any reassurances, but who knows what's going to be right or what's going to be wrong? No one can read the future. The results could be devastating. But that could happen either way. I think if you showed the girl that you're really trying—as a mother or as a friend—to make things work with her, and if you showed her some respect, then she'd be sharp enough to pick up on it and do the rest for herself."

Amé stood there, hands in the pockets of her shorts, and was quiet. Then she said, "You really understand how the child feels, don't you? How come?"

Because I wasn't always on another planet, I felt like telling her. But I didn't.

Amé then said she wanted to give me something as an expression of her appreciation. I told her I'd already received more than enough from her former husband.

"But *I* want to. He's him and I'm me. And *I* want to thank you. And if I don't now, I'll forget to."

"I'd be quite happy if you forgot," I joked.

We sat down on a bench, and Amé pulled out a pack of Salems from her shirt pocket. She lit up, inhaled, exhaled. Then she let the thing turn to ash between her fingers.

Meanwhile, I listened to the birds singing and watched the gardeners whirring about in their carts. The sky was beginning to clear, though I did hear the faint report of thunder in the distance. Strong sunlight was breaking through thick gray cloud cover. In her sunglasses and short sleeves, Amé seemed oblivious to the glare and heat, although several trails of sweat had stained the neck of her shirt. Maybe it wasn't the sun. Maybe it was concentration, or mental diffusion. Ten minutes went by, apparently not registering with her. The passage of time was not a practical component in her life. Or if it was, it wasn't high on her list of priorities. It was different for me. I had a plane to catch.

"I have to be going," I said, glancing at my watch. "I've got to return the car before I check in."

She made a vague effort to refocus her eyes on me. A look I occasionally noted in Yuki. Like mother, like daughter, after all. "Ah, yes, the time. I hadn't noticed," said Amé. "Sorry."

We got up from the bench and walked back to the cottage.

They all came outside to see me off. I told Yuki to cut out the junk food, but figured Dick North would see to that. Lined up in the rearview mirror as I pulled away, the three of them made a curious sight. Dick waving his one arm on high; Amé staring ahead blankly, arms folded across her chest; Yuki looking off to the side and kicking a pebble. The remnant of a family in a makeshift corner of an imperfect universe. How had I ever gotten involved with them? A left-hand turn of the wheel and they were gone from sight. For the first time in ages I was alone.

31

Back at the Shibuya apartment, I went through my mail and messages. Nothing, of course, but petty work-related matters. How's that piece for the next issue coming along? Where the hell did you disappear to? Can you take on this new project? I returned nobody's call. Faster, simpler to get on with the work at hand.

But first, a phone call to Makimura. Friday picked up and promptly turned me over to the big man. I gave him a brief rundown of the trip, saying that Hawaii seemed to be a good breather for Yuki.

"Good," he said. "Many thanks for everything. I'll give Amé a call tomorrow. Did the money hold out, by the way?"

"With lots to spare."

"Well, go ahead and use it up. It's yours."

"I can't do that," I said. "Oh yes, I've been meaning to ask you about your little present."

"Oh, that," he said, making light of it.

"How did you arrange that?"

"Through channels. I trust you didn't stay up all night playing cards, eh?"

"No, I don't mean that. I want to know how you could buy me a woman in Honolulu all the way from Tokyo. I'm just curious how something like that is done."

Makimura was quiet, sizing up the extent of my curiosity.

"Well," he began, "it's like international flower delivery. I call the organization in Tokyo and tell them I want a girl sent to you, at such-and-such a place, at such-and-such a time. Then Tokyo contacts its affiliated Honolulu organization and they send the girl. I pay Tokyo. Tokyo takes a commission and wires the rest to Honolulu. Honolulu takes its commission and what's left goes to the girl. Convenient, eh? All kinds of systems in the modern world."

"Sure seems that way," I said. International flower delivery.

"Very convenient. It costs you, but you save on time and energy. I think they call it worldwide sex-o-grams. They're safe, too. No run-ins with violent pimps. Plus you can write it off as expenses."

"That so?" I said, nodding to myself. "I guess you couldn't give me the number to this organization?"

"Sorry, no go. It's absolutely confidential. Members only, very exclusive. You need glamour and money and social standing. You'd never pass. I mean, forget it. Listen, I'm already talking too much. I told you this much out of the kindness of my heart."

I thanked him for it.

"Well, was she good?" he asked

"Yes, quite good," I admitted.

"Glad to hear it. I asked them to send you the best. What was her name?"

"June."

"June, eh? Was she white?"

"No, Southeast Asian."

"I'll have to check her out next time," he said.

There wasn't much more to say, so I thanked him again and hung up.

Next, I rang Gotanda and got his answering machine. I left a message saying I was back and would appreciate a call. By then it was already getting late in the day, so I hopped in the Subaru and drove to Aoyama to do some shopping before the stores closed. More pedigreed vegetables, the latest shipment fresh from Kinokuniya's own pedigreed vegetable farms. Somewhere in the remote mountains of Nagano, pristine acres surrounded by barbed wire. Watchtower, guards with machine guns. A prison camp like in *The Great Escape*. Rows of lettuce and celery whipped into shape through unimaginably grueling supravegetable training. What a way to get your fiber.

No message from Gotanda when I got back.

The following morning, after a quick breakfast at Dunkin' Donuts, I headed to the library and combed through the last month's newspapers. Checking if there'd been a breakthrough in the investigation of Mei's death. I read the *Asahi* and *Mainichi* and *Yomiuri* with extreme care, but found only election results and a statement by Revchenko and a big piece on delinquency in the schools and how for reasons of "musical impropriety" the White House had canceled a command performance by the Beach Boys. Anyway, not one line about the case.

I then read through back issues of various weekly magazines. And there it was: "Naked Beauty Found Strangled in Akasaka Hotel." A sensationalized, one-page article on Mei. Instead of a photograph, there was a sketch of the corpse by a specialist in criminal art. Next best thing if you didn't have the bloody photo itself. True, the sketch did look like Mei, but then I knew who it was supposed to be. Could anyone else have recognized her? No, Mei had been warm and animated. Full of hopes, full of illusions. She'd been gentle and smooth, fantastic, shoveling her sensual snow. It was the reason we could connect so well, could share those illusions. *Cuck–koo*. She was all innocence.

This lousy sketch made it cheap and dirty. I shook my head. I shut my eyes and sighed slowly. Yet that line drawing, better than any morgue photograph, hammered home the fact that Mei was dead. Extremely, irrevocably dead. She was gone. Her life had been sucked away into black nothingness.

The article fit the drawing. A young woman believed to

be in her early twenties was discovered strangled to death with a stocking in a luxury Akasaka hotel. Completely naked, without identification, an assumed name, et cetera, et cetera. Nothing new to me, except for a one detail: Police were running down probable links to a prostitution ring, an organization that dispatched call girls to first-class hotels.

I returned the magazines to the racks and sat thinking. How had the police been able to narrow their leads to the prostitution ring? Had some hard evidence turned up? Not that I was about to call those two cops to find out.

I left the library and ate a quick lunch nearby, then went for a walk, waiting for a brilliant notion to pop into my head. No such luck. I walked to Meiji Shrine, stretched out on the grass and looked up at the sky.

I thought about the call girl organization. Worldwide sex-o-grams. Place your order in Tokyo and your girl is waiting in Honolulu. Systematic, efficient, sophisticated. No muss, no fuss. Very businesslike. Just went to prove, once you've got an illusion going, it can function on the market like any other product. Advanced capitalism churning out goods for every conceivable niche. Illusion, that was the key word here. Whether prostitution or discrimination or personal attacks or displaced sex drive, give it a pretty name, a pretty package, and you could sell it. Before too long they'll have a call girl catalog order service at the Seibu department store. *You can rely on us*.

I looked up at the sky and thought about sex.

I wanted to sleep with Yumiyoshi. It wasn't out of the question. Just get one foot in her door, so to speak, and tell her, "You have to sleep with me. You *should* sleep with me." Then I undress her, gently, like untying the ribbon on a present. First her coat, then her glasses, then her sweater. Her clothes off, she'd turn into Mei. *Cuck–koo*, she says. "Like my body?"

But before I can answer, the night is gone. Kiki is beside me, Gotanda's graceful fingers playing over her back. The door opens. Enter Yuki. She sees me making love with Kiki.

It's me this time, not Gotanda. Only the fingers are his.

"I can't believe this," says Yuki. "I really can't believe this."

"It's not like that," I say.

"What was *that* all about?" says Kiki for the umpteenth time.

It's not like that, I insist. *The one I want to sleep with is Yumiyoshi.* I just got my signals crossed.

First thing, I have to untangle the connections. Otherwise, I come away empty-handed. Or with someone else's hands. Or even a missing hand.

Leaving the grounds of Meiji Shrine, I went into a backstreet café in Harajuku and had a good strong cup of coffee. Then I walked leisurely home.

In the evening Gotanda rang.

"Sorry, I don't have much time now," he spoke on the fly. "Can I see you tonight around eight or nine?"

"Don't see why not."

"Good, let's have dinner. I'll come pick you up."

While I waited, I put away my suitcase, then went over the receipts from the trip, methodically separating Makimura's charges from my own. Half the meals and the car rental go to him, along with Yuki's personal purchases—surfboard, blaster, swimsuit, . . . I itemized our expenses and slipped the calculations into an envelope together with the leftover travelers cheques, ready to be cashed at the bank and returned to Makimura. I always keep on top of these business details. But not because I like them. I just hate sloppiness in money matters.

After finishing with the accounting, I mixed up some baby whitefish with boiled spinach to go with a bottle of Kirin black label. Then I reread a Haruo Sato short story from years ago. It was a lovely uneventful spring evening. The sky grew darker, painted blue on blue, one stroke at a time, into deeper and deeper shades of night.

When I tired of reading, I put on the Stern-Rose-Istomin Trio playing Schubert's Opus 100, a piece I always reserve for spring. It breathed with the lush sadness of the night. Where off in the depths of gloom drifted six white skeletons. Life was sinking into an abyss, bones hard as memories positioned before me.

32

Gotanda swung by at eight-forty. He was wearing a perfectly ordinary gray V-neck sweater over a perfectly ordinary blue button-down shirt with—you got it—perfectly ordinary cotton slacks. And still he looked striking. Extraordinarily so.

He was curious about my digs, so I invited him in.

"Nice," he said with a shy smile. Such a sweet smile, it made you feel like offering to let him stay for a week.

"Takes me back," he said, as if to himself. "Reminds me of the place I used to have—before I hit it big." From anyone else, the comment would have been an unbearable snub, but from him it was a compliment, straightforward and pure.

I offered Gotanda a big cushion and got out my fold-away low table from the closet. Then I brought us black beer with my spinach-and-whitefish concoction and put on the Schubert again.

"Fantastic!"

"Really? How about something else?"

"I'd love it, but I don't want you to have to go to the trouble."

"No trouble at all. I can whip something up quick and easy. Nothing too fancy, though."

"Can I watch?"

"Sure," I said.

Scallions tossed with salt-plum. *Wakame* seaweed and shrimp vinaigrette. *Wasabi* preserves and grated daikon with sliced fish mousse. Slivered potatoes in olive oil and garlic with minced salami. Homemade cucumber pickles. Yesterday's *hijiki* seaweed plus tofu garnished with heaps of ginger.

"Amazing," sighed Gotanda. "You're a genius."

"Very kind of you to say so, but I assure you, it's real simple. Just throwing together stuff I have around."

"Sheer genius. I could never do it."

"Well, thank you, but I could never imitate a dentist."

"Aaa—," he said, dismissing my return of compliment. "You know, would you mind if we didn't go out tonight? This stuff is great."

"Fine by me."

So we drank and ate. When the beer ran out, we switched to Cutty Sark. We listened to Sly and the Family Stone, the Doors and Stones, Pink Floyd. We listened to the Beach Boys' *Surf's Up*. It was a sixties kind of night. The Loving Spoonful, Three Dog Night. Any self-respecting alien transponding in from Sirius would have thought himself caught in a time warp.

No alien showed, but from ten o'clock it did start to rain. Softly, quietly, barely audible on the eaves. Almost silent as the dead.

As the night wore on, we stopped putting on music. My apartment didn't have the thick walls of Gotanda's condominium, and loud noise after eleven asked for complaints. With the music off, the whisper of the rain underscored the tone of our conversation. The police hadn't made much headway on Mei's case, I lamented. No, they haven't, Gotanda sighed. He'd been checking the newspapers and magazines too.

I opened a second bottle of Cutty Sark, and for the first round we toasted Mei.

"The cops have narrowed their investigations down to prostitution rings," I went on, "so they must have gotten a hold somewhere. I'm worried that'll lead them to you."

"There's a chance," said Gotanda, knitting his eyebrows slightly. "But it's probably okay. I was a little nervous, so I asked the folks at my agency about it. Whether that club's as tight-lipped as they claim. And you know what? Seems the club has a lot of political connections, some pretty big names apparently. So even if the club did spill to the police, they wouldn't be able to go sniffing too far. They couldn't lay a hand on anybody. And for that matter, my agency has a bit of clout too. Some of the bigger stars have very close friends in high places. Sometimes in not-so-nice places. So either way, the cops don't have a lot of room to maneuver. And because I'm a money tree for the agency, they don't want anything to happen to me. I'm a major investment. They don't want to see my value plummet. True, if you'd mentioned my name to the cops, my ass would've been hauled in for sure. All the political connections in Ginza couldn't have kept that from happening. But no fear of that now. The rest is a power play, one system against another."

"It's a dirty world," I said.

"Isn't it, though," said Gotanda. "Dirty to the core."

"Two votes, dirty."

"Say what?"

"Two votes for dirty, motion adopted."

He nodded, then smiled sadly. "Two votes for dirty. No one can be bothered to think about a murder victim. Everyone's busy looking out for Number One," he said. "Myself included."

I went into the kitchen to replenish the ice, bringing out crackers and cheese.

"I want to ask you a favor," I said, sitting down. "Could you call up the organization and ask them something for me?"

He pinched his earlobe. "What do you want to know? Anything to do with this case is out of the question. They'd never crack."

"Completely unrelated. I want to know about a call girl I

met in Honolulu. I've heard a girl overseas could be arranged through the club."

"Who told you that?"

"Someone with no name. I'm willing to bet that the organization this guy was talking about is the same club we're talking about. Because you got to be rich and famous to join. Neither of which I begin to approach, or so I was told."

Gotanda smiled. "Yeah, I think I may have heard about a service like that. One phone call does the trick. I haven't had the pleasure, but it's probably the same setup. So, what about that hooker in Honolulu?"

"I just want to know if the club has a Southeast Asian woman named June working for them."

Gotanda thought about this, but didn't ask anything more. He jotted down the name in his datebook.

"June what?"

"Gimme a break. She's a call girl," I said. "It's just June."

"Got it. I'll ring the place up tomorrow."

"Thanks. I owe you," I said.

"Forget it. After what you've done for me, this is a pittance." He winked and gave me a thumbs-up. "You go to Hawaii alone, by the way?"

"Who goes to Hawaii alone? I went with a girl. She's only thirteen, though."

"You slept with a thirteen-year-old girl?"

"What do you think I am? The kid doesn't even wear a bra yet."

"Then why'd you go with her?"

"To teach her table manners, interpret the mysteries of the sex drive, bad-mouth Boy George, go see *E.T.* You know, the usual."

Gotanda gave me a long look. Then he skewed his lips into a smile. "You really are a little odd, you know?"

Now everyone seemed to think so. Motion passed by unanimous vote.

Gotanda drank some whiskey and nibbled on a cracker.

"I saw my ex-wife a couple of times while you were away," he said. "We're getting along pretty well. Strange to say, but sleeping with your ex-wife can be fun."

"I guess."

"Why don't you try seeing your ex-wife?"

"No way. She's about to get married. Didn't I tell you?"

He shook his head. "Didn't know. Well, too bad."

"No, it's better this way," I said and I meant it. "But what about your ex?"

He shook his head again. "It's hopeless. No other way to put it. Hopeless. A dead end. You know, we make better love than we ever have. We don't have to say a word. We understand each other. It's better than when we were married. *We love each other*, if you want to know. But it can't go on forever like this, meeting in love hotels. I wish we didn't have to hide, but if her family finds out, they'll make my life miserable. As if they haven't already. If it's between me or them, she'll pick them every time. I lose whichever way I turn. . . . God, the things I would give for a normal life with her." Gotanda swirled the ice in his glass, around and around. "Funny isn't it? I can get almost anything I want. Except the one thing I want the most."

"That's how it is," I said. "But I never could get everything I wanted, so I can't really talk."

"No, you've got it wrong," said Gotanda. "You never wanted things to begin with. For instance, would you ever want a Maserati or a condo in Azabu?"

"Well, if somebody forced them on me, . . . But I guess I *can* live without them. My little apartment and my trusty Subaru satisfy me all right. Well, maybe satisfy is an overstatement. But they suit me all right, they're easy to manage, they're not *dis*satisfying anyway. But who knows? Maybe there'll come a time when I need those things."

"No, you're wrong again. That's not what need is. This stuff isn't natural. It's manufactured. Take that place where I live. A roof over your head is the point, not what fancy part of town it's in. But the idiots at the agency say—Itabashi or

Kameido or Nakano Toritsukasei? No status. You big star, you live Azabu. The next thing I know, they've stuck me in that ridiculous condo. What bullshit! What the hell is so great about Azabu? A bunch of rip-off restaurants run by fashion designers and that eyesore called Tokyo Tower and all those crazed women wandering around all night. The same thing with the goddamn Maserati. Who the hell drives a Maserati in Tokyo? It's such bullshit! Subaru or Bluebird or Corona? Nope. Big star no get caught dead in anything but Maserati. The only saving grace of that car is that it's not new; they got it off some *enka* singer."

He poured some whiskey over melted ice, took a sip, frowned.

"That's my world. Azabu, European sports car, first-class. Stupid, meaningless, idiotic bullshit. How did all this . . . this . . . this total nonsense get started? Well, it's very, very simple. You just repeat the message and repeat the message and repeat the message. You pound that baby in. Until everybody believes it. Like a mantra. Azabu, BMW, Rolex, Azabu, BMW, Rolex, Azabu, BMW, Rolex, Azabu, . . .

"That's how you get those poor suckers who actually believe the bullshit. But if they believe that, they're exactly like everybody else. They're blind; they got zero imagination. I'm fed up with it. I'm fed up with this life they have me living. I'm their life-size dress-up doll. Sewed together with loans and mortgages. But who wants to hear this grief? After all, I live in a jet-stream condo in Azabu, I drive a Maserati, I have this Patek Philippe watch—a step up from Rolex, don't you know? And I can sleep with a high-class call girl anytime I feel like it. I'm the envy of the whole goddamn town. I want you to know I didn't ask for any of it. But the worst thing is—boy, this must be getting boring—as long as I keep living like this, I can't get what I really want."

"Like, for instance, love?" I said.

"Yeah, like, for instance, love. And tranquillity. And a healthy family. And a simple life," he ran down the list. Then he placed both hands together before his face. "Look at me, I had a world of possibilities, I had opportunities. But now I'm a puppet. I can get almost any woman I want. Yet the one woman I really want . . ."

Gotanda was getting good and drunk. It didn't show on him, but he sure was letting it all hang out. Which I could appreciate, absolutely, this urge to drink himself silly. We'd been going for almost four hours like this. Gotanda asked if he should get out of here, but I told him I wasn't doing anything special, same as always.

"Sorry to force myself on you," he said. "I don't have anyone else to talk to, to tell you the truth. If I told someone that deep down I'm a Subaru man, they'd think I was stark raving mad, they'd cart me off to a shrink. Of course, it's in fashion, you know, going to a shrink. Amazing bullshit. A show-business shrink is like a vomit clean-up specialist." He closed his eyes. "Seems like I came here just to bitch."

"You've said 'bullshit' at least twenty times."

"Have I?"

"Go ahead, blow it off, if that's what you want."

"No, enough of this. I'm sorry to make you listen to this garbage. It's just that I'm surrounded by all this steaming shit. Makes me want to puke."

"Then go ahead and puke."

"Idiots all around me," Gotanda practically spat out the words. "Bloodsuckers, fat, ugly bloodsuckers, slopping their fat asses around, feeding off the hopes and dreams of decent people. I tell myself it'd be a waste of good energy strangling them."

"Yeah, using a baseball bat would be better. Strangling takes too long."

"You're right," said Gotanda. "But strangling makes the point clearer. Instant death is too good. Why waste kindness on them."

"Ah, the voice of reason."

"Honestly—," he went on, ignoring my irony, then broke off with a sigh and brought his hands together in front of his face again. "I feel so much better."

"Well, now that we've settled that, how about some *o-chazuke?*"

"*O-chazuke?* You're kidding. I'd love some *o-chazuke.*"

I boiled water for tea, tossed together some crumbled *nori* and salt-plum and *wasabi* horseradish, topped two bowls of rice with the mixture, and poured tea over each. *O-chazuke.* Yum.

"From where I sit, seems to me you don't have a bad life," Gotanda said.

I lay back against the wall and listened to the rain. "Some parts, sure. I'm not *un*happy. But I'm like you. I feel like something's missing. I'm living a normal life, I suppose. I'm dancing. I know the steps, and I'm dancing. It's all right. But socially speaking, I've got nothing. I'm thirty-four, I'm not married, I don't have a regular job, I live from day to day. I can't get a public housing loan. I'm not sleeping with anybody. What am I going to be like in thirty years?"

"You'll get by."

"Or else I won't," I said. "Who knows? Same as everyone."

"But with my life, I don't even have parts I enjoy."

"Maybe not, but you look like you're doing pretty well for yourself."

Gotanda shook his head. "Do people who're doing pretty well for themselves pour out such endless streams of grief? Do they come bother you and slosh all over you?"

"Sometimes they do," I said. "We're talking about people, not common denominators."

At one-thirty, Gotanda announced he was leaving.

"You can stay if you like. I've got an extra *futon.* I'll even make you breakfast," I said.

"No, really, but thanks for the offer. I'm sober now, so I might as well go home," he said. "But I've got a favor to ask first. I'm afraid you're going to think it's a little strange."

"Fire away."

"Would you be willing to let me borrow the Subaru for a bit? I'll trade you the Maserati for it. The Maserati is so flashy, I can't go anywhere in peace, especially when I'm trying to see my ex-wife."

"Borrow the Subaru for as long as you like," I said. "But to be honest, I don't know about taking on the Maserati. I keep my heap in a parking lot, so it could easily get banged up at night. And if I dent it or something, I'll never be able to pay for it."

"Don't worry about it. I don't. If anything happens, the agency will take care of it. That baby's insured up the tail pipe. Drive the thing into the sea if you feel like. Honest. They'll only buy me a Ferrari next. There's a porno writer who's got one he wants to sell."

"A Ferrari?" I said limply.

"I know what you're thinking," he laughed. "But you can just shelve it. It's hard for you to understand, but in this debauched world of mine, you can't survive with good taste. Because a person with good taste is a twisted, poor person, a sap without money. You get sympathy, but no one thinks better of you."

So Gotanda drove off in my Subaru, and I pulled his Maserati into the lot. A superaggressive machine. All response and power. The slightest pressure on the accelerator and it practically left the ground.

"Easy baby, you don't have to try so hard," I said with an affectionate pat on the dashboard. But the Maserati wasn't listening to the likes of me. Cars know their class too.

33

The following morning, I went to check on the Maserati. It was still there, untouched. A curious picture, seeing it parked where the Subaru usually was. I climbed inside and sank into the seat, but just couldn't get comfortable. Like waking up and finding a beautiful woman you don't know sleeping next to you. She might be great to look at, but having her there doesn't feel right. Makes you a little tense. You need time to get used to things.

In the end, I left the car alone that day. Instead, I walked, saw a movie, bought some books.

Toward evening Gotanda rang. Thanks for yesterday. Don't mention it.

"About the Honolulu connection," he said. "I made a call to the club. And, well, yes, it is possible to reserve a woman in Hawaii from here. Modern conveniences, you know."

"Uh-huh."

"I also asked about this June of yours. I mentioned someone recommending this Southeast Asian girl to me. They went and checked their files. They made a big deal about their information being confidential, but seeing as how I was such a favored customer, blah blah blah. Not something to be so proud of, let me tell you. Anyway, they did have a listing for a June in Honolulu. A Filipino girl. But she quit three months ago."

"Three months ago?"

"That's what they said."

I thanked him and hung up. This was going to take some hard figuring.

I went out walking again.

June quit three months ago, but I slept with her not two weeks before. She gave me her telephone number, but when I called it, nobody answered. This made my third call girl—first Kiki, then Mei, now June—who'd disappeared. All of them somehow connected to Gotanda and Makimura and me.

I stepped into a coffee shop and drew a diagram in my notebook of these personal relations of mine. It looked like a chart of the European powers before the start of World War I.

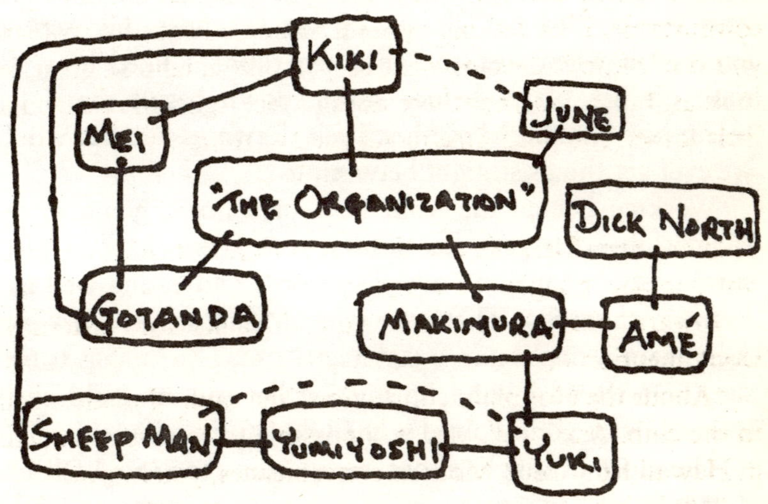

I pored over the diagram, half in admiration, half in despair. Three call girls, one too-charming-for-his-own-good actor, three artists, one budding teenage girl, and a very uptight hotel receptionist. If this was anything more than a network of casual relationships, I sure didn't see it. But it might make a good Agatha Christie novel. *By George, that's it! The Secretary did it!* Only who was laughing?

And who was I kidding? I didn't have a clue. The ball of yarn tangled wherever you tried to unravel it. First there were the Kiki and Mei and Gotanda threads. Add Makimura and June. Then Kiki and June were somehow connected by the same phone number. And around and around you go.

"Hard nut to crack, eh, Watson?" I addressed the ashtray before me. The ashtray, of course, did not respond. Smart ashtray. Same went for the coffee cup and sugar bowl and the bill. They all pretended not to hear. Stupid me. I was the one running amok in these weird goings-on. I was the worn-out one. Such a wonderful spring night, and no prospect for a date.

I went home and tried calling Yumiyoshi. No luck. The early shift? Or her swim club night? I wanted to see her badly. I missed her nervous patter, her brisk movements. The way she pushed her glasses up on her nose, her serious expression when she stole into the room. I liked how she took off her blazer before sitting down beside me. I felt warm just thinking about her. I felt drawn to her. But would we ever get things straight between us?

Working behind the front desk of a hotel, going to her swim club—that gave her satisfaction. While I found pleasure in my Subaru and my old records and eating well as I went on shoveling. That's the two of us. It might work and then again it might not. INSUFFICIENT DATA, PROGNOSIS IMPOSSIBLE. Or would I wind up hurting her too, as I did every woman I ever got involved with? Like my ex-wife said.

The more I thought about Yumiyoshi, the more I felt like flying up to Sapporo to fill in the missing data. At least I could tell her how I felt. But, no, first I had to untie some critical knots. Things were half-done. I didn't want to keep dragging them around with me. A half-gray shadow would cloud my path for the rest of my days. Not entirely ideal.

The problem was Kiki. I couldn't get over the feeling that she was at the heart of it. She was trying to reach me. In my dreams, in a movie in Sapporo, in downtown Honolulu. She kept crossing my path, trying to lead me somewhere, leave me a message. That much was clear. But nothing else. Kiki, what did you want from me?

What was I supposed to do?

I could only wait, until something showed. Same as ever. There was no point in rushing. Something was bound to happen. Something was bound to show. You had merely to wait for it to stir, up from the haze. Call it a lesson from experience.

Very well, then, I would wait.

I got together with Gotanda every few days after that. After a while, it became a habit. And each time we met, he'd apologize for keeping the Subaru so long.

"Haven't plowed the Maserati into the sea yet, have you?" he joked.

"Sorry to say, but I haven't had time to go to the sea," I parried.

Gotanda and I sat at a bar drinking vodka tonics. His pace a little faster than mine.

"I bet it would feel great, though. Plowing it into the sea," he said, raising his glass to his lips.

"Like a cool breeze," I said. "But then you'd only get yourself a Ferrari."

"I'd ditch that too."

"And after the Ferrari?"

"Hmm, who knows? But sooner or later, the insurance company's going to want a word with me."

"Insurance company? Who gives a damn about your insurance company? You got to think big. Go for the grand sweep. This is fantasy, not one of your low-budget movies. Fantasies don't have budgets, so why be middle class about it? Go wild! Lamborghini, Porsche, Jaguar! The sky's the limit! And the ocean's big enough to swallow cars by the thousands. Let your imagination do its stuff, man."

He laughed. "Well, it certainly lightens me up."

"Me too, especially since it's not my car and not my imagination," I said, then asked how things were going with his ex-wife.

He took a sip of his drink and looked out at the rain. The bar had emptied out except for us. The bartender had nothing to do but dust the bottles.

"Things're going okay," he said meekly, under a whisper of a smile. "We're in love. A love affirmed and consummated by divorce. Romantic, isn't it?"

"Isn't it, though. I might faint."

He chuckled.

"But it's true," he said.

"I know," I said.

That was the general drift of conversation each time I saw Gotanda. What we talked about was too serious to treat anything but lightly. Most of the jokes weren't terribly good, but it didn't matter. It was enough that we *could* joke, that there were jokes between us. We ourselves didn't know how serious we were.

Thirty-four is a difficult age. A different kind of difficult than age thirteen, but plenty difficult. Gotanda and I were both thirty-four, both beginning to acknowledge middle age. It was time we did. Readying things to keep us warm during the colder days ahead.

Gotanda put it succinctly. "Love. That's what I need."

"I'm so touched," I said. But the fact was, that's what I needed too.

Gotanda paused to consider what he'd said. I thought about it as well. I also thought about Yumiyoshi. How she drank all those Bloody Marys that snowy night.

"I've slept with so many women, I can't count them. You sleep with one, you've slept with them all. Hell, you go through the same motions," said Gotanda after a while. "Love's what I want. Here I am, baring my sentimental soul to you again. But I swear, the only woman I want to sleep with is my ex-wife."

I snapped my fingers. "Incredible. The Word from Above. O Light Resplendent. You've got to hold a press conference. Make your I-only-want-to-sleep-with-my-wife proclamation. Everyone will be moved beyond tears. You might even receive a citation from the Prime Minister."

"No, this is Nobel Prize material. Not something the common man can do."

"You'll need a frock coat for the ceremony."

"I'll buy it. Put it on my expense account."

"*Sanctus tax deductum.*"

"I'll be on stage with the King of Sweden," Gotanda went on. "I'll declare it for all the world to hear. Ladies and gentlemen, the only woman I want to sleep with is my wife! Waves of emotion. Storm clouds part; sun breaks through."

"The ice cap melts, the Vikings are vanquished, the mermaids sing."

Ah, love. We both lapsed silent, meditating on its grandeur. I had a lot to think about. I had to make sure I picked up some vodka and tomato juice and Lea & Perrins and lemons.

"Or then again, maybe you won't receive an award," I piped up. "Maybe they'll just take you for a pervert."

Gotanda considered that. "Maybe. We're talking neo-sexual revolution here. The masses might rise up and trample me to death," he said. "I'd be a sexual martyr."

"The first actor martyred to the neo-sexual revolution."

"Martyred and never to sleep with his ex-wife again."

Time for another drink.

If he had a spare moment, Gotanda would call and we'd go out or he'd come over to my place or I'd go over to his. The days passed. I'd resolved not to work at all. I couldn't be bothered. The world was doing very well without me. Meanwhile I was waiting.

I mailed Hiraku Makimura the balance of his money and receipts from the trip.

The next day I got a call from Boy Friday, begging me to take it all.

It was too much trouble to go through the whole back-and-forth bow-and-scrape routine, so I gave in. If it made the Master happy, who was I to argue? And before you could say "money in the bank," Makimura had sent me a check for three hundred thousand yen. Also in the envelope was a receipt marked FOR SERVICES RENDERED—FIELD RESEARCH. I signed it, stamped it with my seal, and posted it. Back to the wonderful world of expense accounts.

I placed the check for three hundred thousand yen on my desk to appreciate 8¾% dust.

The Golden Week holidays came and went.

I called Yumiyoshi a number of times. She was always the one who determined the length of the conversation. Sometimes we talked for a long time, other times she'd simply say, "Busy, got to go now," and hang up. Or if a silence hung on the line too long, she'd cut me off without warning. But at least we talked. Exchanged data, a little at a time. And one day, she gave me her home phone number. Progress.

She went to her swim club twice a week. Which I found, to my dismay, still brought on moments of jealousy. Handsome instructors and all. I was as bad as a high school boy and I knew it. And what was worse, I was afraid she knew it. *Jealous of a swim club? That's ridiculous. You're so immature.* I was afraid she'd never want to see me again.

So whenever the subject came up, I held my tongue. Though not talking about it only inflated my paranoia. Visions of the instructor—Gotanda, of course—keeping Yumiyoshi after class for intensive one-on-one sessions. His hands supporting her chest and abdomen as she practiced the crawl. His hands caressing her breasts, easing between her thighs. But it's all right, he says.

It's all right. Don't you know? The only woman I want to sleep with is my wife.

Then he takes Yumiyoshi's hand and puts it on his crotch. She begins to massage it. An underwater erection, like coral. Yumiyoshi is in rapture.

It's all right. Don't you know? The only woman I want to sleep with is my wife.

Idiotic, yet that's what came to mind whenever I called Yumiyoshi. As time went on, the vision got more and more complex, with a whole cast of characters. Kiki and Mei and Yuki put in guest appearances. As Gotanda's fingers stroked her body, Yumiyoshi became Kiki.

"Listen, I'm just a plain, run-of-the-mill person," Yumiyoshi said one night. She seemed particularly drained after a long day's drudgery. "The only difference between me and anyone else is my name. Otherwise I'm the same. I'm just working behind the counter of a hotel day after day, pointlessly wearing down my life. Don't call me any more. I'm not worth the phone charges."

"But I thought you liked hotel work."

"I do."

"But?"

"The work is fine. But sometimes, I think the hotel's going to eat me up. Just sometimes. I ask myself, if I'm here or not, what's the difference? The hotel would still be there. But not me. I'm out of the picture. That's the difference."

"Aren't you taking this hotel business a little too seriously?" I asked. "The hotel's the hotel, you're you. I think about you a lot, and sometimes I think about the hotel. But never together. You're you, the hotel's the hotel."

"You think I don't know that? I know that, but people get confused. My private life and my identity get dragged into this hotel world, and then they get swallowed up."

"It happens to everyone. You get dragged into something and you lose track of where one thing ends and the other begins. You're not the only one. It happens to me too," I said.

"It's not the same thing, not at all," she declared.

"No, maybe not. But I can still sympathize, can't I? Because, I mean, there's something about you that's very attractive."

Yumiyoshi went silent, out there in the telephone void.

"I . . . I'm frightened," said Yumiyoshi, verging into sobs. "I'm frightened of that darkness. I'm frightened that it's going to come again, soon."

"Hey, what's going on with you? Are you all right?"

"Of course I'm all right. What did you think?" She was clearly sobbing now. "So I'm crying. Anything wrong with that?"

"No, nothing at all. I was merely concerned."

"Can't you just be quiet?"

I did as told and Yumiyoshi cried until she couldn't cry anymore, then she hung up on me.

On May seventh, Yuki called.

"I'm back," she announced. "Why don't we go out for a ride?"

I tooled the Maserati to the Akasaka condo. But when Yuki saw the car, she wrinkled up her face unpleasantly.

"What's with this?"

"I didn't steal it, don't worry. My car fell into an enchanted spring and what do you know? The fairy of the spring appeared looking like Isabelle Adjani and asked, 'Was that a gold Maserati or a silver BMW just now?' And I said, 'Neither, that was a copper Subaru,' and—"

"C'mon, bag the stupid jokes," said Yuki. "I'm asking a serious question. Where the heck did you get this thing?"

"I traded temporarily with a friend. He needed to borrow the Subaru, for personal reasons."

"A friend?"

"You may not believe it, but yes, I do have at least one friend."

She climbed into the passenger seat, took a look around inside, then made a funny face. "Weird car," she said. "Dopey."

"Now that you mention it, the owner said the same thing. Although his words were slightly different."

That shut her up.

I pointed the Maserati south, toward Shonan. Yuki wouldn't speak. I played a Steely Dan tape on low and drove with care. The weather was clear and warm, so I was wearing an aloha shirt and sunglasses, and Yuki had on a pink Polo shirt. It was like being in Hawaii again. In front was a livestock truck full of pigs, their red eyes peering through the slats at us. Could pigs distinguish between a Maserati and a Subaru?

"How was it in Hawaii after I left?" I finally asked.

Yuki shrugged.

"Things go all right with your mother?"

Another shrug.

"Get your surfing down?"

Still another shrug.

"You look real healthy. Perfectly tanned. Like café au lait, all smooth and delicious."

Shrug.

You couldn't say I wasn't trying. I was trying everything.

"Is it your period or something?"

The same.

So I shrugged back.

"I want to go home," Yuki said. "Hang a U."

"This is an expressway. Even Niki Lauda couldn't manage a U-turn here."

"Then exit someplace."

I turned to her. She looked exhausted suddenly, her eyes lifeless and unfocused. Perhaps a bit pale too; it was hard to tell through the tan.

"Want to stop and take a rest?"

"I don't want a rest stop. I want to go back to Tokyo. Now!"

We got off at the expressway at Yokohama, then headed back on going in the opposite direction. When we reached Akasaka, Yuki asked if we could go sit somewhere. So I parked the Maserati in the lot, and we walked to the grounds of Nogi Shrine and found a bench.

"I'm sorry," said Yuki, trying to be reasonable. "I felt sick. I didn't want to say anything, so I held it in."

"You don't have to hold it in. I know how girls get. I'm used to it."

"It's not like that!" she shouted. "That has nothing to do with it! What got to me was riding in that car. That *stupid* car!"

"What's wrong with the Maserati? It's not such a bad car. It handles real well, rides pretty nice too. True, a bit too flashy for my simple tastes. Even if I could afford it, I guess I'd never buy a car like that."

"I don't care what brand that car is. The problem's *that car*. Couldn't you feel it? It was *icky*. I was suffocating. I could feel a pressure in my chest, and in my stomach too. You didn't feel it?"

"No," I said. "Although I got to admit, I don't feel one hundred percent comfortable in it. I thought it was because I was used to the Subaru. You know, you like what you're used to, but that's not this pressure you're talking about."

She shook her head. "No, it's not that at all. This is something real *peculiar.*"

"Is this more of your . . . ?" I cut myself short. I didn't want to say anything that sounded condescending.

"Yeah, it's more of that. I *felt* something."

"Well, what was it? What did you sense in that car?"

Yuki shrugged yet again, but this time she was talking. "It'd be easy if I could explain, but I can't. I can't picture it. There's just this feeling—a heavy, dark, awful lump of pressure in me. And it's totally . . ." Yuki searched for the word, hands on her lap. "It's *wrong*! I don't know *what's* wrong.

But *some*thing's wrong. I couldn't breathe in there. I tried to ignore it, I thought maybe it was jet lag or something, but then it got worse and worse. I don't want to ride in that car ever again, you hear me? Get your Subaru back."

"The Curse of the Maserati," I intoned.

"This is no joke. You shouldn't be driving that car," she said, very seriously.

"Okay, okay," I gave in with a smile. "I know you're not kidding. I'll try not to drive the Maserati too much. Or maybe I should go sink the thing in the sea?"

"If possible," said a grave Yuki.

It took Yuki about an hour to recover from this shock to her system. We sat on the bench, and she rested her chin on her hands and kept her eyes shut. People passed through the grounds. Old folks, mothers with children, foreign tourists with cameras strung around their necks. Occasionally, a salesman-type or salaryman would stop and take a breather on a bench near us. Dark suit, plastic briefcase, glassy stare. Ten minutes later, he'd be off beating the pavement again. By most standards, a normal adult should be working at this hour, and a normal kid should be in school.

"What about your mother?" I asked. "Did she come back with you?"

"Mmm." That was Yuki saying yes. "She's up in Hakone with that one-armed guy. Sorting out her photos of Kathmandu and Hawaii."

"And you didn't want to stay in Hakone?"

"I didn't feel like it. There's nothing for me to do there."

"Just thought I'd ask," I said. "Tell me, what exactly is there for you to do on your own in Tokyo?"

One of her patented shrugs. Then, "I can hang out with you."

"Well, I couldn't ask for more myself. However, trying to be realistic, pretty soon I ought to be getting back to work. I can't afford to keep running around with you forever. And I don't want handouts from your father either."

Yuki sneered. "I can understand your not wanting to take handouts from my parents, but why do you have to make such a big deal about it? How do you think it makes me feel, dragging you all around the place like this?"

"So you want me to take the money?"

"If you did, I wouldn't feel so guilty."

"You don't get it, Yuki," I said. "I don't want money for being your friend. I don't want to be introduced at your wedding reception as 'the professional male companion of the bride since she was thirteen.' Everyone would be tittering, 'professional male companion, professional male companion.' I want to be introduced as 'the boyfriend of the bride when she was thirteen.'"

Yuki blushed. "You turkey. I'm not going to have a wedding reception."

"Great. I don't like weddings. All those absurd speeches and the bricks of wedding cake you're supposed to take home. Strains the boundaries of propriety. But all I want to say is, you don't buy friends. Especially not with expense account money."

"That makes a good moral for a fairy tale."

"Wow! You're finally getting the proper gift of gab. With practice we could be a couple of stand-up comics."

Shrug.

"But seriously, folks, . . ." I cleared my throat. "If you want to hang out with me every day, Yuki, I'm all for it. Who needs to work? It's just pointless shoveling anyway. But we have to have one thing clear: I'm not going to accept money for doing things with you. Hawaii was different. I took money for that. I even took the woman thrown in. Of course, I thought you weren't ever going to talk to me again. I hated myself for allowing the whole business about payment for services to happen at all. From now on, I'm doing things my way. I don't want to answer to anybody, and I don't want to be on somebody's dole. I'm not Dick North and I'm not your father's manservant, whatever his name is.

You don't need to feel guilty."

"You mean you'll really go out with me?" Yuki chirped, then looked down at her polished toenails.

"You bet. You and me, we could be this pair of outcasts. We could be quite an item. So, let's just relax and have a good time."

"Why are you being so kind?"

"I'm not."

Yuki traced a design in the dirt with the tip of her sandal. A squared spiral.

"And I'm not a burden on you?"

"Maybe you are and maybe you aren't. Don't worry your pretty little head about it. I want to be with you because I like you. Sometimes when I'm with you, I remember things I lost when I was your age. Like I remember the sound of the rain and the smell of the wind. And it's really a gift, getting these things back. Even if you think I'm weird. Maybe you'll understand what I mean some day."

"I already know what you mean."

"You do?"

"I mean, I've lost plenty of things this far in my life too," said Yuki.

"Well, then, there you are," I said.

She said nothing. I returned to looking at the visitors to the shrine grounds.

"I don't have anybody I can really talk to but you," Yuki spoke up. "Honest."

"What about Dick North?"

Yuki stuck out her tongue. "He's a goon."

"Maybe he is and maybe he isn't. But I think you should know, he does good, and he's not pushy about it. That's pretty rare. He may not be up to your mother's level, and he may not be a brilliant poet. But he genuinely cares for your mother. He probably loves her. He's a good cook, he's dependable, he's considerate."

"He's still a goon."

Okay, okay. Yuki obviously had her feelings on the matter. So I changed the subject. We talked about the good times we had in Hawaii. Sun and surf and tropical breezes and piña coladas. Yuki said this made her hungry, so we went to eat pancakes and fruit parfaits. Then we took in a movie.

The following week, Dick North died.

34

Dick North had been doing the shopping on a Monday evening in Hakone and had just stepped out from the supermarket with a bag of groceries under his arm when a truck came barreling down the road and slammed into him. The truck driver confessed that he didn't know what possessed him to gun full-speed ahead in such poor road visibility. And Dick himself had made a telling slip. He'd looked to his left, but was one or two breaths behind in checking his right. A common mistake among people who have lived overseas for any length of time and have just returned to Japan. You haven't gotten used to cars driving on the left-hand side yet. In most cases, you come away with chills, but sometimes it's worse. The truck sent Dick sailing into the opposite lane, where he was battered again by an oncoming van. He died instantly.

When I heard the news, the first thing that came to mind was going shopping with Dick at a probably similar supermarket in Makaha. How knowledgeably he selected his purchases, how he examined the fruit and vegetables and unembarrassedly tossed a box of Tampax into the shopping cart. Poor bastard. Unlucky to the last. Arm blown off in Vietnam when the guy next to him stepped on a mine. Running around morning to night putting out Amé's smoldering cigarettes. Now dead on the asphalt holding onto a load of groceries.

His funeral saw him returned to his rightful family, his wife and child. Neither Amé nor Yuki nor I attended.

I borrowed the Subaru back from Gotanda and drove Yuki to Hakone that Tuesday afternoon. It was at Yuki's urging. "Mama can't get by on her own. Sure, there's the maid, but she's too old to do anything and she goes home at night. We can't leave Mama alone up there."

"Yeah, it's probably good for you to spend some time with your mother," I said.

Yuki was flipping through the road atlas. "Hey, you remember I said bad things about him?"

"Who? Dick North?"

"Yeah."

"You called him a goon," I said.

Yuki stowed the book in the door pocket, rested her elbow on the window, and turned her gaze to the scenery ahead. "But you know," she said, "he wasn't so bad. He was nice to me. He spent time telling me how to surf and all. Even without that arm, he was a lot more alive than most people with two arms. Plus, he took good care of Mama."

"I know."

"But I said nasty things about him."

"You couldn't help yourself," I said. "It's not your fault."

She looked straight ahead the whole way. She didn't turn to look at me. The breeze blowing in through the window ruffled her bangs.

"It's sad, but I think he was that sort of person," I said. "A nice guy, maybe even worthy of respect. But he got treated like some kind of fancy trash basket. People were always dumping on him. Maybe he was born with that tendency. Mediocrity's like a spot on a shirt—it never comes off."

"It's unfair."

"As a rule, life is unfair," I said.

"Yeah, but I think I did say some awful things."

"To Dick?"

"Yeah."

I pulled the car over to the shoulder of the road and turned off the ignition.

"That's just stupid, that kind of thinking," I said, nailing her with my eyes. "Instead of regretting what you did, you could have treated him decently from the beginning. You could've tried to be fair. But you didn't. You don't even have the right to be sorry."

Yuki looked at me, shocked and hurt.

"Maybe I'm being too hard on you. But listen, I don't care what other people do. I don't want to hear that sort of talk from you. You shouldn't say things like that lightly, as if saying them is going to solve anything. They don't stick. You think you feel sorry about Dick, but I don't believe you really do. If I were Dick, I wouldn't want your easy regret. I wouldn't want people saying, 'Oh, I acted horribly.' It's not a question of manners; it's a question of fairness. That's something you have to learn."

Yuki couldn't respond. She pressed her fingers to her temples and quietly closed her eyes. She almost seemed to have dozed off, but for the slight flutter of her eyelashes, the trembling of her lips. Crying inside, without sobs or tears. Was I expecting too much of a thirteen-year-old girl? Who was I to be so self-righteous? Still, whether or not she was thirteen, whether or not I was an exemplary human being, you can't let everything slide. Stupidity is stupidity. I won't put up with it.

Yuki didn't move. I reached out and touched her arm.

"It's okay," I said. "I'm very narrow-minded. No, to be fair, you've done the best that can be expected."

A single tear trailed down her cheek and fell on her lap. That was all. Beautiful and noble.

"So what can I do now?" she spoke up a minute later.

"Nothing," I said. "Just think about what comes before

words. You owe that to the dead. As time goes on, you'll understand. What lasts, lasts; what doesn't, doesn't. Time solves most things. And what time can't solve, you have to solve yourself. Is that too much to ask?"

"A little," she said, trying to smile.

"Well, of course it is," I said, trying to smile too. "I doubt that this makes sense to most people. But I think I'm right. People die all the time. Life is a lot more fragile than we think. So you should treat others in a way that leaves no regrets. Fairly, and if possible, sincerely. It's too easy not to make the effort, then weep and wring your hands after the person dies. Personally, I don't buy it."

Yuki leaned against the car door.

"But that's real hard, isn't it?" she said.

"Real hard," I said. "But it's worth trying for. Look at Boy George: Even a fat gay kid who can't sing can become a star."

"Okay," she smiled, "but why are you always getting on Boy George's case? I bet you must really like him, deep down."

"Let me think about that one," I said.

Yuki's mother's house was in a large resort-housing tract. There was a big gate, with a pool and a coffee house adjacent. There was even a stop-and-shop minimart filled with junk food. No place someone like Dick North would have bought groceries at. Me either. As the road twisted and turned up the grade, my friendly Subaru began to gasp.

Halfway up the hill was Amé's house, too big for just a mother and daughter. I stopped the car and carried Yuki's bags up the steps to the side of the stone embankment. Down the slope, between the ranks of cedars, you could make out the ocean by Odawara. The air was hazy, the sea dull under the leaden glaze of spring.

Amé paced the large, sunny living room, lit cigarette in hand. A big crystal ashtray was overflowing with bent and crushed Salem butts, the entire tabletop dusted with ashes. She tossed her latest butt into the ashtray and came over to greet Yuki, mussing her hair. She wore a chemical-spotted oversized sweatshirt and faded jeans. Her hair was uncombed, eyes bleary.

"It's been terrible," said Amé. "Why do these horrible things always happen?"

I expressed my condolences and inquired about the details of yesterday's accident. It was all so sudden, she told me, she felt out of control, confused, uncertain. "And of course the maid came down with a fever today and won't be in. Now of all times, a fever! I'm going crazy. The police come, Dick's wife calls, I don't know what they expect of me."

"What did Dick's wife have to say?"

"I couldn't make it out," she said. "She just cried. And when she wasn't crying, she mumbled so I could barely understand what she was saying. And me, in this position, what was I supposed to say? . . . What *was* I supposed to say?"

I shook my head.

"I told her I'd send along Dick's things as soon as I could, but then the woman was crying even more. It was hopeless."

She let out a big sigh and collapsed into the sofa.

I asked her if she wanted anything to drink, and she asked for coffee. For good measure, I also cleared away the ashtray and cocoa-caked mugs, and wiped off the table. While I waited for the water to boil, I tidied up the kitchen. Dick North had kept a neat pantry, but already it was a mess. Dirty dishes were piled in the sink, cocoa had been dribbled across the stainless steel cooktop, knives lay here and there smeared with cheese and who-knows-what, the lid of the sugar container was nowhere in sight.

Poor bastard, I thought as I made a strong pot of coffee. He tried so hard to bring order to this place. Now in the space of one day, it was gone. Just like that. People leave traces of themselves where they feel most comfortable, most worthwhile. With Dick, that place was the kitchen. But even that tenuous presence was on its way out.

Poor bastard.

I carried in the coffee and found Amé and Yuki sitting on the sofa. Amé's head rested on her daughter's shoulder. She looked drugged and drained. Yuki seemed ill at ease. How odd they appeared together—so different from when they were apart—how doubly unapproachable.

Amé accepted the coffee with both hands and drank it slowly, preciously. The slightest glow came to her eyes.

"You want anything to drink?" I asked Yuki.

She shook her head with no expression whatsoever.

"Has everything been taken care of?" I asked Amé. "The business about the accident, legal matters, and all that?"

"Done. The actual procedure wasn't so difficult. It was a perfectly common accident. A policeman came to the house to tell me the news, and that was it. I told them to contact Dick's wife, and she handled everything. I mean, I had no legal or even professional relationship with Dick. Then the wife called here. She hardly said a word, she just cried. She didn't even scream, nothing."

A perfectly common accident.

Another three weeks and Amé wouldn't remember there ever was someone in her life named Dick North. Amé was the forgetful type, and, unfortunately, Dick was forgettable.

"Is there anything I can do to help?" I asked.

"Well, yes. Dick's belongings," she muttered. "I told you I was going to return them to her, didn't I?"

"Yes."

"Well, last night I put his things in order. His manuscripts and typewriter and books and clothes—they all fit in one suitcase. There wasn't that much stuff. Just one suitcase full. I hate to ask, but could you deliver it to his wife?"

"Sure. Where does the family live?"

"I don't know exactly. Somewhere in Gotokuji, I know. Could you find out for me?"

Yuki showed me the study where Dick's things were. Upstairs, a long, narrow garret at the end of the hall, what had originally been the maid's room. It was pleasant enough, and naturally Dick had kept everything in immaculate order. On the desk were arranged five precision-sharpened pencils and an eraser, an unqualified still life. A calendar on the wall had been annotated with meticulous handwriting.

Yuki leaned in the doorway and scanned the interior in silence. All you could hear were the birds outside. I recalled the cottage in Makaha. It had been just as quiet, and there had been birds too.

The tag on the suitcase, also in Dick's hand, had his name and address. I lugged it downstairs. With his books and papers, it was much heavier than it looked. The weight yet another reminder of the fate of Dick North.

"There's not much here to eat," said Amé. "Dick went out to do the shopping and then all this happened."

"Don't worry. I'll go to the store," I said.

I checked the contents of the refrigerator to see what she did have. Then I drove down to town, to the supermarket where Dick had spent the last moments of his life, and purchased four or five days' worth of provisions.

I put away the groceries, and Amé thanked me. I felt like I was merely finishing up the task that Dick had left undone.

The two women saw me off from atop the stone embankment. The same as in Makaha, only this time nobody was waving. That had been Dick's role. The two stood there, not moving, gazing down on me. An almost mythological scene, like an icon. I heaved the gray suitcase into the backseat and slid behind the wheel. Mother and daughter were still standing there when I turned the curve and headed out of their sight. The sun was starting to sink into an orange sea. How would they spend the night? I wondered.

That one-armed skeleton in the eerie gloom of the room in Honolulu, it was now clear, *was* Dick North. So, who could the other five be?

Let's say my old friend, the Rat, for one. Dead several years now, in Hokkaido.

Then Mei, for another.

That left three. Three more.

What was Kiki doing there? Why did she want to show me these six deaths?

I made it down to Odawara and got on the Tokyo–Nagoya Expressway. Exiting at Sangenjaya, I navigated my way into the suburbs of Setagaya by map and found Dick North's house. An ordinary two-story suburban home, very small. The door and windows and mailbox and entry light—everything seemed to be in miniature. A mongrel on a chain patrolled the front door. There were lights on inside the house, the sound of voices. Dick's wake was in progress. At least he had somewhere to come home to.

I took the suitcase out of the car and hauled it to the front door. I rang the doorbell and a middle-aged man appeared. I explained that I'd brought Dick's things; my expression said I didn't know any more than that. The man looked at the name tag and grasped the situation immediately.

"Very much obliged," said the man, stiff but cordial.

And so, with no more resolve than before, I returned to my Shibuya apartment.

Three more, I thought.

In the scheme of things, what possible meaning was there to Dick North's death?

Alone in my room, I mulled it over a whiskey. It happened so suddenly, how could there have been meaning? All these blank spots in the puzzle and this piece didn't fit anywhere. Flip it over, turn it sideways, still no good. Did the piece belong somewhere else entirely?

Even if Dick's death had no meaning in itself, a major change of circumstances seemed inevitable. And not for the better either, my intuition told me. Dick North was a man of good intentions. In his own way, he had held things together.

But now that he was gone, things were going to change, things were going to get harder.

For instance?

For instance, I didn't care for Yuki's blank expression whenever she was with Amé. Nor did I like Amé's dull, spaced-out stare when she was with Yuki. There was something bad there. I liked Yuki. She was a good kid. Smart, maybe a little stubborn at times, but sensitive underneath it all. And I had nothing against Amé, really. She was attractive, full of vision, defenseless. But put the two of them together and the combination was devastating.

There was an energy that mounted with the two females together.

Dick North had been the buffer after Makimura. But now that he was gone, I was the only one left to deal with them.

For instance—

I rang up Yumiyoshi a few times. She was as cool as ever, although I may have detected a hint of pleasure in her voice. Apparently I wasn't too much of a nuisance. She was working every day, going to her swim club twice a week, dating occasionally. The previous Sunday, she told me, a guy had taken her for a drive to a lake.

"He's just a friend. An old classmate, now working in Sapporo. That's all."

I didn't mind, I said. Drive or hike or like, I didn't need to know. What really got to me was her swim club.

"But anyway, I just wanted to tell you," said Yumiyoshi. "I hate to hide things."

"I don't mind," I repeated. "All I care about is that I get up to Sapporo to see you again. You can go out with anybody you like. That's got nothing to do with us. You've been in my thoughts. Like I said before, I feel a bond between us."

Once again, she asked me what I meant. And again, my heart was in my words, but the explanation made no sense. Typical me.

A moderate silence ensued. A neutral-to-slightly-positive silence. True, silence is still silence, except when you think about it too much.

Gotanda looked tired whenever I saw him. He'd been squeezing trysts with his ex-wife into an already tight work schedule.

"All I know is, I can't keep this up forever," he said, sighing deeply. "I'm not cut out for this living on the fringes. I'm a homebody. That's why I'm so run-down. I'm overextended, burned out."

"You ought to go to Hawaii for a break," I said. "Just the two of you."

"Wouldn't I love to," he said, smiling weakly. "Maybe for five days, lying on the beach, doing nothing. Even three days would be terrific."

That evening I'd gone to his condo in Azabu, sat on his chic sofa with a drink in my hand, and watched a compilation tape of the antacid commercials he'd appeared in. The first time I'd ever seen them.

Four office building elevators without walls or doors are rising and falling at high speeds like pistons. Gotanda is in a dark suit, briefcase in hand, every inch the elite businessman. He's hopping back and forth from elevator to elevator, conferring with his boss in one, making a date with a pretty young secretary in another, picking up papers here, rushing to dispatch them there. Two elevators away a telephone is ringing. All this jumping back and forth between speeding elevators is no easy trick, but Gotanda isn't losing his cool mask. He looks more and more serious.

VOICE OVER

Everyday stress builds up in your stomach. Give the business to your busy-ness with a gentle remedy. . . .

I laughed. "That was fun."

"I think so too," he said. "Idiotic but fun. All commercials are nonsense, but this one is well shot. It's a damn sight better than most of my feature films, I'm sorry to say. Ad people have no qualms about spending on details, and the sets and those special effects cost a lot. It's not a bad concept either."

"And it's practically autobiographical."

"You said it," he laughed. "Boy, does my stomach get stressed out. But let me tell you, that stuff doesn't do a damn thing. They gave me a dozen packs to try, and it's a wonder how little it works."

"You really do move, though," I said, rewinding the tape by remote control to watch the commercial again. "You're a regular Buster Keaton. You might have found your calling."

A smile floated across Gotanda's lips. "I'd be interested. I like comedy. There's something to be said when a straight man like me can bring out the humor of a routine like that. You try to live straight in this crazy, crooked, mixed-up world—*that's* what's funny. You know what I mean?"

"I do, I do," I said.

"You don't even have to do anything especially funny. You just act normal. That alone looks strange and funny. Acting like that interests me. That type of actor simply doesn't exist in Japan today. People always overact when it comes to comedy. What I want to do is the reverse. Not act." He took a sip of his drink and looked up at the ceiling. "But no one brings me roles like that. The only roles they ever, ever bring into my agency are doctors or teachers or lawyers. You've heard me go on about this before, and let me tell you, I'm bored, bored, bored, *bored*. I'd like to turn them down, but I'm in no position to reject anything, and my stomach takes a beating."

Gotanda's first antacid commercial had been so well received, he'd made a number of sequels. The pattern was always the same. If he wasn't jumping back and forth between trains and buses and planes with split-second timing, he was scaling a skyscraper with papers under his arms or tightrope-walking between offices. Through it all, Gotanda kept a perfect deadpan.

"At first the director told me to look tired. Like I was about to keel over from exhaustion. But I told him, no, that it'd come off better if I just played it straight. Of course, they're all idiots, they didn't go for it at all. But I didn't give in. I don't do these commercials for fun, but I was sure about the right way to do it. I insisted. So they shot it two ways and everyone liked mine much more. And then, of course, the commercial was a success, so the director took all the credit. He even won some kind of prize for it. Not that I care. What eats me is how they all act so big, as if they thought the whole thing up. The ones with no imagination are always the quickest to justify themselves."

Gotanda switched off the video and put on a Bill Evans record.

"All these idiots think they're so sharp, they got me dancing on their pinheads. Go here, go there. Do this, do that. Drive this car, go out with that woman. It's a bad movie of a bad life. How long can it last?"

"Maybe you ought to just toss it and start again from scratch. If anyone could do it, you could. Leave your agency, and take your time paying back what you owe."

"Don't think I haven't thought about it. If I was on my own, that's what I'd do. Go back to square one, and join some theater group. I wouldn't mind, believe me. But if I did, my ex-wife would drop me, just like that. She grew up under pressure—star-system pressure—and she needs people around her who feel that pressure too. If the atmosphere drops, she can't breathe. So if I want to be with her, I haven't got a choice," said Gotanda, with a smile of resignation. "Let's talk about something else. I could go on until morning and still not get anywhere."

And so he brought up Kiki.

It was because of Kiki that Gotanda and I had become friends, yet he'd hardly heard a word out of my mouth about her. Did I find it hard to talk about her? If so, he wouldn't insist.

No, I told him, not at all.

I told him that Kiki and I got together entirely by chance and that we were living together soon after that. She burrowed into my life so unobtrusively, I could hardly believe she hadn't always been there. "I didn't notice how extraordinary it was at the time. But when I thought it over later, the whole scenario seemed completely unreal. And when I put it into words, it sounds silly. Which is why I haven't told anyone about it."

I took a drink, swirling the ice in my glass.

"In those days, Kiki was working as an ear model, and I'd seen these photos of her ears and, well, I got obsessed, to put it mildly. Her ear was going to appear in this ad—I forget what for—and my job was to write the copy. I was given these three photos, these three enormous close-ups of her ears, close enough to see the baby fuzz, and I tacked them up on my wall. I started gazing at these ears, day in and day out. At first I was fishing for some kind of inspiration, some kind of catchphrase, but then the ears became a part of my life. Even after I finished the job, I kept the photos up. They were incredible—they were perfectly formed, bewitching. The dream image of an ear. You'd have to see the real thing, though. They were . . ."

"Yeah, you did mention something about her ears."

"I had this total fixation. So I made these calls and found out who she was and I finally got ahold of her and she agreed to see me. The first day we met, we were at a restaurant and she personally *showed* me her ears. Personally, I mean, not professionally, and they were even more amazing than in the photograph. They were exquisite! Fantastic! When she exposed her ears professionally—that is, when she modeled them—she *blocked* them, she said. So they were gorgeous but they were different from her ears when she *showed* them. And when she did, it was like the entire world underwent a transformation. I know that sounds ludicrous, but I don't know how else to put it."

Gotanda considered seriously what I'd said. "What do you mean by her 'blocking' her ears?"

"Severing her ears from her consciousness."

"Oh."

"She pulled the plug on her ears."

"Uh-huh."

"Sounds crazy, but it's true."

"Oh, I believe you. I'm honestly trying to understand. Really, no kidding."

I eased back into the sofa and looked at a painting on the wall.

"Her ears had special power. They were like some great whirlpool of fate sucking me in. And they could lead people to the right place."

Gotanda pondered my words again. "And," he said, "did Kiki lead you anywhere? To some 'right place'?"

I nodded, but didn't say more about it. Too long and involved to explain.

"Now," I said, "she's trying to lead me somewhere again. I can sense it, very strongly. For the last few months, I've had this nagging feeling. And little by little I've been reeling in the line. It's a very fine line. It got snagged a couple of times, but it's gotten me this far. It's brought me in contact with a lot of different people. You, for instance. You're one of the central figures in this drama. Still, I can't get a grip on what's going on. Two people I knew have died recently. One was Mei. The other was a one-armed poet. I don't know what's going on, but I know *something* is."

The ice in the bucket had all but melted, so Gotanda fetched a new batch from the kitchen to freshen both our drinks.

"So you see, I'm stuck too," I picked up again. "Just like you."

"No, there you're wrong. You and I are not alike,"

Gotanda said. "I'm in love with one woman. And it's a dead-end kind of love. But not you. Maybe you're confused and wandering in a maze, but compared with this emotional morass I've gotten myself dragged into, you're much, much better off. You're being guided somewhere. You've got hope. There's possibility of a way out. But not for me, not at all. That's the big difference between us."

Well, maybe, maybe so. "Whatever. I've been clinging to this line from Kiki. That's all I can do for now. She's been sending these signals, these messages. So I spend my time trying to stay tuned in."

"Do you think," Gotanda started cautiously, "that there's a possibility Kiki's been killed?"

"Like Mei?"

"Uh-huh. I mean, she disappeared so suddenly. When I heard Mei was murdered, right away I thought about Kiki. Like maybe the same thing happened to her. I didn't want to say it before."

And yet I'd seen her, in downtown Honolulu, in the dim dusk light. I'd actually seen her. And Yuki knew it.

"Just something that crossed my mind. I didn't mean anything by it," Gotanda said.

"Sure, the possibility exists. But she's still sending me messages. Loud and clear."

Gotanda crossed his arms for a few minutes, pensive. He looked so exhausted, I thought he might nod off. Night was stealing into the room, enveloping his trim physique in fluid shadow.

I swirled the ice around in my glass again and took a sip.

That was when I noticed a third presence in the room. Someone else was here besides Gotanda and myself. I sensed body heat, breathing, odor. Yet it wasn't human. I froze. I glanced quickly around the room, but I saw nothing. There was only the feeling of *something*. Something solid, but invisible. I breathed deeply. I strained to hear.

It waited, crouching, holding its breath. Then it was gone.

I eased up and took another sip.

A minute or two later Gotanda opened his eyes and smiled at me. "Sorry. Seems we're making a depressing evening of it," he said.

"That's because, basically speaking, we're both depressing people," I said.

Gotanda laughed, but offered no further comment.

35

Toward the end of May, by chance—as far as I know—I ran into one of the cops who'd grilled me about Mei's murder. Bookish. I was coming out of Tokyu Hands, the department store with everything for the home you ever wanted, and found myself squeezed up against him at the exit. The day seemed like midsummer, yet here he was in a heavy tweed jacket, entirely unaffected by the heat. Maybe police stiffs are trained to be insensitive. He was holding a Tokyu Hands bag like me. I pretended not to see him and was moving past when the undaunted detective spoke directly to me.

"You don't have to be so standoffish, you know," he quipped. "As if we didn't know each other."

"I'm in a hurry," was all I said.

"Oh?" said he, not swallowing the line for a second.

"I have to be getting back to work," I stammered.

"I can imagine," said he. "But surely even a busy man like yourself can spare ten minutes. Let me buy you a cup of coffee. I've been wanting to talk to you, business aside. Honest, just ten minutes of your time."

I followed him into a crowded coffee shop. Don't ask me why. I could've politely said sorry and gone home. But I didn't. We went in and sat down alongside young couples and clusters of students. The coffee tasted horrible, the air was bad. Bookish pulled out a cigarette and lit up.

"Been trying to quit," he said. "But there's something about the job. When I'm working, I gotta smoke."

I wasn't going to say anything.

"The job's rough on the nerves. Everybody hates you. The longer you're in homicide, the more they hate you. Your eyes go, your complexion starts to look like shit. You wouldn't know your own age. Even the way you talk changes. Not a healthy way to live."

He added three spoonfuls of sugar and creamer to his coffee, stirred well, and drank it like a connoisseur.

I looked at my watch.

"Ah, yes, the time," said Bookish. "We still have five minutes, right? Fine. I'll keep this short. So about that murdered girl. Mei."

"Mei?" I asked. I'm not snared that easily.

He twisted his lips, insinuating. "Oh, right, sure. The deceased young woman's name was Mei. Not her real name, of course. Her *nom d'amour.* She turned out to be a hooker, just like I thought. She may not have looked professional, but I could tell. Used to be you could spot the hookers in a second. The clothes, the makeup, the look on their faces. But nowadays you get girls you'd never believe in the trade. It's the money, or they're curious. I don't like it. And it's dangerous. Or don't you think so? Meeting unknown men behind closed doors. There's all types out there. Perverts and nut cases."

I forced a nod.

"But young girls, they don't know that. They think everything's cool. Can't be helped. When you're young, you think you can handle anything. By the time you find out otherwise, it's already too late. You got a stocking wrapped around your neck. Poor thing."

"So did you find the killer?"

Bookish shook his head and frowned. "Not yet, unfortunately. We did discover some interesting facts. Only we didn't publish them in the newspaper. Seeing as how the investigation is still going on. For example, we found out her professional name was Mei, but her real name was . . . Aww, what difference does it make what her real name was. The girl was born in Kumamoto. Father a public servant. Kumamoto's not such a big city, but he was next-to-top there. Family very well-off. Mother came to Tokyo once or twice a month to shop. No financial problems. The girl got a good allowance from them. She told them she was in the fashion business. She had one older sister, married to a doctor; one younger brother, studying law at Kyushu University. So what's a nice girl from a good home like that doing selling her tail? The family had a big shock coming. We spared them the call girl part, but their darling daughter strangled to death in a hotel room was pretty unsettling."

I said nothing and let him continue.

"We looked into the prostitute ring she was involved in. It wasn't easy, but we managed to track it down. How do you think we did it? We staked out the lobbies of some luxury hotels around town and hauled in a few women on suspicion of illegal commerce. We showed them the same photos we showed you and asked a few questions. One of them cracked. Not everyone's got a tough hide like you, heh heh. Anyway, turns out the deceased worked for this exclusive operation. Superexpensive membership. Nothing the likes of you or me can swing. I mean, can you pay seventy thousand yen a pop? I know *I* can't. At that price, I'd just as soon screw the wife and buy the kid a new bike," he laughed nervously. "But suppose I *could* swing the seventy grand, I still wouldn't be good enough. They run a background check, you see. Safety first. They can't afford weird shit from customers. But also they prefer a certain *class* of customer. No way a detective can get membership. Not that law enforcement is necessarily a strike against you. If you're top brass, real top brass, that's another story. You might come in handy someday. But a cop like me, no way."

He finished his coffee and lit up another cigarette.

"So we went to the captain for a search warrant. It took

three days to come through. By the time we set foot in the place, the whole operation had been cleaned out. Spotless. Not a speck of dust. There'd been a leak. And where do you think that leak came from?"

I didn't know.

"C'mon, man, you're not dumb. The leak came from *inside*. I'm talking *inside the police*. Somebody on top. No proof, of course. But we grunts on the street know an inside job when we see one. The word goes out to get scarce. Sorry state of affairs. But predictable. And an operation like that one is used to this sort of thing. They can move in the time it takes us to use the toilet. They are *gone*. They find another place to rent, buy new phone lines, and just like that they're back in business. No sweat off their back. They still got their subscriber list, they still got their girls lined up, they barely been inconvenienced. And there's no way to trace them. The thread's cut. With this dead girl, if we had some idea what type of customer was her specialty, we could do something. But as it is, we gotta throw up our hands."

"Don't look at me," I said.

"You sure you don't know anything?"

"Hey, if she was part of this exclusive call girl setup like you say, they'd know in an instant who killed her, right?"

"Exactly," said Bookish. "So chances are the killer was probably someone not on the list. The girl's own private lover, or else she was turning tricks on the side. We searched her apartment. Not a clue."

"Listen, I didn't kill her."

"I know *that*," said Bookish. "I already told you that. You're not the killer type. I can tell by looking at you. Your type never kills anybody. But you do know something, I know that. You know more than you're letting on. So why don't you come out with it? That's all I want. No hard-lining. I give you my word of honor."

"I don't know a thing," I said.

"Figures," Bookish mumbled, puffing his smoke. "This is going nowhere. Fact is, the boys upstairs aren't crazy about this investigation. After all, it's only a hooker killed in a hotel, no big deal. To them, that is. They probably think a hooker's better off dead anyway. The guys on top, they hardly ever set eyes on a stiff. They haven't got the vaguest idea what it's like to see a beautiful girl naked and strangled like that. They can't imagine how *pitiful* it is. And you can bet that it's not just police brass in on this prostitution racket. There's always a few upstanding public servants got their fingers in the pie too. You can see the gold lapel pins flashing in the dark. Cops develop an eye for this sort of business. We see the least little glint, and we pull in our necks, like turtles. Something you learn from your superiors. So that's how it goes. Somehow, the drift is, our Miss Mei's murder is just going to get buried. Poor thing."

The waitress cleared away Bookish's cup. I still had half of my coffee left.

"It's weird, but I feel close to this Mei girl," said Bookish. "Now why should that be? It doesn't figure, does it? But when I saw her strangled naked on that hotel bed, she did a number on me. And I decided, I made this pledge to her, I was going to get the fucker who did it. Now, I've seen more stiffs than I care to. So what's one more corpse, you say? This one was special. Strange and beautiful. The sunlight was pouring in through the window, the girl lying there, frozen. Eyes wide open, tongue hanging out of her mouth, stocking around her throat. Just like a necktie. Her legs were spread, and she'd pissed. When I saw that, I knew. The girl was asking me for help. Must seem remarkable to you, this soft touch I have. No?"

I couldn't say.

"You, you've been away a while. Got a tan I see," said the detective.

I mumbled something about Hawaii on business.

"Nice business. Wish I could switch saddles to your line of work, instead of looking at stiffs morning to night. Makes a fellow real fun company. You ever see a corpse?"

No, I hadn't.

He shook his head and looked at the clock. "Very well, then, hope you excuse me for wasting your time. But like they say, small world running into you at a place like this. What do you got in your bag?"

A soldering iron.

"Oh yeah? I got some drainpipe cleaner. Sink in the house backed up."

He paid the bill. I offered to pay my portion, but he insisted.

As we were walking out, I asked casually if prostitute murders happened a lot.

"Well, I guess you could say so," he said, eyes sharpening slightly. "Not every day, but not only on holidays either. Any reason you're so interested in prostitute murders?"

Just curious is all.

We went our separate ways, but the queasy feeling in the pit of my stomach still hadn't gone away the following morning.

36

May drifted past, slow as clouds.

It had been two and a half months since I'd worked. Fewer and fewer work calls came in. The trade was gradually forgetting about me. To be sure, no work, no money coming in, but I still had plenty in my account. I didn't lead an expensive life. I did my own cooking and washing, didn't spend a lot. No loans, no fancy tastes in clothes or cars. So for the time being, money was no problem. I calculated my monthly expenses, divided it into my bank balance, and figured I had another five months or so. Something would come of this wait-and-see. And if it didn't, well, I could think it over then. Besides, Makimura's check for three hundred thousand yen still graced my desktop. No, I wasn't going to starve.

All I had to do was keep things at a steady pace and be patient. I went to the pool several times a week, did the shopping, fixed meals. Evenings, I listened to records or read.

I began going to the library, leafing through the bound editions of newspapers, reading every murder case of the last few months. Female victims only. Shocking, the number of women murdered in the world. Stabbings, beatings, stranglings. No mention of anyone resembling Kiki. No body resembling Kiki, in any case. Sure, there were ways to dispose of a body. Weight it down and throw it in the sea. Haul it up into the hills and bury it. Just like I'd buried Kipper. Nobody would ever find him.

Maybe it was an accident? Maybe she'd gotten run over, like Dick North. I checked the obituaries for accident victims. Women victims. Again, a *lot* of accidents that killed a *lot* of women. Automobiles, fires, gas. Still no Kiki.

Suicides? Heart attacks? The papers didn't seem interested. The world was full of ways to die, too many to cover. Newsworthy deaths had to be exceptional. Most people go unobserved.

So anything was possible. I had no evidence that Kiki was dead, no evidence that she was alive.

I called Yuki now and then. But always, when I asked how she was, the answer was noncommital.

"Not good, not bad. Nothing much."

"And your mother?"

"She's taking it easy, not working a lot. She sits around all day, kind of out of it."

"Anything I can do? The shopping or something?"

"The maid does the shopping, so we're okay. The store delivers. Mama and I are just spacing out. It's like . . . up here, time's standing still. Is time really passing?"

"Unfortunately, the clock is ticking, the hours are going by. The past increases, the future recedes. Possibilities decreasing, regrets mounting."

Yuki let that pass.

"You don't sound like you have much vim and vigor," I said.

"Oh really?"

"Oh really?"

"What's with you?"

"What's with you?"

"Stop mimicking me."

"Who's mimicking you? I'm just a mental echo, a figment

of your imagination. A rebound to demonstrate the fullness of our conversation."

"Dumb as usual," said Yuki. "You're acting like a child."

"Not so. I'm solid with deep inner reflection and pragmatic spirit. I'm echo as metaphor. The game is the message. This is of a different order than child's play."

"Hmph, nonsense."

"Hmph, nonsense."

"Quit it. I mean it!" yelled Yuki.

"Okay, quits," I said. "Let's take it again from the top. You don't sound like you have much vim and vigor, Yuki."

She let out a sigh. "Okay, maybe not. When I'm with Mama . . . I end up with one of her moods. It's like she has this power over how I feel. All she ever thinks about is herself. She never thinks about anyone else. That's what makes her so strong. You know what I mean. You've seen it. You just get all wrapped up in it. So when she's feeling down, I feel down. When she's up, I'm up."

I heard the flicking of a lighter.

"Maybe I could come up and visit you," I said.

"Could you?"

"Tomorrow all right?"

"Great," said Yuki. "I feel better already."

"I'm glad."

"I'm glad."

"Stop it."

"Stop it."

"Tomorrow then," I said and hung up before she could say it.

Amé was indeed "kind of out of it." She sat on the sofa, legs neatly crossed, gazing blankly at a photography magazine on her lap. She was a scene out of an impressionist painting. The window was open, but not a breeze stirred the curtains or pages. She looked up ever so slightly and smiled when I entered the room. The very air seemed to vibrate around her smile. Then she raised a slender finger a scant five centimeters and motioned for me to sit down on the chair opposite. The maid brought us tea.

"I delivered the suitcase to Dick's house," I said.

"Did you meet his wife?" Amé asked.

"No, I just handed it over to the man who came to the door."

"Thank you."

"Not at all."

She closed her eyes and put her hands together in front of her face. Then she opened her eyes again and looked around the room. There was only the two of us. I lifted my cup and sipped my tea.

Amé wasn't wearing her usual denim shirt. She had on a white lace blouse and a pale green skirt. Her hair was neatly brushed, her mouth freshened with lipstick. Her usual vitality had been replaced by a fragility that enveloped her like mist. A perfumed atmosphere that wavered on evaporation. Amé's beauty was wholly unlike Yuki's. It was the chromatic opposite, a beauty of experience. She had a firm grasp on it, knew how to use it, whereas Yuki's beauty was without purpose, undirected, unsure. Appreciating an attractive middle-aged woman is one of the great luxuries in life.

"Why is it . . . ?" Amé wondered aloud, her words trailing off. I waited for her to continue.

". . . why is it," she picked up again, "I'm so depressed?"

"Someone close to you has died. It's only natural that you feel this way," I said.

"I suppose," she said weakly.

"Still—"

Amé looked me in the face, then shook her head. "You're not stupid. You know what I want to say."

"That it shouldn't be such a shock to you? Is that it?"

"Yes, well, something like that."

That even if he wasn't such a great man. Even if he wasn't so talented. Still he was true. He fulfilled his duties nobly, excellently. He forfeited what he treasured and worked hard to attain, then he died. It was only after his death that his worth became apparent. I wanted to say that—but didn't. Some things I can't bring myself to utter.

"Why is it?" she addressed a point in space. "Why is it all my men end up like this? Why do they all go in strange ways? Why do they always leave me? Why can't I get things right?"

I stared at the lace collar of her blouse. It looked like pristinely scrubbed folds of tissue, the bleached entrails of a rare organism. A subtle shaft of smoke rose from her Salem in the ashtray, merging into a dust of silence.

Yuki reappeared, her clothes changed, and indicated that she wanted to leave. I got up and told Amé we were going out for a bit.

Amé wasn't listening. Yuki shouted, "Mother, we're going out now," but Amé scarcely nodded as she lit another cigarette.

We left Amé sitting on the sofa motionless. The house was still haunted by Dick North's presence. Dick North was still inside me as well. I remembered his smile, his surprised look when I asked if he used his feet to slice bread.

Interesting man. He'd come more alive since his death.

37

I went up to see Yuki a few more times. Three times, to be exact.

Staying in the mountains of Hakone with her mother didn't seem to hold any particular attraction for her. She wasn't happy there, but she didn't hate it either. Nor did she feel compelled to look after her mother. Yuki let herself be blown along by the prevailing winds. She simply existed, without enthusiasm for all aspects of living.

Taking her out seemed to bring back her spirits. My bad jokes slowly began to elicit responses, her voice regained its cool edge. Yet, no sooner would she return to the house than she became a wooden figure again. Her voice went slack, the light left her eyes. To conserve energy, her little planet stopped spinning.

"Wouldn't it be better for you to be back on your own in Tokyo for a while?" I asked her as we sat on the beach. "Just for a change of pace. Three or four days. A different environment can do wonders. Staying here in Hakone's only going to bring you down. You're not the same person you were in Hawaii."

"No way around it," said Yuki. "But it's like a phase I have to go through. Wouldn't matter where I was, I'd still be like this."

"Because Dick North died and your mother's like that?"

"Maybe. But it's not the whole thing. Just getting away from Mama isn't going to solve everything. I can't do anything on my own. I don't know, it's just the way I feel. Like my head and body aren't really together. My signs aren't so good right now."

I turned and looked out to sea. The sky was overcast. A warm breeze rustled through the clumps of grasses on the sand.

"Your signs?" I asked.

"My star signs," Yuki smiled. "It's true, you know. The signs are getting worse. Both for Mama and me. We're on the same wavelength. We're connected that way, even if I'm away from her."

"Connected?"

"Yeah, mentally connected," Yuki said. "Sometimes I can't stand it and I try to fight it. Sometimes I'm just too tired and I give in, and I don't care. It's like I'm not really in control of myself. Like I'm being moved around by some force. I can't stand it. I want to throw everything out the window. I want to scream 'I'm only a kid!' and go hide in a corner."

Before it got too late I drove Yuki home and headed back to Tokyo. Amé asked me to stay for dinner, as she invariably did, but I always declined. A very unappetizing prospect, the idea of sitting down to a meal with mother dreary and her disinterested daughter, both on the same wavelength, there in the lingering presence of the deceased. The dead-weighted air. The silence. The night so quiet you could hear any sound. The thought of it sank a stone in my stomach. The Mad Hatter's tea party might have been just as absurd, but at least it was more animated.

I played loud rock 'n' roll on the car stereo all the way home, had a beer while cooking supper, and ate alone in peace.

Yuki and I never did much. We listened to music as we drove, lolled around gazing at clouds, ate ice cream at the Fujiya Hotel, rented a boat on Lake Ashinoko. Mostly we just talked and spent the whole afternoon watching the day pass. The pensioners' life.

Once, upon Yuki's suggestion that we see a movie, we drove all the way down to Odawara. We checked the listings and found nothing of interest. Gotanda's *Unrequited Love* was playing at a second-run theater, and when I mentioned that Gotanda was a classmate from junior high school, whom I got together with occasionally, Yuki got curious.

"Did you see it?"

"Yeah," I admitted, "I saw it." I didn't say how many times.

"Was it good?" asked Yuki.

"No, it was dumb. A waste of film, to put it mildly."

"What does your friend say about the movie?"

"He said it was a dumb movie and a waste of film," I laughed. "And if the performer himself says so, you can be sure it's bad."

"But I want to see it anyway."

"As you wish."

"You don't mind?"

"It's okay. One more time's not going to hurt me," I said.

On a weekday afternoon, the theater was practically empty. The seats were hard and the place smelled like a closet. I bought Yuki a chocolate bar from the snack bar as we waited for the movie to start. She broke off a piece for me. When I told her it'd been a year since I'd last eaten chocolate, she couldn't believe it.

"Don't you like chocolate?"

"It's not a matter of like or dislike," I said. "I guess I'm just not interested in it."

"Interested? You are weird. Whoever heard of not *liking* chocolate? That's abnormal."

"No, it's not. Some things are like that. Do you like the Dalai Lama?"

"What's that?"

"It's not a 'what,' it's a 'who.' He's the top priest of Tibet."

"How would I know?"

"Well, then, do you like the Panama Canal?"

"Yes, no, I don't care."

"Okay, how about the International Date Line? Or *pi*? Or the Anti-Trust Act? Or the Jurassic Period? Or the Senegalese national anthem? Do you like or dislike November 8, 1987?"

"Shut up, will you? How can you churn out so much garbage so fast?" she struck back. "So you don't like or dislike chocolate, you're just not interested in it. Happy?"

Presently the movie began. I knew the whole story backwards, so I didn't bother paying a lot of attention. Yuki didn't think much of the picture either, if the way she muttered to herself was any indication.

On screen, the handsome teacher Gotanda was explaining to his class how mollusks breathe. Simply, patiently, with just the right touch of humor. The girl lead gazed at him.

"Is that guy your friend?" Yuki asked.

"Yeah."

"Seems like a real airhead," said Yuki.

"You said it," I said. "But only in the film. In real life, he's a good guy."

"Then maybe he should get into some good movies."

"That's what he wants to do. Not so easy, though. It's a long story."

The movie creaked along, obvious and mediocre plot. Mediocre script, mediocre music. They ought to have sealed the thing in a time capsule marked "Late 20th Century Mediocrity" and buried it somewhere.

Finally Kiki's scene came up. The most intense point in the movie. Gotanda and Kiki sleeping together. The Sunday morning scene.

I took a deep breath and concentrated on the screen. Sunday morning sunlight slanting through the blinds, the same light, same exposure, same colors as always. I'd engraved every detail of that room in my brain. I could almost breathe the atmosphere of that room. Zoom in on Gotanda. His hand moves down Kiki's spine. Sensuously, effortlessly, caressing. The slightest tremor of response runs through her body. Like a candle flame just flickering in a microcurrent of air that the skin doesn't feel. I hold my breath. Close-up of Gotanda's fingers. The camera starts to pan. Kiki's face comes into view. Enter lead girl. She climbs the apartment stairs, knocks on the door, opens it. Once again, I ask myself, why isn't it locked? Makes no sense. But it doesn't have to. It's just a film and a mediocre one at that. The girl walks in, sees Gotanda and Kiki getting it on. Her eyes register shock. She drops her cookies and runs. Gotanda sits up in bed, numbly observing what has transpired. Kiki has her line, "What was *that* all about?"

The very same as always. Exactly the same.

I shut my eyes. The Sunday morning light, Gotanda's hand, Kiki's back, everything floats up with singular clarity. A discrete little world existing in a dimension all its own.

The next thing I know, Yuki was bent forward, head on the backrest of the seat in front, with both arms wrapped around herself as if to ward off the cold. Dead silent, not moving a hair. Hardly a sign of breathing.

"Hey, are you all right?" I asked.

"No, I don't feel very well," Yuki barely squeezed out the words.

"Let's get out of here. Do you think you can manage?"

Yuki half-nodded. I held her stiffened arms and helped her out of the theater. As we walked up the aisle, Gotanda was up on the screen behind us, lecturing the class in biology. Outside, the streets were hushed under a curtain of fine rain. The scent of surf blew in from the sea. Supporting her by the elbow, I walked her slowly to the car. Yuki was biting her lip, not saying anything. I didn't say anything either. The parking lot was scarcely two hundred meters from the theater, but it took forever.

I sat Yuki in the front seat and wound her window open. Soft rain fell, undetectable to the eye, though the asphalt was slowly staining black. There was the smell of rain. Some people had their umbrellas up, others walked along as if nothing was coming down. An outstretched hand would be retracted with only a hint of dampness. It was that fine a rain.

Yuki rested an arm on the door and her chin upon that, the tilt of her neck turning her face half out of the car. She held that pose for a good while, not moving except to breathe. Each tiny rise followed by a tiny fall, the slightest crest and trough of breath. How could anyone look so fragile, so defenseless? From where I sat, it seemed that the least impact would be enough to snap off her head and elbow. Was it merely that she was a child, not hardened to the ways of the world, while I was an adult, who, however inexpertly, had endured?

"Is there anything I can I do?" I asked.

"Not really," said Yuki, swallowing as she spoke face-down. The saliva clearing her throat sounded unnaturally loud. "Take me somewhere quiet where there's no people, but not too far."

"The beach?"

"Wherever. But don't drive fast. I might throw up if we bump too much."

I lifted her head inside onto the headrest, careful as if cradling an egg, and rolled up her window halfway. Then as slowly as the traffic would allow, we headed to the Kunifuzu seaside. We parked the car and walked to the beach, where Yuki vomited onto the sand. There'd been hardly anything in her stomach, only the chocolate and gastric juices. The most excruciating way to get sick. The body is in spasms, but nothing comes. You're wringing out your entire system, until your stomach is a knot the size of a fist. I massaged her back. The misting rain continued, but Yuki didn't notice.

Glyauughhh . . . Yuki's eyes welled up with tears as she retched.

I tried lamely to comfort her.

After ten minutes of this, I wiped her mouth with a handkerchief and kicked sand over the mess. Then holding her by the elbow, I walked her over to a nearby jetty. We sat down, leaning back against the seawall as the rain began to fall. We stared off into the waves, at the cars droning in the background on the West Shonan Causeway. The only people around were standing in the water before us, fishing. They wore slickers and rain hats, their eyes trained somewhere below the horizon, their rods unbending. They didn't turn around to see us. Yuki lay her head on my shoulder, but didn't say a word. We must have seemed like lovers.

Yuki closed her eyes. Breathing so lightly, she seemed to be asleep. Her wet bangs were plastered in a clump across her forehead, her skin still tan from last month. But beneath the overcast sky, Yuki looked sickly. I wiped the rain and tears from her face. Rain kept falling silently over the boundless sea. Self-Defense Force submarine-spotting planes groaned past overhead like dragonflies in heat.

Finally, her head still resting on my shoulder, she opened her eyes and looked at me in soft focus. She pulled a Virginia Slim from her hip pocket and lit up. Or tried to repeatedly—she barely had the strength to light a match. No lectures from me about smoking, not this time. Eventually she got it lit and flicked the match away. Then after two drags on the cigarette, she tossed it away too. It continued burning until the rain put it out.

"Your stomach still hurt?" I asked.

"A little."

"Let's just stay put a while though. You're not cold?"

"I'm fine. The rain feels good."

The fishermen were still transfixed on the Pacific. What was the attraction of fishing? It couldn't be merely catching fish. Was it just one of those acquired tastes? Like sitting out on a rainy beach with a high-strung thirteen-year-old?

"Your friend," Yuki ventured cautiously, her voice cracking.

"My friend?"

"Yeah, the one in the film."

"His real name's Gotanda," I said. "Like the station on the Yamanote Line. The one after Meguro and before Osaki."

"He killed that woman."

I squinted at Yuki, hard. She looked wan. Her breathing came irregularly, like a nearly drowned soul trawled up from the drink. What was the girl saying? It didn't register. "Killed what woman?" I asked.

"That woman. The one he was sleeping with on Sunday morning."

I didn't get it. I couldn't get it. What was she talking about? Half-consciously, I smiled and said, "But nobody dies in the movie. You must be mistaken."

"Not in the movie. In real life. He actually killed her. I saw it," said Yuki, clutching my arm. "It scared me so much I could hardly breathe. That *whatever-it-is* came over me again. I could see the whole murder, sharp and clear. Your friend killed that woman. I'm not making this up. Honest."

My spine turned to ice, I couldn't utter a word. Everything was falling out of place, tumbling down, out of my hands. I couldn't hold on to anything.

"I'm sorry. Maybe I shouldn't have said anything," said

Yuki. She sighed and let go of my arm. "The honest truth is, I don't know. I can *feel* that it's real, but I can't *really* be sure if it's real or not. And I know you'll probably hate me like everyone else for saying so. But I couldn't *not* tell you. Whether it's real or not, I saw it. I couldn't keep quiet about it. I'm really scared. Please don't get angry at me. I can't handle it. I feel like I'm falling apart."

"I'm not mad, so calm down and tell me what you saw," I said, holding her hand.

"It's the first time I've ever seen anything clearly like this. He strangled her, the woman in the movie. And he put the body in the car and drove a long, long way. It was that Italian car you were driving once. That car, it's his, isn't it?"

"Yes, it's his car," I said. "Is there anything else? Slow down and think it over. Whatever comes to mind, no matter how small, tell me. I want to know."

She shook her head tentatively, twice, three times. Then she breathed deeply. "There's really not much more. The smell of soil. A shovel. Night. Birds chirping. That's about it. He strangled that girl to death, loaded her off somewhere in that car, and buried her. That's all. But—and this is the truly strange part—the whole thing didn't seem vicious or horrible or anything. It didn't even seem like a crime. It was more like a ceremony. It was a quiet thing, between the killer and the victim. But a very strange quiet. Like it was out on the edge of the earth or something."

I closed my eyes. My thoughts wouldn't go anywhere. Objects and events in my head were disintegrating, flying like shrapnel through the dark. I didn't believe what Yuki was saying; I didn't disbelieve what Yuki was saying. I let her words sink in. They weren't fact. They were possibility. Nothing more, nothing less, but the force of the possibility was shattering.

Any semblance of order I had come to know over the last few months was shot. Diffuse, uncertain, but it was order, and it had taken hold. No more.

The possibility exists. And in the moment that I admitted

that, something came to an end. Ever subtly, yet decisively, it was over. But what? I couldn't think further. No, not now. Meanwhile, I found myself alone again. With a thirteen-year-old girl, on a rainy beach, desperately alone.

Yuki squeezed my hand.

How long she held it, I don't know. A hand so small and warm it almost didn't seem real. Her touch was more like a tiny replay from memory. Warm as a memory, but it doesn't lead you anywhere.

"Let's go," I said. "I'll take you home."

I drove her back up to Hakone. Neither of us spoke. When the silence became too oppressive, I put on the stereo. There was music, but I didn't hear it. I concentrated on driving. Hands and feet, shifting gears, steering. The wipers going back and forth, monotonously.

I didn't want to have to see Amé, so I let Yuki out at the bottom of the steps.

"Hey," said Yuki, looking in through the passenger seat window, arms crossed tight and shivering, "you don't have to swallow everything I told you. I just saw it, that's all. Like I said, I don't know if it *really* happened. Please don't hate me. I'd die."

"I don't hate you," I said, coming up with a smile. "And I won't swallow anything, unless it's the truth. It's got to come out some time. The fog's got to pull away. I know that much. If what you say turns out to be true, okay, it just means that I got a glimpse of the truth through you. Don't worry. It's something I have to find out for myself."

"Are you going to see him?"

"Of course. I'll ask him if it's true. There's no other way."

Yuki shrugged. "You're not mad at me?"

"No, I'm not mad at you, of course not," I said. "Why would I be mad at you? You haven't done anything wrong."

"You were such a good guy," she said. "I never met anyone like you."

Why the past tense? I wondered. "And I've never met a girl like you."

"Good-bye," said Yuki. Then she took a good, long look at me. She seemed fidgety. As if she wanted to add something more or hold my hand or kiss me on the cheek.

Nervous images of possibility kept floating into my head all the way home. I made myself focus on the mindless music and tacked my attention to the road ahead. The rain let up just as I exited the Tokyo–Nagoya Expressway, but I didn't have the energy to turn off the wipers until I pulled into my parking space in Shibuya. My head was in a shambles. I had to do something. So I sat there in my parked Subaru, my hands glued to the wheel.

39

I tried to put my thoughts in order.

First question: Should I believe Yuki? I analyzed matters on the level of pure possibility, wiping the field clear of emotional elements as far as I could see. This required no great effort. My feelings had been numbed, as if I'd been stung, from the very beginning. *The possibility exists.* The longer I considered the possibility, the more the possibility moved toward probability. I stood in the kitchen making coffee. Then pouring myself a cup, I retreated with it to my bed. By the time I'd finished it, the probability had become a fair certainty. Yes, it was exactly as Yuki had seen it: Gotanda had murdered Kiki, hauled her body away, and buried it.

How absurd. There was no proof whatsoever. Only the dream of an oversensitive thirteen-year-old girl watching a movie. And yet, somehow, what she said could not be doubted. This was shocking. Still my instincts accepted it fully. Why? How could I be so sure?

I didn't know.

Next question: Why would Gotanda kill Kiki?

I didn't know.

Next question: Did Gotanda also kill Mei? Why? What would make Gotanda want to kill her?

Again I didn't know. I wracked my brains, but couldn't

come up with a single reason why Gotanda would kill either Kiki or Mei.

There were too many unknowns.

I had to see Gotanda. I had to ask him directly. I reached for the phone but couldn't bring myself to dial his number. I set down the receiver, rolled over on the bed, and gazed up at the ceiling. Gotanda had become a friend. I would never have guessed how much of a friend. Suppose he did kill Kiki, he was still my friend. I didn't want to lose him. Not like I'd already lost so many things in this life. No, I couldn't call him.

I didn't want to talk to anybody.

I sat, and when the phone rang, I let it ring. If it was Gotanda, what was I going to say? If it was Yuki, or even Yumiyoshi, I didn't care. I didn't want to talk to anybody.

Four days, five days, I stayed put and thought. *Why?* I hardly ate, hardly slept. I didn't drink a drop. I stayed indoors. I lost touch with my body. With all that had happened to me already, I was still losing. And now here I was, alone. It was always like this. In some ways, Gotanda and I were of the same species. Different circumstances, different thinking, different sensibilities, the same species. We both kept losing. And now we were losing each other.

I could see Kiki. *What was that all about?* But was Kiki dead, covered with dirt, in the ground? Like my Kipper? Ultimately, Kiki had to die. Strange how I couldn't see things any other way. The skin of my soul was no longer tender. I tried not to feel anything at all. My resignation was a silent rain falling over a vast sea. Even loneliness was beyond me. Everything was taking leave of me, like ciphers in the sand, blown away on the wind.

So another person had joined the group in that most bizarre chamber of my world. Four down, two to go. Sooner or later, bleached white bones ferried to that room via some impossible architecture. Death's waiting room in downtown Honolulu, connected to the dark chill lair of the Sheep Man in a Sapporo hotel, connected to the Sunday morning bedroom where Gotanda lay with Kiki. Was I losing my mind? Real events, under imaginary circumstances, filtering back, wild, distorted, bizarre. Was there nothing absolute? Was there no . . . reality? Sapporo in the March snow could as easily *not* have been real. Sitting on the beach in Makaha with Dick North had seemed real enough—but a one-armed man cutting bread in perfect slices? And a Honolulu call girl giving me a phone number that I later find in the anteroom to the death chamber Kiki leads me to? Why isn't that real? What could I reasonably admit into evidence without causing my whole world to shake at its foundations?

Was the sickness *in here* or *out there*? Did it matter?

What was the line now? Get in step and dance, so that everyone's impressed. Keeping in step—was that the only reality? Well, dance yourself to the telephone, give your pal Gotanda a ring, and ask him casually: "Did you kill Kiki?"

No way. My hand experienced sudden paralysis. I sat by the phone, numb, shaking, as if I was in a crosswind. Breathing grew difficult. I liked Gotanda, I liked him a lot. He was my only friend, he was part of my life. I understood him.

I tried dialing. I got the wrong number, every time. On the sixth try, I hurled the receiver to the floor.

I never did manage to call. In the end it was Gotanda who showed up at my place.

It was a rainy night. He was wearing a rain hat and the same white trench coat as the night I drove him to Yokohama. The rain was coming down hard, and his hat was dripping. He didn't have an umbrella.

He smiled when he saw me. I smiled back, almost by reflex.

"You look awful," he said. "I called and called but never got an answer. So I decided just to come over. You been under the weather?"

"Under is not the word," I said.

He sized me up. "Well, maybe it's a bad time. I'll come

back when you're feeling better. Sorry to come by unannounced like this."

I shook my head and exhaled. No words came. Gotanda waited patiently. "I'm not sick or anything," I assured him. "I just haven't been sleeping or eating. I think I'm okay now. Anyway I've been wanting to talk to you. Let's go somewhere. I haven't eaten a full meal in ages."

We took the Maserati out into the rainy neon streets. Gotanda's driving was precise and smooth as ever, but the car now made me nervous. The deep soundproofed ride cut a channel through the clamor that rose all around us.

"Where to?" Gotanda asked. "All I care is that it's somewhere quiet where we can talk and get decent food without running into the Rolex crowd." he said. He looked my way, but I said nothing. For thirty minutes we drove around, my eyes focused on the buildings we were passing.

"I can't think of any place," Gotanda tried again. "How about you? Any ideas?"

"No, me neither." I really couldn't. I was still only half present.

"Okay, then, why don't we take the opposite approach?" he said brightly.

"The opposite approach?"

"Someplace noisy and crowded. That way we can relax."

"Okay. Where?"

"Feel like pizza? Let's go to Shakey's."

"I don't mind. I'm not against pizza. But wouldn't they spot you, going to a place like that?"

Gotanda smiled weakly, like the last glow of a summer sun between the leaves. "When was the last time you saw anyone famous in Shakey's, my friend?"

Shakey's was packed with weekend shoppers. Crowded and noisy. A Dixieland quartet in suspenders and red-and-white striped shirts were pumping out *The Tiger Rag* to a raucous college group loud on beer. The smell of pizza was everywhere. No one paid attention to anyone else.

We placed our order, got a couple drafts, then found a

table under a gaudy imitation Tiffany lamp in the back of the restaurant.

"What did I tell you? Isn't this more like it?" said Gotanda.

I'd never craved pizza before, but the first bite had me thinking it was the best thing I'd ever tasted. I must have been starving. The both of us. We drank and ate and ate and drank. And when the pizza ran out, we each bought another round of beer.

"Great, eh?" belched Gotanda. "I've been wanting a pizza for the last three days. I even dreamed about it, sizzling hot, sliding right out of the oven. In the dream I never get to eat it, though. I just stare at it and drool. That's the whole dream. Nothing else happens. What would Jung say about pizza archetypes?" Gotanda chuckled, then paused. "So what was this that you wanted to talk to me about?"

Now or never, I thought. But come right out with it? Gotanda was thoroughly relaxed, enjoying the evening. I looked at his innocent smile and couldn't bring myself to do it. Not now, at least.

"What's new with you?" I asked. "Work? Your ex-wife?"

"Work's the same," Gotanda said. "Nothing new, nothing good, nothing I want to do. I can yell until my throat gives out, but nobody wants to hear what I have to say. My wife —did you hear that? I still call her my wife after all this time—I've only seen her once since I last saw you. Hey, you ever do the love hotel thing?"

"Almost never."

"I told you she and I have been meeting at love hotels. You know, the more you use those places, it gets to you. They're dark, windows all covered up. The place is only for fucking, so who needs windows, right? All you got is a bathroom and a bed—plus music and TV and a refrigerator—but it's all pretty blank and anonymous and artificial. Actually, very conducive to getting down and doing it. Makes you feel like you're really *doing it*. After a while, though, you feel the claustrophobia, and you begin to sort of hate the place. Still, they're the only refuge we got."

Gotanda took a sip of beer and wiped his mouth with the napkin.

"I can't bring her to my condo. The scandal rags would have a field day if they ever found out. I got no time to go off somewhere. They'd sniff it out too anyway. We've practically sold our privacy by the gram. So we go to these cheesy fuck hotels and . . ." Gotanda looked over at me, then smiled. "Here I go, griping again."

"That's okay. I don't mind listening."

The Dixieland band struck up "Hello Dolly."

"Hey, how about another pizza?" Gotanda asked. "Halve it with you. I don't know what it is with me, but am I starving!"

Soon we were stuffing our faces with one medium anchovy. The college kids kept up their shouting match, but the band had finished their final set. Banjo and trumpet and trombone were packed in their cases, and the musicians left the stage, leaving only the upright piano.

We'd finished the extra pizza, but somehow couldn't take our eyes off the empty stage. Without the music, the voices in the crowd became plastic, almost palpable. Waves of sound solidifying as they pressed toward us, yet broke softly on contact. Rolling up slowly over and over again, striking my consciousness, then retreating. Farther and farther away. Distant waves, crashing against my mind in the distance.

"Why did you kill Kiki?" I asked Gotanda. I didn't mean to ask it. It just slipped out.

He stared at me as if he were looking at something far off. His lips parted slightly. His teeth were white and beautiful. For the longest time, he stared right through me. The surf in my head went on and on, now louder, now fainter. As if all contact with reality was approaching and receding. I remember his graceful fingers neatly folded on the table. When my reality strayed out of contact, they looked like fine craftwork.

Then he smiled, ever so peaceably.

"Did I kill Kiki?" he enunciated slowly.

"Only joking," I hedged.

Gotanda's eyes fell to the table, to his fingers. "No, this isn't a joke. This is very important. I really have to think about it. *Did* I kill Kiki? I have to give this very serious thought."

I stared at him. His mouth was smiling, but his eyes weren't.

"Could there be a reason for you to kill Kiki?" I asked.

"Could there be a reason for me to kill Kiki? I don't even know myself. Did I kill Kiki? Why?"

"Hey, how would I know?" I tried to laugh. "Did you kill Kiki, or didn't you kill Kiki?"

"I said, I'm thinking about it. Did I kill Kiki, or didn't I?"

Gotanda took another sip of beer, set down his glass, and propped his head up on his hand. "I can't be sure. Sounds stupid, doesn't it? But I mean it. I'm not sure. I think, maybe, I tried to strangle Kiki. At my place, I think. Why would I have killed Kiki there? I didn't even want to be alone with her. No good, I can't remember. But anyway, Kiki and I were at my place—I put her body in the car and took her someplace and I buried her. Somewhere in the mountains. I can't be sure if I really did it. I can't believe I'd do a thing like that. I just *feel* as if I might have done it. I can't prove it. I give up. The most critical part's a blank. I'm trying to think if there's any physical evidence. Like a shovel. I'd have to have used a shovel. If I found a shovel, I'd know I did it. Let me try again. I buy a shovel at a garden supply. I use the shovel to dig a hole and bury Kiki. Then I toss the shovel. Okay, where?

"The whole thing's in pieces, like a dream. The story goes this way and that way. It's going nowhere. I have memories of *something*. But are the memories for real? Or are they something I made up later to fit? Something's wrong with me. It's gotten worse since my wife and I split up. I'm tired. I'm really . . . lost."

I said nothing.

After a pause, Gotanda went on. "Well, what's real anyway? From what point is it all phobia? Or acting? I thought if I hung around you, I'd get a better grip on things. I thought so from the first time you asked me about Kiki. Like maybe you'd clear away this muddle. Open a window and let some fresh air in." He folded his hands again and peered down at them. "Let's say I did kill Kiki—what would be the reason? I liked her. I liked sleeping with her. When I was down, she and Mei were my only release. So why kill her?"

"Did you kill Mei?"

Gotanda stared at his hands for an aeon, then shook his head. "No, I don't believe I killed Mei. Thank god, I have an alibi for that night. The day she was killed, I was at the studio until midnight, then I drove with my manager to Mito. What a relief. If no one could swear I was at the studio that night, I'd worry that I killed Mei too. But I still feel responsible for Mei's death. I don't know why. I wasn't there, but it's like I killed her with my own hands. I have this *feeling* that she died on account of me."

Another aeon passed while he stared at his fingers.

"Gotanda, you're beat," I said. "That's all. You probably didn't kill anyone. Kiki just vanished somewhere. When we were together, she used to disappear like that. It wouldn't be the first time. You're riding yourself too hard. Don't do it."

"No, it's not like that. Not that simple. I probably did kill Kiki. I don't think I killed Mei, but, yes, I think I killed Kiki. The sensation of the air going out of her throat is still in my fingers. I can still feel the weight of the dirt in the shovel. In effect, I killed her."

"But why would you kill Kiki? It doesn't make sense."

"No idea," he said. "Maybe an urge to self-destruct. It's happened before. I get this gap between me Gotanda and me the actor, and I stand back and actually observe myself doing shit. I'm on one side of this very deep, dark fault, and then unconsciously, on the other side, I have this urge to destroy something. Smash it to bits. A glass. A pencil. A plastic model. Never happens when other people are around, though. Only when I'm alone.

"But once, when I was in elementary school, I knocked into this friend of mine, and he fell off a small bluff. I don't know why I did it. But the next thing I knew, he was down there. It wasn't a big fall, so he wasn't hurt too bad. It was supposed to be an accident. I mean, why would I push this friend of mine over the edge on purpose? That's what everyone thought. I wasn't so sure. Then high school, I set fire to these mailboxes. I'd put a burning rag down the slot. Not just once, not even as a prank. It was like I was compelled to do it. Like it was the only thing that'd bring me to my senses. Unconsciously, that was what I thought. But afterwards I would remember the feel of things. I could still feel it in my hands. And I wouldn't be able to wash it off. God, what a horrible life. I don't know how I can stand it."

Gotanda shook his head.

"How do I check if I killed Kiki?" Gotanda went on. "There's no evidence. No corpse. No shovel. No dirt on my trousers. No blisters on my hands. Not that digging a hole is going to give you blisters. I don't even remember where I buried her. Say I went to the police and confessed, who'd believe me? If there's no body, it's not a homicide. She disappeared. That's all I know for sure. There've been times I wanted to tell you, but I just couldn't. I thought it'd wipe out whatever closeness we had. Whenever I'm with you, I feel so relaxed. I never feel the gap. You don't know how precious that is. I don't want to lose a friendship like ours. So I kept putting off telling you, until you asked, like this. I really ought to have come clean."

"Come clean? When there's no evidence you did anything?"

"Evidence isn't the issue. I ought to have told you first. But I *concealed* it. That's the problem."

"C'mon, even if it were true, even if you did kill Kiki, you didn't *mean* to kill her."

He held out his palms, as if he were going to read them. "No. I didn't mean to. I didn't have a reason. I liked her, and in a small way we were friends. We could talk. I could tell her about my wife, and she'd listen, honestly. Why would I want to kill her? But I did, I think, with these hands. Maybe I didn't do it willfully. But I did. I strangled her. But I wasn't strangling *her*, I was strangling my *shadow*. I remember thinking, if only I could choke my shadow off, I'd get some health. Except it wasn't my shadow. It was Kiki.

"*It all took place in that dark world*. You know what I'm talking about? Not here in this one. And it was Kiki who led me there. *Choke me,* Kiki told me. *Go ahead and kill me, it's okay*. She invited me to, allowed me to. I swear, honestly, it happened like that. Without me knowing. Can that happen? It was like a dream. The more I think about it, the more it doesn't feel real. Why would Kiki ask me to kill her?"

I downed the last of my lukewarm beer. A dense layer of cigarette smoke hovered like an ectoplasmic phenomenon.

"Feel like another beer?" I asked him.

"Yeah, I could use one."

I went to the bar and came back with two mugs, which we drank in silence. The turnover at the place was as busy as Akihabara Station at rush hour, customers coming and going constantly. Nobody bothered listening in to our conversation. Nobody even looked at Gotanda.

"What'd I tell you?" Gotanda summoned up a smile as he spoke. "Not a star in sight." Gotanda swished his two-thirds empty glass around like a test tube.

"Let's forget it," I said quietly. "I can forget it. You forget it too."

"You think I can forget it? Easy to say, but you didn't kill her with your own hands."

"Hey, you hear me? There's no evidence you killed Kiki. Stop blaming yourself for something that might not have even happened. Your unconscious is using Kiki's vanishing act as a convenient way to lay a guilt trip on you. Isn't that a possibility?"

"Okay, let's talk possibilities," said Gotanda, laying his palms flat on the table. "I've been doing nothing but considering possibilities lately. All sorts of possibilities. Like the possibility that I'll kill my wife. Am I right? Maybe I'd strangle her if she allowed me to, like Kiki did. Possibilities are like cancer. The more I think about them, the more they multiply, and there's no way to stop them. I'm out of control. I didn't just burn mailboxes. I killed four cats. I used a slingshot and busted the neighbors' window. I couldn't stop doing shit like this. And I never told anyone about it, until this minute. God," he sighed deeply, "it's almost a relief, telling you.

"What goddamn thing am I going to do next? That gap—it's too big, too deep. Professional hazard, huh? The bigger the gap, the more weird the shit I find myself doing. Is it in my genes? God, I'm afraid that I will just kill my wife. I haven't got any control over it. *Because it won't take place in this world.*"

"You worry too much," I said, forcing a smile. "Forget this nonsense about genes. What you need is a break from work. Stop seeing your wife for a while. It's the only way. Throw everything to the wind. Come with me to Hawaii. Lie on the beach, drink piña coladas, swim, get laid. Rent a convertible and cruise around listening to music. And if you still want to worry, you can do that later."

"Not a bad idea," he said, the folds of his eyes crinkling as he smiled. "We'll get us two girls and the four of us can fool around till morning again. That was fun."

Shoveling that good snow. Cuck–koo.

"I can take off any time," I said. "How about you? How long will it take you to finish up what you're doing?"

Gotanda gave me the oddest smile. "You don't understand a thing, do you? There's no such thing as finishing up in my line of work. All you can do is toss the whole thing. And if I do that, you can be sure I'll never work again. I'd be drummed out of the industry, *permanently*. And, I'd lose my wife, *permanently*."

He drained the last of his beer.

"But that's fine. Back-to-nothing is fine. At this point, I'm ready to call it quits. I'm tired. Time I went to Hawaii and blanked out. Okay, let's scrap it all. Let's go to Hawaii. I can think things over later. I'll . . . become a regular human being. Maybe too late, but worth a try. I'll leave everything up to you. I trust you. Always did, from the time you first called me up. You seemed like such a decent guy. Like what I'd always wanted to be."

"No such decent guy here," I protested. "I'm just . . . keeping in step, dancing along. No meaning to it at all."

Gotanda spread his hands a body-width apart on the table. "And just where, pray tell, *is* there meaning? Where in this life of ours?" Then he laughed. "But that's okay. Doesn't matter anymore. I'm resigned to it. I'll follow your example. I'll hop around from elevator to elevator. It's not impossible. I can do anything if I put my mind to it. I'm sharp, handsome, good-natured Gotanda after all. So, okay, Hawaii. We'll get the tickets tomorrow. First class. It's gotta be first class. It's in the cards, you know. BMW, Rolex, Azabu, and first class. We'll leave the day after tomorrow and land on the same day. Hawaii! I look good in an aloha shirt."

"You'd look good in anything."

"Thanks for tickling what remains of my ego."

Gotanda gave me a good, long look. "You really think you can forget I killed Kiki?"

"Uh-huh."

"Well, one other thing you don't know about me. Remember I told you I got thrown in confinement for two weeks?"

"Yeah."

"That was a lie. I blabbed everything and they let me out right away. I wasn't scared. I wanted, in some sick way, to do something gutless. I wanted to hate myself. I'm such a louse. You didn't know that when you clammed up to save my face, you also saved my rotten hide. You did something for me that I wouldn't do for myself—wash away my dirt. And I was glad, you know. It gave me the chance to finally be honest with myself. I feel like I've come clean at last. Man, I bet it wasn't too pleasant to watch."

"Don't worry about it," I said. *It's brought us closer together*, I wanted to say. But I didn't. I decided to wait for a time when the words would mean more. So I just repeated myself, "Don't worry about it."

Gotanda took his rain hat from the back of his chair, checked to see how damp it was, then put it back. "I got a favor to ask you," he said, "as a friend. I'd like another beer, but I don't have it in me to get up and go get one."

"No problem," I said.

I stood up and went up to the bar. There was a line, so it took me a while. By the time I waded back to the table, mugs in hand, Gotanda was gone. Ditto his rain hat. And no Maserati in the parking lot either. Great, I shook my head, just great.

There was nothing I could do. He had disappeared.

40

The following afternoon they dredged the Maserati out of Tokyo Bay. As I expected. No surprises. As soon as he disappeared, I saw it coming.

Another corpse. The Rat, Kiki, Mei, Dick North, and now Gotanda. Five. One more to go. What now? Who was the next in line to die? Not Yumiyoshi, I wouldn't be able to bear that. Yumiyoshi was not meant to die. Okay, then Yuki? The kid was thirteen. I couldn't let that happen to her. I was going down the list, as if I were the god of doom, dealing out orders for mortality.

I went down to the Akasaka police station to tell Bookish that I'd been with Gotanda the previous night until right before his death. Somehow I thought it was the right thing to do, though naturally I didn't mention Kiki. That was a closed book. Instead, I talked about how exhausted Gotanda had been, how his loans were piling up, the problems with work, the stresses in his personal life.

Bookish took down what I said. Unlike before, he made simple notes. Which I signed. It didn't take an hour. "People dying left and right around you, eh?" he said. "At this rate, you'll never make friends and influence people. They start hating you, and before you know it, your eyes go and your skin sags. Not a pretty prospect."

Then he heaved a deep sigh.

"Well, anyway, this was a suicide. Open and shut case. Even got witnesses. Still, what a waste. I don't care if he was a movie star, he didn't have to go blitzing a *Maserati* into the Bay, did he? Ordinary Honda Civic or Toyota Corolla would've done the job."

"It was insured."

"No sir, insurance never covers suicides," Bookish reminded me. "Anyway, you can go now. Sorry about your friend. And thanks for taking the trouble to come in," he said as he saw me to the door. "Mei's case isn't settled yet. But the investigation's still going on."

For a long time after, I walked around feeling as if I'd killed Gotanda. I couldn't rid myself of the weight. I went back over all the things we'd talked about that night. If only I'd given him the responses he'd needed to save himself, the two of us might be relaxing on the beach in Maui right now.

No way. Gotanda had made up his mind from the beginning. He'd been thinking about plowing that Maserati into the sea all along. He'd been waiting for an excuse. It was his only exit. He'd already had his hand on the doorknob, the Maserati in his head sinking, the water pouring in, choking him, over and over again.

Mei's death had left me shaken, Dick North's death sad and resigned. But Gotanda's death lay me down in a lead-lined box of despair. Gotanda's death was unsalvageable. Gotanda never really got himself in tune with his inner impulses. He pushed himself as far as he could, to the furthest edge of his awareness—and then right across the line into that dark otherworld.

For a while, the weeklies and TV and sports tabloids feasted on his death. Like beetles on carrion. The headlines alone were enough to make me vomit. I felt like throttling every scandalmonger in town.

I climbed into bed and shut my eyes. *Cuck–koo,* I heard Mei far off in the darkness.

I lay there, hating everything. The deaths were beyond comprehension, the aftertaste sickening. The world of the living was obscene. I was powerless to do anything. People came and went, but once gone, they never came back. My hands smelled of death. *I wouldn't be able to wash it off*, like Gotanda said.

Hey, Sheep Man, is this the way you connect your world? Threading one death to another? You said it might already be too late for me to be happy. I wouldn't have minded that, but why this?

When I was little, I had this science book. There was a section on "What would happen to the world if there was no friction?" Answer: "Everything on earth would fly into space from the centrifugal force of revolution." That was my mood.

41

Three days after Gotanda plowed the Maserati into the sea I called Yuki. To be honest, I didn't want to speak to anyone, but her of all people I *had* to talk to. She was vulnerable and lonely. A child. And I may have been the only person in the world who would hear her out. Then again, more importantly, *Yuki was alive*. And I had a duty to keep her that way. At least, that's what I felt.

Yuki wasn't in Hakone. A groggy Amé answered the phone and said that Yuki had left two days earlier to return to the Akasaka condo.

I called Akasaka. Yuki snatched up the receiver immediately. She must have been right beside the phone.

"It's okay for you to be away from Hakone?" I asked.

"I don't know. But I needed to be alone. Mama's an adult, right? She ought to be all right on her own. I wanted to think about myself. Things like what to do from here on. I think it's time I start to get serious about my life."

"Well, maybe so."

"I saw the papers. That friend of yours, he died, huh?"

"Yes, the Curse of the Maserati. As you warned me."

Yuki did not answer. The silence seeped through the wires. I switched the receiver from the right ear to the left.

"How about a meal?" I asked. "I know you've only been eating junk, right? I haven't been eating too well myself. Let's get ourselves a better class of grub."

"I've got to meet somebody at two, but before that I'm okay."

I looked at the clock. A little past eleven.

"Fine. I'll get ready now. See you in about thirty minutes," I said.

I changed clothes, took a swig of orange juice, pocketed my wallet and keys. I'm off, I thought. Or no? Had I forgotten something? Right, I'm always off. I'd forgotten to shave. I ran over my beard with a razor, then sized myself up in the mirror. Could I still pass for a guy in his twenties? Maybe. Maybe not. But did anybody care? I brushed my teeth again.

Outside it was sunny. Summer coming on. If only the rainy season could be put on hold. Sunglasses on, I drove to Yuki's condo. I rang the bell at the entrance to her building and Yuki came right down. She was wearing a short-sleeve dress and sandals, and carried a shoulder bag.

"You're looking very chic today," I said.

"I told you I had to see someone at two, didn't I?" she replied.

"It suits you, your dress. Very becoming, very adult."

She smiled but said nothing.

It was a bit before twelve, so we had the restaurant to ourselves. We filled up on soup and pasta and sea bass and salad. By the time the tide of salarymen washed in, we were out of there.

"Where to?" I asked.

"Nowhere. Just drive around," she said.

"Antisocial. Waste of gasoline," I said, but Yuki let it drop, pretending not to hear.

Instead she turned on the stereo. Talking Heads, *Fear of Music*. When did I ever put that tape in the deck?

"I decided to get a tutor," she said. "That's who I'm meeting today. I told Papa I wanted to study, and he found her for me. She seems like a real good person. Strange, but seeing that movie made me want to learn."

"What movie? *Unrequited Love?*"

"That's right. Sounds crazy, I know. Even sounds crazy to me. Maybe your friend playing the teacher made me feel like studying. At first, I thought, gimme a break, but I must have gotten hooked. Maybe he did have talent."

"Yeah, he had talent. He could act. If it was fiction. Not reality, if you get what I mean."

"I think so."

"You should have seen him as a dentist. He told me *that* was acting. . . . Anyway, wanting to do something is a good sign. You can't really go on living without it. I think Gotanda would be pleased to hear it."

"Did you see him?"

"I did," I said. "I saw him and we talked. We talked a long time. A very honest talk. And then he died, just like that. He was talking with me, then he gunned the Maserati into the Bay."

"Because of me?"

"No, not because of you." I shook my head slowly. "It's not your fault. It's nobody's fault. People have their own reasons for dying. It might look simple, but it never is. It's just like a root. What's above ground is only a small part of it. But if you start pulling, it keeps coming and coming. The human mind dwells deep in darkness. Only the person himself knows the real reason, and maybe not even then."

He'd been waiting for an excuse. He'd already had his hand on the doorknob.

No, it was nobody's fault after all.

"Still, I know you hate me for it," said Yuki.

"I don't hate you."

"You may not hate me now, but you will later."

"Not now, not later. I don't hate like that."

"Well, maybe not hate, but something's going to go away," she murmured, half to herself. "I just know it."

I glanced over at her. "Strange. Gotanda said the same thing."

"Really?"

"Yeah. He said he had the feeling things were disappearing on him. I don't know what kind of things he meant. But whatever they are, sometime they're going to go. We shift around, so things can't help but go when that happens. They disappear when it's time for them to disappear. And they don't disappear until it's time for them to disappear. Like that dress you got on. In a couple of years, it won't fit you, and you might even think the Talking Heads are moldy oldies. You might not even want to go on drives with me anymore. Can't be helped. As they say, just go with the flow. Don't fight it."

"I'll always like you. That has nothing to do with time."

"Makes me happy to hear that, because I want to think so too," I said. "But to be fair, Yuki, you still don't know much about time. It's better not to go deciding too many things now. People go through changes like you'd never believe."

She was silent. The tape auto-reversed to side B.

Summer. Wherever you looked, the town looked like summer. Cops and high school kids and bus drivers were all in short sleeves. There were even women in no sleeves. And to think not so long ago it had been snowing.

"And you really don't hate me?"

"Of course not," I said. "In this uncertain world, that's about the only thing I'm sure of."

"Absolutely?"

"Absolutely 2,500 percent."

She smiled. "That's what I wanted to hear." Then she asked, "You liked Gotanda, didn't you?"

"I liked him, sure," I said. Suddenly my voice caught. Tears welled up. I barely managed to fight them back and took a deep breath. "Each time we met I liked him more. That doesn't happen very much, especially not at my age."

"Did he kill the woman?"

I scanned the early summer cityscape for a moment. "Who knows? Maybe he did and maybe he didn't."

He'd been waiting for an excuse.

Yuki leaned on her window and looked out, listening to her Talking Heads. She seemed a little more grown-up than when we first met, only two and a half months before.

"What are you going to do now?" asked Yuki.

"Yes, what am I going to do," I said. "I haven't decided. I think I've got to go back to Sapporo. Tomorrow or the day after tomorrow. Lots of loose ends up there."

Yumiyoshi. The Sheep Man. The Dolphin Hotel. A place that I was a part of. Where someone was crying for me. I had to go back to close the circle.

I offered to drive Yuki wherever she had to go. "Heaven knows, I'm free today."

She smiled. "Thanks, but it's okay. It's pretty far; the train'll be faster."

"Did I hear you say thanks?" I said, removing my sunglasses.

"Got any problems with that?"

"Nope."

We were at Yoyogi-Hachiman Station, where she was going to catch the Odakyu Line. Yuki looked at me for ten or fifteen seconds. No identifiable expression on her face, only a gradual change in the gleam of her eyes, the shape of her mouth. Ever so slightly, her lips grew taut, her stare sharp and sassy. Like a slice of summer sunlight refracting in water.

She slammed the door shut and trotted off, not looking back. I watched her receding figure disappear into the crowd. And when she was out of sight, I felt lonely, as if a love affair had just broken up.

I drove back up Omotesando to Aoyama to go shopping at Kinokuniya, but the parking lot was full. Hey, come to think of it, wasn't I going to Sapporo tomorrow or the day after? So I cruised around a bit more, then went home. To my empty apartment. Where I plopped down on the bed and stared up at the ceiling.

They've got a name for this, I thought. *Loss. Bereavement.* Not nice words.

Cuck–koo.

It echoed through the empty space of my home.

42

I had a dream about Kiki. I guess it was a dream. Either that or some act akin to dreaming. What, you may ask, is an "act akin to dreaming"? I don't know either. But it seems it does exist. Like so many other things we have no name for, existing in that limbo beyond the fringes of consciousness.

But let's just call it a dream, plain and simple. The expression is closest to something real for us.

It was near dawn when I had this dream about Kiki.

In the dream as well, it was near dawn.

I'm on the phone. An international call. I've dialed the number that Kiki apparently left me on the windowsill of that room in downtown Honolulu. *Beepbeepbeep beep beepbeep beepbeep* . . . I can hear the phone lines connecting. I'm getting through. Or so I think. The numbers are linking up in order. A brief interval, a short dial tone. I press the receiver to my ear and count the muffled reports. Five, six, seven, eight rings. At the twelfth ring, someone answers. And in that instant, I'm in that room. That big, empty death chamber in downtown Honolulu. It seems to be daytime. Noon, judging from the light pouring straight down through the skylight. Flecks of dust dance in these upright shafts of light, bright as a southern sun and sharp as gashes from a knife. Yet the parts of the room without light are murky and cold. The contrast is remarkable. Like the ocean floor, I'm thinking.

I'm sitting on a sofa there in the room, receiver at my ear. The telephone cord trails away over the floor, across a dark area, through the light, to disappear again into the gloom. A long, long cord. Longer than any I've seen. I've got the phone on my lap and I'm looking around the room.

The furniture in the room is the same as it was. The same pieces in the same places. Bed, table, sofa, chairs, TV, floor lamp. Spaced unnaturally apart. And the room has the same smell as before. Stale and moldy, a shut-in air of disuse. But the six skeletons are gone. Not on the bed, not on the sofa, not in the chair in front of the TV, not at the dining table. They've all disappeared. As have the scraps of food and plates from the table. I set the telephone down on the sofa and stand up. I have a slight headache. The kind you get when there's a high-pitched hum in your ears. I sit back down.

I detect a movement from the farthest chair off in the gloom. I strain my eyes. Someone or something has gotten up and I hear footsteps coming my way. It's Kiki. She appears from out of the darkness, cuts across the light, takes a chair at the dining table. She's wearing the same outfit as before. Blue dress and white shoulder bag.

She sits there, sizing me up. She is quiet, her expression tranquil. She is positioned neither in light nor in darkness, but exactly in between. I'm about to get up and go over to her, but have second thoughts. There's still that slight pain in my temples.

"The skeletons go somewhere?" I ask.

"I suppose," says Kiki with a smile.

"Did you dispose of them?"

"No, they just vanished. Maybe you disposed of them?"

Eyeing the telephone beside me, I press my fingers to my temples.

"What's it mean? Those six skeletons?"

"They're you," says Kiki. "This is your room. Everything here is you. Yourself. Everything."

"My room," I repeat after her. "Well, then, what about the Dolphin Hotel? What's there?"

"That's your place too. Of course. The Sheep Man's there. And I'm here."

The shafts of light do not waver. They are hard, uniform. Only the air vibrates minutely in them. I notice it without really looking.

"I seem to have rooms in a lot of places," I say. "You know, I kept having these dreams. About the Dolphin Hotel. And somebody there, who's crying for me. I had that same dream almost every night. The Dolphin Hotel stretches out long and narrow, and there's someone there, crying for me. I thought it was you. So I knew I had to see you."

"Everyone's crying for you," says Kiki, ever so softly, in a voice to soothe worn nerves. "After all, that whole place is for you. Everyone there cries for you."

"But you were calling me. That's why I went back, to see you. And then from there . . . a lot of things started. Just like before. I met all sorts of folks. People died. But, you did call me, didn't you? It was you who guided me along, wasn't it?"

"It wasn't me. It was you who called yourself. I'm merely a projection. You guided yourself, through me. I'm your phantom dance partner. I'm your shadow. I'm not anything more."

But I wasn't strangling her, I was strangling my shadow. If only I could choke off my shadow, I'd get some health.

"But why would everyone cry for me?"

She doesn't answer. She rises, and with a tapping of footsteps, walks over to stand before me. Then she kneels and reaches out to touch my lips with her fingertips. Her fingers are sleek and smooth. Then she touches my temples.

"We're crying for all the things you can't cry for," whispers Kiki. Slowly, as if to spell it out. "We shed tears for all the things you never let yourself shed tears, we weep for all the things you did not weep."

"Are your ears still . . . like they were?" I'm curious.

"My ears—," she breaks off into a smile. "They're in perfect shape. The same as they were."

"Would you show me your ears again, just one more time?" I ask. "It was an experience like I've never known, as if the whole world was reborn. In that restaurant that time, you knocked me out. I've never forgotten it."

She shakes her head. "Maybe sometime," she says. "But not today. They're not something you can see at any moment. It's something to see only at the right time. That was a right time. Today is not. I'll show you again sometime, when you really need it."

She stands back up and into a vertical shaft of illumination from above. She stays there, her body almost decomposing amid the specks of strong light.

"Tell me, Kiki, are you dead?" I ask.

She spins around in the light to face me.

"Gotanda thinks he killed me," says Kiki.

"Yes, he does. Or he did."

"Maybe he did kill me. For him it's like that. In his mind, he killed me. That's what he needed. If he didn't kill me, he'd still be stuck. Poor man," says Kiki. "But I'm not dead. I just disappeared. I do that. I move into another world, a different world. Like boarding a train running parallel. That's what disappearing is. Don't you see?"

No, I don't, I say.

"It's simple. Watch."

With those words, Kiki walks across the floor, headlong toward the wall. Her pace does not slacken, even on reaching the wall. She is swallowed up into the wall. Her footsteps likewise vanish.

I keep watching the wall where she was swallowed up. It's just a wall. The room is silent. There's only the specks of light sifting through the air. My head throbs. I press my fingers to my temples and keep my eyes on the wall. When I think of it, of that time in Honolulu, she'd vanished into a wall too.

"Well? Simple enough?" I hear Kiki's voice. "Now you try."

"You think I can?"

"I said it's simple, didn't I? Go ahead, give it a try. Walk straight on as you are. Don't stop. Then you'll get to this side. Don't be afraid. There's nothing to be afraid about."

I grab the telephone and stand up, then walk, dragging the cord, straight toward the wall where she disappeared. I get wary as the wall looms up, but I do not slacken my pace. Even as I touch the wall, there is no impact. My body just passes through, as it might a transparent air pocket. Only the air seems to change a bit. I'm still carrying the telephone as I pass through and I'm back in my bedroom, in my own apartment. I sit down on the bed, with the phone on my lap. "Simple," I say. "Very, very simple."

I put the receiver to my ear, but the line is dead.

So went the dream. Or whatever it was.

43

When I got back to the Dolphin Hotel, three female receptionists stood behind the front desk. As ever, they were uniformed in neatly pressed blazers and spotless white blouses. They greeted me with smiles. Yumiyoshi was not among them. Which upset me. Or rather, it tipped over all my hopes. I'd been counting so much on being able to see Yumiyoshi right away that I could hardly pronounce my own name when asked. As a result, the receptionist wavered slightly behind her smile and eyed my credit card suspiciously as she ran a computer check.

I was given a room on the seventeenth floor. I dropped my bag, washed up, and went back down to the lobby. Then I sat on the sofa and pretended to read a magazine, while casting occasional glances at the front desk. Maybe Yumiyoshi was on a break. After forty minutes she still had not shown. Still the same three indistinguishable women with identical hairstyles on duty. After one hour, I gave up.

I went out into town and bought the evening paper. Then I went into a café and read the thing from front to back over a cup of coffee, hoping for some article of interest.

There wasn't. Not a thing about either Gotanda or Mei. Notices of other murders, though, other suicides. As I read, I was hoping Yumiyoshi would be standing behind the counter when I got back to the hotel.

No such luck.

Had she for some unknown reason suddenly vanished? Walked into a wall? I felt a terrible uneasiness. I tried calling her at home; no answer. Finally I telephoned the front desk. Yumiyoshi had taken "a leave of absence." She'd be back on duty the day after next. Brilliant, I thought, why hadn't I called her before I showed up?

I'd worked myself up into such a state that it hadn't entered my mind to do something as obvious as that. What a dummy! And when was the last time I'd called her anyway? Not once since Gotanda died. And who knows when before that. Maybe not since Yuki threw up on the beach. How long ago was that? I'd forgotten about Yumiyoshi. I had no idea what might have happened with her. And things do happen.

I was suddenly shaken. What if Yumiyoshi had disappeared into a wall, and I'd never see her again? Yes, one more corpse to go. I didn't want to think about it. I started hyperventilating. I had trouble breathing. My heart swelled big enough to burst through my chest. Did this mean I was in love with Yumiyoshi? I had to see her face-to-face to know for sure. I called her apartment, over and over, so many times my fingers hurt. No answer.

I couldn't sleep. I lay in my hotel bed, sweating. I switched on the light and looked at the clock. Two o'clock. Three-fifteen. Four-twenty. After that, I gave up. I sat by the window and watched the city grow light to the beating of my heart.

Yumiyoshi, don't leave me alone. I need you. I don't want to be alone anymore. Without you I'll be flung out to the far corners of the universe. Show your face, please, tie me down somewhere. Tie me to this world. I don't want to join the ghosts. I'm just an ordinary guy. I need you.

From six-thirty in the morning I dialed her apartment at half-hour intervals. To no avail.

June in Sapporo is a wonderful time of year. The snow has long since melted, the plains that were frozen tundra a few months earlier are dark and fertile. Life breathes everywhere. The trees are thick with foliage, the leaves sway in the breeze. The sky is high and clear, crisply outlining the clouds. An inspirational season. Yet here I was in my hotel room dialing Yumiyoshi's number like a maniac. She'll be back tomorrow—what was my rush? I must have told myself this every ten minutes. I couldn't wait. Who could guarantee she'd come back tomorrow? I sat by the phone and kept dialing. And then I sprawled out on the bed and stared up at the ceiling.

Here is where the old Dolphin Hotel used to stand. It was the pits of a hotel. Untold others stayed there, stepped in the grooves in the floor, saw the spots on the wall. I sat deep in my chair, feet on the table, eyes closed, picturing the old place. The shape of the front door, the worn-out carpeting, the tarnished brass keys, the corners of window frames thick with dust. I'd walked those halls, opened those doors, entered those rooms.

The old Dolphin Hotel had disappeared. Yet its presence lingered on. Beneath this new intercontinental Dolphin, behind it, within it. I could close my eyes and go in. The *cr-cr-crr-creaking* of the elevator, like an old dog wheezing. It was still here. No one knew, but it was here. This place was my nexus, where everything tied together. This place is here for me, I told myself. Yumiyoshi *had* to come back. All I had to do was sit tight and wait.

I had room service bring up dinner, which I accompanied with a beer from the mini-bar. And at eight o'clock I tried Yumiyoshi's number again. No answer again.

I turned on the TV and watched baseball, with the sound off. It was a lousy game. I didn't want to watch baseball anyway. I wanted to see live human bodies in action. Badminton, water polo, anything would have done as well.

At nine o'clock I tried calling again. This time, she picked up after one ring. At first I couldn't believe she was actually there. I was cut to the quick, a lump of air stuck in my throat. Yumiyoshi was actually there.

"I just got back this minute," said Yumiyoshi, utterly cool. "I went to Tokyo to see relatives. I called your place twice, but nobody answered."

"I'm up here in Sapporo and I've been calling *you* like crazy."

"So we nearly missed each other."

"Nearly missed," was all I could bring myself to say, tightly gripping the receiver and peering at the muted TV screen. Words would not come. I was caught off-guard, impossibly confused.

"Hey, are you there? Hello? Hello?"

"I'm here all right."

"Your voice sounds strange."

"I . . . I'm nervous," I explained. "I've got to see you or I can't talk. I've been on edge all day. I've got to see you."

"I think I can see you tomorrow night," she said after a moment's thought. I could just picture her pushing her glasses up on the bridge of her nose.

Receiver fast to my ear, I lowered myself onto the floor and leaned back against the wall. "Tomorrow's a long way off. I kind of think it'd be better to meet tonight. Right away, in fact."

A negative air came to her voice. Even if that voice hadn't said anything yet, the negative came across. "I'm too tired now. I'm exhausted. I just got back. And since I'm on duty tomorrow morning, tonight I just want to sleep. Tomorrow, after I get off, let's get together. How about that? Or won't you be around tomorrow?"

"No, I'll be here for a while. And I do sympathize with your being tired. Only, honestly, I'm worried. Like maybe by tomorrow you'll have disappeared."

"Disappeared?"

"Disappeared. Vanished."

Yumiyoshi laughed. "I don't disappear so easily. I'm not going anywhere."

"No, it's not like that. You don't understand. We keep moving. And as we do, things around us, well, they disappear. I know I'm not entirely coherent, but that's what worries me. Yumiyoshi, I need you. I mean, I really need you. Like I've never needed anything before. Please don't disappear on me."

Yumiyoshi paused for a moment. "Golly," she said. "I promise. I won't disappear. I'll see you tomorrow. So please just wait until then."

"Okay," I said. I had no choice but to be satisfied—though I wasn't—with her assurances.

"Good night then," she said, and hung up.

I paced around the room, then went up to the lounge on the twenty-sixth floor, the lounge where I'd first seen Yuki. The place was crowded. Two young women were drinking at the bar, both very fashionably dressed, one with beautiful legs. I sat, nursing my vodka tonic, and eyed them with no special intentions. Then I turned my gaze to the night skyline. I pressed my fingers to my temples, though I did not have a headache. Then I felt the shape of my skull, slowly tracing the shape of bone matter beneath the skin, imagining the skeletons of the women at the bar. Skull, vertebrae, sternum, pelvis, arms, legs, joints. Beautiful white bones inside those beautiful legs. Pristine, white as clouds, expressionless. Miss Legs looked my way, undoubtedly aware of my stare. I would have liked to explain. That I wasn't looking at her body. That I was only thinking about her bones!

I had three drinks, then returned to my room. Having reached Yumiyoshi at last, I slept like a dream.

Yumiyoshi showed up at three in the morning. The doorbell rang, I turned on the bedside lamp, and looked at the clock. Then throwing on a bathrobe, I went to the door, innocently, three-quarters asleep. I cracked it open. And there she was, in her light blue uniform blazer. She stepped into the room through the narrow opening, like she always did.

She stood in the middle of the room and breathed deeply. Without a sound she removed her blazer and folded it carefully over the back of the chair. The same as ever.

"Well, I haven't disappeared, have I?" was the first thing she said.

"No, it doesn't look like you've disappeared," came my voice from somewhere. I couldn't quite grasp whether this was actually happening or not.

"People don't disappear so easily," she spoke deliberately.

"You just don't know. Lots of things can happen in this world. You name it."

"Perhaps, but I'm here. I haven't disappeared. You *do* admit that, don't you?"

I glanced around the room and looked Yumiyoshi in the eye. This was real waking reality. "Yes, I admit it. You don't seem to have disappeared. But what brings you to my room at three in the morning?"

"I couldn't sleep," she said. "I went to bed right after you called, but my eyes popped wide open at a little past one and I didn't sleep a wink after that. What you said kind of got to me. So I called a taxi and came here."

"Didn't anyone think it was strange, you showing up at three in the morning?"

"Nobody noticed. Everyone's asleep. The hotel keeps going twenty-four hours, but the only people awake at three A.M. are the front desk and room service. Nobody's hanging around the employees' entrance. And nobody keeps track anyway. You can always say you came to sleep in the sleep room. I've done it plenty of times before."

"You've done this before?"

"Yes, when I couldn't sleep. I come and wander around. I know this sounds strange, but it's very restful. And, well, I like it. No one ever notices. It's not a problem. Of course, if they found me in this room, that's another story. But don't worry, I'll stay until morning and slip out to work. Okay?"

"Of course it's okay by me. What time do you have to be on duty?"

"Eight," she said. "Another five hours."

Yumiyoshi nervously removed her watch and laid it down on the table. Then she straightened her skirt. I sat down on the corner of the bed, having slowly awakened to the circumstances. "So now," said she, "did I hear you say you need me?"

"Like crazy," I said. "I've been all around. I've made a complete revolution. And I've come back to the fact that I need you."

"Like crazy," she reminded me, tugging at the hem of her skirt.

"That's right, like crazy."

"Just where all around have you been?"

"You wouldn't believe it if I told you. I've made it back to reality—that's the important thing. I've come full circle. And I'm still on my feet, dancing."

She looked at me quizzically.

"I can't go into details. Just believe me. I need you. That's very important, to me anyway. Maybe it could be important to you too."

"So what do you want me to do?" said Yumiyoshi, with no change of expression. "Fall into your arms? Be moved to tears? Tell you how wonderful it is to be wanted?"

"No, no, nothing like that," I said quickly, but then couldn't find the right words to go on. As if there were right words. "What can I tell you? I've known it all along and never doubted it. I knew that we would sleep together. Only at first we couldn't. The timing wasn't right. It had to wait until it was right."

"So now I'm supposed to sleep with you? Just like that?"

"I know the argument's short-circuited. And I know it's the worst possible way to convince you. But to be honest, that's what it comes down to. I can't help how the words come out. I mean, with me too, if these were normal circumstances, I'd try to do things in the proper order. I'm not that much of a dud. But this is a very simple thing, and this approach is truer. I know it. Which is why I can't express it any other way. I've always known that we would sleep together. It's decided, it's fact. And we shouldn't go fiddling around with that. That might ruin everything. Honest!"

Yumiyoshi eyed her watch. "You do realize you're not making much sense, don't you?" she said. Then she sighed and began to unbutton her blouse. "Don't look."

I lay back on the bed and gazed up at a corner of the ceiling. There's another world somewhere, but now I'm here, in this one. Yumiyoshi undressed slowly. I could hear soft sounds of fabric against skin, then the sound of folding. Then the sound of her glasses being set down. A very sexy sound. And then she was turning out the bedside lamp and sliding under the covers next to me. As quietly as she'd stolen into my room.

We touched. Her body and mine. Smooth, but with a certain gravity. Yes, this was real. Unlike with Mei. Mei had been a dream, fantasy, illusion. *Cuck–koo.* But Yumiyoshi existed in the real world. Her warmth and weight and vitality were real. I caressed her and held her.

Gotanda's fingers trailing down Kiki's back was also illusion. It was acting, light flickering on a screen, a shadow slipping between one world and another. It was not reality. *Cuck–koo.*

My real fingers were stroking Yumiyoshi's real skin.

Yumiyoshi buried her face in my neck. I felt the touch of her nose. I searched out every part of her body. Shoulder, elbow, wrist, palm, the tips of ten fingers. My fingers explored and my lips kissed. Her breasts, her stomach, her sides and back and legs, each form registered and sealed. I needed to be sure. I ran my fingers over her pubis. I moved down and kissed it. *Cuck–koo.*

We did not speak. We held each other. Her breath was warm and wet. Words that were not words hung in the air. I entered her. I was hard, very hard, and full of desire.

Toward climax, Yumiyoshi bit my arm, enough to draw blood. The pain was real. I held her hips and slowly eased into ejaculation. Ever so slowly, sure not to miss a step.

At seven I woke her. "Yumiyoshi, time to get up," I said.

She opened her eyes and looked at me. Then slid out of bed like a fish and stood naked in the morning light. She seemed full of new life, alive. I propped myself on my pillow and admired her. The body I'd registered and sealed a few hours before.

Yumiyoshi showered and brushed her hair with my brush and got dressed. I watched her put on each article of clothing, the care she took doing up each button. Her blazer was next, then she checked in the mirror for wrinkles. She was very serious about these things. Her attitude said "morning." "My makeup is down in my locker," she announced.

"You're beautiful as you are," I said.

"Thanks. But makeup is a part of the job. I don't have a choice."

I gave Yumiyoshi a hug. It was so good to hold her with her glasses and blazer on.

"You still want me, now that it's morning?" she asked.

"I still want you," I said. "I want you more than I wanted you yesterday."

"I've never had anyone want me so much before."

"No one's ever wanted you?"

"Not the way you do," she said. "It's like being in a nice, warm room. Nice and cozy."

"Well, stay put. There's no reason ever to leave."

"Are *you* going to stay put?"

"Yes, I'm going to stay put."

Yumiyoshi pulled back a bit. "Can I come stay with you again tonight?"

"Absolutely. But aren't the risks too high? Wouldn't it be better if I went to your place or stayed in another hotel?"

"No," she said, "I like it here. This is your place, and it's also my place. I want to make love with you here. That is, if it's all right with you."

"I want to make love with you wherever you like."

"Okay, I'll see you this evening. Here." Then she cracked the door open and slipped away.

I felt happy. Yes, I felt happy. And then I wondered if, maybe, it was time to give up the shoveling habit. Do some writing for myself for a change. Without the deadlines. Something for myself. Not a novel or anything. But something for myself.

44

Yumiyoshi came back at six-thirty. Still in uniform, although her blouse was different. She'd brought a bag with a change of clothes and toiletries and cosmetics.

"I don't know," I said. "They're going to find out some time."

"Don't worry, I'm not careless," she said, then smiled and draped her blazer over the back of a chair.

Then we sat on the sofa and held each other tight.

"I've thought about you all day long," she said. "You know, wouldn't it be wonderful if I could work during the daytime, then sneak into your room at night? We'd spend the night together, then in the morning I'd go straight to work?"

"A home convenient to your workplace," I joked. "Unfortunately I couldn't keep footing the tab to this room. And sooner or later, they'll find out about us."

"Nothing goes smoothly in this world."

"You can say that again."

"But it'd be okay for a few more nights, wouldn't it?"

"I imagine that's what's going to happen."

"Good. I'll be happy with those few days. Let's both stay in this hotel."

Then she undressed, neatly folding each article of clothing. She removed her watch and her glasses, and placed them on the table. Then we enjoyed an hour of lovemaking, until we were both exhausted. No better kind of exhaustion.

"Mmm," was Yumiyoshi's appraisal. Then she snuggled up in my arms for a nap. After a while, I got up, showered, then drank a beer. I sat, admiring Yumiyoshi's sleeping face. She slept so nice.

A little before eight, she awoke, hungry. We ordered a sandwich and pasta au gratin from room service. Meanwhile, she stored her things in the closet, and when the bellhop knocked, she hid in the bathroom.

We ate happily.

"I've been thinking about it all afternoon," I began, picking up from our earlier conversation. "There's nothing for me in Tokyo anymore. I could move up here and look for work."

"You'd live here?"

"That's right, I'd live here," I said.

"I'll rent an apartment and start a new life here. You can come over whenever you want to. You can spend the night if you feel like it. We can try it out like that for a while. But I've got the feeling it's going to work out. It'll bring me back to reality. It'll give you space to relax. And it'll keep us together."

Yumiyoshi smiled and gave me a big kiss. "*Fan*tastic!"

"What comes later, I don't know. But I've got a good feeling about it. Like I said."

"Nobody knows what's going to happen in the future. I'm not worried about that. Right now, it's just fantastic! Oooh, the best kind of fantastic!"

I called room service for a bucket of ice, making Yumiyoshi hide in the bathroom again. And while she was in there, I took out the bottle of vodka and tomato juice I'd bought in town that afternoon and made us two Bloody Marys. No lemon slices or Lea & Perrins, but bloody good enough. We toasted. To us. I switched on the bedside Muzak and punched the Pops channel. Soon we were treated to the lush strains of Mantovani playing "Strangers in the Night."

You didn't hear me making snide comments.

"You think of everything," said Yumiyoshi. "I was just dreaming of a Bloody Mary right about now. How did you know?"

"If you listen carefully, you can hear these things. If you look carefully, you'll see what you're after."

"Words of wisdom?"

"No, just words. A way of life in words."

"You ought to specialize in inspirational writing."

We had three Bloody Marys each. Then we took our clothes off and gently made love again.

At one point, in the middle of our lovemaking, I thought I could hear that old Dolphin Hotel elevator *cr-cr-crr-creaking* up the shaft. Yes, this place was the knot, the node. Here's where it all tied together and I was a part of it all. Here was reality, I didn't have to go further. I was already there. All I had to do was to recover the knot to be connected. It's what I'd been seeking for years. What the Sheep Man held together.

At midnight, we fell asleep.

Yumiyoshi was shaking me. "Wake up," she said urgently. Outside it was dark. My head was half full with the warm sludge of unconsciousness. The bedside light was on. The clock read a little after three.

She was dressed in her hotel uniform, clutching my shoulder, shaking me, looking very serious. My first thought was that her boss had found out about us.

"Wake up. Please, wake up," she said.

"I'm awake," I said. "What is it?"

"Hurry up and get dressed."

I quickly slipped on a T-shirt and jeans and windbreaker, then stepped into my sneakers. It didn't take a minute. Then Yumiyoshi led me by hand to the door, and parted it open a scant two or three centimeters.

"Look," she said. I peeked through the opening. The hallway was pitch black. I couldn't see a thing. The darkness was thick, gelatinous, chill. It seemed so deep that if you stuck out a hand, you'd get sucked in. And then there was that familiar smell of mold, like old paper. A smell that had been brewed in the pit of time.

"It's that darkness again," she said.

I put my arm around her waist and drew her close. "It's nothing to be afraid of," I said. "Don't be scared. Nothing bad is going to happen. This is my world. The first time you ever talked to me was because of this darkness. That's how we got to know each other. Really, it's all right."

And yet I wasn't so sure. In fact, I was terrified out of my skin. Thoroughly unhinged, despite my own calm talk. The fear was palpable, fundamental; it was universal, historical, genetic. For darkness terrifies. It swallows you, warps you, nullifies you. Who alive can possibly profess confidence in darkness? In the dark, you can't *see*. Things can twist, turn, vanish. The essence of darkness—nothingness—covers all.

"It's okay," I was now trying to convince myself. "Nothing to be afraid of."

"So what do we do?" asked Yumiyoshi.

I went and quickly got the penlight and Bic lighter I'd brought just in case this very thing happened.

"We have to go through it together," I said. "I returned to this hotel to see two people. You were one. The other is a guy standing somewhere out there in the dark. He's waiting for me."

"The person who was in that room?"

"Yes."

"I'm scared. I'm *really* scared," said Yumiyoshi, trembling. Who could blame her?

I kissed her on her brow. "Don't be afraid. I'm with you. Give me your hand. If we don't let go, we'll be safe. No matter what happens, we mustn't let go. You understand? We have to stay together." Then we stepped into the corridor.

"Which way do we go?" she asked nervously.

"To the right," I said. "Always to the right."

We shined the light at our feet and walked, slowly, deliberately. As before, the corridor was no longer in the new Dolphin Hotel. The red carpet was worn, the floor sagging, the plaster walls stained with liver spots. It was *like* the old Dolphin Hotel, though it was *not* the old Dolphin Hotel. A little ways on, as before, the corridor turned right. We turned, but now something was different. There was no light ahead, no door leaking candlelight. I switched off my penlight to be certain. No light at all, none.

Yumiyoshi held my hand tightly.

"Where's that door?" I said, my voice sounding dry and dead, hardly my voice at all. "Before when I—"

"Me too. I saw a door somewhere."

We stood there at the turn in the corridor. What happened to the Sheep Man? Was he asleep? Wouldn't he have left the light on? As a beacon? Wasn't that the whole reason he was here? What the hell's going on?

"Let's go back," Yumiyoshi said. "I don't like the darkness. We can try again another time. I don't want to press our luck."

She had a point. I didn't like the darkness either, and I had the foreboding feeling that something had gone awry. Yet I refused to give up.

"Let's keep going," I said. "The guy might need us. That's why we're still tied to this world." I switched the penlight back on. A narrow beam of yellow light pierced the darkness. "Hold on to my hand now. I need to know we're together. But there's nothing to be afraid of. We're staying, we're not going away. We'll get back safe and sound."

Step by step, even more slowly and deliberately, we went forward. The faint scent of Yumiyoshi's hair drifted through the darkness, sweetly pricking my senses. Her hand was small and warm and solid.

And then we saw it. The door to the Sheep Man's room had been left slightly ajar, and through the opening we could feel the old chill, smell the dank odor. I knocked. As before, the knock sounded unnaturally loud. Three times I knocked.

Then we waited. Twenty seconds, thirty seconds. No response. Where is he? What's going on? Don't tell me he died! True, the guy was not looking well the last time we met. He couldn't live forever. He too had to grow old and die. But if he died, who would keep me connected to this world?

I pushed the door open and pulled Yumiyoshi with me into the room. I shined my penlight around. The room had not changed. Old books and papers piled everywhere, a tiny table, and on it the plate used as a candle stand, with a five-centimeter stub of wax on it. I used my Bic to light it.

The Sheep Man was not here.

Had he stepped out for a second?

"Who was this guy?" asked Yumiyoshi.

"The Sheep Man," I said. "He takes care of this world here. He sees that things are tied together, makes sure connections are made. He said he was kind of like a switchboard. He's ages old, and he wears a sheepskin. This is where he's been living. In hiding."

"In hiding from what?"

"From war, civilization, the law, the system, . . . things that aren't Sheep Man-like."

"But he's not here. He's gone."

I nodded. And as I did a huge shadow bowed across the wall. "Yes, he's gone. Even though he's supposed to be here."

We were at the edge of the world. That is, what the ancients considered the edge of the world, where everything spilled over into nothingness. We were there, the two of us, alone. And all around us, a cold, vast void. We held each other's hand more tightly.

"Maybe he's dead," I said.

"How can you say a thing like that in the dark? Think more positively," said Yumiyoshi. "He could be off shopping, right? He probably ran out of candles."

"Or else he's gone to collect his tax refund." Even in the candlelit gloom I could see Yumiyoshi smile. We hugged each other. "You know," I said, "on our days off, let's drive to lots of places."

"Sure," she said.

"I'll ship my Subaru up. It's an old car, but it's a good car. It runs just fine. I like it better than a Maserati. I really do."

"Of course," she said. "Let's go everywhere and see lots of things together."

We embraced a little longer. Then Yumiyoshi stooped to pick up a pamphlet from the pile of papers that was lying at her feet. *Studies in the Varietal Breeding of Yorkshire Sheep*. It was browned with age, covered with dust.

"Everything in this room has to do with sheep," I explained. "In the old Dolphin Hotel, a whole floor was devoted to sheep research. There was this Sheep Professor, who was the father of the hotel manager. And I guess the Sheep Man inherited all this stuff. It's not good for anything anymore. Nobody's ever going to read this stuff. Still, the Sheep Man looks after it."

Yumiyoshi took the penlight from me and leafed through the pamphlet. I was casually observing my own shadow, wondering where the Sheep Man was, when I was suddenly struck by a horrifying realization: I'd let go of Yumiyoshi's hand!

My heart leapt into my throat. I was not ever to let go of her hand. I was fevered and swimming in sweat. I rushed to grab Yumiyoshi by the wrist. *If we don't let go, we'll be safe.* But it was already too late. At the very moment I extended my hand, her body was absorbed into the wall. Just like Kiki had passed through the wall of the death chamber. Just like quicksand. She was gone, she had disappeared, together with the glow of the penlight.

"Yumiyoshi!" I yelled.

No one answered. Silence and cold reigned, the darkness deepened.

"Yumiyoshi!" I yelled again.

"Hey, it's simple," came Yumiyoshi's voice from beyond the wall. "Really simple. You can pass right through the wall."

"No!" I screamed. "Don't be tricked. You think it's simple, but you'll never get back. It's different over there. That's the otherworld. It's not like here."

No answer came from her. Silence filled the room, pressing down as if I were on the ocean floor.

I was overwhelmed by my helplessness, despairing. Yumiyoshi was gone. After all this, I would never be able to reach her again. She was gone.

There was no time to think. What was there to do? I loved her, I couldn't lose her. I followed her into the wall. I found myself passing through a transparent pocket of air.

It was cool as water. Time wavered, sequentiality twisted, gravity lost its force. Memories, old memories, like vapor, wafted up. The degeneration of my flesh accelerated. I passed through the huge, complex knot of my own DNA. The earth expanded, then chilled and contracted. Sheep were submerged in the cave. The sea was one enormous idea, rain falling silently over its vastness. Faceless people stood on the beachhead gazing out to the deep. An endless spool of time unraveled across the sky. A void enveloped the phantom figures and was encompassed by a yet greater void. Flesh melted to the bone and blew away like dust. *Extremely, irrevocably dead*, said someone. *Cuck–koo*. My body decomposed, blew apart—and was whole again.

I emerged through this layer of chaos, naked, in bed. It was dark, but not the lacquer-black darkness I feared. Still, I could not see. I reached out my hand. No one was beside me. I was alone, abandoned, at the edge of the world.

"Yumiyoshi!" I screamed at the top of my lungs. But no sound emerged, except for a dry rasping in my throat. I screamed again. And then I heard a tiny click.

The light had been switched on. Yumiyoshi smiled as she sat on the sofa in her blouse and skirt and shoes. Her light blue blazer was draped over the back of the chair. My hands were clutching the sheets. I slowly relaxed my fingers, feeling the tension drain from my body. I wiped the sweat from my face. I was back on this side. The light filling the room was real light.

"Yumiyoshi," I said hoarsely.

"Yes?"

"Are you really there?"

"Of course, I'm here."

"You didn't disappear?"

"No. People don't disappear so easily."

"It was a dream then."

"I know. I was here all the time, watching you. You were sleeping and dreaming and calling my name. I watched you in the dark. I could see you, you know."

I looked at the clock. A little before four, a little before dawn. The hour when thoughts are deepest. I was cold, my body was stiff. Then it was a dream? The Sheep Man gone, Yumiyoshi disappearing, the pain and despair. But I could remember the touch of Yumiyoshi's hand. The touch was still there within me. More real than this reality.

"Yumiyoshi?"

"Yes?"

"Why are you dressed?"

"I wanted to watch you with my clothes on," she said.

"Mind getting undressed again?" I asked. It was one way to be sure.

"Not at all," she said, removing her clothes and easing under the covers. She was warm and smooth, with the weight of someone real.

"I told you people don't just disappear," she said.

Oh really? I thought as I embraced her. No, anything can happen. This world is more fragile, more tenuous than we could ever know.

Who was skeleton number six then? The Sheep Man? Someone else? Myself? Waiting in that room so dim and distant. Far off, I heard the sound of the old Dolphin Hotel, like a train in the night. The *cr-cr-crr-creaking* of the elevator, going up, up, stopping. Someone walking the halls, someone opening a door, someone closing a door. It was the old Dolphin. I could tell. Because I was part of it. And someone was crying for me. Crying for me because I couldn't cry.

I kissed Yumiyoshi on her eyelids.

She snuggled into the crook of my arm and fell asleep. But I couldn't sleep. It was impossible for my body to sleep. I was as wide awake as a dry well. I held Yumiyoshi tightly, and I cried. I cried inside. I cried for all that I'd lost and all that I'd lose. Yumiyoshi was soft as the ticking of time, her breath leaving a warm, damp spot on my arm. Reality.

Eventually dawn crept up on us. I watched the second hand on the alarm clock going around in real time. Little by little by little, onward.

I knew I would stay.

Seven o'clock came, and summer morning light eased through the window, casting a skewed rectangle on the floor.

"Yumiyoshi," I whispered. "It's morning."

Also available in Vintage

HARUKI MURAKAMI

Norwegian Wood

'Murakami must already rank among the world's greatest living novelists'
Guardian

'Evocative, entertaining, sexy and funny; but then Murakami is one of the best writers around'
Time Out

'Such is the exquisite, gossamer construction of Murakami's writing that everything he chooses to describe trembles with symbolic possibility'
Guardian

When he hears her favourite Beatles song, Toru Watanabe recalls his first love Naoko, the girlfriend of his best friend Kizuki. Immediately he is transported back almost twenty years to his student days in Tokyo, adrift in a world of uneasy friendships, casual sex, passion, loss and desire – to a time when an impetuous young woman called Midori marches into his life and he has to choose between the future and the past.

'This book is undeniably hip, full of student uprisings, free love, booze and 1960s pop, it's also genuinely emotionally engaging, and describes the highs of adolescence as well as the lows'
Independent on Sunday

VINTAGE BOOKS
London

Also available in Vintage

HARUKI MURAKAMI

The Wind-up Bird Chronicle

'Mesmerising, surreal, this really is the work of a true original'
The Times

'Murakami writes of contemporary Japan, urban alienation and journey's of self-discovery, and in this book he combines recollections of the war with metaphysics, dreams and hallucinations into a powerful and impressionistic work'
Independent

Toru Okada's cat has disappeared and this has unsettled his wife, who is herself growing more distant every day. Then there are the increasingly explicit telephone calls he has started receiving. As this compelling story unfolds, the tidy suburban realities of Okada's vague and blameless life, spent cooking, reading, listening to jazz and opera and drinking beer at the kitchen table, are turned inside out, and he embarks on a bizarre journey, guided (however obscurely) by a succession of characters, each with a tale to tell.

'Murakami weaves these textured layers of reality into a shot-silk garment of deceptive beauty'
Independent on Sunday

'Deeply philosophical and teasingly perplexing, it is impossible to put down'
Daily Telegraph